BROKEN

Karin Fossum

Broken

TRANSLATED
FROM THE NORWEGIAN
BY

Charlotte Barslund

Harvill *Secker*
LONDON

Published by Harvill Secker 2008

2 4 6 8 10 9 7 5 3 1

First published with the title *Brudd* in 2006
by J.W. Cappelens Forlag A.S., Oslo

First published in Great Britain in 2008 by
HARVILL SECKER
Random House, 20 Vauxhall Bridge Road
London SW1V 2SA

www.randomhouse.co.uk

Addresses for companies within The Random House Group Limited can be found at:
www.randomhouse.co.uk/offices.htm

The Random House Group Limited Reg. No. 954009

A CIP catalogue record for this book is available from the British Library

This edition was published with the financial assistance of NORLA
ISBN 9781846552113 (hardback)
ISBN 9781846550614 (trade paperback)

The Random House Group Limited supports The Forest Stewardship
Council (FSC), the leading international forest certification organisation. All our titles
that are printed on Greenpeace approved FSC certified paper carry the FSC logo. Our
paper procurement policy can be found at www.rbooks.co.uk/environment

Mixed Sources
Product group from well-managed
forests and other controlled sources
www.fsc.org Cert no. TT-COC-2139
© 1996 Forest Stewardship Council
FSC

Typeset by SX Composing DTP, Rayleigh, Essex
Printed and bound in Great Britain by
CPI Mackays, Chatham ME5 8TD

To Herdis Eggen, my editor

CHAPTER 1

I see them in the porch light.

A long queue of people waiting on the drive outside my house; on closer inspection they turn out to be a mixture of the old and the young, men, women and children. They are patient, their heads are bowed, they are waiting for their stories to be told and it is I who will tell them, I am the author. I watch them for a long time, partly hidden behind my curtain, all the time thinking about the challenge ahead of me. But I am tired now; it is midnight, tomorrow maybe, I think, yawning. I need a few hours' sleep, it is hard work to give life to new characters every single day, it is not as if I am God, I am just a tired, middle-aged woman trying to keep going.

I watch the ones whose faces are in the shadows. There are so many of them, they are hard to count, and what happens to the ones whose stories I never get to tell, who will look after them? I press my nose against the window, my breath makes the glass steam up, I draw a little heart. At the front of the queue is a young woman cradling a small bundle, it is a baby swaddled in a blue towel. She clutches the baby to her chest, her face is racked with guilt. What can be haunting her so terribly? She is awfully young, emaciated, early twenties probably. She is wearing a dark coat with a hood and she wears high-heeled ankle boots. She stands as if rooted to the spot, with the baby in her arms and her head bowed towards her chest. Behind her stands a man. He looks somewhat puzzled, his hands are folded. An unassuming man in his early forties, thinning hair, he stoops slightly. He is not a religious man, though he might be praying to me; it seems as if he is beckoning me, that he has attached himself to the fringes of my consciousness. Behind him stands a very old man, scrawny and withered. There is no glint in his eyes, he has one foot in the grave and nobody notices him. But God knows he needs to be noticed, I think and scrutinise him. Inside his concave chest beats the noblest of hearts. Behind him is a woman, a little thin, greying hair, could she be me, will I tell my own story one day? I realise that it is midnight and I make an effort to tear myself away. I have to turn my back on them, I'm exhausted. I have drunk a bottle of burgundy and I have just taken a Zyprexa for anxiety, a Cipralex for depression and a Zopiclone to make me sleep, so I need my rest now. But it is so hard to turn my back on them, they continue to disturb me. At times they stare at my window in an intense and compelling way. How many of them are there? I lean against the window and try to count them. More than eleven, that means it will take me at least eleven years to get through them all. At the same time I know that as soon as I have dispatched the young woman with the baby and the man with his hands folded, new characters will arrive in a steady stream, I don't believe it will ever stop. This is how my life has turned out. I walk down the stairs every morning, then across the floor to the computer; I delve into the fate of a new character oblivious to everything around me. Time stands still, I feel neither hunger nor thirst, I am fixated by the blue glare from the computer. After several hours' work I finally resurface. The telephone rings and brings me back to life. It is busy outside, a real world with laughter and joy, with death, misery and grief. While I am absorbed by fiction, I pull the strings like a puppeteer; I make things happen, it's a passion and a lifelong obsession.

My cat appears on the veranda; I let him inside where it is warm. This agile grey animal is one of the most beautiful creatures in the world, I think; he walks across the parquet floor silently, softly and elegantly.

'Are you sleeping on my bed tonight?' I ask.

He fixes his green eyes on me and starts to purr. Then he heads for the stairs. Together we walk up the fifteen steps to the first floor and into my bedroom. It is small, cool and dark. There is my bed, my bedside table with the blue lamp. An alarm clock, an open book. I open up the window completely, the cool November air wafts in. By the bed is an old armchair, I place my clothes on the armrest. Then I slip under the duvet, curl up like a child. The cat jumps up, settles at my feet, a warm, furry ball of wool. For a moment everything is wonderfully quiet, then faint noises start to come through the window. Rustling from the cluster of trees outside. A car drives by; its headlights sweep ghostlike across my window. The house sits solidly on its foundation, resting like an ancient warrior. I close my eyes. Normally I am asleep the second my head hits the pillow and I remember nothing else. But now I am disturbed by a sound. Someone is trying to open the front door; I'm not hearing things. My eyes open wide and I struggle to breathe, fear surges through my body because this is really happening. The sound was very clear, it could not be misinterpreted. Did I forget to lock the door? Frantically I look at my alarm clock, the green digits glow, it is past midnight. The cat raises his head and I sense his movement through the duvet, this means the noise is not a figment of my imagination because cats are never wrong. What happens next is terrifying and eerie. The stairs creak; I hear slow, hesitant steps. I lie rigid in my bed. Then all goes quiet. I'm breathing too fast, my fists are clenched, I brace myself, I lie still, listening to the silence, praying to God that I'm hearing things. It could have been the trees outside, or a deer, perhaps, stepping on dry twigs. I calm myself down and close my eyes. Finally the sleeping pill kicks in; I drift off and only a tiny fragment of my consciousness is present. That is when I awake startled. Someone is in the room; I sense another human being. A pulse, a smell, breathing. The cat arches his back, he sniffs the darkness and in the dim, grey light from the window I see the outline of a man. He takes a few steps towards me and sits down on the chair next to my bed. I hear the creaking of the chair and the rustle of clothing. For several long minutes I lie very still under the duvet; the situation is bizarre, every single cell in my body is trembling. Neither of us speaks or moves, times passes, my eyes acclimatise to the dark.

A man is in the chair by my bed. The light reflects in his moist eyes. For a moment I am paralysed. Then I force myself to break the silence, my voice is devoid of strength.

'What do you want?' I whisper.

It takes a while before he answers, but I hear how he shifts in the chair, I hear his breathing and the sound of his shoes scraping against the floor. Finally he clears his throat cautiously, but no words come out. I'm not someone who takes the initiative, I remain immobile, but my fear is so overpowering that my entire system is on the verge of collapse. Terror rips through my body, my heart contracts violently, then stops, then beats, three or four wild beats. Again a soft cough and finally he says in a deep and modest voice:

'I do apologise for intruding.'

Silence once more, for a long time. I fight my way out of my comatose state and half sit up in bed. I squint through the darkness, he is only a metre away.

'What do you want?' I repeat.

He struggles to find the words, squirms a little in the chair.

'Well, I would hate to be a nuisance. I have absolutely no wish to intrude, I'm not normally like this. But the thing is, I've been waiting for so long and I just can't bear it any longer.'

There is a note of desperation in his voice. I frown, confused. I consider the situation from an outsider's point of view: a middle-aged woman, a cat and a mysterious intruder.

'What are you waiting for?' I ask. My voice is back to normal, I might be about to die, but then I have always been aware of that.

Yet again he changes his position in the chair, he crosses one leg over the other having first hitched up the fabric to prevent creases. This manoeuvre seems calming, this is how an educated man behaves, I think, I am still panting, my body's need for oxygen is constantly increasing.

'I'm waiting for my story to be told.'

I fall back into my bed. For several long seconds I lie there feeling my heartbeat return to normal.

'Turn on the light,' I ask him softly.

He does not reply, does not stir, his body is still in the chair. So I raise myself up on my elbow and turn on the light. I stay in this position watching him in amazement. He sits with his hands folded. The light causes him to blink fearfully, his grey eyes avoid looking at me.

'You've jumped the queue,' I say.

He bows his head in shame. Nods his heavy head.

'I recognise you,' I say. 'You're second. There is a woman with a baby in front of you.'

'I know!' he groans, his face contorting with pain. 'There's always someone ahead of me, I'm used to that. But I can't bear it any longer, I'm exhausted. You have to tell my story now, you have to start this morning!'

I sit upright and smooth my duvet. I lean against the headboard. The cat jumps up and listens, his ears perked up, he does not know how to react either.

'You're asking me to make you a promise,' I say, 'I can't. The woman has been waiting too, she has been waiting for many years and she is deeply unhappy.'

He rocks restlessly in the chair. Moves his hands to dust off something from the knees of his trousers, then his fingers rush to the knot of his tie, which is immaculate.

'Everyone is unhappy,' he replies. 'Besides, you can't measure unhappiness, the pain is equally great in all of us. I have come forward to ask for something, to save my own soul. I'm using the last of my strength and it has cost me a great deal.' And then in a thin voice: 'Should that not be rewarded?'

I give him a look of resignation; I'm filled with conflicting emotions. I'm not a naturally commanding person, but I try to be firm.

'If you have been waiting that long,' I say, 'you can wait another year. The woman with the baby will be done in twelve months.'

He is silent for a long time. When he finally speaks, his deep voice is trembling.

'This assumes that you live that long,' he says eventually. His voice is very meek, he does not look me in the eyes.

'What do you mean?' I ask, shocked.

'I mean,' he says anxiously, 'you might die. Then I'll have no story, I'll have no life.'

The thought that I might die soon does not upset me, I live with it daily and every morning I'm amazed that I'm still alive. That my heart beats, that the sun still rises.

'But then that applies to all of you,' I reply in a tired voice. 'I can't save everyone. Have you seen the old man behind you in the queue? He is way past eighty. He is valuable to me. The very old know more than most people, I want to hear what he has to say.'

He gives a heavy, prolonged sigh. Glances at me, a sudden touch of defiance in his grey eyes.

'But I've summoned the courage,' he says, 'I've come all the way to your bedroom, I've taken action. I'm begging you! And I want you to know something; this is terribly difficult for me. It goes against my nature, because I'm a very humble man.'

I watch him more closely now. His eyes are downcast once again, his face tormented. His hair is thinning and a little too long, it sticks out inelegantly at the back, he is wearing a slate-grey shirt, a black narrow tie and a black jacket. Grey trousers, black well-polished shoes with even laces. He is very clean and neatly groomed, but old-fashioned-looking, a man from another age.

'A very humble man,' he repeats.

I exhale; my breath turns into a sigh.

'I'm completely awake now,' I say. 'I won't get any sleep tonight.'

Suddenly he cheers up. The pitch of his voice rises.

'Well,' he says excitedly, 'if you make the decision now that you will get up in the morning and start my story, then you will be able to sleep, I'm certain of that. You need structure and I can give you that.'

'And what about the woman with the child?' I ask. 'She's first in the queue, you know, and has been for a long time. It's extremely hard to pass people over, I can't handle that.'

At that he looks me straight in the eye. It comes at a price, his breathing quickens.

'I think it is too late for her anyway,' he says quietly.

I reach for the cat, draw him to me, hold him tight.

'What do you mean, too late?'

He nods his heavy head.

'I think the child is dead.'

I shake my head in disbelief.

'Why do you say that? Have you spoken with her?'

Once again he brushes his trousers, I imagine it is a kind of reflex, which he cannot suppress.

'You write crime novels, don't you?' he mumbles. 'So the child will have to die. Her story is about the child's fate, about what happened to it. Did she find her child dead? Did she kill it herself? Was the child killed by its father, was it ill? Things like that. She would get picked by someone else anyway. Whereas I'm not interesting like her, no one else would pick me. Do you see?'

His voice is timid and pleading.

'You're wrong,' I state.

'No, I'm not. Please don't tell me that I have to go outside again, please don't ask me to go back to that wretched queue!'

His voice falters.

'I know lots of people who would pick you if you came their way,' I say, 'greater writers than me.'

'But this is where I've come,' he says, hurt.

'Why?'

'Why?' He shrugs. 'You must have summoned me, I was driven here, it's already been three years. For three long years I've been waiting under the porch light.'

'I never summon anyone,' I say in a firm voice. 'I haven't invited you. Suddenly you appeared as number two in the queue. And yes, I've known you were there for a long time, I've seen you very clearly, but there needs to be some sort of system, otherwise I lose control.'

The cat has curled up once more in my lap and is purring unperturbed.

'What's the cat's name?' he asks suddenly.

'Gandalf,' I reply. 'Gandalf, after Tolkien's wizard.'

'And what about me?' he goes on. 'Give me a name too, please, if nothing else.'

'What if I have a cruel fate in mind for you?' I ask him. 'Painful, difficult? Filled with shame and despair?'

He juts out his chin. 'I thought we might have a little chat about that. And agree the bigger picture.'

I narrow my eyes and give him a dubious look.

'So you're going to interfere too?' I shake my head. 'That's not going to happen, I'm very sorry, but I'm in charge here. No fictitious character ever stands by my bed telling me what to do. That's not how it works.'

'All the same,' he pleads, 'hasn't it occurred to you that I might make your job easier?'

'How?' I reply sceptically.

'There will be two of us making the decisions. If you get stuck I can tell you what I would like to happen; don't push me away, think about it, please.'

'I never get stuck,' I declare. 'I need to sleep now, it's night-time and I need to get up early.'

'A name, please!' he begs. 'Is that too much to ask?'

'Right, I'll name you,' I say, 'and before I know it, you'll want something else. A profession. Somewhere to live. A girlfriend.'

'No girlfriend,' he says quickly.

'Really? Why not?'

He becomes evasive once more. He falters. 'I don't need one, let's keep it simple.'

'So you're already interfering?'

Suddenly he looks wretched. 'I'm sorry, so sorry, I didn't mean to, but I'm scared! If you die soon, I will be lost for eternity.'

'I'm not going to die,' I comfort him.

'You are! All of us out there are worried about it and for good reason. Several members of your family have died from cancer. You smoke forty cigarettes a day, you drink too much red wine in the evenings, you're addicted to millions of pills, you eat too little, you work too hard, so you're clearly not going to live to be an old lady.'

I ponder this. 'Very well, you may be right. I can only do what I do and death is never convenient. However, I'm only fifty-one and you are second in the queue.'

'Name me,' he pleads again.

I pull up my knees. My shoulders are freezing cold, and my temples are starting to throb.

'Come closer to the light.'

He gets up and lifts the chair; he moves closer to the bedside table. He sits down again and folds his hands.

'You have a sensitive face,' I say inspecting him. 'You're gentle, poetic with a tendency towards melancholy. You come from a small, unassuming family of hard-working people. They all have this humility, this awareness of nuances, with the exception of your mother, perhaps, I'm not quite sure about her. I can picture them, they are fair-skinned and you can see their veins like fine, green threads.'

He pulls up the sleeve of his jacket and studies his wrist.

'You have large grey eyes,' I go on. 'However, your gaze is often defensive; if anyone talks to you, you'll look away. Your hair is thinning; it bothers you because in your own way you're vain despite your self-proclaimed modesty. You have dreams, they will never come true. Yet you're patient. You've always been patient. Right up until now.'

'And my name?'

'Give me a little time. Names are very important. If I rush, it will be wrong and I doubt that you'll be content with just anything.'

'I'm sorry I interrupted you,' he says, 'please continue, I'm listening.'

'Your hands,' I state, 'are really quite small. Your shoe size is thirty-nine, which is small for a grown man. You're clean, you watch what you eat and you're good at saving money. You're never ill, and you drink moderately. You have a green thumb, you're very fond of music. You notice how the light changes outside your window, you watch people and they fascinate you in a way you don't understand, yet you don't feel connected to them. You never approach anyone, you live your life without involving anyone else. You never complain, you don't shout, you never object to anything, you never get stressed; you make yourself go on like a carthorse. What do you think of Torstein?'

He gives me an uncertain look. 'It's not terribly poetic.'

I think again. Names fly through my mind and with each one I observe him closely. I hold the name up to his face, trying to make it fit.

'I would have to agree with you. Besides, Torstein is a strong man's name, resourceful and decisive. And I don't want to hurt your feelings, but you're a bit spineless.'

He bows his head and blushes scarlet in the light from the lamp on the bedside table.

'You must forgive me,' I say, 'but it was your idea to enter my house and I'm in charge here.'

'I know, I know. I will take what I'm given, I mean that from the bottom of my heart.'

'Then let's continue.'

I think again, I close my eyes.

'You sleep well at night, you sleep like a baby. You get up early and are always equally content with each new day. However, this serenity of yours, this meticulousness is actually very fragile. No one is allowed to disturb it, enter into it or distract you. You need to be in control and have a clear overview of absolutely everything that will happen.'

New names fly by. Names full of gravity and poetry.

'How about Alvar?' I suggest.

'Is that a name?' He looks at me quizzically.

'Of course it's a name. Though better known in Sweden than here in Norway. Attractive, too, in my opinion. Think it over.'

'I am. What about my surname? I suppose I'll be given one of those too?'

'Of course. Personally I favour monosyllabic names. Like Krohn. Or Torp. But I want to give you more than that.' I close my eyes again. Search through a myriad names.

'Your surname is Eide,' I say with absolute conviction.

'Alvar Eide,' he says quietly. 'That's good, I'm very grateful.'

He straightens his back and smiles.

'So you'll be starting tomorrow?'

I rest my head against the headboard, I shrug with resignation. Never, in all my life, have I experienced anything like this.

'Because now that I am visible to you, you won't be able to wait. I'll have a word with the woman holding the dead child, I'm sure we can come to an understanding.'

'Well, if you've been reassured now, would you kindly leave and find your place in the queue? I need some sleep, it's very late now.'

'Yes!' He nods adamantly. His grey eyes have lit up. 'There's just one small thing.' He raises his hand, he is begging. 'Am I a good person?'

I smile and shake my head at this. The way he is looking at me makes me laugh, and I concede that he has won.

'Of course you're a good person, Alvar Eide, you're as good as gold. Now leave me alone, I'm tired.'

Finally he gets up; he carefully puts the chair back in its place. Turns off the light, bows politely and exits. I hear his footsteps on the staircase, I hear the door being closed. I put my head on my pillow, I feel dizzy.

'Goodness gracious me,' I say out into the darkness. 'What do you make of this, puss?'

The cat is asleep, his paws twitching, he is hunting.

'Gandalf,' I whisper, 'listen to this. There is mutiny in the queue outside the house!'

The cat sleeps on determinedly. I turn on to my side and pull up my knees. What does it mean that I no longer have an orderly system? This has never happened before. What will happen in future, if they start arguing about the sequence? Is there a moment far into the future where this flow of people ends? Where will I turn then? Will I have to settle for people who have created their own lives, real people? Lives I have no control over, lives I cannot shape the way I always have? I can find no peace. I don't like this night, this turn that my life has taken, I'm used to a certain amount of control, a certain order. But now Alvar Eide has wedged himself into my life. I turn to the wall and I want to go to sleep, but I'm troubled by words flying through my head. I want to enter the room where Alvar lives, but the door is shut and locked. I don't find the key until the early-morning hours.

CHAPTER 2

I'm a good person.

So thought Alvar Eide, just as he was putting on his coat. He stood in his hall studying his face in the mirror. This thought, that he was a good person, seemed to comfort him, as if he had suddenly realised that he had not amounted to much else in this world. He had never distinguished himself, never caused a stir. Not that he had wanted to either, but the years were mounting up, he had started to think about the end. At the age of forty-two he was thinking about the end. Perhaps because his father, Emmanuel Eide, had only lived to fifty-three. Then without warning his heart had stopped beating never to start again. Alvar found it hard to believe that he himself would live past this age; he imagined his death was programmed into his genes like a time bomb and that it would go off in eleven years. But there was now one thing to comfort him, one cool morning in November just as he was about to walk the two kilometres to his place of work: I have never achieved anything major, I have never distinguished myself, but deep down I know I'm a good person.

He stuck his arms through the sleeves and reached for a camel-coloured woollen scarf he liked to wear wrapped around his neck. The scarf lay beautifully and neatly folded on the chest of drawers beneath the mirror. His gloves lay in a drawer; he pulled them on, they were slightly too big. He knew they kept his hands warmer that way. On his head he wore nothing. Even so, he glanced at the mirror to check that his hair was in place, gently combed over from his right temple and all the way across to his left. There was no breeze outside.

He grabbed the door handle. Pushed it down and went out into the cool air; it felt clean and fresh against his cheeks. The light caused him to squint. Alvar Eide lived in the upstairs flat of a house in Nøste outside Drammen; his neighbours, the Green family, owned the ground-floor flat. He did not know them very well. They came and went and he nodded briefly by way of acknowledgement; but he did everything he could to avoid having to make small talk. Alvar Eide was a shy man. Green, however, could be intrusive; sometimes he would linger downstairs by the letter boxes wanting to chat about everyday matters. The weather, the price of petrol, interest rates, the new government. And as Alvar liked to think of himself as a good person, he was never curt so that his behaviour might be interpreted as frosty or arrogant. Yet he kept Green at arm's length, gave monosyllabic answers to every question, while smiling politely the whole time and speaking in a low, educated voice. But is that goodness? he suddenly started to wonder and felt upset. Am I really a good person after all? I have never hurt anyone, but does that make me good? Surely you're meant to do good deeds, go the extra mile, make sacrifices in order to earn the label 'a good person'.

He struggled with these questions as he walked down the steep hill into town. The fjord gleamed metallically in the low sun. He felt weighed down by gloom. How impossible it was to know anything about yourself, something you could be certain of. And he had never been severely tested. Of course he donated to charity, modest sums. It never occurred to him to refuse. The thought of this brightened his mood instantly. Many people said no. They said, no, actually I wouldn't dream of helping, the hungry will just have to fend for themselves, the same goes for drug addicts. And cancer, well, that's never affected our family, I'll probably be struck down by other things and when the time comes I will make my contribution to whatever charity will benefit me and my own health. It's everyone for themselves. It's not my fault that people starve in Africa, that there's a war in Iraq. Maybe that's what they said holding their heads high, looking right at the face of the child with shiny eyes, perhaps, who might be standing outside their front door holding out a sealed collecting tin. Some, possibly, said nothing at all, they simply slammed the door with a bored look. Or even worse, they never even bothered to open it. He always opened the door whenever someone rang the bell even though he found it very difficult. Not a great deal happened in his life, he saw no one and had no family, no friends, no wife and child. So he went to the door when the bell rang even though it made his stomach lurch. He became very nervous when the shrill tone of the bell rang out through the rooms, at the mere thought that someone might want something from him. Might demand things, beg. Break into his neat, ordered world. On one occasion he had happened not to have any money on him; he had found that terribly embarrassing. Having to close the door without having helped, to close the door with downcast eyes and flushed, burning cheeks. Had they even believed him when he said he was out of cash? Or had they walked off, angrily denouncing him as a skinflint? The very thought of it tormented him because he regarded himself as generous, if only people would give him the chance. He usually found some kroner in a pocket or the bowl in the kitchen where he would store excess change from his wallet. Heavy wallets ruined the cut of his clothes, his mother had taught him that. He continued walking into town feeling troubled. He no longer felt good about himself. He gave money because it was embarrassing to say no. He never went back into his living room with the feeling of having contributed something, it felt more like a game and he was simply playing by the rules. Perhaps it's because I don't give enough, he thought. If I gave a thousand kroner, I might feel differently. But that would be too much. Surely there was something ostentatious about giving one thousand kroner? The whole point of charity appeals was that many people donated and everyone gave a small amount.

A cool gust of wind from the fjord hit his face. The comb-over, which lay loosely across his scalp threatened to fly up. He braced himself against the wind and hoped for the best. He looked down towards the light-bulb factory with its giant dome, which was lit up at night. The dome with its bright yellow glow was a landmark.

Often in the evening he would stand by the window staring at its strong light. He saw the busy port, the silos belonging to Felleskjøbet, the bridges and the trains with their green and red carriages. Now he was turning left, reaching Engene. He would walk along until he had Bragernes church on his right, then he would pass the grandiose old fire station, past Harry's Café before reaching Albumsgate. And Gallery Krantz, where he worked. The time was a quarter to ten. Now it was the wind from the river which nipped his cheeks; he kept on walking, swinging his arms rhythmically.

Whenever anyone came walking towards him on the pavement, he would make way for them in plenty of time. I enjoy walking through the town, Alvar thought, I like watching other people and wondering about them. Many walked around in pairs. Sometimes three or four walked together, some formed small groups on corners where they would chat. Voices and laughter flew through the air. Alvar Eide observed this phenomenon with a certain degree of bemusement. People had an indefatigable urge to socialise. It was something he personally had never done, he had gone through his life alone. But it was not a nagging loneliness. It was the life he preferred, because it gave him clarity and control. On top of that it was convenient, no demands, no unpleasantness. No agreements to fulfil, no promises to keep, no intrusive questions, how are you, Alvar? How are you really? It seemed that friends had some sort of right to know how you were. Consequently he never had company, it just so happened that he was perfectly happy minding his own business. He liked the peace and quiet of the flat, he enjoyed listening to Bach's 'Toccata and Fugue', quite loud, if he wanted to. He liked sleeping on his own. He considered sleep to be something terribly intimate and he shuddered at the thought of another person being able to watch him in this condition, as he lay curled up with his eyes closed and his mouth open. There had been times when he had considered getting a cat, but it had remained a thought. Cats probably needed all kinds of things, food, vaccinations and a tag, and even neutering if he chose a tom or contraceptive implants if he chose a female. He would have to take the animal to the vet's and deal with all of these things. Not that he would be incapable of that, he was a very competent man and he had a way with words when it was required of him. After all, he dealt with customers in the gallery. But still the thought of having to sort all this out, everything he would have to remember and take care of, had so far prevented him from getting a cat, even though he did, in fact, really want one. And it might get ill as well, it might come home with worms. When he was a boy, their neighbour had a cat. A heavy, tabby tomcat without a tail. One day it came into the living room and started vomiting violently. And the pile on the rug had started to squirm. Inside the revolting mess there was twitching and writhing. Alvar had been sent next door by his mother, holding a cup with no handle to borrow some sugar, and the sight of worms in the vomit had haunted him from that day on. That's just what cats are like, the neighbour had assured him, Alvar, don't worry about it. But Alvar knew that he would not be able to stomach an experience like that. And then there were fur balls, which they kept bringing up. So no cat.

Alvar kept on walking. He knew every courtyard, every street, every single shop in the heavily trafficked road. He returned to the question of being good. He had always believed that he was a good person. So how come this doubt had appeared like a bolt out of the blue and why would it not leave him alone? He realised that he had never, ever in all his life done anything which could be considered a good deed. He had never saved anyone's life, never intervened, never made the first move. Well, apart from the spare change he handed out whenever the doorbell rang. Or, preferably, to the Salvation Army officer who often stood outside the entrance to the shopping centre, silent and dignified, his uniform immaculate, holding a tin. Sometimes he had pushed a fifty-krone note through the slot and felt very pleased. Pleased, but not good. In a way the officer did the work for him. If I had stood there myself holding the tin, Alvar thought, then I would have felt better, that could have been deemed an active contribution. And I have a lot of my life left to live, or eleven years at any rate, and I can continue doing good work. Sponsor a child in India, perhaps, in Peru or Zimbabwe? He dismissed the thought instantly. A sponsored child would want letters and presents and he did not know how to relate to a foreign child in a country far away, a country he would know nothing about anyway. He had no experience of foreign cultures. But it would have been a good thing to do. Perhaps he would receive a photo of the child which he could hang on the wall above the fridge, a beautiful brown child with white teeth. Suddenly another thought cropped up, it came out of nowhere, like a bolt of lightning, possibly because a man was coming towards him, a very obese man struggling to walk, his cheeks flushed with exertion. What if this man collapsed from a heart attack right there and then on the street, what would he do? Stand there petrified, unable to move? He did not know first aid, he did not own a mobile phone, he would not even be able to phone for help. He visualised the grim scene, him standing there paralysed, his arms hanging limply. Others would come running and deal with it. The image instilled profound despondency in him. A sensation of worthlessness. The feeling was so painful that it stopped him in his tracks. He stood there, still staring at his newly polished shoes, as a car raced past, causing his coat to flap; it billowed like a sail. And then his tuft of hair stood up, something which always sent a shiver down his spine. A feeling of having been revealed as a fraud. For a long time he stood like that, but snapped out of his trance as a lady passed him on the outside of the pavement. Quickly he averted his eyes.

He walked on thinking, once I get myself to the gallery and the paintings then I'll be myself again. Because the paintings, these frozen moments, always filled him with serenity. Finally he could see the front of the stately building where he worked. A three-storey, twentieth-century villa, very well maintained and exclusive, painted a warm, creamy shade of yellow with a few details in red. Columns fronting the entrance, large arched windows and a double, reddish-brown oak front door with magnificent carvings. He did not earn a huge salary from his work there; however, he could manage on very little. He had inherited the flat in Nøste from his mother and the mortgage had been paid off ages ago. In the yard behind the house stood an old Mazda, which he would use if the weather was awful or if he fancied seeing a little of the surrounding countryside. He was very good at saving money and he had no expensive habits.

The owner of the gallery was an art dealer called Ole Krantz. He had run it for years and had many regular customers. Then suddenly at the age of fifty he had started to paint himself. It was going surprisingly well, he painted with latex on thick, high-quality watercolour paper. Decorative, colourful, easy-to-sell pictures. The subject might be the wing of a bird, a pansy, a bowl of strawberries, the kind of images people like having on their walls. Ole Krantz had become a child again following the amazing discovery that he had a talent for painting. Though, when discussing his own work, he said that it hardly counted as great art and this was consequently reflected in the price, which was moderate. The pictures went for anywhere from five to ten thousand kroner. Alvar truly felt at ease in the gallery. He enjoyed visual art, it was a subject he was well versed in and comfortable with, and he was a good salesman. He was patently good because during his long career there had not been a single instance where a customer had regretted a purchase and had come back to return a painting. Ole Krantz had a different sales technique, however. He sold huge quantities of paintings, but had to accept that several would be returned. He sold by seducing the customers, by stressing the rise in value, the unique features of the painting, the beneficial influence of a particular shade of blue, how this very picture would fill a void and, yes, it was pricey, but you can always pay in instalments. And so on and so forth in a steady persuasive stream. He was quick to spot what the customers wanted and roughly what they could afford. This one can stretch to a Willibard Storn while that one over there will probably have to make do with a Halvorsen. However, when Alvar sold a painting it was always based on mutual understanding and profound respect. The customer should always be left with the feeling that he had made a choice he would not regret.

Even though he was only an employee in the gallery, no sooner had he entered and disabled the alarm by pressing three-three-four-two, than he felt he owned the whole building. This was his castle, his kingdom, his undisputed domain. He instantly took in the smells, the familiar aroma of oil and turpentine and the meticulously washed stone floor. Yes, this was his territory, he revelled in the feeling and he was the master of this house. Alvar Eide was a man of few words. However, when it came to art he was practised at expressing himself and he was confident, he knew the terminology. He had long conversations with the customers and it was no effort at all as long as there was a painting between him and the other person. A kind of wall that he could hide behind. He never spoke about personal matters.

Now he switched on the light on the ground floor before going upstairs to the first floor. Onwards into the kitchen which doubled up as the break room. There he switched on the monitors; the cameras were aimed at the important areas of the gallery, primarily the ground floor where the most expensive paintings were hung. He had an Ekeland, a Revold and a Gunnar S. downstairs, and from time to time a Weidemann or a Sitter. They usually hung there for a while, the price tag was high. He poured water into the coffee-maker and measured coffee into the filter, seven level spoonfuls. It was two minutes to ten in the morning and the gallery closed at five in the afternoon. They were comfortable working hours with a free Saturday every other week when Ole himself staffed the gallery and handled any sales. He did not want to lose contact with his customers altogether. Alvar found a mug in the cupboard and sat down at the table. He stared at the three monitors. They showed the gallery in black and white, and while the images were not particularly sharp, at least they gave him the chance to keep an eye on things. There was no denying that the building contained pieces of staggering value. On a few occasions people had popped their heads round the door to inspect the gallery, then noticing the cameras attached to the ceiling, had spun round and disappeared. He did not know what that meant. Perhaps they had just dropped by out of sheer curiosity and then realised that the prices were too high. Though sometimes he entertained the notion that they were casing the place, planning a raid. The thought of this sent a chill down his spine. However, nothing serious had ever happened during the time he had been working there and he always felt safe and contented throughout the whole day.

Every day he spent some of his time framing pictures. Not the major paintings, not the ones by Knut Rumohr or Nerdrum, Ole Krantz dealt with those as he was a trained frame maker. But other things, smaller items. He cut the glass and the passepartout, he brushed dust and grit off the surface of the painting, he cut lists and joined them with tags, he made the fixings. There were small lithographs, which sold for a thousand kroner, or paintings, which people had handed in for framing. Drawings or photos, or something they had bought on their holidays abroad. It was pleasant work and he felt at ease in the framing workshop, which was at the back of the gallery on the ground floor. It smelled of wood, cardboard and glue. He had a radio in there, which was always tuned to P2, the arts channel. By now the coffee had filtered through and Alvar poured himself a cup. Ole Krantz had spared no expense when it came to the kitchen, it was equipped with a fridge, dishwasher and a microwave. In the fridge were several bottles of sparkling white wine; whenever he made a good sale Krantz was in the habit of opening a bottle so he and the customer could toast the painting. Alvar never did that. Partly because he was shy. One glass of wine could lead him astray. Also he would rather that the customer left with the painting, went home, hung it on their wall and then had a glass of something to savour the moment and their own excellent choice, their own good taste. That was how he thought it ought to be. Alvar could tell immediately if Ole Krantz had sold a valuable painting on one of his Saturdays because there would be two wine glasses standing on the worktop.

Alvar drank his coffee and kept an eye on the monitors. The big building was very quiet, there was not a sound to be heard, only his own slurping as he drank the strong coffee. This wasn't a place people flocked to, sometimes one, two hours passed between customers. Then he would sit and ponder, ponder life and himself, and at regular intervals he would take a walk through the building. He would start on the second floor, which housed all the foreign art, names unknown to most people, but the paintings were of a high quality. Prints were on the first floor, some of them French, but mainly good, Norwegian prints. The Norwegian paintings were lined up on the ground floor; most were oils, but every now and again an artist would experiment with acrylics, which created a rather bold and vivid impression. There was something about acrylics, they commanded your attention more than oil did, Alvar thought, shuffling from picture to picture, his hands folded behind his back. He had a personal relationship with each and every one of these paintings, he made sure to develop that as soon as they arrived at the gallery. So when a customer's attention was caught by a painting, a Ruhmor for example, he could find the right words instantly. Words which would guide the customer inside the painting, help the customer understand and respect the work. If they asked whether it would increase in value, he deftly avoided the question by asking, what is important to you? Why don't you simply buy the painting because you like it, because it gives you something unique? Why don't you simply buy the painting because you think it was meant for you?

He knew that Ole Krantz appreciated him and his contribution, he knew that his job was secure. A better person could not replace him; he was absolutely convinced of that. Pleased at the thought of this he went down to the workshop to check out what was lying on the worktop waiting to be framed. A photo of giggling, chubby toddlers. Their father had taken the photo, he regarded the result as particularly successful and had decided to have it enlarged and now framed. He has asked for a red passepartout, something which vexed

Alvar. The way he looked at it, one should never, ever, regardless of what type of picture it was, choose anything other than an off-white passepartout. Only the picture should speak, not its frame. The red passepartout would sap the photo of its strength. But the customer is always right, he thought and calmly began his work. He lifted up the sheet of glass and placed it carefully on the worktop. Found the cutting diamond and the ruler and started cutting with a steady hand. He liked the sound of the hard stone, he enjoyed snapping the offcuts, the crispy sound, like brittle caramelised sugar. He worked slowly and with concentration. But all the time parts of his mind were preoccupied with other things. He was alone, no colleagues disturbed him and his thoughts freewheeled. Was he really a good person deep down? Why was it starting to haunt him like this? Selling art to people was a fine thing to do, it was honest work, he did it diligently, he did it with conviction, respect and love. He was doing well in life, he donated to charities. He led an orderly life, he did not hurt anyone. So why had this strange feeling come over him?

CHAPTER 3

I turn off the computer and go into my kitchen.

The cat follows and starts to beg; he is hoping for a prawn, perhaps, or a bowl of tuna. He pleads silently with his green eyes. I give him pellets and fresh water. I hear his sharp teeth crunch the dry feed.

So, I think, he's really got to me, Alvar Eide, indeed he has. I have taken off and I'm in the air. I need a bite to eat before I go back to work; I open the fridge and look inside, spot a scrap of salami, a curled-up piece of brown cheese, four eggs, a tube of mayonnaise. And a wheel of Camembert cheese. I take an egg and the Camembert from the fridge, find a bowl and a fork. Crack the egg on the rim of the bowl and whisk it forcefully. I find some stale bread in the bread bin. I crumble it on the breadboard and unwrap the Camembert. Then I hear footsteps in the hall, soft, cautious steps. Alvar enters my kitchen. He stands in the doorway with his hands folded across his stomach watching me with meek, apologetic eyes.

'I'm sorry to disturb you,' he says and looks down.

'What is it?' I ask him, surprised. I lean against the kitchen counter and look at him with curiosity.

'Just wanted to stop by,' he says shyly.

He spots the cheese and the egg. Chews his lip. His voice is a mere whisper. 'Shouldn't you be working?'

I let my arms fall and give him a stern look.

'You won't even allow me to stop for lunch?' I reply. 'I can't think when I'm hungry. Don't you understand?'

He slumps on a kitchen chair. Dusts off the knees of his trousers even though they are immaculate.

'Of course,' he says quickly. 'I didn't come here to make a fuss, I don't want to cause you any trouble. Really, I don't.'

He looks at my food on the breadboard. The cheese, the bowl with the beaten egg, the breadcrumbs.

'Why don't you just wolf down a sandwich? You normally do, you stand by the counter when you eat. This is going to take time. But, don't get me wrong, I'm not telling you how to organise your day, I'm just very keen to get started.'

I cut two thick wedges of cheese with a sharp knife. Find a frying pan in a cupboard, put it on the cooker.

'Now calm down, Alvar,' I say, 'you're inside now. Right inside as a matter of fact,' I say, tapping my temple. 'Besides, you're only forty-two. Think about the old man; I do.'

I put a lump of butter on the pan, immediately it starts gliding towards the edge; the cooker tilts slightly towards the wall.

'And I do, I really do,' Alvar says. 'He's really very patient, he stands there like a post, waiting. No one in the queue minds that I jumped it. You must believe me.'

I dip the wedges of cheese in the beaten egg and coat them with the breadcrumbs.

'What about the woman with the child?' I ask. 'What does she say?'

He bows his head, I see his chest heave.

'It was like I said. She is unable to say anything, because the baby is dead.'

I look at him and sigh. 'She's just standing there with a dead child, waiting?'

'Yes. She's incapable of action, I presume. It upsets me, really it does. I feel it here.' He places a hand on his chest.

'So it should,' I say, placing the cheese wedges now coated in egg and breadcrumbs in the frying pan. The butter is golden yellow, it sizzles temptingly, the smell of melting cheese begins to fill the kitchen.

'It upsets me too,' I say. 'And I have thought a great deal about this. Whether it's acceptable to anticipate events in this way.'

Slowly the wedges of cheese turn golden. I go to the fridge for cranberry sauce, find a plate, a knife and a fork.

'Well, I stand by my decision. But nevertheless something about it troubles me. Now take it easy, Alvar, and don't put too much pressure on me.'

I turn the cheese over, the wedges are perfect.

'I do like my flat,' he says. 'I'm very pleased about my job at the gallery. It's almost more than I dared hope for, I could have ended up in a dirty workshop with a gang of noisy, crude men, I would not have enjoyed that.'

'If you're so pleased,' I say, 'why are you here? I think you're too quick to interfere, I've only written one chapter.'

He squirms a little on the chair. I look at his black shoes, they are so shiny you can see your face in them.

'The thing is, I'm worried,' he says. 'I'm forty-two years old and I am starting to question my own worth. My goodness, which I have always taken for granted. And pardon me for mentioning this, but from what you've written so far it's starting to look suspiciously like a midlife crisis.'

I stop what I am doing and my eyes widen.

'Surely I'm not destined for that kind of story?' he asks nervously. Then he smiles apologetically and lowers his head.

I lean back and fold my arms across my chest.

'If this is going to work at all, we have to trust each other,' I say. 'Last night you said that you would accept whatever fate you were given. Do you stand by that?'

Alvar is embarrassed, but he nods. I look at his folded hands, they lie like a knot in his lap.

'Why do you always sit with your hands folded?' I ask him out of curiosity.

'I can't put them in my pockets,' he says quickly, 'it ruins the cut of my trousers, my mother taught me that.'

I nod and I understand. I remove the wedges of cheese from the frying pan and slide them onto my plate, arrange the cranberry sauce next to them and carry everything into the dining room. Alvar follows me softly. He pulls out a chair.

'You will go back to work when you've finished eating, won't you? There's still much of the day left.'

I rest my chin in my hands. 'Would you kindly let me eat in peace?'

He falls silent. His grey eyes flicker around the room, he looks at the pictures on my walls.

'Death,' he says all of a sudden. 'You have a picture of Death on your wall.'

I nod and spear a slice of cheese with my fork.

'Why is that?'

'He's an old friend.'

He shakes his head at this. Gives me an uncertain look. 'What's that supposed to mean? An old friend?'

I cut a piece off the melted cheese and dip it in the cranberry sauce.

'Well, how can I put it? He feels familiar, like an old, faithful friend. When I can't manage any more, he comes and takes me away. Maybe he'll put me on his lap, just like the picture.'

'It's a drawing by Käthe Kollwitz,' Alvar says. '*Death with a Maiden on his Lap*.'

'That's right. It's beautiful. Look how gentle he is, see how delicately she rests against his chest. Sometimes when I work, Death comes into my room. He places a hand on my shoulder.'

'That would chill me to the bones,' Alvar says. 'Doesn't it frighten you?'

'No. It's more like a gentle caress. Not now, I tell him calmly, not now, I'm in the middle of a book and I have to finish it.'

'There's never a good time for dying,' Alvar says. 'We know that we all have to and it's a fate we carry with dignity as long as it doesn't happen today. Or tomorrow, because there are a few things we were hoping to do.'

'That's how it is,' I reply. 'However, I prefer to maintain a degree of contact with Death. It's an exit, which is always open. At night I play a game. I go to bed and feel my sleeping pill wash over me like a wave. Suddenly I'm on a beach and a man dressed in black comes rowing. I stand completely still waiting while he moors the boat. The water ripples over the stones, the old woodwork creaks.'

'Do you get in?' Alvar asks me earnestly.

'Yes, I do. The water is like a mirror. Death turns the boat round and rows with steady strokes, he knows where we are going, he knows these waters and he is confident.'

'Is it night and is it dark?' Alvar wants to know.

'No,' I say. 'It's twilight. And Death rows until we have reached the middle of the fjord; then he places the oars at the bottom of the boat and looks at me firmly. "Tomorrow is another day," he says. "Do you want it?" I think about this for a long time. I have been in this world for over fifty years; I suppose I can manage one more day. So he turns the boat round and rows me back, and I disembark. Back on dry land for a new day, which was never a certainty. Because every night I have to choose.'

Alvar is silent for a long time. Again he looks at the paintings on my wall.

'You also have a Lena Cronquist,' he enthuses, pointing to a painting above the television.

'I do. Do you know her?'

'Of course. I pride myself on being well informed when it comes to modern art.'

I eat more cheese, it tastes delicious. And while I eat, my thoughts are drifting. What do we people have in common? I wonder. Well, we're born. Not because we want to be, but because someone else wanted it. We grow up and we don't know where we're going or what we'll get. We think we can make our own decisions, that we can plan things. And so we can to a certain extent, but fate can be very capricious. A late-running bus can change a whole life, it can steer us towards another fate. We stumble on the kerb, someone rushes to our aid, we catch someone's eyes for a brief second and lightning strikes. A glance can lead to marriage and children, suddenly we've ended up in a totally different place from what we imagined. Alvar doesn't have much, not at the moment. A flat, a job, and a very sensitive personality. This sensitivity, I decide, watching him secretly, that will be his fate. He wants to be a good person; however, we don't live in a world where good people are rewarded, but he doesn't know that.

Alvar follows each mouthful with his eyes. I finish eating and clear up after myself, then I sit down in the living room, I light a cigarette; Alvar follows me. He comes into the room hesitatingly and finds a chair for himself.

'Please don't let anything happen to Ole Krantz,' he says out of the blue. Again he looks down as if every time he says something he instantly regrets his words.

I blow a column of smoke across the coffee table, it hovers there swirling in the light from the lamp.

'I'm not allowed to let anything happen to Krantz?'

'No, because he's a fine man, he doesn't deserve it.'

'My dear Alvar,' I say in a patronising voice, 'there can be no dramatic tension if I'm not allowed to make anything happen. I would have thought you understood that.'

Again he is embarrassed. There are red patches on his throat and his grey eyes blink.

'You're mine now,' I continue, 'you're not responsible for the other characters. I'm the one who'll be taking care of them, it's a matter of honour with me.'

'That's your twentieth cigarette today,' he points out shyly.

'So you're keeping count?'

'I don't have any bad habits like that.' He says this with pride.

'I'm sure you don't. But we all have our crosses to bear. You can die from so many things. Perish for any number of peculiar reasons.'

I flick the ash off the cigarette and stare out of the window; the azalea by the entrance sways in the wind. I can't decide what fascinates me the most. His badly concealed eagerness, his spotless character, the light in his grey eyes.

'Dear God,' he says terrified, 'are you going to let me perish?'

CHAPTER 4

The oak door opened and the bell rang out.

The bell had a fragile and wistful ring to it, which Alvar really liked. It announced that someone had arrived, someone who needed his expertise and his always impeccable service. He was sitting in the gallery's kitchen with a list of names. Krantz wanted to arrange a special exhibition in the new year, the preparations were underway, brochures would be printed and sent out to all their regular customers. Alvar looked through a pile of colourful photographs. The artist's best painting would adorn the cover together with a brief biography about his achievements so far. In this case, the artist being Knut Rumohr, these comprised fifteen large paintings, which were all outstanding. Alvar looked closely at the photos. He felt he could vouch for every single one of them and this was not always the case. Most artists were inconsistent. Rumohr, however, never disappointed and every painting was unique, there was strength and radiance in all of them. Besides, he was an unassuming man, private and polite, friendly and modest, a man after Alvar's own heart. He often visited the gallery wearing green wellies and with a sturdy sheath knife hanging from his belt. A craftsman, almost a labourer.

However, the bell had rung and Alvar looked up. On the left monitor he could see a woman entering. She was tall, slim and wore a dark coat. He let her wander around, it was not Alvar's style to charge in, the customer needed to be given time. His coffee had gone cold so he poured it into the sink. He went over to a mirror on the wall to check that his hair was in place. He looked at himself for a long time. His head was heavy, he took after his father. His features, however, were clean and fine, his dark brows strong and straight. He arranged his thinning hair across his scalp and then he went slowly down the stairs to the ground floor. She noticed him as he took the last few steps, nodded and smiled at him. A minute elegant nod of her head. She was an attractive, well-groomed woman, a little older than him, and, judging from her clothes, she was well off. She probably owned some works of art already. Alvar greeted her in a friendly manner, but remained standing, a little defensive, with his hands folded across his stomach. He did not recognise her, perhaps she had only recently moved to the town, or she might be passing through, he was not sure which, but he had a number of regular customers whose names he knew. Or the artists themselves popped in to see if anything was going on. He enjoyed talking to the artists. He had quickly made the discovery that the vast majority were down-to-earth, hard-working people.

However, here was a woman in a dark coat. She wore a foxtail around her neck and gloves of fine brandy-coloured leather. She wore boots with buttons. Alvar became almost besotted by them, they were black and pointy with high heels and, like his own shoes, polished to a shine. She continued to wander around; Alvar stayed in the background. It was easy for him to spot whether the customer had any knowledge of art. This woman stopped in front of a painting by Axel Revold, to Alvar's intense joy; however, the painting was so expensive that it was unlikely that she would be in a position to buy it. You do not sell a Revold just like that, a Revold is an event. So Alvar thought while he watched the woman furtively. She had moved on to a painting by Gunvor Advocat. An Advocat would be a respectable choice, too. But no, she carried on and after a few minutes she disappeared up to the first floor to the prints. He followed her, but went into the kitchen, he did not want to pester her with his enthusiasm. Because that was what he experienced at every sale: enthusiasm, selling a painting was like finding a home for a stray dog. A work of expressive art would finally find its place and give daily joy.

The woman seemed self-assured as well as determined. He could tell from looking at her that she wanted something specific and he felt quite sure that he would shortly secure a sale, because of the purposeful way she was moving around. While he waited, he followed her on the middle monitor. She walked from picture to picture, came back again, took a closer look, read the artist's signature, leafed through some brochures which lay on a table. Then she straightened up and approached a picture, stood calmly in front of it. At this precise moment Alvar got up from his chair and joined her. She had stopped in front of a work by Jon Bøe Paulsen. A small picture modestly priced. Alvar sold a great deal of Jon Bøe Paulsen, people liked his beautiful lines and a few even said, I like Bøe Paulsen, because at least I can see what it's meant to be. The pictures could resemble photographs; they were darkly lit and full of atmosphere. The print depicted a svelte, but graceful woman seen from behind. She had lifted up her long hair and was piling it up on the top of her head, so that her body arched and all her curves and muscles were clearly and attractively displayed.

He stopped behind her and cleared his throat.

'The appeal of Bøe Paulsen,' he said, 'is his gentleness. His delicate hand, his light strokes. No strong expression, but softness.'

She nodded and smiled at him.

'Yes,' she said, 'it's lovely. But it's not for me,' she added, 'I'm looking for a present for a friend who's turning fifty. She'll probably like this.'

She said this in a tone, which clearly indicated that her own taste differed. She did not dismiss the print, but it was not her type of art.

'Personally I prefer a somewhat stronger expression,' she admitted.

Alvar nodded.

'Have you seen the paintings by Krantz?' he asked, thinking that she might enjoy the strong latex pictures.

'Yes, they're impressive,' she said, 'but they won't last.'

Alvar agreed completely, but he did not say so. Ole Krantz's painting got your attention instantly, but what they had to say, they said in a moment.

She had made up her mind and decided on the print. As the picture was a present he took it downstairs to the workshop to gift-wrap it. He cut a piece of corrugated cardboard and folded it around the picture, then he wrapped it in tissue paper. Finally he covered it in wrapping paper and made a rosette from some gold ribbon. She paid with a credit card as people always did, then she said goodbye and Alvar was once more left to his own devices. If only Ole Krantz had heard that, he thought, that he won't last. On the other hand it was unlikely that he would have been offended, because Krantz did not consider himself to be a proper artist, more a decorator. Alvar poured himself another cup of coffee and pondered his lack of goodness once more. The thought kept returning and had now begun to torment him in earnest. Here he was sitting by the kitchen table enjoying a cup of coffee, he was at work, he performed his job well in every way, so why would he reproach himself on account of his absent goodness? He who had never hurt a fly.

He drank big gulps of coffee as his brain began to spin. Was there anything he could do about it? And if he were to do something, would that make the thought go away or would it grow worse? You could never be certain when it came to human psychology. After all, weren't there stories about aid workers who became totally caught up by all the misery they witnessed in foreign countries? They ended up consumed by despair at the world's bloodthirsty injustice and when they returned to Norway developed huge problems just eating a meal without feeling racked with guilt. He did not want his life upset like that.

He got up and decided to start work on some frames. He left the kitchen and went down to the workshop, to the little pile of small pictures. The chubby children were ready and he thought the photo was good, but not striking. The children had round cheeks and large soft mouths. He had never understood the appeal of children or why people became so fascinated by them. Children always made him feel anxious and awkward and they had a habit of gawping at him in a cannibalistic manner. When it came to children he felt as if they shone a spotlight directly at him and they stared with large, bright eyes right into his soul. Obviously he did not believe that they had this power, but that was how they made him feel. He preferred adults, if he was forced to deal with other people. But most of all he preferred the elderly. The secretive, wrinkled faces, the slow movements. Nothing unpredictable ever happened in their company. That in turn made him relaxed and calm, it meant he was in control.

He selected another picture. It was a drawing, made by an amateur, who clearly felt that he had surpassed himself given that he had asked for the drawing to be framed. The subject was a very muscular horse. And it was presumably these muscles which had inspired him to make the drawing to begin with, perhaps it was his own horse, or his daughter's, because in the bottom left-hand corner he had written in pencil underneath his signature 'Sir Elliot, 4 June 2005'. The paper had a faint yellow tint, which meant that it was good quality, and the drawing was not at all bad. However, the actual soul of the animal was lost in the formidable mass of muscles and that was the proof that he was, in fact, not a good artist at all. Alvar cut glass and cardboard for the picture. The customer had requested a gold frame. Alvar was not a huge fan of gold frames, personally he would have chosen a narrow black or grey list for the picture. However, he always sided with the customer and would give him what he had asked for. He finished framing the drawing and returned to the kitchen. He felt like having his packed lunch now, it was half past twelve and he had not eaten since breakfast. He had three open sandwiches with slices of cold cuts and slivers of cucumber wrapped in greaseproof paper. He made another pot of coffee and found a plate in the cupboard, placed his sandwiches on a chopping board and halved them. Just then the downstairs bell repeated its fragile and wistful greeting. A young man entered. Alvar saw him on the left monitor, he was wearing a fashionable light-coloured coat. Once more he left the kitchen and went downstairs.

The man had stopped in front of a painting by Reidar Fritzwold. He was looking at it closely now, his hands in his coat pockets, leaning slightly forward, eager. The painting was challenging: it depicted a roaring waterfall with chunks of ice and snow in the surrounding landscape. It was magnificent, Alvar thought, impressive and grand in every way, but it needed a lot of space. As a result it had been in the gallery for a long time. The man appeared to be in his early thirties. He had taken a few steps back and placed his hands on his hips. Now he was standing with his legs apart inspecting the painting.

'Quite overwhelming, don't you think?' Alvar nodded, indicating the foaming water. You could almost feel the spray from the waterfall in your face. The colours were extraordinary, all shades of blue, green, turquoise, purple, yellow and white.

'Is it by a Norwegian artist?' the man wanted to know. He filled out the light-coloured coat. He had broad shoulders, a trendy short haircut with a few blond highlights in it. Alvar nodded.

'Norwegian born and bred,' he said. 'Name's Fritzwold. He paints landscapes. This is one of his most dramatic paintings. He usually paints mountain scenes, calm, blue paintings with a great deal of harmony.'

'I'm buying a painting for my living room,' the man said, 'and I would like the painting to be a good investment. My point being that if it's not going to go up in value, it's of no interest.'

Alvar moved forward very cautiously. He recognised the man's attitude and prepared for battle.

'But you like it?' he said lightly.

'Christ, yeah,' the man said, moving closer. 'Very, very good,' he muttered, nodding to himself. His eyes grew distant as if he had disappeared into another room and Alvar understood that he had mentally gone to his own living room where this painting might hang one day. Now he was trying to visualise it. The ice-cold torrents of water cascading down his wall.

'There are times when it is very important to make a good

investment,' Alvar said in that light, amiable voice he always used. 'However, it's terribly important that you like the painting, that it gives you something unique. Always follow your heart,' he said, 'don't intellectualise the process. Remember it's a relationship for life, it might even be passed on to the next generation.'

'It's huge at any rate,' said the younger man, 'it's bound to create a stir.'

Right, Alvar thought to himself. He wants attention, possibly from the guests, who would enter his living room and see the roaring waterfall, clap their hands with excitement, as they toasted their host's exquisite and dramatic taste.

'Surely it's possible to buy with your head as well your heart,' he ventured, giving Alvar a challenging look. His eyes were blue and sharp.

'Indeed it is,' nodded Alvar. 'But the fact is that this painting is not primarily a good investment.'

The young man fell silent for a moment and his brows contracted while he thought hard. His eyes, however, could not bear to leave the colossal water masses on the wall.

'So why isn't it a good investment?' he demanded to know. His voice had acquired a sulking touch, he hated that things were not going his way. He had taken a fancy to the painting now and it felt like his living room would be nothing without this work of art.

'It will most certainly increase in value,' Alvar stated, 'but not to the same extent as other paintings. Partly because it is not an oil painting,' he continued. 'It's an aquarelle and it has been painted using an opaque technique.'

The man was taken aback, but did not want to admit to his ignorance when it came to the visual arts.

'I see.' He hesitated. 'I was wondering why the painting was behind glass.'

'Plexiglass,' Alvar said. 'Regular glass would have been too heavy. And watercolours need more protection than oils.'

'Watercolours?' He gave Alvar a confused look.

'They're sun-resistant,' Alvar said quickly, 'but the painting ought to hang on a wall which is never exposed to direct sunlight.'

Once again the man visualised his living room, as if to check out the light conditions.

'A picture with glass is difficult to hang,' Alvar said calmly, 'precisely because of the glass. I'm only telling you this now so that you have all the information.'

The man had fallen silent. He squirmed a little and seemed troubled at his own indecisiveness.

'Why didn't he paint it in oil?' he asked as if Alvar would know.

'Fritzwold has always worked with a range of techniques,' he explained patiently. 'Many artists do. And this is a very successful piece of work, in my opinion.'

The waterfall continued to cascade in front of them. Suddenly the man started to walk backwards. He walked almost as far as the opposite wall.

'You can't tell that it's not oil,' he argued, 'even from a short distance.'

Alvar could easily tell that it was, but he did not say so.

'I mean, it's not as if I have to tell anyone.'

Alvar had to smile at this so he bowed his head to conceal his reaction.

'It's a very fine painting indeed,' he said. 'Its surface is more delicate than an oil painting's, but you have nothing to fear. The waterfall will last,' he smiled, 'the waterfall has timeless appeal.'

Once again the man walked up close to the painting. He had reached the most important point.

'The price?' he said softly. Alvar could see he was nervous now.

'Thirty thousand,' Alvar replied. 'Plus the usual three per cent, but I'm sure you're aware of that.'

The man breathed a sigh of relief.

'I can afford that,' he said. 'I could actually do this.' He stood there admiring the painting a little longer. It did not lose its impact, it went on roaring, he liked the forces and the play in the torrents of water. He liked the fact that the painting was huge, almost overwhelming, as he had never seen a watercolour of this size, and in his living room the painting would almost reach the ceiling. Everyone who entered the room would instantly be met with all this force.

'But,' he then said, 'why isn't it primarily a good investment?' He had wanted to make a good investment and he was annoyed that he couldn't have everything his way.

'For several reasons,' Alvar said. 'It's not an oil painting and it's not a typical Fritzwold. Fritzwold's forte is calmer landscapes than the one he has painted here. In some respects this painting is an exception to his style. As though for once he wanted to go to town. Indeed, he normally paints far smaller paintings. His paintings sell quickly, but this one needs a special buyer. If you like the painting then you will form a special bond with it and thus you will have made a good emotional investment. That's valuable too.'

The man exhaled and took a few steps back.

'Yes,' he said. 'I'll go for it. Why the hell not?' He laughed and seemed instantly happy as if he had finally come out of the shade and ended up in the sun. 'But how am I going to get it into my car?' he wondered, looking at the parking bay outside the gallery. A dark blue Audi, the latest model, was parked there.

'Mr Krantz, who owns the gallery, will drive it home to your house,' Alvar said. 'He has a Blazer Chevrolet and it'll take most paintings. However, I can't promise you that it'll be today. It depends on how busy he is, he does all sorts of things. If you would like I can call him and find out right now.'

The man nodded enthusiastically even though the light in his eyes went out because now he could not wait to have the painting in all its glory up on his wall. He paced up and down restlessly while Alvar ran upstairs to telephone.

'Krantz,' Alvar said down the receiver, 'you won't believe this, but I've sold the waterfall!'

'Really,' said an elated Krantz down the other end, 'I have to hand it to you, Eide, I really do. Let me guess. It's a man. He's under forty. Wants to show off.'

'Correct.'

'Ask him if he works in advertising. Or, he might be an estate agent.'

Alvar could not help but smile. Krantz had a good nose after all his years in the business.

'And I'll bet he frequents some gym or other. And I'm sure he's the type who likes to do a line of coke or two at the weekend.'

'Is there anything else?' Alvar asked him, still smiling.

'He prefers red wine to beer.'

They chatted for a few minutes then Alvar went downstairs again.

'He'll deliver it tomorrow,' he said cheerfully. 'That's not too bad, is it? After all, you'll need to make room for the painting or do you have a big empty wall just waiting to be filled?'

'No,' the man had to smile, 'I don't,' he admitted. 'I have some old photos and other stuff that I need to take down.'

'And you need to get a very strong hook,' Alvar said. 'It's a heavy painting; the frame alone weighs a good deal. Please make sure that you buy the right fixings or the waterfall will land on your head.'

He nodded and followed Alvar to pay for the painting. As he took out his card, Alvar detected the minute hesitation, which occurred from time to time. However, a moment later the man seemed content once more.

'Are you local?' Alvar asked.

'Yes, I live out at Bragernes,' he said. 'Do you want me to write down my address?'

He found a pen and a piece of paper and wrote the address in very neat handwriting. He was a little edgy, the way people are when they have spent a considerable amount of money, or what they would regard as a considerable sum. A thirty-thousand-krone painting was still a modest sum in Alvar's eyes, he had sold paintings worth two hundred thousand.

'So, tomorrow afternoon it is,' he said smiling to the younger man. 'Go home and make room for the magnificent painting.'

Oh yes, he would go home immediately and make some room. He thanked Alvar for his help, and went on his way happily; he even threw a pining glance at the painting as he went out to the Audi. Alvar heard him rev up the engine. He returned to the kitchen on the first floor. He felt very pleased with himself. He had sold a huge Fritzwold and he had been honest the whole time. He immediately sank his teeth into a sandwich. He was now so hungry that his stomach was rumbling. He ate slowly as he listened to a radio programme. Half the day had already gone. Life's not too bad, he thought, I enjoy it here, I do. I haven't achieved a great deal, but then again not everyone does. Some stick their necks out, they choose to take risks, others seek the path of least resistance. He was suddenly reminded of his parents and how they had lived their lives. It's none of our business, his mother always said, whenever anything happened. Her attitude to life was that people should take care of themselves. She did not want her life upset.

His father had been a silent and shy man who never showed any initiative; Alvar had barely known who he was. And thus I became a decent, but very defensive man, he thought, and that is fine. It makes life simple, no conflicts, no unexpected events. A little flat, perhaps, a little dull. But comfortable. In the evening I can relax with a good book and sometimes I treat myself to a sherry. Only one, but it's a large one. I sleep well. I have no friends, but then again no enemies either. He swallowed coffee in between mouthfuls of sandwich and looked out of his window onto the street below. A steady stream of cars was heading for the town centre. Having finished his lunch, he returned to the workshop. He wanted to frame a few more pictures, he enjoyed tinkering downstairs.

On the wall hung a picture by Danilo. The painting was in the gallery's workshop as it was still drying. Krantz had been visiting the artist in his studio, he had bought it instantly and brought it to the gallery to allow it to dry. Danilo was easy to sell. It was quite a charming picture, not one of his more impressive ones, but nevertheless, reasonably well executed and it was priced at ten thousand. Alvar went over to the picture, stopped, legs apart. The subject was a bowl of strawberries. It had been tipped over, the red glistening berries had rolled out onto a rustic wooden table. The berries were so ripe, so juicy that you felt like sinking your teeth into them. Alvar stood there looking at the moist, shiny surface. And then suddenly, like a bolt from the blue, he raised his right hand. Then he planted his thumb right in the middle of a strawberry. The paint smeared. He quickly withdrew his hand and jumped as if he had received an electric shock. What kind of behaviour was this? And his thumb covered in red paint. Terrified, he moved closer. He could clearly see the lines of his thumbprint. For a moment he was paralysed. Where had that impulse come from, and what did it mean? He was not someone who felt the need to draw attention to himself in any way, surely? Baffled, he went looking for a bottle of turpentine. It was easy to remove the paint from his finger. He stared at the painting once more. Look, there was the Danilo with his own thumbprint. Someone would buy that painting and hang it in their living room, but they would never know about this print, Alvar Eide's secret signature. He began cutting glass, cardboard, he sawed lists. He tagged and he glued. He hummed to himself, but he was disturbed. It was only a sudden impulse, he thought, trying to reassure himself and calm his pounding heart.

Nothing to fret about.

CHAPTER 5

It was five in the afternoon when Alvar left the gallery.

First he checked in the mirror to make sure his hair was in place. He put the plate and his mug in the dishwasher, he checked that every room was clear of customers. He locked the door and activated the alarm. He took the first right and wandered down towards Albumsgate, came out at Bragernes Square and strode purposefully across the large open space. Pigeons were sneaking around hunting for crumbs. He noticed the old man who always sat on a bench with a bag of stale bread, leaning forward, his hands trembling and a confusion of birds between his legs. He saw several of the town's homeless people stagger around, their eyes vacant. The sight of them made him feel despondent, they were so pathetic and shabby, every single one of them pricked his conscience. He sneaked past them averting his eyes, turned into the pedestrian area and headed for the Cash and Carry; he wanted to get himself something quick and easy for dinner. Something simple, something from the deli counter he could reheat in his microwave. The store was big, he preferred the smaller shops, but they didn't have a deli counter like the Cash and Carry.

He took a number and queued patiently and quietly. When it was finally his turn, he hesitated. Hotpot, lasagne or casserole? He opted for the lasagne, he knew it was good. He bought a large piece and had it wrapped in foil before moving on with his basket. He found a bag of ground coffee and a half-litre of milk. That was everything he needed, the modest shopping basket of a bachelor. He went to the checkout and joined another queue. And it was while he was waiting that he started to look at the trolleys around him. People shopped to excess, the trolleys were loaded. He looked at his own purchases and felt how sad they looked, surely anyone would guess that he lived alone. That no one was waiting for him, that his flat was empty. He did not mind living on his own, but right now he minded that it was so obvious to other people. That man over there, they might be thinking, he's never found someone, there's probably something wrong with him, a loner, an outsider. Finally it was his turn to be served and he placed his modest purchases on the belt, paid and left the shop. He turned left, passed the light-bulb factory and began the long, slow ascent to his home. The Green family in the ground-floor flat had two teenage children, a boy and a girl. He would sometimes see them in the morning on their way to school. They were both laden down with heavy rucksacks as they walked out through the gate, and every time he saw them it struck him that it was hard to tell them apart. They were wearing the same type of clothing, they were exactly the same height. Perhaps they're twins, it suddenly occurred to him, he had never thought of that before.

He walked calmly and contentedly up the hill and arrived at the front garden. Let himself in and carefully hung up his coat in the hall. He went into the kitchen. He unwrapped the lasagne and put it in the microwave, then he laid the table in the living room for dinner. He placed the newspaper he had just bought next to his plate and poured water into a jug. Three minutes later the microwave emitted a ping and he burned his fingers as he lifted out his plate. He ate extremely slowly, alternating between reading the newspaper and looking out of the window. The large room had four windows, which let in plenty of light, and he had several green plants, they were lush and verdant. The furniture was the same as when his mother had been alive, it was heavy and solid and he would never manage to wear it out. It didn't bother him that it was old-fashioned. It was comfortable to sit in and he thought it was nice. There was also a large fireplace made from soapstone. On the mantelpiece stood seven crystal trophies, which his father had won at bridge. They were not particularly attractive, but he could not make himself throw them out, in some way they were a family heirloom. A family which would cease to exist when he himself died. In eleven years' time when the bomb went off. As he was sitting there quietly minding his own business, he heard a sudden bang. Something had happened in the street outside, glass was shattering, metal screeched and he jumped out of his chair and ran to the window. Two cars had collided. He stood, as if nailed to the spot, staring at the accident. The cars had come to a stop diagonally across the street; the tarmac was covered with shards of glass. A distressing silence followed. A couple who had been walking on the pavement now came rushing across the street to help. One of the car doors was opened and an elderly man staggered out. He supported himself against the car, slumping helplessly against the metal. Then the other driver stepped out. He, too, just stood there looking lost and cradling his head with both hands. For a while they remained there staring at one another, incapable of action. Alvar's heart was pounding and suddenly the memories came flooding back. They knocked him sideways and he staggered across to the sofa, collapsed onto it and leaned forward over the coffee table. He sat there breathing heavily, trying to pull himself together, but to no avail.

His cheeks were scarlet with shame. The shame that was the reason he would never be able to connect with another human being. To him this shame was visible, his eyes glowed with it and that was why he always averted his eyes whenever anyone looked at him. Even now, after so many years. As the memories overwhelmed him, something inside him ripped open and began haemorrhaging. They had gone for a drive in his father's lemon-coloured Anglia. A Sunday one spring. How old was I then, he thought, seven, maybe eight years old? He was sitting alone in the back looking out of the windows. He could hear his mother chatting in the front. His father drove and said nothing.

'Look at that garden, Emmauel,' he heard, 'look at those roses. They must be Nina Weibull, they're thriving. I think we should consider planting Nina Weibull around the house, they're so hardy.

It's some house, I must say. Why do people need so much extra space? I'm so glad I'm not living in a tower block, those flats look like nesting boxes, don't you think? Look at that awful plastic pool in those people's garden. It makes you wonder what people are thinking, it looks so tacky. Oh, a whole wall of clematis! I've often thought that we ought to plant clematis on the west wall, Emmauel, what do you think?'

His father was still silent. He leaned forward and hugged the steering wheel. By now they had reached the countryside and the houses were fewer and far between. The landscape glided past. Alvar sat in the back quietly enjoy the reassuring hum of the engine. He sat with his hands folded and stared; here were some chubby-looking sheep, over there a herd of fat, red cows. From time to time, but not often, a car coming from the opposite direction would pass them.

'Those people have a double garage, would you believe it?' he heard his mother say. 'I can't imagine how people can afford to have two cars. But I suppose they have to. And look, there's also a rusty old wreck blighting their farm. I don't know why people don't have their old cars towed away.'

'Perhaps they need it for spares,' his father mumbled from behind the wheel.

His objections were meek and drained of strength. Alvar's ears pricked up. His parents did not seem aware that he was present in the car, they were in an adult world of their own, and if he wanted to snap them out of that, he would have to ask them something. He did not do that, he was a polite child, he sat very still watching everything they drove past. Some people were out walking their dogs, he saw a couple of cyclists.

After they had been driving for a while they spotted something ahead of them on the road. Alvar sat bolt upright, craned his neck trying to get a good look. It was a car crash. It must have just happened as there were neither police nor ambulances in attendance. One car was lying off the road on its roof, another was crushed and had ended up diagonally across the road. His father slammed on the brakes. The Anglia swerved to the right and came to a halt. People were standing around the wrecked cars screaming. One man had blood pouring from his forehead, another was still in his car, slumped across the wheel. A woman spotted them and came staggering towards them, blood gushing from her head.

Then something happened that Alvar found utterly incomprehensible. His mother started screaming.

'No, no!' she cried. 'We're not going to stop, I'm sure they've already called an ambulance, there's nothing we can do, Emmauel, drive on. Drive on right now!'

Her voice was so panicky that Alvar's heart froze. All three of them remained in the car staring, horrified, at the injured people and the damaged vehicles. The woman with the head wound was approaching the Anglia, Alvar could hear her pleading voice, he curled up on his seat in a foetal position. Again his mother screamed that they should drive on, she was banging the dashboard with one hand; he had never seen her so frenzied. His father clung to the steering wheel struggling with his conscience, torn between the urge to help and the strong woman in the passenger seat who had such power over him. Alvar was now pressing his face against the rear window staring at the injured woman. She stared frantically back at him and stretched out her white hands as if trying to get hold of him.

'Drive on, Emmauel, now!' his mother screamed again.

'But,' his father stuttered, 'they're badly hurt!'

She spun round in her seat. 'So you're a doctor now, are you? Do you know anything about what to do in an emergency situation? No? Now drive! The ambulance is on its way, I'm sure I can hear it coming! I want you to drive now.'

His father put the car in gear; Alvar held his breath. The woman had now reached their car, she was still staring at Alvar with pale, frightened eyes and blood was pouring down her cheeks. Alvar stared back horrified because his parents were running away from it all and he felt a sudden pang in his chest as if a cord had been severed. The magnitude of their betrayal nearly knocked him unconscious. He buried his face in his hands and huddled in a corner, he felt a shame so great that his entire body burned with it. The woman had seen him. He knew he would never forget her eyes and her white outstretched hands, hands he never got to take. His father pushed the accelerator and changed into second gear, the car leapt forward.

'Someone else will deal with this,' his mother shouted, 'it's not our problem!'

'But,' his father said in his meek voice, 'running away like this –'

'We're not running away,' his mother interrupted him, 'we realise that there's nothing we can do. Do you know how to do chest compressions, can you stop bleeding? No, you can't and neither can I.'

'All the same,' his father stuttered, hunched over the wheel, 'perhaps we could have helped them in some other way.'

'And what way would that be? Can you do mouth-to-mouth resuscitation? No, you can't. And we don't even have a first-aid kit in the car, not as much as a single plaster, so how would we be able to help them?'

Alvar held his breath. His mother had become hysterical, she was rocking backwards and forwards in her seat, there were red patches on her cheeks.

At that moment they finally heard the sirens, faintly at first, then they grew stronger.

'I told you so,' his mother said triumphantly. 'Someone's on their way who'll know how to deal with this; we're ordinary people, Emmauel, we can't get involved with such terrible things, we would only make it worse. You're not supposed to lift an injured person, they could become paralysed. Do you hear, Alvar?' Suddenly she turned towards the back seat and looked at him, her face was flustered. Alvar kept silent, he was terrified. His father gritted his teeth and drove on. At a slightly lower speed now, shaken by what had happened.

Alvar sat on the sofa remembering this incident. And it occurred to him that he had inherited his mother's cowardice. It was linked to an inability to take action and it was sown in him at that very moment. The moment when the woman staggered across the road stretching out her hands and his father had sped away. And Alvar felt that something inside him had been snapped clean off. That was why as an adult he was incapable of connecting with another person. Why he discreetly, but at the same time very efficiently, blocked any attempt at conversations with others. He hated using the telephone, for example. He could barely manage to make a call should a situation arise which he could not manage on his own. Whenever the telephone rang his heart leapt into his mouth. It was ridiculous, and yet it was real. He just wanted to be alone in his own universe, without having to deal with anything. He got up and returned to the window, peering out nervously. A police officer had arrived; he was making notes on a pad.

Later, as Alvar sat in front of his television watching the news, he pondered this cowardice again. It was mankind's worst feature. Everyone sat, like him, watching misery on a global scale while they all thought that somebody else ought to do something about it. His thoughts made him feel depressed and he found a book on the shelf, turned off the television and made himself comfortable. Reading was always comforting. He instantly disappeared into a world of fiction and everything around him was forgotten. He read for two hours, then he went to the bathroom and had a shower. Afterwards he made his packed lunch for the next day, put four shirts and some underwear in the washing machine and returned to his seat in front of the television. He watched a programme until the washing machine had finished. Then he hung his shirts on hangers, turned off all the lights in the living room, cleaned his teeth and went to bed. His eyelids began to close. He thought about this day which was now over. The crash outside his window, the disturbing memories. Nevertheless, he thought, quietly contented, no big, nasty surprises, no situations he was incapable of dealing with. No great joys either, but he was okay, in good health and sleepy. He had sold two pictures. And tomorrow would come and it would be exactly like today, filled with the same activities in the same order. The years would pass and the days would remain the same, broken into short segments, which he would live through one by one. In time he would start to slow down, become more sluggish. His vision would deteriorate, as would his hearing. So his life would proceed until the fifty-three years, which he believed he had been allocated, were up.

Suddenly a thought struck him like someone throwing a spear at his chest. The feeling made his eyes widen. What was this? A distressing feeling of panic. Surely he was not going to start having trouble sleeping now? He had never had any problems with that. Perhaps it was his age, was he about to go through a midlife crisis, like some men did when they reached their forties? He turned over onto his side and pushed the spear away. He felt as if it had scratched him. He exaggerated his breathing, making it deep and even and felt how tired he was. Of course, it was naive to think that nothing would ever happen to him, something happened to most people, surely he was no exception. But what would happen to him? He sensed unease, a touch of dread. But he could see nothing in his future to fear. He sat upright in bed. Went out into the bathroom and drank a glass of water. That was it, he thought, it was thirst, nothing more. He returned to his bed and lay down, closed his eyes. Surely there was an interference in the silence, which he had never been aware of before? Why had he suddenly started noticing things? Perhaps there's something missing in my life? A distraction. He kept thinking about the cat. He wanted a grey one. He wanted a tom. He could put an ad in the paper, or he could think about it, at any rate. Again he turned over in his bed. It was strange. Something in his life was upsetting him, he had a premonition of upheaval. And he could not understand it.

However, the next morning everything was as it always had been. He contemplated the night before and remembered his uneasiness, but it had passed. He shaved in front of the mirror in the bathroom. The growth of his beard was exceedingly modest, but he enjoyed the ritual even though strictly speaking he could get away with shaving every other day. He used a razor. He liked going out into the fresh air and feeling the unique sensation which newly shaven skin always gave him. The weather was a little overcast and he walked along easily and contentedly. A steady flow of people was heading for the town centre. Big wheels turning, he thought, we keep this machine in motion, we don't give up, it's touching. What if we all were to lie down and give up? It was inconceivable. It was a question of keeping death at arm's length. It will come to us, but we pretend it won't, because it's obviously not going to happen today, and probably not tomorrow either, and definitely not next week. That too is touching, he thought. He was not scared of dying. But on one occasion he had articulated the following thought to himself: the last thing you lose is your hearing. So it was possible that he could be lying in a bed and someone would be sitting by his side checking that his breathing and heartbeat had ceased, someone who would then say: he's gone. That he might, in fact, lie there for several seconds knowing that he had just died. What would that be like? Was it the case that some people experienced such a moment? A moment they could never tell anyone about? As far as his own death was concerned he had few wishes, but he hoped that he would be lying in his own bed when it happened. It was less important to him whether he was alone or might have a carer sitting beside his bed. Many died alone.

He walked on and began to wonder why he was so preoccupied with death. Perhaps it was the previous day's uneasiness manifesting itself after all? No, he was in the midst of life and that was the time when such thoughts arose. Children and the young are immortal, he thought, and that is their privilege, but in the end it comes to us all. I'm of an age where I start to reflect and it is a good age. I'm better off now as an adult than I was as a child. Not that I had a bad childhood, not at all. My parents were kind and loving. True, they were shy bordering on awkward. He could find nothing to reproach them for, yet something had been missing. A sense of belonging. He remembered Magnus, a friend from his childhood, who had moved away the summer they both turned thirteen and whom he had never seen again. After Magnus he never made another friend. But he managed fine on his own. Again he thought about other people and how they sought each other out. Not to mention men and women and their eternal search for love. He did not comprehend that either. Did they consider themselves incomplete without a partner? And then there was sex. He realised that he lacked something that many others had. However, many people went without sex, it was perfectly possible to live a celibate life. What if I tried sex, he thought, blushing instantly, would I then start to need it? Maybe. Perhaps it was something you could become addicted to, like food and drink.

He had reached the church and he looked up at the cemetery. This is where I'll end up one day, he thought, and it's beautiful. On a hill above the town. He had put money aside for his funeral and he also had some savings. Seventy thousand kroner. He was a regular saver. He was not saving up for anything in particular, but it was always good to have something set aside for a rainy day. During the time he had worked at Gallery Krantz he had bought some prints and a few drawings. Not expensive items, but pictures that he really appreciated. He had often dreamt of finding the one painting that was destined for him. Because he believed it existed, he had seen it happen many times in the gallery. A customer would enter and stop in their tracks in front of a picture mesmerised. And they would be rooted to the spot, they would be incapable of returning to their home without this painting. The painting was something they had been searching for, something they had been missing. He never thought it was an act, but a precious moment. A unique meeting between the artist and the spectator, a singular language, which would be understood by a chosen one and would seduce him. Personally he had never encountered such a picture.

He greatly appreciated the coal drawings of Käthe Kollwitz, but Kollwitz was out of reach both in terms of price and in other ways. But something along those lines, he thought. In fact, the artist's name was less important; however, the impact had to match that of

Kollwitz if it were to move him. Few artists had such an impact. But if he were ever to spend his seventy thousand kroner on anything it would surely have to be a painting. He had often thought that he might do a bit of travelling, but it had remained a thought. Although he fancied a trip to Copenhagen at some point, a weekend break perhaps. Potter about in the friendly Danish atmosphere, eat warm open sandwiches with liver pâté and crispy bacon, have a Tuborg and a snapps or a 'lille en', as Danes called it. However, he preferred his flat, and from this base he went for walks in the town and surrounding area. For example, he often drove up to Spiralen and went for long walks through the forest. There were people and dogs he could watch, there was nature with its smells and mild breezes. There was a view. And last but not least a lovely café where he would buy a roast beef sandwich with remoulade. On a few occasions someone had struck up a conversation with him and he had stopped and replied politely, but he never encouraged a lengthy conversation. He went to the cinema from time to time. He studied the film reviews in the newspaper and whenever he came across something interesting, off he would go to buy a ticket. He had seen many excellent films. He liked sitting in the dark cinema with all the other people he would never have to talk to. And munching some chocolate, a Cuba bar perhaps. He even liked the adverts, he found them entertaining. He liked going out into the street afterwards, filled with this experience, if the film had been a good experience and it had been on some occasions. He never got tired of playing Mozart's Requiem on his stereo. He thought the best paintings were good enough to hang on a living-room wall a whole lifetime, and would last into the next generation. Though if he were to buy a picture there would be no one to leave it to; however, this did not worry him unduly, after all, when you are dead you are dead and he was not troubled by how strangers might dispose of his property. A retirement home? he thought next. No, not a retirement home, not at any cost. True, his mother had spent three years in a retirement home and been looked after very well, but there was no way he was going there. He wanted to stay in his home. He was going to die in his own bedroom even if he did end up needing home care. He could not imagine it any other way.

There, he had reached the gallery. He entered the code and disabled the alarm, opened the door and went inside. All the pictures hung there. They were like old friends to him. Selling a picture was always an ambiguous experience. It meant it disappeared and he would never see it again. Pictures he had been studying for several months could suddenly be snatched away. But then a joyful event followed, which never failed to lift his spirits. Ole Krantz would hang a new one. Today the waterfall was leaving and Alvar would miss its roaring water torrents.

CHAPTER 6

'I'm starting to feel a little worried,' Alvar says, stopping in the middle of the floor. 'I didn't mean to disturb you, you know it's not in my nature; but as I said, I'm worried. I have trouble sleeping. I can't handle that. Suddenly I'm lying in my bed overcome with panic.'

His voice is troubled.

I am sitting in front of the computer, my fingers skate quickly across the keyboard. There are times it becomes flexible like a ribbon in my hands and I can bend and twist the language any way I please. Alvar comes up behind me, shifting nervously from one foot to the other.

'Are you really going to burden me with your sleeping problems and anxiety?'

I turn round and give him a somewhat patronising look.

'Everyone struggles with anxiety,' I say. 'Can you feel how it eats away at you? In here, behind your ribs?' I tap my chest with my finger. 'A cowardly rat sits in here gnawing its way through your ribs. It hurts.'

'But I'm a decent man,' he says, 'I always keep my affairs in order.'

I turn off the computer, turn round in my chair and look at him again. 'Yes, that's true. At the same time you're all alone. It's dangerous to go through life without someone you can lean on. In certain circumstances it might well prove to be extremely dangerous for you.'

'In certain circumstances,' he echoes, 'that you are about to put me in?'

I get up from my desk and go to my armchair, sit down and light up a cigarette.

'What will be will be,' I say to him over my shoulder. He follows me. He stands with his hands folded. It is grey outside the windows. Heavy and wet, no hint of wind or movement.

'That rat,' I continue, 'which gnaws at us all, it never feels satisfied. We constantly seek relief in every way possible. And on rare occasions it allows us a brief respite. Do you know what it's like when everything suddenly falls into place, when that feeling floods your body? It's like taking off from a great height. We float through the air and everything around us is warm. For a few brief seconds we think how great life can be. You'll have such moments too, I promise you.'

He sits down on the sofa, on the edge as usual.

'Are people supposed to settle for a few brief moments of happiness?' he asks, dismayed.

'That's a good question. It's up to each and every one of us to decide. The majority spend most of their day looking for some kind of relief. A cigarette, a bottle of red wine. A Cipralex, going for a run. I won't deprive you of sleep, Alvar, I promise you. But you have come to my house. I have seen you close up and some events are inevitable. At this point in the story I'm no longer free, there is a clear structure and I have to work within it.'

'That doesn't make any sense,' he says. 'You can use your imagination. It may not be boundless, but you have artistic licence.'

'Think of my imagination as a lake with a thousand outlets,' I say. 'Rivers, streams and waterfalls. I flounder in this lake while I look around for an outlet. If I drift in a certain direction then I am swept along by the current. It may carry me towards a waterfall or towards a peaceful pond. The point I'm making is that as I'm drifting I cannot turn and choose another route. From then on all I can do is describe what I see on my way. That particular landscape, the vegetation and the people I pass.'

'So you're drifting?' he says anxiously. This revelation makes him blink.

'Yes,' I say. 'I'm drifting. But I do have some tools. Because other people have an ability to intervene, interfere or cause change. Someone might build a dam and divert the river. A waterfall is directed through pipes. Farmers discover the stream and use it to water their fields. So I might end up somewhere completely different from where I had imagined.'

'Nevertheless, you can choose to give me a happy ending,' he pleads. 'You can determine in advance that everything will turn out all right. All this talk of drifting is making me nervous.'

'There are many things which are hard to accept, Alvar. And true, there are people who are masters of their own destinies. But you're not one of them. You're not a proactive person. Neither am I.'

'But you work several hours every single day,' he objects. 'You make things happen. You can dole out love and happiness.'

'Yes,' I reply, 'it's like blowing on embers in a fire, they flare up instantly. But I am watching you from a distance and I describe what I see. It's rare for me to act. We are very like each other, you and I. And that's why it's possible for me to tell your story. In some ways you live your life through the pictures in the gallery. You live in a fictitious world of people and landscapes. I live my life through all the characters I invent. If it's any comfort I do know how you feel.'

He buries his head in his hands. 'No, there's no comfort in the fact that others feel the same way, it's no consolation that others are worse off. I watch people as I walk through the town, they drift around Bragernes Square. Drug addicts. Stiff-legged and pale with glassy eyes. I see that they are in pain, but they're none of my business. The strength I have I need for myself. To live a decent life that no one can find fault with. People come into the gallery every day, they chat to me, but these are brief conversations and then they leave; I have no need to expose myself, I don't want to get involved with them. I don't want to know if they are feeling bad. I am probably selfish and it troubles me. Why did you have to mention that rat? Now that image is in my head for ever. Now it's gnawing at me too.'

'Perhaps it's a sign of things to come?' I say. 'Now, try to take it easy. You're at the front of the queue now, it's finally your turn. You have questions and they will be answered. Consider yourself privileged. I can delete unpleasant things as well. If only you knew what I would give to erase certain chapters from my own life.'

He gets up from the sofa and paces the room restlessly.

'Please may I ask you a question?' he says.

'Feel free.'

'When you're in bed at night, I mean before you fall asleep and everything in the house is quiet, do you think about me then?'

'Every single night,' I reply. 'I follow you with my mind's eye.'

'How much do you see?'

'Everything.'

'So you're inside my very home?'

'Further than that,' I say. 'I follow you into your bedroom, I watch you when you sleep.'

'And you have your own ideas?'

'Yes, I have my own ideas. Every day I notice something new. A minor observation that tells me something about who you really are and what is going to happen. For example, I see you turn off the lights in your flat. You carry your coffee cup to the kitchen, or your glass if you have treated yourself to a sherry, you rinse it under the tap. Next you go into the bathroom where you brush your teeth and wash your hands before turning off the light in there as well, you like saving electricity. You continue into your bedroom and you undress. You fold your clothes neatly and place them on a chair. I watch you slip under the covers and set your alarm clock. Then you allow yourself to sink into the mattress as you give yourself a few minutes to think about the day that has just gone. You're about to turn off your bedside lamp when you notice that you did not fold your trousers properly, they will crease in the wrong place, so you get out of bed to refold them. As you have got out of bed anyway, you go over to the window. You look out into the street, which lies so silently outside, perhaps you see a lonely person wander by in the darkness and you count yourself lucky that you can hide behind the curtain and won't ever have to know how it feels to be the person wandering in the night on his own. You go back to bed, you always lie on your side with your knees pulled up. You don't pray because you know no God, but then again you feel no emptiness either. The alarm clock ticks. You like the silence and the darkness and your thoughts move on to the next day. You trust that everything will be fine, that you will be able to do everything which is expected of you. Your eyes glide shut, your breathing slows down. At that moment I always feel a great sense of calm. I let you rest for a long time and when I feel my own strength returning I wake you up to a new day. Then I take your hand and we continue the journey together.'

He lets the air out of his lungs.

'Do you see anyone else apart from me?' he asks shyly.

I smile a little. 'How do you mean?'

'I mean it's a long queue outside. Your computer is full of drafts, unresolved fates hanging in the air. Does it ever happen that your eyes are drawn in another direction? Might you follow someone else and forget about me?'

'That would be such a relief,' I admit, 'if I could forget about you for one moment. But you're very persistent, you don't make it easy for me, and that surprises me because you're a mild-mannered person. However,' I add, 'we all wish to be seen. Even a lone wolf hungers for a brief glance. He only shuns other people because he has abandoned all hope that they'll notice him, but the longing for a warm hand on our shoulder is there all the time. Someone who stops you in your stride and asks how are you, do you need anything, anything I can give you? You think of yourself as a man of few needs. You make no great demands, all the time you take what you're given and that's not a lot. But you've shown your true colours by stepping out of the queue, Alvar, because you do need something and that requires a certain amount of courage. Now I'm rewarding you just like you asked me to. And now I'm asking you to leave so I can think in peace.'

But he does not leave, he lingers. He examines the objects in my living room, the angel on the bookshelf with its wings outstretched, the icon on the wall, my pictures. The small wooden casket on the top of the chest of drawers.

'That's a beautiful casket,' he says stepping forward to study it more closely.

'Yes,' I say. 'Hand-carved. From Indonesia. I'm fond of that casket, it's important.'

'What do you keep in it? Letters?'

I shake my head. 'The casket is filled with worries.'

His eyes widen. 'What do you mean? Bills?'

His literal thinking makes me laugh.

'No, it's like I say. The casket is filled with worries, all kinds of worries. I write them down and place them in the casket and then I slam the lid shut. So they can lie there in the darkness and never materialise.'

'May I take a look?' he asks cautiously.

I shrug in resignation. 'If you want to. Even though I think worries are very personal.'

He lifts up the lid. Looks at the little heap of white scraps of paper. Picks one of them up. Reads it.

'"This novel won't be good enough. I'm going to get slaughtered."'

'Precisely,' I say earnestly. 'That's how it is. That's what I think.'

He takes another one, holds it up.

'"I probably won't grow very old."'

'That's something I've always known,' I explain. 'And I can live with that, it's fine.'

'"Alvar Eide won't make it."'

He shudders and looks at me in horror.

'There, there,' I say, 'it was just a spontaneous outburst. As I told you, I follow the current and I promise you that I will use all the literary skill I possess to save you from destruction.'

But now he is deeply worried. He slams the lid shut, goes to the window. Stares out at the azalea by the entrance.

'Not a single leaf is moving,' he says, 'even though there must be thousands of them, gossamer-thin leaves on stems as delicate as silk. Not one movement, not a tremor. Where is nature's overwhelming force?'

He turns round and looks me in the eye. 'Is it the calm before the storm, I wonder?'

CHAPTER 7

The waterfall was swiftly replaced by a merry-go-round.

Ole Krantz had hung it in the space that had belonged to Reidar Fritzwold, and the change in the room was striking because the painting was smaller and darker. When Alvar let himself into the gallery, he stopped short, took it in. The painting was unusually detailed. One metre square, with an extravagant gilded frame. Thin layers of paint, fine brushstrokes and gaudy colours. Alvar stood still, staring at the painting with one hand under his chin, leaning forward slightly with squinting, peering eyes. A big, old-fashioned merry-go-round from a fair, with black-and-white horses, snorting, galloping on shiny hooves. There was a rider on each horse, dressed in bizarre clothing. The picture lacked a focus, a centre that the eyes would be drawn to; he felt how his eyes flittered, jumping about looking for something, a point, a revelation. On his journey around the painting he noticed all the details, the reins of the horses, a boot with a shiny buckle, a broad-brimmed hat with a feather. A glove-clad hand, a whip, a spur, a velvet jacket with gold buttons. The canopy above the merry-go-round was beautifully decorated; there were red and green lanterns, an elegant cast-iron structure which held it all together. His eyes kept jumping about looking for somewhere to settle.

Finally, after a very long time, he made an unexpected discovery. It made him step back. The riders sitting on the horses were all dead. He had not spotted that at first, all he had seen was the merry-go-round, the horses and the long, colourful garments. Now he could see that the riders were ghosts, they grinned at him with yellow teeth. Their eye sockets were black holes and they cracked their whips and rode the horses in ecstasy and with malicious joy. He stepped back a bit further to get a better perspective. What was there to say about this picture? he thought perplexed; someone might want to buy it and it was vital to have some observations ready. A skilled art dealer would never stand dumbfounded in front of a picture. Well, he could highlight the element of surprise, that the merry-go-round was ridden by ghosts, that at first sight they looked as if they were enjoying themselves, a colourful experience, until the truth was brutally flung in your face. Death rides a merry-go-round, he thought, how disturbing. Once this discovery was made the picture became more of a clever display. Painted with a confident hand, that much was true, with a precision bordering on photographic, but apart from that the picture lacked soul. He narrowed his eyes and considered it. Many years in the gallery had turned Alvar into a connoisseur.

The picture was priced at eighteen thousand kroner and was likely to be sold quickly. To someone with little knowledge of art. Some-one young. A man. No more than thirty-five years old. Someone it was easy to impress, someone who enjoyed gimmicks. Here I will need to highlight the painter's striking technique and the fine strokes, Alvar thought. The richness of detail, the colours. As he leaned forward again he noticed to his amazement that a few of the skulls had tiny white dots in their sockets. You had to be very close to detect them and it required a great deal of light. This was something he would need to mention to the future buyer. This painting needs a picture light above it if you are to see all the details, he would have to say. It varied from painting to painting. Some lit up all on their own, such as those by Advocat or Sitter. He went upstairs to make coffee. The merry-go-round haunted him for a few minutes; he started to think it might be an omen. After all, death had been on his mind a fair amount the last few days and now it had followed him into the gallery. But he dismissed it. No, it's only human to ponder death. They always had pictures with elements of death in them, this was merely a coincidence. Slowly he drank his coffee while he leafed through the local paper. Every now and again he looked up at the monitors.

The first customer arrived at eleven in the morning and entered briskly and purposefully. A woman of about fifty wearing a sea-green knitted coat. She smiled softly and in recognition as he came down the stairs; she had been there often, he knew her well. No, not *knew*, because he knew no one, but he was aware of how she behaved and this gave him a sense of calm. She was one of those mature women who were at ease with themselves and their lives, and Alvar could relax. Now she took off her gloves and looked around the gallery. Took a few steps forward and stopped.

'What a ghastly picture,' she laughed, taking in the merry-go-round. 'Who painted that?'

'An Englishman,' Alvar replied. 'His name's Wilkinson.'

He suppressed a comment to the effect that he did not like it either; it was a risk he could not afford to run, his primary purpose was to sell it, after all. But the way he saw it, it was vital that it was sold to the right buyer and this woman was not the right one. Although she might not like the picture personally she might want to give it to someone else; he always had to bear such things in mind.

'I don't like it,' she admitted. 'There's something wrong with this picture. Don't you think?'

Alvar exhaled deeply. Now he could relax and answer her question honestly.

'It doesn't come alive,' he explained. 'The painter wants to depict a jarring moment, but his expression is frozen, almost stylised. This subject should be generating a great deal of noise, but notice how silent it is.'

'But it's a picture of ghosts,' she smiled, 'they're not meant to be alive, are they?'

'No, perhaps not,' he smiled back. 'But there's something about this painter, he's missing something. The way I see it it's nothing but a clever display.'

She agreed with him, yet remained standing in front of the merry-go-round for a long time.

'Some yuppie will come along and buy it,' she stated.

'Yes, that was my thought too,' he admitted. 'Someone who likes to show off a bit.'

He looked at her politely. 'So what can I do for you today?'

'Nothing at all,' she said. 'I just wanted to pop in to see if you had anything new. Something exciting.'

'I've sold the waterfall,' he told her.

'Yes, of course, it's gone!' She spun round and stared open-mouthed. 'I'll really miss that,' she said. 'That waterfall was here for a long time.'

'Two and a half years,' he said.

'Who bought it?' she wanted to know.

'A yuppie,' Alvar smiled and they both laughed conspiratorially at this. Afterwards she wandered around for a long time visiting all three floors and Alvar left her to it. He returned to the kitchen and watched her on the monitors every now and again. She probably knew that he was doing this, but it did not bother her, she moved around confidently and calmly and gave herself plenty of time for each picture. At half past twelve he ate his three sandwiches. Up until now my life has been fine, he thought, once his hunger had started to abate. Nothing unforeseen has happened. No big surprises, no unexpected turns. Other people are struck down by all sorts of things and here I am eating my lunch without a care in the world. He thought that it would last. He was once more lost in his newspaper when he heard the bell downstairs. He raised his eyes and looked at the right-hand monitor. Something resembling a grey shadow had entered the gallery.

A grey shadow.

Alvar remained sitting staring at the monitor as he watched it slip quietly through the door. Then it stopped and stood immobile on the stone floor. A shadow, strange, blurred. He narrowed his eyes in order to get a better look and it occurred to him that it was obviously a person. A small person, he thought, as she glided towards the wall. A woman. He thought it was a woman, but could not understand why she moved so oddly, she was rigid and fluid at the same time. Something told him instantly that this was no ordinary customer. He straightened up, scratched his cheeks nervously. But the shadow did not appear to be interested in the pictures. It was supporting itself against the wall and now it stood there motionless. The seconds ticked away and she did not move. Alvar left the kitchen and went quietly down the stairs, his heart beating faster. When he reached the ground floor she came into focus. A young woman, skinny and dressed in grey clothes. She wore tight, pointy ankle boots with incredibly high heels. A grey jacket, which came down to the middle of her thighs. It had a trim of filthy, tatty fur. Her legs, too, were very thin. Her hair was blonde and matted, wisps of it hung over her cheeks and her roots were dark. Her eyes were heavily made up. Her doll-like face was pinched and pale and all he could see were these panda eyes. They were staring at him. He stopped. What was it about her eyes? Her pupils were as tiny as pinheads. And how she trembled, she was actually shaking, as she stood there slumped against the wall. Alvar had never in all his life seen anyone as cold and translucent as this young woman. He stopped some distance away and kept watching her. His heart was pounding as he tried to get a grip on the situation.

'It's bloody cold outside,' she said feebly.

He nodded automatically. At the same time it began to dawn on him what kind of creature she was. She was a drifter, there were so many of them in this town. They normally hung out around Bragernes Square where they wandered about aimlessly. But this one here had found her way to Albumsgate and the gallery.

'Just trying to warm up,' she whispered.

She seemed both lethargic and excited at the same time. Trembling and quivering, yet she spoke slowly, slurring her words, and he realised that she had to be on something, he did not know what, but she was only partly present. Her eyes were distant, they rolled and then she closed them. She leaned upright against the wall next to the merry-go-round and she had clearly forgotten all about him. Alvar did not know what to do. He saw her thin, narrow hands and the pointy ankle boots and thought that she ought to be wearing thick-soled boots and thick woollen socks and a padded jacket and a woollen cap rather than wander around in such thin clothes, after all it was November and very cold. He saw her tiny mouth and her pretty snub nose and thought that she was in fact quite nice. And yet so incredibly ravaged. She had dark circles under her eyes, her lips were drained of colour. And she was just standing there, far away in her own world and not even aware of him. What was it Ole Krantz had told him again and again? If any drug addicts come in here, you've got to get rid of them straight away, Eide. Sometimes they come in here to shelter and you just can't trust them. Don't start talking to them, just show them the door. But she was not doing anything. She was just standing there borrowing a little of their central heating. In his head he could hear the three words he needed to say to get rid of her. Please go away. However, he was unable to open his mouth and say them. He had never ever said anything so dramatic to another human being. And as far as he was concerned she could stay there. There were no other customers in the gallery, no one who might take offence at this wretched creature.

He moved away and headed for the workshop; he could stay in there and watch her from a distance. Krantz was undoubtedly right: people like that could not be trusted. But he found it hard to imagine that she might suddenly stir, snatch a picture off the wall and then push open the door as she escaped. She doesn't even look as if she could lift a carton of milk, he thought. She was only just managing to remain upright. Suddenly he was frightened that she might collapse. He had heard that they often did that. In which case he would have to call the police. But it seemed to him to be quite ridiculous that he, a grown man, would need help to get rid of a young woman, that two broad-shouldered police officers would have to turn up to remove a girl weighing forty kilos. And even to ring a public authority would be beyond his capabilities. She looked to be less than twenty years old and her skin was transparent like delicate paper. When he had been standing in front of her, he had noticed the veins in her temples, a delicate blue-green web. At least there was real blood coursing through her body, he thought, though she looked like a zombie. Her skin was waxen. And cold. He stood in the workshop watching her through the doorway. No, she could stand there. And if a customer were to enter, he would just go over to her and politely but firmly escort her to the door. He doubted that she would resist, she seemed without a will of her own. Alvar reached for a bottle of glass polish and started polishing some graphics, which strictly speaking were in no need of being polished, but at least it gave him something to do. He kept looking at her furtively. He wanted to leave her alone. After all he was a good person. But if it had been Ole Krantz who had been working in the gallery that day she would have been turfed out instantly, Alvar was sure of that, and probably been given a piece of Ole's mind as well. There would have been swearing. Krantz was not known to be merciful. Alvar kept on polishing the pictures.

The young woman kept leaning against the wall, but suddenly she squatted down on her heels. She started blowing into her hands. Oh, dear God, how cold she is, Alvar thought, he could hardly bear to watch her. And there was the familiar nagging of his conscience again. He remembered that he had some coffee left in the coffee machine upstairs in the kitchen. Quietly he walked up the stairs and when he reached the top step he turned round and looked at her again. Some coffee. A warm mug to hold in her hands. It was a tiny gesture, it cost him nothing and after all he was a good person. He found a clean mug in the cupboard and filled it right up to the brim. He went back down the stairs. Hesitated. When he stood in front of her she looked up at him indifferently. She spotted the mug and took it without thanking him. Perhaps he had been expecting a small word of thanks, yet at the same time he understood that she had very little surplus energy for good manners. She drank the coffee greedily.

He thought that she would burn her tongue. But she did not, she carried on drinking until the mug was empty. He had never seen anyone drain a mug of hot coffee so quickly. When the mug was empty she held it out to him. A big blue mug.

'Feeling better?' he asked cautiously, taking it from her. Then something strange occurred. She held on to it. One of her fingers was hooked around the handle and a strength he would not have credited her with prevented him from getting hold of it. He stood there desperately trying to snatch the mug. Her eyes fixed him with sudden lucidity and just as he was about to let go, she released the mug and he took an involuntary step backwards. This manoeuvre wrong-footed him. She put her hands, which had now been warmed up a little by the mug, on her cheeks. Her white, cold cheeks. He thought, you have to go now. You've been here a while, someone might come. But she did not go. She stayed squatting with her hands on her cheeks and Alvar stood there utterly helpless. She's almost like a child, he thought, even though she was eighteen, yes, she had to be eighteen and thus of age. An adult. But incapable of looking after herself. So why had she come? Was she homeless? He could not imagine that she might not have a room or a home somewhere, after all she was so young. Homeless people were older, at any rate he thought so.

'Thanks,' she said suddenly. He was startled, her words were so unexpected. She had thanked him after all and he felt a tiny warm spark of joy inside.

'It was nothing,' he said softly. And then after a while: 'Are you starting to warm up?'

She looked up at him again and he noticed that her make-up-smeared eyes were actually very pale. They were bluish, like thin ice.

'I'll be gone in a minute,' she said, lowering her head again. He stared down at her dark roots. He wanted to say that she was welcome to stay, but that would not be entirely true. Besides, he was feeling rather pleased with his efforts. He was not a man to turn people away, he had a heart. And this much he knew: that many businesses in the town would not even hesitate when it came to people like her. He looked at her and said: 'I've got some work I have to do.' Then he returned to the workshop. He polished more glass. He kept glancing furtively out of the door the whole time. After fifteen minutes she got up. She staggered for a while trying to find her feet. Then, as she turned round, she noticed the paintings. It was as if she had not seen them until that moment. She'll go now, he thought, and she did. She shuffled towards the door. He had never seen a young body as ravaged as hers. She was like a doll, fragile and slender as a reed. She leaned all of her forty kilos against the door and slowly forced it open. Then she was gone.

Alvar rushed out of the workshop and over to the window. From there he watched her stumble down the street on her high-heeled ankle boots. He guessed she was heading back down to Bragernes Square in search of more drugs. That was how it was for those wretched creatures, they had to have drugs all the time. As it left their bodies, the hunger for more returned. He stood there watching her for a long time. Then she turned left and disappeared at the crossing and he lost sight of her. The large room was empty once again. He returned upstairs to the kitchen and sat down, contemplating what had just passed. How would she spend the rest of her day? And night? Did she have somewhere she could sleep? Perhaps she was a vagrant who would eventually collapse somewhere, on a bed he hoped, where she would sleep a dreamless sleep. She had to have someone. Parents or brothers and sisters. He sincerely hoped that this was the case.

He tried to read his paper again, but was unable to concentrate. He kept thinking about the kohl-black eyes, and the thin fingers, frozen blue like icicles. How do such people make it through the winter, he wondered, being outside freezing like this month after month? He was able to return to a warm flat, a hot shower. A fireplace and a bed with a feather duvet. He could not get her out of his mind. People visited the gallery, they admired all his pictures, the hours ticked away.

When the working day was over and he had tidied up after himself and locked the door, he crossed Bragernes Square to look for her, he could not help himself. To his great surprise he spotted her outside the Narvesen kiosk. She was with a man and counting coins, which she held in the palm of her hand. He did not want her to recognise him, so he walked past her at a distance. He wondered what her name might be. He wondered about the man standing next to her, he was older, thirty maybe. Scruffy and dishevelled. He hoped that she was not a prostitute, but did not want to be naive either. Addictions cost money. A lot of money. Once again he went to the Cash and Carry, as always he went to the deli counter, and bought a meal for one. A heat-and-serve casserole. God only knows when that girl last had a decent meal. Alvar walked home slowly. He heated up the food and sat down by his dining table; he felt terribly privileged. Yes, he really did. He was all alone in the world, but at least he was able to take care of himself. Not everyone was. However, it did not follow that she was a bad person, that much he understood. At the same time he was a little nervous. She had unsettled him. She had clung on to the blue mug and her glance had demolished his defences.

He thought about her a great deal in the days that followed.

Not all the time, but in brief snatches he remembered her frozen body and her kohl-black eyes. The spiky, thin fingers, the pointy ankle boots. Every time the gallery bell went he would glance quickly at the monitor, but she did not return. It was not that he hoped she would come back, but he was unable to forget her ice-blue eyes. She looked like a fallen angel, he thought, with her blonde strands of hair and her frail shoulders. She had to belong to someone. Surely someone as young as her could not be all alone in the world, he refused to believe that. Every day when he left the gallery he looked out for her on Bragernes Square, but it was as if she had vanished into thin air. Other lost souls wandered restlessly around begging alongside the pigeons. From time to time they managed to get a few crumbs too, a five or a ten kroner. In the course of a long day it probably added up to one shot of relief. A miserable but simple existence, Alvar thought, with only a single aim: more drugs.

Alvar was getting ready for Christmas. He always spent Christmas on his own and he knew how to pamper himself. He bought ribs, sausages and sauerkraut. He placed poinsettias on his windowsill, he lit candles. He burned incense; he enjoyed its sweet smell. On his door he hung a wreath of the kind normally placed on graves, they were his favourite kind. He enjoyed listening to Christmas carols on the radio; he liked the lights and decorations in town. Christmas never highlighted his loneliness, he simply pampered himself with a little extra. Sometimes he bought a chocolate yule log, cut it into thin slices and placed the slices in an elegant fan shape on a plate. He also made glühwein for the customers in the gallery. Sales increased dramatically. In fact, the last two days before Christmas were usually their best days in the whole year. When people came at the last minute they parted with their money more easily. Ole Krantz had invested in some beautiful shiny wrapping paper and the small lithographs sold like hot cakes. Life's good, Alvar thought, I can't complain, I'm doing fine. I'm a very contented man.

The new year brought cold temperatures and an abundance of fireworks over the town. Even the dome of the light-bulb factory paled in comparison with the colourful visions in the night sky. He went to bed at half past midnight. A new year had begun. He did not think that it would bring any exciting changes as far as he was concerned, but on the other hand he was not looking for exciting changes. Though minor, unexpected events were not to be sniffed at.

You never could tell.

CHAPTER 8

'Hello, it's me again, sorry to disturb you. Shouldn't you be working?'

I nearly jump out of my chair. Alvar appears behind me. He leans forward and reads a few lines on my screen.

'I'm writing a letter to a good friend,' I reply tartly. 'Is that all right with you?'

He nods, a little contrite.

'Just wanted to drop by as soon as possible to say thank you,' he says politely.

I turn round and look him in the eye.

'Thank me? For what?'

'For the girl. The poor freezing girl you sent me.'

I feel a prickle of guilt and look away.

'I mean,' he says enthusiastically, 'I got the chance to do a good deed. Of course, there is no reason to make a song and dance about a mug of coffee, but afterwards I was pleased that I did what I did.'

'That's good, then,' I say and look at the screen again.

'I'm not one to start chatting to people like that,' he goes on, 'in fact, I'm quite surprised at myself. But my own circumstances became so clear to me. How lucky I really am. And as you know, if you're well off, you have a duty to do good. Don't you think so?'

'Alvar,' I make my voice firm. 'I need to finish this letter, it's important to me. It needs to be posted today and the last post is at three thirty this afternoon.'

He folds his hands and shifts from one foot to the other. 'You're starting to get a little cross, aren't you? I spot things like that straight away. But I just wanted to mention something: I've always considered it a matter of honour to be respectful. Or to have good old-fashioned manners, if you like. But the thing is that we have a relationship, you and I, and you can't expect me to just sit back and wait when it concerns my own fate; you know I'm someone who needs to be in control.'

'Yes,' I say drily, 'I've noticed that.'

'And that's why,' he carries on, 'I must admit that I was terribly upset when this girl came into the gallery.'

'Whatever for?'

He coughs nervously covering his mouth with his hand. 'Well, we've talked about relationships. For one awful moment I thought you were going to turn us into a couple.'

I give up trying to finish the letter. I fold my arms across my chest instead and study him.

'My dear Alvar,' I say in a kind voice, 'I'm well aware that you prefer men.'

I am totally unprepared for his reaction. He flushes deeply all the way from his throat and up his cheeks. He takes a step sideways to recover his balance. Then he buries his face in his hands.

'You thought I didn't know?' I ask softly.

He does not reply, he groans. Frozen in this desperate position with his hands over his face. He wants to speak, but cannot find his voice.

'Please don't be so upset,' I comfort him.

He exhales deeply and gasps. Turns away in shame.

'Do you have to tell them that?' he whispers.

'You mean, do I have to include it in the story? We can talk about it. I obviously know more about you than what I put in the book. However, we can't prevent those who meet you from speculating. Don't underestimate people. You will never be able to control their thoughts.'

Finally he straightens up, but he finds it difficult to look me in the eye.

'I'm begging you on my knees,' he stutters. 'Please, please cut that bit, it's not as if it's important.'

I ponder this. Reluctantly. 'No, I'm not going to cut it, but I can treat it with respect.'

He begins to relax a little. He breathes a sigh of relief. 'I want to put the record straight,' he says suddenly. 'I have no such feelings for Ole Krantz. Just so you know.'

I have to smile. 'I know.'

'So we understand one another,' he says, reassured. 'And please forgive all my interventions, but I'm very shy, you know that. The idea that people can read me like an open book is unbearable.'

'It's not as scary as you think,' I reply, 'people knowing who you are. Wasn't that why you jumped the queue? You jumped the queue because you wanted to be noticed.'

'I did,' he admits instantly. 'But they don't need to know every-thing.'

'True,' I concede. 'Of course I make choices. But readers can be very perceptive, they add to the story and complete the picture. Ultimately you're protected by the boards of the book.'

Again he looks relieved.

'Will my story be several hundred pages?'

'Oh, no,' I reply immediately, 'it will be a modest story about a modest man. As I said before. If you're looking for volume, you'll have to go elsewhere.'

He runs his hand across his head, but takes care not to disturb the comb-over, which does not move. 'In other words: you don't think I'm very important? What about the woman and her dead child? They'll get more space, won't they?'

'Perhaps. I don't know yet, I've got my hands full with you. And my head,' I add, 'and my heart.' I place my hand on my chest. He smiles bashfully and looks at the floor.

'That's almost more than I had hoped for,' he says, 'that I can truly move another person. You. It's a wonderful feeling!'

Again I have to smile.

'But I'm not funny,' he warns me. 'Don't add humour to this story, it wouldn't work.'

'I don't have a sense of humour,' I confess, 'so you have nothing to fear. I'm looking for depth and drama.'

'Drama? That sounds disconcerting. Why do you have to have so much of that?'

'Drama makes the blood run faster through your veins. When the story reaches its peak that's when I feel most alive. You could do with a shot of adrenaline, you know, it's a fantastic high and totally addictive.'

'I think I'll stick with sherry,' he replies and smiles. 'There's something else. Where did you find the girl?'

'On Bragernes Square. There were several of them, all I had to do was choose one. And the one I picked stood out. She was so skinny and pale and translucent that she appeared to be almost ethereal. Did you notice her eyes? They're like ice. Her hair is like cotton grass. Her skeleton as fragile as a bird's. I felt I could snap her in half with one hand like a twig. I was taken with her frailty. She reminds me of Royal Copenhagen china.'

'That was beautifully put,' Alvar says.

'Thank you, I do try.'

'But she should be wearing something else on her feet for this time of year. Did you see her ankle boots? I've never seen such high heels, she could barely walk in them. And those boots aren't terrible warm either, did you know that? I'm sure they're synthetic, only plastic. What do you think?'

'Mm. They're plastic.'

'I mean, they must be very uncomfortable, on top of everything else. For example, she can't run in such boots, should she have to.'

'Heroin addicts don't run, Alvar, in fact they're very, very slow.'

He looks at me for a long time. 'So if something were to happen to her, she wouldn't be able to escape?'

I do not reply. I look at the screen again and my half-finished letter. I rest my chin in my hands.

'You've suddenly gone very quiet,' Alvar says. 'I'm convinced that you've thought of something, that you've just had an idea of what's going to happen.'

'That's correct. And I can't tell you what it is, I'm sure you understand.'

I look at him, he is twisting his fingers. There's something very virginal about him. A man of forty-two with his innocence intact. A man who has hidden himself away his whole life. It feels as if I'm about to throw him to the wolves. His unease is totally justified, he senses that something is about to happen. I force myself to be tough and push ahead with my plan even though I know I will cause him a great deal of pain.

'What are you thinking about?'

He looks directly at me.

'I'm thinking of everything we humans have to suffer. Restless hours filled with anxiety and distress. Sleepless nights, pain. I'm thinking of the bravery dormant in us all. How we grit our teeth and carry on. Some go with God. And those of us who don't have that option, those of us who don't lift our heads towards heaven, we walk on all the same with our heads bowed, right until our own end.'

'I can visualise what you've just said,' Alvar says. 'It's a powerful image. If I were a painter that is the very subject I would have chosen. Two people going to their deaths, one with and one without God.'

'Have you ever dreamt of being a painter?' I want to know.

'Oh, no, not ever, I don't have the talent. I'm perfectly happy just admiring the work of others. Whenever I stand in front of a painting, I can always find the words. Then I'm able, despite my shyness, to have long, in-depth conversations with another human being. However, when I'm outside on the street and someone stops me to ask directions, then I'm helpless.'

'Because there isn't a painting between you?'

'That's right. Of course, I give them a reply, but only a very brief one, and then I hurry on as quickly as I can. But in the gallery I can stand in front of a painting and talk for an hour.'

'You're an enigma,' I smile.

'Perhaps I'll surprise you along the way,' he says, looking terribly pleased with himself.

No, Alvar my dear, I think to myself, you're the one who is going to be surprised.

I turn my back on him so I can finish my letter. He stands behind me for a few minutes; I sense his presence like a shadow and I find it hard to concentrate.

'Do you ever dream about me at night?' he asks out of the blue. I sigh deeply, save the last sentence and turn round again with resignation.

'No, never. I dream vividly every single night, but I have never dreamt of you.'

He looks disappointed.

'May I ask you what you dreamt about last night?' he asks cautiously. 'I mean, if you don't think I'm being too forward?'

I lean back in my chair. I recall last night's events and the very unpleasant dream which still haunts me.

'I dreamt I was living in a city with narrow streets,' I tell him. 'I was drifting around this city; I had no mission, no purpose. Everyone was busy doing their own thing, but I wandered through the day with nothing to do. Then an important delegation came to the city, five grave-looking men dressed in black. They walked in procession through the streets carrying their heavy suitcases. One of the men was carrying a small bundle, but I couldn't see what was in it. They soon spotted me. They stopped and looked at me solemnly.

' "We have an important task for you," the man with the bundle announced. "We're here for five days, we have something very important to discuss and during those five days you must take care of this." He passed me the bundle, which was wrapped in a piece of filthy cloth. I unwrapped it and inside I discovered a baby.'

Alvar listens attentively, never taking his grey eyes off me.

'It wasn't a normal baby,' I say, 'it was the tiniest baby I'd ever seen. Three pounds at most and stark naked. Baffled, I looked at the child and the man fixed me with his eyes, then he said in a stern voice, "This is your responsibility. We will come back to collect it in five days." Then they left with their suitcases, they disappeared into the town hall and I lost sight of them. I was left standing on the cobbled street with the baby in my arms. And it wasn't just any baby, Alvar, it was slippery and smooth like a bar of soap and it immediately started to squirm, you know, like a cat struggles when it no longer wants to be held. I tried to tighten my grip on it, but despite my best efforts, it slipped from my hands and hit the cobbled street head first. I felt a sudden attack of dizziness as if I was about to pass out. Strange gurgling sounds were coming from the child's mouth, and its head on its fragile neck looked sickeningly as if it was loose. I felt nauseous with fear when I bent down to lift it up. But it was alive. It had shrunk a little, but I could see from its tiny chest that it was breathing. I started walking to a small hideaway with a simple bed and a blanket. I went inside still holding the baby and quickly lay down on the bed. There I felt safe in the knowledge that nothing would happen. We lay there until the next day. From time to time the baby made sucking noises and I realised that it needed food. I got out of bed. Very carefully I held the naked baby and went over to a bench where I had access to fresh water. I found a cup, filled it halfway and tried to pour the water into its tiny, tiny mouth; it didn't go very well. The baby began to squirm and wriggle again and in an unguarded moment it hit the ground for the second time. I heard its tiny skull smack against the floorboards. My heart skipped a beat. There was no doubt that the child had been injured, and it was as if its neck had been stretched into a long thin thread; its head was barely connected to its frail shoulders.'

I look at Alvar; he returns my gaze breathlessly.

'Again I lay down on my bed. But I understood that you can't spend your whole life in bed, you have to get up and face the world and thus risk exposing yourself and those you love. So I went out into the streets clutching the baby, pressing against the walls, looking left and right. Again the baby started to squirm, again it hit the cobbles, and when I lifted it up I thought it was dead. But I detected a weak pulse, and its head was still hanging by that thin thread that its neck had become. I crossed the square, ashamed because I had failed this simple task entrusted to me. Another four days passed and I knew that the important delegation would soon come out of the town hall to collect the child. I stared at it and could see that it had shrunk a great deal. For the fourth time I dropped the baby and I felt that hope was fading. Finally I slumped against a stone wall, leaned my head against it, clung on to the child, closed my eyes and just wanted the time to pass. And it passed, and the delegation came walking down the street with their black suitcases. I felt relieved that everything would be over soon and I could hand back the uncontrollable baby that kept squirming. They stopped a metre away from me, formed a semicircle and watched me with their black eyes.

' "The child," they said gravely.

'I handed them the bundle. My hands were shaking; I couldn't give it back soon enough. One of the men reached out to receive it. At that very moment it began to squirm violently; it shot out of my hands like a bar of soap in the shower and smashed against the cobbles. It lay there and did not stir; its neck was now as thin as a nail, and its head partly bashed in. They stood there looking at me accusingly and I was at my wits' end as to what I should do. I was weighed down by guilt and despair.

' "We gave you a simple task," they said. "And you failed."

'I could give them no answer. The baby had been in my care and I had failed. Suddenly they vanished and I was left alone.'

I stop speaking. Alvar is gawping.

'And then?' he asks eagerly. 'What happened next?'

'I woke up,' I reply. 'And thanked my lucky stars that it was only a dream. But that sense of failure has haunted me the whole day.'

I turn to the computer again; I want to finish my letter.

'But what does it mean?' he insists.

I shrug. 'Perhaps it is about you after all. I'm scared that I won't manage to hold on to you. Scared you'll slip out of my hands, that we won't make it to the end.'

'I won't squirm,' he says quickly.

I have to smile at this. 'That's true. And you're not slippery and smooth either. But you're a lot heavier than the baby. I have to carry you for a whole year and that's hard.'

'No one has ever held me like you,' Alvar says.

CHAPTER 9

January and freezing cold.

It was five to ten in the morning when Alvar let himself into the gallery. He walked across the room, stopped and looked around. He immediately made a breathtaking discovery, as if he had unexpectedly reached a hilltop and a new and unknown landscape had opened up inside him. Ole Krantz had acquired a new painting. Alvar felt a chill down his spine. Suddenly he was gripped by a force field. The painting had not been hung yet, but was propped up against the wall, beautifully lit by the big arched window in the middle. A large oil painting, strangely dark and powerful. Alvar stood as if struck by lightning while his eyes took in the subject. At first all he could see was the faint outline of a building in a dark fog, something black slowly emerging from a deep canyon. He felt the hairs on the back of his neck stand up. Now what was this? He moved closer, shaking his head. A bridge, he realised, a heavy bridge. A bridge, which disappeared into murky darkness. But it was not just a bridge. It was an unfinished construction; it ended abruptly, halfway across the void, as if the project had been halted. The bridge did not reach the other side. Or, it struck him, it had been severed; he could make out some jagged beams jutting into the fog. So the bridge led nowhere. Alvar gasped. It was a huge and violent painting and he surrendered to it. The bottomless void, the steep mountainsides, the mysterious, hazy light. This severed bridge, so majestic. But a beautiful construction, nonetheless, he could see that, simple but ingenious, beautiful and arched, delicate yet strong. But also amputated. He stood as if paralysed, staring at the bridge. Who had painted this picture? Which artist had had the idea of painting a severed bridge? He walked closer, but he was unable to read the signature. He got hold of the top of the painting and tried to tilt it. Perhaps its title was on the back? The painting was heavy even though it was as yet unframed. He leaned the painting forwards and wiggled behind it so as to get a better look. And there was the title scribbled with a charcoal pencil. *Broken*, 1997. He put the painting against the wall and once more took a few steps backwards. It certainly was broken. Perhaps a ship had miscalculated the height of its masts and torn the bridge in half, that had to be it, he understood it now. But what was it about this bridge, why was he drawn towards this painting as if by an inexorable force? Because it's my painting, Alvar thought, I've been looking for this, this is the one for me. It speaks to me in all its gloomy silence. He turned away for a moment because it was all becoming too much for him. He stood there with his back to the painting while thoughts welled up in him, wild and raging. He must ring Ole Krantz instantly; he had to know who the painter was. What if it turned out to be a commission, imagine if the painting was not even for sale? he thought, with something bordering on desperation. The picture had not been hung, or priced. It's expensive, Alvar thought, this is a fairly expensive painting, not everyone will be able to afford it. I have a chance. I have seventy thousand in the bank. He tried to tear himself away. He went upstairs to the kitchen and made coffee. Then he had to go back downstairs for a second look. It probably would not have the same powerful effect on him this time, some of its force would diminish, since he had studied the painting in depth once already. But when he came downstairs the picture took hold of him with the same violence. It drew him in, he was swallowed up by the fog, he saw the broken surfaces, the severed bridge, beams and wires bristling in the darkness, and he gasped for air. He ran up the stairs and called Ole Krantz.

'Happy New Year,' he croaked into the receiver.

'Have you caught a cold?' Krantz asked. 'It sounds like you've lost your voice.'

Alvar shook his head. He cleared his throat. 'No, I just had something stuck.'

A moment's silence followed while they waited for each other. Alvar checked the monitors, he did not want any customers now, he had to find out about this picture, this violent force on the ground floor. He struggled to control himself, he wanted to come across as professional and mature, but it was impossible, he was quivering with excitement.

'Did you see the bridge, Eide?' Krantz said out of the blue.

Alvar jolted. 'Yes,' he stammered, 'and it's overwhelming, Krantz, utterly overwhelming.' He could not help it, his voice was falsetto. 'Don't you think?'

At the other end Krantz chuckled. 'I suspected that you would like it.'

Alvar held his breath. Focused and took off.

'Where does it come from?'

'An unknown chap,' Krantz said. 'His name's Lindstrøm. I came across the painting in Stockholm and had it sent back here. I'm sure we'll be hearing a lot more about him.'

An unknown chap, Alvar thought. Perhaps the painting won't be so expensive after all. Unknown painters could not expect high prices, there were rules for these things which had to be respected, it took a long time before they finally made it. The breakthrough that they all dreamt about. *Broken* could be such a breakthrough, literally.

'If anyone happens to ask,' Alvar said, trying to keep his voice at a steady pitch, 'what kind of price are we talking about?'

Again he held his breath. Krantz thought about this for a long time.

'I'm thinking seventy thousand.'

Alvar reeled. He felt like giving up. Seventy thousand kroner. All his painstakingly compiled savings, his entire life insurance. For an unknown painter. How could he even contemplate something like that?

'Did you say the painter was an unknown?' he stammered, clutching the handset. His ear flattened against his temple.

'He is, he is. But what a picture! It's monumental. It's worth seventy thousand.'

Alvar pondered this amount. This bizarre coincidence. Could it be a sign from above?

'We'll have it in the gallery for a long time, then,' he said out loud, nursing a faint hope, because he needed time. He was not an impulsive man and he was not used to feeling spellbound as he did today. He was composed, measured. A man who always thought before he acted.

'Let me put it this way,' Krantz said, 'if anyone makes us an offer, we'll consider it.'

I want to make you an offer, Alvar thought, but he did not say it out loud. He wanted to hang up, he wanted to return to the picture, stand in front of it and feel the strange sensation that the picture portrayed him, his very core. This was how he had always felt, he had never connected with other people, something inside him had been severed.

'Someone will be completely smitten with this picture,' Krantz went on, 'and this one person will be prepared to pay the price. Just you wait and see. I'm right about this, mark my words.'

I already know you are, Alvar thought. He managed to conclude the conversation. He went back downstairs, walking hesitatingly down the steps, and over to the picture. He remained in front of it for a long time. He was scared that someone might come. He was scared that someone might appear in the doorway, spot the picture, fall completely in love with it and take it away from him. He was overcome by a childish urge to hide it in the workshop so that no one would ever see it. There is no other way, he thought, I'll just have to buy it, it's that simple. And I must buy it now. There is no time to lose. If I don't buy it, someone else will and this picture was meant for me. But it costs seventy thousand; it's everything I have in the bank. It'll clear me out. Poor as a church mouse, he thought, and shivered at the thought. On the other hand, he argued, money is there to be spent. And I'll never find a picture like this ever again. But seventy thousand kroner. Then he would have nothing put by for sudden expenses and that in itself was extremely risky. On the other hand he was a good customer at the bank, so if any unforeseen expenses were to crop up, it was likely that the bank would offer him a small loan. If he were to dent the car or break a tooth. Anything could happen, Alvar thought; he was a man with a lot on his mind. Right now he was infatuated by the picture. He felt quite faint. He was experiencing a dizzying joy. This was art at its best, this was happiness. At that very moment the doorbell rang. His heart leapt to his throat. Was it happening already? Was someone coming to take the picture away from him?

He recognised her instantly.

The young woman in the high-heeled ankle boots. She stopped in the open doorway and looked at him. She looked better than last time. Her eyes were brighter, she was composed and her movements were steady, she was not staggering as before. She let the door close behind her and took a few steps across the stone floor. Looked at him with her ice-blue eyes and said, 'Hi, only me. Could you spare a cup of coffee?'

Alvar gawped. He had almost forgotten her, no, not forgotten her, but she had been out of his thoughts for a long time. It had never occurred to him that she might come back, not after all this time.

'Coffee.' He hesitated. Right away he experienced a deep, disconcerting resistance. If he were to give her a cup of coffee, what would happen then, where would it lead? But it was hard to say no to such a simple request. How could he suddenly be mean when he had previously been so compassionate? That would not look very good and he was a decent man.

'Very well,' he mumbled reluctantly, 'I suppose I could.' He turned round mechanically and went up the stairs. She followed him. In the midst of it all he experienced a bizarre sense of relief. She was not here for the picture, she just wanted some coffee. She stood in the opening to the kitchen and stared at him while he complied with her simple request. He found the same blue mug from before and filled it right up to the brim.

'It's cold outside,' he said, watching her white fingers. She took the mug and drank. Her lips were thin and bluish white, but her eyes, which he recalled as being dull were suddenly as sharp as glass. 'Bloody cold,' she said, looking at him over the rim of the mug.

No, it struck him as he watched her, she had to be older than he had first assumed. She was probably in her early twenties, he detected some fine lines around her eyes. She was wearing the same clothes as the last time. Perhaps she had never taken them off. It horrified him that a young person could look so dreadful, but of course her body was totally ravaged by drugs.

'Where do you live?' he blurted out.

'Here and there,' she replied indifferently. 'It's not very strong your coffee, is it?'

'Oh.' Alvar was disappointed. He had always believed that he made a decent cup of coffee. He could not allow this; he would have to do something about it later.

'You here every day?' she asked, looking around the large building. Her question made him smile.

'Yes, every day. Year in, year out,' he replied.

'That sounds utterly boring,' she stated.

'Oh no, not at all,' he assured her, folding his hands across his stomach as was his habit.

She kept hold of the mug and started wandering around the rooms on the first floor. He followed her. She looked at the pictures. Shook her head, screwed up her eyes. I don't suppose she knows much about art, Alvar thought.

'Is that expensive?' she asked, pointing at a picture.

'Terribly,' he admitted. 'Well, some of them are, not all of them. But that one, however, by Nerdrum, that's expensive, you wouldn't be able to afford it.'

She laughed a delicate and tinkling laugh, the way little girls laugh.

'You don't have anyone to talk to in here,' she pointed out, and he stared down at the toes of his shoes as if she had humiliated him. 'Or perhaps you talk to the pictures?' she teased.

She looked directly at him now, and he tried to meet her eyes, she was only a girl and a cheeky one at that.

'I don't have a great urge to talk,' he explained and cleared his throat. He was thinking about the bridge. If you had a painting like that on your wall, it would no longer be necessary to say anything else in this life. Somewhere there was an artist who had imagined this landscape. The depths, the sea stacks, the fog. And its impact on him had been so strong; it was like being hit by a gale-force wind. That was how he felt it. He was suddenly overcome by an urge to show it to her, just to see what would happen.

'Do you know anything about art?' he asked watching her. She yawned.

'Is there anything to know?' she said. 'You either like a picture, or you don't. Is there anything more to say?'

'There's a great deal more to say,' he replied.

'There is?' She staggered a bit and drank from the mug, greedily, the way a thirsty child gulps down a glass of milk.

'Come with me, I want to show you something!'

She followed him down the stairs to the ground floor. He went straight over to the wall and gestured towards the bridge with one grand, solemn gesture. She gazed at it attentively still holding the blue mug. She drank a few gulps, she took in the picture. Then she licked the corners of her mouth with the pink tip of her tongue.

'Right,' she said eventually. 'A bridge going nowhere. Amazing.'

'Yes, don't you think?' he said, pleased because he could see that the painting had moved her and it made him feel that there might be hope for her after all, that behind all this devastation there was a sentient human being.

'What's it called?' she asked with curiosity.

'*Broken*,' said Alvar dramatically.

She swallowed the rest of her coffee in one big gulp and handed him the mug.

'Nice title. Do you know, that's the only name it could have.'

He declared that he was in total agreement with her.

'I saw you on Bragernes Square a little while ago,' he said all of a sudden. He did not know why he said it, it just came out.

'Aha?' she replied.

'You were together with a man. A dark-haired man, older than you. Long hair. Perhaps it was your brother?'

She looked at him and then she burst out laughing.

'My brother? I don't have any brothers, or sisters for that matter.'

'How about parents then?' he wanted to know.

'No parents either,' she said sullenly and turned away from him. She started pacing in a circle on the stone floor. 'They've all gone.'

'Gone?' He did not understand.

'Gone away. Scattered by the four winds. That's all right. I'm not too bothered by it, family is just trouble. Folks you have to see just because you're related to them. Do you have any family?' she asked.

Alvar had to tell her the honest truth, which was that he was all alone in the world.

'No kids? No wife?' she said.

'No,' he said. It sounded lame. He felt interrogated, but on the other hand he had been the one to start it all off.

'And why not?' she said looking at him. Her blue eyes dissected him.

'It's just never happened,' he said. 'I can offer you no other explanation. I'm fine with it,' he added, looking back at her.

'You ought to get a haircut,' she said suddenly. 'Comb-overs are out.'

'Comb-over?' He touched his scalp. 'I'd better look after the little I've got left.'

'You'd look much better without it,' she stated.

She really is very cheeky, he thought, so very cheeky. I have never seen the like.

'Thank you for the coffee,' she said. 'I've got to go.'

'Have you?' he said and felt pleased about that. At the same time something happened inside him. He could not fully explain what it was, but it was becoming too much for him, this girl, the painting. Seventy thousand kroner. I need time to think, he told himself, I need to sleep on it. I want to have another look in the morning. If it has the same strong effect tomorrow, then I will buy it.

'I'm thinking of buying that picture,' he said, pointing once more to the bridge.

'How much is it,' she asked swiftly.

'Seventy thousand kroner.'

She rolled her eyes wildly. 'You have that much money?'

'I've got a bit put away,' he said proudly. 'I've been saving up for years.'

For one moment he thought he saw a flicker of light in her eyes.

'I see,' she said. 'You want the damaged bridge. That's all right. Bloody great picture,' she smiled. Her ravaged face cracked up and softened. He had a feeling that she was secretly laughing at him. He liked her and yet he did not like her, he was confused.

'Got to run,' she said firmly.

She staggered off on her high heels. She leaned against the oak door, forcing it open. Then she was gone. This time he didn't watch her from the window. In a sudden moment of despair because he had exposed himself in a way which was uncharacteristic for him, he carefully touched the top of his head. The lock of hair was still in its place.

When he left the gallery he took the route via Bragernes Square. He crossed into the pedestrian area, and as he passed Magasinet something strange happened. He felt driven by a sudden impulse and as he came to Saxen, a hairdressing salon, he went straight in. He had just ended up there, the urge had surprised him. It felt like floating. He looked down at his shoes, checking that he was still in contact with the floor. A young woman was busy cutting the hair of a small, long-haired boy. She looked up at him and smiled. Studied his old-fashioned hairstyle with a look of professional determination.

'Would you have time to cut my hair?' he asked. He instantly stroked his head, terrified. It had never occurred to him to have what little hair he had left cut off. He would be bald. All he'd have left would be a modest semicircle of hair at the back of his head.

'Yes,' she smiled, still watching him, 'if you can wait ten minutes. Have a seat please, I won't be long.'

He thought that she looked remarkably young, as if she ought to be in school. Her hair was cut short, it stuck out wildly and was dyed in several different shades. Her ears were heavily decorated with rings and studs and at the back of her head she had a small tattoo of a unicorn.

Alvar took a magazine, which he leafed through while he waited. He had to sit on a pouffe, it was horribly soft, he had no back support. Thus he sat, almost slumped, like a man with bad posture. On the pouffe next to him sat a woman, probably the boy's mother. She looked awfully pleased whenever the boy's hair landed softly on the floor. Alvar's pulse was rising. It was too late to leave now, after all he had sat down, and it would not do to storm out of the door at this point, even though this was precisely what he felt like doing. What had he started? A casual remark from a stranger had pushed him over the edge and now he would look like an idiot if he were to leave. If he walked off like some feeble-minded, gutless coward. He kept leafing through the magazine, but managed only to look at the pictures. The boy in the chair had now acquired a short haircut; finally his neck was brushed and he was allowed to get down. His mother paid with a note and they both left. Alvar let the magazine fall to the floor. He was told to sit down by the sink. He did so, resting his head on the neck support. This position, with his throat exposed, made him think of lying on the scaffold. The hairdresser tested the temperature of the water and started washing his hair; he liked the feel of her fingers massaging his scalp, they were strong and soft at the same time, she moved her hands in circles across his head.

He enjoyed it as best he could while he tried to convince himself that he had made the right decision. All the same he was shocked. How could he allow himself to be controlled by a young, blonde drug addict? A woman he did not even know. Because he knew that it was her comment about comb-overs being old-fashioned which had caused him to end up in this chair. He knew no other women. He was not used to people commenting on his appearance. And what would happen if she turned up at the gallery again and noticed that he had in fact done what she had said? Perhaps she would collapse in a heap of wild, uncontrollable giggling, slap her pointy knees and poke fun at him?

'Shall we get rid of the bit on the top?' the hairdresser asked diplomatically.

Alvar was seated in front of the mirror. He nodded. He sat looking miserable in his chair and watched the long tuft of hair fall to the floor. His scalp appeared, shiny like a mirror. He instantly looked older. It might very well be more modern, more contemporary, but it definitely aged him. But then again at least he would be spared the constant trips to the mirror to check that the tuft of hair was still in place. Now there was not a single hair on his head long enough to move or sway in the wind. He had enjoyed having his scalp touched. She smelled good, something sweet and mild. His regular barber kept his distance, he was formal, talked about the weather. But this young woman chatted away in a soft, feline voice. Alvar replied with brief sentences, but he did not feel threatened by her. Now she was using the hair trimmer at the back of his neck.

'There you are,' she said, brushing away any loose hairs. 'Nice and tidy.'

Alvar had to agree. When he thought about it, he did feel good after all. He was not pretending to have more hair than he really did. His baldness was plain for all to see, no more pretending. He straightened his shoulders, thanked her and paid, went outside on the freezing cold day. Hair or no hair, even young men shaved their heads, it was fashionable. It was masculine. And there was nothing wrong with the shape of his head. In fact, the back of his head was nicely rounded, a head he could be proud of. Perhaps this was an appropriate day to treat himself to something extra special for dinner? A fillet of beef, perhaps, or a piece of salmon? Again he went to the Cash and Carry, where he took a number as always at the deli counter. When it was finally his turn, he decided on an elk steak, and on the condiment shelf he found a jar of mountain cranberries. That's the thing, he thought, and headed homeward with this small exclusive meal in a carrier bag.

He let himself into his flat and went straight into the bathroom. He hesitated as he walked over to the mirror. He saw his bald head and was startled. Because this was his own mirror and the man looking back at him was him. The man he had seen in the mirror at the hairdresser's had not been him; we only see ourselves as we really are in our own mirrors, he thought, and this is the honest truth. Alvar Eide with no hair. Alvar Eide aged forty-two, with a modest band of hair at the back of his neck. It will take me a year to grow out my hair again, he thought, and this period, before his hair was long enough to be combed all the way over to the right side, would be an awful time. He tried to laugh at himself and went out into the kitchen. Unwrapped the elk steak and wiped it with a piece of kitchen towel so that the meat would be completely dry when it hit the browning butter in the frying pan. He found salt and pepper. He went into his living room and turned on the radio. He saw that Green from next door was coming home from work. When the meat was frying he stood there inhaling the wonderful smell. He even hummed a tune the name of which he could not remember, but it was played incessantly on the radio and he could not get it out of his head. Like a buzzing, persistent insect he could not be bothered to chase away.

He set the table in the living room. He sat down and ate while his eyes wandered around the room. Where would he hang the severed bridge? Above the fireplace, of course. Oh, how it would tower over the room almost like a monument, he thought. Seventy thousand kroner. Every single krone he had saved up. It was quite extravagant. Why did he have such a desire to own this painting? After all he could see it every day in the gallery. The picture might even hang there for months, and perhaps he might get sick of it after a while and want a different one. He knew that was not true. This was Alvar being sensible, practical, prudent Alvar. The part of him that kept him in check, the part of him that had kept him on the right course his entire life. On his own, but taking care of himself. But then there was another voice, a strong seductive voice. It pushed common sense aside and made him weak. The painting is meant for you, the voice said, it illustrates your very soul, this severed bridge in the mute darkness. The picture will complement your flat, the picture will soothe the unrest you sometimes feel at night, because all your fears have finally been articulated by an unknown painter. A soulmate. Someone who knows exactly how you feel. Thus the painting will become your most treasured possession. Everyone who enters this room will see it and wonder. At its audacity, the elegance of the construction, while they simultaneously shiver at the drama because it disappears into a silent, dark fog. They will see that you have taste, that you are a real connoisseur. But no one ever comes here, he suddenly thought. Salespeople only come as far as the hall, and my neighbour has never been in here, no one but me will ever get to see it. But surely you're buying the painting for yourself, the voice replied. And even if the painting is not of very high quality, it is nevertheless a good investment, isn't it? Yes, but I've never really been very interested in investments. I've always believed that when it comes to art you have to go with your gut instinct. True, but is it not your gut instinct talking to you now? Buy it, Alvar, buy it! Get up now and go to the telephone, call Ole Krantz. Tell him you're buying the painting. Then it's done, once and for all. I have to sleep on it, he thought then, it's not like it's going to go anywhere overnight. Unless a burglar turns up and swipes it from under my very nose. But they had never had any break-ins at Gallery Krantz. Touch wood, he thought, tapping the table. What is going on with me? I'm behaving like a little child. Of course I should buy that painting. I'm all over the place and there is a reason for that. You have to take these things seriously. You should always listen to your intuition; it too has its own inner voice. The body needs sustenance, food, drink and sleep. However, the soul needs nourishment too. He finished eating and went over to the fireplace. Above it hung three unassuming lithographs, now he took them down and carried them out into the hall. Then he went back into the living room and stood there looking at the empty wall. Yes, it would fit there. It would not only fit, the painting would also be beautifully lit by the windows in the middle facing it. It would look as if it had always hung there. When he closed his eyes he could visualise it clearly. But as he had already told himself, he ought to sleep on it. And tomorrow he would go to the gallery and see how he would feel then. Perhaps nothing would happen, perhaps it would be an anticlimax. It had happened to him before. The painting would cry out to him at first sight only to lose its impact later. It was a strange mechanism, but he preferred pictures that grew on him over time. Seventy thousand kroner. He forced himself to move away from the bare wall and carried his plate and cutlery out into the kitchen. Rinsed off the leftover gravy and cranberries, then sat down in his chair in front of the television. Touched his scalp and felt dizzy. None of the terrestrial channels were showing anything worth watching, so he picked up the newspaper and checked the satellite listings. Perhaps there would be something on National Geographic. '9 p.m.,' he read, '*When Expeditions Go Wrong*. 10 p.m., *Deadly Heat*. 11 p.m., *Seconds From Death: The Bhopal Tragedy*. 11.30 p.m., *The Eruption of Mount St Helens*. 12 a.m., *Trapped Undersea*.' This list of disasters made him feel anxious. Perhaps the severed bridge was a warning.

CHAPTER 10

'There was something I wanted to talk to you about,' Alvar says as he softly crosses my floor. 'And I don't mean to be rude, it's not in my nature, not in any way. But this is completely inappropriate!'

I look over my shoulder at him. His voice is falsetto.

'I'm not in the habit of chatting to people like that, volunteering personal information, I don't think it's appropriate and I certainly don't want total strangers to know. And I have never been dissatisfied with my appearance, that visit to the hairdresser's was entirely out of character. I've ended up looking like a fifty-year-old.'

He is genuinely upset. His newly shaven cheeks are flushed.

I tilt my head and look at him.

'Calm down. You look good. Trust me.'

He runs his hand over his naked scalp.

'Why did you reintroduce her?' he asks. 'I had almost forgotten about her, I was waiting for something else to happen.'

'It's not easy to change track once I've made a decision,' I reply. 'Let's wait and see where it takes us. There's no point in worrying about something that hasn't happened yet.'

'But,' he objects, 'so much is happening at the same time. You've created a longing in me that I never knew existed. That severed bridge won't leave me alone, I can't relax. If I buy the painting I spend all of my savings. That in itself is a huge risk and I never splash out. If I don't buy the painting I have to live with the loss of it. That awful feeling when the painting goes to another.'

'In other words, you're being forced to make a decision,' I reply drily. 'And you have to make it quickly.'

He collapses uninvited into a chair and folds his hands.

'Why are you putting all this pressure on me? Does it all have to happen so quickly? It unsettles me.'

I look at him across the desk.

'Well, that's how it's turning out. This is a short narrative, I don't have many pages at my disposal.'

'Not many pages? But why not? Surely that's up to you. Whether you want to write a hundred and fifty pages or six hundred?'

'No, it's not up to me. And I realised that as soon as I began. You're a modest man, this will be a modest tale.'

The thought of this depresses him.

'I am, in other words, not terribly important?'

I sigh heavily.'Of course you're important. And surely you're not saying that a short life is less important than a long one? The real question is: does anyone see us while we are here on earth? I see you clearly. I'm showing you to others. But it would seem that you're still not satisfied?'

He blushes once again. Strokes his forehead with a trembling hand. 'I'm sorry, but I'm still worried. People will be able to judge me. My actions and my values. It's a frightening thought. Dear God, what will they think, what will they say?'

'Some might take you to their hearts,' I reply, 'others will pass by unmoved. That's how life is. The point is that you have to give them a chance. If you want to be seen, you have to put yourself out there, it's that simple.'

'But why does it have to be through a drug addict?'

I light a cigarette, I inhale. Get up and let the cat in, he has been scratching at the back door.

'That's just how it's turning out.'

He shakes his head. 'Your replies confuse me. It's as if you have no will of your own. You could have chosen someone different. You must have had a reason. Consciously or subconsciously. Can't you outline the plot so that I can relax?'

'No, not really,' I reply frankly. 'However, I needed a conflict. Your relationship with Ole Krantz is clear, there is nothing for me to explore. I needed a contrast. Someone who lives their life in a completely different way from you. The door to the gallery opened and there she was. I could see her very clearly. For the time being I am watching you from a distance waiting to see what will happen. And to be honest, I like being surprised. Perhaps I'll end up in a different place from where I originally intended. Perhaps you'll do better than I fear at the moment. You've had your hair cut,' I say to him, 'and I see how much you fret about this one spontaneous act. But changing your hairstyle does not make for very interesting reading. Anyway, it really suits you. More manly, somehow. And exchanging a few words with a stranger shouldn't exactly knock you sideways. Most people are well intentioned towards you. Let yourself go a little, Alvar, and see what happens.'

'So you're saying I should buy the painting?'

'That's not what I'm saying, I've merely offered you the chance. Now don't force me to analyse it too deeply, I need to be flying free in order to write.'

'There are times,' he objects feebly, 'when I wish I had called on someone else. On a writer with a better overview, more control.'

'Well, we've already discussed that,' I say. 'But as it happens you're here with me.'

He relaxes his shoulders. Gives me a sidelong glance.

'I guess I'm a complete nuisance,' he says. 'I suppose I ought to be pleased about what you've done so far rather than throw a spanner in the works. That was never my intention. That really was not what I meant. That was not what I meant at all.'

'You're not a spanner in the works. We're a team now, you and I, it's called letting things happen. You have no experience of that and that's why you're feeling afraid. So am I, I live with it every day. But my heart is still beating, as is my pulse, the minutes pass one by one. The sun will come up tomorrow, I'm absolutely certain of that. I really do pity mankind,' I say, 'we don't have the ability to live in the moment. Soon other things will happen, difficult things, they will happen tonight or next week. And even though we're not there yet, our thoughts race ahead like horses through an open gate. In other words, only genuine contemplation can stop this clock inside us ticking and ticking towards our death. A painting, a piece of music, an engrossing book, a chat to a good friend. Bad things will always happen, but they are not going to happen today. Because today the sun is shining and we get out of bed. We put our feet on the floor and breathe. There is actually a good deal of courage in you, Alvar, I'm absolutely convinced of that. But, of course, I'm worried that you've chosen to isolate yourself. If something goes wrong, you've got no one to turn to. Do you ever think about that? Do you understand what that means?'

His eyes become distant, they seek out the window.

'I've been thinking a great deal about dying,' he admits. 'Who will arrange my funeral, will anyone mourn me? Who'll clear out my flat, what will happen to my furniture and all my other belongings? But then again I'm only forty-two. And all sorts of things might happen before I grow old. I hope that time will take care of it for me.'

'It won't,' I say gravely. 'If you want things to change, you have to change them yourself. I'm with you all the way, but I rely on you grabbing the opportunities I give you. Otherwise we're never going to get anywhere. Do you understand what I'm saying to you?'

He gets up and goes over to the window. He stares out across the Lier Valley.

'You authors are a funny lot,' he says with his back to me.

'No, we're like most people. We work hard, we have a profession. We have office hours, we toil.'

'I can see all the way to Fjell,' he says over by the window.

'Yes, you can.'

'And all the greenhouses. They glow like gold bullion in the dark.'

'It's pretty, don't you think?'

'Does all this beauty inspire you?'

'No.'

He turns round. 'Really?'

'I would have preferred a cell in a basement.'

'You're not serious?'

'Yes. A single solitary source of light. No windows. A spartan room. Where no external influences can penetrate my mind. In spring, living as I do here, it's unbearable, with the pretty valley in front of the house and the woods right behind it.'

'What's wrong with the woods?'

'The birds just won't shut up! Doves cooing, cuckoos singing, and the woodpeckers, they drive me crazy. But I do like the cows when they start to low at five in the morning. You know, Alvar,' I explain, 'for human beings to be in balance, their external landscape must match their internal one. That's why I like fog. Darkness and storms. Northern lights, a full moon. Shooting stars. Heavy, persistent rain, leaves falling.'

'If that's your attitude then I worry that you're about to tell quite a dark story,' he says anxiously.

'Yes, it's in my nature.'

He comes back and finds his seat on the sofa.

'There's something I have to ask you,' he says. 'Do you like your work?'

'I love it. It's a passion.'

'But you're all alone. In front of your screen. Year in, year out.'

'That's correct. But I never think about it. There's no room for second thoughts once I've started. Then time stands still, it's like being on the crest of a wave. And then, when that day's work is done I'm spat out into reality where everything is equally intense. Then I find out that there's a war on in Iraq, that a vast number of people on this planet continue to starve, that there's still unrest in the Middle East. And that what I spent my time on has no importance whatsoever.'

'But surely as a writer you must feel that you matter somehow?'

'Sadly, no. But I don't want you to think I'm going to treat you and your destiny lightly. I take this very seriously. But I should have been in Africa building wells.'

He smiles sadly.

'Have you put any worries in your box?' he asks softly.

'Obviously,' I say in a tired voice. 'They come to me in a steady stream; I'm a terribly anxious person. When my alarm goes off in the morning I am overwhelmed by everything that might go wrong. I can barely find the courage to put my feet on the floor; this world will never be a familiar place to me, every day I have to navigate it as a beginner. The fifteen steps downstairs, the walk to the computer. But once I see the blue light from the screen, the tension within me subsides and I am back on familiar ground. I honestly don't know how to handle the real world, I stagger through my day, my heart beats unsteadily and I struggle to breathe. If the telephone rings, my heart skips a beat. If I see an unknown car on my drive I hide behind my curtains while staring like crazy at the stranger heading for my door. I look for fixed points the whole afternoon and when night-time finally comes I'm utterly disorientated. Because I lasted a whole day, because the disaster never happened. I take nothing for granted. Not the rest of my life, not tomorrow. Or you. And when the disaster finally strikes,' I say, 'I know what I'll say.'

'And what will you say?' asks Alvar gently.

'I always knew this would happen.'

CHAPTER 11

The next day when he let himself into the gallery, his entire body was brimming with tremendous excitement. He practically walked sideways across the floor in an attempt not to look at the painting. What if the bridge had gone? What if Ole Krantz had let himself in after the gallery had closed and taken the painting home to keep for himself? But it was there, in exactly the same spot, leaning against the wall, monumental and overwhelming. Alvar slowly walked up to it. He instantly felt a sense of inner calm, the painting made him feel whole. The severed bridge was somewhere he could deposit all those feelings he would never be able to articulate. Oh, he enjoyed reading books, he liked seeing himself reflected in the characters in them. But this. This wordless art, the immediate impression, how it could have such an effect on him, it was inconceivable. And I'm not an emotional person, he thought, I'm a quiet man with my life under control. I sleep well, I'm content. On my own, admittedly, but I'm nevertheless a hard-working and valid member of society. Not terribly interested in politics, or social issues for that matter, but I take good care of myself and I do my duty. So why do I need this painting so badly? How can this artist know how I feel?

He forced himself to walk away from the painting and went upstairs to the kitchen to make coffee. As he opened the cupboard he spotted the blue mug. He chose a different one, settled down by the table and opened the newspaper, which had been delivered to his flat earlier that morning. Every now and then he would look up at the three monitors. It was impossible to enter Gallery Krantz without the doorbell ringing, but as a precaution he kept an eye on the rooms all the same. Seventy thousand kroner, he thought. After all it's only money, mere digits in a computer, I've never actually seen it. Why don't I just ring Krantz right now and tell him that I want to buy the painting? Perhaps he'll give me an employee discount? Perhaps I can pay for the painting by instalments so I don't have to part with all my money at once? Surely we'll find a way around it? Will it make me happy? he wondered. Wasn't it rather that the painting had created a desire in him that he never thought he would experience? A desire to connect with other people? It felt as though he had been willing it to happen, he had longed for such an experience. Finding this one crucial painting. And now it was here, sitting downstairs. Why could he not just accept that and buy it? He drank his coffee slowly while he waited for the first customer of the day. He kept running his hand across his naked scalp, he could not get used to his bald head.

The first customers of the day turned out to be a young couple. Alvar put them somewhere in their twenties and they were clearly very much in love. He noted such things with great composure. It never made him feel embarrassed or insecure, or shy. Anyway, a young couple arrived. A slender, dark-haired woman and a tall blond man. They entered the gallery and as he sat there watching them on the left monitor, he realised that they rarely visited galleries. The way they moved around the space was hesitant. Nor had they realised that the paintings had been hung so as to present themselves most favourably, the intention being that you would begin by the left-hand wall and then move clockwise until you reached the staircase. That would take you to the first floor, if you were interested in looking at prints. They meandered from one wall to another. He let them wander around for a few minutes before he went downstairs. The moment he appeared they became shy, but he gave them a reassuring smile and he immediately knew that this couple would never be mesmerised by the severed bridge. Besides, they were unlikely to be able to afford it; he was safe – for now.

'Just take your time,' Alvar said, 'there are two more floors. On the second floor you'll find mainly foreign art if you have an interest in that.'

They nodded and continued to wander around, holding hands all the while. Alvar rearranged some silk roses in a jar; he displayed some brochures on a table. The couple moved from painting to painting, they did not speak, but studied the pictures with genuine interest. Finally the young woman stopped and remained in front of a picture for a long time. A sketch. Alvar suppressed a smile, women invariably stopped in front of this picture. At first glance it was an insignificant image in pale shades. It depicted a bird's nest and in the nest lay four turquoise eggs. The young woman was utterly taken with it.

'You have to see this,' she said, looking at the man. A frown instantly appeared on his forehead.

'Well,' he said, trying not to hurt her feelings, he was a considerate man, 'it's very pretty, but you can barely make it out. I mean, if we're going to have a painting above the sofa it should be a bit bigger, shouldn't it?'

'Yes,' she agreed, but continued to gaze at the picture all the same. 'I just really like it.' However, she already knew that it was a lost cause. They wandered on. Alvar fetched a duster so that he could potter about and do some work in the knowledge that his presence would be unobtrusive and yet he would remain accessible. They had reached the merry-go-round. The young man stopped and squatted in front of it.

'Now there,' he said, 'just take a look at this one!'

The woman joined him. She stared carefully at the painting with the skeletons for a long time. Then she wrinkled her nose.

'I think it's a bit gross,' she said.

'Gross?' He glared down at her, he was at least a foot taller than her and now it was his turn to look surprised; he simply did not understand why she found the painting gross.

'They've got maggots crawling out of their eyes,' she shuddered. 'Look.' She pointed. He leaned towards the painting.

'But you can hardly see them,' he argued. 'Only close up.'

'We can't buy a painting that we only like as long as we don't look at it close up,' she countered. This logic silenced the man.

'Anyway, it would be far too expensive,' she said. 'It's an oil painting.'

'But that's what we're looking for,' he said. 'If we wanted to buy a print we might as well have gone to IKEA. That's why we've come here.'

They reached no consensus and walked on.

'*The Merry-go-round* costs seventeen thousand kroner,' Alvar informed them from the corner where he was wiping dust off a frame.

The woman rolled her eyes. The man looked put out. But Alvar did not want to sell them the merry-go-round. They deserved something else, something better, he felt.

'How about this?' he said, walking over to a painting on the furthest wall, which faced the car park. It was a drawing by Bendik Sjur. The couple followed him enthusiastically. They looked at the picture for a long time. A creature was seemingly crawling towards them on a dark wooden floor. A strange creature, skinny, and soft and thin, like something out of the underworld. It looked right into the eyes of the observer with a devil-may-care look. Alvar was a great admirer of Bendik Sjur.

'Christ,' the young man said, 'he looks like Gollum. Gollum from *Lord of the Rings*,' he explained and looked at Alvar. Once more they were silent as they watched the strange creature. It was drawn with a delicate, light touch, it had a soul and a distinctive character. It simultaneously exuded calm and tension. The young couple was lost, they gazed spellbound at the painting and squeezed each other's hands. But they moved on, they were not the type to be rushed into anything. So while they slowly and patiently walked through both the first and second floors, Alvar went back into the kitchen and drank another cup of coffee. When he saw that they had returned to the ground floor and had stopped in front of the drawing once more, he went downstairs.

'Yes, we're interested in this,' the young man said pointing at Sjur's drawing. 'We think it's really cool.'

Well, Alvar thought. A cool picture. He supposed that was one way of putting it. Yet they still seemed to be hesitating. Money was probably an issue.

'Four thousand,' Alvar said. The man instantly brightened up. That would do nicely. He looked at his beloved. She, too, liked the creature from the underworld, if that was where he came from, he defied definition in any way; he was half-human, half-beast or rather a type of insect with deranged eyes. They bought it. Alvar took it down from the wall, wrapped it and wrote them a receipt. The man carried the picture out. The couple had frowned when they had seen the severed bridge; they had never been a real threat. Yet Alvar felt his body tense up every time the doorbell rang. At any moment someone might walk in, stand there open-mouthed staring at it, just like he had done. Why don't I just buy it, he wondered, am I really that gutless? I who have always claimed that you should follow your heart and not your head when it comes to buying art.

He went back upstairs to the kitchen and unpacked his lunch. Three open sandwiches with pastrami ham and slivers of cucumber. He halved the slices and placed them on a plate; he ate quietly. At times he thought about the young woman who had visited the gallery twice. But she had not come back, even though it was starting to get colder now. Perhaps she's got herself some warmer clothes, he thought. Some more sensible footwear. He went to the toilet after finishing his lunch and was once again confronted by his naked head in the mirror. His hair was so short at the back of his head that it pricked his palm. Ah, well. Nothing to fret about, *sic transit gloria mundi*. And I don't look all that bad, he comforted himself, and once again he marvelled at how a total stranger could make one throwaway remark about his hair which caused him to rush off to have it cut. What about the rest of his appearance? He looked at his reflection in the mirror, with his checked shirt and the black tie. He had never had much fashion sense and had never aspired to. He liked not standing out. In the autumn he wore a grey trench coat and in the winter a woollen coat, which at the time had been a great expense, but a good investment because it was a very fine quality and warm. In addition he wore smart, pressed trousers and black shoes. Brown leather gloves on his hands. A thin woollen scarf around his neck. He never took his car to work, he needed the exercise, so he always dressed warmly. As he came out from the lavatory he heard the bell ring. Ole Krantz came up the stairs with a picture tucked under his arm. He put it down in the kitchen and looked at Alvar. At the same time he planted his feet firmly on the floor and put his hands on his hips. He was a tall, broad man, masculine and ruddy.

'Good heavens,' he said, 'you've had a summer haircut in November.'

Alvar thought he detected a quick smile flash across his face, so he stared down at the floor while he ran his hand across his head in an apologetic fashion.

'I thought it was a good idea,' he said.

'Absolutely,' Krantz said assuredly.

And that was all that was ever said on the matter. He went to the cupboard to fetch a mug and poured himself some coffee.

'So what else is new?' he wanted to know. He knew the gallery was in the best of hands.

'I've sold a Bendik Sjur,' he said.

'Well done,' Krantz said as he sat down by the kitchen table. 'Who bought it?'

'A young couple.'

'I thought so.'

In the silence that followed Alvar thought about the bridge. He decided to make his move.

'That painting,' he hesitated, 'the severed bridge. I've been thinking about it.'

'Aha?' Krantz said and waited for him to continue.

'I've been wondering if I should buy it.'

Krantz raised his eyebrows. 'Really?' he said, surprised. 'It's expensive,' he added.

'I know,' Alvar said. 'But I have some money put aside.'

'Really?' Krantz said once again.

'It was just something I've been thinking about,' Alvar said, wanting to retract. It was very expensive. It would clear him out, it would put him in a financially vulnerable position that he had not been in for years. Where an unexpected dental bill would have the power to throw his monthly budget. Was it really worth it? Yes, it was worth it, it meant so much, this work of art was worth the price which Krantz and the artist together had assigned to it.

'I need a few days to make up my mind,' Alvar said, experiencing a sudden burst of initiative.

'I'm sure it'll be here for a while,' Krantz said, 'so there's no need for you to rush. We'll sell it sooner or later, it's a unique painting.'

As if Alvar did not already know. But he did not want to share his feelings for the picture with Krantz, he felt it was too intimate. So he spoke in the appropriate language for an art dealer.

'A rare picture,' he declared drinking his coffee. 'They are few and far between. Just consider the concept. What do you think inspired the picture? I mean, is there actually such a severed bridge?'

'Perhaps in a war zone somewhere,' Krantz suggested. 'They're always blowing up bridges. I don't know an awful lot about Lindstrøm, he's the quiet type. But he travels extensively, that I do know. The picture needs plenty of light, but I'm sure you've thought of that.'

'Of course,' Alvar said.

'And it's gathered plenty of dust,' Krantz continued. 'Buy a fresh loaf of bread and make a ball from the crumbs. Work your way across the whole painting in circular movements. Best way to clean an oil painting. Bread absorbs well and you return a little fat to the painting's surface.'

'Fresh bread,' Alvar said. 'I'll bear that in mind.

That evening he poured himself a sherry.

The painting was never out of his thoughts. The bare wall above the fireplace was ready and waiting for the most breathtaking work of art. Am I ever going to take a single risk in my life, he wondered, follow my instinct for once? I never have. I wander around the town and I look at displays in shops. I look at beautiful furniture and rugs. But there's nothing wrong with what I already have. There's nothing wrong with it, I tell myself, it's too good to be replaced, it will last me years. I can't in all clear conscience buy a new armchair because there's nothing wrong with the one I have. Besides, I like this chair. He patted one of the armrests as if to reinforce his argument. He drank more sherry and thought further. But there's only one painting. No painting has ever captivated me like this, I've never been captivated by anything else. A Weidemann or an Ekeland has never had such an effect on me. It might never happen again, I'm past forty, this is my chance.

The sherry warmed his stomach and he sensed that he was moving towards a final decision. He poured himself another sherry, a large one. Of course, he could pay for the painting in instalments, thus avoiding having to part with all his money at once. On the other hand he had never liked the idea of paying by instalments, so he dismissed the idea as quickly as it had emerged. He would buy the painting and pay cash or he would not buy it at all. I'm going to buy it, he told himself, I'm going to buy it tomorrow. I'll go to the gallery and put a red sticker on the painting, then I'll go to the bank and transfer the money. Ole Krantz will give me a hand transporting the painting home. I want it. If I don't buy it, I'll regret it till the day I die. Regret it keenly and bitterly. Why does it have to be so hard? What a coward I am. And the sherry is starting to cloud my judgement. You should never make any important decisions when you're drunk, never ever. I need to sleep on it.

He cleaned his teeth and went to bed after having folded his clothes neatly. He closed his eyes and fell asleep. That night he had a strange dream. He dreamed that he went to the bank. He took out all his savings and put them in a bag. A brown bag, with a press stud at the top. He left the bank and made his way towards the gallery.

Suddenly he tripped on the pavement and fell. The bag split open and the notes flew off in all directions, seized by an unexpected and violent gust of wind. He got back on his feet and started chasing them, he found a note here another there, he clawed them back feverishly. His heart pounded fast as he scrambled for the notes. But they were impossible to catch. They surged in the wind, they were carried far, far away and he was left with just a few crumpled notes in his hand. The bag was empty. At that point he woke up, fraught and distressed. Then he had to laugh. What a ridiculous dream, he thought. But afterwards he began analysing what the dream might actually have meant. Perhaps it was telling him that he should not buy the painting. That he was literally throwing money away. That he ought to spend his money on something else. But what? There was nothing else he wanted. Irritably he tried to go back to sleep. When he woke up later he could still recall the dream and it continued to disturb him.

He was in two minds as he made his way to the gallery that morning. I'll leave it to fate, he thought eventually; he was rapidly losing patience with the whole business. Why was this painting, which he had fallen in love with at first sight, starting to become a problem for him? Presumably the only solution was to buy it. Could it be that simple? He passed the courthouse and realised that he was cold. Then he remembered that he had forgotten his woollen scarf. He pulled his coat tighter at the throat and walked faster to warm up. He decided to turn up the radiators in the gallery, it was important that people got a pleasant feeling of warmth when they stepped inside, when they put their feet on the stone floor. He let himself in, looked at the bridge with a mixture of reverence and misgiving and ran upstairs to the kitchen.

CHAPTER 12

I put the cat on my lap and force his jaws apart.

He instantly starts to scratch and kick me, his razor-sharp claws dig into the delicate skin on my arms and make my eyes water. I grit my teeth and endure it. How can a four-kilo cat have this much strength? I wonder. It's incredible, he's fighting for his life. Even though I'm doing this for his sake. I take the tiny pill from the table, drop it down his throat and force his jaws shut. I massage his neck and throat with my other hand until the cat swallows the pill. Alvar is watching me, petrified.

'What are you doing?' he croaks.

'Something entirely necessary. I'm worming him,' I reply. 'He's lost a bit of weight recently, he might have worms.'

'Oh,' he says, taking a step back. I seize the moment to let the cat go, he jumps down on to the floor and races to the garden door, he wants to get out. I open the door for him and watch him disappear into the bushes.

'So how are you?' I ask Alvar. 'Why don't you sit down?'

He perches on the very edge of the sofa, picking at his nails.

'I need an honest answer,' he says fixing me with his eyes. 'Am I miserly?'

I sit down again, dig out a cigarette from the packet on the table.

'I don't think so. No, you're not miserly. But you're wondering why you can't make a decision about the painting, aren't you? The severed bridge you so desperately want?'

He nods in agreement. 'Yes. I think there has been enough procrastination. In fact, I'm genuinely disappointed with myself because I can't act. Other people buy things they want whereas I've still got all my old furniture, most of which I've inherited from my mother. And I have enough money.'

'In other words,' I say, lighting the cigarette, 'you have everything you need in order to buy the painting. And now you don't understand what's holding you back?'

He hitches up his trousers before crossing his legs; he flexes his feet in the shiny shoes.

'I keep asking myself,' he says pensively, 'whether the money might be intended for something else.'

'What would that be?' I say, feigning innocence. I am no longer able to meet his eyes.

'Well, if only I knew. I can't think what it might be, but something is holding me back. Something vague and intangible. What do you think?' he says, looking at me. His gaze is terribly direct.

'Deep down you have an inkling,' I say. 'You know that something is bound to happen further into the story and subconsciously you're thinking that the money will come in useful later. That's why you haven't got the courage to spend it. You're waiting. You feel restless. If you buy the painting you will have achieved precisely what you wanted and everything will grind to a halt. And we're only about one hundred pages into your story. You want more space, so you let the painting stay in the gallery. While you're waiting for something else to happen.'

He watches me suspiciously; there is a deep furrow between his brows.

'True, a hundred pages isn't much to get excited about,' he concedes. 'So perhaps you're being brutal enough to show me the painting, yet you won't let me own it. I think that's hard for me to deal with because it's an important painting.'

'I understand,' I console him. 'But you'll just have to learn how. I once desperately wanted a painting by Knut Rose. I found it many years ago and it's called *The Helper*. I never came to own it, but it no longer drives me crazy. Let me put it this way: it's a mild grief.'

'A mild grief,' he echoes. 'Which you think I ought to tackle without whining?'

'Exactly.'

'But I'm not very good at dealing with emotions,' he says.

I flick the ash from my cigarette. 'Do they frighten you?'

'Yes. I don't want too many of them and I don't want them to be very strong. I prefer it when everything is slow and steady.'

'What about happiness?' I smile. 'That's an emotion too. Don't you want that?'

He shrugs shyly. He is actually a well-built man, but he never straightens up, never lets anyone see his broad shoulders.

'I suppose so. If it should come my way.'

'Come your way? Happiness is not some bird, Alvar, which suddenly lands on your shoulder, though poets like to put it that way. You need to set something in motion to achieve the good things in life. You have to act.'

He finds a speck of dust on his trousers and brushes it off.

'But you'll help me, won't you? That's why I came here. Do you see any happiness in my future?'

I close my eyes and concentrate. A host of images appears on my retina.

'Perhaps.'

He blinks. 'What do you mean, perhaps? That doesn't sound terribly reassuring.'

'A half-finished story is a delicate thing,' I explain. 'Never anticipate events, it's dangerous. Everything can burst like a bubble. Besides, I don't want to give you false hopes, or make promises I can't keep.'

'Can you give me anything at all?' he pleads.

I consider this. 'Yes, I can actually. There is one thing that has been on my mind a long time. But I don't know if it'll make you feel better, perhaps it'll only cause you more anxiety. It's a small, but well-intentioned gesture. Something which might turn out to be useful.'

He looks at me with anticipation. I get up from my chair and walk over to my desk. Scribble something on a yellow Post-it note, return and hand it to him. He grabs it hungrily.

'A telephone number?' he says, baffled.

I nod. 'Put this note by your phone and make sure you don't lose it.'

He folds the paper and puts it in his jacket pocket.

'A telephone number,' he repeats pensively. 'That's not a lot, is it?'

I protest fiercely. 'You're wrong. This number will lead you to another human being who will answer when you call. Someone who can think and act. A compassionate person. This number can save your life, Alvar.'

He is startled. He looks scared and his eyes widen.

'Are you going to test me?' he whispers.

'Alvar my dear,' I reply patiently, 'you're worse than a child. And I know that you're in a tricky place right now. It's like you're half finished. You're dangling, literally, in thin air. But if it's any comfort, Alvar, I'm dangling too. I'm halfway through my story, I'm still in the deep end. I'm struggling to sustain my faith in my own project. Doubt creeps up on me like an invisible gas, it goes to my head and it fills me with fear. Now what's this? I ask myself. Who would want to read this? Can I expect to demand my readers' time and attention with this story? Have I drawn you so clearly that they can see you as well as I can, that they will come to care about you? Have I found the right words?'

'But you love your work, too, you said so the other day.'

'I'm a very inconsistent person,' I declare. 'Yes, I love it, I hate it, I struggle. When it's at its best it sends shivers of delight down my spine, at its worst I'm tearing my hair out. I get up in the morning and I go over to the mirror. I look at my weary face and I tell myself that I can't do it, that it's too hard.'

He frowns. He looks sulky, he is pouting.

'So you don't think I'm worth it?'

'It might be the case that you're only important to me. And perhaps that's enough.'

'I know that I'm not important or amazing or exciting. But there's only one Alvar Eide,' he says, a little hurt.

'That's true. And I've always been of the opinion that every single one of us has a whole novel inside. Every single person you meet has their own life-and-death drama. Just take a look at people, Alvar, as you wander through the town. Look at their eyes, at how they bow their heads; their brisk, but also slightly hesitant, walk. Their anxieties. Their secrets. Oh, I want to stop every single one of them, lift up their chins and look them in the eyes. What do you carry, what do you hide, what do you dream about, please would you tell me so I can write it down, please let me show you to the world?'

'And then you can only pick a few,' he nods. 'What you can manage in your own lifetime. Now I'm starting to feel honoured because you chose me.'

'May I remind you that you anticipated events and made your own way into my house,' I say.

'True, but I was second in the queue anyway. My time would have come regardless.'

'Probably. So, is it time for us to move on? We have to go out into the cold, Alvar, it's the middle of winter.'

He gets up from the sofa. Takes a few steps towards the door.

'I really value our conversations.'

'So do I,' I reply, 'but I might end up deleting them.'

'What?'

He looks shocked.

'They might turn out to be superfluous. You might manage just fine with your own story and your own drama.'

He opens the door, turns one final time.

'It's freezing cold,' he says and shivers. 'Can you feel it?'

He walks down the steps and pauses on the drive for a while. The porch light shines on his bald head.

'I've felt so cold ever since I had my hair cut,' he says.

CHAPTER 13

It was the middle of January and still very cold.

The town was bathed in pale sunlight, white, glazed and shiny. She arrived at half past four in the afternoon just as Alvar was getting ready to close up. This time she was looking ravaged, pale and purple with cold. She looked at him with her kohl-black eyes, they were watering from exhaustion and the frost. She wore no gloves. Her thin neck was bare, a weak stem with thin, blue veins. Alvar rushed off to get her a cup of coffee, it didn't occur to him not to, but he felt a deep sense of unease, it was like sliding towards something unknown, something unmanageable. She took the mug with stiff fingers and went over to the staircase, where she sat down on the second step.

'You ought to get yourself some gloves,' he said, 'and a scarf.'

'I know,' she said indifferently, slurping her coffee. 'But I can't be bothered.'

'Can't be bothered?' he said, surprised because he did not think putting on a scarf was a major challenge. For a while he pondered. Then he decided that he wanted to do something nice for her, something more than just getting her a cup of coffee. After all, she had decided to come back, so events would have to run their course. He made up his mind to act on this whim, even though it was not in his nature. He went up to the kitchen where his outdoor clothes hung and returned with his thin woollen scarf. She accepted it reluctantly. Then she pressed it against her nose and inhaled it for a long time.

'It smells good,' she said, 'it smells of aftershave.'

He nodded. 'It's long,' he said, 'you can wrap it around your neck several times.'

She did so. It looked good on her. The scarf was camel-coloured wool and it suited her. It contrasted beautifully with her pale skin and her ice-blue eyes.

'My gloves are too big for you,' he said, 'so I'll keep them for myself.'

She nodded and drank her coffee, drank it quickly and greedily until she had emptied the mug. Then she put the mug on the step and began staggering around the gallery on thin, unsteady legs. Alvar watched her. He did not mind her being there, she was not making any trouble. She looked somewhat haggard, but she could pass for an ordinary customer if you didn't look at her too carefully. But up close you could tell. The fine veins in her temples, her lips drained of colour. Her ankle boots clicking against the stone floor. She had reached the bridge.

'You said you were going to buy it,' she challenged him.

He shrugged.

'I'm still thinking about it,' he said truthfully.

'And you can't make up your mind?'

'Well, it's expensive,' he said, 'that's why. It's a lot of money to spend in one go.'

'But you can afford it,' she said, 'you said you'd been saving.'

'Yes,' he said, 'I have been saving up. I've been saving for a rainy day. If I buy the painting, I have nothing to fall back on.'

She tasted the words 'fall back on'.

'Is that important?' she smiled. Mockingly, he thought.

'I've nothing to fall back on,' she admitted, 'I live from hand to mouth.'

He gave her a puzzled look. 'So how do you survive? Do you work?'

She laughed out loud. 'God, no,' she hiccupped, 'I can't be bothered with that. People work because they think they have to. I'd rather claim benefits.'

'That can't be very lucrative,' Alvar declared, 'when you can't even afford to buy yourself a scarf and a pair of gloves in the winter.'

'Of course I can afford to buy clothes,' she said, 'but I prefer to spend money on other things. It's all about your priorities.'

'Really?' He looked at her once more. At her incredibly thin legs and the pointy high-heeled boots. Perhaps she was one of those women who sold themselves when their benefit money ran out. He did not like the thought of it, so he instantly pushed it from his mind. But that was how they got money for drugs, he had read about it in the papers. It was truly awful. She was a lovely young woman, with a doll-like face and a tiny pale mouth. She was practically a child, he thought. Could she really be one of those women who got in and out of cars? At night, down on Bragernes Square, where they all congregated? He did not want to judge her. She might have been driven to it by some terrible event. Perhaps she had had an awful childhood, perhaps her father had hit her, or something worse, he didn't know what it could be, but his imagination was starting to run away with him. He didn't think of her as second-rate. But it upset him that she lived in such wretched circumstances when in all likelihood she was just as bright as he was in every possible way. She should have been living another life. But she did not seem to think so. She just drifted from one day to the next without purpose or meaning, without hopes or dreams. And perhaps this was enough for her, as long as she got her drugs, as long as she found relief. Her body was slowly breaking down, but it didn't seem to trouble her. True, it was not as if he knew her well and understood everything, but she did not seem doomed like so many of the others.

'I need to go,' she said suddenly. She handed him the mug and thanked him. She had to step to the side to regain her balance. He watched her disappear.

Later that day, while he was eating a simple meal at the table in the living room, he started thinking about her again. He wondered what her name was, where she lived, things like that. She had said she lived all over the place. There was something ephemeral about her, something transient. He wondered why she kept returning to the gallery. Was it really just to get a cup of coffee? Perhaps that was all there was to it. And he had welcomed her, even though he could have told her to get out. He was just about to leave the table when the doorbell rang. This did not happen often, and when it did it was his neighbour asking to borrow something, or a salesman. He composed himself and went out into the hall. He opened the door and gasped. She was standing outside, in her grey coat with his old woollen scarf around her neck. Alvar was speechless. He stood in the doorway staring at her as if he was hypnotised. She laughed when she saw his surprise, tilted her head and cackled, and he saw her teeth clearly, they were tiny and sharp.

'Hi,' she said cheerfully. 'I thought you might be in.'

Alvar had lost the power to speak. He rocked backwards and forwards on the threshold as he clung to the door frame with one hand.

'You're *here*?' he eventually managed to stammer. A dart of unease pierced his chest. A myriad bewildering thoughts rushed through his mind.

'Yes,' she said simply, letting her hands drop. It looked as though she was expecting to be invited in. Alvar did not want to let her in. He would never have believed that this could happen. Her coming to the gallery was one thing. It was open to everyone and he had been unable to make himself throw her out. But here. In his flat, his home, his castle. He hesitated. She stood there rubbing her cold hands, impatiently, in the doorway.

'How did you know I lived here?' he asked, baffled. He didn't mean to be rude, but he didn't have a clue what was going on.

'I followed you,' she said. 'A few days ago. I saw you go into this flat. And you didn't notice,' she added, 'you don't notice anything.'

She looked at him with her ice-blue eyes. 'Your name is Alvar Eide,' she stated.

'Yes,' he stuttered. He was still clinging to the door frame. His brain was throbbing violently, trying to find a solution.

'Can I come in, please?' she asked directly. And he thought, no, no you can't come in, this is my flat, my boundary is this threshold, I don't want you to intrude. But he did not have the strength to say it to her face. A skinny, fragile young woman was standing at his door wanting to come in. And he was not a cruel man, and he didn't look down on women like her. Nor did he think that she was out to cause him any trouble either, it didn't seem to be her intention. Perhaps she just wanted another cup of coffee. Or to warm up. He opened the door fully and she entered the hall. She gave no indication of wanting to take off her coat. Alvar liked that. That suggested that she would only be staying a little while.

He went into the living room, still marvelling at her presence, and she followed him and sat down on his sofa without waiting to be asked. She sat down as if it was the most natural thing in the world and inspected the room. Alvar collapsed in an armchair. Then he leaned forwards and started tidying away the newspapers, he didn't know what else to do. She followed him with her eyes. He grew nervous. He started to think she was laughing at him. Suddenly she put her feet on his coffee table. He looked directly at the narrow, spiky heels of her ankle boots. Alvar had never put his feet on the coffee table, he thought it was a nasty habit, and besides, she was wearing boots. But he said nothing, he just sat there waiting for something to happen. Perhaps there was a reason for her visit? Was there something specific she wanted? He decided that maybe he ought to make some coffee, as you do when you have guests. But he did not, he stayed in his armchair with a strong feeling of appre-hension coursing through his body. He felt invaded in his own home, yes, indeed he did. She was calmly sitting there staring at him as if he were an exhibit in a museum. When she had finished staring at him, she started looking around the room. She looked at his furniture and his possessions with an open, curious gaze.

'So this is where your painting will go?' she asked out of the blue. She pointed at the vacant space above the fireplace.

'Yes,' he said, turning in his armchair. 'That's what I had in mind. But I need a few days to think it through properly.'

'You'd better hurry up,' she suggested. 'Or it'll be sold.'

I know that, he said to himself, but he did not want to appear argumentative. Instead he decided to ask her a few questions. He felt he had a right, given that she had come all the way into his living room in this brazen manner.

'What's your name?' he asked as he folded his hands in his lap.

'Lindys,' she replied.

'Lindys,' he repeated. He had never heard of such a name.

'Or Merete,' she said. 'Or Elsa. It depends.'

He was confused. 'Depends on what?'

'Well,' she said, flexing the pointy toes of her boots, 'it depends what I feel like that day.'

He lowered his head slowly. He was not feeling very well.

'I see,' he said and could clearly hear that his voice sounded tart. 'So what do you prefer today?'

She thought about it briefly. 'Helle,' she said.

'Very well,' he said. 'Helle. That's settled then.'

'So your name's always the same?' she asked and smiled playfully. She revealed her sharp teeth again.

'Of course,' he said earnestly. 'People usually keep the same name their entire life. And I know you're only joking.'

She laughed once more. Suddenly she took her feet off the coffee table. He experienced an instant sense of relief.

'You got any sweets?' she asked.

Alvar was taken aback. Sweets? Was she being serious?

He hesitated again. 'Sweets?'

'Yes. Sweets, fruit gums, chocolate,' she explained. A little perplexed because he was being so dim.

'No, no, I don't have any sweets,' he replied, shaking his head.

'None at all?' she pressed.

He felt his irritation rise again as he carefully tried to recall the contents of his kitchen cupboards.

'I might have a packet of raisins,' he remembered.

'Raisins?' She mimed munching them. 'Yeah, all right. Can I have them? I need sugar and I need it now.'

He sat there gawping at her. She was demanding that he fetched her some raisins. He did not begrudge her the raisins, but he was not entirely sure where she was going with this. He went out into the kitchen and found the packet. It was one of those snack boxes you put in children's packed lunches. He returned and handed it to her and she opened it immediately. She dug her greedy fingers into the contents.

'Chocolate is better,' she said, 'but raisins will have to do.'

Yes, they certainly will, Alvar thought. He sat watching her as she ate the raisins. She ate all of them and tossed the empty packet onto the coffee table. Again he felt a surge of irritation. She was so careless. She was his guest, but she was acting as if she owned the place. She certainly made herself at home. I guess I'm just being petty, he thought, I'm not used to having guests. I scarcely know how guests would behave. At the same time a chill passed through him. He was always alone and he was always in control and now he was being overpowered by a skinny girl and he did not have the guts to stand up to her. He decided to ask her where she lived. Even though he had asked her before and she had replied, 'Oh, all over the place.' All the same, he was sure that she lived somewhere, she was just unwilling to tell him. He felt very awkward in her presence. Surely his knees were too sharp and his arms too long?

He changed his mind and instead he asked her, 'How old are you?'

'How old? Well, how old do you think?'

Having to guess made him feel uncomfortable. Then he thought, I don't have to guess, I can tell her that I've no idea. But then he looked at her again and estimated her to be twenty.

'Eighteen,' she replied.

Alvar nodded. Perhaps she was lying about this too, like she lied about her name. She was still smiling and he noticed that she had bits of raisins stuck between her teeth. It didn't look attractive, but he couldn't tell her that. He was restless. He wondered how long she intended to sit there lounging on his sofa.

'You're over forty, aren't you?' she said, watching him.

'Forty-two,' he replied truthfully.

'Isn't it about time you got married and started a family?'

He squirmed in his armchair. He was not enjoying this conversation and he refused to expose himself.

'Don't do it,' she said the next moment. 'Family equals trouble. Responsibilities. No money. Endless guilt and a life of drudgery.'

'Does it?'

She ran her fingers through her hair, which was sticking out like a bristle brush.

'I prefer brief acquaintances,' she said. 'Same as you, I can tell from looking at you.'

'Can you?'

She looked around his flat, her ice-blue eyes scanned his possessions and his furniture. 'Christ, you're tidy. Potted plants and embroidered cushions, would you believe it.'

Alvar was feeling increasingly uncomfortable. It was weird that she was sitting there; she had flown right through his door like some strange bird. Even though he wanted to chase her away there was a big knot of resistance inside him which stopped him.

She had walked over to the window. She stared down at the light-bulb factory.

'The Mazda parked down behind the house, is that yours?'

'Yes.'

He squeezed his hands in his lap and tried to be patient.

'I don't have a car,' she said. 'Too much hassle. Who lives downstairs? Do you ever talk to them?'

'The Greens,' he explained. 'We exchange a few words every now and then.'

'Making polite conversation,' she said, 'how awful.'

He nodded in agreement.

'You're really wound up because I'm here, aren't you?'

He was shocked. His instinctive reaction was to protest, but he could not manage it.

'You're one of those loners who keep everyone else at arm's length. That's quite all right, I'm the same.'

'You just took me by surprise,' he said cautiously. 'I don't get many visitors,' he added.

'None,' she said, looking at him. 'No one ever comes here, not a living soul. Am I right?'

Alvar blushed. She was so direct and so forward that she took his breath away.

'You don't need to make excuses,' she went on. 'People come in all shapes and sizes, and I'm the pot calling the kettle black. But most of the time I feel sorry for people. They make it so hard for themselves to be who they really are.'

'And you don't?' he asked before he could stop himself.

She walked over and sat down on the sofa again. 'My life isn't easy,' she said, 'but it is really straightforward. I live one hour at a time. Right now I'm in your cosy living room and I'm enjoying it. I've no idea where I'll be spending the night. But I'm not worried about it. Whereas you,' she said watching him, 'you're already thinking about tomorrow. You're making plans and you'll stick to them. Rather than living in the moment. Am I right? I know I'm right.'

Alvar bowed his head. He could not see how there was anything wrong with making plans. But her presence was really getting on his nerves now and he was desperate for a way to end the conversation.

'No,' he said abruptly and patted the armrests on his chair, 'and anyway, I've got things to do.'

He could not look her in the eyes as he said it, but he got up from his armchair to signal that her visit was over. She just looked at him with wide eyes.

'Really?' she said, puzzled. She did not get up. 'What is it you need to do?'

'Well,' he hesitated. 'Some paperwork.'

She considered this. To his immense relief Alvar saw that she was getting up. He thought, she'll be gone soon and I'll be on my own again and if she rings the doorbell another time, I won't let her in. I won't open the door because I'm in charge here. Then he realised that he would not be able to see who was outside. He did not have a spyhole in his door. Never mind. He decided not to open his door to anyone. No one ever turned up anyway, and if someone did ring the doorbell in the next few days it would probably be this Lindys. Or Elsa. Or Helle. Whatever her name was. She went out in the hall and he followed her. Suddenly she stopped, turned and fixed her eyes on him.

'Could you lend me a grand?'

Alvar gasped for air. Was she out of her mind? Were there no limits to her importunity?

'I don't think I have that much cash on me,' he blurted out. He made an apologetic gesture. She kept looking at him.

'Can't you check?' she asked. 'I'm totally skint and I need a fix.'

Alvar started shaking. His wallet was in his coat pocket, it hung in the hall less than a metre from where they were standing. And he did not understand why he acted as he did. At that moment all he could think of was getting her out of his flat at any cost. He stuck his hand in the inside pocket and pulled out his wallet. She watched it hungrily. He opened the note section and quickly counted the contents. Seven hundred and fifty kroner plus a bit of loose change in the coin compartment. He pulled out the notes. She stared at them. And before he had time to blink she had snatched them from him. He was left startled and empty-handed. Go, he was screaming inside, just go. Please, please go!

She placed her hand on the door handle and opened the door.

'You're all right, Alvar,' she said softly. Her voice was suddenly tender and almost feline.

Alvar melted instantly. It had been a very long time since anyone had last paid him a compliment. Had anyone ever done so? He was not feeling very well. Yet at the same time he was moved.

Then she was gone. She practically darted around the corner of the house like a squirrel. He remained in the hall for a while to calm himself down. I'll never see that money again, he thought. He was well aware of it. Yet he worried all the same. She would spend it on drugs. Yes, of course she would, he thought, in which case I haven't done a good deed after all, I'm contributing to her ruin, that's what I'm doing. He went into his living room and walked over to the window. Leaned against the windowsill and gasped for air. He watched her disappear down the hill. He followed her with his eyes. He could not shake off the feeling that he had done something very stupid. That's it, he thought, you'll never get rid of her now. You let her into your warm home. You go looking in the cupboard for raisins, you lend her money. You can't let her in ever again or you'll be trapped. At the same time it was a rare experience for him that someone actively sought his company. Although it was not his company she was interested in. She wanted his money. He collapsed back into his chair and ran his hand over his bare scalp. She had not commented on his new hairstyle and for that he was deeply grateful.

CHAPTER 14

Another icy morning.

A day when the earth was a frozen shell, impenetrable. He snatched the newspaper from his letter box and set off down the hill towards Engene. He was wearing his winter coat, it was warm, but he missed his scarf. The chill gripped his neck tightly like a claw. He marched on and gradually his body began to warm up. Yesterday's discomfort was beginning to lift, but he was still feeling uneasy. There's no point in worrying about what might happen, he reasoned with himself, because it probably never will, I worked that one out long ago. However, this argument did not make him feel much better. I'm on thin ice, he thought, I have to tread carefully, not lose my head. Stay in control, maintain a firm grip. Thirty minutes later he let himself into the gallery. He was still feeling unsettled, as if he was expecting Lindys, or Elsa, or Helle to turn up at any moment. Something inside him was waiting for her. He did not want her to come, she was a disruption in his life, something unpredictable. But here, in the gallery, he could not refuse to open the door; she could open it herself and walk right in. Having allowed her in the first time it would be difficult to refuse her now. How stupid he had been, how naive.

He went into the workshop to find something to occupy himself with, he needed to be distracted. He cut glass and cardboard, he polished and glued and tagged. He tried to enjoy this tinkering, but he wasn't able to. Weidemann's painting with his own thumbprint had dried ages ago and now it hung out in the gallery next to the bridge. He kept peeking furtively outside. First she would appear like a shadow outside the window, then the bell would ring. But he saw no one. The hours passed. Perhaps I was worrying about nothing, he thought. Perhaps she was just in a tight spot, but she'll stay away from now on. She won't be coming here any more. She is far too unstable to form a bond with anyone. This logic comforted him. Other customers came and went, he made polite conversation with them, maintaining his usual defensive stance. You should never underestimate a customer, he thought, the most unassuming individual might turn out to possess an impressive knowledge of Norwegian art. His approach was always cautious, a kind of tentative dance. He did not initiate a conversation with a customer until they had exchanged a few pleasantries.

The customers started to thin out and he seized the opportunity to eat his packed lunch. He spent the afternoon replacing a number of light bulbs, there was a spotlight positioned above every single painting. He felt terribly pleased at the end of the day because she hadn't showed up. The painting of the bridge had begun to take second place in his mind; it seemed as if Lindys was taking up all the space, as if she was standing inside his head shouting in a manner that was impossible to ignore. As he was about to leave he paused a metre from the painting. The pillars and a stump jutting out above the void, a dense, mystical fog. Faint contours of rocks and the mainland, but no horizon, no divide between sky and sea. The painting consumed him once more; it seemed to re-establish his inner balance.

He avoided Bragernes Square on his way home. He thought she might be drifting around there together with the dark-haired man who was not her brother. Have I really let a prostitute into my life? he thought as he walked home. No, I haven't let her in, she won't be coming back, I'm certain of this, those people are so restless. That day he shopped in Rimi. He bought fish fingers, which he would eat with potatoes and tartar sauce. Cheap and good for you, Alvar thought. He put his shopping in a bag and went back out into the street and started walking up the steep hill to his flat. At the letter box he met Green, his neighbour, who nodded to him briefly; Alvar nodded briefly back. Had he seen Lindys the previous day when she came to his door? Seen her slumped there in all her wretchedness? What must he have thought? She looked like a mere child, but the life she was living had so obviously left its mark on her. The Greens were probably gossiping at long length about her over dinner. He shuddered at the thought. He loathed the idea that other people might be discussing him, might be thinking about him, because it was beyond his control. For a moment he felt unwell, he felt disjointed and awkward, it was like falling apart. Then he pulled himself together and let himself in.

As he entered the flat he was suddenly filled with a sense of purpose, it rose within him like mercury in a thermometer. He went straight to the telephone and called his bank to find out the balance of his savings account.

'The available balance is: seventy thousand three hundred and sixty-seven kroner and thirty øre,' the voice announced. Alvar was delighted. Tomorrow morning he would go straight to his bank and transfer the money to Gallery Krantz. He would do it before he went to work. He would call his boss and ask him to drive the painting over to his flat, he would hang it on the wall. He would pull his armchair over to the fireplace, pour himself a sherry and sit down to look at the painting for the whole evening. Drown in it, lose himself in it, possess it. The thought filled him with joy. Then he thought of Lindys again. From now on whenever he saw a blonde head in the street, he knew he would jump. He was certain her name was Lindys. Alvar possessed a little insight into other people. The first name she had given him was her real name. The others were just to wind him up. Banter. She was like that. He decided to think of her as Lindys. When he thought of her. Because he was thinking of her and he did not understand that either. He was unaccustomed to another human being occupying his consciousness, someone just appearing and destroying his protracted and meticulous way of thinking. Again his thoughts were drawn to the painting. An extravagance, it struck him, the greatest in my life. A turning point. What will it be like to have the painting in my home? Perhaps it will drive me crazy? Now while it's hanging in the gallery I pine for it. But once it's on my own wall perhaps it will be different. Once it's here all the time, every time I lift my eyes and look above the fireplace. When I come into the living room in the morning and in the evening. Always this severed bridge. This dark, mysterious bridge, which ends abruptly in nothingness. Will it make me happy? Yes, a voice inside him said, it will make me happy.

CHAPTER 15

'Now I understand it all,' Alvar says, 'I'm no longer confused. She's my challenge, this Lindys.'

He assumes a dramatic mien. Contrary to all his good habits, he stuffs his hands into the pockets of his newly pressed trousers.

I look up from my newspaper. I nod.

'It certainly looks that way,' I say. 'Are you disappointed?'

He pulls his hands out of his pockets.

'I'm nervous. I'd been expecting something else. We don't speak the same language, she and I, and she makes me feel incredibly inept.'

I cannot help but smile.

'You *are* inept,' I say. 'But you can learn how to interact with other people. God knows you need the practice. I gave you a young, damaged woman because I needed a contrast. I needed something that might turn nasty.'

'Is she nasty?' he asks swiftly. His grey eyes darken.

'Not at all,' I assure him. 'But she lives in a rough world and she has been hardened by that. I would advise you to proceed with caution, Alvar. She probably knows a lot of people you wouldn't be able to handle.'

'Will there be more of them?' he asks.

'I'm not sure yet. I'm still thinking about it.'

His eyes look haunted. He takes a seat on the sofa, brushes the knees of his trousers. He is immaculately dressed as always, his shirt is white and freshly ironed.

'I suppose it's for the best if I break off all contact with her immediately,' he says after a pause. 'That I toughen myself up. That

I don't let her in, especially not into my flat. Do you know something? She puts her feet on my coffee table. It's a flame birch table from 1920. My mother would turn in her grave.'

I give him a wistful smile. 'Do you really think you can manage that? You don't have it in you, Alvar, you're not able to turn anyone away. Especially not a fragile young woman. Did you know,' I continue, 'at the start I contemplated sending you a child? A chubby, cheeky child.'

He looks up.

'A child? That wouldn't have worked very well,' he declares. 'I'm not good with children, I don't know how to behave in front of them. They always stare at you, it's like they're spying on you, and then they drool.'

'Yes, they do, don't they?'

He leans forward across the table and rests his hands on his thighs.

'In that case I'm really pleased that you changed your mind,' he says, relieved. 'I'll just have to manage as best I can. One day at a time. But am I allowed to make a wish?'

I hesitate. I fold my newspaper.

'As long as you don't wish for a happy ending,' I say eventually.

He runs his hand across his head. Still somewhat surprised at his baldness.

'No, I'm not asking for anything specific. A pleasant interlude, perhaps. A moment, an experience. Anything.'

'It won't be easy,' I reply, 'you're not terribly spontaneous, Alvar, and consequently not much happens in your carefully organised life.'

'But what if I make an effort?'

I nod. 'Let's go for it, let's see what happens. I'll offer you some bait and we'll see if you take it.'

'There was one other thing,' he remembers. 'I don't mean to be pushy, but when do you think we'll finish?'

I shrug. I mull it over. 'We're talking about a year probably. But this assumes I'm allowed to get on with my work without too many interruptions.'

'You think I'm pushy, don't you?'

I nod. 'You're pushy in a very disarming way,' I reply. 'I'll make an exception this time, but I've no intention of making it a habit. You spotted an opening, Alvar, and caught me off guard. Now I want to let events unfold, and I hope we both make it to the end. And please forgive me for saying this, but I never intended for you to be an ambitious project.'

He frowns and his face droops.

'So what was I meant to be?' he asks feebly.

'Well,' I venture, 'a lesser work. Something charming, unpretentious. A fleeting joy, a pleasant acquaintance. A minor literary game.'

'In other words,' he says, 'not a masterpiece?'

I am taken aback. 'That's asking for too much. Now you're making me nervous.'

'Allow me to add,' he says quickly, 'that I'm quite happy so far, I really am. I would hate to complain. But I suppose I had a faint hope that I might be heroic. In some way.'

'You are,' I tell him, 'in your everyday life. The question is what you'll do when you're tested.'

He looks at me closely.

'What does your gut instinct tell you?' he asks.

Again I cannot help but laugh. It is liberating, I laugh till the tears roll down my cheeks. 'You're unbelievable, you really are,' I hiccup. 'I've never experienced such pestering, you're worse than a spoiled child. Now please be patient, Alvar, I have a good feeling about you, I'll admit that much, and that's a good sign. All the same,' I add, 'based on my past records I can be quite brutal. Besides, I need to resolve something within myself along the way. Your weakness, this tendency to keep your distance from everyone and everything, your inability to act, your bashfulness, your modesty, your meticulousness, how do I honestly feel about that? Where do I place you in terms of morality, what do I think about the way you live your life? Are you a coward, are you arrogant, are you socially maladjusted or are you an attractive man with a pure heart? You have a fair amount of resources and talents, but you've isolated yourself and you're terrified of going off the rails.'

'So you want to derail me? You want me to crash?'

'I'm afraid you're right,' I reply.

Alvar turns pale. He takes a handkerchief out of his shirt pocket and wipes his forehead.

'But that doesn't mean that you won't recover,' I add. 'Perhaps you'll get back on another, an even better track. What do you say to that?'

'I'm not very fond of changes,' he admits.

'Me neither,' I say honestly. 'I know how you feel, Alvar, I empathise. But sometimes I get frustrated. You stay within the confines of your safe existence and as your audience I get fed up with it. Just let yourself go a little, I urge you; swear out loud, tell a customer to clear off, start slamming some doors.'

'That wasn't the done thing when I was growing up,' he says quickly.

'But you're a grown man now,' I retort.

He folds the handkerchief neatly and returns it to his shirt pocket.

'I'm no good at confrontation,' he says quietly. 'I like it here with you,' he adds, 'you never lash out.'

'I'm afraid to,' I say. 'Like you, I'm simply too scared.'

'Why, what do you think would happen?' he asks.

'There are times when I just want to scream, but I'm afraid to because I think the windows would shatter.'

'Why?' he insists.

'Because the scream would be so loud.'

He goes silent again, he looks distant.

'Do you want me to leave?'

'Yes, I do actually. If that's all right with you. I want to do another hour of work or two.'

He gets up from the sofa.

'Like I said,' he emphasises, 'we all have free will and I have chosen an ordered life with fixed routines. You're saying you want to derail me, but you'll have to expect that I will protest.'

'Really?'

'You'll just have to wait to see if I can take care of myself, if I can scope out the territory and watch my own back.'

CHAPTER 16

February came and took the edge off the worst of the cold.

Ole Krantz had finally hung the painting of the severed bridge on the wall and angled a spotlight to illuminate it properly. Alvar was still debating whether or not to buy it. The decision had to come from somewhere deep inside him; he oscillated between hope and fear. Hope that one day he would own it. Fear that someone would snap it up before his very eyes. He obviously wanted to buy it and possess it, he just had to get into the right frame of mind, it was a huge and important purchase. It was one thing to buy a print by Jarle Rosseland, people did that without a second thought. However the painting *Broken* was something else, so overwhelming, enormous and dramatic. At seven minutes past five he left the gallery and made his way as usual to the Cash and Carry. He headed straight to the delicatessen and bought the home-made meatballs with pickled gherkins and paprika. Then he continued around the big store and picked up some coffee, a packet of sandwich biscuits and a newspaper. He paid and was just about to leave when he spotted the large noticeboard on the wall by the exit. On the spur of the moment he decided to read the notices, as if an awareness of other people's lives had suddenly flickered in his consciousness. He put down his bag and started going through them.

Childminder in Bragernes available. Non-smoker. Good with
    kids of all ages.
For sale: two-seater sofa in brown leather, slightly worn,
    bargain buy.

Yoga course starting now. Beginners and Intermediates.
Have you seen Pilate? Green parrot missing since January.

Alvar kept on reading. The noticeboard was completely covered with scraps of paper and he realised that he would be unable to tear himself away until he had read every single one of them.

Home-made griddle cakes and marzipan horns made from traditional recipes. We bake to order.
Bric-a-brac needed for charity sale on the 20th.
Fancy singing in a choir?

Alvar took a step back. No, he did not fancy singing in a choir, absolutely not, he had no talent for singing. The thought of mingling with so many people was also quite impossible for him to entertain. Then he stepped forward again and read another note.

Free kittens. Four females and one male, house-trained and ready for collection.

And then a photo of them, five tiny fluff balls in a basket. Alvar felt his heart beat tenderly. A cat, he thought, I've always wanted a cat. But I have never done anything about it, it's embarrassing. A cat could look after itself and it would offer him silent companionship, precisely what he was looking for. True, a cat was a commitment, but he had only himself to look after and he had plenty of spare time. It was also true that he had absolutely no clue how to care for an animal, but he would learn by doing. And there was a veterinary surgery only ten minutes' walk from his house where he could get all the help and guidance he needed; in case the cat fell ill or required injections. A cat, soft and warm. A cat slinking around his flat, a cat lying on his sofa purring. A cat sleeping at the foot of his bed at night.

Maybe. He kept looking at the photo. He liked the grey one the best, but he was adamant that he wanted a tom. If the grey one turned out to be the tom, he would get it. If they had not already found new homes for them; there was no date on the note, it could have been up there a long time. There was both an address and a telephone number. Haugestad Farm in Frydenlund. It was ten minutes in the Mazda. There's no harm in looking at them, he thought, I can go there to see them and then give myself a few days to make up my mind. But to have a cat. Someone to chat to, someone waiting for me, when I come home from work. And if I worm it then I'll avoid those disgusting regurgitations that I was so repulsed by as a child. He stood for a while looking at the small fur balls. They would probably need a few bits and pieces, it occurred to him. A basket to sleep in, toys. Vitamins. He pondered this for a long time. Then he snapped himself out of his trance and started walking home.

He let himself in and put his shopping on the kitchen counter, then he went over to wash his hands. That was when his doubts resurfaced. A pet ties you down, after all. If he wanted to go to Copenhagen for a weekend, for example, he would not be able to do that. Not that he had ever spent a weekend in Copenhagen, but if he wanted to one day, then the cat would have to be left on its own. But of course there was always Green downstairs. True, they never really spoke, but it was surely acceptable to ask his neighbour to please put some cat food in a bowl and top up the water over the weekend. Green's teenage children would do it for him, he was convinced of that. A cat, he thought, that would be bouncing around happily, it would be a joy every day.

He took the meatballs out of the bag, placed them on a plate. He put the plate in the oven. Now the seed had been planted it gave him no peace at all. To top it all the cat was free, so it could not be deemed an extravagance. He was so excited he ate his food in record time, carried his plate to the kitchen, rinsed everything off and went to the bathroom. There he washed his hands and combed the small semicircle of hair with a fine-toothed comb. He took his car keys from a hook in the hallway and left. He wondered if the Mazda would even start, he did not drive it very often. Sometimes he started it and let the engine run for fifteen minutes so it would not stop working altogether.

He got in and turned the key. Heard the engine splutter to life. He was ready to go. He pressed the accelerator, but it was not enough. He turned the key again, revving the engine harder, and finally the engine started to hum. He sat in his seat for a while waiting for the engine to warm up. He had no complaints about his car. The Mazda had never let him down. Then he drove out through the gate and onto the road. A cat. If they still had any left. Perhaps he should have phoned in advance, it occurred to him, but there was always someone around on a farm. He turned left at the light-bulb factory, found the right lane and kept an eye on the traffic behind him in his rear-view mirror. He considered himself to be a good driver. He always drove slightly below the speed limit just to be on the safe side, and he always drove defensively. He had the fjord on his right, it was blue grey in colour and there were ripples in the water caused by the evening breeze. His heart was racing. If they had no more kittens left, he would be terribly disappointed. Because now, halfway through his life, he was finally ready for this event. He had no trouble locating the farm and swung onto the driveway. Stayed in his car and looked around. A dog came padding towards him, it looked like a setter. A woman appeared in the doorway; she waved. Then she leaned against the door frame expectantly. Alvar stepped out of his car. He started walking towards the whitewashed farmhouse.

'I'm here about the cats,' he said, 'I saw the picture of them in the Cash and Carry. But perhaps they've all gone?'

She smiled broadly and gestured to him.

'No, don't worry, I've still got some left. Do come in. Come on, in you come!' she said warmly and opened the door wide. Alvar walked slowly up the steps. They shook hands and he was ushered into a warm farmhouse kitchen with a long table, a fireplace and curtains with colourful pelmets.

'I've got three left,' the woman said, 'they're all over the place; you see, they're already nine weeks old. But why don't we go into the living room and see if we can find them?'

He followed her. Noticed an adult cat on a chair. Curled up next to her were the kittens. Dear Lord, Alvar thought, how tiny they are. How fragile.

She picked up a black kitten with a white chest. Alvar remained standing, fiddling with his fingers, not even sure that he had the courage to hold it. He could see himself dropping it on the floor out of sheer fright. The woman put the kitten on the table and it staggered around. Its tail was short and stuck right out, and its eyes were blue.

'And then we've got the grey one,' she said, lifting up another one. Alvar recognised it from the photo. 'It's a tom,' she said, 'the only one in the litter. Which do you prefer?'

'The tom,' he said swiftly. 'I can't risk it having kittens, I know nothing of such things.'

'Then that's the one for you,' she said happily, 'and when it's eight months old you take it to the vet's and have him neutered, then he won't stray. And he'll fight less with other cats. There you are,' she said, holding out the kitten, 'do you want to hold him?'

Alvar held out his hands. She placed the kitten in them. It sent shivers down his spine. It was so soft. It was so light and warm. He felt a faint vibration in the palm of his hand.

'He's purring,' the woman said excitedly, 'he's taken to you already. The kids call him Bugs Bunny.'

'Bugs Bunny?' Alvar shook his head baffled. 'Why?'

'Because he's grey and white,' she explained. 'But you can decide on a name yourself, he's your cat. That's right, isn't it? He's your cat now?'

Alvar nodded. He was in awe. My cat, he thought, is most certainly not going to be called Bugs Bunny.

'I'll get you a box,' the woman said. 'With a lid. And some holes for ventilation. Place it next to you in the car and drive carefully on your way back.'

'Does he need injections right away?' he asked solemnly.

'Injections?' she chuckled. 'Here on the farm we don't worry too much about injections. If they're going to make it, they'll make it, after all we've got plenty of them. But if you want to do it properly then just call a vet and they'll tell you all you need to know.'

'What kind of food does he eat?' he enquired.

'Buy pellets. And buy the cheapest brand. I know the vets say it's old, pulped IKEA furniture, but the cats seem to love it.'

'IKEA furniture?' Alvar gave her a horrified look.

'Well, vets too have their contacts which they have to keep sweet, don't they?' she laughed. 'No, give him what you like, for God's sake. Leftovers, slices of bread with liver paste. But always make sure he has plenty of fresh water. And if I were you I'd buy a tray with cat litter. Yes, it's a bit messy, but soon the cat will claw at the door when he wants to go outside. He's practically house-trained already.'

She walked briskly back to the kitchen. Alvar followed her. Holding the cat firmly all the time. She lifted the seat of a bench and pulled out a grey box. Then she grabbed a roll of kitchen towel, tore of a few sheet and lined the box with them. 'In case he pees on the way back,' she explained. Alvar put the kitten in the box. Immediately he started squeaking like a mouse. The lid had three large holes, he could see the kitten's head in the semi-darkness.

'Just give me a call if you've got any questions,' she said cheerfully.

'Well, I'm sure I'll be fine,' he said, holding the box carefully against his chest. 'Where would I get cat litter?'

'From the pet shop in Bragernes. You'll find everything you need there. And you don't have to worry about bad smells, because the cat litter they make these days is very good.'

He nodded. Held out his hand and thanked her. She escorted him to his car and watched him as he placed the small box on the seat beside him.

'Go easy over the speed bumps,' she ordered him.

Alvar nodded. 'I will.'

Then he started the car and turned out into the road. The woman stood on the steps watching him.

Alvar drove.

He could hear how the kitten clawed frantically inside his box.

The poor thing was sitting in there in the dark, brutally torn away from his mother. How merciless, Alvar thought, but that's what human beings do. And he will soon get used to me. Perhaps he will sleep on the rug by my bed, that would be cosy. The box was rocking, he noticed, the little creature was trying to escape and he realised that he was beginning to feel stressed. What if the kitten got sick? Or run over? Or some other dreadful thing happened to it? He drove into the town centre and left the kitten in the car while he bought a tray, some cat litter and some dry food.

'I want a good quality cat food,' Alvar stated firmly. 'None of that pulped IKEA rubbish, if you don't mind.'

The girl behind the desk laughed at him. 'Then you'll want this one,' she said. 'Royal Canin. The very best. But it's pricey.'

'Never mind. Can't be helped,' he said and paid without blinking. He was remarkably flash with his money, nothing but the best for his cat. He carried everything out into his car and packed it in the boot. Shortly afterwards he pulled in to his own backyard. First he carried his purchases upstairs, then he got the kitten. He pressed the box carefully to his chest. At this point his neighbour appeared. He stared at him. There was something about the grey box which aroused his curiosity.

'Got yourself a hamster?' he chuckled.

Alvar shook his head fiercely. 'Oh, no. It's a kitten.'

'Really? A kitten?' Green sighed. 'That's it, I'll never hear the end of it now, the kids have been pestering me for years to get a cat. Really?' he said again. 'How much did you have to pay for it?'

'Nothing at all,' Alvar said. 'But I had to get some equipment, you know, trays and whatnot. And that was fairly expensive.'

His neighbour came over to him. Very carefully Alvar lifted the lid and they both looked down at the terrified animal.

'What a gorgeous little thing,' his neighbour said.

Alvar agreed. He made as if to leave but his neighbour remembered something.

'There was someone at your door today.'

'Oh?'

'A young girl. Or a woman, I should say. I'm not quite sure. Skinny and blonde. She rang the bell for a long time.'

Alvar felt his stomach lurch. His neighbour scrutinised him as though waiting for further explanation.

'That doesn't sound like anyone I know,' he lied and headed for his own front door.

'Are you sure? I could swear that I've seen her before,' his neighbour persisted. 'In fact, I recognise her from Bragernes Square,' he added.

Alvar's cheeks burned. He tucked the box under one arm and unlocked the door with his other hand.

'Of course,' his neighbour said eventually, 'it's none of my business, but you can't give those people an inch. They'll just take a mile.'

Alvar felt an icy chill down his spine. 'I'll bear that in mind,' he said, averting his eyes. Then he went into the hallway. He put the box with the kitten on the kitchen table and lifted the lid. Lifted the little bundle out. It stood up on trembling legs looking confused. He thought the kitten was absolutely perfect. It had a white chest, but was otherwise grey with a tiny pink nose. Tiny, tiny paws. Bright blue eyes that soon would turn yellow or green, he guessed. Then he remembered that it might be thirsty. He put the kitten on the floor and found a bowl in his kitchen cupboard, which he filled with water. The kitten came over straight away to drink. This was a momentous occasion for Alvar. He was responsible for this tiny animal, he had to look after it, take care of it, feed it, and these were things he had hardly ever done for another living creature. He sat down on the floor and watched it as it drank. And you need a name, too, he thought. And given that art is my passion, I'll name you after a painter.

How about Rembrandt? he thought. No, it was too big and cumbersome. Picasso was out of the question; da Vinci? No, that was conceited. How about the Norwegian painters? he wondered. Kittelsen, how funny would that be? Or Heiberg, perhaps. He instantly dismissed it as ridiculous. He stood up again and thought on. Started preparing a litter tray for the kitten. It would have to go in a corner of the kitchen for the time being. Suddenly he felt deeply moved by everything that had happened. And how quickly it had all come about. From the minute he had gone over to the noticeboard up to this moment when he was standing in his own kitchen with his very own kitten. It was really so unlike him to let himself go like this. He spread out the sand so it lay evenly in the tray and then he pushed it up against the wall. The kitten grew curious, it soon climbed into the tray and did its business. Alvar sank down onto a kitchen chair, cupped his chin in his hands and admired the little bundle. I'm going to treat myself to a sherry tonight, he decided, as the cat bounced around. In his mind he was flicking through great sections of art history. Finally he decided to name the kitten Goya.

At this very moment someone rang the doorbell hard.

Alvar jumped in his chair, he grabbed the kitten and he ran into the living room. His heart was pounding. Was it her again, Lindys? Or a salesperson, perhaps, or his neighbour? He stood petrified, clutching the kitten to his chest. If he just kept totally still whoever it was would eventually go away; right now he did not want to be disturbed. The bell rang again, sharply this time. His heart leapt to his throat. Why had she come to his flat, what did she want? What had he done wrong? Why did she have to blight his peaceful existence? The bell rang for the third time. Whoever it was, was leaning on the bell, the sound cut through the flat. His cheeks were hot with despair. Then it struck him how ridiculous it all was; him standing there shaking with fright just because someone was ringing his doorbell, and how pathetic he had become. It was a simple case of refusing to open the door, she would give up eventually. Because now he was quite certain that it was Lindys on the other side of the door. The bell rang for the fourth time. Or, he thought, I'll open the door and I'll ask her to go away once and for all. He rehearsed the words in his head. Go away once and for all. Suddenly everything went quiet, he thought he heard voices. Had his neighbour gone out? He went over to his kitchen window and looked out. Then the bell started ringing again. He could not bear it any longer; he clutched the kitten and went to open the door.

'Christ,' she said, putting her hands on her hips, 'what took you so long? You were here the whole time!'

Then she spotted the kitten. She melted instantly.

'Oh, but just look at you,' she said taking the kitten from him. She simply snatched it from his hands and pressed it confidently to her pale cheek.

'So when did you get this one? What's his name? Is it a boy? How old is it?'

Alvar struggled to deal with four questions simultaneously.

He cleared his throat nervously. 'I got him today. He's nine weeks old. His name is Goya.'

'Goya,' she repeated dubiously. 'Why?'

'Because,' he said, 'I named him after the Spanish painter. Francisco de Goya.'

'Right.' She still did not quite follow. 'Can I come in?' she asked then.

'I was just about to go out,' he spluttered. He reached out for his kitten, but she refused to give him back.

'I just need a few minutes,' she said, and before he knew it, she had stepped past him and into the hall. Alvar bit his lip.

'He's got blue eyes,' she said joyously.

He looked at her kohl-black eyes. She did not seem to be high and she was not slurring her words, that was always something.

'They'll turn green eventually,' he explained. She sat down on the sofa and put her feet on the coffee table. Alvar remained standing, clenching and unclenching his fists in frustration. She had clearly never been taught manners of any sort and her ankle boots were far from clean.

'You're lovely, you are,' she said, kissing the kitten on his pink nose. Alvar stood in the middle of the floor watching them. The kitten dangled like a toy in her hands.

'Don't squeeze him too hard,' he warned her. He couldn't bear it that she had taken the kitten from him.

'Oh, cats can cope with anything,' she said. 'They've got nine lives, didn't you know?'

'I have to correct you there,' Alvar said, 'they only have one, actually. And this kitten is my responsibility.'

She laughed at him. She stroked the head of the kitten with her fingers.

'So you're going out?' she said then. 'Where are you going? Are you taking the car?'

He nodded. 'I've got some business to attend to. In Oslo,' he lied.

'Cool!' she burst out. 'Can I come with you?'

He took a step back as he inwardly cursed himself and he started babbling. 'Yes, no,' he gibbered, 'I'm not leaving right now. I'm not altogether sure when, I need to go into town first, I've got some shopping to do there.'

She fixed him with her ice-blue eyes. 'Good God, you're a busy man,' she said. Then she laughed again, her laughter was shrill and loud.

'Well, I've got several things to do,' Alvar said again, 'in several different places. You'll just be bored waiting for me here, there and everywhere. It would be better if you took the bus,' he said rapidly. 'Or the train.'

She put the cat down on the table. Alvar leapt forward and grabbed it immediately.

'I didn't think you'd be so dull,' she said then.

Dull? Am I dull? Alvar thought. No, I certainly am not. But I'm floundering, how am I going to get this person out of my house?

'Do you have any more raisins?' she asked.

He shook his head firmly. 'No raisins. No chocolate. Nothing at all.'

Suddenly she started patting the pocket of her grey coat.

'One fag, that's all I need, I'm not staying long. You can get ready in the meantime. Do you leave the cat on his own when you go out? Then always remember to put the toilet seat down when you've been to the loo. I had a cat once and one day I found it drowned in the loo.'

Alvar was shocked. 'So,' he said when he had recovered, 'it only had eight lives left then?'

She made a face at him. Stuck a cigarette in her mouth, fished out a lighter advertising a convenience store.

'I was trying to give you a piece of advice,' she said, 'but if you're not interested then that's no skin off my nose.' She blew a column of smoke out into the room. Alvar hated it, he was not used to the smell of smoke, he did not even own an ashtray, so he went into the kitchen and found a bowl. Put it in front of her on the coffee table. She immediately flicked the ash off her cigarette.

'Don't you have something you should be getting on with?' she said. He sat down in his armchair. He felt he ought to make conversation, but at the same time he wanted her to leave.

'What have you done with the scarf?'

'The scarf?' She gave him a perplexed look.

'Yes,' he said, 'the scarf I gave you. The Mulberry scarf. It's a very fine scarf.'

She shrugged. 'Not a clue,' she said. 'It's not so cold any more, just as well.'

Alvar felt deeply depressed. It was an expensive scarf, and she had discarded it carelessly and he had been taught a lesson. His neighbour had been right, you could not trust those people.

'Why haven't you bought the painting?' she asked, nodding towards the blank wall above the fireplace.

'Ahem, I haven't got round to it,' he replied.

'Got round to it?' She laughed again. 'The painting is hanging in your workplace. All you have to do is unhook it. You're not very quick off the mark, are you?' she stated. 'You really wanted it. Are you that indecisive, Alvar?'

He could feel his cheeks burning again. He certainly was not indecisive, on the contrary he was controlled and organised. Yes, he was going to buy the painting, but not because she was pushing him. It would happen of its own accord, he would know when the time was right, when he was ready to act.

'My mum could never make a decision,' she said suddenly.

'Oh?' Alvar enquired.

'Yes. She had a phobia. And this phobia was so great that it paralysed her. All she could do was sit in her chair all day. She couldn't manage any decisions, she never ate. She couldn't leave her room, she never left the house.'

'What was she scared of?' Alvar asked.

'Dying,' she said. 'She was so scared of dying that she wasn't able to live life like other people. She ended up killing herself with some pills the doctor had given her.'

'She was so scared of dying that she killed herself?'

Alvar was perplexed. He could see no logic in this.

'Weird, don't you think?' she said, inhaling. 'People can be so strange.'

Alvar's living room was now dense with cigarette smoke. He detested it. The stress was building up in him and he was certain that she was aware of it, but she pretended not to notice.

'Do you have any spare cash?' she asked, stubbing out her cigarette in the bowl.

Alvar jerked. 'No,' he said brusquely. 'Absolutely not. I have no cash.' He got up and stood next to his chair.

'But you've got a cashpoint card?' she said in a commanding voice. Her eyes had lit up in a way that scared him.

'A card? Yes, of course I've got a card.'

'Good, since you're going to Oslo anyway you can give me a lift to the Cash and Carry, where there's a cash machine. You can get some money out. You'll probably need to get some for yourself as well,' she declared.

Alvar paled. Were there no limits to her impudence? He put the kitten down on the chair and inhaled deeply as he got up.

'Don't get your knickers in a twist,' she said, 'I was just asking you a question. I'll meet you downstairs. I'll be waiting by your car.'

His head was turbulent with chaos. On top of everything it seemed impossible to abandon the kitten, which had only just arrived. The kitten was running around confused in a strange house. Overwhelmed by concern he lifted up the little bundle, carried him out into the kitchen, put him in the box and replaced the lid. Then he went outside. She was hanging around by the car.

'It's open,' he coughed. She went round and got in. He got in behind the wheel. I can't believe this is happening to me, he thought, I can't believe I'm doing what she tells me to do. He started the engine and pulled out into the road. Changed gears and drove down the hill.

'Well,' she said, looking around the car, 'it's not exactly a Jaguar, is it?'

Alvar did not reply. He had nothing more to say, he just wanted her to leave and he would never, ever open his door the next time someone rang the bell. He drove right up to the cashpoint. Got out, found the card in his wallet.

'I need a thousand!' she called from the car. Alvar's fingers trembled, she was watching him like a hawk. He inserted the card and entered his PIN number, glancing quickly over his shoulder to see if she was getting out. She was. Her boots clicked businesslike against the tarmac. The machine ticked and whirred. Then his card came out and shortly afterwards his money. He held it in his hand for a moment as if frozen solid. She snatched it from him and stuffed it in her pocket.

'You're a dear,' she exclaimed joyfully. Suddenly she leaned forward and kissed his cheek, a big sloppy kiss. Then she walked across the road and was gone.

CHAPTER 17

Lindys has entered my life.

This was what Alvar was thinking as he opened the gallery at five to ten on a Monday morning in late February. She has entered my life and I need to make a decision. Whether I want her there or not. If I want her in my life I need to have a strategy in place for dealing with her. If I don't want her there, I need to get rid of her. And I have to devise a strategy in order for that to happen. In other words, I need to make a choice. Does she need me? he asked himself. Maybe. But he could not know for certain. She had kissed him on his cheek, but surely that was just an affectionate gesture, he thought, and not an expression of love or devotion. That was how the young behaved these days; they would kiss anyone and not be the least bit embarrassed about it. The cynical part of him was utterly convinced that she was only interested in him for his money, but he did not like to be so cynical. Rather, he decided, she was looking for several things. Companionship and warmth, and money for drugs. She had even opened up to him, she had told him that her mother had killed herself because of her phobia. Her confiding in him had genuinely moved him. But he also felt disturbed. She was so unpredictable, she only showed up when she wanted to. She never cared if it was convenient for him. Alvar decided that if they made a proper date, if for example she said, 'I'll be back again on Friday around six o'clock in the evening,' then he would be prepared and everything would be easier. Of course he could also ask her, he could mention it in passing, are you thinking of dropping by one of these days? But that sounded like an invitation and he certainly did not want to invite her. Then it might spiral into something he would have no control over whatsoever and the very thought made him cold with fear.

The trip to the cashpoint had left him feeling very tense because he was finding it hard to accept that he had acted the way he had. He had walked like a servant to his car, driven by a vague sense of duty, quite simply because the word 'no' was so difficult to articulate. No. I don't want to, you won't make me, we can't do this, it's out of the question, are you out of your mind? He had all these words in his head, but they were too deep inside. In addition he found it terribly hard to get angry. He was not used to people wanting something from him and even less used to them asking for what they wanted in such a direct manner. What would happen if he gave in? And how could people around him make themselves so accessible? They gave out their telephone numbers without a moment's hesitation, they gave out their email address and their home address, they travelled abroad and met foreigners whom they invited to Norway, why not? If you're ever in this part of the world, do drop by. Had they no idea of the risks they were running? And when it came to Lindys she was a damaged person on top of everything else and the circles she moved in were even worse. For all he knew she might be a thief, a prostitute, a liar. She might have been to prison, she might have been a drug dealer and that was a criminal offence. Of all the people he could have run into in this world, it had turned out to be someone like her. Was this significant? At the same time it was also an opportunity. All of his deepest feelings and values were tested. Others would have handled this in a far more straightforward manner, it struck him, others would have turned their back and cut the tie with a machete. Ole Krantz would have lifted her up and carried her out into the cold, dumped her in a gutter outside perhaps, and he would not have thought twice about it. But I'm not Ole Krantz, he thought, I'm Alvar Eide. I might lack something that other people possess. What could it be? A sense of entitlement? Do other people have rights which I don't award myself? And if this is the case, why is it so?

He struggled with these thoughts as he walked around the gallery. Stood in front of the severed bridge and stared at it. Out of the darkness and the fog he saw the construction rise, soar, beautiful and brutally severed, just as his ties to other people had been cut. Can such damage be mended? he asked himself. Can you regrow the stumps, can you become whole again? Once more the bridge had this healing effect on him, he was transfixed. Was there communication between people which could bypass distance, time and culture? He had never met this painter, Lindstrøm. And the bridge was in every way a direct message to him personally. He was aware though that other people might be equally mesmerised by the painting, even though it had not happened yet. Then the doorbell rang and he spun round. Ole Krantz came striding in with a frame tucked under his arm.

'Look at you standing there drooling,' he smiled. 'Like a kid in a sweet shop. So, what's it gonna be?'

Alvar hesitated. 'Well,' he said reluctantly, 'of course, I'll have to buy it. If I don't I'll regret it for the rest of my life.'

Krantz squatted down. He was wearing green wellies and he had rolled down their tops.

'This painting is a good investment, I can promise you that.'

He wiped a drop of moisture from under his nose with the back of his hand, got up and planted his hands firmly on his hips. So stands a man who owns his own world, Alvar thought. He did not mention that he was not at all interested in the investment aspect.

'I can drive the painting over to your place today,' Krantz said, 'then you can hang it and keep it for a couple of weeks. That way you'll get a sense of how it affects you. If you then decide to hold on to the painting, you'll pay me, let me see, we'll knock a bit off, let's say sixty thousand. If you don't like it as much as you thought you would, I'll just come and pick it up.'

Alvar hesitated. This was one of Ole Krantz's standard sales pitches and he used it frequently. Initially it sounded reasonable, but when push came to shove most people found it hard to hand back a painting which had found a space in their living room. A painting they had fallen for for some reason. Hardly anyone returned their paintings, they did not like the emptiness that followed when the painting was taken down. But these customers never became regulars. They felt tricked and went to another gallery in future.

'No, thank you,' he said after a pause. 'I'd rather give myself a deadline. Let me see, I'll make up my mind before Friday.'

'So what will you do if a buyer turns up on Thursday?' Krantz wanted to know. He tilted his head and smiled a proper salesman smile.

Alvar thought long and hard about that. 'In that case I'll have to take my punishment,' he said presumptuously.

Krantz shook his head. He had little faith that Alvar Eide was the kind of man who could take his punishment.

The familiar sound of the doorbell startled him again. Up until now he had always enjoyed this sound and would enjoy going down the stairs to be of service. Now he hesitated and stared nervously at the monitor. It might be Lindys and now it had become utterly impossible to get rid of her. No, this was a taller person, it was the outline of a man. He was tall and broad and solid. A relieved Alvar left the kitchen. The man was standing in front of the bridge and when Alvar appeared on the stairs he bowed to him in an old-fashioned way.

'Lindstrøm?' he said, pointing at the painting.

'Yes. Yes, exactly,' Alvar stuttered because here was a customer who was familiar with the name of an artist Alvar had only just heard of.

'I've seen his work before,' the man stated. 'If I remember rightly, he's very popular in the States.'

Alvar gawped. Was he perhaps standing in front of another Nerdrum? An artist who was unappreciated at home, but celebrated abroad?

'Lindstrøm's style's somewhat dramatic,' the man went on. 'He shouts rather than speaks, if you know what I'm saying.'

'Indeed,' Alvar whispered. He was growing anxious. 'However, I don't think that he takes it too far, nor does he merely paint for effect either, not the way I look at it.'

He dug his fingers into his palms behind his back. He watched the customer furtively.

'Perhaps,' the man hesitated, 'he borders on shouting too loud. I mean, here we have a bloody deep canyon and a massive severed bridge. And all of it clouded in some sort of medieval mist. A bit over the top, don't you think?'

Alvar could feel how his cheeks were starting to get hot. It felt like the customer was analysing his own love affair with the painting, but then he realised that he was merely overreacting.

'True, he's good,' the man went on, 'there's no doubt about it. I have a good feeling about this painting, I really do. But as to hanging it on my living-room wall,' he paused and a frown appeared on his forehead as he considered it. 'I'm not sure I'd go that far. But it would look impressive in the hall. There is no furniture and the ceiling is high. This bridge needs to be kept far away from curtains and floral cushions. This painting is a monument.'

Alvar cleared his throat. 'Well, we're all different,' he said, managing a weak smile. 'Floral motifs always sell well. Or Norwegian mountain landscapes. And most people think it's important to have a nude, in their bedroom perhaps. But I agree, this is a very powerful painting. There needs to be a certain order in the room where it will hang.'

The man walked right up to the canvas, studied a few details before stepping back again.

'A painting like this can almost darken your mood,' he suggested. 'One thing that does occur to me when I look at it is that some enormous and irreparable damage has been done here.'

'Really?'

Alvar's cheeks paled. He had never viewed it in this way, he had regarded the bridge as an image of his deepest self. Irreparable damage? he thought uneasily. Am I irreparably damaged?

'I've discussed it briefly with Ole Krantz,' Alvar said. 'Do you think his inspiration might have come from some war-torn country?'

The man shook his head. 'I doubt it,' he said. 'This is wholly symbolic. And this Lindstrøm, he has a few problems of his own, I know something about that.'

Alvar's eyes widened as he listened.

'He satisfies all the requirements for the struggling artist. They say he's in his studio working up to twenty hours without a break. He forgets to eat, he forgets to sleep. At times he has collapsed on the floor from exhaustion only to get up and continue painting. And he drinks too much. He won't live to be an old man. I'm passionately interested in art,' he said, smiling broadly, 'but I've never understood why it's necessary to live on the edge, like Lindstrøm does. Anyway, let's hope he succeeds in painting several good pictures before he finally kills himself.'

Alvar was shocked. 'Might he do that?'

'Absolutely,' the man assured him. 'He lives a hard life. And the fact that he's fairly successful abroad doesn't make it any easier, he can't handle it. He's like a wild animal in a cave. He only comes out to fight.'

'Life's not easy,' Alvar said, gesticulating clumsily.

'No, indeed it isn't.'

The man looked at the painting again. 'It's terribly good, of course. Imposing even. But dark, really very dark. It beckons you and scares you at the same time. How much is it?'

Alvar shuddered, suddenly consumed by fear. 'Seventy thousand.'

'I see. Seventy thousand? Fancy that. Who would have thought it? Seventy thousand for a Lindstrøm, that's nothing. In New York this painting would have sold for two hundred thousand.'

'Is that possible?' stammered Alvar.

'In five years he'll command the same prices at home, I'm

convinced of it. I really ought to buy it, purely because it's such a good investment.'

Alvar held his breath. Was it about to happen, right before his eyes? A man with better knowledge of Lindstrøm than him was calmly considering the painting, with a pensive look on his face. A man who furthermore did not value the painting for the right reason; he was nowhere near as mesmerised as Alvar. He was impressed. Though he thought the painting was average, he believed buying it would be a sound investment. Alvar exhaled. Should such a man be blessed with that which he himself so desperately desired?

'Do you know what, I'll give it some thought,' the man said. 'I'll take a couple of days. I'll pop by, I want to view it a few more times.'

Alvar nodded and gulped.

'Like I said, it would look good in the hall. Anyone who comes into my house will have a very dramatic entrance, you can't deny that.'

'No, precisely,' Alvar mumbled.

'In terms of colour it will match the ivory walls and the grey stone floor.'

'Undoubtedly,' Alvar said quietly.

'And then I'll have a touch of red as well, preferably near the painting. In the form of red candles in tall candlesticks or a bouquet of roses. That would be the finishing touch.'

'It sounds great,' stuttered Alvar.

'And as far as the frame is concerned,' he continued, 'I was thinking of charcoal grey. Not too dark, just a shade darker than the painting. You frame paintings here as well, don't you?'

'We do,' said Alvar restlessly.

'Well, well.' He took a few steps backwards and started studying the other paintings in the room. Alvar dragged himself towards the staircase. He disappeared into the kitchen and sat down at the table. He followed the man on the monitor. Was this how it was going to turn out? Would he end up in the workshop cutting lists, tagging and gluing them, framing the painting for another person purely because he lacked the fundamental ability to make a decision?

CHAPTER 18

It was three days before she reappeared.

Alvar was sitting in front of his fireplace staring at the naked wall where the bridge was going to hang if only he could make up his mind. The kitten was lying in his lap, curled up into a fur ball, he could feel it warming his thighs. It was nine in the evening when the doorbell broke the silence. His heart leapt to his throat, then he lifted the kitten carefully and put him on the floor. He thought, it's Lindys, I guess. I don't have to open the door. What will the neighbours be thinking of her coming and going? How was he going to stop it? By refusing to open the door, he told himself firmly. The doorbell rang again, longer this time, she was holding the button down. It hurt his ears. Finally he buckled and went out into the hall to open the door. She was standing outside with a swollen black eye and make-up running down her face.

'For God's sake,' she exclaimed, 'what took you so long? I know you're in!'

'Have you hurt yourself?' he stuttered in a frightened voice.

She marched past him and into the living room without waiting to be asked. Peeled off her grey jacket and left it in a heap on the floor.

'I got beaten up,' she muttered, touching her eye.

He closed the door and followed her, alarmed.

'Beaten up? By whom?'

She turned round and looked at him. She was as white as chalk and her eye really looked very nasty, she could barely see out of it. It had swollen up into a purple ball and he thought it might burst at any moment.

'By a bad-tempered creditor,' she said. 'I owe him some money.'

Alvar felt his heart sink.

'You've got to go to A&E,' he told her.

'Nope,' she said, shaking her head. 'There's no way I'm going to A&E. They don't want us, anyway, so I'm bloody well not going to bother them.'

He ignored her swearing and watched as she made herself comfortable on his sofa. She put her feet on the coffee table straight away.

'Could I stay the night?' she asked him.

Alvar gasped for breath. Had he heard her correctly? Stay the night, here in his flat? A woman, a total stranger?

'I'm not really sure,' he began, squirming like a worm on a hotplate. He was still standing with his hands folded across his stomach. He thought the room was starting to sway.

'On your sofa,' she said, watching him with her undamaged ice-blue eye.

'But,' he stammered, 'don't you have your own place?'

'Yes,' she said, putting her hand over her swollen eye. 'But he'll find me there and he's very upset. I need to keep out of his way until he's calmed down. Sod it, I tried to outrun him, but it's no good running in these boots.'

'Who's after you?' Alvar asked.

'Rikard. A dealer. I owe him twenty grand.'

Alvar gave her a horrified look. 'How much did you say?'

'I've no hope of ever finding that kind of money,' she groaned. 'And if I can't get it, he's going to beat the crap out of me.'

Alvar bit his lip. 'But you've got to find some sort of solution,' he said feebly.

'You think I don't know that?' she replied sarcastically. Then she sighed deeply and sincerely and dug a packet of cigarettes out of her pocket. Alvar instantly went to the kitchen to find a bowl for the ash. Eventually he managed to sit down. He watched her as she lit her cigarette, watched her damaged face in horror.

'Can you see out of that eye?' he asked quietly.

'Are you thick or something?' she replied simply.

'Does it hurt?'

'I can handle it, I'm no sissy.'

'So what are you going to do?' he asked.

She shrugged. 'No idea. But I'm probably going to hell eventually and I've always known that. Bloody stupid idea to buy drugs on credit, but I had no choice. And then the tosser has added a ton of interest. I guess he'll break my nose next time. Or my front teeth. His right hook is like a piston.'

She looked at him again. 'Can I stay the night?'

Alvar felt that he had crossed a line and a vast void was opening up. Now he was clinging to the edge and he clenched his fists so hard his knuckles ached. The word 'no' was ringing in his ears, filling his mouth, but it was refusing to come out.

'Well,' he said in a little voice, 'I can probably find a blanket somewhere. One night wouldn't hurt, I suppose.'

He stressed the word 'one'. At the same time he was horrified at this development. She is devouring me, he thought, where will it end?

'You're one of the good guys,' she said suddenly.

Her smile reached up to her healthy eye.

Alvar felt warm all over.

'Others would have said no,' she said, as if this surprised her.

'Well,' he said modestly, 'it's no big deal to let you have the sofa just for the one night.'

Again he stressed the word 'one'.

'By the way, sleeping on that sofa is not a bad idea, I sometimes have an afternoon nap on it,' he confessed, 'and I never end up with a bad back or anything like that.'

She began laughing. She puffed blue smoke out into the air looking quite comical with her swollen eye.

'You're really quite all right,' she said.

Her voice was both teasing and affectionate.

'All right how?' he wanted to know.

'You know. A bit different. Like an old woman.'

Alvar tightened his lips. What sort of description is that? he thought. I'm not effeminate, I never have been, I'm one metre eighty-seven tall and fairly broad-shouldered.

'Are you hurt?' she smiled.

'Certainly not,' he lied, crossing one leg over the other and brushing away a speck of dust.

Suddenly she put her feet on the floor and got up from the sofa. She had spotted the kitten. Now she went over to pick him up and take him back with her to the sofa.

'He's such a sweetie,' she said, stroking the kitten's head. 'When I was a little girl I always wanted to have a kitten, but I never got one. Those people gave me nothing.' Her voice was angry, bitter. 'But I can pretend that he's mine. Hello, kitty,' she chirped, 'I'm going to visit you lots and lots and you will be mine. I'll fuss over you and take care of you for ever and ever.'

Her words sent a chill down Alvar's spine. Had she not just declared that she would keep coming back, to his flat, to his kitten? What had he started?

She leaned her head back and closed her eyes. The kitten settled on her lap and started purring.

'Do you know what I fancy right now?' she said, looking at him. Alvar was tormented by her bruised eye. He shook his head nervously.

'Hot chocolate,' she said softly. 'Hot chocolate with lots of sugar. Please would you make me some, please, please, please?'

Alvar was not sure if he had any cocoa as he preferred tea or coffee. But there might be something in a packet somewhere, probably well out of date. He got up to check, driven by her needs in a way he resented. Again he felt like a servant. And this confused him, because he was in charge of his own life. Now with her simple request she had switched their roles. He opened the cupboard and had a look inside. Searched among bags of flour and spaghetti and rice for the brown cocoa packet. And there in the furthest corner he discovered some Kakao Express. Well, why not? he thought. It'll warm her up and she probably needs that. And they had to do something to pass this long evening. He found some milk in the fridge and poured it into a saucepan. Put it on the stove. Found a mug and a teaspoon and a bowl of sugar. From where he was standing he could see into the living room. Help, he thought, there's a stranger in my flat and she'll be here right until tomorrow morning. I can't find the words, I won't be able to talk to her, she has taken all my power from me and I'm helpless. He added cocoa powder to the milk and stirred with a wooden spoon; steam quickly started to rise. We're in a labyrinth, Lindys and I, and now we've run into each other on one of the many crooked paths, and we can't get past each other, everything has ground to a halt. My breathing, my heart, what am I going to do, move to a hotel for two weeks, so she'll think I've sold the flat? He instantly realised how ludicrous this idea was, as he struggled to find a solution. The milk was starting to boil, so he took the saucepan off the hob and poured the milk into a mug. Added a few extra spoonfuls of sugar and brought her the drink.

She let go of the kitten and grasped the hot drink eagerly.

'Christ, it's hot,' she burst out and licked the corners of her mouth with her pointy, pink tongue. 'But it's delicious, Alvar, it really is.'

He sat down again, touched by hearing the sound of his own name. He rarely heard his name spoken by others and he was filled with conflicting thoughts. Now she was stroking the kitten with her left hand and holding the mug in her right.

'You're probably thinking that I've made a right mess of my life,' she said in between gulps of cocoa.

He could not think of anything to say in reply, so he raised his eyebrows instead, as a sign that she could go on.

'On drugs, shooting heroin. Unemployed, battered and miserable. You probably think I'm the lowest of the low. A pathetic, broken creature who doesn't deserve to live in a welfare state.'

Alvar gave her a startled look. 'No,' he practically cried out, 'I've never ever thought that!'

'You haven't?' She looked at him sharply and narrowed her healthy eye.

'I don't know much about these things,' he said reluctantly, 'but you probably haven't had an easy life.'

His reply caused her to look serious.

'No,' she said in a tired voice, 'I haven't had an easy life. My mum was always ill, she spent most of her time in bed and my dad travelled the world selling ankle socks which don't cut off your blood supply when you wear them.'

Alvar, who had been studying his hands, looked up.

'So you were on your own a lot of the time,' he said softly.

'Practically all the time,' she said. 'And whenever she did get out of bed she would sit in a chair shaking like a rag doll because of her phobia. Have you ever seen phobia close up? It looks like someone's being electrocuted. She took a lot of pills, not that they seemed to do her any good. The curtains in our house were always drawn because she was scared of the light. She was scared whenever someone rang our doorbell, she was afraid of the telephone. We never had any visitors, she was scared of people. I could never bring any friends round.'

'But,' said Alvar, shaken to his core, 'when your father came home, what happened then?'

'Then he would drink,' she said simply. 'Binge drinking two to three weeks at a time. He would turn into someone I couldn't recognise. I had to cook my own meals, no one ever helped me with my homework. When my mum took an overdose, my dad got so scared he left the country. And I was taken into care.'

Alvar leaned forward a little to show his sympathy.

'What was it like there? Were they nice to you?'

She smiled an acid smile.

'Sometimes,' she said and suddenly became indifferent.

Alvar did not understand.

'Either they were nice to you or they weren't.'

'It was too late,' she said, 'I was fifteen years old by then. The damage had already been done.'

Damaged, Alvar thought, broken like the severed bridge. A strange feeling of solidarity filled his heart. Here he was talking to a total stranger, and yes, they were having a real conversation. He suddenly thought he was observing the scene in his own living room from a distance. A skinny girl with a mug of cocoa and a kitten on her lap. He in an armchair, the adult, being supportive. Peace and mutual understanding. Snow melting outside.

'But,' he said, suddenly feeling very reckless, 'surely you could get help somewhere? Couldn't you ask to go into rehab?'

She looked at him with mild reproach.

'And lose the only thing that gets me through the day? I wouldn't dream of it. It might sound crazy to you, but this is how I want it, I don't want to be on this merry-go-round any more. It's riddled with ghosts.'

Alvar recalled the painting and nodded.

'But,' he said, raising his voice because he was beginning to engage deeply, 'you're so young. You might get a job one day, and a flat and a kitten. Wouldn't that be something?'

At that she smiled broadly. 'But I've already got that,' she said, nodding down at the kitten. Alvar started to feel dizzy. He got up from his chair, he felt in urgent need of a large sherry. Did she want to join him?

She shook her head adamantly.

'Growing up with a drunk teaches you to stay clear of alcohol, if nothing else,' she said, sipping her cocoa demonstratively.

This made complete sense, Alvar thought, even though her argument seemed somewhat flawed given that she had substituted alcohol with heroin. But he said nothing. He fetched the bottle from the cupboard and poured himself a large glass. Fell back into his armchair and tasted the golden liquid.

'You're very tidy,' she said, watching him.

He clutched his glass.

'Yes,' he conceded after a long pause, 'I like to know where everything is.'

'Or you'll start to fret?' she teased him, scrutinising him from head to toe.

He shrugged and put the glass on the table.

'That's who I am,' he said simply. 'I can't stand mess. It makes it impossible to find anything.'

She laughed and threw back her head. 'So what are you looking for then?' she said, her voice filled with laughter. 'We're all set on the same path, the one that leads to death. Just in case you didn't know that.'

That irked him. He did not like that she was talking about death, nor did he feel that he was on the same path as her.

'I'm just talking rubbish,' she consoled him. 'My life's chaotic. Getting high, getting beaten up, desperation and strange disgusting men, that's all I have. I bet you have a lot that I'll never have. A well-paid job. Family and friends.'

Alvar looked down. He had none of those things.

'Is it all right if I take a shower?' she asked.

Alvar jumped again. 'I suppose so,' he said.

'I feel so filthy and grimy,' she explained, 'and it's not often I get the chance because I don't have a shower in my room.'

He nodded again. Once more he felt that she was devouring him, but, having given her cocoa, offered her sherry and a bed for the night, it felt impossible to deny her a shower. She leapt out of the sofa and placed the kitten on his lap.

'I know where it is,' she called out and made a beeline for the bathroom. Again he sat there with his heart in his throat. He could feel his cheeks burning. A woman would be standing behind a thin wall with no clothes on. The water would wash over her. The same room where he carefully washed and got himself ready every morning and evening. Her smell, her hair in the plughole. He gulped down more sherry, he could think of no other solution.

At eleven he switched on the TV to watch the late-night news. Lindys was lying on the sofa, her hair was damp. The kitten had snuggled up to her chest and had fallen asleep. She was not interested in the news, she lay calmly with her eyes closed. Her swollen eye worried him, but it did not seem to bother her. Alvar was halfway through his second sherry. Human beings can cope with far more than we think, he decided, as a mild level of intoxication reached his head. There's a woman lying on my sofa and I haven't panicked. I'm taking it all in my stride, I'm a self-assured man. After a while he could see that she was asleep. She had neither a pillow nor a blanket, so he got up and went to a cupboard in the hallway where he kept a pure wool Berger blanket. He returned to the sofa. Stood there for a moment watching her. Her blonde, almost white hair had fallen over her cheek where the skin was stretched tightly over her cheekbones. The swollen eye looked truly nasty. He could not understand how anyone could have the heart to hurt such a defenceless girl. His initial thought had been to spread the blanket over her, but it seemed such an intimate gesture that he did not dare. Instead he laid the blanket over her feet. Perhaps she might wake up during the night and pull it all the way up. What would tomorrow bring? he wondered. What might she get up to while he slept? Could he trust her? No, Ole Krantz would have said, you can't trust people like that. Get rid of them, Alvar, get rid of them! He switched off the light, turned off the TV and went to the bathroom. He remembered that he had forgotten to provide her with a clean towel, so she had used his. He noticed black stains from her eye make-up, too. He took a clean towel from the linen cupboard, brushed his teeth and washed his hands. Left the bathroom light on and the door ajar, so she could find her way in the dark in case she woke up during the night. Then he quickly went out into the hall to retrieve his wallet from his coat pocket. He brought it into his bedroom and placed it in the drawer of his bedside table, and this small precaution felt like a nasty sting.

*

When he woke up she was standing by his bedside.

He yanked his duvet up under his chin. Her eye looked even worse, he thought, and what time was it anyway?

'Like I said,' she spoke firmly, 'I need twenty grand. If I go back into town without that money, he'll kill me.'

Alvar sat up in his bed. He could not believe his own ears.

'As long as I owe him that money, I'm fair game. I can't even return to my room.'

She stuck her chin out and planted her hands on her hips.

Alvar ran his hand across his bare head. He had been ambushed, it felt unbearable.

'But,' he moaned, 'you'll never be able to pay that back.'

'Oh, sure,' she said confidently, 'I can sell some drugs. Spring's coming, that means I can start working the streets again. I always make a lot of money this time of year.'

Alvar rubbed his eyes.

'I've made coffee,' she said proudly. 'And then we're going to the cashpoint.'

He looked at her in disbelief. Hugged his duvet tightly.

'I don't even have that much money in my account,' he tried in a desperate attempt to escape the humiliation she was subjecting him to.

'But you've got seventy thousand,' she said. 'You've been saving, you told me all about it.'

'It's for the painting,' he objected feebly.

'But you haven't bought it. That wall in there,' she nodded towards the living room, 'is still bloody empty!'

He wanted to get out of bed, but he could not bear the thought that she might see him in his underwear, even though his boxer shorts were perfectly acceptable.

'It's in another account,' he said, 'a savings account. I don't have a card for that.'

She rolled her blue eyes. 'Then we'll go to your bank,' she said lightly. 'They open at nine.'

She went back into the living room.

'I let the cat out,' she called to him over her shoulder.

Alvar forgot all about his embarrassment and jumped out of bed. 'What did you just say? You let him out?'

She came back in, stopped in the doorway.

'Yes, of course I did. Don't tell me you're keeping that poor little creature cooped up in here all day.'

Alvar reached for his neatly folded clothes on the back of the chair near his bed.

'But what if he can't find his way home?' he said miserably. At this she burst into a fit of laughter.

'What are you on about? I've never heard anything like it. Of course he'll find his way home. And he's not as helpless as you think. When you come home from work today, he'll be waiting on your doorstep, he's not stupid either, he knows who feeds him. Now get a move on, the bank opens in thirty minutes.'

He got dressed. He went to the bathroom. He stared at his terrified reflection in the mirror. If he did not give her the money, she would get another beating. If he gave her the money she would become indebted to him and then she would have to walk the streets to pay him back. Both options were unthinkable. If he swore at her and told her to get the hell out of his flat, he would not be able to live with himself; after all, he was a good person. He went through his usual morning ritual; he lingered and dawdled as much as he could. There was music coming from the living room, she had turned on the radio. Finally he came out. She was sitting on the sofa with a cup of coffee and she had put out a cup for him too. They drank their coffee in silence.

'I'm not going to come with you inside when we get to the bank,' she said after a long pause. 'I'll wait outside. I'll sign an IOU,' she added, 'if you want me to.'

He shook his head. 'No, what would be the point of that?' he said dully. There was no way she was ever going to pay him back. Now she had become something he had been lumbered with. He looked at her, he looked at his coffee cup, which she was holding in her hands as if it was the most natural thing in the world. And the kitten outside now on his own, he might get run over. Alvar moaned inwardly.

'Don't be scared,' she said all of a sudden.

'What do you mean?' he asked.

'You're always so scared, you don't have to be. You see, there's nothing to be scared of.'

He bowed his head again. He could no longer see a way out. He could barely imagine this day ending. From now on everything was up in the air and he could not handle it. Days needed to follow like pearls on a string, even, round and smooth. Safe, measured days that he had complete control of. Now he could only see as far as the bank.

She got up. 'Come on,' she said, 'we're going.'

He got up too. Went out into the hall and put on his coat. She slipped out before him. They'll see us, he thought, my downstairs neighbours, they'll see us walk down the road together, and they'll talk.

God help me.

There were no other customers in the bank.

The cashier looked up at him with a welcoming smile. He asked to withdraw twenty thousand and even though it was his own money and even though he was going to give it away he felt greedy. He folded the notes and put them in his pocket. Signed for them and left. She was waiting outside. When he gave her the notes she crumpled. It was like watching butter melt in the sun.

'Thank you,' she said and burst into tears. 'Thank you, thank you, thank you! You've taken such a load off my mind. Oh, you're so nice, so nice!'

Again she gave him a big wet kiss on his cheek. Alvar felt her soft lips on his skin. He was so overcome by emotions that he had to look away. She stuffed the notes into the pocket of her grey jacket and started walking towards Bragernes Square. He followed her tiny figure with his eyes. Then it dawned on him that he no longer had enough money to buy the severed bridge. He also realised he might never see her again. That this was what she had been building towards the whole time. Settle her debt so she would be left in peace. He stood there for a while, wondering about himself and life's twists and turns. The strange direction his life had taken. A feeling of anxiety made his chest ache.

CHAPTER 19

He drags himself across my floor with heavy footsteps.

'So,' I say, 'there you are.'

'Yes,' he says, 'here I am. And you might get angry with me now. Because I keep interrupting you, but I can't help it.'

He glances at the table. 'You're relaxing with a glass of wine, I see. Rather a large glass, I must say. It's practically a bowl.'

He looks fraught. 'I'm up to my neck in problems. I've tried to escape, but it's gone too far.'

I point towards the sofa, ask him to sit down.

'You sound as if it's the end of the world,' I say. 'You've found yourself in unfamiliar territory and it frightens the living daylights out of you.'

He rubs his tired face.

'That's not to say there are no solutions,' I say, 'but you need to act. When you're in a situation involving another person, you need to take a stand. There's nothing wrong with listening, supporting and encouraging. But don't lose sight of your own interests. You've been swallowed up by her needs and her greed. She is walking all over you. You need to start asserting yourself. That doesn't mean you can't help her, but in my opinion you're entitled to make certain demands.'

'Like what?' he asks quickly.

'I think you should demand one hundred per cent honesty, for example.'

He looks at me suspiciously. Raises his eyebrows.

'Where are you going with this?'

I look at him gravely. 'She's told you her life story. Illness. Neglect, alcoholism, foster homes and violent drug dealers.'

'Yes. It's just awful,' he says.

'Indeed it is. If it's true.'

He is startled. 'Is she lying?'

'I don't know. What do you think? It strikes me that you take everything at face value. That she's a victim, that she never had a chance to become anything other than a heroin addict. You've had little experience of dealing with other people,' I continue. 'God knows you don't know much about human nature. If you did you might have questioned her in more detail and perhaps found out that she may not be who you think she is.'

He braces himself as if hit by an icy wind.

'What you're saying now doesn't exactly make me feel any better,' he says.

'I understand that completely. But you've come to me with your questions and you have to accept what you're given. That was the deal we made, wasn't it?'

He contemplates this for a long time. He rests his chin in the palm of his hand.

'It all began so promisingly, I did everything right. She entered the gallery and she was freezing, I decided to do a good deed. In my heart of hearts I didn't think I had the right to throw her out into the cold. So I gave her a mug of coffee. And that coffee,' he agonises, 'was probably my first mistake.'

He hugs himself. 'What kind of a world is this? Where good leads to bad? How are we meant to behave when there are no consequences, no logic or justice? And not only that. Imagine if I had indeed sent her packing the very first time I met her, then she would simply have gone somewhere else and another person would have made the same mistake. There is no solution to this, none at all. And what will this experience do to me? It'll mean that the little goodwill I still possess will just dissolve and evaporate. In the end, I'll just think of her the same way she already thinks of herself. A crooked human being, who's a pain and a burden to everyone.'

I have to smile in response to his reasoning.

'Do you think she's a crooked human being?'

'No,' he says, 'are you mad? I don't think of people like that, never. But I'm having to deal with her and I'm getting really irritated. But only with myself, because I can't find a way out. Do I have to be lumbered with her now, I wonder, is there no way out of this mess?'

'Alvar,' I say watching him, 'you won't find a way out of this mess until you open your ears and eyes.'

'You mean I haven't?'

I raise my glass and drink. 'No, you haven't. You're actually quite self-obsessed when you're with other people. You spend all your energy fretting about how you behave and how you come across, how important it is that you remain polite, and correct and nice. And that's why you miss what's really going on.'

'You've lost me,' he whimpers. 'I've no idea what you're talking about.'

I light a cigarette and blow the smoke towards the ceiling; I follow the blue column with my eyes, the smoke spirals under the lamp.

'She stayed the night in your flat.'

'Yes,' he nods. 'But only on my sofa. With a blanket.'

'Did you check if anything was missing from your flat when you got up this morning?'

Alvar looks sick.

'Did she steal something? That's not possible, she's not like that, I'm certain of it. She wanted money and that's bad enough, but I've no cash lying around the place, only some change in a bowl in the kitchen. And let me add, given that you've brought up my boundless naivety, that I hid my wallet in my bedroom when I went to bed. I have no other valuables.'

'We'll see,' I say. 'But I'll continue to argue that you're naive, even if you don't like it.'

'That doesn't surprise me,' he says. 'But it's better than being a cynic. I've been standing outside your house for years, I've seen people go through a great deal.'

I burst into a hearty laugh. 'I care about everyone who comes to my house,' I say, 'you all grip me in different ways. If I was indifferent to you there would be no story. And I certainly don't feel indifferent towards you, Alvar, I think about you night and day. I hope you'll cope, that you'll do the right things. I may not be able to promise you happiness, but I can promise you hope. Besides, you need to understand that once I've written the last page then you're on your own. With the tools I've given you.'

'Tools?' he says, baffled. 'What tools have you given me?'

'Of course I've given you tools. I'm trying to open your eyes, I'm trying to force you out into the real world, which you've never been a part of. You've been given a name, a job, a voice and I've placed you on a well-lit stage. If we're lucky you'll have an audience too and they will judge you mercilessly. But some might recognise themselves in you and be touched. Others might smile at your defensive and very cautious nature, some might get up and leave halfway through the show. But you've been given something that many people will never have. The chance to show yourself and be seen.'

'But I don't want an audience,' he protests.

'Oh, of course you do. Even if you're not aware of it; you think of yourself as modest, and you can't even bear to entertain the idea. But we need other people, we need to mirror ourselves in them. Naturally there's a risk that we might run into individuals we don't want to meet, but that's part of the price we have to pay.'

'Yes,' he says despondently, 'I'm paying, literally. Twenty thousand kroner, to be precise, left my account today.'

'Because you were incapable of saying no.'

'I didn't think I had the right.'

'Who took that right away from you?'

'I've never had it.'

'Why were you never given it?'

'I don't know. Who hands it out?'

'Your parents,' I say. 'And after them your brothers and sisters and your friends.'

'My parents were very stingy,' he says, 'and I've never had any friends to speak of.'

'In other words,' I say, 'you need to get yourself some friends. They'll give you what you need.'

He gives me a defeated look. 'If you've intervened in order to help me establish a friendship with someone, why have you sent me a heroin addict who's spending all my money?'

'I can understand that you feel used. This isn't what you wanted, you don't need this kind of person.'

'Correct. I don't.'

'But she needs you.'

His grey eyes blink.

'I need to look after the interests of everyone in the book,' I explain. 'You're only concerned with your own part. I'm responsible for the whole story, for everyone involved.'

'But you're on my side, surely?' he asks anxiously.

'That goes without saying,' I reply.

He ponders this for a while, he narrows his eyes.

'You're saying something has gone missing from my flat. That she's taken something. Are you going to tell me what it is?'

I take another sip of my red wine, which is just the right temperature.

'There's a time and a place for everything, Alvar. Think of this book as an equation. It all needs to add up in the end, that's the idea.'

'And if it doesn't add up, what then?'

'Then there'll be no story.'

'But what about me and what you've started?'

'I'll put you on ice. I put many ideas on ice. Four years ago full of enthusiasm I started a new book. It was about three inmates who absconded from Ila security prison. They escape in a van and drive to Finn forest, where they hide out in an old cabin.'

'And then what happens?'

'They're still there. I never managed to move them on.'

He looks disgusted at this thought.

'I'm leaving now,' he announces, 'so that you can finish your work!'

He leaps up from the sofa and goes to the door. 'I just have one small favour to ask you,' he pleads. 'Please forgive me for mentioning this, I don't mean to interfere in your business, but I can't stop myself.'

'No, you can't, can you?' I say. 'What is it?'

'You need to get up early tomorrow morning; you've got work to do. So don't drink so much that you make yourself sick.'

CHAPTER 20

Ten long days passed before Lindys reappeared.

At that point Alvar had started to relax and become his old self again. His shoulders were no longer hunched, his nerves had calmed down. What a fool he had been. He had been thinking this invasion would be permanent. Him, Alvar Eide. The loner. The oddball. Ultimately he was not a very interesting person, so she had probably found someone else to attach herself to, someone else she could fleece. He walked through the town with a spring in his step. He had finished work for the day. His life was once again his own, order and control ruled supreme. The snow melted, it trickled everywhere, people unbuttoned their coats and enjoyed the sun. He quickly popped into the Cash and Carry for some food before making his way up the hill to his flat. Outside he met Green who was emptying his letter box. Alvar nodded briefly, he didn't feel like talking. Green didn't say anything either, but he gave Alvar an odd look. Green's hand appeared holding a pile of junk mail whereupon he went to his own front door and vanished into his flat. Alvar felt a dart of something. What did that look signify? It was such a condescending look, as if his value as a human being had suddenly tumbled. He felt an instant, inexplicable sense of discomfort. He fumbled for the key in his pocket and stuck it in the lock. He tried turning it clockwise, but the key refused to budge. Now what was this? Had the lock caught? He tried again, this time with more force, but was at the same time scared of twisting the metal. Out of sheer frustration he turned the key anticlockwise. He heard a sharp click. What's this? he gasped. He turned the key clockwise again and there was another click. He turned the door handle and the door opened. The explanation revealed itself to him in its full horror. He had left his flat without locking his front door. He went into the hall with a strong sense of unease. He stopped and listened.

'Hiya!' It came from the living room. He froze instantly.

'I let the cat in,' he then heard. 'And afterwards I took a shower. You don't mind, do you?'

Several seconds of silence followed. 'You don't mind, do you, Alvar?'

He wanted to take a step forward, but he was paralysed. Finally he forced himself to move. She was lying on his sofa under a blanket. She propped herself up on her elbow, supporting her head in her hand.

'You can stop staring at me,' she said, 'I'm not a ghost.'

'But,' he struggled to find the words. 'But,' he said again and could manage nothing else.

She sat up on the sofa and arranged the blanket across her lap.

'I just needed some time out,' she explained. She reached for a mug on the coffee table. The kitten was asleep in an armchair. Alvar was speechless.

'I've made myself a cup of tea,' she went on, drinking from the mug. She slurped the tea. 'Well, go on, sit down. I don't bite.'

'But,' he said for the third time. He looked out into the kitchen, he stared out of the window, he did not understand a word of it.

'You can relax,' she said drily, 'there's no one else, only me.'

'Did I leave the door open?' he croaked.

'No, why would you think that? You're not absent-minded, Alvar. I've got a key.'

She picked up something from the coffee table. The metal gleamed in the light.

He took a step closer to the sofa. He was indignant now because he could not understand how that had happened, he could think of no explanation.

'But how did you get hold of that?' he finally managed to ask.

'From the key cupboard in the hall,' she said lightly. 'Most people have more than one set. I took it the last time I was here. I thought I could let myself in and out. You don't mind, do you?'

She peeked up at him with her ice-blue eyes.

He finally collapsed into a chair. The kitten was purring. Lindys drank her tea. Alvar sat like a log, trying to compose himself. Her eye had healed, he noticed. The grey jacket she always wore lay in a heap under the coffee table. He closed his eyes. Unable to take in what had happened.

'For Christ's sake,' she said suddenly, 'you don't need to make such a drama out of it, I'll leave soon, I promise.'

'But the key,' he whispered. 'You can't just help yourself to things like that, people just don't do that.'

'Yes,' she said. 'I do. I help myself. Whereas you never do.' She smiled, showing her sharp teeth.

'I've been thinking of moving,' he said abruptly. It just burst out of him.

She laughed out loud.

'Oh, you're so naive, matey!'

He bowed his head.

'Now take off your coat. Do you want me to make you a cup of tea?'

He shook his head. No, he was screaming on the inside, no, no, no!

'You're nervous,' she said more mildly this time. 'I can tell. But surely you can see that I'm not high?' She spread out her hands and beamed at him.

No, she was not high. And she was more brazen than ever, he thought.

'But you know,' she carried on, 'that's not something that can continue for very long.' She smoothed the blanket a little. 'I need a grand.'

He shook his head, terrified. She narrowed her eyes.

'You know what will happen if you say no,' she said, suddenly sounding vulnerable. 'I'll go cold turkey, and that's not a pretty sight.'

He bit his lip. Gave her a doubting look, wrung his hands in his lap.

'But don't you worry about that, I can always turn tricks. I would have to, anyway, in order to pay back what I owe you. You're thinking you won't ever see that money again, you think I'm robbing you blind and that I'll never repay you. You don't think very much of people like me.'

Her lower lip protruded, she was sulking.

'I'm not really sure,' he began.

'Exactly. You're like all the others. With your fine flat and your job and your cat and your savings while the rest of us are on the street living hand to mouth.'

He shook his head again.

'I don't want to be mean,' he said then. It felt as if he was falling down a pit. He fumbled for his wallet in the inside pocket of his coat, opened it and looked into the notes compartment.

The painting, he despaired. If this goes on, I'll never be able to afford it. It's like the bridge is sliding away from me and another person with a more forceful character will snatch it right before my eyes. A staunch, resolute man. A man who makes decisions without even blinking.

'I've only got five hundred in cash,' he whispered.

She turned her head angrily. 'Bloody plastic,' she said fiercely. 'I've got friends begging on the streets of Oslo and that's all they ever hear. *I don't carry cash*. I'm gonna get one of those little Visa terminals,' she said, 'and I'll swipe their bloody cards until they light up like a Christmas tree.'

He put the notes on the table for her, his hand was limp. She snatched them greedily.

'Just finishing my tea,' she said.

Has she stopped saying thank you? he wondered. Are we where I thought we would end up? Suddenly he felt exhausted. He rested his head in his hands and closed his eyes.

She immediately slammed her mug on the table with a bang. 'Why are you looking so tormented? You look like you're on your deathbed and you're clearly not.'

'I'm just a little tired,' he explained. He looked at the kitten. He wanted to lift him up and stroke his back, but he could not do it while she was looking, as if stroking the kitten was something terribly intimate.

'What have you got to be tired about?' she demanded.

He merely gave her a deep sigh in return.

'Oh, I get it, the picture,' she said, leaping up from the sofa. 'Anyway, it was nice to have a shower. I'm going to go now so you can get some peace. You don't need to get so stressed out just because you come home and find someone in your flat. Most people can handle that,' she claimed.

She retrieved her jacket from under the coffee table and put it on. Stood unsteadily on the high-heeled ankle boots. She went out into the hall. Alvar sat as before, immovable, with his head in his hands.

'See ya,' she called from the hall. He heard the door slam. Nevertheless he remained on his chair. And then a new wave of despair rolled over him. He had not got his key back.

Eventually he snapped out of his trance.

He fetched his shopping bag, which he had abandoned in the hall and went out into the kitchen with heavy steps. There he stopped and stared aimlessly at the worktop. Parts of him were still paralysed, he was unable to lift his hands. She had got him now. She had him in a vice, she was spending his money and using his bathroom, she was drinking his tea. She had the key to his flat in her pocket. She could have ten copies made of it and hand it out on Bragernes Square, it was only a matter of time before they would all be going to his flat and he risked coming home from work to find them there, perhaps a whole gang of them with their feet on the coffee table. And her with the kitten on her lap. He shuddered. This prospect almost brought him to his knees.

He lifted the shopping bag onto the worktop and unpacked the food. For weeks, he thought, for months, for years she would burden him, what am I going to do? These thoughts distressed him deeply. They circled places he did not want to go to. How do you get rid of someone you do not want? What would his neighbour think? Would he end up drifting around the town himself, too scared to go back to a flat filled with strangers, would he end up being forced out of his own home? No! a voice inside him screamed. Fate can't be that cruel. I don't deserve this. Though he did not believe in justice. Misfortune could strike anyone, he realised, and now it's my turn. Or I've got it the wrong way round, she's the unfortunate one. She needs heroin; she walks the streets in thin clothes. He clasped his head with both hands while he stared at a coil of Cumberland sausage. Suddenly he had an idea. The solution was so obvious, so brilliant in all its simplicity, and in addition totally achievable; he just had not thought of it until now. When my mind is darkened my thoughts go around in circles. I'll replace the lock, he exclaimed joyously, I'll do it right away. And get new keys. Then she won't be able to let herself in. And I'll never open the door when the bell rings!

The plan energised him and he hurried into the living room where he snatched the Yellow Pages from the shelf. Looked up a locksmith. Ran to the telephone to punch in the number. He lifted the handset cautiously and heard the dialling tone. It took a lot out of him to make the call. Asking for anything was so terribly hard for him that he wavered. He inhaled deeply several times before dialling the number. He heard the ringing tone. At the same time he looked at his watch. They were obviously closed, it was almost six in the evening. He would have to wait until tomorrow. He left the Yellow Pages open on the floor and went back to the kitchen to prepare his dinner. While he cooked he visualised her face the next time she would be standing outside his door with a key that no longer fitted. He could imagine disbelief, disappointment and rage, he saw anguish and desperation. But sod it, he thought and was startled by his own language, even though he had not said it out loud. I need to take charge here, before everything goes completely off the rails.

He put butter in the frying pan and watched it melt. After a while it started to sizzle, then it turned golden and later nut brown and that was when he cut up the sausage and placed it in the pan. He opened a packet of sauerkraut and heated it in the microwave. He arranged the food attractively on his plate and carried it into the living room. He felt awfully pleased with himself. Something was stirring inside him now, a completely new sensation, and he would never have believed he could feel this good. He was angry, pure and simple. He was angry with Lindys, he was angry with himself, he was angry with drug dealers and he was angry at the injustice of the world. The food tasted delicious. Afterwards he lay on the sofa, filled with a deep sense of calm. He felt serene and determined. The kitten jumped up and settled by his feet.

At exactly nine o'clock the next morning he rang the locksmith. When he had finished the call he felt very proud of himself. He had carried out his plan in a firm voice, employing a polite and friendly tone, it had gone like clockwork. The locksmith would arrive at six in the evening with a new safety lock and two keys, the cost of which would be two thousand three hundred kroner including fitting the lock. Alvar's peace of mind returned and on his way to the gallery he felt the sun warm his face. Of course solutions could be found, of course he was a man of action. He clenched his fists out of sheer joy and punched the air because he felt so strong. He unbuttoned his coat and savoured the faint touch of spring in the air. He was even capable of looking at people he passed in the street, looking at them with an open and friendly face. He straightened his back, he lowered his shoulders, he strode on, imbued with energy. Then he remembered the severed bridge. Which he could no longer afford to buy. This thought depressed him. Then he tried to trivialise it. It had only been a fleeting infatuation, he told himself, and these things always pass. Perhaps he would fall for another painting sometime in the future. Human beings are so unpredictable, he thought, they change, they let you down. Take Lindys, for example, there was no way you could trust her. And when it came to Ole Krantz, well, he was a nice enough chap and he meant well, but when push came to shove he would inevitably look after number one. That's how it is, Alvar Eide thought, as he walked through the town. He reached the gallery at two minutes to ten. He disabled the alarm and went inside. He stopped in front of the painting of the severed bridge. Suddenly it struck him how sombre it was, how dark, almost brutal. On the other hand he had no eye for bright, colourful pictures of naked rocks, glittering lakes or pretty flowers. Beauty, he thought, is all well and good, but it's not what we base our lives on. He continued up the stairs and into the kitchen where he started making coffee. He opened his newspapers and bent over to read.

The locksmith was on time and went to work straight away. Alvar made himself comfortable in an armchair and listened to the drone of the drill. A new lock, he thought, delighted. From now on only I can get in, no one else can disturb my peaceful life. He switched on the television and watched the news. Pope John Paul II was dying. The locksmith worked on. Alvar's heart beat like a drum, he felt empowered in a new way. He was also very good at his job, even if he did think so himself. He could see only clear skies ahead. Everything will be fine from now on, he thought, because I've taken control. Then the locksmith finished and Alvar tried the new lock. He inserted the shiny new key and turned it. A sharp, precise click sounded.

'That's excellent,' he enthused. He thanked the locksmith profusely and settled his bill. The locksmith left. He decided to celebrate his newly discovered vigour with an early evening sherry. Now she could ring his doorbell for as long as she liked, he had shut her out once and for all. Then he turned and looked straight at Lindys.

She had come out from his bedroom, her hair all tangled and messy. Alvar could feel himself starting to sway, he had to steady himself by putting his hand on the wall.

'Christ Almighty,' she said, 'what a racket. What is going on here?'

She stared at him with wide-open eyes, her clothes were crumpled.

Alvar was struck dumb. He just stood there supporting himself against the wall, staring at her in disbelief. At the same time he also felt as if she had caught him with his hands in the till.

'Was that you drilling?' she asked.

He opened his mouth in an attempt to breathe.

'What's your problem?' she said in an exasperated voice. 'I told you I would be coming and going. I wanted to have a nap so I locked the door. That mattress of yours is rock hard, I don't know how you sleep on it.'

He was still incapable of uttering a single word.

'Now just calm down,' she told him, 'it's not like it's a crime to have a nap.'

He opened his mouth, not a sound came out.

'I could hear that you had visitors,' she said, 'and I didn't want to disturb you. What on earth were you doing?'

He was still leaning against the wall, while his heart pounded wildly. She took a few steps into the living room; she scanned it with sharp eyes. However, she found nothing unusual in the bright room. Then something occurred to her. She briskly walked into the hall. Alvar held his breath.

'Bloody hell,' he heard, 'you've replaced the lock! You've only gone and replaced the bloody lock!'

Alvar's knees turned to jelly and he blushed crimson from shame. She returned. Stopped in front of him and planted her hands on her hips and jutted out her chin.

'What's wrong with you?' she raged. 'Cat got your tongue? If you don't want me here you can just tell me to go to hell. Just tell me straight to my face, because that's what you really want to do, isn't it!'

Alvar inhaled. No, he did not want her to go to hell, he just wanted to be left in peace. But he could not find the words.

'Is that what you want?' she challenged him. 'You just want me to piss off because you can't bear the sight of me? Well, if that's the case, why don't you just tell me?'

He shook his head in despair. He tried to straighten up, but his knees threatened to give way. All his vigour deserted him. He was weak, he had shrivelled up and he felt mortified. His chest was hurting too, he realised, as if someone had jabbed a potato peeler into his heart and was now twisting it slowly.

'So we're cool?' she asked in a milder voice. 'I mean, surely we can sit down and be honest with each other. Can't we?'

'Yes, of course,' he said, still upset by everything that had happened.

'So, you're saying we're cool?' she repeated.

'Yes,' he whispered, 'we're cool.'

She was silent. For several long seconds. Then her voice sounded bright and cheerful again.

'That's all right then,' she said, relieved. 'So I'll just have a quick shower and I'll be off.'

She marched into the bathroom, slamming the door behind her. Alvar was still leaning against the wall. Then he tried to stagger over to his armchair. His knees continued to tremble, his heart was starting to calm down, but the pain in his chest still scared him. I'm going to cause a scene, he thought, perhaps I'll collapse and I'll be discovered by a drug addict, lying face down on the floor, no pulse, not breathing. He collapsed into his armchair and clung to the armrests; he could hear the shower running in the bathroom. Now he had really been pushed over the edge. What's your problem? she had asked him. Well, what was his problem, why did his own will evaporate like mist before the sun, whenever it was confronted with another person's determination? An eternity later he heard her turn off the water and then a few minutes of silence followed. She came back out again, bright and cheerful, smiling broadly.

'I feel much better now,' she said running her fingers through her hair, which ended up sticking out all the same. She looked at him and pursed her lips.

'Have you still not got your act together?'

Alvar was afraid to look her in the eyes. 'Of course,' he coughed, but his voice told a different story.

'I need to go out,' she said and headed for his bedroom where she had left the grey jacket she always wore.

'I need another shot,' she declared, 'I'm starting to crave it. In here.' She put her hand on her chest. 'You got any money for me?'

'No,' he said without thinking.

She froze. Then she gawped at him.

'Really? You don't have any money?'

'No,' he said for the second time. The word felt foreign, but also liberating.

'You're telling me that you have spent everything that you own? You're skint? Your bank account has been cleared out and your savings have gone?'

He pressed his lips together. Refused to reply.

'You're lying,' she said fiercely. 'Of course you've got money. But if you don't want to give it to me, then that's another matter, so why don't you just tell me? Didn't we promise each other that we would be honest?'

He lowered his head. He could not fight this creature and her logic; he could not find the words or the strength. Wearily he went out into the hall where his coat hung. He found his wallet, opened it and took out the notes.

'Six hundred,' he muttered and went back. She instantly snatched them from him.

'You're a star!' she declared and kissed his cheek. She went out into the hall. 'And I'll take one of the keys for the new lock. If that's all right with you.'

Alvar was gobsmacked. He could not believe his ears; she spoke these words so casually that it took his breath away.

He ran out into the hall; she already had her hand in the key cupboard.

'You can't just help yourself like that,' he stammered and yanked the key from her. In the confusion he accidentally scratched her hand. Her eyes bored into him. Her jaw dropped.

'This is my flat,' he continued, 'and I need to have some control over who comes and goes here.'

'But you never get any visitors,' she argued.

'All I'm saying,' he said feeling like a complete idiot, 'is that I would like to be in charge of my own home.'

'But you are, aren't you?' she objected with big, wide eyes. 'All I'm doing is sitting on the sofa while you get on with whatever you're doing.'

'Yes, but you know, a key,' he said, 'a key might get lost, I need to have a certain amount of control.'

Her head dropped to her chest, an ominous silence followed.

Alvar had to look down too while he struggled to find the words.

'It's nice that you pop in every now and again,' he said cautiously. 'But there needs to be some order. And you know, you don't give a key to just anyone. Only to close friends.'

That was when she lifted her head and looked him straight in the eyes.

'So I'm not a close friend?' she said pitifully. Her lower lip quivered. 'I'm an unwanted friend, is that what you're saying?'

'No, no,' he protested fiercely, 'but we don't know each other all that well. Not yet.'

She tilted her head as she considered this. 'So what you're saying is that after a while when we know each other better, then I can have a key?'

He was struggling to keep up with her, let alone be ahead.

'Yes,' he shrugged. 'Something like that.'

'How much time are we talking about?' she asked him directly.

Again he shook his head in confusion.

'So how long does it take before two people have become good friends?' she insisted.

'Well, that depends, I'm not really sure, I don't have a lot of experience,' he admitted.

'I think of you as a friend,' she said quietly. She lowered her head gain. 'But I was wrong.' She turned away from him, turned her back on him. 'I always end up getting rejected,' she whispered, hurt.

'But I'm not rejecting you,' he assured her, 'I'm just saying that I need more time!'

'That's easy for you to say. You're not going down the drain like me and I haven't got time. This might be the last time you ever see me!'

He took one step forward. He raised one hand and wanted to place it on her shoulder, but he was afraid.

'Now don't be like that,' he comforted her, 'I'm sure you'll be all right, you always are.'

'You might end up regretting saying those words,' she said. 'People like me drop dead all the time. You know that, we're at risk. You'll probably just breathe a sigh of relief, lock your door and lie down on your sofa and forget all about me.'

'Oh no,' he said quickly. 'Not at all, don't think like that. I'd be beside myself if anything happened to you, I really mean that.'

'So you do care about me a little?' she said softly.

'Of course,' he said firmly.

'But not enough?'

'What do you mean?'

'Not enough to give me a key?'

Alvar went totally quiet. It dawned on him that he had run out of words, that he would never win this battle. So he held out his hand and gave her the new key. She instantly closed her fingers and gripped it. A second later the front door slammed.

He stayed in his armchair for a very long time.

The television was droning on in the background, but he did not even notice it. She is like a pebble in my shoe, he thought, every single step I take hurts. She is like burdock, you cannot pull it off without hurting yourself, she is like an itch that gets worse and worse. She spreads likes a disease, she grows like a tumour, she makes me want to scream. His vicious thoughts frightened him. He was not a violent man, not at all. He was angry with her, but his anger instantly ricocheted back on himself. He felt faint when he thought about his own incompetence. He would never hit her, he did not know how to argue, he had never been taught how and he never felt the desire. And yet he could still feel pressure building up inside his chest. He listened carefully to it. Yes, it was a roar, there could be no doubt. He had never heard himself roar and he was terrified of letting it out. He imagined a wild animal in there baring its teeth, hurling itself against the bars of its cage, desperate to get out. Then he started to sob. It was a dry, pathetic sob and it made him crumple as he sat there in his armchair. Alvar Eide is sobbing, he thought, my life has become so dramatic that I have lost my self-control. He dried his tears, but he was unable to get up from his chair. A sherry, he thought, that's what I need to calm my nerves. He pulled himself together and made himself go into the kitchen to get the bottle. His hands were shaking, the tears were flowing. He felt like a nervous wreck. And all because of a girl of forty-odd kilos. He found a milk glass and filled it almost to the brim. Raised it to his mouth and drank. He leaned against the worktop gulping sherry, and suddenly he had to laugh. He observed himself through the eyes of another. A lonely man reduced to drinking sherry from a milk glass with tears streaming down his face, just because some girl had been to his home. The whole business was so demeaning it made him cringe. He continued to laugh, louder now, it began to resemble a kind of braying, sounds he did not know he was capable of making filled the whole kitchen. Every now and then he would pour himself another sherry, swigging it as if it were juice, followed by more outbursts of his braying laughter. With his free hand he gripped the worktop tightly.

This, he realised, is the end of the road for me.

CHAPTER 21

'I'm already beaten,' Alvar says.

It is hard for him to accept this realisation, and his back is bent. His eyes shine from too much sherry and his hands are shaking badly.

'Sit down,' I order him. 'Let's talk about it.'

'No one in my family ever had a drink problem,' he adds.

'Is that right?'

'I just wanted you to know that. It's not a path I wish to take and I don't usually knock back sherry like this.'

'I'll bear that in mind,' I reply. 'So let's say that you needed to let off some steam very badly, but that it's not going to become a habit.'

'Thank you.'

He lets himself fall onto my sofa. There are beads of sweat on his shiny forehead and hints of dark shadows under his eyes.

'There's something I've been meaning to ask you,' he says in a tired voice.

'Fire away.'

'Is she the strong one or am I?'

I consider his question. 'What do you think?'

He shakes his head. 'I don't know. But I need to take my share of the blame for the situation I've ended up in. At the same time she is so slippery, like an eel between my hands. I try to find a way out, but as things stand now, I can't see it. There are times when I just feel like giving up. Leave the responsibility for everything to you. Just drift along while you let things happen, whatever those things might be. It's not as if it can get any worse, can it? Can it get any worse?'

'What precisely are you scared of?' I ask.

He thinks about it. 'Well, many things, I guess. Perhaps I'm scared of losing my mind. Sometimes it feels like that might happen and I'm frightened that the fragile thread that I have with the outside world might snap. Though there is no history of mental illness in my family either, not as far as I know, anyway. And I'm also scared that I might act on impulse.'

'Why is that scary?'

'Surely that's obvious,' he exclaims. 'We can't allow ourselves to be controlled by impulses.'

'Which particular impulse did you have in mind?' I ask.

'The one that controls your temper,' he says darkly.

I lean forward across the table. I look him straight in the eye.

'Alvar. Dear Alvar. I know you, you wouldn't be able to hurt a fly.'

'I've always thought so too,' he says, somewhat relieved. 'I've always striven to behave as calmly as possible. But sometimes I get this gut feeling. It tightens and it spreads to my arms in a horrible way. And before I know it I clench my fists ready to fight. Because everything around me is exploding and because I can't find the words, so I lose my footing and I stumble over the edge. Are you turning a peaceful man into a thug, is that your plan?'

'No, Alvar, calm down. God knows you're a peaceful man,' I say, 'and I'm not going to tamper with this feature. Mankind's tragedy, however, is that too much peacefulness can sometimes lead to disaster. You ought to read Zapffe,' I suggest, 'he's your kind of philosopher. I've got his essays here on my bookshelf, if you want to borrow them.'

'Thank you.'

'Incidentally, I have always believed that you ought to judge people on the basis of their actions,' I continue, 'not on what they say, think or mean. There are plenty of people ready to shoot their mouths off.'

'But I'm not that type either,' he says quickly. 'I don't act and I don't judge. All I'm doing is pacing up and down this labyrinth looking for the exit. Like a lab rat. A repulsive, trained lab rat.'

'I think you're being very hard on yourself.'

'You're the one being hard, it's your book.'

'Our book,' I correct him. 'Don't underestimate your own part in this collaboration. I listen to you, I can be influenced. Especially at this point, when we're well into the book.'

'It's going to be dramatic, isn't it? That's what I'm picking up from you. We've peaked and now we're going to start running down the hill. And I can't even pray because you haven't given me a God.'

'Would you like a God?'

'I imagine all lost souls would. It's the loveliest fairy tale in the world,' he adds, looking sad. 'Reserved only for the few.'

'Try to believe in yourself,' I say, 'believe that you're worth something. That you can do something. That you possess great reserves which you can draw on in times of crisis.'

'You believe in me,' he said miserably. 'But I'm scared that I might end up letting you down. That I can't run the race you have entered me in.'

I look at him solemnly and say sincerely, 'It has never, ever happened that one of my characters has let me down.'

'There's always a first time.'

'With that sort of attitude you might well be right. It takes a lot out of me too, don't forget that. I'm worn out.'

He gets up from the sofa and takes a walk across the floor. His head is bowed, his hands are behind his back. Then he stops, he has remembered something.

'In some strange way I actually like Lindys,' he says, somewhat surprised by his own, stumbling admission.

'Tell me more.'

'She doesn't give a damn about anything. She doesn't follow any rules, she helps herself to whatever she wants. She doesn't care what people think of her. She never tries to please anyone and she doesn't care about consequences. Her attitude is devil-may-care and perhaps that's a kind of freedom. She's on heroin, she lives her life one hour at a time. Whereas I, on the other hand, am trapped inside myself. I have order and control and structure, but I can't get out.'

'And deep down that's what you want? To finally show yourself as you really are, warts and all?'

'I never used to think so,' he says, 'but now I can see that this is what it's all about. I'm fed up with being careful. Anonymous. Correct.'

'What do you think we would see if you finally escaped?'

He stops. He folds his arms across his chest.

'That's the problem, this is what truly worries me. Perhaps I have nothing to show, perhaps what you see in front of you standing here on the floor is all there is to see. Or, I might open up only to discover terrible things.'

'Such as?'

'Cowardice. Brutality. Panic.'

'But no great passion,' I smile, 'no bubbling joy, no heartache, no wild and uncontrollable laughter.'

He goes over to the window and stares out of it. His shoulders sag.

'I can see all the way into town.'

'Yes, it's beautiful.'

'All the lights,' he adds, 'street lights, lights from the houses, they glow.'

'Everything looks beautiful at a distance, doesn't it? Even when seen through shimmering, polluted air.'

'When will the battle commence?' he asks, abruptly turning round.

I shift slightly in my chair, 'Are you asking me for an actual date?'

'Why not? There's no escape for me anyway.'

'November,' I propose. 'The eighteenth.'

'Why November exactly?'

'I need rainstorms and fairly cool air. I need rotting leaves and muddy roads. The kind of shivering quality that characterises November. The grey, naked landscape stripped of everything that grows and comforts us, but not yet blessed with white, icing-sugar snow. A bleak time in many ways, a brutal time. It is as if everything surrenders in November and we huddle in corners and light candles. I love November.'

'But why?' he repeats.

'I was born in that month, on the sixth. It was a wild night, God-awful weather, when I saw the world for the first time. November is in my blood, a darkness, a melancholy. A permanent feeling of sadness. My hands are like bare branches, I have fog in my head and storm in my heart. You were born in September,' I tell him, 'and you are marked by that, the summer was drawing to a close when you were born. The holidays had ended, but the harvest had yet to come and Christmas was far away. No expectation,' I say, 'just an orderly, eventless time between bright sunshine and crisp frost. But I love all the months, each has its own tone, its own hue. Imagine this wheel. January, for example, bright blue and white and a trumpet with clear, sharp notes. February, almost identical, with the sun a little more yellow and I hear a cornet. March, grey and white, I hear a viola, there lies a faint hope in its deep note. April, yellow and white. Violins,' I say, 'with a hint of trapped despair. May, yellow and green. People dancing around a maypole. June, airy and sky blue, accordion. A big flaming bonfire, sparks flying off out into the night. July is a deep yellow, the colour of sand, the sound of a radio. August, the summer is fading, I hear a faint guitar. Then comes your month, September. It is the colour of earth and now I hear a cello. October,' I continue, 'rusty red and with a strong beat. Someone is playing an oboe. November, as I mentioned just now, bare. In November I hear kettledrums and a moaning trombone. Then we finally reach December, with candles and tinsel. And so the years pass, in an ever-recurring circle. If you live to be eighty, Alvar, you will have existed nearly thirty thousand days. Or, approximately seven hundred thousand hours, if you like.'

He pales. 'And how many minutes is that?'

'Forty-two million. It's almost three hundred million heartbeats.'

Alvar comes over and steadies himself against my chair.

'You mustn't say such things. Now I too can feel every single heartbeat.' He places his hand on his chest.

'It's fine,' I say, 'it's fine that you can feel your heart. I think we need to feel alive, I think we need to expose ourselves to pain. But in our society this is not acceptable. People have always used their shrewdness and imagination to relieve pain. Today everything must be easy and it mustn't take time. I hate disposable cutlery,' I confess, 'and ready meals. Parboiled rice. Powdered hot chocolate and instant coffee. Part-baked bread. Things like that. Living takes time. We need to give each other time.'

He finds his place on the sofa. 'November,' he says lamely. 'It's eight months away and from now on I'll be aware of every second. Lindys has knocked through my shell and left a gaping hole. I feel the cold differently now and nearly all sounds have become noises. I'm not used to such sensitivity.'

'It's about time your body found out what it means to be alive,' I say. 'And yes, it hurts. But that's also how you'll learn to let in a little joy.'

'I don't need very much of that,' he claims, 'I prefer security. And you have taken it away from me.'

'In order to give you something else,' I say. 'Experience.'

CHAPTER 22

The days passed, and the weeks.

Alvar carried out his job with the same diligence and pride as he always had done. He was friendly, correct and polite, and when he framed pictures in the workshop it was with great care and attention to detail. But in the late afternoon, when it was nearing closing time, he was consumed by a nagging anxiety. What if she was lying on his sofa, or even worse, in his bed? Perhaps she was having a shower in his bathroom now? Perhaps she had robbed him blind? Though he had no valuables to speak of. He had acquired another idiotic habit. He always stopped by the cashpoint outside the Cash and Carry on his way home. As long as he had money, she would take it and go, it was the only way he was able to get her out of the flat quickly. His savings dwindled slowly and steadily. One day there would be no more, he thought, one day I'll be as poor as a church mouse. What's she going to do then?

He left the gallery at five in the afternoon. The knot in his stomach grew as he walked through the streets to the Cash and Carry. He got to the cashpoint, he took out his wallet and found his card, which he stuck in the machine. The card was checked, please enter your PIN. He entered the code and all the time a voice inside was telling him that this was insane, but he was unable to stop himself. The money was his only weapon and with it he bought back his own freedom. He took out six hundred kroner, put the notes in his wallet and headed home. The cat was sitting on his doorstep and he experienced a brief moment of bliss. His front door was locked, but then she usually locked it from the inside, presumably so she could hear when he came back. He unlocked the door and went in. He spotted her immediately; she was lying on the sofa under the blanket without moving. He took a few more steps towards her. Then, to his horror, he saw something on the coffee table. A syringe, he realised, and a thin light grey rubber tube. He clasped his mouth in fear. He stared at her for a long, long time, but all he could see was a bit of her cheek and locks of her blonde hair falling over her forehead. Out of sheer desperation he coughed violently to see if she would react. She did. She turned her head and opened her eyes, her gaze was unfocused.

'You can't bring this back here,' he yelped, pointing at the table, at the syringe and the tube, which frightened the living daylights out of him. She grunted something incomprehensible and closed her eyes. He remained where he was while his brain was working overtime. He had put up with so much from her, but now he was overcome by an irresistible urge to put his foot down. To tell her that there were limits to what he was willing to tolerate.

'Lindys,' he said louder this time, 'you can't bring drugs in here!'

Again she opened her eyes and she gazed at him dully. 'Why are you calling me Lindys?' she slurred. 'My name's Rikke.'

He let out a soft groan. 'I'm not having it!' he said, still in a tone of voice bordering on falsetto. She sat halfway up, turned and lay down with her back to him. Alvar waved his hands in the air. It felt as if he was fighting a shadow, which kept slipping away so that he would never be able to punch it. He looked at the syringe on the coffee table and shuddered. Here, in his living room. A girl on heroin. Had his neighbours seen her arrive, and what might they be thinking? He spun on his heel abruptly and went out into the kitchen. Stood for a while leaning against the worktop while he thought furiously. I need to eat, he thought, I need to eat to get through this, I mustn't panic. I need to talk to her when she wakes up, properly. I need to be firm and decisive and resolute. Yes, he thought, I need to stop giving her money. I will make this a condition. She will not get another krone if she brings drugs into my living room. It's that simple.

Cheered by this resolution he opened the door to the fridge and found a box of eggs. An omelette was what he needed, he could grate some cheese and sprinkle it on top, have some bread with it. The cat appeared for a drink of water. There were no sounds coming from the living room. He tried to ignore the fact that she was in there. Then he cracked two eggs against the edge of a bowl. She'll be gone soon, he told himself, and perhaps I'll get several days without a visit. Again he had another flash of inspiration and an idea began to take shape in his head. She had taken his spare key, perhaps it was in the pocket of her grey jacket? He took a few steps and looked into the living room. Yes, it was in a pile on the floor. And Lindys was still sleeping. Or Rikke, or whatever her name was. What if he stole it back? What if he gave her a taste of her own medicine for once, used her own methods? This is what it means to be shrewd, he realised, and now there was a time and a place for it.

He tiptoed into the living room. His heart began to pound, but she was clearly on a different planet, he could not even hear her breathing. Then he got hold of the collar of her jacket and pulled it carefully towards him. First he tried the left pocket, but there was nothing but fluff. Then he eased his hand into the right pocket and there it was. His key. He snatched it and put it in his trouser pocket and he instantly felt like a thief. He replaced the jacket on the floor and went back to the kitchen. I had no idea I could be this devious, he thought, amazed. Soon she'll wake up and rub her eyes. Then she'll ask me for money and then she'll leave. Still thinking that the key is in the pocket of her jacket. Two to three days will pass and then she'll return, but she won't be able to let herself in. There'll be trouble, he thought anxiously, what am I going to do if she starts hammering on the front door with her fists, what will the neighbours say? He started to worry, unable to live with what he had done. Perhaps it was best if she had her own key anyway? Then he became massively irritated at his own indecisiveness, he was perfectly entitled to retrieve his key.

He whisked the eggs with a fork and added salt and pepper to the mixture. He poured the eggs into a frying pan, and they started to congeal instantly. He grated some cheese and sprinkled it onto the eggs, he sliced some bread and buttered it. When the meal was ready he carried it into the living room. Again he looked at the syringe and the tube. He felt ill at ease. Something like that was dangerous, he knew, the papers wrote all sorts of things about infection, and here he stood with his freshly cooked food which he was just about to eat. He rushed back out into the kitchen and found a pair of Marigold gloves, pulled them on and went over to the coffee table. Picked up the tube and the syringe, went over to the bin under the worktop and dropped them into it. Finally he could breathe more easily and he went over to eat. He switched on the television and still she did not stir. Where are you now? he wondered, and looked at her blonde hair. In some kind of paradise? A place free from hurt, worries and discomfort? A place with no concept of time, no pain? A place where you float? Perhaps it's like being in warm water, the light is low and the silence complete. Soon she would wake up and then what would happen? He ate quietly, taking care to breathe steadily and calmly the whole time; unless he focused on his breathing, he would whip himself into a state of frenzy within seconds. When he had finished he clinked his cutlery a little to see if she would react. She did. She rolled quietly onto her back and faced him. Her eyes were black.

'Hi,' she said softly.

He did not reply. He was not sure whether she was present in the same way he was, and if she wasn't then there would be no point in trying to have a conversation with her.

'Christ, I'm so thirsty,' she said, 'do you think you could get me a glass of water?'

She brushed her hair away from her face with a drawn look.

He looked at her, but still did not reply. He carried out his plate and cutlery, found a glass in the cupboard and got some water from the tap for her and carried it back. She sat up on the sofa, grabbed the glass and drank greedily; he could hear how the water glugged down her narrow throat.

'Your neighbour,' she said eventually, 'he's a very bad-tempered man.'

Alvar looked at her.

'He started asking questions when I was outside. As if it's any of his business what we get up to.'

Are we getting up to anything? Alvar wondered.

'He told me you were out,' she went on, 'and I told him I had my own key. You should have seen the look he gave me. As if I was a piece of rubbish someone had thrown on his lawn.'

'You can't bring your drugs in here,' Alvar said abruptly.

She looked up. Suddenly she looked sulky.

'No, I suppose you would prefer it if I sat in a doorway and shot up for everyone to see.'

He could think of no answer to that.

'But,' he objected, 'I don't want to get mixed up in anything like that.'

She drained her glass and slammed it down on the coffee table. 'You're not mixed up in anything,' she stated irritably. 'I don't row with you, I don't make you take drugs, do I?'

'No.'

'So what are you whingeing about?'

'Well,' he whimpered, 'I don't mean to whinge. But it makes me a little nervous.'

'That's because you're a sissy,' she declared.

'But, Rikke!' he moaned.

'Rikke?' She gave him a baffled look.

'I've got some cash for you,' he said before he could stop himself. 'Six hundred kroner. You can have it, but then you have to do this somewhere else. I make this a condition,' he said, his voice getting louder. He instantly felt his strength return.

Her jaw dropped.

'You're blackmailing me,' she said, hurt. 'You know I'm desperate and now you're putting pressure on me.' She buried her face in her hands. He thought he could hear her snivelling. Her slender shoulders jolted.

'But you have your room?' he said. 'Isn't that right?'

'I don't have a room,' she sobbed.

'But then where do you sleep?' he exclaimed.

'Here, there and everywhere,' she cried. 'Surely you can understand that people in my line of work don't have all the stuff that normal people have. A bed. Food. A regular pay cheque. I've got none of those.'

He scanned her face for tears, but found none.

'I don't think I'm asking for much,' she said, 'and I don't know what your politics are, but I thought you were a decent person.'

'Of course, I'm a decent person,' Alvar said. 'Look here.' He got out his wallet. 'Here's some money.'

She snatched it as swiftly as she always did and scrunched it up in her hand.

'If you cut me off then I'll have no one,' she said in tears. 'You know I'm going straight to hell and it would have been nice to have some company for the last bit of the journey.'

'You're not going to hell, are you?' he asked, perturbed.

'Don't be so bloody naive!' she screamed.

'Hush!' he said quickly. 'You mustn't shout, not in here!'

His heart had started pounding again. He found it unbearable when people shouted, his whole body shrank.

'I don't think you've got it in you,' she claimed, looking defiant. She got up from the sofa and ran her fingers through her hair. She stumbled then regained her balance.

'But I'm going to go now and leave you in peace. Pour yourself a sherry, Alvar, let yourself go a little, why don't you?'

She picked up her jacket from the floor; Alvar's heart skipped several beats. In the distance he thought he could hear the faint roll of drums slowly getting louder. She put on her jacket, buttoned it and quickly brushed herself down. Then she stuck her hands in her pockets and Alvar held his breath. She searched for a while, then her eyes widened.

'The key,' she said dully. For a moment she looked confused. Alvar froze.

'The key, it's gone.' She looked at him with disbelief and anger. Then she exploded.

'You've pinched it!' she shouted. 'You've pinched my bloody key!'

Alvar felt as if he was being melted down and poured away, his cheeks were burning hot.

'I see.' She folded her arms across her chest, her face hardened. 'So you've finally shown your true colours, it took you long enough. So this is what all your supposed goodness boils down to. You were just faking, you were just pretending to be a good person. You're the most deceitful person I've ever met. The most cowardly, the most devious!'

Alvar started to shake in his armchair.

'You're just as bad as all the others,' she went on, her voice jarring. 'You'll open your door to some sorry creature, but that's all. That's fine by me, I'll get out of your way once and for all and you'll never see me again. I'm going to get myself another hit, a big one, which will make me forget this bloody shithole which is all this world really is!'

'No. No!' Alvar screamed, getting up from his chair. 'Don't say things like that! Look, look, here is the key.' He pulled it out of his trouser pocket. 'I don't mind you coming here, I really don't; I'm not going to throw you out, that's not what I meant. Please don't get angry, it's just me, I get really anxious sometimes,' he stuttered.

She accepted the key. Studied the new, shiny metal and looked at him with narrow eyes.

'The problem is,' she said slowly, 'it's a bit difficult for me to believe what you're saying. Because now I don't know if you really mean it.'

'I mean it,' he pleaded, 'please, please forgive me, I'm such an idiot.'

'God knows,' she said, somewhat appeased now. 'Well, well. I'm counting on you then. I'm relying on the fact that you've finally made up your mind and that you'll keep your word.'

She went out into the hall. Alvar stared after her. She opened the door and turned one last time. Then she sent him a look that made him wince. I know who you are all right, the ice-blue eyes said. I know how to handle you and I'm much stronger than you. The door slammed shut.

CHAPTER 23

In April, May and June she came and went as she pleased.

Alvar went about his business with a knot in his stomach. He thought of the knot as a grey tumour and imagined how it would spread to the rest of his body. How it would devour him from the inside, wrap itself around his internal organs and strangle them. He was always overwhelmed by relief whenever the flat was empty. When it was not he mobilised all his remaining strength to deal with her. Keep some kind of conversation going, give her money and get her out of the door as quickly as possible. His savings were dwindling dangerously fast and at times he caught himself longing for the moment when he would withdraw his last krone. Then it would all be over and she would have to go elsewhere. At the same time he knew that as long as he gave her money then she would not have to walk the streets, something he could not bear to think about. She would not have to make her frail body available to complete strangers, in an alleyway, in the back of a car or in some disgusting room.

She had kept her part of their bargain and he had not once returned to find her syringe on the coffee table. But she was often high. Then her eyes were so distant that he knew she must be in another universe where he was unable to reach her. If she were, he would wait in his armchair until she came round and then they would chat about everyday stuff. Often he was appalled at how little she knew about what went on in the real world. Her existence was narrow and dark, and it was all about satisfying her violent addiction to heroin. Nothing else mattered. She disappeared on a few occasions. Once she was gone fourteen days and Alvar became strangely restless. He did not understand why. Perhaps she has gone to another town, he used to think, or she might simply be sick. Not that he downright missed her, but he could not handle the uncertainty of it.

His neighbour, Green, had stopped talking to him; whenever they met, he would merely nod and disappear into his flat. They were probably wondering what on earth was going on, but Alvar did not have the energy to worry about it, and he could not cope with arguments or conflicts, so he nodded politely in return and pretended that everything was just fine.

He had become very fond of his cat. The kitten had grown in record time and turned into a fine, handsome animal. Of course, he ought to have him neutered, but he could not find it in himself to call the veterinary surgery and have this brutal procedure carried out. He could not bear the thought of witnessing the operation. He just did not have the strength, it was that simple. As a result the cat often came back home with cuts and tears all over his body from fights with other cats in the neighbourhood. And he clearly had an inbuilt alarm clock because he always sat on the stairs waiting for Alvar when he came home from work. If he was not there it usually meant that Lindys or Rikke or whatever her name was had let herself into the flat and let the cat in at the same time.

As he walked up the drive he could not see the cat. He waited for him on the bottom step for a while; he called out a few times to see if he would turn up. And then something grey and white stirred in the bushes. And the cat came towards him. He unlocked the door and went inside; the cat followed him. There was no one on his sofa. So she was probably not going to turn up today either; that would make it six days since he saw her last. The cat walked around the floor, sniffing. He followed him with his eyes, but when he went to lift him up, he hissed furiously at him. He was shocked. The cat had never hissed at him before. Perhaps he was hurt. He checked him for cuts and bruises, but he looked unharmed and healthy. He went out into the kitchen with the shopping he had just bought. Some bacon, a leek, a litre of milk, a loaf of bread. The cat followed him and went over to his bowl straight away and started to eat his pellets. Alvar diced the bacon with a sharp knife. He chopped up the leek and fetched eggs from the fridge; he wanted to cook himself a really delicious omelette. The cat ate until he was sated, then he returned to the living room where he was in the habit of settling down in an armchair or on the corner of the sofa. But today he did not do that. He stopped in the middle of the floor and started miaowing plaintively. Alvar followed and looked at him. He had a strong feeling that something was wrong, but he couldn't pinpoint what it was.

'Why don't you want to go on the sofa, Goya?' he asked. The cat miaowed again. So he went back to finish his cooking. That was when he heard someone open and slam the front door shut. And there she was, dressed in a pink angora jumper and leggings so washed out they hardly had any colour. The same ankle boots with those ghastly heels.

'Hi. What are you making?'

He glanced at her sideways from the kitchen and nodded. She joined him immediately and asked for a glass of cold water.

'I'm thirsty all the time,' she explained, leaning her head back as she drank. He nodded a second time. He did not really understand addicts, but suddenly it was rather nice that she had turned up. And she never stayed for long, he had to give her that. Most of the time she was simply sleeping on his sofa while he got on with his business. Also, she was not high and her ice-blue eyes were completely clear. How bright they are, he thought, as hard as jewels. Yet again he was struck by her transparency, her green veins, her pale cheeks, her skin stretched tightly across her bones. She put down her glass on the worktop and went into the living room. She settled down on her regular spot on the sofa. She called the cat immediately; her voice was soft and enticing. Alvar whisked eggs. He put the diced bacon and the leeks into a frying pan. The smell of bacon and leek began to fill the kitchen. Did she want anything to eat? No, she never wanted anything to eat. He did not believe that she ever ate. He would estimate that she weighed around forty kilos, a frail skeleton stripped of muscles. He peeked into the living room. She had got up again, and she walked across the floor to get the cat. He hissed aggressively at her. She straightened up, folded her arms and looked at Alvar, who had poked his head round the door.

'So what have you gone and done now?' she asked.

He had no idea what she meant. He rushed back to the stove to turn the heat down.

'What have I done wrong now?' He gave her a baffled look.

'The cat,' she said, looking at him and shaking her head at the same time.

'Yes, he's a bit odd today,' Alvar said, watching the cat. He had jumped up onto the windowsill where he was trying to hide behind a potted plant.

'Odd?' she said, exasperated. 'Is he odd?'

'What I'm trying to say,' he replied, 'is that he's been behaving a little strangely today. I think he might have been in a fight. He won't let me pick him up.'

Suddenly she walked up to him with long striding steps.

'But dear God,' she said loudly, 'haven't you got eyes in your head?'

'Yes,' Alvar hesitated. 'Of course I have.'

'No, you bloody don't. Take a look at him, go on!'

She pointed towards the windowsill, her finger quivering. Then she began to laugh out loud.

'Just look at the cat!' she ordered him.

'But what about the food,' he whimpered.

She quickly moved the frying pan away from the heat and nudged him into the living room. Alvar felt confused. But he did as he was told; he went into the living room and over to the window where the cat was pressing itself against the pane. His eye teeth were bared, they were sharp as needles.

'Is he pregnant?' he asked sheepishly.

At that she threw back her head and laughed heartily.

'Pregnant? Are you out of your mind? It's a tom, for God's sake!'

'But, something's wrong,' he said perplexed, shaking his head, 'and I don't know what it is.'

'It's not your cat,' she laughed.

'Eh?'

He let his hands drop and he wriggled his fingers nervously.

'You've dragged someone else's cat into the flat.'

'No,' he said quickly.

'Yes! Surely you can see it's not Goya. Goya has a white chest and grey paws. This one has a grey chest and white paws. It's also smaller and it's frightened out of its wits because it doesn't know you. It wants to get out, but it can't find the way. Alvar, go and open the door. I bet you Goya is sitting out on the step wanting to get in.'

Alvar stared at the strange cat, his arms still hanging limply. He felt like a complete idiot. She was still laughing. A silvery, playful laughter tinged with superiority.

'You really are something else,' she hiccupped. Alvar wanted to laugh, but he could not manage it. He went out into the hall and opened the door. Goya shot in. The strange cat darted across the floor like an arrow and was gone in a flash. Alvar's cheeks flushed scarlet. That he could be so absent-minded, it was unbearable. Angrily he marched out into the kitchen and put the frying pan back on the heat; he heard the butter starting to sizzle again and added the eggs. He frantically began talking about other things. How much he needed a holiday and how he was thinking about maybe going away for a few days. He peered furtively at her to see how she would react.

'I can look after your flat for you,' she suggested enthusiastically. 'And water your plants. Can I stay overnight? It's so comfy. I won't bring anyone here, I promise.'

He didn't reply, but he thought about what she was saying.

'And I can clean the floors and collect your post.'

He folded the omelette and eased it out of the frying pan with a spatula.

'But do you think you could leave me some money before you go away?'

He sighed. Found cutlery and poured himself a glass of milk, placed everything on a tray and carried it into the living room. She followed him.

'And I can feed the cat. You can't just leave him, you know, he needs his food.'

'I could put him in a home,' he argued.

'Oh, but that's so expensive,' she replied.

'You won't lose the key, will you?' he asked. 'I'm scared that it might fall into the wrong hands.'

'I'll take good care of the key,' she said. 'Look. It's around my neck on a piece of string.

She stuck her hand down the pink angora sweater and pulled out a blue string and there was the key.

'I won't let anyone else in, I won't talk to your neighbours and I won't tell anyone that you've gone away; I'm not stupid, Alvar.'

He believed her. In spite of everything there was a part of her that wanted to be honest.

'Where will you go?' she asked, flopping onto the sofa.

He pulled his chair closer to the dining table and started eating.

'Well, not far. Only a few days. A short break, to Copenhagen possibly. Or maybe Sweden, where they have all these hostels.' As he said it he realised that the idea of sharing accommodation with a group of total strangers did not appeal to him in the least. 'Or I might find a cheap hotel,' he said. 'I might drive around in the Mazda for a bit and see the countryside. Värmland, for example, is said to be very pretty, and a change is as good as a rest.'

'Yes, it is, isn't it?' she replied warmly. 'I fancy a change as well. I hate this town,' she went on, 'all those people staring at you, young guys fighting the whole time, I'm fed up with it. And it's so bloody cold in the winter, there's a wind from the river, it's like someone pinching your cheeks with icy fingers. Have you ever felt it, Alvar?'

Yes, he had. All the same one of his favourite things about the town was the river running through it. The bridge, the boats. The promenade where he liked to go for walks on Sundays.

'You're so good at managing on your own,' she said abruptly.

He looked up.

'You cook proper food. And it's always so neat and tidy in here, and so clean. Your plants thrive, all lovely and green.'

He shook his head, slightly embarrassed by her praise.

'I mean, single men are usually so messy.'

'Really?'

'I know a lot about that,' she said, 'I've visited a lot of them.'

I don't doubt that, Alvar thought, drinking his cold milk.

'Don't you have any vices at all?' she asked.

He considered this. 'I drink sherry,' he said, 'in moderate quantities.'

'Then it's not a vice,' she stated. 'Merely a harmless habit. It doesn't mean that you are genetically disposed towards dependency.'

'There is such a gene?' he asked.

'I swear on my life,' she said. 'In fact, addicts like me are innocent victims. You must realise that, Alvar.'

'I'm not judging anyone,' he said, hurt.

'I know,' she said softly. 'You're a sweetheart.'

Alvar choked on his milk and was overcome by a violent coughing fit.

'And you press your trousers,' she laughed. 'I don't know anyone else who does that.'

Alvar ate the rest of his omelette in silence. From time to time he glanced up at her, there was something he was dying to ask her. She lit a cigarette; he went into the kitchen as he always did to fetch her a saucer. He returned and placed it on the coffee table.

'What's your real name?' he asked, bending down.

She threw her head back and laughed. 'It's Ella,' she said, 'Ella Margrethe Riis.'

'And what will it be tomorrow?' he asked.

'Well, let me see, Linda, perhaps. Or Britt. You can call me what you like.'

'Heidi,' he suggested.

She snorted. 'What? That's just so naff.'

He pouted and pretended to look stern. 'You were the one who wanted to play name games so you'll just have to put up with it.'

'All right, all right then,' she conceded. 'My name's Philippa.'

'And I'm supposed to believe that?'

She shrugged. 'I'm supposed to believe that your name's Alvar. Even though I think it's a weird name. What were your parents thinking when they gave you that name?'

'How would I know?' he said. 'I imagine it's a family name of some sort,' he added. 'It might have been the name of my great-uncle or something, and I was named after him.'

She inhaled her cigarette.

'Do you have any family?' he wanted to know.

She was quiet for a long time. 'Perhaps. But I never see them.'

He frowned at her reply. 'Either you have family or you don't.'

'Of course. That's what I was just saying. I might have some family, but I don't know what they're doing.'

He sighed. 'You're not easy to get on with,' he said then.

'Is that what it's all about?' she asked. 'Being easy to get on with? I think you have turned being nice into a full-time job. I bet you're nice even when you're on your own.'

'Of course,' he said. 'Should I be nasty to myself?'

'Some people are,' she said. 'Some people are at their worst when they're alone. They get plastered, they overeat, they cut themselves, they bang their head against the wall, they play their stereo at full blast and blow their eardrums, they stand by the window and howl at the moon.'

'Do they?' he said, horrified. 'Why?'

'To relieve their despair, obviously. You know about despair, don't you?'

'No, not really. Not much,' he admitted. 'And surely raging against it won't make it any better?'

'Yes, it will. It gets the adrenaline flowing,' she said, 'and that's a great rush. You ought to try it sometime.'

'It's not in my nature,' he said.

'You're just scared,' she claimed, 'you're scared of what you'll find and where it will take you.' She looked around the tidy living room.

'If I were going to go mad in here, I would throw all those glass sports trophies at the wall. Oh, they would make a great sound and my ears would ring. Haven't you ever wanted to?'

He looked at the sports trophies on the mantelpiece. 'No. And please don't go mad in here,' he said, horrified.

She laughed again. 'No, no. Nothing will happen as long as you do what I say. That's my basic technique. It works on almost everyone.'

'But not on Rikard?'

She looked at him quickly. 'Who's Rikard?'

'The man who sells you the drugs?'

'Oh. You mean Roger. No, it doesn't work on him. Nothing works on him, he's a nasty piece of work.' She got up suddenly and lifted the cat onto her lap. She caressed his head.

'Oh, you gorgeous Goya munchkin,' she said softly. 'You have no worries. If I get to live my life all over again I hope I'll come back as a beautiful cat. Who can curl up on someone's lap. Have you felt his heart?' she asked. 'It beats so swiftly and so lightly. His nose is cold, is it meant to be cold? And his paws, they're all pink. And so lovely to touch. Tiny, tiny strawberry-flavoured chewy sweets. I wish I had a cat.'

Alvar sat still listening to her. Her bright, light voice filled his ears. Now, when she was sitting with the cat on her lap she reminded him mostly of a lost little girl. Impossible to handle, but very sweet in the pink sweater with the puffy sleeves.

CHAPTER 24

He saw less of her in July and August.

The thought had crossed his mind that everything would feel strange and empty if she vanished altogether. He was slowly beginning to enjoy her chatting to him from the sofa. The way she stroked the cat, her laughter, so silvery and bright. He also liked it when she lay quietly sleeping. Then he would sit down in his armchair with his newspaper or a good book. Or he would treat himself to an evening sherry, which he would enjoy slowly. Then he would watch her and be filled with a kind of serenity. The cat would often lie at her feet, a grey, curled-up fur ball. The two of them, he thought, are all I have in the world. But it's enough, it's more than enough. Yet a new worry had entered his life. There was hardly any money left in his savings account. It had trickled away in a steady stream and the inevitable moment was approaching. The day he would have to say, I don't have any more money, it's over, we've spent it all. Her eyes, her ice-blue eyes, would darken and fill with hatred. Some nights he could hardly sleep. In dreams he lived this moment over and over, her disbelief, her rage, his despair. Then he would awaken with a gasp. He kept pushing the reality aside. The severed bridge still hung in the gallery. How naive he had been to think that he would ever own it. It puzzled him that no one else had bought it, that no one else had fallen for the drama of the great painting. Now it served as a reminder of his own weakness, his capricious nature, and he could no longer bear to admire it, delight in it or pine for it. He scowled at it, like at forbidden fruit.

She turned up again in the middle of September and from then on her visits became more frequent. She was sometimes gentle and chatty, but more often she was silent and grumpy; and then she would throw herself on the sofa and turn her back on him. He said nothing. He tiptoed around, terrified of upsetting her. After all, she had so much to deal with, and he wanted to be considerate.

Autumn arrived; October was dark and dense and rainy, November was freezing cold, windswept and sombre. On the eighteenth day of the month she returned to his flat. On this day she was in very bad shape, she was unable even to unlock the door on her own, she just leaned on the doorbell until he came out to let her in. He found her slumped against the wall, her knees trembling. She was pale and damp and her pupils filled her irises.

'Where have you been!' she screamed hysterically.

Alvar was alarmed. He glimpsed his own pallid reflection in the mirror above the chest of drawers, he held his breath as his thoughts raced around his head.

'I was waiting for you yesterday, on the sofa, I waited for hours! I needed a fix and I was broke!'

Alvar opened his mouth. His voice was feeble. 'I went to a late movie,' he explained, 'the movie finished at ten past one. I went to see *The Exorcism of Emily Rose*.'

She was trying to focus on his face, a little saliva trickled from the corner of her mouth.

'You went to the movies,' she said accusingly, 'and I was scared shitless because I thought you had gone away. To bloody Värmland or somewhere even worse. And I wouldn't be able to get any money and so I wouldn't be able to get a fix!'

She paused to catch her breath.

'You could have left me a note telling me when you would be back, Alvar! You can't do this to me! You're always here. You have to be here all the time!'

She collapsed again, she clung to the door frame. Alvar felt torn apart by distress.

'I feel bloody awful,' she gasped. 'Haven't had a fix for three days. I'm completely broke.'

He held the door open for her, but she did not move from the wall. His trip to the cinema seemed like a mortal sin and his knees felt weak.

'I can't walk,' she groaned. 'I can't stop shaking.'

Alvar was unaccustomed to physical contact with other human beings. He could barely remember the last time he had touched someone, he had never even escorted an old lady across the street. Now he held out an arm to support her as she came in. She staggered across the floor on her high heels and collapsed onto the sofa. The cat jumped up next to her, but she seemed unaware of it. Her eyes were watering and she kept curling up in a foetal position as if she was in pain.

'I've got no one but you!' she screamed. 'You can't just go out and not tell me!'

'I'm so sorry,' Alvar stuttered. 'I've always been on my own and I'm not used to thinking of other people. I'm so, so sorry!'

She stood up and swayed dangerously; it seemed as if she wanted to go to the bathroom. He had never seen her so wasted. She was slurring her words, wobbling, her arms were flailing as though she was pushing aside dense vegetation. Her body began to seize as though in the grip of fever, a sea of pain and discomfort he could not begin to imagine, but it took his breath away. Finally she closed the door behind her and Alvar stood horrified in the middle of the floor, his mind racing. Withdrawal, he thought, petrified. The poison was leaving her body, and now every cell was screaming out for more heroin. The true horror of the situation finally dawned on him. She could not be saved; she was heading for the abyss. His first impulse was to get her more drugs, he could not bear to see her like this, it hurt him too, and he was not used to feeling anyone else's pain. As soon as he had this thought a new fear overcame him. He started pacing the floor, while anxiously listening out for noises from the bathroom. What was she doing in there? It had gone very quiet. Finally he heard the sound of water running. She came out shortly afterwards, her fringe was wet and her mascara was smeared pathetically all down her cheeks. On her way back to the sofa she tripped over her own feet and fell flat on her face; she remained prostrate on the floor, struggling between the coffee table and the sofa.

'Oh God,' she slurred, 'oh God, oh God, I feel like shit!' Alvar rushed over. Again he was reluctant to touch her, but his heart was beating so fast, and he felt so distraught that he had to do something. He stuck his hands under her armpits and lifted her up. He dragged her over to the sofa and laid her down. She curled up in pain instantly. Then she started to shake again, the fits came and went.

'Can I get you a drink of water?' he asked anxiously. She did not reply, she just lay there shivering. A strange sound was coming from her mouth and he realised that her teeth were chattering. He quickly went into his bedroom and found a blanket. He returned and tucked her in, but she did not seem to notice and it made no difference either. He had never seen another human being in such distress and the sight of her terrified him. He collapsed into an armchair. There he remained while his heart pounded as he watched her being ripped apart. Soon she started sweating profusely, tiny beads formed on her upper lip and on her forehead. Suddenly she gagged violently, but nothing came up. She fell back onto the sofa and clasped her hand over her mouth.

'Why don't we go to see the doctor?' Alvar asked.

She still did not reply.

'I've taken out one thousand kroner, are you able to walk down to Bragernes Square?'

He was shocked at his own words, that he could even think along these lines. But seeing her like this was torture for him, so much so that he seriously contemplated going there himself, finding her dealer, buying her a hit and giving it to her so that she could get some relief. So that her hysterical body could calm down. Because he was feeling so distressed, he went out into the kitchen and poured her a glass of water which he placed in front of her. She took no notice of that either. She was shivering. She was shaking. She groaned, she wiped snot and tears away, she wiped away the sweat.

'A small sherry, perhaps?' he suggested out of sheer desperation.

He received no reply. Then he jumped up again and went out into the bathroom. Found a clean face cloth, dipped it in warm water, wrung it and returned.

'Look here,' he was practically pleading, 'you can wipe your face with this.' She did not take it. Then he pushed aside all his shyness, leaned forward and started cleaning her cheeks with the wet, warm cloth. She said nothing, she closed her eyes and Alvar let the cloth glide over her forehead, her nose and her chin, very lightly as though she was made of glass. He thought she began to relax a little. He stayed like this, bent over the sofa with the cloth in his hand, and he was filled by a strange sensation, it was something he had never experienced before. The satisfaction of easing another person's pain. Reaching out a hand and seeing how her features softened. If only she could fall asleep and sleep through it all, he thought, but she was unable to fall asleep. She started shivering and shaking again, it came in vicious fits. Suddenly she spoke in a laboured voice.

'My heart,' she said weakly.

Alvar pricked up his ears. 'Yes,' he said breathlessly, 'what about your heart?'

She groaned again, pressed both hands against her chest. 'It's going to burst out, I've got to keep it in place!'

He shook his head. 'No, it's not going to burst out,' he said quickly. 'It's not!'

'It feels that way,' she said hoarsely. 'I've got to keep it in place, it's going to explode. I can feel it oozing out between my ribs.'

'Do you want some paracetamol?' he asked helplessly.

She laughed a bitter laugh at his suggestion. 'Is that all you can offer me? Paracetamol?'

Her voice was brimming with pain and disdain.

He wrung his hands in desperation.

'What are we going to do?' he asked sheepishly. 'You can't lie here like this.'

She brushed her damp hair away from her face.

'I can't do this any more,' she said weakly. 'I haven't got the energy to live this life any longer.'

Alvar tore himself away and went over to the window. He stared down at the light-bulb factory and at the dome, which glowed. It competed with the grey November light.

'There's got to be someone who can help you,' he said.

'There are not enough places,' she replied from the sofa. 'I've tried lots of times. Not enough places, I don't get methadone, or subutex. Nothing. I haven't been using long enough.'

Alvar closed his eyes. Then she had another seizure and she howled into the sofa to cope with the pain. Every single fibre in Alvar's body tensed up.

'No one should have to feel like this!' he screamed into the glass. 'It's not right!'

He looked over at her thin body.

'Do you want me to go down to Bragernes Square?' he asked. 'Do you want me to try to get something for you?'

She was silent for a long time. Her breathing was irregular, he thought, her whole body fighting a huge battle.

'Do you think you could get me a fix?' she whispered. 'I'm shaking so badly that I don't think I can manage to go myself.'

Get her a fix? Was she asking him to inject her? He gasped at the thought.

'It's easy,' she whispered. 'I'll tell you what to do.'

He instinctively shook his head. There was no way he would inject drugs into another human being. Especially not a tiny girl, no matter how ill she might be. She had another fit, her voice was close to breaking point.

'Go find Roger,' she asked him, 'he usually hangs out by the quay at Skutebrygga. Long hair, green parka. Go now, please, Alvar, please! I'm begging you!'

Alvar clenched his fists. He felt a sudden urge to slap his own cheeks; he seemed unable to think straight. He ran out into the hall, driven by a mixture of desperation and determination. Put on his coat, snatched his keys from the key cupboard and left. Started the Mazda, drove down the hill and into Engene. Turned left at the fire station and then took another left so he had the river on his right. Pulled into a car park, locked the car and ran out. His eyes flashed in all directions, but there was no one on the quay, no dealer in a green parka. He checked the cars and the people in town, kids, old people, the cooing pigeons. The taxis lined up on Bragernes Square. But he could not see any drug dealers; it was as if they had all gone with the autumn wind. Helplessly he stood there looking around. He became aware that others were watching him. He probably had a look of panic in his eyes, a madness clear for all to see and everyone was wondering about him.

He began walking across the cobbled square, all the way to St Hallvard's fountain. There were some benches there; they were empty. He stared down the side streets, to see if there were any dealers there. But today, the eighteenth of November, only respectable people were out and about, the town's down-and-outs were nowhere to be seen. Exhausted, he let himself fall down on a bench. He rested his elbows on his knees, buried his face in his hands, hunched up to avoid the freezing wind. He had never in all his life felt as lost as he did now. He could see no way out of this mess, he could not return to her without something that would relieve her pain. Then he heard low voices. Someone had approached the bench, he was being watched.

'Having a bad day, mate?' a rusty male voice asked him. Alvar looked up. He saw a group of three people. Two men and a woman, dressed a little shabbily, were watching him.

'Are you Roger?' Alvar asked him hopefully, looking at the gangly man, who had long hair and was wearing a green parka.

'Who wants to know?' he replied, giving Alvar a doubtful look.

'Philippa needs heroin. She needs it now!'

They looked at him doubtfully, exchanged glances.

'We don't know anyone called Philippa.'

'She's blonde,' he said, touching his own bald head. 'She's very thin, her hair's almost white, she's ill, she's lying on my sofa and it's awful!'

They continued looking at him in a doubtful way.

'You mean Blondie?'

'Yes,' Alvar said swiftly. Of course she would tell them her name was Blondie, he was sure of that.

'I don't have any heroin,' the man said, 'but I've got something else.'

Alvar's heart sank.

'Will it help?' he asked anxiously.

The three people started to giggle as they sent each other telling glances. Roger dug his hand down into the parka's pocket.

'This works for everything,' he said, nodding. 'You got any money?'

Alvar fumbled to get his wallet out and showed them his money.

'All right,' Roger said. 'Come on, we're going down under the bridge.'

Together they walked across Bragernes Square. Alvar felt strange in such scruffy company; he trailed behind them like a little lost child, eyes fixed on the street, hands deep in his pockets. They gathered under the bridge, there was a walkway there, it was covered with syringes and other rubbish. A small sachet was shoved in Alvar's hand, he paid and thanked them. How easy it is, he thought, how easy it is to throw your life away if that's what you want. He put the small sachet in his pocket, followed the group with his eyes as they disappeared across the walkway. He ran back to the car park, all the time checking that the small sachet was safe in his pocket. He started the car and drove back to his flat. He had only one thing on his mind: getting her to a place of peace. He let himself in and went over to the sofa. She opened her eyes and looked at him.

'Find my gear,' she ordered him, 'it's in my pocket.'

Alvar bent over her and rummaged through the pockets of her grey jacket. In a leather purse he found a syringe and a rubber tube. Then he opened the small sachet and made a discovery. It contained a handful of tiny white pills. He put them on the table. She got up on her elbow and stared at them in surprise.

'What did he give you?'

'I don't know,' he cried, 'they didn't have anything else, but they said these work for everything. Perhaps you can take two?'

She shook her head in disbelief, sent him a wounded look and picked up the pills with trembling fingers. He thought he could hear her bones rattle, he thought he could see the red muscle of her heart force its way through her ribs. Before he had time to do anything, she had tipped all the pills into her mouth and was reaching for the glass of water.

'Oh no,' he exclaimed, 'you mustn't take them all at once! They might be strong and we don't know what they are!'

She had already swallowed them. She half fell back onto the sofa and stayed there without moving. Her mouth was half open, her face contorted. She finally closed her eyes. Alvar collapsed in his armchair from exhaustion, he watched the enormous transformation which slowly began to take place before his very eyes. After one minute she stopped moving, after two her breathing became more regular. It was as if her frail body sank into the sofa. A faint smile spread across her face. The smiled lasted, it was a beautiful smile and he saw clearly how lovely she was, fragile like an angel, he thought, and waves of relief washed over him, it was over now, for the time being anyway. And he hoped that wherever she had gone she would be there for a long time. The cat came creeping towards them and snuggled down next to her. Alvar let his head fall back onto the headrest and closed his eyes. He pushed aside anything the future might bring. At this very moment in time all he did was enjoy the silence, relieved that she was feeling fine, that her breathing was steady. There was something very reassuring about that, something that made him feel sleepy. Just a quick nap, he told himself. I'm exhausted.

Darkness outside, now. Silence.

He woke up and realised that he was cold.

The house rested heavily on its foundation, it was as if everything had ground to a halt. He imagined a machine which had suddenly been switched off and the steady hum he was used to had ceased.

He had been asleep for more than two hours.

With a jolt he jumped out of his chair, a half-strangled groan coming from his throat. He glanced over at the sofa where she lay motionless. Her eyes were half open. It seemed as though she was semi-rigid, her immobility was terrifying. He could not hear her breathing, there was something missing in the room. An absence. Her ice-blue eyes were vacant, covered, it seemed, by a film of frost. The cat had moved and was now lying in a corner of the room. Alvar rushed out into the bathroom and closed the door behind him. Now she was out of sight, he could convince himself it had all been a bad dream, a nightmare, he thought with his back to the door. He stayed there for a long time. Then he sneaked over to the mirror, and clung on to the sink. He blinked repeatedly, no, he was not dreaming, this was real, something dreadful had happened. No, he had to be mistaken. She'll wake up now, he thought, running back out again, she'll wake up if I shake her and call her name. But I don't know what her name is. He tiptoed over to the sofa. But shaking her was pointless, there was no life left in her frail body, no heartbeat, no pulse, no warmth. November, he suddenly realised. It's the month of November and it's an evil month.

He started pacing the flat with rasping breath, he went from room to room, he wrung his hands so hard his knuckles cracked, he saw that her face had contorted into an ugly grimace. Her jaws had locked, her eyes were raw and dry. Every now and then he would peek over at the sofa; he was waiting for her to wake up, he was waiting for his old life to return, the life he had always taken for granted. She continued to lie there. He went back to the bathroom and washed his face with cold water, his eyes were bloodshot. He came back out and she was still lying there. He went to the kitchen and poured himself a sherry with trembling hands, stood in the doorway, drinking it, she continued to lie there. She was a stranger now who had staggered into his home and then lay down to die on his sofa, that was what had happened, was it not? Death had turned her into a stranger and she was no longer any of his concern. But he had opened the door, he had gone down to Bragernes Square and bought the pills, put them in front of her, fetched water for her and sat there watching her as she swallowed them. His actions throughout the past year, his well-meaning and apparently good intentions, piled up in front of him and turned into a mountain of guilt. He, Alvar Eide, had displayed a degree of negligence which had led her right to her death. He started to sink onto the floor; he could never hold his head up high again, not after this. Imagine that this was how his life would end, tainted by guilt and shame and horror; why had he not been able to see where it was all leading? He lay prostrate on the floor digging, clawing his fingers into the parquet, trying to gather his scattered thoughts. And they gathered themselves and turned into a sly plan, which almost took his breath away, the ultimate proof that he had never been a good person. He realised that she had been right all the time, all he knew was pretence and cowardice, he had never been a hero. Merely spineless. Defensive, pathetic. And the vile plan which was slowly taking shape was all he had to cling to, it made his body obey, it made his heart beat at a normal rate.

I've got to get rid of her, he thought, I've got to carry her out of the house, I can't have her here, what will people say, what will they think? Will they put me away for this, will I be branded a criminal? I'll never be able to look anyone in the eye. I can't manage anything at all after this, he thought, why was I not tougher with her? If I'd been tough, she would have been alive now. Perhaps. He groaned in despair, his distress roared like a waterfall in his ears. What am I going to tell the police? I can't go to the police, it struck him, I can't tell them what has happened, they'll blame me. It was I who financed her addiction, I drove her to her death. It's all my fault. There is no God, there is no forgiveness. I was only trying to help her, I couldn't bear to see her in such pain, because I'm weak, I'm full of flaws and shame. Time will pass, he thought feverishly, time will pass, soon I'll be in another moment, an even worse one because she is still lying there with her gaping mouth and blind eyes. Why did she pick me? Can you tell from a distance that I'm a pushover; does it show in my pathetic eyes, am I betrayed by my nervous hands? Thoughts rained through his head like a shower of arrows. He concentrated on his plan. He put his palms on the floor and attempted to push himself up, but they were too weak. Blood rushed to his head, his pulse beat in his ears. A thought occurred to him, a wretched idea. He would put a blanket over her and cover her up. He pushed off again and stood up laboriously. Reluctantly he went over to the sofa, got hold of the blanket and arranged it so it covered her head and her body. But it offered him no relief, the contours of her thin body were still visible. Again he went over to the window. He stared out at the town, saw cars crawling through the streets, and the lights, yellow, red, green, people were heading home, it was rush hour. He stood there holding on to the trivial activities outside as the plan continued to grow in his head, slowly, from deep inside him: no one knows anything. No one can see into my living room, can see that there is a dead body on my sofa. Or that I'm responsible. That it is I, Alvar Eide, who pushed her into the abyss. I'll wait until night-time, he thought, then I'll carry her outside. I'll leave her somewhere, so she'll be found, and people can think what they like. I need to tidy my living room, I can't have things like that lying around.

A faint hope grew in him, a simple, cynical thought.

Perhaps I'll get away with it. After all, so many of them die, they call it an overdose, she's clearly one of them. She's been seen on Bragernes Square, the police will probably recognise her. They wouldn't make a big deal of it. I need to wait until later in the evening. When everyone has gone home. When will everyone be asleep? Between three and five in the morning. That's when I'll carry her outside and put her in the back of the car, I'll drive out into the woods with her, I'll cover her with the blanket. I never asked for this awful business to happen, I was just trying to help her. He forced himself to snap out of it and went to his bedroom where he lay down fully dressed on his bed. Turned over onto his side and pulled up his knees. He closed his eyes, but they opened again. He kept looking at the lamp on his bedside table, a cold glass dome.

He fell into a perplexing dream.

It was difficult to breathe.

He was crawling around on an ice-cold surface, on all fours, like a wounded animal, and the air was dense and raw, it was like inhaling thick porridge down his lungs. At the same time he sensed a cool breeze further ahead, a freezing draught from a hole in the ice. He struggled to find his way, fighting to breathe the whole time, it was like a lead weight on his chest, he had to use every muscle in his upper body to make his lungs open and take in air, every breath was a struggle. His hair and his cheeks were damp, and he worked out that he was in a thick fog, which was approaching from all sides, it surrounded him, made him invisible to the rest of the world. Still he crawled on, centimetre by centimetre, the cold breeze grew stronger and he thought he heard a faint murmur, a grinding sound, but he did not recognise the sound and it was too dark to see anything. Then his hand reached out into thin air. He stopped and froze, waved his hands in front of him in terror, there was nothing, he had reached the edge and a fierce, freezing cold wind hit from the void.

He woke up and gasped for air. There was still a weight on his chest, and breathing a sigh of relief, he finally realised what it was. Goya, his cat, was lying on his chest purring. He nudged him off and lay there staring at the ceiling.

At a quarter past three in the morning he got up and went into the living room.

His saliva tasted of blood and metal. There was not a sound coming from the house, the streets outside were empty. The yard was surrounded by a fence. Would Green hear him start his car? Would he turn over in his bed, check the time and wonder? He forced himself not to worry about that. He went out into the hall, put on his coat and shoes. Turned round, saw the tiny body under the blanket. Boot or back seat? he asked himself. It would have to be the back seat. He could hide her under the blanket. He sneaked out into the yard, unlocked the car, put the key in the ignition. Got out again and opened the door to the back seat, looked inside. There was plenty of room for her tiny body. Then something happened to his heart, it started beating violently and his legs buckled and he had to support himself against the car as the reality of his gruesome errand dawned on him. He automatically looked up at the sky, no stars were visible, it was cloudy and overcast.

He went back inside, stopped in the middle of the living room. Now he would have to touch her, hold her close. It felt like an insurmountable task. He did not want to feel her cold cheek against his own. He went over to the sofa, pulled the blanket off her and spread it out on the floor. Don't think, he decided, just act, be strong. Get her out of the living room once and for all. I should have done it a long time ago. He moved the coffee table to reach her more easily. Stood for a while stretching out his fingers as he often did.

She was lying flat on her back with her mouth open, her irises were starting to look cloudy. Alvar held his breath and prepared himself. Counted to three and lifted her. He froze. Her body was completely rigid. It was like lifting a log and one of her arms stuck out like the branch of a tree. He swayed violently for a moment, he nearly keeled over. Then he remembered that several hours had passed, and of course he had heard of rigor mortis. Nevertheless he felt paralysed; he stood holding her dead body for a long time as though his feet were nailed to the floor.

He finally pulled himself together. Reluctantly, with awkward, hesitant steps, he inched away from the sofa and over to the blanket. There he put her down. He wrapped her in the blanket, got up, wiped his brow. Then he went back out into the hall and jammed the door open with a shoe. Listened out into the darkness for sounds. It would take him a few seconds to settle her in his car, a few fateful seconds of his life. He breathed in and bent down again, lifted her up and started to walk. He was watching himself from afar. Here goes Alvar Eide with a dead body in his arms. It's three thirty in the morning, everyone is fast asleep. How did this happen, where did I go wrong? He walked with short, stumbling steps out into the hall and again sideways out through the front door. Then he walked as fast as he dared over to the car, bent forward and placed her inside head first, diagonally across the back seat. She lay like a wooden plank, her outstretched arm pointing accusingly at him. Carefully he closed the door without slamming it. Then he went back to close the front door and lock it. He felt revitalised now, it was nearly over. He quickly got in the car and started it, his hands were shaking so badly he almost couldn't turn the key in the ignition. Finally he got the car into gear, rolled past the letter boxes and out through the gate.

Down the hill he passed a car; it felt weird. It drove past him indifferently. Will I ever be able to sleep after this? he wondered. Will I be able to smile or laugh? Eat a meal, will I be able to swallow? He turned right at the Central Hospital. He drove further on, up towards the ridge, he intended to drive right to the top. Many tourists came there and there were always plenty of people; she would be found quickly, that was his plan. He could not bear to turn round and look at her, he drove quietly in the darkness, crouched over the wheel. To his right were a couple of houses with no lights on. Finally he reached the top. It was a viewpoint. He stayed in his car for a while, letting the engine run, staring out at the glittering town. A car had been abandoned in the car park, it worried him, but he could see no people. Then he drove into the car park and left the car as close as he could to the beginning of the path. A sign was visible in the beams of his headlights. *Åsa Pond, 11 kilometres.* It was a narrow path, but there was room for one car. He drove on for one hundred metres and then stopped. He sat there a few seconds to gather strength. Then he opened the car door and got out; he felt the cool November air on his face. The leaves were rustling, the trees murmured in a menacing breeze, he felt as though he was being watched. Then he walked round the car and opened the door to the back seat. Glanced frantically over his shoulder, got hold of her and pulled her out. Carried her a few metres before laying her down. He took a few steps back. The bundle was barely visible in the darkness, but the sun would rise soon and some unsuspecting person would walk by.

He drove away hastily.

Then he heard a low drumming.

The volume of the sound was increasing rapidly. The sound startled him, someone was coming through the woods, he sensed, and he clutched the wheel. In a flash he identified the sound. Sudden and violent raindrops started to splatter against his windscreen. The skies opened, rain came down like a grey, compact wall. It almost forced him off the road. Her tiny body would be soaked in a matter of minutes, the rain would go straight through the blanket, freezing cold and raw. He slammed on the brakes, buried his face in his hands. Was there no end to this misery? But she's dead, he thought, she won't feel anything. Nevertheless it was pouring down and he did not have the strength to push the thought out of his mind. Her skinny body at the side of the path and the rain washing down on her mercilessly. No one should lie like that, he thought, and it is I, Alvar Eide, who is responsible for all of this. He forced himself to drive on. He met no cars, the streets were empty now, he drove through them at a snail's pace, visibility was nearly zero.

Ten minutes later he rolled into his yard. He turned off the ignition and got out. The intensity of the rain had escalated. He carefully closed the car door and quickly entered his flat. He locked the door behind him and stopped. And then it all got to him, everything that had happened and the rain, which pelted the windows like a punishment from God. I can't bear it, he thought, she's lying out there getting wet. Someone else needs to take over now and help me. Then something occurred to him. He went over to the telephone, stopped and stared at it. He saw the yellow Post-it note with a number on it, which he himself had stuck to the telephone a long time ago. With his hand trembling he lifted the receiver and punched in the number. After three rings there was a reply.

'You're through to the Red Cross emergency helpline. This is Marie speaking, how can I help you?'

Alvar opened his mouth, supporting himself with one hand on the chest of drawers, his voice barely audible.

'I've done something truly awful,' he sobbed.

Silence. He could hear her breathing.

'Do you want to tell me about it?'

A female voice. So light and friendly. Alvar held his breath. He was overcome by fear of what was about to happen. Marie. Perhaps this really was her name, or perhaps she just called herself this when she was working, why should he trust her? Young women just made stuff up.

He carefully replaced the receiver.

CHAPTER 25

At this point in the story I lean back and sigh heavily.

I stare at the screen in despair. It's all my fault. I wanted to test Alvar and now I can see that he'll fail. So I imitate him. I get up and wander across the floor. I go over to the window and stare outside. I'm responsible; I have to get him through this. His despair is my despair, his shame is my shame, I don't know how it's going to end now. I begin to worry about his mental state and what he might end up doing, he has nowhere to go, no one who can help him. Yes, it was a difficult situation, but now he has made it worse, it's a disaster. The way things stand I don't see how he can avoid going to prison, and I don't think he can handle that. Then I think of his father who died at the age of fifty-three from a heart attack. I drift aimlessly through the rooms as I struggle to find a solution. Am I really omnipotent? That's not how it feels. There's only one way out, but I can't see it. How easy it is, I think, putting someone on a stage. Focusing a spotlight on them, getting them started, letting events unfold without a second thought. Suddenly you hit a wall and the audience waits expectantly like children, with their mouths hanging open waiting for the conclusion. I like to end my novels on a succinct, merciless remark.

My front door opens, I cease my restless wandering. I hear dragging footsteps in the hallway, a door slamming. Alvar Eide enters, grey-faced and with rings under his eyes. Without saying a word he collapses onto my sofa, then he slumps over the coffee table and hides his face in his hands. I watch him for a while as thoughts churn in my head. What does he need now, what am I going to say? He beats me to it. It's hard for me to make out what he's saying because his face is hidden.

'I can't find a way out. I'll have to kill myself.'

In the silence that follows I can feel my pulse throb in my throat. Alvar breathes heavily; he's rocking himself backwards and forwards. I'm standing there feeling I've been utterly cruel, but there is nothing else I can do.

'You can't,' I state calmly. 'Then there'll be no story.'

He does not reply. I go over to him, I place a hand on his shoulder.

'Marie,' I say. 'Marie who answered the helpline, she would have helped you. She would have told you what to do. But you didn't let her.'

I can hear some half-strangled sobs. I let myself fall into a chair, I watch his desperate figure and rack my brains for some words of hope and comfort.

'If I send someone to help you,' I ask him, 'will you let them?'

He finally looks up at me, he folds his hands on the table.

'As I see it,' he says, 'it's best that I remove myself from this earth once and for all. I can't handle this game, which life ultimately is, I don't understand the rules.'

'You can learn them,' I say, hurt.

He shakes his heavy head.

'I'm going to hook up a hose to the exhaust pipe and lie down in my car,' he groans. 'It'll be over in a few minutes.'

'Then you'll be letting down everyone who's followed you up until now,' I say, 'those who hope that you'll get through this.'

He looks at me darkly. 'Why should I care about them? I don't know them.'

'But they know you,' I reply, 'they've followed you every step of the way, you can't run off now.'

In the silence that follows I can hear the wind in the trees outside. A magpie lands on my veranda, it sits there bobbing its tail, a car drives past, the seconds tick away.

'I just want to sleep,' he says. 'It won't take very long and then I'll be gone.'

I sigh deeply at his words. 'Is that what you think will happen? You think you'll fall asleep and be dead in a few minutes?'

He looks up, he starts to waver. 'Exhaust fumes are very poisonous,' he says, 'I've always known that. I've heard they make you sleepy.'

I bite my lip. 'Yes, you're right. They're poisonous as well as deadly. But your death won't be that straightforward. It doesn't work like that.'

'Could it be simpler?' he asks, looking at me in disbelief. 'I'll be sitting in the car inhaling exhaust fumes, I'll sit very still with my hands in my lap.'

'You think you'll be able to sit completely still?'

He is growing more uncertain. He gives me a searching look.

'I'm not sure where you're going with this.'

I lean across the table and look at him sincerely.

'Everyone can flirt with the idea of suicide,' I say, 'but there's a big gap between thought and action. And even though you seem to think that it's a swift and easy death, I'm sorry to have to tell you that you're very much mistaken.'

'Why do you say that?'

'Because I know.'

'What do you know?'

I can't sit still any longer, I have to move. I walk softly up and down the room.

'True, exhaust fumes are very poisonous,' I say, 'but do you know how they kill?'

He shakes his head. He waits for me. His grey eyes are guarded.

'The fumes attach themselves to haemoglobin in your blood and prevent the blood from circulating oxygen. You will, in other words, suffocate from within. Literally.'

He is starting to look anxious.

'And it doesn't take a few minutes,' I say, 'it takes many hours. On your way to death you will need to go through several stages. Do you really want to know this, Alvar?'

He nods softly, he squeezes his hands in his lap.

'First you'll experience trouble breathing. You'll develop a severe migraine-like headache. Then you'll feel nauseous; your body will dispose of its stomach contents. Disorientation and hallucinations follow. Perhaps you'll start clawing at the door handle as your body desperately struggles. Before you finally pass out. Hours can pass between the time you faint and your actual death. When you're found your airways will be filled with foam. Your lungs will turn into two large oedemas, as will your brain. And you'll be found in your own vomit. There will not be much left of the imposing man you once were. In other words, you won't die in your sleep, you'll be fighting all the way until you die.'

He shakes his head in disbelief. His cheeks are pale.

'But how do you know these things?'

'I have been where you are now,' I reply.

He looks dubiously at me. 'You? Why?'

'I had my reasons,' I reply, 'and I thought they were valid. I'd done my homework carefully, I'd read all I could find on exhaust poisoning. I wanted to know how it happened, what I would have to go through. It was in March,' I continue. 'Everything stopped. I was overcome by fear, I couldn't manage anything. I couldn't eat, couldn't sleep, I couldn't even move. My fear came in violent attacks, like electric shocks.'

Alvar sits listening to me.

'I realised after a few days that I couldn't live like that, I wouldn't be able to handle it. So I got off the sofa and I went downstairs to the basement.'

'What were you keeping there?' he asks.

'A hose,' I explain. 'I brought the hose upstairs to the kitchen, where I kept a roll of parcel tape in a drawer. I went out into the garage to my Mercedes. Then I squatted down and examined the exhaust system. Inside the pipe itself were two smaller pipes and I went back inside and cut the hose into two equal parts of approximately three metres each. Then I went back to the car. I opened the window on the driver's side very slightly. I attached the hoses to the exhaust pipes, trailed them along the car and fed them through the gap in the window. Then I went about sealing every crack, so the inside of the car would be airtight. My plan was to achieve the highest concentration of the exhaust fumes in the shortest possible space of time. And given that the risk of vomiting is relatively high I decided to stop eating in the time I had left, because the thought of being found in a pool of my own vomit was unbearable. When the hoses were properly attached to the exhaust pipe and the window had been sealed, I went back into my house and upstairs to my bedroom. I took my duvet and my pillow and carried them to the car. I reclined both seats and arranged the bed linen as neatly as I could. I wanted to create the illusion that I was dying in my own bed. Because that's ultimately what we all want, isn't it?'

Alvar's eyes widened.

'Then I selected some music,' I told him. 'K. D. Lang would sing "Hallelujah". It was the most beautiful song I could think of. I inserted the CD into the player. Then I returned to the flat, it was late morning. I fixed a time,' I continued. 'My exit would be at three in the morning. In other words, it was only a matter of hours. The seconds ticked by quickly. I found a bottle of whisky and started drinking as I counted the minutes. It was so dark everywhere, in my mind, in my living room, I could barely see the furniture. I could see no future. It was like being in a tunnel that was growing more and more narrow. I took off my watch and put it on the coffee table. Next to it I put my credit cards, one Visa and one Mastercard. Then I let myself flop down again and drank more whisky. My fear was now so powerful that it occurred to me that I might have severe difficulties actually getting to the car because my legs would be unable to carry me. Ah, well, I thought, I'll just have to crawl. Crawl across the gravel on the drive to my final resting place. And because my fear came in bursts, I needed to act quickly. I had to leave the house between fits, if I was to get into the car at all.'

I stop speaking. Alvar looks at me across the table.

'But here you are,' he says. 'What happened?'

'I drank whisky all afternoon and evening,' I tell him. 'It dulled some of my pain, but it strengthened my resolve to kill myself. Everything felt right and inevitable. I was committed to a course of action, I could not stop. I kept looking at the hands of the clock. When it was ten in the evening, I thought: now I've got five hours left. Three hundred minutes. They passed quickly, I tell you. The fear of death nearly suffocated me, I was so terrified I could taste blood in my mouth. And even though I was lying on this sofa, in this room,' I say, 'the room seemed as small as an attic.'

Alvar nods earnestly.

'Then,' I tell him, 'the telephone rang.' I nod in the direction of my desk, where the telephone is. 'The telephone rang, and I was so startled that I nearly ended up on the floor. It rang angrily as if it was urgent. I staggered over and stared at it. It rang a third time, a fourth, a fifth, I couldn't see who it was, the number was being withheld. But there is something about a ringing telephone, it's impossible not to answer it. I had the chance to hear a voice, be connected again to life and other people. So I answered it.'

'Who was calling you?' he asks breathlessly.

'A friend,' I say. 'A very dear friend. "How are you?" he asked.

' "I'm in a very bad way," I replied. "I'm going to end it all at three o'clock tonight."

'It went silent down the other end. I could hear he was thinking.

' "You can't stop me," I said. "I can't take it any more."

'He was still thinking because he is a wise man. He weighed his words.

"I can tell from your voice that you are serious," he said. "But there's something I want you to do for me."

'I held the telephone close to my ear and listened to his reassuring voice. "And what would that be?" I asked anxiously.

' "That you postpone it," he said. "That you grant yourself another day, and that you'll come over and see me tomorrow. We'll go for a walk in the woods. You ought to allow yourself that. You deserve another day."

'I clutched the telephone and thought about what he had said. A walk in the woods. I glanced out at the drive, towards the garage. Where my Mercedes had been turned into a gas chamber.

'"Are you there?" he asked.

'"Yes," I whispered.

'"Is that a promise?"

'I had to support myself on the desk with my other hand. "Yes, I'll be there."

'"I'm trying to get you to agree to something. Will you come over tomorrow?"

'"Yes," I said dully.

'"Are you sure?" he asked.

'"Absolutely," I replied. At that moment I felt that something had changed inside my chest. It felt as if a warm substance was trickling down it, as if something was melting.

'"Then I expect you to come," he said. "I'll be waiting for you. If you kill yourself tonight, I will feel that you have let me down. And you don't want to let down a good friend, do you?"

'I considered what he had just said. No, I didn't want to let him down. The feeling of warmth continued to spread through my body.

'"Then I'll see you tomorrow," he repeated.

'"Yes," I replied. "You'll see me. Thank you for calling. Goodnight."'

Alvar smiles a feeble smile.

'So what did you do once you had hung up?' he asks.

'I stood there for a long time trying to get my breathing under control,' I say. 'And my fear, which had held me in its vice for so long, finally let me go. Because I had avoided death by answering the telephone. I had given myself a rain check, I had plans. So I went to the garage. I tore loose the tubes, fetched my bedlinen and carried it upstairs. I lay down in my bed under the floral duvet. Whisky and exhaustion made me fall asleep instantly. And when I woke up the next morning everything felt strange.'

'In what way strange?' Alvar wants to know.

'The sun was so yellow,' I say. 'The light was so bright. It was an extra day, a very special day. A day I was not meant to have, and it felt wondrous. I had come back into the light after such a long time in the dark. I went out and started the car. K. D. Lang sang "Hallelujah", and it was entirely appropriate. And I walked with my friend in the woods. We talked about all sorts of things. And when we said goodbye, he wanted to fix another time, of course. And so it continued until I had returned to life completely.'

I look at Alvar across the table. 'And now,' I say, 'I want a promise from you. We can't say goodbye like this.'

'I don't have a friend who'll call me in the evening,' he says and looks down.

'But you have me,' I say. 'And I want to see you again. Come back to me when it's all over. We need to end this properly, we've known each other more than a year, I think I deserve that. With friendship,' I add, 'with friendship comes obligation; you, too, have to give something up when I ask you.'

Again he hides his face in his hands. But then he removes them and manages a brave smile.

'Alvar,' I say earnestly, 'you're not going to let me down, are you?'

CHAPTER 26

All day Saturday he stumbled around in a distracted and distressed state of mind. The modest universe which was Alvar, a normally very steady and controlled human being, was experiencing a frantic, turbulent rebellion. It raged through him, it tore him to pieces, a frenzy which whipped him from room to room. He staggered from the kitchen into the living room, from the living room to the bathroom, where he looked at himself in the mirror, pale with fear. He hunched over the sink, clinging to the porcelain basin. He prayed to God, whom he did not even believe in, he prayed for help, for relief and forgiveness, he prayed for a way out, he prayed for mercy. At the same time he felt deeply ashamed of this pathetic manoeuvre, but he had no one else to turn to. He did not even have a family he could bring shame on. A war was being waged inside his muddled head. He would have to go through everything that was about to happen on his own and people would read the newspapers and judge him. Because now he could see how absurd his actions had been.

Finally he collapsed onto his bed after several hours of manic pacing round the flat. He stayed there staring at the wall while he wrung his fingers till they nearly broke. Whimpering sounds came from his mouth, from time to time a hoarse sigh, noises he did not have the strength to suppress. So he lay, hour after hour. He only got up to use the loo or to fetch himself a glass of water, which he would gulp down with trembling hands. He waited, he listened. He tried to calm his frantic heart, but it beat unruly behind his ribs. It continued to rain, but it was easing off. A few faint noises from outside penetrated the bedroom, he was listening out for cars. So he lay, trapped, gripped by fear. He wanted to switch on the radio to find out if she had been found, but he did not have the courage. He was hyperventilating and he felt dizzy. He also felt hungry, but he couldn't manage to eat anything. The doorbell would ring, he didn't know when, but the doorbell would ring soon and there would be someone outside who would point the finger at him.

The hours ticked by so slowly. Now and then he would doze off for a few minutes only to wake with a gasp. He kept seeing her, her tiny body by the path. Like a parcel someone has discarded, alone and abandoned in the rain. He curled up in agony. Pulled up his knees, tucked his hands under them and locked them; he lay like a convulsing knot of bones and muscles. How cruel life could be. What a coward he was, he could not take this like a man. All he felt was guilt and shame, and a degree of self-hatred that made him want to throw up. An inferior human being, that was what he was. Something pathetic, something worthless. Here he was lying curled up and whimpering like a baby, when what he ought to do was make a telephone call and get it over with. I need to rest, he thought, tossing and turning in his bed, I need to rest. I must gather strength for everything that's to come. I mustn't explain it away, I need to tell it like it is. Even though the truth is odious. How will I be able to carry this burden? I'm already broken. Someone who never pays their way, a stowaway, you could say. The world is filled with suffering and I've never done anything to alleviate it. Other people act, others rush in when disaster strikes. I stand in the wings and shudder. And he lay beating himself up the whole day, it was as if he was flagellating himself till his blood started flowing, he wanted to atone. The light faded and evening approached. The room was filled with shadows and whispering voices. Look, there's Alvar Eide, he's an idiot. They pointed their fingers at him, they snickered, they whispered nasty comments to each other, a swarm of accusations whirled around him from all directions. He fell asleep in the early-morning hours only to wake up with a scream after a series of nightmares. It grew light again, but he could not get out of bed. Today's Sunday, he thought, a day of rest. The worst day of my life.

Then the shrill sound of the doorbell pierced the rooms. Even though he had been expecting it, even though he was prepared, a jolt of fear, so forceful he could not help but call out, shot through him. They were here already, perhaps there were many of them. But he hadn't heard a car, he didn't understand that. He got out of bed and stumbled out into the hall. His shirt was crumpled and hung loosely over his trousers. His throat felt tight and he did not know for certain if he would be able to say anything. It's starting now, he thought. The nightmare. Then he opened the door. Green was outside waving the Sunday paper.

'Have you seen this?'

Alvar stared at the paper, which his neighbour was holding up in front of his face, a picture of a young, smiling girl with thin, blonde hair. She seemed familiar. Of course she was familiar. But in the picture she was happy, with round cheeks he had never seen her like this.

'Katrine Kjelland,' Green said, tapping the picture with his finger. 'Found dead up at the viewpoint yesterday morning. Wrapped in a blanket. Would you believe it?'

The newspaper flapped in Green's hand. Alvar swallowed hard.

'Katrine?' he asked, perplexed.

'She must have been murdered,' his neighbour went on. 'You know her, don't you? She was always coming to see you. The last time I saw her here was Friday, she came to your door.'

Green stood rocking backwards and forwards on the doorstep, his blue eyes sparkled with excitement.

Alvar was unable to reply. His knees started to tremble; he instinctively planted a hand on the wall to steady himself.

'You must call them,' Green said, his voice sounding a little too enthusiastic, 'the police are asking the public to help them. Have you phoned them?'

Alvar shook his head. He wanted to reply, but he still couldn't locate his voice.

'For God's sake, you have to ring them! They need all the information they can get, and she has been coming to see you for months. What's wrong with you, are you ill? You're white as a sheet.'

Green lowered the newspaper and scrutinised him.

Alvar nodded. Yes, he was very ill. He had to concentrate very hard on staying on his feet.

'My guess is that someone gave her an overdose,' Green said in a businesslike way, 'and then they panicked. Wrapped her in a blanket and drove her up there. If I were you I'd call the police straight away. If you don't and they find out she's been coming to your flat, then they'll think it's suspicious that you haven't come forward. That's my advice.'

Green gave him a bossy look. Alvar nodded again. He was trying to collect his thoughts, articulate a reply, but he did not have the strength.

'Anyway, how did you get to know her?' Green asked nosily. 'She was not exactly your type. And so very young, only sixteen, would you believe it.'

Alvar swallowed a second time. 'Sixteen? I didn't know her,' he said weakly. 'Not really.'

'But she came here for a year. She even had her own key!'

Alvar was lost for words. He wanted to close his door, he did not want to explain anything to Green, whom he didn't even know well. Resolutely he reached for the door handle. His neighbour backed off.

'Well, I'm sorry to trouble you, but I do think this is very strange. I just wanted to make sure you knew what had happened. So I'll be expecting you to call. We need to call.'

He folded the newspaper. Retreated a little.

We? Alvar thought. He pulled the door so only a tiny gap was left.

'Yes,' he whispered. 'I'll make the call.' Then he closed the door completely, turned the key and went over to the telephone. He glared down at the numbers. How was he supposed to be able to call and explain anything? He could not even speak. He escaped to his bedroom again and fell onto his bed, exhausted and shivering. Again he felt hungry, but he did not want to eat. He did not deserve food, he did not deserve something to drink. He did not deserve sleep. The seconds ate their way through him, his agony grew hour by hour. Then it struck him that all the pain he was going through could be ended once and for all if only he would make that call. He would just have to stand there coughing and spluttering until they came to his door. Then the disaster would be a known fact, but he would also reach a different stage. He stared out into space with aching eyes. What was he going to say? Hello, my name's Alvar Eide. This Katrine Kjelland, she came to see me last Friday. She overdosed on my sofa and I panicked. I carried her out in the middle of the night and drove off with her. Because I couldn't handle the consequences. It was very stupid, but then I'm a very stupid man.

He reflected on these words, whether he would be able to say them out loud. Even he could hear how idiotic they sounded. What if they jail me? he wondered. Would I manage on my own in a cell? Am I now a criminal? How did this happen? Is there any hope of redemption for me? He lay on his bed struggling with these dark thoughts. Many hours passed, he slipped in and out of sleep. When the doorbell rang for the second time, he sat up dazed and confused, terrified and drowsy. He suddenly realised that Green would have called the police. Alvar planted his feet on the floor. He rubbed his tired face and staggered out into the hall. He opened the door quietly. There he was, the police officer. A mountain of a man, dark and broad, with dense, thick eyebrows. He took up the whole doorway and threw a menacing shadow into the hall.

'Alvar Eide?'

He nodded and clung to the door frame. His heart contracted and a rush of blood went to his cheeks.

'I'm a police officer. May I come in, please?'

Alvar still had no voice. He opened the door fully and walked ahead of him into the living room. Stood by the window looking down at the floor. The officer followed him, and stood calmly in the living room. An almost explosive silence followed.

It's happening now, Alvar thought. My entire miserable existence takes its revenge on me. My cowardice, my submissive nature, my total inability to take action. I thought I could live outside society, but that's impossible. Everyone gets involved sooner or later, in an incident, with another person.

'Do you know why I'm here?' the officer asked. He took a few steps forward, his voice was deep and authoritative.

'I think so,' Alvar stuttered.

'So you've seen today's paper?'

Alvar still had his back to him. He muttered against the pane. 'My neighbour came, he showed it to me. I suppose he was the one who called you?' He said this without turning.

The police officer took his time. He weighed his words carefully.

'Yes, we've received some information and now we're following it up. Is it the case that you knew Katrine Kjelland?'

'Yes, but not very well,' he mumbled. 'And she did not call herself Katrine. She called herself whatever she wanted to, every day it was something different.'

'When did you last see her?'

Alvar struggled to control his voice which was stuck at a very high pitch. 'Friday night. She was here. She lay on my sofa and slept.'

The police officer listened calmly.

'And when did she leave?'

Alvar bowed his head. The truth had become impossible.

'Well, I can't say for sure. She stayed quite a while,' he whispered.

'One hour. Two?'

'As I said, I'm not sure.'

'Was she under the influence of anything when she arrived?'

He half turned but avoided the other man's eyes. 'Yes, I suppose she was behaving strangely.'

'In what way strange?'

'Well, she was shaking somewhat.'

The police officer came up and stood next to him; now they were both staring out of the window.

'What was your relationship with her?'

'It wasn't a relationship,' he said swiftly. 'There was no relationship at all.'

'So she just came to visit you?'

Alvar grabbed hold of the windowsill with both hands.

'She came to borrow money.'

'Did you give her any?'

'Yes.'

The police officer pondered this for a while.

'Did anything unusual happen between you last Friday?'

'No.'

'When she left where was she going?'

'She never said, she just drifted. Around Bragernes Square.'

'You've got a cat, I see,' he said, diverting Alvar's attention.

'Yes, I've got a cat.' Alvar looked at Goya. The cat lay curled up on the sofa.

'He's very handsome. But he moults quite a lot, I can imagine?'

'I'm not bothered about that,' Alvar said, baffled by this question.

'You ought to be.' The police officer circled the floor, stuck his hands in his pockets.

'Katrine Kjelland was discovered up at the viewpoint yesterday. On a path, close to the car park. Dead, wrapped in a blanket. The blanket was covered in small, white hairs. If we can match them to your cat, then you've got a problem.'

CHAPTER 27

They told him he had a great deal to explain.

He crumbled instantly.

They told him his situation was serious and that he risked a custodial sentence, that there was much that warranted investigation and had to be examined in greater detail. They told him that Katrine was sixteen years old and that her family lived at Bragernes Ridge, her father was a dentist, she had two brothers; they knew she was a heroin addict and they had feared the worst. She rarely visited them and then she would talk about him, about Alvar Eide, about how she sometimes stayed with him. That he was a kind of friend, the only one she had.

They told him they found it hard to believe him, they kept asking him to repeat his story and there were many unanswered questions. But why, Eide, they asked him, baffled, why didn't you call us? Alvar was not used to explaining himself to others. He stuttered and stammered, he sat in the bare interrogation room looking at the floor. There were no windows here, just naked, cold walls. A camera was attached to the ceiling, there were a table and some chairs. The walls were painted white, there was a fluorescent tube in the ceiling giving out an almost blue-white light.

'That's just the way I am,' he ventured. 'I removed the problem from my house, my parents taught me to do this, it's the only way I know and I'm a useless man.'

Did he have any addictions?

He shook his head vigorously.

Had he ever suffered from mental health problems?

'No, no, I'm not one of those people, I just lost my head. It's only happened that one time!'

The two officers questioning him exchanged glances. As if they were not quite sure of what they were actually dealing with. They were calm, but very serious. Had he, at any point, wanted her out of his life?

Yes, there had been times. But as time passed, he had grown accustomed to her, she came and went as she pleased.

'Did she ever steal from you?'

'Only a key. I let her keep it, she carried it on a string around her neck.'

'Do you understand how serious it is, Eide? That the money you gave her led directly to her destruction?'

'It was like sliding,' he replied then. 'The speed accelerated and I couldn't slam on the brakes. I closed my eyes and let it happen. I waited for the big crash.'

'Now it's happened. She's dead,' they said.

'I've been expecting it,' he said. 'I knew it would end like this, she said it was what she wanted.'

'She was sixteen years old, she should have been saved. Did you try to get help for her?'

'She said that no one was prepared to help her, that there were no beds, that she was too young. I don't know much about these things, but I thought she wanted to be an outsider. She didn't enjoy being with other people and neither do I.'

'We don't completely understand your actions, Alvar Eide. It appears that you're intelligent and well adjusted.'

'It might seem like that. If you don't look too closely.'

'According to your boss, Ole Kristian Krantz, you're reliable and solid as a rock. You're brilliant at your job. Your flat is in good condition and well looked after and so are you.'

'Yes. I know. What I can't handle are the streets filled with people. There I have no control and anything can happen. How badly can this end?' he blurted out.

They cited the Penal Code.

'Section two hundred and thirty-nine. "Anyone who by means of threats, or in a motor vehicle, or by any other means causes the death of another," we repeat, "by any other means causes the death of another, will be punished by up to three years' imprisonment, or in aggravating circumstances up to six years. If mitigating circumstances exist a fine may be imposed." '

He placed his hands on the bare table.

'I'm actually a good person,' he said. 'You've got it all wrong.'

'They all say that,' they replied. 'We deal with facts. You were the last person to see her alive, you carried her out of your flat. The postmortem will tell us how she died, and we will then decide what to charge you with. You never called for help, you never resuscitated her.'

He looked at them in disbelief.

'Her eyes were covered by a film. I could see at once that it was too late. I was scared that I would be blamed.'

'And you think you shouldn't be?'

This silenced Alvar for a long time.

'Have you ever witnessed withdrawal close up?' he asked eventually.

Yes, they had seen it. A lot of screaming and shouting, they admitted, but nothing that they couldn't handle.

'I can't bear to see others suffer,' Alvar said, 'and that's why I keep everyone at a distance.'

'Katrine was an exception?'

'She got a hold over me, I've never experienced anything like it.'

'We're talking about a sixteen-year-old girl,' they stated.

'Oh,' he burst out, 'but she had so much power, such will! If she was in the room with us now, you would have felt her force, like a magnetic field.'

The two officers exchanged looks.

'Did the two of you ever share the same bed?' they asked suddenly.

Alvar's jaw dropped.

'I wouldn't have dreamt of it. I'm sorry to have to say this, but you're barking up the wrong tree completely.'

'You say that you gave her money. Didn't you ask for anything in return?'

'No.'

'Do you expect us to believe that?'

'I ask you to believe it because it's true.'

'And she never came on to you?'

'Never.'

'Would you have said yes? If she'd suggested something like that?'

'No.'

A long pause followed. Alvar tried to breathe calmly, he was scared of walking into a trap. He had heard that the police might try to entrap you.

'You seem very sure of this. Even though you've just told us that she was like a magnetic field.'

Alvar looked them in the eye. There was nothing left to lose. He quickly glanced up at the ceiling, he noticed the camera in the corner. The camera, which would capture his face and his voice right now, capture a few simple words he had never said out loud. The lens would capture his final confession.

'The thing is,' he said quietly, 'I prefer men.'

Again they exchanged glances. But his remark did not lead to scorn or contempt, they just shrugged, that was all. Left it there and changed the subject. Alvar was beginning to wonder if he had any rights at all. A lawyer. Was it not the case that he could simply refuse to answer any questions unless his lawyer was present? He was not entirely sure. He supposed they would have told him if this was the case, surely they were obliged to read him his rights.

'If it's true,' they asked, 'that you keep away from other people and that you're a shy man, then why did you pick a heroin addict when you finally made contact with someone?'

'She picked me,' Alvar said. 'She said she was all alone in the world, that her mother had committed suicide, that her father had left the country. I thought she was telling the truth. I'm not used to people lying. Now I've learned my lesson,' he added.

'And what about you. Are you telling the truth?'

'Every single word.'

'We hear what you're saying, we believe the actual circumstances, but we find it hard to understand them.'

'When it comes to being with other people, then I'm unfit,' he said quietly. 'I accepted that a long time ago and I have to live with the consequences. Everything that has happened is incomprehensible to me too. It's as if forces outside me have taken control, it's like heading for disaster. I won't shirk my guilt. Nor will I blame her, she was a helpless victim, she needed a strong man. She did not get that, she got me.'

'The tablets that you gave her. You never asked what they were. Can you explain that?'

'They told me they would fix everything, that was all I needed to know. I don't take drugs, I'm not interested. It was best not to know, was what I thought. Besides, I didn't have the time, her heart was about to jump out of her chest!'

At this they exchanged a very long look.

'But one thing I can tell you,' he added. 'No matter what I'd come back with, she would have taken it, she was unstoppable, she was desperate. No one would ever have stopped Katrine, she had made up her mind.'

'What about responsibility, Eide?' they said darkly. 'Do you consider yourself to be a responsible person?'

'I always have done. Now I don't know any more, perhaps I don't even know what being responsible means. The way I saw it, I was the one keeping her alive. How could I have been so wrong!'

CHAPTER 28

His defence counsel entered.

It happened so elegantly that Alvar thought he could hear a fanfare in the distance. Benedict Josef Lind entered the room with a spring in his step. Dressed in a dark suit and a snow-white shirt with a narrow bottle-green tie which matched his eyes. He was slim and long-limbed, about the same age as Alvar, and he carried a black briefcase. He stopped. Took a good look at Alvar. His gaze was steadfast, his handshake firm and warm. Then he held up the briefcase and pressed the locks. A sharp snapping sound was heard as they both sprang open at the same time, a carefully studied gesture, a ritual. He took out some papers. Stood for a while peering at the words, put the papers back in his briefcase.

'Eide. Delighted to meet you. How are you?' he asked with authority. His voice was powerful and deep. 'Have they given you something to eat?'

Alvar shook his head, he was confused. He could not remember the last time he ate, but he did not feel hungry. Only giddy, it felt as if he was floating.

'I'll take you downstairs to the canteen,' Lind said resolutely. 'If you're going to get through this, you'll need a decent meal.'

'But,' Alvar faltered, 'I need to explain myself! It's such a long story, you see, I need time!'

Lind looked at him.

'You'll have all the time in the world, Eide, I give you my word, but you need to take care of yourself. You look exhausted, you've ended up in a difficult situation.'

There was no point in protesting. Alvar closed his mouth.

Suddenly it felt good that someone else was taking charge. He, who up until now had never wanted to let go, now surrendered completely to his commanding, confident lawyer in the dark suit. It was a totally new sensation, a feeling of falling, of melting like butter, becoming pliable. Because could it get any worse? He had a vision of himself lying on a bed with his hands behind his head. A small window with bars in front of it. A desk, a simple chair, a shuttered door. Uprooted from the community. Though it occurred to him then that he had never been part of the community.

'The canteen makes first-class sandwiches,' Lind said. 'And Magda, the cook, can make a cup of coffee that will wake us both up. Come on, let's go. We can talk while we eat.' Lind nodded in the direction of the door; Alvar got up from his chair and followed him. Together they went down the corridor, Alvar with his head bowed, Lind with his chin up. They took the lift, they stood close to each other. A faint smell of aftershave filled the tiny space.

'Everything can be explained,' Lind said. 'There's a logical explanation for even the most incomprehensible action.'

'Exactly!' Alvar burst out. 'If only they'll believe me. If only they can understand!'

'It's my job to make sure they believe you, but I'll obviously need your help.'

Alvar nodded. The lift had stopped, they exited. Lind strode into the canteen, he knew his way around and was completely at ease. Alvar trailed after him, while he looked fearfully at the other diners. But no one even glanced at him twice, they had their own problems to contend with, he thought.

'Here, Eide. By the window,' said Lind, pointing.

He had stopped at a table for four; now he pulled a chair out for Alvar. This tiny gesture moved him, he had never been attended to in this way. It made him study Lind furtively.

'What can I tempt you with, Eide?' Lind asked. 'Rissoles? Prawns? Roast beef?'

'Rissoles, please,' Alvar said modestly. Suddenly he felt starving.

He remained at the table while Lind went over to the well-stocked sandwich counter. He poured two cups of coffee, paid, and returned. Carried the laden tray with the greatest of ease. Alvar stayed in his seat, staring at Lind's well-groomed hands; his fingers were long, his nails completely clean. No ring on his finger, though that meant nothing, the man was probably married and had children like everyone else. No, a little voice told him, not this man. He is different. His feelings took him by surprise; he stared down at the table. Grabbed his knife and fork, he could not think of anything to say.

Lind sat down. His manners were exquisite, as though he had been a winner his entire life, someone who could cope with anything life threw at him.

'So this Katrine Kjelland,' he said, 'whom it appears you knew, if I've understood it correctly, for a whole year. Do you blame her?'

Alvar looked up. He shook his head fiercely.

'Oh, no,' he said sincerely, 'I don't blame her for a second. She was a lost soul. She was trapped in the mire and she couldn't get out. That's how I look at it.'

Lind kept watching him. Alvar felt that his bare head shone like a bowling ball. Lind frowned.

'But she put you in a very difficult situation, surely we can agree on that?'

While he waited for Alvar to reply, he cut off the corner of his open prawn sandwich and put it in his mouth. His teeth were white and flawless.

'Well,' Alvar pondered, 'I suppose it takes two. I was naive. I always have been.' He stuck his knife into the rissole, it was very tender.

'That's not a crime,' Lind said with emphasis. He washed down the prawn with a mouthful of coffee. 'And your intentions were probably good.'

'Good intentions?' Alvar looked at him across the table. Every time he looked into those green eyes, he felt perplexed. Because everything about this man seemed so familiar. He sensed a kind of trust, as if they were on the same side. And so they were, but there was something more than that, something that made him blush.

'You bought drugs for her,' Lind said, 'because you couldn't bear to see her suffer. That's a good intention, don't you think?'

Alvar nodded. He drank his coffee and wiped his mouth with a napkin.

'I've always kept people at a distance,' he admitted. 'I can't bear it if they suffer. I can't bear the responsibility. I'm a coward deep down. The mess I'm in now stems from my own cowardice. It's my only explanation, my only excuse.'

Lind studied him closely. His green eyes grew sharp.

'Why don't you blame her at all?' he asked directly. 'She forced her way into your life, she exploited all your weaknesses. She manipulated you, emptied your bank account, slept in your bed, drank your coffee, died on your sofa?'

Alvar dropped his knife and fork.

'But she had no proper control over herself,' he said, trying to make excuses for her. 'Everything she did was controlled by heroin. Addicts are not themselves, you know that.'

Lind listened, resting his chin on his hand.

'True,' he conceded. 'In a way you were victims of each other. You both did something right, you both did something wrong. I want the blame shared, Eide, what do you say to that?'

Alvar hesitated. 'Sharing the blame? Only one of us is alive, surely that says it all?' Suddenly he felt utterly despondent. Lind chatted on undisturbed.

'Her family doesn't hold you responsible; they could see where she was heading. They don't blame you,' he said softly.

'I don't understand,' Alvar said. 'How can they be so magnanimous given what's happened?'

Lind looked at him sternly. 'It was her lifestyle that killed her,' he stated. 'Not you, Alvar Eide. Don't you see?'

'I contributed,' he argued weakly. 'I went to Bragernes Square and I was careless. I should have checked what it was I bought for her.

Suspected that it might be harmful. I was just trying to ease my own discomfort, I'm actually very selfish.'

'But she took the pills herself,' Lind said. 'She grabbed them and washed them down with water.'

'While I was watching her,' Alvar said. 'Passively. Terrified. And what happened afterwards is unforgivable.'

'Tell me about it,' Lind asked him.

Alvar looked down. 'I felt deeply ashamed. It's a well-known feeling for me, I grew up with it. It's in my veins, let me put it that way. It was like being dragged along by the current. The feeling that I could never hold my head up high again.'

Lind pushed his plate aside and kept listening to him.

'How people would gossip, the story splashed all over the front pages. Suggestions that I might have been taking advantage of her, but I didn't!'

'I know,' Lind said calmly.

'But worst of all was the fear. As I sat in the car driving through town with her dead body on the back seat, I suddenly had the feeling that I didn't know myself at all. That I had a cunning and devious side to me that I had never known about until then.'

'You're not cunning and devious,' Lind said softly.

Alvar folded his hands in his lap. 'I probably won't manage very well in prison,' he said feebly.

'If you're convicted, I'll make sure it's a suspended sentence. We will claim mitigating circumstances.'

'No,' Alvar shook his head in despair. 'You won't be able to get me off this one. I'm touched that you have faith in me, but I'm a grown man of forty-two and she was a sixteen-year-old girl. The jury will expect a certain degree of maturity, which I clearly don't possess. And that's humiliating, it's unbearable.'

Lind leaned forward. His voice was low and sincere.

'But you had your reasons for acting the way you did,' he said. 'We need to tell the jury what they were. We will show them in such a way that the whole sequence of events seems inevitable and logical.

You took her in for a whole year. She considered you to be her friend, her family will testify to that. The way I look at it, your chances are good, but you have to believe that, too. I'll be with you all the way.'

His last sentence echoed in Alvar's head. *I'll be with you all the way.*

'There's a story behind this tragedy,' Lind said. 'Twelve long months when she was a part of your life. You need to tell this story, Eide, right down to the last detail. What you thought, what you felt, how you were. How she got this hold over you, which she clearly had. She did have a hold on you, didn't she?'

'I can't stand up in court and speak ill of her,' Alvar said quickly. 'I've no right to do that and you can't make me.'

'You don't need to speak ill of her, but you need to tell it like it was. That she was stronger than you. I presume that she was?'

'She wasn't scared of anything,' he said in a tired voice. 'Not until that Friday when she turned up in withdrawal. I think of her as a brave soldier, she went to war every single day. While I, big coward that I am, sat safe and sound in my own comfortable castle.'

'You're very hard on yourself,' Lind said. 'Why is that?'

Alvar relaxed his shoulders. 'I should have seen where it was going. I should have turned her away, then she would still be alive.'

'No,' Lind said calmly. 'She was already on her way down and she took you with her.'

Then he folded his arms and rested them on the table. 'Tell me this,' he asked. 'Will you miss her?'

A wounded smile escaped from Alvar's lips. 'Yes,' he said, 'I will miss her. No one else comes to my flat.'

This revelation made him blush a second time.

'If you've had enough to eat,' Lind said, 'I suggest we start work. Is there anything else you want to tell me, anything that's important?'

'My cat,' Alvar said suddenly. 'My cat's probably sitting on my doorstep waiting to be let in. I'm sure he's hungry.'

'You have a cat?' Lind smiled. His white teeth sparkled. 'I'll look after your cat. Give me your keys, I'll stop by your house when we've finished.'

Alvar rummaged through his pocket for the key. He got up and pushed his chair. Lind gestured in the direction of the lift.

'Together we'll build a defence,' he said. 'You need to do your part. Do you understand?'

Alvar stared at the floor.

'Those who will be judging you need to know who you are. This means that you need to make yourself vulnerable and tell them all those things, it means you've got to trust me, you must believe that I want what's best for you.'

Alvar swallowed hard. 'I've never been in the habit of talking about myself in great detail,' he said quietly.

'What are you scared of?' Lind wanted to know.

'That they'll laugh, I think. That they'll despise me. That they'll call me a pathetic loner.'

'Don't be so negative,' Lind said firmly, 'chin up! Talk about yourself, start giving people a chance. People are much better than their reputation. Now you've got the opportunity to make a new discovery.'

'Perhaps they'll reject me,' Alvar said, deeply worried.

'Perhaps they'll find you not guilty,' Lind said.

The lift door closed. The space felt intimate.

'How did it start?' Lind asked. 'When did you first meet her?'

Alvar closed his eyes and remembered. Suddenly it all became clear to him. His first, but oh-so-fateful mistake.

'It was late last November, and it was cold. She came into the gallery where I work, staggering on her high-heeled boots, and she was freezing cold. I've never in all my life seen anyone so cold. Someone had to do something,' he said. 'For once in my life I decided that it was going to be me. So,' he sighed, 'I went up to the kitchen and got her a cup of coffee.'

CHAPTER 29

A man jumped the queue.

He was second in line, but he could not wait. He came into my house, all the way to my bedroom, he demanded to be heard. I carried him for twelve months. He has been in my thoughts every single day. His despair was my despair, I have felt responsible for him every single minute. Now I am standing by my window looking out at the world, the world I forget about for long periods of time when I am preoccupied with my writing. The azalea by my front door sways in the wind. Every now and then there is a sudden and forceful gust. It looks as if the whole crown of the tree is dancing a mournful dance, it bends, it surrenders. It has been standing there for more years than I have been alive, and it will still be there the day I die. That day may not be far away, I live a hard life. One day my teeth will be grinning in my skull, while the azalea dances.

The wide Lier Valley spreads out in all its glory. I can see farms, cows out to pasture, and now and then I can hear lowing, mild, woeful complaints in the stillness. I let the cat in, he goes to the kitchen for some food. I stroke his head lightly, feel his small skull underneath his fur. It is autumn, it is dark November. This season which I love most of all, the time when everything settles down. The outer landscape matches my inner one, it is gloomy and windswept. I go over to the computer, pull out my chair and sit down, pondering in the blue light. I have left Alvar Eide in the care of Benedict Lind. He does not need me any more, he can manage the remainder of the race himself, but I have given him some tools. He has been given his own story and he needs to tell it to those who will judge him. I hope they don't judge him harshly, I certainly don't. Yet there is one more detail before we finish. I feel that it belongs in the story. I want to give Alvar a final, friendly send-off. So I make myself comfortable and type, swiftly and fluently, a last important page. Just then I hear a sound from the corridor. Cautious steps, a door creaks. Alvar enters in his usual, shy way. He stops, he folds his hands. Looks at me across the room with mild eyes.

'Why are you still writing? I thought we'd finished?'

His eyes are unusually bright. I don't comment, I don't want to embarrass him.

'Yes,' I reply, 'but I have one important thing left to do.'

'What is it?'

He is intrigued

'I thought you might be interested,' I say. 'It's the post-mortem report.'

At this he goes white as a sheet.

'I don't know if I will be able to make sense of it,' he says, embarrassed. His grey eyes start to flicker, he shrugs helplessly.

'Then let me explain.'

I continue typing, my fingers run briskly across the keyboard. Alvar waits, I can hear his breathing.

'According to the pathologist Katrine Kjelland died from a cerebral haemorrhage,' I declare.

He gives me a frightened look.

'And what does that mean?'

'Bleeding in her brain,' I reply. 'What happens is that a vein bursts. It can occur in young people and can be caused by high blood pressure, or stress. In other words, she didn't die as a result of the pills you gave her, it was not a fatal dose, but they made her fall asleep. Thus you are not to blame for the death of Katrine Kjelland.'

Alvar cries out in relief. He buries his face in his hands, his knees look as if they might buckle.

'It that possible?'

'It says so here in black and white.'

The colour starts to return to his cheeks.

'But what did I give her then?' he asks quickly.

'Morphine,' I reply. 'She was probably experiencing some sort of blissful state when her heart stopped beating. And in her last moments someone wiped her brow with a warm cloth. She died on the sofa of a good friend,' I add. 'I might not be that lucky.'

He circles the floor. He clearly wants to shout for joy, but controls himself as always.

'But I drove off with her,' he recalls, 'that's unforgivable, what will people think?'

'I've got an old copy of the Penal Code here,' I say. 'If you like I can read it out to you.'

He nods silently. He waits.

'Section three hundred and forty-one. "Anyone who unlawfully or secretively either destroys the body of a deceased person or disposes of it so that it cannot be examined appropriately, or who refuses to inform the authorities of the whereabouts of a child or other incapacitated person they have in their care or who participates in so doing will be punished by a fine or up to six months' imprisonment."'

'Six months' imprisonment?'

He turns pale again.

'Let's hope they let you off with a fine,' I say. 'Now give people a chance.'

He nods again. Looks at me kindly as if he is seeing me for the first time.

'And what about you?' he asks. 'How are you doing? You've reached the end of the road. Are you happy?'

I shake my head. 'I haven't reached the end, Alvar, the worst is yet to come.'

'What's that?' he asks quickly.

'The book needs to reach an audience. I can barely find the courage. So I'll go over it a few more times. Adding, deleting a sentence here and there. And I still have to read the proofs, that's pure torture. Is that really all I did? I think, battling hard with myself, while I plan my next book. The book where I'll finally succeed once and for all.'

'Are you saying that you're disappointed with this one?' he asks nervously.

'Well,' I say, 'I'm not ecstatic. But that's the way life is. My dissatisfaction drives me to act, to write another book.'

I look up at him. I smile.

He nods. 'Do you wish me luck?'

'That goes without saying. You're on your own now. Trust those who will be judging you. Believe that they are compassionate people who'll understand.'

'I'll do my utmost,' he says. 'I want to thank you, you've been very generous.'

'You paid a high price,' I say, 'for the events you're about to face. But friendship is never free, you have to do your share.'

'It was worth it,' he says firmly. 'Besides, I'm wiser now.'

'How about Ole Krantz?' I ask. 'Have you spoken to him?'

'Yes. Benedict helped me explain. Krantz doesn't blame me and the job in the gallery is still mine.'

'What about the severed bridge?' I ask.

He smiles. He tilts his head. 'The bridge has been sold,' he says calmly.

'Is that right?' I say, giving him a big blue-eyed look of innocence. 'How do you feel about that?'

He juts out his chin. 'I don't need the bridge any more, not for anything. Because I have finally connected with another person. Benedict Josef Lind will be a friend for life.'

He walks quietly towards the door. I know that I'll never see him again and I'm filled with a sudden surge of grief. The door will never creak again, he'll never return to the room we shared for so long. Then he is gone and it goes very quiet. I switch off my computer, get up from my chair. I stand in the empty living room, left to my own devices, to a reality which is almost unbearable. Dear God, this silence, all I can hear is my own heart and I no longer have a destiny to cling to. My hands are empty. Who can I turn to, where can I go? I walk softly over to the window. I look out at the long queue of people still waiting on my drive. The woman with the dead child is still at the front. I watch her for a while, she doesn't move. She doesn't appear to have noticed me, she seems paralysed. I go out into the corridor, I put my shoes on, I open the front door. I walk down the drive, crunching the gravel. For a while I stand underneath the porch light studying them one by one. A couple of them look up at me hopefully. Some poke at the gravel with their shoes. They stand there with all their problems, all their guilt and shame. They stand there with hope of happiness and true love. I take the last few steps towards the woman with the child. I stop in front of her and give her a kind look.

'Hello. Do you want to come inside?'

She does not reply. Her eyes are apathetic. There is no doubt that her child has died, his small face is lightly marbled, his eyes are sunken.

'What happened?' I ask, trying to get her to look me in the eye. 'Did you find your child dead?'

Still no reply. Only silence, only her vacant eyes.

'I really want to help you,' I say, 'but you need to talk. If you don't talk, I won't be able to help you. Do you understand what I'm saying?'

A Place Called Home

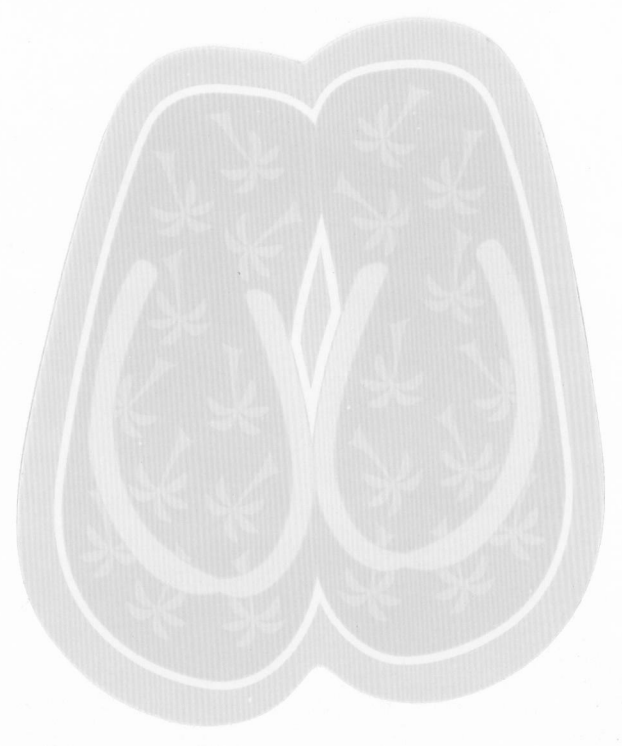

A Place

Called Home

Writings on the Midwestern Small Town

EDITED BY

RICHARD O. DAVIES

JOSEPH A. AMATO

DAVID R. PICHASKE

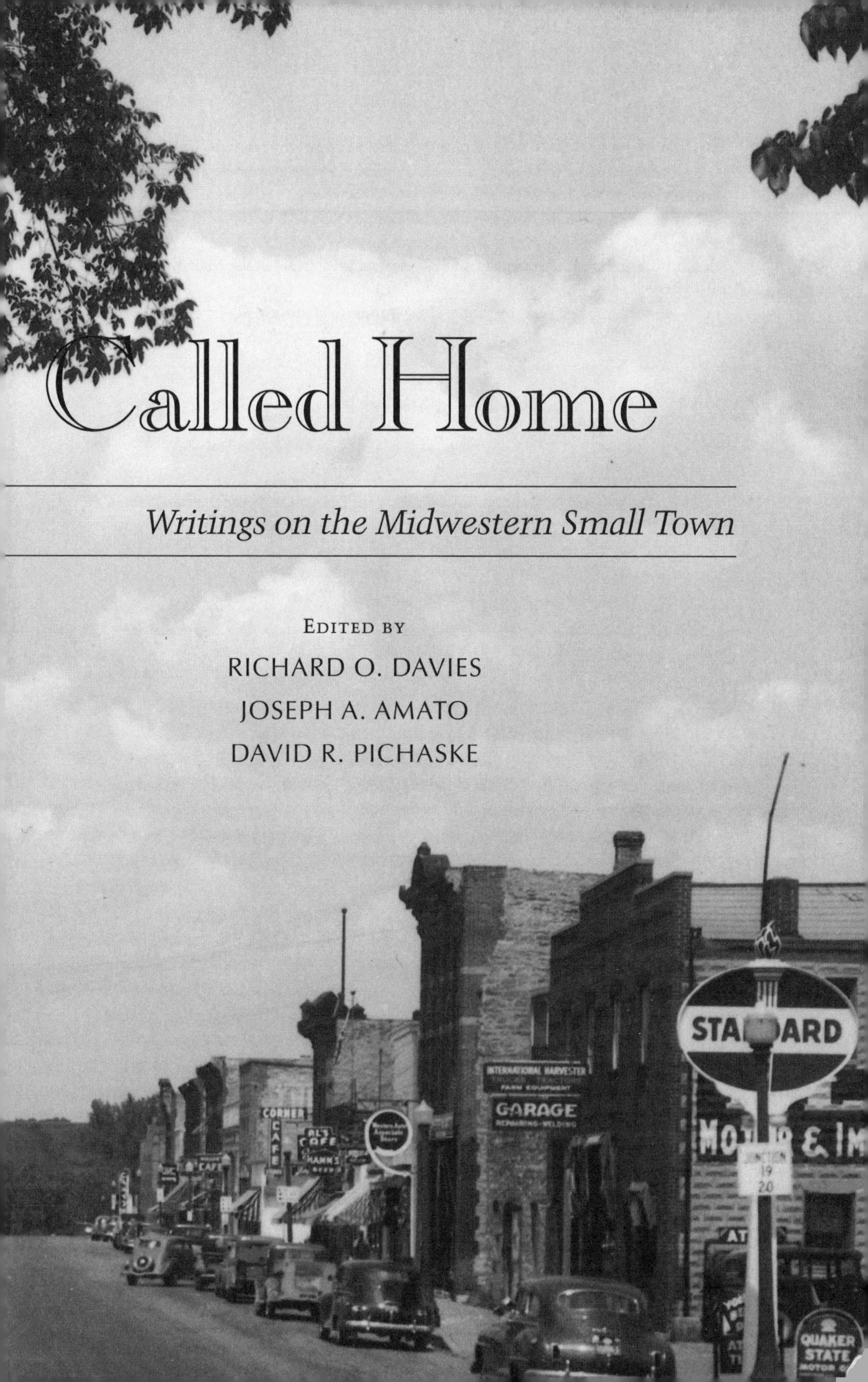

Credit information for previously published material appears at the back of the book.

Borealis Books is an imprint of the Minnesota Historical Society Press.

www.borealisbooks.org

Manufactured in the United States of America

10 9 8 7 6 5 4 3 2 1

♾ The paper used in this publication meets the minimum requirements of the American National Standard for Information Sciences—Permanence for Printed Library materials, ANSI Z39.48-1984.

International Standard Book Number 0-87351-451-3 (paper)

Library of Congress Cataloging-in-Publication Data
A place called home : writings on the midwestern small town / edited by Richard O. Davies, Joseph A. Amato, David R. Pichaske.
p. cm.
Includes bibliographical references and index.
ISBN 0-87351-451-3
1. American literature—Middle West. 2. City and town life—Literary collections.
3. Middle West—Social life and customs. 4. Middle West—Literary collections.
5. City and town life—Middle West. I. Davies, Richard O., 1937– II. Pichaske, David R.
III. Amato, Joseph Anthony.

PS563 .P58 2003
810.8′0321734—dc21
2002151825

Table of Contents

A Place Called Home

Introduction

Small Towns, Of Thee We Sing

T HE MIDWESTERN SMALL TOWN has been overwhelmed by change of every sort. It has lost its claim as a distinct place, a particular locale, or a unique community. Ever more penetrated by outside goods, technologies, ideas, peoples, and agencies, the small town, weakened at every point, has little autonomy and independence left.

In truth, the midwestern small town was never free of change. It was founded in the second half of the nineteenth century by railroads transforming the nation. In the early decades of the twentieth century, it crystallized around a belief in commerce and progress. Today it is changing beyond recognition.

Change came to the small town from all directions. Cars and roads, expanding the grid set down by settlement and railroad, reshaped rural body and mind. Catalogues, movies, and radio incrementally diverted the attention of small-town and farm dwellers to urban markets, expectations, and fantasies. The draft requisitioned the rural boys—especially farm hands and small-town day laborers—for two world wars and later the Korean and Vietnam Wars, proving among other things that you can't keep them "down on the farm" once they have been to the city. The GI Bill convinced two generations of veterans that they didn't need to go back home, and the chance for better wages and opportunities for a better life attracted small-town and rural dwellers to nearby metropolitan centers throughout the century.

At the same time, those who stayed behind focused increasingly on the city and insisted on its goods. They too wanted the best in medical treatment, fire protection, sanitation and running water, and schooling. They wanted swimming pools, bright water-filled contemporary kitchens, paved tennis courts, and green fairways. If they couldn't go to the city, they would bring the city to them.

Goods multiplied, prices diminished, and surplus cash surfaced in the countryside. Rural travel increased, shopping became a matter of choice, and small towns diminished as larger shopping centers grew. Honeymoons and vacations took more and more local people farther and farther away. Over time distant affiliations of every sort played a role in reshaping small-town lives.

Small markets irreversibly gave way to larger markets. In every way available, the rural consumer proved his loyalty to distant markets. Workers and professionals moved out of smaller rural centers. Political subordination followed economic diminution. In increasing numbers, starting in the final decades of the twentieth century, towns were annexed, discarded, or turned into bedroom communities. Correspondingly, metropolitan areas expanded into the countryside. Federal and state funding constituted an ever greater part of the town's economic survival, and rural legislators were forced to try to shake larger crumbs from bigger tables.

No longer could anyone say that the small town stood balanced between the farm and the metropolis. Both center city and remote village were bypassed by distant markets. Suburb by suburb, mobile society avoided both village and downtown. Americans chose to live in neither city nor country but in the city-country. Society sought to fuse country living with city advantage. Rural inhabitants left smaller settlements for larger rural towns and, in turn, they abandoned Main Street to live on the periphery of towns small and large. They built their commerce—principally service industries—in bright shiny strips along edges of town and in industrial parks. The wealthiest, who were often newcomers in town, sought their privacy and built castles, singularly and in housing developments, in the nearby surrounding and scenic countryside, amidst hills and dales, along river edges and on lake fronts.

By the end of the twentieth century, small towns knew that they no longer marched hand in hand with progress and nation. The 1980s definitively called off the parade; the decade's farm crisis tolled a death knell for the small town. However one counted numbers, money, and power, the tally was the same: the small town was manifestly diminished. Its streets had fallen apart; it commercial class had vanished. Its principal client—agriculture—despite ever growing productive powers, belonged to an aging and dwindling group. There were more musicians on the air than farmers on the land.

This situation requires a dramatic accounting: the midwestern town can be pronounced stone dead. The small town is as dead as the entirety of traditional Western European rural life and the peasantry. Indeed, future historical perspectives may conjoin their deaths, judging them victims of the annihilation of space and the accompanying destruction of local and rural life everywhere.

City and town, our funeral sermon suggests, have become one, equal parts of homogenizing mass, commercial, and national society. Talented and ambitious young people have abandoned the small town for a lifetime. Their parents now also leave town annually to be with their children and to spend warmer winters and cooler summers. Exoduses of every sort—of body and mind, permanent and seasonal—have already occurred or are under way. Nursing homes and elderly-care establishments replace schools.

Deserted main streets challenge memory to reconstruct noisier days when children and commerce filled corridors along which people really cared, if only for gossip and coffee-klatch reasons, about one another's comings and goings.

In the countryside, even ethnic farming communities (the hardest kernels of rural farm and small village) have now lost their character. And more and more individuals and agencies advocate preserving land, waters, and wild animals at the expense of agriculture. The latter's conquest of water and land is assumed and then forgotten. The atoms of midwestern society have disintegrated.

We may inventory Main Street's missing stores and personalities more specifically. Schools, churches, and fire and police departments have merged, consolidated, or vanished altogether. In the last twenty years, local institutions of every sort—from banks, hospitals, law firms, dentists, and co-ops—have gone regional, joining state and national chains. Along Main Street one counts among new businesses antique, second-hand, rummage, and junk stores (which often form a descending progression), while hardware shops, grocery stores, shoe stores, bakeries, movie theaters, and pool halls close. Talk about revitalization and economic development becomes a second kind of "weather talk." Thriving small towns—whose populations are several thousand or more and which are commonly county seats and regional service centers—lay computer cable and add new indoor skating rinks, libraries, parks, and bike trails. They cannot relent in their efforts to add amenities that will attract new and retain old businesses. They must make desperate efforts to stay even, or they will fall still further behind.

Yet no stacking and piling of metaphors or compounding of numbers can describe what has been lost. Nostalgia—admittedly so often a search for the sensual plenitude of youth's first impressions and experiences— helps us depict the sinking of yesteryear's small town. Nostalgia has it that inhabitants carried out their lives, as ever fewer do today, in a single spot. They conducted the majority of their transactions, great and small, in a single place. They played out their lives and fates on ground they knew to be home. In the confines of a relatively stable, if not fixed circle, they shared events, stories, and suspicions. At all times they knew to the bone the other players on the stage. For them, space, place, locale, community, and home were one. They formed a single microcosm composing nation, world, and humanity.

Critics of Main Street like Sinclair Lewis and his followers moved in the opposite direction. For them, Main Street's narrow and straight ways reflected a band of narrow, straight, and dull shopkeepers. They and their wives led the righteous way in church, club, and committee—in both progressive cause and moral reaction. This elite molded town life to serve self-interest, vanity, and glory, driving the rest to the town's edges and clandestine niches.

Nostalgia and criticism aside, select small towns (especially those with a courthouse) became lead communities, serving as commercial and government centers. They functioned as outposts for the distant metropolis and nation. They instructed town and county inhabitants on what to buy, what not to drink, and what was new and progressive. During wartime, they taught, often with the help of state agencies, how one should most patriotically serve the nation.

On another level, the small town (taking advantage of one of its principal assets) drew to itself cheap labor. It offered workers near and far poorly paid, non-unionized jobs. Without a large and diverse job market, small towns forced workers and their mates—those who chose to stay—to live out their lives at minimum or close to minimum wages, enjoying in turn the benefits of family, safety, and usually lower-cost housing. However, starting in the second half of the twentieth century, the most energetic and ambitious workers left the small town for the metropolitan center, where pay is better and work opportunities more abundant.

Yet this sort of philosophizing begins to ring hollow in its generalization and in the face of the definitional questions it raises. First, we must ask of the uniqueness of the midwestern town itself. Do its character and plight differentiate it from the small towns of other national regions? In fact, might not productive comparisons be made with the small towns of Europe and the world in this age of national and global forces? Does not the twentieth century require a global or trans-regional perspective on the rural and small everywhere? Certainly an affirmative answer is required if only on the basis of a single book, Gert Mak's *Jorwerd: The Death of the Village in Late 20th Century Europe*. Writing of a single Dutch village in Friesland, he describes how in the course of the last fifty years contemporary technology, markets, society, and government have metamorphosed small, thriving, autonomous agricultural villages. Once filled with stores, bulging with associations, and occupying the lives and minds of its people, Jorwerd has become principally a residence for individual families of commuters in a town almost without store and craft and in a region where agriculture has become a remote, lonely, regulated, and centralized activity. Jorwerd, still a village, is no longer a place and less than half a home.

A second question—which moves us in a different direction—pivots on the size of the small town itself. Should we allow the number 2,500 and below (a division used by the U.S. Bureau of the Census) to define the small town? Surely, a village or hamlet of 100 or fewer (which had few stores and associations even when it flourished) is not a village of 500, which in its heyday of fifty or so years ago would have had a variety of stores and services, including a co-op and bank. In turn, the village of 500 was and is dissimilar to a town of 1,000 which—if it resembles thriving Cottonwood, Minnesota, in 1968—had a Main Street of few blocks holding competing restaurants and grocery stores, a furniture store, a hardware store, tractor sales, and bars, in addition to a movie theater, a doctor, a dentist, a small industry, a large insurance company, many active churches, and a very large Lions Club. Yielding even greater differences and distinctions would be comparisons between towns of 1,000 and those of 2,500, 5,000 and 10,000.

The Minnesota town of Marshall, with a population of 10,000 in 1980, has continued even in the last two decades to have a slightly growing population, reaching almost 13,000 in the 2000 census. Serving as a county seat and a regional service center for twenty to thirty miles in every direction, it houses a four-year educational institution, a major food industry, and many other businesses and industries. In addition to downtown and the mall, its principal east-west bypass has major retail chains and motels, while its central east-west road between downtown and the college has a several-block strip of fast-food emporiums, motels, and regional and national franchises. Thanks largely to a meat-cutting factory and a few computer parts plants at which immigrants from Mexico, Somalia, and Laos worked in considerable numbers, the rate of population turnover in Marshall between 1990 and 1995 exceeded that of the Twin Cities proper.

In fact, demographers and students of small-town commerce resort to a far finer hierarchy than 2,500 and below. They distinguished hamlets, composed of a gas station, café, and grocery store (which increasingly have been combined into a single convenience store); a minimum convenience center; a full convenience center; a partial shopping center (with four to eight specialized shops); the complete shopping center (with nine or more); and—the heavyweight of heavyweights—the primary wholesale-retail center, which incorporates all the functions of the previous and contains more than one hundred businesses.

Places gathered and divided in this way are of course more than representatives of a typology. They have a history. They do not pass through time with fixed mass on constant orbit. Influenced by a variety of separate and interdependent local factors, organizations, and personalities, small towns (always of distinguishing size, shape, composition, and relationship to the immediate periphery) respond to alterations in regional business and demography. They also have been shaped by vacillations in consumer purchasing power and demand; the introduction of new technologies, especially laborsaving devices; alterations in transportation and communication industries; and overall trends in the national and global economies. In sum, change in any one place might require micro- and macro-analysis. Explanation may have to focus simultaneously on rivalry with a nearby town; on a hometown business's choice; on a trend in a national agricultural or even commercial or industrial market; or upon a decision by state government to locate a public institution or expand a highway.

As Joseph A. Amato and John W. Meyer explain in *The Decline of Rural Minnesota*, several general factors determine the fate of towns of different sizes. By analyzing the 1990 census, they established (for rural Minnesota) that agriculture was in a state of demographic decline; that is, smaller numbers of farm families inhabited larger acreages. It followed, as numbers illustrated, that the more rural a county (the more it was composed of farms and small towns of 5,000 or fewer) the older and greater the decline, the origins of which could be traced as far back as the 1950 census. Only three of Minnesota's counties, which had towns of approximately 10,000 or more, escaped demographic decline. Decline, reaching as high as 18 percent in Minnesota's most rural counties, doubled the average percentage of decline in the 1960s and 1970s and was matched by the aging of farm and small-town population. The American farmer's median age of sixty years was replicated in select smaller towns and villages throughout Minnesota. The most severe cases of decline in rural Minnesota—as shown by the 1995 census—showed natural decline in a dozen counties in which deaths outnumbered births. The flight of youth, the end of Main Street, and the death of small town and farm—this whole doleful litany of small town decline, vividly apparent in agricultural Minnesota—characterized all the agricultural regions of the Midwest in the 1980s and 1990s.

Working just to the west of Minnesota, in *Plains Country Towns*, John Hudson convincingly shows that decline reached the prairie in North Dakota at the time of settlement itself. Competing railroads overbuilt lines and towns. Indeed, countless imagined towns died on the drafting board, becoming instant ghost towns. Others, if not ploughed in the ground, are now materially vanishing in dry winds and swirling dust on the prairie, having reached their demographic apex of a handful of people in the very first year of their existence. Surely, decline reached the agricultural west early when, in 1900, the population of North and South Dakota declined in absolute numbers.

Working its way east, decline started to crisscross small-town America in the 1920s, conveyed by the automobiles that took rural citizens, body and mind, out of their own small villages to nearby towns and cities. Decline became generalized in succeeding decades, as youth in ever greater numbers left farm and town, county bank assets accumulated in regional centers, and small service centers served fewer with less. By the 1990 census, even the most ardent boosters were stymied in their attempts to deny this exodus and the pessimistic trends associated with it.

There could be exceptions. A small town could have a brilliant entrepreneurial son who stayed home and built a food industry. It could be situated on a large lake, drawing a recreation and a retirement community, or along a major expressway, or close to a regional center or an expanding metropolitan center. If numbers alone counted, optimists could overlook the fact that even towns that grew had lost their functions as a community and been transformed into a bedroom community or remade into suburb.

The censuses of 1990 and 2000 confirmed a dark story: the nation's agricultural regions and its small towns were on a treacherous slippery slope. They were now only smaller pieces of the whole; they were distant and cold bodies in a contracting universe. Midwestern agriculture and its small towns were simply following the same path, yielding to the same economic laws that brought down mining, lumbering, and farming in the course of the century. However venerated the nation's heartland, its small towns had served merely as vehicles for an economic colossus on its way to national, continental, and global economic empires. Each in his own way, geographers John Borchert and John Hudson and historians William Cronon, Hal Barron, and Richard O. Davies offer a century-long path describing the rise and fall of the small town.

The 2000 census makes it clear that the small town—defined as 2,500 or fewer, or even 10,000 or fewer—continues to decline in the Midwest as percentage of total population. Paralleling the more than two-century-old eclipse of countryside by city and rural by urban life, the decline of small towns has taken place for the last hundred years, and at accelerating rates for the last fifty.

Specific calculations from the census exist for just two states, Ohio and Iowa, and suggest, if only as hypothesis, that steeper decline proceeded from east to west. Small towns arguably decline where populations are more dense, key cities are bigger, more numerous, and proximate, and connecting systems of highways and interstates are more abundant. Small towns at the eastern end of the Midwest have more quickly been transformed into burgeoning suburbs on the one hand, or drained of population and services by adjacent metropolitan markets, influences, and opportunities on the other. In either case, small towns in the populous quarters of the eastern band of the Midwest, or more precisely, small towns—whatever their compass location—in the vicinity of large urban centers have been more rapidly metamorphosed than those more distant from a metropolis.

This line of speculation contradicts our earlier identification of decline with the West and the Dakotas. There, it was argued that the smaller the spur along which a settlement occurred, the more likely it never took root at all or began to decline sooner after founding. The further west a settlement was and the later the date of incorporation, the greater likelihood the town would be not only small but also vulnerable. As if it were the runt of a civilization's litters, it started life imperiled.

To accept the truth of both of these theories suggests that the optimal place for the settlement, survival, and longevity of small towns was somewhere in the middle of the Midwest. It was not along the more populous eastern zones that quickly absorbed and integrated the land, population, society, and small towns. Nor was it in the more arid, more remote, and far less populated zones of the Midwest, bordering on the high prairie that was not as welcoming to agriculture and carried with it a standing cost for shipping goods and a comparative scarcity of amenities.

It can further be conjectured that optimal conditions for a varied and long small-town existence occurred along a band reaching from southwestern Wisconsin, Minnesota, and eastern South Dakota south to Iowa and western Nebraska to central and eastern Kansas, Missouri, and western Illinois. Settled and defined by agriculture in the decades immediately following the Civil War, these areas flourished thanks to available water and good soils. Outside markets, though accessible and stimulating, were not overwhelming in their intrusions. In this zone, agriculture and market found a truce—a kind of rough and shifting equilibrium. For more than a century, farmers and small towns fashioned their lives around the reality and illusion that, as tillers of the land and practitioners of free enterprise, they had a covenant with the nation—and, indeed, they more than any other group were its essence.

Small towns have now entered, as suggested at the beginning of this essay, a period of differentiation, transition, and metamorphosis. Like the proverbial soldier, they don't die, they just seem to fade away. Without a viable Main Street business core and with only a house and trailer or two, they are no longer by any measure a town, a village, and a community. They are stopping-off places for a day, a few years, or a decade or two on the way to somewhere else. Transformed into bedroom communities, resort spots, or suburbs, they are no longer the kernel communities of experience and association they once were.

Depicting their differentiation and transformation will be the principal task of new breeds of historians and writers. Their best students will have to seek multiple ways to explore the external dimension of this change. At the same time, as suggested in Joseph A. Amato's *Rethinking Home* and so well illustrated by John Radziłowski's *Prairie Town*, they will have to dedicate themselves to understanding in detail the diverse subjects associated with the contemporary metamorphosis of the local. They will have to scrap older ideas that the midwestern small town constituted a single structure and a common experience. They will have to seek the sense of lives and places that have multiple meanings; they will have to study villages filled with worlds, microcosms bursting with macrocosms.

The story of the small will be global. It will be intertwined with region, nation, and world. It will be about markets and democracy. It will also be about humanity that lives less and less bounded by space and increasingly independently of place. It will be about a world in an era of whirling change—when, not dissimilar to the subjects of peasant and countryside, farm and barns, the small town will be an artifact by which we seek to reconstruct past minds and communities.

I

The Formative Years
1790–1900

As WHITE SETTLEMENT PROCEEDED from Ohio across the fertile prairie land and onto the high plains—a process that encompassed much of the nineteenth century—approximately 4,000 permanent towns were established in the Midwest, comprised of all or parts of the thirteen states that stretch from eastern Ohio westward to central Kansas and Nebraska and upward to the Canadian border. Designed to serve as service centers for the surrounding farmland, these towns were located along rivers and creeks and manmade canals, along primitive trails that would someday become paved highways, along the early lines of the expanding railroad network. Speculators and planners in Ohio, Indiana, and Michigan relied primarily upon access to navigable bodies of water for the location of new towns, but beginning in Illinois the determining factor was often location along a newly constructed railroad line. Railroad executives understood that new towns were crucial to their company's future profits, as they would generate demand for passenger and freight services. The towns that the railroads established also generated profits from the sale of land. During the early 1850s, for example, the Illinois Central Railroad created such town sites now occupied by the substantial communities of Centralia, Kankakee, Champaign, and La Salle. By 1870 it had created eighty-one new towns along its lines with a total population of 172,000.

Stimulated by the spectacular financial success of the Illinois Central, other railroads devised their own town promotions. None were as successful as the Illinois Central, but Iowa, for example, was dotted with small towns promoted by the Chicago, Burlington & Quincy. One land agent of the Burlington, Charles Perkins, sardonically commented to his wife in 1864 about the process: "Towns they are on paper, meadows or timber land with here and there a house, in reality." Two years later this intrepid promoter remarked, "I shall have two or three more towns to name very soon. . . . They should be short and easily pronounced. Frederic, I think is a very good name. It is now literally a cornfield, so I cannot have it surveyed, but yesterday a man came to arrange to put a hotel there. This is a great country for hotels." Historians have tended to overlook the crucial role of railroads and land speculators in the creation of the midwestern urban and town network. Although promoters tended to proclaim, "Tell them we are building a great city," in reality few of these towns ever became a thriving metropolis, but small towns all across the Midwest owe their existence to the work of land speculators and promoters, only some of whom could be called "scrupulous." The historian Richard Wade once commented that the truly influential "frontiersmen" who settled the Midwest were not the Indian fighters and early explorers. Rather, they were those intrepid promoters who aggressively sold the promise of a future metropolis located in a cornfield to anyone who would listen to their pitch.

Whatever their origins, the physical appearance of midwestern towns took on a reassuring sameness all across the region. Planners embraced the grid pattern for purposes of efficiency, but also because it provided a visual image of permanence and security. Along the town's central corridor— almost invariably called Main Street—settlers set about building replicas of the towns of the eastern seaboard states from which they had come.

Because the towns matured relatively quickly, it is difficult to realize that initially they were little more than primitive outposts carved out of the woods and prairie. Small ramshackle wooden structures with dirt floors provided shelter for settlers; in the treeless regions in Nebraska, Kansas, and the Dakotas sod houses were cut out of the soil. Modest general stores, crude taverns, livery stables, feed stores, and granaries soon began to fill up some of the space along the modest-sized commercial corridor. If the village survived—and many did not—within a few years a cluster of professionals had opened their doors for business: physicians, blacksmiths, butchers, barbers, coopers, jewelers, insurance agents, bakers, and undertakers. The commencement of a weekly newspaper usually came somewhat later in the town-building process and provided an important symbolic milestone in the emergence of a stable, mature community with viable long-term prospects. Brick buildings usually appeared within a decade or two after a town's founding, symbolizing a sense of permanence, a tangible sign that anticipated a long and hopeful future. Not surprisingly, small and often poorly capitalized locally owned banks, seeking to reflect an impression of economic strength, were among the first brick buildings to appear along Main Street. Over the years many of the initial wooden business structures were replaced by brick ones, often after a devastating fire wiped out large swaths of the frame buildings along the business district.

In those towns settled by New Englanders a central square often became the focal point. In those communities designated as a county seat, these squares became the location of the county court house, which usually featured a neo-classical federal architectural style. Just off of the main business corridor planners allocated space for churches and a school. Residential streets extending away from the central corridor were typically identified in one of three ways. There were the names of popular presidents: Washington, Jefferson, Hamilton, Madison, Jackson, Van Buren; soothing names of bucolic trees: Maple, Oak, Pine, Elm, Cedar, Hickory; and the ubiquitous, if less imaginative utilitarian numbers, with First Street invariably being located adjacent to the town's core. Railroad promoters had often named the streets of an entire town on their drawing boards before the first residents ever arrived.

As the community matured, the initial primitive cottages were replaced by much more permanent frame and brick structures, many of which remain inhabited today. All across the Midwest, two-story box-like wooden frame houses, invariably painted white and often encumbered with ornate Victorian bric-a-brac, proved popular. Although similar in style, each had its distinguishing features; fortunately the towns were spared the numbing look-alike formula of post–World War II suburban tract housing developments. The town's more prosperous families tended to opt for similarly styled, albeit larger, houses constructed out of red brick with white trim. The midwestern towns broke with a common eastern seaboard tradition of building houses with adjoining walls that were set close to the street. In the Midwest, befitting the vast expanse of open land, houses were typically set well back from the street, their fronts dominated by a large covered porch that provided a popular venue for relaxing on hot summer evenings. An extensive expanse of grass required constant attention in the summer months, and out back a vegetable garden and fruit trees attested to the town's close connection to the surrounding farmland. Along the back alley were located the privy and small horse barn and perhaps other storage buildings.

The prosperity of the towns depended upon the state of the agricultural economy. Economic conditions of Main Street rose and fell with the fluctuations of the commodities markets. The town's population depended upon location. A railroad main line or primary highway tended to attract more commercial venues, thereby boosting population. However, the size of a town was also influenced by the number of farm families living within its immediate range. East of the Mississippi River towns were generally established about eight to ten miles apart, the distance dictated by the ability of a farmer's horse and wagon to make a round trip to town. This pattern slowly broke down beyond the Mississippi River due to the greater influence of the railroads in laying out the sites of future towns; they wanted a reasonable distance between towns to reduce the number of stops their trains would have to make. Thus in the western regions of the Midwest the distance between towns tended to range between ten and twenty miles. By 1900, some 4,000 towns in the Midwest had taken permanent root. While many new suburban communities emerged during the decades of extensive growth after World War II, the number of towns has changed little in the last century.

As the historian Robert Wiebe points out, although connected to a regional town and urban network via dirt roads, waterways, and railroads, these agricultural towns remained essentially "island communities" well into the twentieth century. Within those communities, however, the establishment of complex social and economic systems occurred surprisingly quickly as these frontier outposts were readily transformed into viable, reasonably complex communities. Public schools were established within years, if not months, of the arrival of the first settlers. Churches were erected with even greater alacrity. Lending libraries appeared somewhat later but were viewed with considerable community pride because they symbolized a town's commitment to serious cultural pursuits. A town government—chartered by the state legislature—provided for maintenance of public streets and buildings, and it appointed a town marshal and a justice of the peace to provide law and order in communities where serious crimes occurred only infrequently. Volunteer fire departments were established as an antidote to the many tinderbox structures that, in an age of open fireplaces and kerosene lanterns, were vulnerable to raging fires that could destroy a full town block. Fire companies also provided a source of socialization and status for the men selected for membership.

By the 1880s every town that considered itself a progressive place had its own baseball team and community band. In the summer months a community's hopes and aspirations were carried on the shoulders of the team as it competed fiercely on weekend afternoons with rivals from nearby communities. The "town ball" tradition would survive until the 1950s, when this institution was undercut by nationally televised major league baseball games. Regarding the community band, the writer Sherwood Anderson once commented, "What does a band mean to a town? Better to ask what is a town without a band?" Most towns took immense pride in their peppy town band, dressed out in snappy uniforms and playing at patriotic events and community celebrations. The band, usually comprised of a dozen or so musicians, often made an appearance on warm summer Saturday evenings when the streets were filled with farm families doing their weekly shopping. The importance of the town band provided the basis for Meredith Willson's enduring *Music Man*, located in the fictional Iowa town of River City. Like the baseball team, the town band fell victim to changing social and economic conditions around the time of World War II.

Although outward appearances gave every indication that the midwestern town was homogenous in its racial and ethnic composition and that its citizenry was unified in what everyone called the "middle class," closer examination reveals that such was not the case. To be certain, few midwestern towns were home to people of color. The towns were overwhelmingly white and often dominated by one particular immigrant or religious group. Although the dominant immigrant heritage was from Great Britain, towns across the region took pride in their ethnic and national uniqueness, whether Swedish, Dutch, German, Belgian, or Czechoslovakian. Certain religious groups, such as the Amish, clustered together in towns and the surrounding farmland in states ranging from Ohio to Iowa. This homogeneity was widely accepted and fostered through local religious, political, and educational institutions, including the holding of summer festivals that invoked the European origins of the residents.

Even within the racially homogeneous towns, there existed widely recognized social distinctions. Many factors determined an individual's place in the town's social pecking order: profession, income, education, and family reputation. The many organizations that sprang up in the towns were frequently pointed to as evidence of a community-wide spirit of cooperation, but these organizations often served to divide the community along subtle but important class lines. A manual laborer or small farmer seldom received an invitation to join the prestigious Masonic Order, where bankers, businessmen, and professionals met not only to conduct the business of their Order, but also to share ideas, cut business deals, and plot political strategies. Their wives naturally dominated the Order of the Eastern Star and carefully monitored memberships in prestigious ladies' bridge, literary, and charity organizations. Clustered in the lower echelons of the middle class were day laborers, schoolteachers, handymen, store clerks, and artisans. They often enjoyed each other's company in organizations that began as mutual insurance and burial societies, such as the Elks and Moose, while their wives usually shared potluck meals at Bible study and sewing groups organized out of their churches. One reliable indicator of a family's social status was whether or not the family secured the services of a part-time maid and sent out its laundry to a working-class woman.

During the nineteenth century and well into the twentieth century, these 4,000 communities, ranging in size from several hundred to 10,000 residents, collectively played a dominant role in the politics and economy of the Midwest. Residents of the towns, together with the farm population they served, constituted a majority of the residents of each of the thirteen states comprising the Midwest. Although already economically subservient to the growing urban network and to the steadily nationalizing trend of the economy, these towns nonetheless wielded considerable political clout in statehouses as well as in Washington, D. C. Political leaders ignored them at their peril.

The Economic Base

FROM *The Urban Frontier*

RICHARD C. WADE

POPULAR MYTHOLOGY has long held that the American westward movement was led by intrepid explorers like Daniel Boone who shunned organized communities and moved on whenever they could see the smoke rising from their nearest neighbor's fireplace. These explorers-pioneers were then replaced by families seeking to take advantage of inexpensive land prices and establish permanent farms.

Contrary to popular myth, however, from the very beginning the new immigrants from east of the Appalachian Mountains set about establishing towns as centers for defense against Indian reprisals and for handling commercial shipping. The movement into the Midwest that began with a trickle of settlers in the 1790s became a veritable flood during the early years of the nineteenth century. Marietta, Ohio, became the first white settlement in the Northwest Territory when pioneers from Massachusetts built a crude fort at the confluence of the Muskingum and Ohio Rivers in 1788; soon thereafter a succession of small towns were founded downstream on the Ohio River. Ohio was admitted to statehood in 1803 and was soon followed by Indiana (1816) and Illinois (1818).

Professor Richard C. Wade created a new historical perspective about the process of settlement other than the frontiersman–pioneer–Indian fighter saga when he explored the role of towns and small cities in *The Urban Frontier: The Rise of the Western Cities, 1790–1830*, published in 1959. He found that settlements such as Cincinnati and Louisville provided departure points for settlers moving into the rich farmlands of Ohio, Kentucky, Indiana, and Illinois. From the very first the towns of the Midwest were designed to serve a vital economic role in the development of the region. Although developers of most towns dreamed of making themselves rich by establishing the foundations of a future metropolis, only a very few of these frontier outposts ever achieved urban status. However, as the following selection indicates, as early as 1815 a few rough-hewn towns had matured as commercial centers to the point that they were already making the transition from town to small city.

o   o   o

Though each town evolved an economy peculiar to its own location and re-sources, some elements were shared by all. The central nexus of the urban-ization of the West was commerce. All towns sprang from it, and their growth in the early years of the nineteenth century stemmed from its expansion. The Ohio River was the chief agent of this development, and the towns on its banks were the initial beneficiaries. Remoter places did not participate in this prosperity, and even Lexington found its landlocked sit-uation an increasing handicap. But other factors too played an important part in laying the economic foundations of frontier urbanism, notably the influence of the army, the tide of immigration, the emergence of manufac-turing, the development of banking, and, most spectacular of all, the com-ing of the steamboat.

Though the army was never popular in Western towns except in time of danger, its influence on the economics of these communities was immense. Not only did the troops protect infant settlements against Indian raids and foreign incursions, but, more important, their purchases provided a con-stant stimulus to urban expansion. "The increase of Pittsburgh was not rapid until 1793," a contemporary observed, but in the next year the Whisky Rebellion brought 15,000 soldiers into the region, "throwing into circula-tion a good deal of public money," and giving the town "a new and reviving impulse, it having since that time progressed very rapidly."[1] Throughout the nineties Pittsburgh served as a supply headquarters for troops in the North-west, and when war came in 1812 the young manufacturing city provided Western forces with ordnance and shot. For better than two decades the army was the town's best customer, and many local fortunes were built on this trade.

Cincinnati, too, from its very first days, profited from federal military spending. Since it served as an outfitting depot for operations against the Indians and later the British, the army leaned heavily on the town's mer-chants. During the war this dependence deepened. Troops rendezvoused in the Queen City before heading to the front, and left behind hard money badly needed in the town. Indeed, government buying became so great in 1813 and 1814 that local prices suddenly rose, contributing to the general optimism that launched the overly ambitious manufacturing drive in the war years.[2] Though no estimate can be accurate, the total amount of this spending was immense, and its abrupt cessation undoubtedly contributed to the sharpness of the postwar decline.[3]

The role of the military in the economic development of other Western towns is a similar story. An exposed settlement such as St. Louis still looked to federal troops for protection, and in time of war became a garrison site. In addition, it benefited in peacetime from supplying the line of forts that the army strung along the Western rivers to pacify the Indians and control fur trading. Curiously enough, during the War of 1812, the navy rather than the army patronized Lexington, whose hemp manufacturers replaced foreign providers of marine and sail cloth for oceangoing vessels. One factory alone filled a $12,000 order for sails, and in the last two years of the conflict Kentucky manufacturers provided over 180 tons of yarn and rope.[4] In some cases this military purchasing was smaller and irregular, but the government was always the most sought-after customer, because its payments were prompt and in specie. In immature economies this priming stimulated commerce and often provided the surplus needed for modest beginnings in manufacturing.

In 1815 most adults in Western cities were immigrants. They came largely from the older sections of the country, but an increasing number arrived directly from Europe without loitering in the East. The population growth of these urban centers reflected the magnitude of the human stream that moved across the mountains into the West. The immigrant impact on their youthful economies, however, is not encompassed merely in numerical increase. These people did more than create an expanding local market; they also brought with them skills to perform new jobs and capital to invest in new enterprises. Choosing cities as carefully as farmers selected land, mechanics and entrepreneurs sought the place of maximum opportunity and brightest future. And Western towns competed for these urban migrants, advertising openings for profitable enterprise and specific types of employment.

As the cities grew, some turned to industry. By 1815 manufacturing had transformed the economic structure of Pittsburgh, made great strides in Lexington, and found advocates in Cincinnati and Louisville. Other towns, more modest in their hopes, embarked only on limited projects, usually for local purposes. Travelers, however, were astonished to see this remarkable development in an area so recently rescued from the wilderness. Some of this industrial growth proved artificial, having been stimulated by embargoes and war which kept foreign goods off the American market. In the depressions that rocked the West at the close of hostilities many business firms failed, factories closed down, and widespread distress resulted. Yet even after this fat had been pared away, an impressive achievement remained. And the increasing adoption of steam power in Western factories strengthened the established urban pattern by concentrating manufacturing in the larger towns where labor and capital could be readily secured.

This development, remarkable as it was, might have been even more extensive if so much urban capital had not been drained off into land speculation. Most of the towns were older than the surrounding country, and capitalists tended to invest in nearby tracts, low in price, whose value was "certain to rise." Only in Pittsburgh, where much of the hinterland was either already appropriated or of poor quality, did commercial profits readily seek industrial channels. In other places the most successful merchants, finding land "a powerful inducement," tended to avoid manufacturing because of the high costs and uncertain returns. Daniel Drake, an influential spokesman for industrialization in Cincinnati, noticed this in his own city. "The conditions which . . . constitute the basis of manufacturing establishments, have not . . . existed in the same degree as if the town had been *younger* than the adjoining country."[5]

The towns were not only the commercial and industrial centers of the West, but its financial leaders as well. Though capital constantly streamed across the mountains into land or commercial enterprises, the new areas continually complained of a kind of colonial status, in which money always seemed to be moving eastward. Soon commercial interests began to demand some kind of banking facilities to increase the volume of money. But banks were unpopular, and new states hesitated to grant charters for issuing notes. Hence banking came to the West through the back door as part of the operations of insurance or trading companies. In 1802 the Kentucky Insurance Company of Lexington was given certain privileges of note issue in connection with its marine insurance, and subsequently put out a large circulation. Similarly, the Miami Exporting Company in Cincinnati, capitalized at $150,000 in 1803 as a trading company, turned four years later exclusively to banking. Pittsburgh's Ohio Company, organized in 1802 for Mississippi commerce, became a branch of the Bank of Pennsylvania within two years and dropped completely its earlier objectives. All these companies were composed of leading merchants, an indication of the intimate relationship between commerce and early financial institutions.

Soon Western states chartered banks directly. By 1815 Cincinnati had three, one without a charter, and all seemed thriving. The Miami Exporting Company had a "reputation and notoriety . . . equal to that of any bank in the western country," its dividends fluctuating between 10 and 15 per cent. The Farmers' and Mechanics' Bank with $200,000 of capital paid between 8 and 14 per cent, and even the unauthorized Bank of Cincinnati issued notes of "excellent credit."[6] These returns were so handsome that merchants began to circulate their own notes, usually without state sanction. In the same period Pittsburgh supported four banks. Indeed, during the war the whole West outgrew its antagonism to banks and developed a policy of easy incorporation. The issues of these institutions broke the log jam of scarcity and soon flooded the Western country with paper, most of whose value was questionable.

Nothing, however, accelerated the rise of the Western cities so much as the introduction of the steamboat. Expanding commerce offered attractive

opportunities in new towns, and manufacturing created an increasing demand for skilled labor, but steam navigation, by quickening transportation
and cutting distances, telescoped a half-century's development into a single generation. It was an enchanter's wand transforming an almost raw
countryside of scattered farms and towns into a settled region of cultivated
landscapes and burgeoning cities. The steamboat, observed James Hall,
"has contributed more than any other event or cause, to the rapid growth
of our population, and an almost miraculous development of our resources." The French Minister of Marine in 1824 also noted its impact on
the urbanization of the Western country. "In the brief interval of fifteen
years, many cities were formed . . . where before there were hardly the
dwellings of a small town. . . . A simple mechanical device has made life
both possible and comfortable in regions which heretofore have been a
wilderness." Another contemporary, Morgan Neville, added his enthusiastic testimony. "The steam engine in five years has enabled us to anticipate
a state of things, which in the ordinary course of events, it would have required a century to produce. The art of printing scarcely surpassed it in beneficial consequences."[7]

Though developed in the East, the steamboat had a peculiar importance for the West. "The invention of the steamboat was intended for us,"
observed the editor of the *Cincinnati Gazette*. "The puny rivers of the East
are only as creeks, or convenient waters on which experiments may be
made for our advantage." The successful run in 1815 of the *Enterprise*
up the Mississippi and Ohio from New Orleans to Pittsburgh established
the practicability of steam navigation on inland waters, though the trip of
the *Washington*, a larger ship, two years later, seemed more conclusive to
contemporaries.[8]

The flow of commerce downriver was now supplemented by a northward
and eastward movement, giving trade and manufacturing new opportunity
for expansion and growth. "To feel what an invention this is for these regions," wrote Timothy Flint, "one must have seen and felt . . . the difficulty
and danger of forcing a boat against the current of these mighty rivers, on
which progress of ten miles a day, is a good one." The shift was not only one
of direction, but of speed. "You are invited to a breakfast, at seventy miles'
distance. You get on board the passing steam-boat and awake in the morning in season for your appointment."[9]

The coming of the steamer in 1815 wrought such basic changes that it
might be said to have ended the first era in the urban history of the west.
The watershed might be fixed a little earlier or later, but this technological
innovation altered all the conditions of transmontane development . . .

Notes

1. S. Jones, *Pittsburgh in the Year Eighteen Hundred and Twenty Six* (Pittsburgh, 1826), 26. For example, see *Liberty Hall* (Cincinnati), May 6, 1812; September 25, 1812; October 27, 1812; March 25, 1813.

2. W. S. Merrill, Diary, Oct. 16, 1820, MS, Merrill Collection (Historical and Philosophical Society of Ohio, Cincinnati).

3. In November 1812, the War Department sent $200,000 for the purchase of supplies in Cincinnati. J. Findlay to Office of Discount and Deposit, Pittsburgh, November 16, 1812, MS, Torrence Papers (H.P.S.O., Cincinnati).

4. J. F. Hopkins, *A History of the Hemp Industry in Kentucky* (Lexington, Kentucky, 1951), 153–54; *Niles' Register*, June 11, 1814.

5. D. Drake, *Natural and Statistical View of Cincinnati and the Miami Country* (Cincinnati, 1815), 142.

6. Drake, *Statistical View*, 150.

7. J. Hall, *The West: Its Commerce and Navigation* (Cincinnati, 1848), 10; M. Marestier, *Mémoires sur les bateaux à vapeur des Etats-Unis d'Amerique* (Paris, 1824), 9–10; M. Neville, "The Last of the Boatmen," in J. Hall, ed., *The Western Souvenir, A Christmas and New Year's Gift for 1829* (Cincinnati, 1828), 108.

8. Quoted in L. C. Hunter, *Steamboats on the Western Rivers: An Economic and Technological History* (Cambridge, Massachusetts, 1949), 4; 19.

9. Timothy Flint, *Recollections of the Last Ten Years* (Boston, 1826), 106; 108.

It Answers Well for a Village

FROM *Sugar Creek*

JOHN MACK FARAGHER

URING THE FIRST HALF of the nineteenth century speculators and promoters established thousands of towns across the Midwest, the line of white settlement extending northward to Minnesota and westward into Iowa and eastern Nebraska. Although some of these towns, like Chicago or Indianapolis, were destined for major urban status, most were doomed to the rank of rural village. Many settlements, such as Sugar Creek, Illinois, never survived the formative processes of community building. The fate of such settlements was often determined by their location (or not) on navigable bodies of water; during the period from 1830 to 1850 many towns (especially in Ohio) built their own artificial rivers in the form of canals, but they were rendered obsolete before the Civil War by the railroads. From the earliest days of settlement, newly arrived residents strove to establish reliable transportation systems to connect them to the outside world. From primitive wagon to stagecoach to steam-powered boats to railroads, the forces of the transportation revolution quickly changed the relationships between neighboring (and rival) towns as well as between towns and the emerging midwestern urban network.

This complex process is captured in the following selection taken from the award-winning study of Sugar Creek by the historian John Mack Faragher. As he points out, the forces of modernity and technology eradicated the once viable town of Sugar Creek; the nearby rival community of Wineman (renamed Auburn by the Illinois legislature) emerged the victor in the struggle for town survival when it attracted the main line of the Chicago and Alton Railroad. The earliest of settlers established themselves along the sluggish Sugar Creek in 1818, and by 1860 their children had ready access to goods shipped only a few days earlier from the East Coast.

о о о

In the spring of 1840, Daniel Wadsworth, a forty-year-old carpenter from Hallowell, Maine, rode the St. Louis Road to Sugar Creek. During the winter a carpenter could find little work in Maine, so, in keeping with his annual custom, Wadsworth had signed on as ship's carpenter on a Kennebec River schooner the previous fall and plied his trade in the Gulf Coast port of Mobile. Rather than returning by his usual coastal route, however, this year instead he bought a ticket on a northbound Mississippi steamboat so he could "see the elephant"—the American "Far West"—for himself. Wadsworth's old friend David Eastman, and his brother-in-law, George Eastman, had moved from Maine to Sangamon County with their wives and children, parents and siblings several years before, and the carpenter planned to visit with them for a few weeks before he returned east. Disembarking in Alton, Illinois, he caught the north-bound Springfield stage and two days later rattled into Sugar Creek, where he found the Eastmans living along the stage road in a newly laid out village called "Auburn," five or six dwellings clustered about a rough-cut public square of bluestem grass, on a slight knoll at the entrance to Drennan's Prairie.[1]

The Eastmans convinced Wadsworth that Auburn needed a skilled carpenter and offered to sell him good, cheap land. Almost on impulse he paid David Eastman sixty dollars out of his winter earnings for ten acres on the south side of the square and began to build a frame house of his own on the road near the Eastman dwellings. In late summer he left to fetch his family, and by mid-November, after three weeks of travel by ferry, railroad, canal boat, Ohio River stern-wheeler, and farm wagon, he returned with his wife, Margaret, daughter Emily, and son Moses. Margaret never knew what convinced her husband to migrate, although she told her daughter that his prolonged winter absences made it easier for him to leave the lifetime haunts and relations of Maine. His children remembered Daniel as a loving but unexpressive father; as granddaughter Mary Wadsworth Jones later wrote, although he rarely lost his temper or fell into bad humor, Daniel "always seemed a serious person," and "none of his children ever remembered seeing him laugh, though at times he engaged in a chuckle." Margaret told granddaughter Mary how her "heart failed her many times" during the first years in Illinois, "particularly when she saw her children suffering from chills and fever, as did all the settlers for years until the land was drained and cultivated," and often openly lamented "the beauty and security of the older community which she had left so far behind."

Auburn, Illinois, certainly was not Hallowell, Maine, but by comparison with life in the open countryside it seemed a bit of transplanted New England, and there in the house Daniel built on the stage road the Wadsworths spent the next half-century. Before the railroads introduced factory-milled pine lumber into central Illinois, Daniel made his living by building houses from hand-hewn oak and walnut cut from the creek's timber, and by selling cuttings from the russet, northern spy, early harvest, and other varieties of northeastern apples he raised in a small nursery on his place. Her children remembered Margaret making apple butter or soap in a large kettle over an open fire in the backyard, like any other farm wife, but always with one eye on the traffic along the road. In 1841 Daniel became postmaster of the third-class office in Auburn, a position he held for better than a decade. The counter and post boxes filled an entire wing of the family dwelling, turning it topsy-turvy with the comings and goings of Sugar Creek society, but both husband and wife preferred this busy round to the slower and lonelier life of the farm.

Auburn represented western land speculation as much as it did the traditions of village living. When Wadsworth's friends came to Illinois from Maine in 1830, David Eastman's aging father, Thomas, had capital to invest, and with sons Asa and George he bought into a milling business in Morgan County, west of Sangamon. In mid-decade his boys began to accumulate land along Sugar Creek, buying nearly eight hundred acres between them and concentrating their purchases in the prairie lands of township 13/6. On this land, in 1835, Asa and George surveyed and laid out a village, which their sister Hannah named for Auburn, Maine, a county seat near the Eastman family home. Next to the Sugar Creek tanyard David Eastman opened in 1836, Asa and George built a steam-powered flour mill, planning to export the produce of the rich Illinois soil.[2]

The Eastmans were participating in the unprecedented boom in western land sales that peaked in 1836 and 1837, when over thirty-eight million public acres of American congress land passed into private hands. Since most Sugar Creek land claims filed before 1835 were to timber or timber margin acreage, enormous tracts of prairie, used by the community for common grazing, remained on the market, and during the boom, land speculators staged what historian Paul Gates calls "a mass attack" upon these common lands. In these years the Springfield office did the biggest business in the state, issuing patents to over seven million acres. After 1835, prairie land accounted for 84 percent of Sugar Creek land claims.[3]

Several speculators tried to develop and sell town lots on these prairie plots. "As the settlers all want to get wood on their farms, they settle all around the borders of the prairie," one Illinois investor wrote, "& leave the center—which may be taken at government prices—& answers well for a village." In the 1830s western investors platted hundreds of these "paper villages," hoping to sell lots in towns yet unborn to tradesmen and merchants willing to take a risk. In Sangamon County alone, speculators laid out at least twelve villages from 1835 to 1838. Auburn was one.[4]

As capitalist ventures, however, these prairie villages proved disappointing. After several years of promotion, Auburn contained but a handful of residents. The Eastmans sold a number of lots, including several to William Swaney, who ran a roadside tavern and rented space to John Smith for his blacksmith shop on the ground level. Swaney frequently left his large family in Auburn when he traveled to Illinois River towns in his fancy two-horse carriage. Local gossips rumored that he was a professional gambler, and the neighborhood fairly buzzed with speculation when Swaney failed to return from a trip in 1843. In this case, rumor was close to truth, for after several weeks Mrs. Swaney learned that a disgruntled loser at the gaming tables had murdered her husband. At the estate auction held to dispose of Swaney's nearly $1,800 in accumulated debts, Smith bought the shop and tavern and Thomas Black a parcel of outlying timberland, but in the absence of any great demand, the Eastmans had to reclaim Swaney's other Auburn properties. That same year Daniel Wadsworth's friend David Eastman died, and for lack of outside interest, Asa Eastman had to buy up his brother's town lots at the estate sale.[5]

From a developer's point of view, then, the Eastman project in Auburn failed. Unable to drum up sufficient business among subsistence-oriented Sugar Creek farmers, Asa and George closed their steam mill in 1841 and moved the machinery to Springfield, where their families soon joined them. In Springfield the Eastmans did a much better business, and by the 1860s Asa had acquired a reputation as the "grain and flour king" of central Illinois. But the Eastman removal left the village an even smaller place, with only six households headed by a carpenter, a joiner, a blacksmith, and three farmers. Although mobility changed several village faces over the next few years, the population in 1850 remained unchanged from ten years before.[6]

If the failure of Auburn to fulfill the speculative hopes of its founders was commonplace, however, the village's survival into the forties was not. Most Sangamon County "paper villages" faded quickly into obscurity. The village of "Mazeppa," for example, platted in the prairie, east of Sugar Camp, boasted a militia ground and a "grocery" that dispensed its own brand of corn whiskey; but by 1840 the village, in Edgar Lee Masters' phrase, "as a poplar tree, had thrived / And aged too soon, and died." "Mazeppa never had a post office," a later chronicler wrote, "and of course could not flourish, for what place without mail privileges could ever exist?" There could be no mail without a mail stage, no mail stage without a post road. In short, Auburn struggled along because it had succeeded John Drennan's Stage Stop as the Sugar Creek embarcation on the stage line from St. Louis to Springfield.[7]

A stage company had begun fortnightly "wagon" service from St. Louis to Springfield in 1822, and in 1834 it upgraded the line with twice-weekly Concord coaches. These four-horse stages carried the mail to Springfield where settlers could pick it up, a great inconvenience to people living in Sugar Creek, fifteen to twenty miles of poor roads south. In 1827 another line opened the "Macoupin Point Road," which forded Sugar Creek a few miles north of its headwaters, forging a trace through the margin of the westside timber, past Crow's Mill, the meeting and schoolhouse, and up the east side of Drennan's Prairie to Drennan's stage stand, where drivers changed teams and dropped the Sugar Creek mail. The Macoupin Point Road reinforced factors of geography, community, and kinship, placing Drennan Prairie at the center of Sugar Creek life.[8]

Families at The Sources, however, remained eight to ten miles from their mail, and as an inducement to a revised stage route, Jacob Rauch, Micajah Organ, Samuel McElvain, and others of the southernmost neighborhood built a fifty-foot oak span across the creek at Rauch's mill in 1838. From this bridge north in the spring of 1839, the stage line blazed a new road directly across the prairies, cutting at least six miles off the old route to Springfield and replacing Drennan's stage stand with Auburn as the location of the Sugar Creek post office. Auburn was small, a capitalistic failure, but the new Alton-to-Springfield road kept the town busy serving the needs of the surrounding countryside. By 1840, William Caldwell, supervisor of the road district, reported to the county commissioners that "the mail stage crosses the Bridge every day in the year except Sundays," and in 1848 postmaster Wadsworth complained to his congressman, Abraham Lincoln, that since he and Margaret had to "get up twice every night or *fourteen times a week*" to receive the mail, the government ought to increase his salary.[9]

More and more, as one incident from Auburn's early history suggests, the concerns of the Sugar Creek community focused on this road. One winter evening in 1842, as the stage driver was delivering the Sugar Creek mail to postmaster Wadsworth, a passenger discovered that his trunk, filled with clothing, money, and fine cigars, had been stolen from the rear baggage compartment of the coach. Rumors about this first "road crime" in Sugar Creek flew across the countryside, but there were no clues as to the identity of the thief. Then, as Moses Wadsworth remembered it, "John Kennedy, a young man of about eighteen, living with his parents on the Harlan place, was very liberal with a lot of fragrant Havanas at the Cumberland Church the next Sunday, dividing them around among the irreverent boys who made a practice of going punctually to meeting and remaining out of doors to discuss horseflesh during service." When Daniel caught Moses with a cigar, the boy told where he had gotten it, and the postmaster suddenly recalled the Kennedy boy had been hanging around the post office the afternoon of the robbery, asking questions about the stage's arrival. Confronted with this circumstantial evidence, Kennedy finally confessed to cutting the trunk from the rest of the baggage as the stage slowly forded Panther Creek, near his father's cabin, and he then led a posse of men to a corn shock where he had cached his booty. Constable James Easley took the culprit into custody, but Kennedy somehow managed to escape, stole a horse, and fled south down the road to St. Louis and out of Sugar Creek history. All this created "great excitement throughout the country," Moses wrote. The road and its stories had become the biggest thing about Sugar Creek.[10]

In the competition for transportation links, the success of one site often marked the demise of another. When the stage company abandoned the Macoupin Point line and dropped Drennan's as a stage stop in 1839, for example, men from Drennan's Prairie and farms down the western margin of Sugar Creek timber petitioned the county to declare the old stage route a "county road" so that they might maintain it with their roadwork. The commissioners quickly agreed. This petition was the first of many efforts on the part of citizens over the next twenty years to alter and improve not only the arterial roadways but also the lanes and cartpaths that linked the farms of the community together. Increasingly, during the 1840s and 1850s, farm owners oriented their work to the production of agricultural commodities, and Sangamo men appeared to be more and more convinced that transportation development offered the best way to break into the market economy. The agitation for better transportation soon turned to the prospect for railroads.[11]

Early promoters of transportation development believed, as one booster wrote in 1823, that the Sangamon River could, "at a trifling expense, be made navigable for nearly 200 miles," but these hopes expired after the steamboat *Talisman* nearly foundered on the river's sandbars and shallows in 1832. In the early 1840s, driven by a passion for "internal improvements," the state invested nearly a million dollars in a rail line from Springfield to the Illinois River, but poor engineering, shoddy construction, and a lack of demand from farmers still committed to self-sufficiency doomed the line. By the mid-forties the state had auctioned it for scrap. But the success of railroads elsewhere demanded that they be introduced into Illinois, and in 1847 the state chartered the "Alton and Sangamon Rail Road Company" to build a line from American Bottom to Springfield, following the same general route that Pulliam had taken in 1817.[12]

Everyone knew that the route selected would greatly affect the future of Sugar Creek, just as the course of the stage road had. No topological barriers prevented the line from passing through Auburn, and most residents expected that it would bring great things to the fledgling village. In early 1851 the Alton and Sangamon Company made the long-awaited announcement of its route: they would build on the west side of the creek, paralleling the stage road south to Macoupin County, but would bypass Auburn to the east by a mile. Disappointed but not yet defeated, village men began "a vigorous and persistent effort" to convince the company to locate a water tank and station on the line due east of the village, expecting that Auburn could eventually incorporate the intervening territory. It soon became clear, however, that the Alton and Sangamon had cut a deal with local landowner Phillip Wineman, who had purchased nearly two hundred acres a mile south of Auburn and had offered the railroad donations of land in the midst of a new paper village he platted there and named after himself.

A "long and fierce" struggle ensued between community factions aligned with either Wineman and his new town or with the Eastmans and Auburn. "It seemed a pity, " Moses Wadsworth later wrote, "that so pretty a site as that of the old town should be abandoned for so unpromising a one as the north-east quarter of section 10 then appeared—much of it a mere swamp—but railroad corporations possess no bowels of compassion, the practical more than the beautiful being their object." The first cars rumbling into Wineman station on September 10, 1852, delivered a death sentence for the village of Auburn. The cars on the Chicago and Alton Railroad, as the company had renamed its line, averaged better than thirty miles per hour, cutting the trip between the Mississippi and Springfield from over two days to under twelve hours, and the accompanying telegraph line that ran along the railroad right of way suddenly brought Sugar Creek into almost instant communication with the eastern United States. Within a year the stage line closed its operations and the federal government relocated the post office in Wineman. Daniel Wadsworth lost his position, Auburn lost its purpose. The next year Asa Eastman bought up the lots of all those who wished to sell and sold the town site to farmer Madison Curvey, who plowed up blocks, public square, and all, and planted corn in their place. Although the Wadsworths stubbornly remained in their house, most residents yielded to the inevitable and relocated south, many dragging the buildings Wadsworth had built with them on ox-drawn sledges, setting them up on lots purchased from Wineman. The stage road had made the village of Auburn. The railroad unmade it.[13]

The railroad changed other things along Sugar Creek. The Springfield papers regularly reported stock mangled by engines, derailed cars along the line, and sometimes the deaths of engineers and firemen; in July 1855, the five-year-old daughter of a prairie farmer was run down and killed as she was crossing the tracks south of Chatham. The average engine on the line hauled twenty cars, with space for fifty to one hundred passengers, bringing new and unfamiliar faces into town. Even more important, the construction and maintenance of the road introduced groups of Irish workmen into the community. In April 1851, as they worked on the grade north of old Auburn, the laborers went out on strike for better wages. James Irwin, an eighteen-year-old Irish immigrant, took work on the Harlan place during the strike and stayed on as a tenant farmer. Three years later he married Silas Harlan's fourteen-year-old daughter. After Rachel Harlan Irwin came into her inheritance, Harlan's Grove gradually became "Irwin's Grove" in deference to the owner, who continued to allow its use as a place for community assembly, opening it "for any national, religious, or social gathering."[14]

During the 1850s the attention of the Sugar Creek countryside focused on the entrepôt of Wineman where, by 1860, nearly two hundred and fifty people lived in over forty households, transacting business in more than twenty establishments, including five grocery and general stores, two farm implement establishments, a furniture store, two hotels, and two saloons. Increased traffic on the road during the Civil War added more residents and businesses, and by 1866 the town's population had grown to three hundred and fifty. Families from the surrounding countryside made regular trips to the town, or to the nearby railroad villages of Chatham or Lowder five miles north and five miles southwest, respectively. By the early 1870s, no Sugar Creek farmer was farther than five miles from a freight depot.[15]

By offering an outlet for farm products, by importing commodities from Michigan pine lumber to Long Island oysters, and by linking farmers to the outside world by iron rails and electrified steel wires, the railroad ushered in a new reality with profound implications for Sugar Creek. In 1865 the Illinois legislature incorporated Wineman's substantial town on the railroad. But in a departing gesture to the failed village on the stage road, the legislators rejected the name Wineman and christened the new town Auburn—much to Phil Wineman's chagrin and Daniel Wadsworth's delight. After the Civil War, no one spoke any longer of the "Sugar Creek" community, but only of "Auburn," the railroad town, and its surrounding countryside.[16]

NOTES

1. This account of the Wadsworths is drawn from [Mary Wadsworth Jones,] "Moses Wadsworth and Hannah Stevens. Their Ancestral Lines and Their Descendants," (typescript, 1941, Illinois State Historical Society, Springfield); Moses G. Wadsworth, "Auburn," in *Sangamon County Gazetteer* (Springfield: John C. W. Bailey, 1866), 13–16; Wadsworth, "The Sugar Creek Country in 1840" (typescript, 1880, Illinois State Historical Society); Wadsworth, "Auburn and Vicinity Forty Years Ago," in *History of Sangamon County, Illinois: Together with Sketches of Its Cities, Villages and Townships, Educational, Religious, Civil, Military, and Political History; Portraits of Prominent Persons, and Biographies of Representative Citizens* (Chicago: Inter-State Publishing Company, 1881), 174–79, 750–52; "Moses Goodwin Wadsworth" (typescript, 1905, Illinois State Historical Society); "Wadsworth" (vertical file, Illinois State Historical Society).

2. John Carrol Power, assisted by Mrs. S. A. Power, *History of the Early Settlers of Sangamon County, Illinois: "Centennial Record"* (Springfield: Edwin A. Wilson, 1876), 276–77; Joseph Wallace, *Past and Present of the City of Springfield and Sangamon County*, 2 vols. (Chicago: S. J. Clarke, 1904), 823–24; *Early Federal Land Sales Within the Present Boundaries of Sangamon County, Illinois* (Springfield: Sangamon County Genealogical Society, 1978), 4; 1838 tax list in "Taxable Lists for Sangamon County, 1832–1838" (microfilm, Illinois State Archives, Springfield, reel #30/157); Wadsworth, "The Sugar Creek Country in 1840," 6–7.

3. R. Carlyle Buley, *The Old Northwest: Pioneer Period, 1815–1840*, 2 vols. (Bloomington: Indiana University Press, 1951), 2:147; Paul Wallace Gates, *Landlords*

and Tenants on the Prairie Frontier (Ithaca: Cornell University Press, 1973), 56, 113–14, 149; Theodore C. Pease, *Frontier State, 1818–1848* (Springfield: Illinois Centennial Commission, 1918), 175–77; *Illinois State Register* (Springfield), April 29, 1836; Horace Q. Waggoner, "The Illinois Prairies Purchasing Pattern" (typescript, n.d., Sangamon State University Archives, Springfield); *Early Federal Land Sales.*

4. Illinois investor, quoted in Douglas R. McManis, *The Initial Evaluation and Utilization of the Illinois Prairies, 1815–1840* (Chicago: University of Chicago Press, 1964), 87; *History of Sangamon County,* 750, 792, 830, 854, 864, 875–76, 914, 920, 932, 940, 963, 1047.

5. *History of Sangamon County,* 751; William Swaney and David Eastman documents, in Sangamon County, Office of Circuit Court, Case Files, Boxes 13 and 14.

6. Wadsworth, "The Sugar Creek Country in 1840," 7; Wallace, *Past and Present,* 283; manuscript schedules of population census for Sangamon County, 1840, reprinted in *Federal Census, 1840, Sangamon County Illinois,* comp. Ruth Z. Marko (Springfield: Sangamon County Genealogical Society, 1980), 40.

7. Edgar Lee Masters, *The Sangamon* (New York: Farrar and Rinehart, 1942), 191; *History of Sangamon County,* 792.

8. Sangamon County Commissioners' Court, Minutes, A:3–9; Pease, *Frontier State,* 10; John Leslie Tevebaugh, "Frontier Mail: Illinois, 1800–1830" (M.A. thesis, University of Illinois, 1952), 83, 101; *Sangamon Journal* (Springfield), January 26 and May 18, 1833, and January 11, 1834; John Mason Peck, *A Guide for Emigrants, Containing Sketches of Illinois, Missouri, and the Adjacent Parts* (Boston: Lincoln and Edmands, 1831), 298.

9. John Mason Peck, *The Traveller's Directory for Illinois* (New York: Colton, 1939), 207–208; Wadsworth, "The Sugar Creek Country in 1840," 6; *History of Sangamon County,* 177; "William Caldwell, Report," in Sangamon County Commissioners' Court, Proceedings Files, Box 2; Daniel Wadsworth to Abraham Lincoln, January 25, 1848, quoted in Don E. Fehrenbacher, "The Post Office in Illinois Politics," *Journal of the Illinois State Historical Society* 46 (1953), 62n.

10. *History of Sangamon County,* 178–79; manuscript schedules of population census for Sangamon County, 1840.

11. Road petition, 1838, Sangamon County Commissioners' Court, Proceedings Files, Box 2.

12. *Beck's Gazetteer of Illinois and Missouri* (1823), quoted in Newton Bateman and Paul Selby, eds., *Historical Encyclopedia of Illinois and History of Sangamon County,* 2 vols. (Chicago: Munsell Publishing Company, 1912), 2:617; Paul Angle, *"Here I Have Lived": A History of Lincoln's Springfield, 1821–1865* (New Brunswick, New Jersey: Rutgers University Press, 1935) 54–55, 144–48; *Charter of the Chicago and Mississippi Rail Road Company, Originally Incorporated by the Name of the Alton and Sangamon Railroad Company* (New York: William C. Bryant & Co., 1854), 3, 11; *History of Sangamon County,* 751–52.

13. *History of Sangamon County,* 751–52; Wadsworth, "The Sugar Creek Country in 1840," 6; *Illinois Daily Journal* (Springfield), January 19, 1854.

14. For typical accidents see: *Illinois Daily Journal,* July 19 and November 1, 1853, June 28, 1854, and August 25, 1855; the Chatham girl's death was reported on July 10, 1855; *Daily State Register* (Springfield), October 17 and November 9, 1853, January 30, 1855. On Irwin see *History of Sangamon County,* 839–40.

15. Wadsworth, "Auburn," 14; manuscript schedules of population census for Sangamon County, 1860, reprinted in *Federal Census, 1860, Sangamon County, Illinois* (Springfield: Sangamon County Genealogical Society, 1982).

16. *History of Sangamon County,* 1029; *Private Laws of the State of Illinois,* 2 vols. (Springfield: Boke and Phillips, 1865), 2:362–69.

The Autobiography of Mark Twain

Selections

THE MOST FAMOUS AMERICAN AUTHOR to come out of the Midwest village is probably the most famous writer to come out of America: Mark Twain. Twain's talents and careers were enormous and varied: he was a printer, a riverboat captain, a journalist, an author; he lived in Missouri, Louisiana, Nevada, California, Connecticut, Europe. The range of his writing extends across continental America to Hawaii and Europe and back in time to the Middle Ages. However, Twain is best remembered for a pair of books set in his fictionalized hometown of Hannibal, Missouri: *The Adventures of Tom Sawyer* and *Adventures of Huckleberry Finn*.

These works are an odd set of bookends. *Tom Sawyer* is a romantic hymn to the endless summer of childhood, a collection of dreams, pranks, adventures, and childhood romances which ends with Tom and Huck and Becky safe, sound, and wealthy in the snug confines of Happy Village. "I'll stick to the widder [Widow Douglas, Huck's guardian] till I rot," Huck Finn tells Tom Sawyer at the book's conclusion, "I reckon she'll be proud she snaked me in out of the wet." *Huck Finn*, on the other hand, presents a much darker picture of the Midwest village, of human nature, and of civilization; it ends with the famous lines that are Huck's indictment of small-town America: "But I reckon I got to light out for the Territory ahead of the rest, because Aunt Sally she's going to adopt me and sivilize me and I can't stand it. I been there before." Episodes of both books—Tom Sawyer trading the "privilege" of white-washing a fence for an apple, a kite, a dead rat, a tin soldier, and other treasures; the Duke and Dauphin playing "The Royal Nonesuch" or bilking Peter Wilks's heirs out of their inheritance—have become staples of high school American literature classes.

But Twain mined his small-town boyhood for material in other books, including his rather positive description of a string of Mississippi River towns in *Life on the Mississippi* ("From St. Louis northward there are all the enlivening signs of the presence of active, energetic, intelligent, prosperous, practical nineteenth-century populations. The people don't dream; they work") and his much more cynical "The Man That Corrupted Hadleyburg" ("Go, and reform—or, mark my words—some day, for your sins, you will die and go to hell or Hadleyburg—TRY AND MAKE IT THE FORMER"). Some-

where in between are Twain's last words on his boyhood villages of Florida
and Hannibal, Missouri, dictated to Albert Bigelow Paine for what became
his *Autobiography*. Twain transects time easily and carelessly in these reminiscences, but one senses that he is being entirely honest. His portraits of
Florida and Hannibal are valuable descriptions of the earliest frontier villages in their initial stages of development.

o o o

I was born the 30th of November, 1835, in the almost invisible village of
Florida, Monroe County, Missouri. My parents removed to Missouri in the
early 'thirties; I do not remember just when, for I was not born then and
cared nothing for such things. It was a long journey in those days and must
have been a rough and tiresome one. The village contained a hundred people and I increased the population by one per cent. It is more than many of
the best men in history could have done for a town. It may not be modest
in me to refer to this but it is true. There is no record of a person doing as
much—not even Shakespeare. But I did it for Florida and it shows that I
could have done it for any place—even London, I suppose.

Recently some one in Missouri has sent me a picture of the house I was
born in. Heretofore I have always stated that it was a palace but I shall be
more guarded now.

The village had two streets, each a couple of hundred yards long; the rest
of the avenues mere lanes, with railfences and cornfields on either side.
Both the streets and the lanes were paved with the same material—tough
black mud in wet times, deep dust in dry.

Most of the houses were of logs—all of them, indeed, except three or
four; these latter were frame ones. There were none of brick and none of
stone. There was a log church, with a puncheon floor and slab benches. A
puncheon floor is made of logs whose upper surfaces have been chipped flat
with the adz. The cracks between the logs were not filled; there was no carpet; consequently, if you dropped anything smaller than a peach it was likely
to go through. The church was perched upon short sections of logs, which
elevated it two or three feet from the ground. Hogs slept under there, and
whenever the dogs got after them during services the minister had to wait
till the disturbance was over. In winter there was always a refreshing breeze
up through the puncheon floor; in summer there were fleas enough for all.

A slab bench is made of the outside cut of a saw-log, with the bark side
down; it is supported on four sticks driven into auger holes at the ends; it
has no back and no cushions. The church was twilighted with yellow tallow
candles in tin sconces hung against the walls. Week days, the church was a
schoolhouse.

There were two stores in the village. My uncle, John A. Quarles, was proprietor of one of them. It was a very small establishment, with a few rolls of "bit" calicoes on half a dozen shelves; a few barrels of salt mackerel, coffee and New Orleans sugar behind the counter; stacks of brooms, shovels, axes, hoes, rakes and such things here and there; a lot of cheap hats, bonnets and tinware strung on strings and suspended from the walls; and at the other end of the room was another counter with bags of shot on it, a cheese or two and a keg of powder; in front of it a row of nail kegs and a few pigs of lead, and behind it a barrel or two of New Orleans molasses and native corn whisky on tap. If a boy bought five or ten cents' worth of anything he was entitled to half a handful of sugar from the barrel; if a woman bought a few yards of calico she was entitled to a spool of thread in addition to the usual gratis "trimmin's"; if a man bought a trifle he was at liberty to draw and swallow as big a drink of whisky as he wanted.

Everything was cheap: apples, peaches, sweet potatoes, Irish potatoes and corn, ten cents a bushel; chickens, ten cents apiece; butter, six cents a pound; eggs, three cents a dozen; coffee and sugar, five cents a pound; whisky, ten cents a gallon. I do not know how prices are out there in interior Missouri now, but I know what they are here in Hartford, Connecticut.[1] To wit: apples, three dollars a bushel; peaches, five dollars; Irish potatoes (choice Bermudas), five dollars; chickens, a dollar to a dollar and a half apiece, according to weight; butter, forty-five to sixty cents a pound; eggs, fifty to sixty cents a dozen; coffee, forty-five cents a pound; native whisky, four or five dollars a gallon, I believe, but I can only be certain concerning the sort which I use myself, which is Scotch and costs ten dollars a gallon when you take two gallons—more when you take less.

Thirty to forty years ago, out yonder in Missouri, the ordinary cigar cost thirty cents a hundred, but most people did not try to afford them, since smoking a pipe cost nothing in that tobacco-growing country. Connecticut is also given up to tobacco raising, today, yet we pay ten dollars a hundred for Connecticut cigars and fifteen to twenty-five dollars a hundred for the imported article.

In the small town of Hannibal, Missouri, when I was a boy everybody was poor but didn't know it; and everybody was comfortable and did know it. And there were grades of society—people of good family, people of unclassified family, people of no family. Everybody knew everybody and was affable to everybody and nobody put on any visible airs; yet the class lines were quite clearly drawn and the familiar social life of each class was restricted to that class. It was a little democracy which was full of liberty, equality and Fourth of July, and sincerely so, too; yet you perceived that the aristocratic taint was there. It was there and nobody found fault with the fact or ever stopped to reflect that its presence was an inconsistency.

Chapter 8

My school days began when I was four years and a half old. There were no
public schools in Missouri in those early days but there were two private
schools—terms twenty-five cents per week per pupil and collect it if you
can. Mrs. Horr taught the children in a small log house at the southern end
of Main Street. Mr. Sam Cross taught the young people of larger growth in
a frame schoolhouse on the hill. I was sent to Mrs. Horr's school and I remember my first day in that little log house with perfect clearness, after
these sixty-five years and upwards[2]—at least I remember an episode of that
first day. I broke one of the rules and was warned not to do it again and was
told that the penalty for a second breach was a whipping. I presently broke
the rule again and Mrs. Horr told me to go out and find a switch and fetch
it. I was glad she appointed me, for I believed I could select a switch suitable
to the occasion with more judiciousness than anybody else.

In the mud I found a cooper's shaving of the old-time pattern, oak, two
inches broad, a quarter of an inch thick, and rising in a shallow curve at one
end. There were nice new shavings of the same breed close by but I took this
one, although it was rotten. I carried it to Mrs. Horr, presented it and stood
before her in an attitude of meekness and resignation which seemed to me
calculated to win favor and sympathy, but it did not happen. She divided
a long look of strong disapprobation equally between me and the shaving;
then she called me by my entire name, Samuel Langhorne Clemens—
probably the first time I had ever heard it all strung together in one procession—and said she was ashamed of me. I was to learn later that when a
teacher calls a boy by his entire name it means trouble. She said she would
try and appoint a boy with a better judgment than mine in the matter of
switches, and it saddens me yet to remember how many faces lighted up
with the hope of getting that appointment. Jim Dunlap got it and when he
returned with the switch of his choice I recognized that he was an expert.

Mrs. Horr was a New England lady of middle age with New England
ways and principles and she always opened school with prayer and a chapter from the New Testament; also she explained the chapter with a brief
talk. In one of these talks she dwelt upon the text, "Ask and ye shall receive," and said that whosoever prayed for a thing with earnestness and
strong desire need not doubt that his prayer would be answered.

I was so forcibly struck by this information and so gratified by the opportunities which it offered that this was probably the first time I had heard
of it. I thought I would give it a trial. I believed in Mrs. Horr thoroughly and
I had no doubts as to the result. I prayed for gingerbread. Margaret Koone-
man, who was the baker's daughter, brought a slab of gingerbread to school
every morning; she had always kept it out of sight before but when I finished
my prayer and glanced up, there it was in easy reach and she was looking the

other way. In all my life I believe I never enjoyed an answer to prayer more than I enjoyed that one; and I was a convert, too. I had no end of wants and they had always remained unsatisfied up to that time, but I meant to supply them and extend them now that I had found out how to do it.

But this dream was like almost all the other dreams we indulge in in life, there was nothing in it. I did as much praying during the next two or three days as any one in that town, I suppose, and I was very sincere and earnest about it too, but nothing came of it. I found that not even the most powerful prayer was competent to lift that gingerbread again, and I came to the conclusion that if a person remains faithful to his gingerbread and keeps his eye on it he need not trouble himself about your prayers.

Something about my conduct and bearing troubled my mother and she took me aside and questioned me concerning it with much solicitude. I was reluctant to reveal to her the change that had come over me, for it would grieve me to distress her kind heart, but at last I confessed, with many tears, that I had ceased to be a Christian. She was heartbroken and asked me why.

I said it was because I had found out that I was a Christian for revenue only and I could not bear the thought of that, it was so ignoble.

She gathered me to her breast and comforted me. I had gathered from what she said that if I would continue in that condition I would never be lonesome.

Chapter 10

In Hannibal when I was about fifteen I was for a short time a Cadet of Temperance, an organization which probably covered the whole United States during as much as a year—possibly even longer. It consisted in a pledge to refrain, during membership, from the use of tobacco; I mean it consisted partly in that pledge and partly in a red merino sash, but the red merino sash was the main part. The boys joined in order to be privileged to wear it—the pledge part of the matter was of no consequence. It was so small in importance that, contrasted with the sash, it was in effect nonexistent. The organization was weak and impermanent because there were not enough holidays to support it. We could turn out and march and show the red sashes on May Day with the Sunday schools and on the Fourth of July with the Sunday schools, the independent fire company and the militia company. But you can't keep a juvenile moral institution alive on two displays of its sash per year. As a private I could not have held out beyond one procession but I was Illustrious Grand Worthy Secretary and Royal Inside Sentinel and had the privilege of inventing the passwords and of wearing a rosette on my sash. Under these conditions I was enabled to remain steadfast until I had gathered the glory of two displays—May Day and the Fourth of July. Then I resigned straightway and straightway left the lodge.

I had not smoked for three full months and no words can adequately describe the smoke appetite that was consuming me. I had been a smoker from my ninth year—a private one during the first two years but a public one after that—that is to say, after my father's death. I was smoking and utterly happy before I was thirty steps from the lodge door. I do not now know what the brand of the cigar was. It was probably not choice, or the previous smoker would not have thrown it away so soon. But I realized that it was the best cigar that was ever made. The previous smoker would have thought the same if he had been without a smoke for three months. I smoked that stub without shame. I could not do it now without shame because now I am more refined than I was then. But I would smoke it just the same. I know myself and I know the human race well enough to know that.

In those days the native cigar was so cheap that a person who could afford anything could afford cigars. Mr. Garth had a great tobacco factory and he also had a small shop in the village for the retail sale of his products. He had one brand of cigars which even poverty itself was able to buy. He had had these in stock a good many years and although they looked well enough on the outside, their insides had decayed to dust and would fly out like a puff of vapor when they were broken in two. This brand was very popular on account of its extreme cheapness. Mr. Garth had other brands which were cheap and some that were bad, but the supremacy over them enjoyed by this brand was indicated by its name. It was called "Garth's damnedest." We used to trade old newspapers (exchanges) for that brand.

There was another shop in the village where the conditions were friendly to penniless boys. It was kept by a lonely and melancholy little hunchback and we could always get a supply of cigars by fetching a bucket of water for him from the village pump, whether he needed water or not. One day we found him asleep in his chair—a custom of his—and we waited patiently for him to wake up, which was a custom of ours. But he slept so long this time that at last our patience was exhausted and we tried to wake him—but he was dead. I remember the shock of it yet.

In my early manhood and in middle life, I used to vex myself with reforms every now and then. And I never had occasion to regret these divergencies for, whether the resulting deprivations were long or short, the rewarding pleasure which I got out of the vice when I returned to it always paid me for all that it cost.

NOTES

1. Written in 1877.   2. Written in 1906.

A Private Lesson from a Bulldog

FROM *The Hoosier School-Master*

I N ONE CHAPTER OF *Main Street*, Sinclair Lewis has his heroine Carol Kennicott survey small-town American literature. She discovers "only two traditions of the American small town. The first tradition, repeated in scores of magazines every month, is that the American village remains the one sure abode of friendship, honesty, and clean sweet marriageable girls. . . . The other tradition is that the significant features of all villages are whiskers, iron dogs upon lawns, gold bricks, checkers, jars of gilded cat-tails, and shrewd comic old men who are known as 'hicks' and ejaculate 'Wall I swain.' This altogether admirable tradition rules the vaudeville stage, facetious illustrators, and newspaper humor, but out of actual life it passed forty years ago."

Edward Eggleston's *The Hoosier School-Master: A Story of Backwoods Life in Indiana* was published nearly a half-century before *Main Street*. It is largely responsible for that second literary tradition. Eggleston was not the first Midwest author to set a story in a specific, recognizable locale and populate it with individuals who spoke a specific, recognizable language. However, he antedated Midwest realists Mark Twain and Hamlin Garland by several years, and publication of *The Hoosier School-Master* in 1871 is generally held to have inaugurated the realist period in midwestern and American literature.

Considerable romantic gloss remains in his portrait of simple-but-shrewd country folk and in the inspirational lessons taught by the book's first chapter, and Eggleston's own narration is far from the language of spoken (Indiana) English. The book was, after all, serialized in the magazine *Hearth and Home* before publication as a book. However, Eggleston writes of life as he knew it and heard it (the story is based on his brother's experience while teaching at a school near Madison, Indiana), and he presents his characters with sympathy and understanding. They speak in their own almost illiterate dialect. And life is not painted in soft pastels. Eggleston's description of small-town Indiana schools in 1871 is hard and unflattering—realistic. It sounds very much like a passage written by one Colin Goodykoontz, quoted by William Gass in his story "In the Heart of the Heart of the Country": "Ignorance and her squalid brood. A universal dearth

of intellect. Total abstinence from literature is very generally practiced. . . ."
Eggleston gave his readers small-town Indiana without the gloss.

---

o o o

"Want to be a school-master, do you? You? Well, what would *you* do in Flat
Crick deestrick, *I'd* like to know? Why, the boys have driv off the last two,
and licked the one afore them like blazes. You might teach a summer
school, when nothin' but children come. But I 'low it takes a right smart
man to be school-master in Flat Crick in the winter. They'd pitch you out
of doors, sonny, neck and heels, afore Christmas."

The young man, who had walked ten miles to get the school in this district, and who had been mentally reviewing his learning at every step he
took, trembling lest the committee should find that he did not know
enough, was not a little taken aback at this greeting from "old Jack Means,"
who was the first trustee that he lighted on. The impression made by these
ominous remarks was emphasized by the glances which he received from
Jack Means's two sons. The older one eyed him from the top of his brawny
shoulders with that amiable look which a big dog turns on a little one before shaking him. Ralph Hartsook had never thought of being measured by
the standard of muscle. This notion of beating education into young savages in spite of themselves dashed his ardor.

He had walked right to where Jack Means was at work shaving shingles
in his own front yard. While Mr. Means was not making the speech which
we have set down above, and punctuating it with expectorations, a large
brindle bulldog had been sniffing at Ralph's heels, and a girl in a new
linsey-woolsey dress, standing by the door, had nearly giggled her head off
at the delightful prospect of seeing a new school-teacher eaten up by the
ferocious brute.

The disheartening words of the old man, the immense muscles of the
young man who was to be his rebellious pupil, the jaws of the ugly bulldog,
and the heartless giggle of the girl, gave Ralph a delightful sense of having
precipitated himself into a den of wild beasts. Faint with weariness and discouragement, and shivering with fear, he sat down on a wheelbarrow.

"You, Bull!" said the old man to the dog, which was showing more and
more a disposition to make a meal of the incipient pedagogue, "you, Bull! git
aout, you pup!" The dog walked sullenly off, but not until he had given Ralph
a look full of promise of what he meant to do when he got a good chance.
Ralph wished himself back in the village of Lewisburg, whence he had come.

"You see," continued Mr. Means, spitting in a meditative sort of a way,
"you see, we a'n't none of your saft sort in these diggin's. It takes a *man* to
boss this deestrick. Howsumdever, ef you think you kin trust your hide in

Flat Crick school-house I ha'n't got no 'bjection. But ef you git licked, don't come on us. Flat Crick don't pay no 'nsurance, you bet! Any other trustees? Wal, yes. But as I pay the most taxes, t'others jist let me run the thing. You can begin right off a Monday. They a'n't been no other applications. You see, it takes grit to apply for this school. The last master had a black eye for a month. But, as I wuz sayin', you can jist roll up and wade in. I 'low you've got spunk, maybe, and that goes for a heap sight more'n sinnoo with boys. Walk in, and stay over Sunday with me. You'll hev' to board roun', and I guess you better begin here."

Ralph did not go in, but sat out on the wheelbarrow, watching the old man shave shingles, while the boys split the blocks and chopped wood. Bull smelled of the new-comer again in an ugly way, and got a good kick from the older son for his pains. But out of one of his red eyes the dog warned the young school-master that *he* should yet suffer for all kicks received on his account.

"Ef Bull once takes a holt, heaven and yarth can't make him let go," said the older son to Ralph, by way of comfort.

It was well for Ralph that he began to "board roun'" by stopping at Mr. Means's. Ralph felt that Flat Creek was what he needed. He had lived a bookish life; but here was his lesson in the art of managing people, for he who can manage the untamed and strapping youths of a winter school in Hoopole County has gone far toward learning one of the hardest of lessons. And in Ralph's time, things were worse than they are now. The older son of Mr. Means was called Bud Means. What his real name was, Ralph could not find out, for in many of these families the nickname of "Bud" given to the oldest boy, and that of "Sis," which is the birthright of the oldest girl, completely bury the proper Christian name. Ralph saw his first strategic point, which was to capture Bud Means.

After supper, the boys began to get ready for something. Bull stuck up his ears in a dignified way, and the three or four yellow curs who were Bull's satellites yelped delightedly and discordantly.

"Bill," said Bud Means to his brother, "ax the master ef he'd like to hunt coons. I'd like to take the starch out uv the stuck-up feller."

"'Nough said," was Bill's reply.

"You durn't do it," said Bud.

"I don't take no sech a dare," returned Bill, and walked down to the gate, by which Ralph stood watching the stars come out, and half wishing he had never seen Flat Creek.

"I say, mister," began Bill, "mister, they's a coon what's been a eatin' our chickens lately, and we're goin' to try to ketch the varmint. You wouldn't like to take a coon hunt nor nothin', would you?"

"Why, yes," said Ralph, "there's nothing I should like better, if I could only be sure Bull wouldn't mistake me for the coon."

And so, as a matter of policy, Ralph dragged his tired legs eight or ten miles, on hill and in hollow, after Bud, and Bill, and Bull, and the coon. But the raccoon climbed a tree. The boys got into a quarrel about whose business it was to have brought the axe, and who was to blame that the tree could not be felled. Now, if there was anything Ralph's muscles were good for, it was climbing. So, asking Bud to give him a start, he soon reached the limb above the one on which the raccoon was. Ralph did not know how ugly a customer a raccoon can be, and so got credit for more courage than he had. With much peril to his legs from the raccoon's teeth, he succeeded in shaking the poor creature off among the yelping brutes and yelling boys. Ralph could not help sympathizing with the hunted animal, which sold its life as dearly as possible, giving the dogs many a scratch and bite. It seemed to him that he was like the raccoon, precipitated into the midst of a party of dogs who would rejoice in worrying *his* life out, as Bull and his crowd were destroying the poor raccoon. When Bull at last seized the raccoon and put an end to it, Ralph could not but admire Bud's comment, "Ef Bull once takes a holt, heaven and yarth can't make him let go."

But as they walked home, Bud carrying the raccoon by the tail, Ralph felt that his hunt had not been in vain. He fancied that even red-eyed Bull, walking uncomfortably close to his heels, respected him more since he had climbed that tree.

"Purty peart kind of a master," remarked the old man to Bud, after Ralph had gone to bed. "Guess you better be a little easy on him. Hey?"

But Bud deigned no reply. Perhaps because he knew that Ralph heard the conversation through the thin partition.

Ralph woke delighted to find it raining. He did not want to hunt or fish on Sunday, and this steady rain would enable him to make friends with Bud. I do not know how he got started, but after breakfast he began to tell stories. Out of all the books he had ever read he told story after story. And "old man Means," and "old *Miss* Means," and Bud Means, and Bill Means, and Sis Means listened with great eyes while he told of Sinbad's adventures, of the Old Man of the Sea, of Robinson Crusoe, of Captain Gulliver's experiences in Liliput, and of Baron Munchhausen's exploits.

Ralph had caught his fish. The hungry minds of these backwoods people were refreshed with the new life that came to their imaginations in these stories. For there was but one book in the Means library, and that, a well-thumbed copy of "Captain Riley's Narrative," had long since lost all freshness.

"I'll be dog-on'd," said Bill, emphatically, "ef I hadn't 'ruther hear the master tell them whoppin' yarns than to go to a circus the best day I ever seed!" Bill could pay no higher compliment.

What Ralph wanted was to make a friend of Bud. It's a nice thing to have the seventy-four-gun ship on your own side, and the more Hartsook ad-

mired the knotted muscles of Bud Means the more he desired to attach him
to himself. So, whenever he struck out a peculiarly brilliant passage, he anxiously watched Bud's eye. But the young Philistine kept his own counsel. He
listened, but said nothing, and the eyes under his shaggy brows gave no sign.
Ralph could not tell whether those eyes were deep and inscrutable or only
stolid. Perhaps a little of both. When Monday morning came, Ralph was
nervous. He walked to school with Bud.

"I guess you're a little skeered by what the old man said, a'n't you?"

Ralph was about to deny it, but on reflection concluded that it was best
to speak the truth. He said that Mr. Means's description of the school had
made him feel a little down-hearted.

"What will you do with the tough boys? You a'n't no match for 'em." And
Ralph felt Bud's eyes not only measuring his muscles, but scrutinizing his
countenance. He only answered:

"I don't know."

"What would you do with me, for instance?" and Bud stretched himself
up as if to shake out the reserve power coiled up in his great muscles.

"I sha'n't have any trouble with you."

"Why, I'm the wust chap of all. I thrashed the last master, myself."

And again the eyes of Bud Means looked out sharply from his shadowing
brows to see the effect of this speech on the slender young man.

"You won't thrash me, though," said Ralph.

"Pshaw! I 'low I could whip you in an inch of your life with my left hand,
and never half try," said young Means, with a threatening sneer.

"I know that as well as you do."

"Well, a'n't you afraid of me, then?" and again he looked sidewise at
Ralph.

"Not a bit," said Ralph, wondering at his own courage.

They walked on in silence a minute. Bud was turning the matter over.

"Why a'n't you afraid of me?" he said presently.

"Because you and I are going to be friends."

"And what about t'others?"

"I am not afraid of all the other boys put together."

"You a'n't! The mischief! How's that?"

"Well, I'm not afraid of them because you and I are going to be friends,
and you can whip all of them together. You'll do the fighting and I'll do the
teaching."

The diplomatic Bud only chuckled a little at this; whether he assented to
the alliance or not Ralph could not tell.

When Ralph looked round on the faces of the scholars—the little faces
full of mischief and curiosity, the big faces full of an expression which was
not further removed than second-cousin from contempt—when young
Hartsook looked into these faces, his heart palpitated with stage-fright.

There is no audience so hard to face as one of school-children, as many a man has found to his cost. Perhaps it is that no conventional restraint can keep down their laughter when you do or say anything ridiculous.

Hartsook's first day was hurried and unsatisfactory. He was not master of himself, and consequently not master of anybody else. When evening came, there were symptoms of insubordination through the whole school. Poor Ralph was sick at heart. He felt that if there had ever been the shadow of an alliance between himself and Bud, it was all "off" now. It seemed to Hartsook that even Bull had lost his respect for the teacher. Half that night the young man lay awake. At last comfort came to him. A reminiscence of the death of the raccoon flashed on him like a vision. He remembered that quiet and annihilating bite which Bull gave. He remembered Bud's certificate, that "Ef Bull once takes a holt, heaven and yarth can't make him let go." He thought that what Flat Creek needed was a bulldog. He would be a bulldog, quiet, but invincible. He would take hold in such a way that nothing should make him let go. And then he went to sleep.

In the morning Ralph got out of bed slowly. He put his clothes on slowly. He pulled on his boots in a bulldog mood. He tried to move as he thought Bull would move if he were a man. He ate with deliberation, and looked everybody in the eyes with a manner that made Bud watch him curiously. He found himself continually comparing himself with Bull. He found Bull possessing strange fascination for him. He walked to school alone, the rest having gone on before. He entered the schoolroom preserving a cool and dogged manner. He saw in the eyes of the boys that there was mischief brewing. He did not dare sit down in his chair for fear of a pin. Everybody looked solemn. Ralph lifted the lid of his desk. "Bow-wow! wow-wow!" It was the voice of an imprisoned puppy, and the school giggled and then roared. Then everything was quiet.

The scholars expected an outburst of wrath from the teacher. For they had come to regard the whole world as divided into two classes, the teacher on the one side representing lawful authority, and the pupils on the other in a state of chronic rebellion. To play a trick on the master was an evidence of spirit; to "lick" the master was to be the crowned hero of Flat Creek district. Such a hero was Bud Means; and Bill, who had less muscle, saw a chance to distinguish himself on a teacher of slender frame. Hence the puppy in the desk.

Ralph Hartsook grew red in the face when he saw the puppy. But the cool, repressed, bulldog mood in which he had kept himself saved him. He lifted the dog into his arms and stroked him until the laughter subsided. Then, in a solemn and set way, he began:

"I am sorry," and he looked round the room with a steady, hard eye—everybody felt that there was a conflict coming—"I am sorry that any scholar in this school could be so mean"—the word was uttered with a sharp emphasis, and all the big boys felt sure that there would be a fight with Bill Means, and perhaps with Bud—"could be so *mean*—as to—shut up his *brother* in such a place as that!"

There was a long, derisive laugh. The wit was indifferent, but by one stroke Ralph had carried the whole school to his side. By the significant glances of the boys, Hartsook detected the perpetrator of the joke, and with the hard and dogged look in his eyes, with just such a look as Bull would give a puppy, but with the most suavity in his voice, he said:

"William Means, will you be so good as to put this dog out of doors?"

Railroad Towns

FROM *Plains Country Towns*

JOHN C. HUDSON

THE NINETEENTH CENTURY was the century of mighty engines, vast excavations, and colossal building projects. No machine better expresses that century's conquest of earth, land, and space than the locomotive. In a matter of decades, starting in the 1830s and at vastly accelerating rates from the 1860s, the railroad lines moved ever westward. By 1869 the Atlantic and Pacific coasts had been linked with the completion of the lines of the Union Pacific and Central Pacific. Thereafter it was a rush to fill in and complete the American grid, a project that was essentially finished by the early 1900s.

Railroads supplemented and eventually displaced canal systems and traditional roadways, becoming synonymous with the Industrial Revolution. They marked new human orders of speed and movements of people, goods, and news as the distribution of newspapers, books, and telegraph lines accompanied railroad expansion. Railroads defined national power insofar as they accelerated production and commerce and demarcated government's capacities to concentrate material for warfare.

The settlement story of the Trans-Mississippi West is inseparable from the pioneering railroads. Underpinning the railroad era was an incredible narrative of public and private financing, major advances in engineering skills, and the essential contributions by hundreds of thousands of laborers. All of this occurred within a frenzied atmosphere of political intrigue and brazen greed as deals were cut regarding the issuance of stocks, granting of government lands, determination of points of departure and terminus, location of rights-of-way, building of bridges, and division of markets.

In the decades following the Civil War, railroads inaugurated a new era of white settlement to the high plains. The structure of life on the prairie was sharply defined by the plans and promises of urban railroad barons. Some projected townsites never left the corporate drawing boards, while others, despite their booster's shilling, were stillborn. Yet other railroad towns— Johnnies-come-lately—were formed too late, on too minor a spur, to ever thrive. Conversely, a few railroad hubs were destined to become dominant midwestern metropolises. The role of the railroads in determining the movement of people, supplies, and fashions made these urban outposts on the prairie "colonies of inland empires," to use the term employed by the historian William Cronon in his *Nature's Metropolis: Chicago and the Great West.*

From Illinois westward, the intricate relationship between town, city, and countryside was mandated by the decisions emanating from the offices of the railroad companies. This complex process is explained by the geographer John C. Hudson as it occurred in North Dakota.

---

o o o

In his monumental history of the Chicago, Burlington & Quincy Railroad, Richard C. Overton argued that the relations between railroads, townsites, and the men of influence who connected one with the other produced a generally beneficial result. By following their own interests, railroad-affiliated townsite promoters created an orderly, permanent development that benefited the local citizenry as much as it did the promoters. "Whether the new towns and farming areas which these companies fostered could have been developed without speculative capital, or whether their development was premature, are moot points," Overton wrote.[1] His generally favorable evaluation balanced a popular view that railroad townsite promotion was little more than a saga of greed and corruption, but neither his analysis nor those of others are sufficient to render moot the question of corporate involvement in the town business.

The record of railroads and their townsites varies from company to company and, thereby, from region to region, but in no instance was the involvement passive. Railroad townsite strategies were most aggressive when independent parties or competing railroads threatened to usurp what was taken as a corporate prerogative—to plant towns where and when the railroad wished. If independent townsites found a permanent home somewhere along a line, it was only because the railroad allowed it; and they did so only when they judged as poor the prospects for success of a town at a given location at a given time. Whether through their own promotions or by what might have seemed benign neglect, all railroad companies watched with extreme care any attempts to promote towns on or near their lines.

The model of town settlement adopted by the railroads was one that had evolved gradually in the course of European and American urbanization. The same model had been used by the many independent townsite boomers who hoped to interest a railroad in their plans. *Structure* assumed priority over *activity* in the railroad town. A site was selected first and was then platted as a series of streets and separated blocks divided into building lots. Only after the structure was completely specified were any townlike activities allowed to locate there.[2]

It was not an ingrained belief in the virtues of urban design that led to a mapped prefiguration of a town, but rather an imperative to control development. Unlike the speculative townsite, whose promoters anticipated profit from real estate sales, the railroad town was a device for organizing the traffic that would come to the company as a result. Also unlike its other local predecessor, the inland town, railroad strategy was to make all parcels of land other than those they wished to control unfit for business activity. This was easily accomplished by the transportation cost advantage that railroad town merchants were known to enjoy over their inland counterparts.

Town Building

Railroad companies engaged in townsite activity whenever and wherever they built new lines. Agreements made with townsite affiliates effectively lapsed once those lines were completed. Some companies (such as the Soo) maintained a long-term arrangement with outside parties who platted and sold their towns, but more commonly railroads reorganized their townsite affiliations when new construction was projected. The work of various townsite agents is thus demarcated more by time than by place. . . .

The birth of a Great Plains railroad town was attended by a circle of admiring well-wishers. There were high hopes for individual success and, beyond that, a shared spirit of civic pride that emerged before the first balloon-frame, false-front store building was raised. Town lot buyers often were strangers to one another, but they were confronted by a common task. It remained for them to translate the surveyors plat into a living, breathing trade center town, to fulfill the predetermined design the townsite company had provided. The process that transformed one into the other was not reinvented every time a new town was born, nor even was the plat itself any more likely than a copy of the last few the surveyor had made, granting only the barest of concessions to local topography. What moved from one site to the next was a set of ideas held in the minds of designers, buyers, and sellers of space about the proper form and function of towns.

Plats had to look like credible towns. Their "common" look, while often criticized, also had a reassuring effect that grander innovations might not have provided. The late-nineteenth-century conventions of urban design that guided them held that the simple grid pattern was sufficient for smaller cities and towns, that alleys were desirable, and that the functions of various city streets should govern their width.[3] These principles were accepted by railroad town builders, although another popular idea, that city blocks should be oblong rather than square, generally was not. Square blocks, with deeper lots, allowed a clutter of small buildings to form along the back alleys, whereas longer but shallower blocks forced buildings to the front. The sparse, uneven look of residential sections that developed in many towns can be attributed to the design.

The standard railroad-town block was 3000 feet square, with lots 140 feet deep and backed by a 20-foot alley. Block faces were divided into six residential lots (50 feet wide) or into twelve 25-foot business lots. The narrow lots, which sold at two or three times the price of residential lots, gave the impression of activity to a business district before there was any. Long, narrow lots on Main Street also guaranteed that the first buildings would assume a uniform size and shape, which, in turn, favored the presence of many small, independent merchants.

The width of the streets on a plat suggested where the greatest activity would congregate. If Main Street was 100 feet wide, the principal cross street was generally 80 feet and residential streets 60 feet, establishing a clear hierarchy. Few railroad town plats showed parks or other public spaces, although these amenities often were created later from unsold land, which unfortunately kept green space out of the town center and on the periphery.

The sizes of town lots, the widths of the streets, and the position of the railroad were thus the principal cues new residents had in choosing a location on the townsite. Three distinct morphologies, characterized by street patterns, placements of the business district, and railroad location, differentiate the entire history of the railroad town from the 1850s to the 1920s throughout North America.[4]

The earliest idea, and one popularized by the Illinois Central Associates, was a parallel arrangement with the railroad track as the axis of symmetry. The prototype is obscure, although possible precedents include the canal towns of western New York state where business houses were lined facing the waterway. Such an arrangement, with the railroad as centerpiece, made passage of the iron horse a daily public display of the new age of transportation.

There were two business streets in the symmetric railroad town, with buildings facing each other across a 300-foot railroad right-of-way designed for elevators, lumberyards, and other enterprises needing direct rail access. Land along the tracks was underused, and eventually some towns acquired a portion of it for parks. The two business streets rarely developed equally, especially in the smaller places. In plan, the two halves of the town were separate but equal, and in railroad towns of the southern states the design was a convenient demarcation of black and white that gave a built-in assist to segregationist practices. Outside the South, the distinction was economic. If First Avenue North was the principal business street, First Avenue South was literally "the other side of the tracks," with a row of saloons and cheap hotels.

The Northern Pacific Railway was responsible for most of the symmetric plats in the northern Great Plains, including New Rockford, Minnewaukan, and Sykeston in the study area. Only New Rockford fulfilled the original design, however. Sykeston and Minnewaukan developed along their Main Streets, perpendicular to the tracks. The adjustment in practice reflected the undesirability of having a strip of land a block wide separating the two parts of the business district. Inserting the railroad led to additional congestion where it was least desirable. Symmetric plats were used rarely after the 1890s, perhaps victim to the fading, Victorian-era fascination with steam railroads.

The orthogonal plat, placing businesses on both sides of the same street, was favored by many western railroads. The depot generally was located near the Main Street crossing, in the middle of the townsite. It was such a commonplace of town morphology that incoming merchants were confused by deviations. Railroad field engineers, however, cared little about the cues provided by such an arrangement, and preferred to locate the depot where access to the water tank used to service steam locomotives was convenient. Where townsite agents saw a thriving town, with Main Street lots commanding $200–$250 apiece, railroad men saw a servicing facility, and their different objectives sometimes conflicted.

A. A. White was astonished when he arrived at Rugby in 1886 to find the depot nearly completed at a site well west of Main Street. The same plan was already underway at Towner. He wrote Solomon Comstock an anguished letter:

> I have spent the past three days in trying to overcome the difficulty of the location. At first I thought we should have to abandon the Main St., as some parties threw up their locations on Main St., but I have succeeded in getting everything on to Main St. as intended and have not made any concessions in prices. Everything will be all right only there is not much money here, and the businessmen are rather light weight.[5]

He pleaded with Comstock to use his influence to prevent the same development at Towner, otherwise he could "not hold the business on Main St." there. It seems reasonable to conclude that White's problem was not isolated, and that there were many other towns where business people might have located on cheaper lots away from the designated Main Street had not the townsite agents urged and cajoled them to the high-priced locations.

Despite the platting of a single business street at right angles to the track, towns tended to develop more on one side of the railroad than on the other. Practice once again led planning, so that by the late 1890s most towns were not even planned to straddle the railroad. In the newer designs, Main Street began at the tracks, creating an arrangement in which the railroad formed the bar of a T-shaped configuration. This proved to be a stable solution, more acceptable both to railroads and to townspeople. The elimination of crossings in the business district was a relief to increasingly accident-cautious railroads, and the isolation of the tracks to one side of town made them less conspicuous to residents. A later Great Northern official observed that "we want to so arrange the property that we can compell all of the town developments to be on one side of the track," and he advocated the railroad's purchase of a strip along the outside of its line to prevent developments that might lead to subsequent demands for crossings.[6]

The single business street of the T-town lacked sufficient differentiation along its length to permit one intersection to stand out as more important. In 1905, the Soo Line began a variation on the T-town form by platting business lots a few blocks up the cross street away from the principal intersection; the Great Northern's towns also soon reflected the idea.[7] The "crossed-T" form was a better anchor on business locations and produced a tighter cluster nearest the center, where lots were most expensive. Banks were almost forced to locate on one of the corner lots at this intersection, following the popular idea that this is where they belonged.

Once the railroad had been moved to the side of the plat, it was possible to reintroduce a point focus, such as a center square, to replace the linear focus imposed by a bisecting railroad line. Central squares and greens were known and admired by Americans familiar with towns that predated the railroad, and thus their reintroduction in some of the later railroad towns is not surprising. D. N. Tallman created four North Dakota towns (Antler, Maxbass, McCumber, and Sarles) around a scaled-down Philadelphia-style center square designed to contain his banks. The Soo Line platted Kenmare, Plaza, Columbus, Ryder, and Imperial with a somewhat similar central focus but with city parks rather than a shrine of business as the centerpiece.[8] Such devices can hardly be called innovations. They do suggest that tastes in urban design changed slowly enough to allow parks and squares to reemerge after intervening ideas, such as the symmetric railroad town, had been discarded.

The evolution of town form proceeded from the undifferentiated grids platted by early speculators to the detailed modifications of the T-town. Each shift was informed by experience. Styles changed to accommodate the railroads' wishes, to be sure, but the tendency toward plats richer in cues about town development reflected what townsite agents had learned from their pricing strategies. Simultaneously, those who platted towns were learning to estimate more accurately how much growth each might sustain, although it was not until the beginning of the twentieth century that townsite agents were skilled enough to create plats of realistic size.

The boom of the 1880s in northern Dakota witnessed many attempts to create great cities in true speculator's fashion, that is, simply by announcing that rapid growth was soon to commence. An extensive gridiron of city blocks on the plat was a simple and inexpensive way to suggest what the future would bring. The tendency to overestimate was not confined to the wildest of speculators: railroad towns were begun with equally grandiose ambitions, following a pattern common to cities elsewhere in the Great Plains. In the 1880s, the average townsite platted in the study area contained forty city blocks, but the poor record of many railroad towns, plus the outright failure of the speculators' schemes, dampened further enthusiasm for gargantuan designs.

The depression of the 1890s was probably responsible for the reversal. Plats first recorded during this period averaged a mere seven or eight blocks each. Such modest ventures seemed unlikely candidates to stimulate the interest of others, and many did not. As confidence was restored in the early 1900s, the average size of plats inched upward once more to a size of ten or twelve blocks, realistically large enough to attract investors but small enough to prevent the tax burden of unsold lots. . . .

The success or failure of a townsite company was measured not in terms of the success or failure of merchants who located in a town, but rather in terms of the number of lots sold. The railroad company, in turn, measured town success in terms of whatever traffic it did not lose to a competitor as a result of the town's presence.

The speculative capital that railroad townsite companies invested at various locations could equally well have been invested by others. In many cases outsiders did desire a role, but they were rebuffed by railroad companies that wanted to control the business for their own purposes. A railroad allowed independent townsites only when there was no competition from another railroad. They created too many towns in the vicinity of their competitors' lines, too few elsewhere.

That the railroads were able to launch so many new towns scarcely was testimony to their wisdom in doing so, although the record speaks well of townsite agents as salesmen. Town plats eventually were scaled in proportion to the sales each site might generate, which, in turn, was evidently a function of the size and productivity of the trade area. Competition for trade, which commenced as soon as a new town was platted near an existing center, worked against the new-town merchant, especially if his town's trading area was insufficiently large. The decline of many small centers, so often linked with the advent of automobile ownership, thus began well before the shift from rail to road networks.

A definitive statement on the success of railroad towns as a type thus can be given only in terms of the criteria held by the various interests involved. If lot sales are taken as the measure, then the rate of failure was comparatively low. Townsite agencies were able to recover their investment with the sale of a fraction of the platted lots and dump the rest to avoid taxes. The most generous definition of success was that held by railroad companies, whose needs were met if the site had no more than a single grain elevator in operation to serve the purpose of traffic capture. Population growth and economic stability were the merchants' concerns, and neither followed just because people purchased town lots and commenced business activity at a site. A successful town, by these criteria, required the emergence of coherent economic and social relationships within the community. . . .

Notes

1. Richard C. Overton, *Burlington West: A Colonization History of the Burlington Railroad* (Cambridge, Mass.: Harvard University Press, 1941), 182.

2. John W. Reps, *Cities of the American West: A History of Frontier Urban Planning* (Princeton, N.J.: Princeton University Press, 1979), x.

3. W. H. Dorsey, "The Laying Out of Towns," *Engineering News* 26 (1891): 192–93, and J. J. Donovan, "The Laying Out of Cities and Additions Thereto," *Engineering News* 26 (1891): 605, summarize late nineteenth-century planning ideas in the practical terms of the engineer.

4. John C. Hudson, "Towns of the Western Railroads," *Great Plains Quarterly* 2, no. 1 (1982): 47–48. The three types had many variations, depending especially on the angle formed between the railroad line and the township-and-range survey grid. There are also many examples of "proposed designs" for railroad towns found in the literature, but the more intricate the design, the less likely it was to be used. See, for example, the proposal of Sanford Fleming (1877) shown in J. Edward Martin, *Railway Stations of Western Canada* (White Rock, British Columbia: Studio E, 1980), 4–5.

5. White to Comstock, 31 August 1886, Solomon Gilman Comstock papers, Northwest Minnesota Historical Center, Moorhead State University, Moorhead, Minn., box 57, folder 5.

6. C. R. Gray to J. T. Maher, 11 April 1913, Presidents' Subject Files, Great Northern Railway Collection, Minnesota Historical Society, Division of Archives and Manuscripts, St. Paul, Minn., 5188; M. C. Byers, "Standard Station Grounds for Use in Prairie Country," MS in Presidents' Subject Files, Great Northern Railway Collection, 5865; R. Budd to Byers, 2 July 1913, Presidents' Subject Files, Great Northern Railway Collection, 5856.

7. The "crossed-T" form, distinguished by incorporation of a business cross street, first appeared in the study area in the plat of Kramer, surveyed in early June 1905 by C. F. Bode for Minnesota Loan and Trust (Soo Line) and in the plats of the nearby towns of Deep and Newburg, surveyed the same week by T. M. Fowble for the Dakota Development Company (Great Northern); Bottineau County, Register of Deeds, plat book. The same idea was used in every subsequent town platted by the two railroads in 1905.

8. Edward T. Price, "The Central Courthouse Square in the American County Seat," *Geographical Review* 58 (1968): 29–60. Tallman's central squares followed the Philadelphia style identified by Price, although they were only eight feet square in size. Kenmare's square was a standard city block (block 2 of the original townsite) with business lots arranged facing it on three sides. Ryder and Plaza had central city parks, two-hundred feet square, with business lots facing on two sides only. Bottineau, Ward, and Mountrail counties, Register of Deeds, plat books.

A "Good Fellow's" Wife

FROM *Main-Travelled Roads*

HAMLIN GARLAND

E VEN WITH THE MANY FRAGMENTS of the past that still litter small towns, it is difficult to subtract from contemporary American life the amenities and institutions to which we have become accustomed and to imagine life as it was a century ago—life without e-mail and internet; without television, telephones, or radio; without automobiles or even paved roads; without McDonald's or Wal-Mart or True Value Home Center; without central heating and flush toilets; without accessible hospital care, retirement homes, unemployment insurance, and Social Security; without automatic cash machines, federally insured bank accounts, or even banks in which to have an account.

Hamlin Garland gives us a portrait of the Midwest village in its raw infancy. Garland grew up on a sequence of small farms and villages, starting in western Wisconsin and ending in eastern South Dakota, as his father moved the family constantly west in search of cheap, fertile land and the gold ring on the merry-go-round of homesteading. Upon reaching maturity, Garland headed immediately east, then returned to South Dakota to try homesteading a claim of his own, then sought employment as a teacher in various Dakota and Minnesota towns, and finally returned to Boston, where he became a famous writer and one of the key figures in American realism. Truth is a higher quality in literature than beauty, he concluded, and spreading the reign of justice should be the writer's principal goal. In his most important work of fiction, *Main-Travelled Roads*, Garland described as accurately as he could life in what was then known as "The West," especially the "ugliness, the endless drudgery, and the loneliness" of farmers, whom he—like Sinclair Lewis—saw as a class exploited by small-town merchants. In particular Garland distrusted bankers and absentee landlords—those who, he claimed, "farmed the farmer."

The final story of *Main-Travelled Roads* describes one such banker who, with the help of a major crisis and his supportive wife, manages to become a useful and productive member of society. James Sanford arrives in Bluff Siding the object of much suspicion, well warranted as events prove. He opens a bank in a town that has none—although it does have a newspaper—and for a time lives well on other people's money. When his risky investments in the copper mines of Michigan's Upper Peninsula turn inexplicably sour, he reveals an "inherent moral weakness" in trying to sneak out of town; when the investments pay off (in an equally mysterious manner), he swells with pride. Sanford's wife displays genuine integrity when she insists that Sanford remain in Bluff Siding, face his creditors, and own up to his debts. She provides a model of the virtuous small-town entrepreneur when she opens a small store, works long hours, builds her business slowly and solidly, and serves the community. Originally recognized for her looks alone, then merely an object of town sympathy, she gains the respect of both the community and her husband as a partner in the town and a partner in the marriage.

Sanford and his wife are opposite personalities: he the gambler, always looking for the "big money" up around Duluth and Ashland; she the conservative, opting for the safety of Bluff Siding. Townspeople are a variety of types, most no better than James Sanford, the banker they alternately glad-hand and threaten to lynch: promoters, farmers, loafers, small-town merchants, grandmothers, Yankees, Norwegians. This is a story of small-town types. But finally this is a story of male roles and female roles, and an early feminist declaration: men and women can be true lovers only when they are equal partners. Garland's tale is a story as much of character as of place.

o o o

Life in the small towns of the older West moves slowly—almost as slowly as in the seaport villages or little towns of the East. Towns like Tyre and Bluff Siding have grown during the last twenty years, but very slowly, by almost imperceptible degrees. Lying too far away from the Mississippi to be affected by the lumber interest, they are merely trading-points for the farmers, with no perceivable germs of boom in their quiet life.

A stranger coming into Belfast, Minnesota, excites much the same languid but persistent inquiry as in Belfast, New Hampshire. Juries of men, seated on salt-barrels and nail-kegs, discuss the stranger's appearance and his probable action, just as in Kittery, Maine, but with a lazier speech-tune, and with a shade less of apparent interest.

On such a rainy day as comes in May after the corn is planted—a cold, *wet* rainy day—the usual crowd was gathered in Wilson's grocery-store at Bluff Siding, a small town in "The Coally Country." They were farmers, for the most part, retired from active service. Their coats were of cheap diagonal or cassimere, much faded and burned by the sun; their hats, flapped about by winds and soaked with countless rains, were also of the same yellow-brown tints. One or two wore paper collars on their hickory shirts.

McIlvaine, farmer and wheat-buyer, wore a paper collar and a butterfly necktie, as befitted a man of his station in life. He was a short, squarely made Scotchman, with sandy whiskers much grayed, and with a keen, intensely blue eye.

"Say," called McPhail, ex-sheriff of the county, in the silence that followed some remark about the rain, "any o' you fellers had any talk with this feller Sanford?"

"I hain't," said Vance. "You, Bill?"

"No; but somebody was sayin' he thought o' startin' in trade here."

"Don't Sam know? He generally knows what's goin' on."

"Knows he registered from Pittsfield, Mass., an' that's all. Say, that's a mighty smart-lookin' woman o' his."

"Vance always sees how the women look. Where'd you see *her*?"

"Came in here the other day to look up prices."

"Wha'd *she* say 'bout settlin'?"

"Hadn't decided yet."

"He's too *slick* to have much business in him. That waxed *mus*tache gives 'im away."

The discussion having reached that point where his word would have most effect, Steve Gilbert said, while opening the hearth to rap out the ashes of his pipe, "Sam's wife heerd that he was kind o' thinkin' some of goin' into business here, if things suited 'im first-rate."

They all knew the old man was aching to tell something, but they didn't purpose to gratify him by any questions. The rain dripped from the awning in front, and fell upon the roof of the storeroom at the back with a soft and steady roar.

"Good f'r the corn," McPhail said, after a long pause.

"Purty cold, though."

Gilbert was tranquil—he had a shot in reserve.

"Sam's wife said *his* wife said he was thinkin' some of goin' into a bank here—"

"A bank!"

"What in thunder—"

Vance turned, with a comical look on his long, placid face, one hand stroking his beard.

"Well, now, gents, I'll tell you what's the matter with this town. It needs a bank. Yes, sir! *I* need a bank."

"You?"

"Yes, me. I didn't know just what *did* ail me, but I do now. It's the need of a bank that keeps me down."

"Well, you fellers can talk an' laugh, but I tell yeh they's a boom goin' to strike this town. It's got to come. W'y, just look at Lumberville!"

"Their *boom* is our *bu'st*," was McPhail's comment.

"I don't think so," said Sanford, who had entered in time to hear these last two speeches. They all looked at him with deep interest. He was a smallish man. He wore a derby hat and neat suit. "I've looked things over pretty close—a man don't like to invest his capital" (here the rest looked at one another) "till he does; and I believe there's an opening for a bank."

As he dwelt upon the scheme from day to day, the citizens warmed to him, and he became "Jim" Sanford. He hired a little cottage, and went to housekeeping at once; but the entire summer went by before he made his decision to settle. In fact, it was in the last week of August that the little paper announced it in the usual style:

> Mr. James G. Sanford, popularly known as "Jim," has decided to open an exchange bank for the convenience of our citizens, who have hitherto been forced to transact business in Lumberville. The thanks of the town are due to Mr. Sanford, who comes well recommended from Massachusetts and from Milwaukee, and, better still, with a bag of ducats. Mr. S. will be well patronized. Success, Jim!

The bank was open by the time the corn-crop and the hogs were being marketed, and money was received on deposit while the carpenters were still at work on the building. Everybody knew now that he was as solid as oak.

He had taken into the bank, as bookkeeper, Lincoln Bingham, one of McPhail's multitudinous nephews; and this was a capital move. Everybody knew Link, and knew he was a McPhail, which meant that he "could be tied to in all kinds o' weather." Of course the McPhails, McIlvaines, and the rest of the Scotch contingency "banked on Link." As old Andrew McPhail put it:

"Link's there, an' he knows the bank an' books, an' just how things stand"; and so when he sold his hogs he put the whole sum—over fifteen hundred dollars—into the bank. The McIlvaines and the Binghams did the same, and the bank was at once firmly established among the farmers.

Only two people held out against Sanford, old Freeme Cole and Mrs. Bingham, Lincoln's mother; but they didn't count, for Freeme hadn't a cent, and Mrs. Bingham was too unreasoning in her opposition. She could only say: "I don't like him, that's all. I knowed a man back in New York that curled his *mus*taches just that way, an' he wa'n't no earthly good."

It might have been said by a cynic that Banker Sanford had all the virtues of a defaulting bank cashier. He had no bad habits beyond smoking. He was genial, companionable, and especially ready to help when sickness came. When old Freeme Cole got down with delirium tremens that winter, Sanford was one of the most heroic of nurses, and the service was so clearly disinterested and magnanimous that every one spoke of it.

His wife and he were included in every dance or picnic; for Mrs. Sanford was as great a favorite as the banker himself, she was so sincere, and her gray eyes were so charmingly frank, and then she said "such funny things."

"I wish I had something to do besides housework. It's a kind of a put-terin' job, best ye can do," she'd say, merrily, just to see the others stare. "There's too much moppin' an' dustin'. Seems 's if a woman used up half her life on things that don't amount to anything, don't it?"

"I tell yeh that feller's a scallywag. I know it buh the way 'h walks 'long the sidewalk," Mrs. Bingham insisted to her son, who wished her to put her savings into the bank.

The youngest of a large family, Link had been accustomed all his life to Mrs. Bingham's many whimsicalities.

"I s'pose you can *smell* he's a thief, just as you can tell when it's goin' to rain, or the butter's comin', by the smell."

"Well, you needn't laugh, Lincoln. I *can*," maintained the old lady, stoutly. "An' I ain't goin' to put a red cent o' my money into his pocket—f'r there's where it 'ud go to."

She yielded at last, and received a little bank-book in return for her money. "Jest about all I'll ever get," she said, privately; and thereafter out of her brass-bowed spectacles with an eagle's gaze she watched the banker go by. But the banker, seeing the dear old soul at the window looking out at him, always smiled and bowed, unaware of her suspicion.

At the end of the year he bought the lot next his rented house, and began building one of his own, a modest little affair, shaped like a pork-pie with a cupola, or a Tam-o'-Shanter cap—a style of architecture which became fashionable at once.

He worked heroically to get the location of the plow-factory at Bluff Siding, and all but succeeded; but Tyre, once their ally, turned against them, and refused to consider the fact of the Siding's position at the centre of the county. However, for some reason or other, the town woke up to something of a boom during the next two years. Several large farmers decided to retire and live off the sweat of some other fellow's brow, and so built some houses of the pork-pie order, and moved into town.

This inflow of moneyed men from the country resulted in the establishment of a "seminary of learning" on the hillside, where the Soldiers' Home was to be located. This called in more farmers from the country, and a new hotel was built, a sash-and-door factory followed, and Burt McPhail set up a feed-mill.

All this improvement unquestionably dated from the opening of the bank, and the most unreasoning partisans of the banker held him to be the chief cause of the resulting development of the town, though he himself modestly disclaimed any hand in the affair.

Had Bluff Siding been a city, the highest civic honors would have been open to Banker Sanford; indeed, his name was repeatedly mentioned in connection with the county offices.

"No, gentlemen," he explained, firmly, but courteously, in Wilson's store one night; "I'm a banker, not a politician. I can't ride two horses."

In the second year of the bank's history he went up to the north part of the state on business, visiting West Superior, Duluth, Ashland, and other booming towns, and came back full of the wonders of what he saw.

"There's big money up there, Nell," he said to his wife.

But she had the woman's tendency to hold fast to what she had, and would not listen to any plans about moving.

"Build up your business here, Jim, and don't worry about what good chances there are somewhere else."

He said no more about it, but he took great interest in all the news the "boys" brought back from their annual deer-hunts "up north." They were all enthusiastic over West Superior and Duluth, and their wonderful development was the never-ending theme of discussion in Wilson's store.

II

The first two years of the bank's history were solidly successful, and "Jim" and "Nellie" were the head and front of all good works, and the provoking cause of most of the fun. No one seemed more care-free.

"We consider ourselves just as young as anybody," Mrs. Sanford would say, when joked about going out with the young people so much; but sometimes at home, after the children were asleep, she sighed a little.

"Jim, I wish you was in some kind of a business so I could help. I don't have enough to do. I s'pose I *could* mop an' dust, an' dust an' mop; but it seems sinful to waste time that way. Can't I do anything, Jim?"

"Why, no. If you 'tend to the children and keep house, that's all anybody asks of you."

She was silent, but not convinced. She had a desire to do something outside the walls of her house—a desire transmitted to her from her father, for a woman inherits these things.

In the spring of the second year a number of the depositors drew out money to invest in Duluth and Superior lots, and the whole town was excited over the matter.

The summer passed, Link and Sanford spending their time in the bank—that is, when not out swimming or fishing with the boys. But July and August were terribly hot and dry, and oats and corn were only half-crop, and the farmers were grumbling. Some of them were forced to draw on the bank instead of depositing.

McPhail came in, one day in November, to draw a thousand dollars to pay for a house and lot he had recently bought.

Sanford was alone. He whistled. "Phew! You're comin' at me hard. Come in to-morrow. Link's gone down to the city to get some money."

"All right," said McPhail; "any time."

"Goin' t' snow?"

"Looks like it. I'll haf to load a lot o' ca'tridges ready f'r biz."

About an hour later old lady Bingham burst upon the banker, wild and breathless. "I want my money," she announced.

"Good-morning, Mrs. Bingham. Pleasant—"

"I want my money. Where's Lincoln?"

She had read that morning of two bank failures—one in Nova Scotia and one in Massachusetts—and they seemed providential warnings to her. Lincoln's absence confirmed them.

"He's gone to St. Paul—won't be back till the five-o'clock train. Do you need some money this morning? How much?"

"*All* of it, sir. Every cent."

Sanford saw something was out of gear. He tried to explain. "I've sent your son to St. Paul after some money—"

"Where's my money? What have you done with *that?*" In her excitement she thought of her money just as she had handed it in—silver and little rolls and wads of bills.

"If you'll let me explain—"

"I don't want you to explain nawthin'. Jest hand me out my money."

Two or three loafers, seeing her gesticulate, stopped on the walk outside and looked in at the door. Sanford was annoyed, but he remained calm and persuasive. He saw that something had caused a panic in the good, simple old woman. He wished for Lincoln as one wishes for a policeman sometimes.

"No, Mrs. Bingham, if you'll only wait till Lincoln—"

"I don't want 'o wait. I want my money, right now."

"Will fifty dollars do?"

"No, sir; I want it all—every cent of it—jest as it was."

"But I can't do that. *Your* money is gone—"

"Gone? *Where* is it gone? What have you done with it? You thief—"

"'Sh!" He tried to quiet her. "I mean I can't give you your money—"

"Why can't you?" she stormed, trotting nervously on her feet as she stood there.

"Because—if you'd let me explain—we don't keep the money just as it comes to us. We pay it out, and take in other—"

Mrs. Bingham was getting more and more bewildered. She now had only one clear idea—she couldn't get her money. Her voice grew tearful like an angry child's.

"I want my money—I knew you'd steal it—that I worked for. Give me my money."

Sanford hastily handed her some money. "Here's fifty dollars. You can have the rest when—"

The old lady clutched the money, and literally ran out of the door, and went off up the sidewalk, talking incoherently. To every one she met she told her story; but the men smiled and passed on. They had heard her predictions of calamity before.

But Mrs. McIlvaine was made a trifle uneasy by it. "He *wouldn't* give you y'r money? Or did he say he *couldn't?*" she inquired, in her moderate way.

"He couldn't, an' he wouldn't!" she said. "If you've got any money there, you'd better get it out quick. It ain't safe a minute. When Lincoln comes home I'm goin' to see if I can't—"

"Well, I was calc'lating to go to Lumberville this week, anyway, to buy a carpet and chamber set. I guess I might 's well get the money to-day."

When she came in and demanded the money, Sanford was scared. Were these two old women the beginning of the deluge? Would McPhail insist on being paid also? There was just one hundred dollars left in the bank, together with a little silver. With rare strategy he smiled.

"Certainly, Mrs. McIlvaine. How much will you need?"

She had intended to demand the whole of her deposit—one hundred and seventeen dollars—but his readiness mollified her a little. "I did 'low I'd take the hull, but I guess seventy-five dollars 'll do."

He paid the money briskly out over the little glass shelf. "How is your children, Mrs. McIlvaine?"

"Purty well, thanky," replied Mrs. McIlvaine, laboriously counting the bills.

"Is it all right?"

"I guess so," she replied, dubiously. "I'll count it after I get home."

She went up the street with the feeling that the bank was all right, and she stepped in and told Mrs. Bingham that *she* had no trouble in getting her money.

After she had gone Sanford sat down and wrote a telegram which he sent to St. Paul. This telegram, according to the duplicate at the station, read in this puzzling way:

E.O., Exchange Block, No. 96. All out of paper. Send five hundred note-heads and envelopes to match. Business brisk. Press of correspondence just now. Get them out quick. Wire.
                              Sanford

Two or three others came in after a little money, but he put them off easily. "Just been cashing some paper, and took all the ready cash I can spare. Can't you wait till to-morrow? Link's gone down to St. Paul to collect on some paper. Be back on the five-o'clock. Nine o'clock, sure."

An old Norwegian woman came in to deposit ten dollars, and he counted it in briskly, and put the amount down on her little book for her. Barney Mace came in to deposit a hundred dollars, the proceeds of a horse sale, and this helped him through the day. Those who wanted small sums he paid.

"Glad this ain't a big demand. Rather close on cash to-day," he said, smiling as Lincoln's wife's sister came in.

She laughed. "I guess it won't bu'st yeh. If I thought it would, I'd leave it in."

"Bu'sted!" he said, when Vance wanted him to cash a draft. "Can't do it. Sorry, Van. Do it in the morning all right. Can you wait?"

"Oh, I guess so. Haf to, won't I?"

"Curious," said Sanford, in a confidential way. "I don't know that I ever saw things get in just such shape. Paper enough—but exchange, ye know, and readjustment of accounts."

"I don't know much about banking, myself," said Vance, good-naturedly; "but I s'pose it's a good 'eal same as with a man. Git short o' cash, first they know—'ain't got a cent to spare."

"That's the idea exactly. Credit all right, plenty o' property, but—" and he smiled and went at his books. The smile died out of his eyes as Vance went out and he pulled a little morocco book from his pocket and began studying the beautiful columns of figures with which it seemed to be filled. Those he compared with the books with great care, thrusting the book out of sight when any one entered.

He closed the bank as usual at five. Lincoln had not come—couldn't come now till the nine-o'clock accommodation. For an hour after the shades were drawn he sat there in the semi-darkness, silently pondering on his situation. This attitude and deep quiet were unusual to him. He heard the feet of friends and neighbors passing the door as he sat there by the smoldering coal-fire, in the growing darkness. There was something impressive in his attitude.

He started up at last, and tried to see what the hour was by turning the face of his watch to the dull glow from the cannon-stove's open door.

"Supper-time," he said, and threw the whole matter off, as if he had decided it or had put off the decision till another time.

As he went by the post-office Vance said to McIlvaine in a smiling way, as if it were a good joke on Sanford:

"Little short o' cash down at the bank."

"He's a good fellow," McIlvaine said.

"So's his wife," added Vance, with a chuckle.

III

That night, after supper, Sanford sat in his snug little sitting-room with a baby on each knee, looking as cheerful and happy as any man in the village. The children crowed and shouted as he "trotted them to Boston," or rode them on the toe of his boot. They made a noisy, merry group.

Mrs. Sanford "did her own work," and her swift feet could be heard moving to and fro out in the kitchen. It was pleasant there; the woodwork, the furniture, the stove, the curtains—all had that look of newness just growing into coziness. The coal-stove was lighted and the curtains were drawn.

After the work in the kitchen was done, Mrs. Sanford came in and sat awhile by the fire with the children, looking very wifely in her dark dress and white apron, her round, smiling face glowing with love and pride—the gloating look of a mother seeing her children in the arms of her husband.

"How is Mrs. Peterson's baby, Jim?" she said, suddenly, her face sobering.

"Pretty bad, I guess. La, la, la—deedle-dee! The doctor seemed to think it was a tight squeak if it lived. Guess it's done for—oop 'e goes!"

She made a little leap at the youngest child, and clasped it convulsively to her bosom. Her swift maternal imagination had made another's loss very near and terrible.

"Oh, say, Nell," he broke out, on seeing her sober, "I had the confoundedest time to-day with old lady Bingham—"

"Sh! Baby's gone to sleep."

After the children had been put to bed in the little alcove off the sitting-room, Mrs. Sanford came back, to find Jim absorbed over a little book of accounts.

"What are you studying, Jim?"

Some one knocked on the door before he had time to reply.

"Come in!" he said.

"'Sh! Don't *yell* so," his wife whispered.

"Telegram, Jim," said a voice in the obscurity.

"Oh! That you, Sam? Come in."

Sam, a lathy fellow with a quid in his cheek, stepped in. "How d' 'e do, Mis' Sanford?"

"Set down—se' down."

"Can't stop; 'most train-time."

Sanford tore the envelope open, read the telegram rapidly, the smile fading out of his face. He read it again, word for word, then sat looking at it.

"Any answer?" asked Sam.

"No."

"All right. Good-night."

"Good-night."

After the door slammed, Sanford took the sheet from the envelope and reread it. At length he dropped into his chair. "That settles it," he said, aloud.

"Settles what? What's the news?" His wife came up and looked over his shoulder.

"Settles I've got to go on that nine-thirty train."

"Be back on the morning train?"

"Yes; I guess so—I mean, of course—I'll have to be—to open the bank."

Mrs. Sanford looked at him for a few seconds in silence. There was something in his look, and especially in his tone, that troubled her.

"What do you mean? Jim, you don't intend to come back!" She took his arm. "What's the matter? Now tell me! What *are* you going away for?"

He knew he could not deceive his wife's ears and eyes just then, so he remained silent. "We've got to leave, Nell," he admitted at last.

"Why? What for?"

"Because I'm bu'sted—broke—gone up the spout—and all the rest!" he said, desperately, with an attempt at fun. "Mrs. Bingham and Mrs. McIlvaine have bu'sted me—dead."

"Why—why—what has become of the money—all the money the people have put in there?"

"Gone up with the rest."

"What've you done with it? I don't—"

"Well, I've invested it—and lost it."

"James Gordon Sanford!" she exclaimed, trying to realize it. "Was that right? Ain't that a case of—of—"

"Shouldn't wonder. A case of embezzlement such as you read of in the newspapers." His tone was easy, but he avoided the look in his wife's beautiful gray eyes.

"But it's—*stealing*—ain't it?" She stared at him, bewildered by his reckless lightness of mood.

"It is *now*, because I've lost. If I'd 'a' won it, it 'ud 'a' been financial shrewdness!"

She asked her next question after a pause, in a low voice, and through teeth almost set. "Did you go into this bank to—steal money? Tell me that!"

"No; I didn't, Nell. I ain't quite up to that."

His answer softened her a little, and she sat looking at him steadily as he went on. The tears began to roll slowly down her cheeks. Her hands were clenched.

"The fact is, the idea come into my head last fall when I went up to Superior. My partner wanted me to go in with him on some land, and I did. We speculated on the growth of the town toward the south. We made a strike; then he wanted me to go in on a copper-mine. Of course I expected—"

As he went on with the usual excuses her mind made all the allowances possible for him. He had always been boyish, impulsive, and lacking in judgment and strength of character. She was humiliated and frightened, but she loved and sympathized with him.

Her silence alarmed him, and he made excuses for himself. He was speculating for her sake more than for his own, and so on.

"Choo-choo!" whistled the far-off train through the still air.

He sprang up and reached for his coat.

She seized his arm again. "Where are you going?" she sternly asked.

"To take that train."

"When are you coming back?"

"I don't know." But his tone said, "Never."

She felt it. Her face grew bitter. "Going to leave me and—the babies?"

"I'll send for you soon. Come, good-by!" He tried to put his arm about her. She stepped back.

"Jim, if you leave me to-night" ("Choo-choo!" whistled the engine), "you leave me forever." There was a terrible resolution in her tone.

"What do you mean?"

"I mean that I'm going to stay here. If you go—I'll never be your wife—again—never!" She glanced at the sleeping children, and her chin trembled.

"I can't face those fellows—they'll kill me," he said, in a sullen tone.

"No, they won't. They'll respect you, if you stay and tell 'em exactly how—it—all—is. You've disgraced me and my children, that's what you've done! If you don't stay—"

The clear jangle of the engine-bell sounded through the night as with the whiz of escaping steam and scrape and jar of gripping brakes and howl of wheels the train came to a stop at the station. Sanford dropped his coat and sat down again.

"I'll *have* to stay now." His tone was dry and lifeless. It had a reproach in it that cut the wife deep—deep as the fountain of tears; and she went across the room and knelt at the bedside, burying her face in the clothes on the feet of her children, and sobbed silently.

The man sat with bent head, looking into the glowing coal, whistling through his teeth, a look of sullen resignation and endurance on his face that had never been there before. His very attitude was alien and ominous.

Neither spoke for a long time. At last he rose and began taking off his coat and vest.

"Well, I suppose there's nothing to do but go to bed."

She did not stir—she might have been asleep so far as any sound or motion was concerned. He went off to the bed in the little parlor, and she still knelt there, her heart full of anger, bitterness, sorrow.

The sunny uneventfulness of her past life made this great storm the more terrifying. Her trust in her husband had been absolute. A farmer's daughter, the bank clerk had seemed to her the equal of any gentleman in the world—her world; and when she knew his delicacy, his unfailing kindness, and his abounding good nature, she had accepted him as the father of her children, and this was the first revelation to her of his inherent moral weakness.

Her mind went over the whole ground again and again, in a sort of blinding rut. She was convinced of his lack of honor more by his tone, his inflections, than by his words. His lack of deep regret, his readiness to leave her to bear the whole shock of the discovery—these were in his flippant tones;

and every time she thought of them the hot blood surged over her. At such moments she hated him, and her white teeth clenched.

To these moods succeeded others, when she remembered his smile, the dimple in his chin, his tender care for the sick, his buoyancy, his songs to the children—How *could* he sit there, with the children on his knees, and plan to run away, leaving them disgraced.

She went to bed at last with the babies, and with their soft, warm little bodies touching her side fell asleep, pondering, suffering as only a mother and wife can suffer when distrust and doubt of her husband supplant confidence and adoration.

IV

The children awakened her by their delighted cooing and kissing. It was a great event, this waking to find mamma in their bed. It was hardly light, of a dull gray morning; and with the children tumbling about over her, feeling the pressure of the warm little hands and soft lips, she went over the whole situation again, and at last settled upon her action.

She rose, shook down the coal in the stove in the sitting-room, and started a fire in the kitchen; then she dressed the children by the coal-burner. The elder of them, as soon as dressed, ran in to wake "poppa" while the mother went about breakfast-getting.

Sanford came out of his bedroom unwontedly gloomy, greeting the children in a subdued manner. He shivered as he sat by the fire, and stirred the stove as if he thought the room was cold. His face was pale and moist.

"Breakfast is ready, James," called Mrs. Sanford, in a tone which she meant to be habitual, but which had a cadence of sadness in it.

Someway, he found it hard to look at her as he came out. She busied herself with placing the children at the table, in order to conceal her own emotion.

"I don't believe I'll eat any meat this morning, Nellie. I ain't very well."

She glanced at him quickly, keenly. "What's the matter?"

"I d'know. My stomach is kind of upset by this failure o' mine. I'm in great shape to go down to the bank this morning—and face them fellows—"

"It's got to be done."

"I know it; but that don't help me any." He tried to smile.

She mused, while the baby hammered on his tin plate.

"You've got to go down. If you don't—I will," said she, resolutely. "And you must say that that money will be paid back—every cent."

"But that's more'n I can do—"

"It must be done."

"But under the law—"

"There's nothing can make this thing right except paying every cent we owe. I ain't a-goin' to have it said that my children—that I'm livin' on some-body else. If you don't pay these debts, *I will*. I've thought it all out. If you don't stay and face it, and pay these men, I won't own you as my husband. I loved and trusted you, Jim—I thought you were honorable—it's been a ter-rible blow—but I've decided it all in my mind."

She conquered her little weakness, and went on to the end firmly. Her face looked pale. There was a square look about the mouth and chin. The iron resolution and Puritanic strength of her father, old John Foreman, had come to the surface. Her look and tone mastered the man, for he loved her deeply.

She had set him a hard task, and when he rose and went down the street he walked with bent head, quite unlike his usual self.

There were not many men on the street. It seemed earlier than it was, for it was a raw, cold morning, promising snow. The sun was completely masked in a seamless dust-gray cloud. He met Vance with a brown parcel (beefsteak for breakfast) under his arm.

"Hello, Jim! How are ye, so early in the morning?"

"Blessed near used up."

"That so? What's the matter?"

"I d'know," said Jim, listlessly. "Bilious, I guess. Headache—stomach bad."

"Oh! Well, now, you try them pills I was tellin' you of."

Arrived at the bank, he let himself in, and locked the door behind him. He stood in the middle of the floor a few minutes, then went behind the rail-ing and sat down. He didn't build a fire, though it was cold and damp, and he shivered as he sat leaning on the desk. At length he drew a large sheet of paper toward him and wrote something on it in a heavy hand.

He was writing on this when Lincoln entered at the back, whistling boyishly. "Hello, Jim! Ain't you up early? No fire, eh?" He rattled at the stove.

Sanford said nothing, but finished his writing. Then he said, quietly, "You needn't build a fire on my account, Link."

"Why not?"

"Well, I'm used up."

"What's the matter?"

"I'm sick, and the business had gone to the devil." He looked out of the window.

Link dropped the poker, and came around behind the counter, and stared at Sanford with fallen mouth.

"Wha'd you say?"

"I said the business had gone to the devil. We're broke—bu'sted—petered—gone up the spout." He took a sort of morbid pleasure in saying these things.

"What's bu'sted us? Have—"

"I've been speculatin' in copper. My partner's bu'sted me."

Link came closer. His mouth stiffened and an ominous look came into his eyes. "You don't mean to say you've lost *my* money, and mother's, and Uncle Andrew's, and all the rest?"

Sanford was getting irritated. "——it! What's the use. I tell you, *yes!* It's all gone—every cent of it."

Link caught him by the shoulder as he sat at the desk. Sanford's tone enraged him. "You thief! But you'll pay *me* back, or I'll—"

"Oh, go ahead! Pound a sick man, if it'll do you any good," said Sanford, with a peculiar recklessness of lifeless misery. "Pay y'rself out of the safe. Here's the combination."

Lincoln released him, and began turning the knob of the door. At last it swung open, and he searched the money-drawers. Less than forty dollars, all told. His voice was full of helpless rage as he turned at last and walked up close to Sanford's bowed head.

"I'd like to pound the life out o' you!"

"You're at liberty to do so, if it'll be any satisfaction."

This desperate courage awed the younger man. He gazed at Sanford in amazement.

"If you'll cool down and wait a little, Link, I'll tell you all about it. I'm sick as a horse. I guess I'll go home. You can put this up in the window, and go home, too, if you want to."

Lincoln saw that Sanford was sick. He was shivering, and drops of sweat were on his white forehead. Lincoln stood aside silently, and let him go out.

"Better lock up, Link. You can't do anything by staying here."

Lincoln took refuge in a boyish phrase that would have made any one but a sick man laugh: "Well, this is a ——of a note!"

He took up the paper. It read:

BANK CLOSED

To my creditors and depositors

Through a combination of events I find myself obliged to temporarily suspend payment. I ask the depositors to be patient, and their claims will be met. I think I can pay twenty-five cents on the dollar, if given a little time. I shall not run away. I shall stay right here till all matters are honorably settled.

James G. Sanford

Lincoln hastily pinned this paper to the window-sash so that it could be seen from without, then pulled down the blinds and locked the door. His fun-loving nature rose superior to his rage for the moment. "There'll be the devil to pay in this burg before two hours."

He slipped out the back way, taking the keys with him. "I'll go and tell uncle, and then we'll see if Jim can't turn in the house on our account," he thought, as he harnessed a team to drive out to McPhail's.

The first man to try the door was an old Norwegian in a spotted Makinac jacket and a fur cap, with the inevitable little tippet about his neck. He turned the knob, knocked, and at last saw the writing, which he could not read, and went away to tell Johnson that the bank was closed. Johnson thought nothing special of that; it was early, and they weren't very particular to open on time, anyway.

Then the barber across the street tried to get in to have a bill changed. Trying to peer in the window, he saw the notice, which he read with a grin.

"One o' Link's jobs," he explained to the fellows in the shop. "He's too darned lazy to open on time, so he puts up notice that the bank is bu'sted."

"Let's go and see."

"Don't do it! He's watchin' to see us all rush across and look. Just keep quiet, and see the solid citizens rear around."

Old Orrin McIlvaine came out of the post-office and tried the door next, then stood for a long time reading the notice, and at last walked thoughtfully away. Soon he returned, to the merriment of the fellows in the barber shop, with two or three solid citizens who had been smoking an after-breakfast cigar and planning a deer-hunt. They stood before the window in a row and read the notice. McIlvaine gesticulated with his cigar.

"Gentlemen, there's a pig loose here."

"One o' Link's jokes, I reckon."

"But that's Sanford's writin'. An' here it is nine o'clock, and no one around. I don't like the looks of it, myself."

The crowd thickened; the fellows came out of the blacksmith shop, while the jokers in the barber shop smote their knees and yelled with merriment.

"What's up?" queried Vance, coming up and repeating the universal question.

McIlvaine pointed at the poster with his cigar.

Vance read the notice, while the crowd waited silently.

"What ye think of it?" asked some one, impatiently.

Vance smoked a moment. "Can't say. Where's Jim?"

"That's it! Where *is* he?"

"Best way to find out is to send a boy up to the house." He called a boy and sent him scurrying up the street.

The crowd now grew sober and discussed possibilities.

"*If* that's true, it's the worst crack on the head *I* ever had," said McIlvaine. "Seventeen hundred dollars is my pile in there." He took a seat on the windowsill.

"Well, I'm tickled to death to think I got my little stake out before anything happened."

"When you think of it—what security did he ever give?" McIlvaine continued.

"Not a cent—not a red cent."

"No, sir; we simply banked on him. Now, he's a good fellow, an' this may be a joke o' Link's; but the fact is, it *might* 'a' happened. Well, sonny?" he said to the boy, who came running up.

"Link ain't to home, an' Mrs. Sanford she says Jim's sick, an' can't come down."

There was a silence. "Anybody see him this morning?" asked Wilson.

"Yes; I saw him," said Vance. "Looked bad, too."

The crowd changed; people came and went, some to get news, some to carry it away. In a short time the whole town knew the bank had "bu'sted all to smash." Farmers drove along, and stopped to find out what it all meant. The more they talked, the more excited they grew; and "Scoundrel," and "I always had my doubts of that feller," were phrases growing more frequent.

The list of the victims grew until it was evident that nearly all of the savings of a dozen or more depositors were swallowed up, and the sum reached was nearly twenty thousand dollars.

"What did he do with it?" was the question. He never gambled or drank. He lived frugally. There was no apparent cause for this failure of a trusted institution.

It was beginning to snow in great, damp, driving flakes, which melted as they fell, giving to the street a strangeness and gloom that were impressive. The men left the sidewalk at last, and gathered in the saloons and stores to continue the discussion.

The crowd at the railroad saloon was very decided in its belief. Sanford had pocketed the money and skipped. That yarn about his being at home sick was a blind. Some went so far as to say that it was almighty curious where Link was, hinting darkly that the bank ought to be broken into, and so on.

Upon this company burst Barney and Sam Mace from "Hogan's Corners." They were excited by the news and already inflamed with drink.

"Say!" yelled Barney, "any o' you fellers know anything about Jim Sanford?"

"No. Why? Got any money there?"

"Yes; and I'm goin' to git it out, if I haf to smash the door in."

"That's the talk!" shouted some of the loafers. They sprang up and surrounded Barney. There was something in his voice that aroused all their latent ferocity. "I'm goin' to get into that bank an' see how things look, an' then I'm goin' to find Sanford an' get my money, or pound——out of 'im, one o' the six."

"Go find him first. He's up home, sick—so's his wife."

"I'll see whether he's sick 'r not. I'll drag 'im out by the scruff o' the neck! Come on!" He ended with a sudden resolution, leading the way out into the street, where the falling snow was softening the dirt into a sticky mud.

A rabble of a dozen or two of men and boys followed Mace up the street.

He led the way with great strides, shouting his threats. As they passed along, women thrust their heads out at the windows, asking, "What's the matter?" And some one answered each time, in a voice of unconcealed delight:

"Sanford's stole all the money in the bank, and they're goin' up to lick 'im. Come on if ye want to see the fun."

In a few moments the street looked as if an alarm of fire had been sounded. Half the town seemed to be out, and the other half coming— women in shawls, like squaws; children capering and laughing; young men grinning at the girls who came out and stood at the gates.

Some of the citizens tried to stop it. Vance found the constable looking on, and ordered him to do his duty and stop that crowd.

"I can't do anything," he said, helplessly. "They ain't done nawthin' yet, an' I don't know—"

"Oh, git out! They're goin' up there to whale Jim, an' you know it. If you don't stop 'em, I'll telephone f'r the sheriff, and have you arrested with 'em."

Under this pressure, the constable ran along after the crowd, in an attempt to stop it. He reached them as they stood about the little porch of the house, packed closely around Barney and Sam, who said nothing, but followed Barney like his shadow. If the sun had been shining, it might not have happened as it did; but there was a semi-obscurity, a weird half-light shed by the thick sky and falling snow, which somehow encouraged the enraged ruffians, who pounded on the door just as the pleading voice of the constable was heard.

"Hold on, gentlemen! This is ag'inst the law—"

"Law to——!" said someone. "This is a case f'r something besides law."

"Open up there!" roared the raucous voice of Barney Mace, as he pounded at the door fiercely.

The door opened, and the wife appeared, one child in her arms, the other at her side.

"What do you want?"

"Where's that banker? Tell the thief to come out here! We want to talk with him."

The woman did not quail, but her face seemed a ghastly yellow, seen through the falling snow.

"He can't come. He's sick."

"Sick! We'll *sick* 'im! Tell 'im t' come out, or we'll snake 'im out by the heels." The crowd laughed. The worst elements of the saloons surrounded the two half-savage men. It was amusing to them to see the woman face them all in that way.

"Where's McPhail?" Vance inquired, anxiously. "Somebody find McPhail."

"Stand out o' the way!" snarled Barney, as he pushed the struggling woman aside.

The wife raised her voice to that wild, animal-like pitch a woman uses when desperate.

"I sha'n't do it, I tell you! *Help!*"

"Keep out o' my way, or I'll wring y'r neck f'r yeh."

She struggled with him, but he pushed her aside and entered the room.

"What's goin' on here?" called the ringing voice of Andrew McPhail, who had just driven up with Link.

Several of the crowd looked over their shoulders at McPhail.

"Hello, Mac! Just in time. Oh, nawthin'. Barney's callin' on the banker, that's all."

Over the heads of the crowd, packed struggling about the door, came the woman's scream again. McPhail dashed around the crowd, running two or three of them down, and entered the back door. Vance, McIlvaine, and Lincoln followed him.

"Cowards!" the wife said, as the ruffians approached the bed. They swept her aside, but paused an instant before the glance of the sick man's eye. He lay there, desperately, deathly sick. The blood throbbed in his whirling brain, his eyes were bloodshot and blinded, his strength was gone. He could hardly speak. He partly rose and stretched out his hand, and then fell back.

"Kill me—if you want to—but let her—alone. She's—"

The children were crying. The wind whistled drearily across the room, carrying the evanescent flakes of soft snow over the heads of the pausing, listening crowd in the doorway. Quick steps were heard.

"Hold on there!" cried McPhail, as he burst into the room. He seemed an angel of God to the wife and mother.

He spread his great arms in a gesture which suggested irresistible strength and resolution. "Clear out! Out with ye!"

No man had ever seen him look like that before. He awed them with the look in his eyes. His long service as sheriff gave him authority. He hustled them, cuffed them out of the door like school-boys. Barney backed out, cursing. He knew McPhail too well to refuse to obey.

McPhail pushed Barney out, shut the door behind him, and stood on the steps, looking at the crowd.

"Well, you're a great lot! You fellers, would ye jump on a sick man? What ye think ye're all doin', anyhow?"

The crowd laughed. "Hey, Mac; give us a speech!"

"You ought to be booted, the whole lot o' yeh!" he replied.

"That houn' in there's run the bank into the ground, with every cent o' money we'd put in," said Barney. "I s'pose ye know that."

"Well, s'pose he has—what's the use o' jumpin' on 'im?"

"Git it out of his hide."

"I've heerd that talk before. How much *you* got in?"

"Two hundred dollars."

"Well, I've got two thousand." The crowd saw the point.

"I guess if anybody was goin' t' take it out of his hide, I'd be the man; but I want the feller to live and have a chance to pay it back. Killin' 'im is a dead loss."

"That's so!" shouted somebody. "Mac ain't no fool, if he *does* chaw hay," said another, and the crowd laughed. They were losing that frenzy, largely imitative and involuntary, which actuates a mob. There was something counteracting in the ex-sheriff's cool, humorous tone.

"Give us the rest of it, Mac!"

"The rest of it is—clear out o' here, 'r I'll boot every mother's son of yeh!"

"Can't do it!"

"Come down an' try it!"

McIlvaine opened the door and looked out. "Mac, Mrs. Sanford wants to say something—if it's safe."

"Safe as eatin' dinner."

Mrs. Sanford came out, looking pale and almost like a child as she stood beside her defender's towering bulk. But her face was resolute.

"That money will be paid back," she said, "dollar for dollar, if you'll just give us a chance. As soon as Jim gets well enough every cent will be paid, if I live."

The crowd received this little speech in silence. One or two said, in low voices: "That's business. She'll do it, too, if any one can."

Barney pushed his way through the crowd with contemptuous curses. "The——she will!" he said.

"We'll see 't you have a chance," McPhail and McIlvaine assured Mrs. Sanford.

She went in and closed the door.

"Now *git!*" said Andrew, coming down the steps. The crowd scattered with laughing taunts. He turned, and entered the house. The rest drifted off down the street through the soft flurries of snow, and in a few moments the street assumed its usual appearance.

The failure of the bank and the raid on the banker had passed into history.

V

In the light of the days of calm afterthought which followed, this attempt upon the peace of the Sanford home grew more monstrous, and helped largely to mitigate the feeling against the banker. Besides, he had not run away; that was a strong point in his favor.

"Don't that show," argued Vance, in the post-office—"don't that *show* he didn't intend to steal? An' don't it show he's goin' to try to make things square?"

"I guess we might as well think that as anything."

"I claim the boys has a right t' take sumpthin' out o' his hide," Bent Wilson stubbornly insisted.

"Ain't enough t' go 'round," laughed McPhail. "Besides, I can't have it. Link an' I own the biggest share in 'im, an' we can't have him hurt."

McIlvaine and Vance grinned. "That's a fact, Mac. We four fellers are the main losers. He's ours, an' we can't have him foundered 'r crippled 'r cut up in any way. Ain't that woman of his gritty?"

"Gritty ain't no name for her. She's goin' into business."

"So I hear. They say Jim was crawling around a little yesterday. I didn't see 'im."

"I did. He looks pretty streak-id—now you bet."

"Wha'd he say for himself?"

"Oh, said give 'im time—he'd fix it all up."

"How much time?"

"Time enough. Hain't been able to look at a book since. Say, ain't it a little curious he was so sick just then—sick as a p'isened dog?"

The two men looked at each other in a manner most comically significant. The thought of poison was in the mind of each.

It was under these trying circumstances that Sanford began to crawl about, a week or ten days after his sickness. It was really the most terrible punishment for him. Before, everybody used to sing out, "Hello, Jim!" or "Mornin', banker," or some other jovial, heart-warming salutation. Now, as he went down the street, the groups of men smoking on the sunny side of the stores ignored him, or looked at him with scornful eyes.

Nobody said, "Hello, Jim!"—not even McPhail or Vance. They nodded merely, and went on with their smoking. The children followed him and stared at him without compassion. They had heard him called a scoundrel and a thief too often at home to feel any pity for his pale face.

After his first trip down the street, bright with the December sunshine, he came home in a bitter, weak mood, smarting, aching with a poignant self-pity over the treatment he had received from his old cronies.

"It's all your fault," he burst out to his wife. "If you'd only let me go away and look up another place I wouldn't have to put up with all these sneers and insults."

"What sneers and insults?" she asked, coming over to him.

"Why, nobody 'll speak to me."

"Won't Mr. McPhail and Mr. McIlvaine?"

"Yes; but not as they used to."

"You can't blame 'em, Jim. You must go to work and win back their confidence."

"I can't do that. Let's go away, Nell, and try again."

Her mouth closed firmly. A hard look came into her eyes. "*You* can go if you want to, Jim. I'm goin' to stay right here till we can leave honorably. We can't run away from this. It would follow us anywhere we went; and it would get worse the farther we went."

He knew the unyielding quality of his wife's resolution, and from that moment he submitted to his fate. He loved his wife and children with a passionate love that made life with them, among the citizens he robbed, better than life anywhere else on earth; he had no power to leave them.

As soon as possible he went over his books and found out that he owed, above all notes coming in, about eleven thousand dollars. This was a large sum to look forward to paying by anything he could do in the Siding, now that his credit was gone. Nobody would take him as a clerk, and there was nothing else to be done except manual labor, and he was not strong enough for that.

His wife, however, had a plan. She sent East to friends, for a little money at once, and with a few hundred dollars opened a little store in time for the holiday trade—wall-paper, notions, light dry-goods, toys, and millinery. She did her own housework and attended to her shop in a grim, uncomplaining fashion that made Sanford feel like a criminal in her presence. He couldn't propose to help her in the store, for he knew the people would refuse to trade with him, so he attended to the children and did little things about the house for the first few months of the winter.

His life for a time was abjectly pitiful. He didn't know what to do. He had lost his footing, and, worst of all, he felt that his wife no longer respected him. She loved and pitied him, but she no longer looked up to him. She went about her work and down to her store with a silent, resolute, uncommunicative air, utterly unlike her former sunny, domestic self, so that even she seemed alien like the rest. If he had been ill, Vance and McPhail would have attended him; as it was, they could not help him.

She already had the sympathy of the entire town, and McIlvaine had said: "If you need more money, you can have it, Mrs. Sanford. Call on us at any time."

"Thank you. I don't think I'll need it. All I ask is your trade," she replied. "I don't ask anybody to pay more'n a thing's worth, either. I'm goin' to sell goods on business principles, and I expect folks to buy of me because I'm selling reliable goods as cheap as anybody else."

Her business was successful from the start, but she did not allow herself to get too confident.

"This is a kind of charity trade. It won't last on that basis. Folks ain't goin' to buy of me because I'm poor—not very long," she said to Vance, who went in to congratulate her on her booming trade during Christmas and New Year.

Vance called so often, advising or congratulating her, that the boys joked him. "Say, looky here! You're goin' to get into a peck o' trouble with your wife yet. You spend about half y'r time in the new store."

Vance looked serene as he replied, "I'd stay longer and go oftener if I could."

"Well, if you ain't cheekier 'n ol' cheek! I should think you'd be ashamed to say it."

"'Shamed of it? I'm proud of it! As I tell my wife, if I'd 'a' met Mis' Sanford when we was both young, they wouldn't 'a' be'n no such *present arrangement.*"

The new life made its changes in Mrs. Sanford. She grew thinner and graver, but as she went on, and trade steadily increased, a feeling of pride, a sort of exultation, came into her soul and shone from her steady eyes. It was glorious to feel that she was holding her own with men in the world, winning their respect, which is better than their flattery. She arose each day at five o'clock with a distinct pleasure, for her physical health was excellent, never better.

She began to dream. She could pay off five hundred dollars a year of the interest—perhaps she could pay some of the principal, if all went well. Perhaps in a year or two she could take a larger store, and, if Jim got something to do, in ten years they could pay it all off—every cent! She talked with business men, and read and studied, and felt each day a firmer hold on affairs.

Sanford got the agency of an insurance company or two, and earned a few dollars during the spring. In June things brightened up a little. The money for a note of a thousand dollars fell due—a note he had considered virtually worthless, but the debtor, having had a "streak o' luck," sent seven hundred and fifty dollars. Sanford at once called a meeting of his creditors, and paid them, pro rata, a thousand dollars. The meeting took place in his wife's store, and in making the speech Sanford said:

"I can tell you, gentlemen, if you'll only give us a chance, we'll clear this thing all up—that is, the principal. We can't—"

"Yes, we can, James. We can pay it all, principal and interest. We owe the interest just as much as the rest." It was evident that there was to be no letting down while she lived.

The effect of this payment was marked. The general feeling was much more kindly than before. Most of the fellows dropped back into the habit of calling him Jim; but, after all, it was not like the greeting of old, when he was "banker." Still the gain in confidence found a reflex in him. His shoulders, which had begun to droop a little, lifted, and his eyes brightened.

"We'll win yet," he began to say.

"She's a-holdin' of 'im right to time," Mrs. Bingham said.

It was shortly after this that he got the agency for a new cash-delivery system, and went on the road with it, travelling in northern Wisconsin and Minnesota. He came back after a three weeks' trip, quite jubilant. "I've made a hundred dollars, Nell. I'm all right if this holds out, and I guess it will."

In the following November, just a year after the failure, they celebrated the day, at her suggestion, by paying interest on the unpaid sums they owed.

"I could pay a little more on the principal," she explained, "but I guess it'll be better to use it for my stock. I can pay better dividends next year."

"Take y'r time, Mrs. Sanford," Vance said.

Of course she could not escape criticism. There were the usual number of women who noticed that she kept her "young uns" in the latest style, when as a matter of fact she sat up nights to make their little things. They also noticed that she retained her house and her furniture.

"If I was in her place, seems to me, I'd turn in some o' my fine furniture towards my debts," Mrs. Sam Gilbert said, spitefully.

She did not even escape calumny. Mrs. Sam Gilbert darkly hinted at certain "goin's on durin' his bein' away. Lit up till after midnight some nights. I c'n see her winder from mine."

Rose McPhail, one of Mrs. Sanford's most devoted friends, asked, quietly, "Do you sit up all night t' see?"

"S'posin' I do!" she snapped. "I can't sleep with such things goin' on."

"If it'll do you any good, Jane, I'll say that she's settin' up there sewin' for the children. If you'd keep your nose out o' other folks' affairs, and attend better to your own, your house wouldn't look like a pig-pen, an' your children like A-rabs."

But in spite of a few annoyances of this character Mrs. Sanford found her new life wholesomer and broader than her old life, and the pain of her loss grew less poignant.

VI

One day in spring, in the lazy, odorous hush of the afternoon, the usual number of loafers were standing on the platform, waiting for the train. The sun was going down the slope toward the hills, through a warm April haze.

"Hello!" exclaimed the man who always sees things first. "Here comes Mrs. Sanford and the ducklings."

Everybody looked.

"Ain't goin' off, is she?"

"Nope; guess not. Meet somebody, prob'ly Sanford."

"Well, somethin's up. She don't often get out o' that store."

"Le's see; he's been gone most o' the winter, hain't he?"

"Yes; went away about New-Year's."

Mrs. Sanford came past, leading a child by each hand, nodding and smiling to friends—for all seemed friends. She looked very resolute and business-like in her plain, dark dress, with a dull flame of color at the throat, while the broad hat she wore gave her face a touch of piquancy very charming. Evidently she was in excellent spirits, and laughed and chatted in quite a carefree way.

She was now an institution at the Siding. Her store had grown in proportions yearly, until it was as large and commodious as any in the town. The drummers for dry-goods all called there, and the fact that she did not sell any groceries at all did not deter the drummers for grocery houses from calling to see each time if she hadn't decided to put in a stock of groceries.

These keen-eyed young fellows had spread her fame all up and down the road. She had captured them, not by beauty, but by her pluck, candor, honesty, and by a certain fearless but reserved camaraderie. She was not afraid of them, or of anybody else, now.

The train whistled, and everybody turned to watch it as it came pushing around the bluff like a huge hound on a trail, its nose close to the ground. Among the first to alight was Sanford, in a shining new silk hat and a new suit of clothes. He was smiling gaily as he fought his way through the crowd to his wife's side. "Hello!" he shouted. "I thought I'd see you all here."

"W'y, Jim, ain't you cuttin' a swell?"

"A swell! Well, who's got a better right? A man wants to look as well as he can when he comes home to such a family."

"Hello, Jim! That plug'll never do."

"Hello, Vance! Yes; but it's got to do. Say, you tell all the fellers that's got anything ag'inst me to come around to-morrow night to the store. I want to make some kind of a settlement."

"All right, Jim. Goin' to pay a new dividend?"

"That's what I am," he beamed, as he walked off with his wife, who was studying him sharply.

"Jim, what ails you?"

"Nothin'; I'm all right."

"But this new suit? And the hat? And the necktie?"

He laughed merrily—so merrily, in fact, that his wife looked at him the more anxiously. He appeared to be in a queer state of intoxication—a state that made him happy without impairing his faculties, however. He turned suddenly and put his lips down toward her ear. "Well, Nell, I can't hold in any longer. We've struck it!"

"Struck what?"

"Well, you see that derned fool partner o' mine got me to go into a lot o' land in the copper country. That's where all the trouble came. He got awfully let down. Well, he's had some surveyors to go up there lately and look it over, and the next thing we knew the Superior Mining Company came along an' wanted to buy it. Of course we didn't want to sell just then."

They had reached the store door, and he paused.

"We'll go right home to supper," she said. "The girls will look out for things till I get back."

They walked on together, the children laughing and playing ahead.

"Well, upshot of it is, I sold out my share to Osgood for twenty thousand dollars."

She stopped, and stared at him. "Jim—Gordon Sanford!"

"Fact! I can prove it." He patted his breast pocket mysteriously. "Ten thousand right there."

"Gracious sakes alive! How dare you carry so much money?"

"I'm mighty glad o' the chance." He grinned.

They walked on almost in silence, with only a word now and then. She seemed to be thinking deeply, and he didn't want to disturb her. It was a delicious spring hour. The snow was all gone, even under the hedges. The roads were warm and brown. The red sun was flooding the valley with a misty, rich-colored light, and against the orange and gold of the sky the hills stood in Tyrian purple. Wagons were rattling along the road. Men on the farms in the edge of the village could be heard whistling at their work. A discordant jangle of a neighboring farmer's supper-bell announced that it was time "to turn out."

Sanford was almost as gay as a lover. He seemed to be on the point of regaining his old place in his wife's respect. Somehow the possession of the package of money in his pocket seemed to make him more worthy of her, to put him more on an equality with her.

As they reached the little one-story square cottage he sat down on the porch, where the red light fell warmly, and romped with the children, while his wife went in and took off her things. She "kept a girl" now, so that the work of getting supper did not devolve entirely upon her. She came out soon to call them all to the supper-table in the little kitchen back of the sitting-room.

The children were wild with delight to have "poppa" back, and the meal was the merriest they had had for a long time. The doors and windows were open, and the spring evening air came in, laden with the sweet, suggestive smell of bare ground. The alert chuckle of an occasional robin could be heard.

Mrs. Sanford looked up from her tea. "There's one thing I don't like, Jim, and that's the way that money comes. You didn't—you didn't really earn it."

"Oh, don't worry yourself about that. That's the way things go. It's just luck."

"Well, I can't see it just that way. It seems to me just—like gambling. You win, but—but somebody else must lose."

"Oh well, look a-here; if you go to lookin' too sharp into things like that, you'll find a good 'eal of any business like gamblin'."

She said no more, but her face remained clouded. On the way down to the store they met Lincoln.

"Come down to the store, Link, and bring Joe. I want to talk with yeh."

Lincoln stared, but said, "All right." Then added, as the others walked away, "Well, that feller ain't got no cheek t' talk to me like that—more cheek 'n a gov'ment mule!"

Jim took a seat near the door, and watched his wife as she went about the store. She employed two clerks now, while she attended to the books and the cash. He thought how different she was, and he liked (and, in a way, feared) her cool, business-like manner, her self-possession, and her smileless conversation with a drummer who came in. Jim was puzzled. He didn't quite understand the peculiar effect his wife's manner had upon him.

Outside, word had passed around that Jim had got back and that something was in the wind, and the fellows began to drop in. When McPhail came in and said, "Hello!" in his hearty way, Sanford went over to his wife and said:

"Say, Nell, I can't stand this. I'm goin' to get rid o' this money right off, *now!*"

"Very well; just as you please."

"Gents," he began, turning his back to the counter and smiling blandly on them, one thumb in his vest pocket, "any o' you fellers got anything against the Lumber County Bank—any certificates of deposit, or notes?"

Two or three nodded, and McPhail said, humorously, slapping his pocket, "I always go loaded."

"Produce your paper, gents," continued Sanford, with a dramatic whang of a leathern wallet down into his palm. "I'm buying up all paper on the bank."

It was a superb stroke. The fellows whistled and stared and swore at one another. This *was* coming down on them. Link was dumb with amazement as he received sixteen hundred and fifty dollars in crisp, new bills.

"Andrew, it's your turn next." Sanford's tone was actually patronizing as he faced McPhail.

"I was jokin'. I ain't got my certificate here."

"Don't matter—don't matter. Here's fifteen hundred dollars. Just give us a receipt, and bring the certif. any time. I want to get rid o' this stuff right now."

"Say, Jim, we'd like to know jest—jest where this windfall comes from," said Vance, as he took his share.

"Comes from the copper country," was all he ever said about it.

"I don't see where he invested," Link said. "Wasn't a scratch of a pen to show that he invested anything while he was in the bank. Guess that's where our money went."

"Well, I ain't squealin'," said Vance. "I'm glad to get out of it without asking any questions. I'll tell yeh one thing, though," he added, as they stood outside the door; "we'd 'a' never smelt of our money again if it hadn't 'a' been f 'r that woman in there. She'd 'a' paid it alone if Jim hadn't 'a' made this strike, whereas he never 'd 'a'—Well, all right. We're out of it."

It was one of the greatest moments of Sanford's life. He expanded in it. He was as pleasantly aware of the glances of his wife as he used to be when, as a clerk, he saw her pass and look in at the window where he sat dreaming over his ledger.

As for her, she was going over the whole situation from this new standpoint. He had been weak, he had fallen in her estimation, and yet, as he stood there, so boyish in his exultation, the father of her children, she loved him with a touch of maternal tenderness and hope, and her heart throbbed in an unconscious, swift determination to do him good. She no longer deceived herself. She was his equal—in some ways his superior. Her love had friendship in it, but less of sex, and no adoration.

As she blew out the lights, stepped out on the walk, and turned the key in the lock, he said, "Well, Nellie, you won't have to do that any more."

"No; I won't *have* to, but I guess I'll keep on just the same, Jim."

"Keep on? What for?"

"Well, I rather like it."

"But you don't need to—"

"I like being my own boss," she said. "I've done a lot o' figuring, Jim, these last three years, and it's kind o' broadened me, I hope. I can't go back where I was. I'm a better woman than I was before, and I hope and believe that I'm better able to be a real mother to my children."

Jim looked up at the moon filling the warm, moist air with a transfiguring light that fell in a luminous mist on the distant hills. "I know one thing, Nellie; I'm a better man than I was before, and it's all owin' to you."

His voice trembled a little, and the sympathetic tears came into her eyes. She didn't speak at once—she couldn't. At last she stopped him by a touch on the arm.

"Jim, I want a partner in my store. Let us begin again, right here. I can't say that I'll ever feel *just* as I did once—I don't know as it's right to. I looked up to you too much. I expected too much of you, too. Let's begin again, as equal partners." She held out her hand, as one man to another. He took it wonderingly.

"All right, Nell; I'll do it."

Then, as he put his arm around her, she held up her lips to be kissed. "And we'll be happy again—happy as we deserve, I s'pose," she said, with a smile and a sigh.

"It's almost like getting married again, Nell—for me."

As they walked off up the sidewalk in the soft moonlight, their arms were interlocked.

They loitered like a couple of lovers.

II

Main Street Ascendant
1890–1930

As the twentieth century began, the midwestern town played a pivotal role in the grand order of things. Fully 60 percent of the nation's population lived in towns or on the farmland they served. Although the towns remained influential, their dominance was being undercut with the growth of cities. It now appeared that the American future was inevitably an urban one. As the cities loomed ever more powerful, anti-urban sentiment began to rise along Main Street. William Jennings Bryan, a spokesman for the interests of the American farmer and a resident of the frontier town of Lincoln, Nebraska, perhaps best summarized such sentiments in his famous "Cross of Gold" speech before the Democratic national convention in 1896: "The great cities rest upon our broad and fertile prairies. Burn down your cities and leave our farms, and your cities will spring up again as if by magic; but destroy our farms, and the grass will grow in the streets of every city in the country." Thirty-five years later, the publisher of a small-town Ohio newspaper commented in a similar vein: "Several writers have advanced the argument that the 'small town is doomed.' We get a good laugh out of that, those of us who live in Camden and in thousands of towns like it. For we know that living conditions in our smaller communities are far in advance of what they were 10 years ago, while they have been growing constantly worse in the cities."

During the early decades of the twentieth century towns everywhere were affected by the introduction of the automobile. Because of the compact nature of the towns, most nineteenth-century residents had usually walked as they went about their daily routines. Walking had its limitations, however, and so the large and sometimes unpredictable horse provided the primary means of power and transportation—pulling plows in nearby fields and moving coaches, produce wagons, and buggies. Livery stables were an essential part of the local economy, providing feed and care for the many animals upon which the citizenry relied. The community's major source of transportation, however, deposited each day a substantial amount of manure and urine on the town's unpaved streets and byways. The resulting aroma was an unpleasant daily fact of town life. Because the health hazards were only dimly perceived, street cleaning was usually haphazard at best.

This natural accumulation was exacerbated by the fact that few streets—even Main Street—were paved. Thus melting snows in winter and cloud-bursts in summer turned the dirt streets into hopeless passageways, com-mingling mud with excrement, making the streets a formidable obstacle for pedestrians. At other times dry weather created a haze of dust that filtered into every nook and cranny of each building in town. It is, then, little won-der that the American people so quickly and enthusiastically embraced the automobile early in the twentieth century; it freed them not only from the very real dangers of cantankerous and sometimes runaway horses but from the stench and filth that had been a constant ever since the town was first established. Incredible as it may seem today, Americans perceived the auto-mobile to be a major advance in improving the environment of town and city alike.

Only during the 1920s did local politicians authorize extensive paving of town streets; they did so only in response to the growing numbers of auto-mobile owners who insisted upon better in-town driving conditions. Not surprisingly, at the same time the improvement of farm-to-market roads be-came a major political issue for county commissions and state legislatures. Many towns first paved their main thoroughfares with brick, and nearly a century later some of those original attractive brick-lined streets remain in service. By the end of the 1920s horses had largely disappeared from town streets, and by the mid-1930s work crews had extracted from Main Street the once ubiquitous hitching posts.

The towns and farms of the Midwest produced many of the men and women who helped transform America into a prosperous and power-ful nation. Out of the towns and into the mainstream of American life there flowed an incredible stream of talented young men and women—businessmen, teachers, physicians, entrepreneurs, writers, artists, scien-tists, politicians, scholars, and an inordinate number of skilled laborers. Many political leaders, including such future presidents as Herbert Hoover, Harry Truman, Dwight Eisenhower, and Ronald Reagan, grew up in mid-western towns. In the final chapter of the novel *Winesburg, Ohio,* about his northwestern Ohio home of Clyde, Sherwood Anderson took note of this phenomenon when he described himself, in the form of newspaperman George Willard, departing for Chicago to build a new career. As the train conductor punches his ticket, he smiles, because he "had seen a thousand George Willards go out of their towns to the city." Taking a final glance at the small town in which he had grown to adulthood, Willard recognizes that "his life there had become a background on which to paint the dreams of his manhood."

When he wrote these words in 1918, Anderson unknowingly identified the essential phenomenon that would bedevil the midwestern town for the remainder of the century. As the cities grew in size and influence, the superior cultural and economic opportunities they offered attracted the best and the brightest of the small towns' high school graduates. Better jobs, myriad cultural events, and greater social opportunities were obvious attractions that the towns could not match.

As early as the mid-1920s a few perceptive observers were taking note of the "lure of the city," but it would not become widely recognized until well after World War II. For most midwestern towns the 1920s constituted the high tide of their existence, a time of generally good economic times and modest population growth. Up and down Main Street a sense of well-being was recognized as the towns enjoyed good times. Infrastructures were markedly improved. Not only were streets paved, but modern water systems replaced individual wells and back-porch cisterns. The central water system not only provided a better and healthier water supply, but also made possible the luxury of indoor plumbing. Backyard privies were removed as public health took a quantum leap forward with modern sewer and waste-disposal systems. Electric lighting had made its initial appearance by illuminating town streets in previous decades, but during the 1920s the wonders of this new source of power were used to improve the quality of life in many ways. Housewives marveled at the laborsaving advantages of refrigerators, vacuum cleaners, electric stoves, and kitchen appliances. The rapid spread of telephone lines improved business and private communications, and in the process facilitated the transmission of the news of the local gossip mill, always a powerful force in the maintenance of community standards. Increased leisure time was filled by listening to the radio and viewing motion pictures at the local theater.

It is not surprising, then, that with business activity humming along, by the end of the decade town leaders exhibited a certain smugness, dismissing out of hand such literary figures as Sherwood Anderson, Edgar Lee Masters, H. L. Mencken, and Sinclair Lewis, whose writings were interpreted as critical of Main Street America. Urban-based intellectuals—many of whom like Lewis and Anderson were themselves products of small towns—had for a decade showered criticism upon the towns. This "revolt from the village" emphasized the lack of cultural sophistication, the racial and cultural intolerance, and the powerful conforming influence wielded by religious zealots and small-minded men and women over the free flow of ideas. That this new literary trend coincided with the 1920 census, which revealed for the first time that the urban population had exceeded the rural, was not coincidental.

Whatever smugness the leaders of the midwestern towns might have exhibited, however, soon faded in the wake of the national economy's collapse. The Great Depression of the 1930s would severely test the resilience of the towns and their residents, but even greater challenges lay ahead once difficult economic times had been overcome.

Belonging to the Community

FROM *Main Street on the Middle Border*

LEWIS E. ATHERTON

SETTLERS TO THE MIDWEST set about creating a working community almost immediately. Although the *raison d'etre* of the town was its commercial function serving the surrounding farmland, the men and women who established residence in the towns devoted a great deal of time and effort to the creation of complex personal and group relationships with their neighbors. It did not take long for observers to notice that the towns were governed by a body of unwritten law and customs to which everyone adhered. Casual observers initially tended to identify the behavior as producing a positive sense of "togetherness," but during the 1920s a new generation of commentators, led by novelists Sherwood Anderson and Sinclair Lewis, saw it in the more negative light of enforced conformity that bred mediocrity.

The following selection, written by a pioneering historian of the midwestern town, focuses upon the period of the late nineteenth century, a time when most towns had already moved beyond their frontier period into an era of social and economic maturation. While most villagers tended to identify the majority of residents as part of an amorphous and expanded middle class, membership in specific churches and lodges, one's political affiliation, along with income and property ownership closely connected each resident to a clearly recognized social standing within the community.

Certain activities, however, transcended class lines and sought to unify the community. Such events as the county fair, patriotic celebrations, ice cream socials with the town band providing the entertainment, baseball games with rival towns, religious holidays, and heated political campaigns all tended to produce a sense of participation that gave each resident a feeling of belonging to a community. The following selection has been excerpted from historian Lewis E. Atherton's classic history of the midwestern town, published in 1954.

o   o   o

"Togetherness"

Since citizens knew the color and shape of every home in town, and could even direct strangers by such means, streets and houses went unmarked until towns grew large enough to obtain house-to-house delivery, at which time federal regulations required people to post street names and house numbers. Here was tangible evidence of the closely knit character of village life, of the satisfaction of being so well-known as to need no identifying numbers, of belonging to a neighborhood, of achieving membership in a community simply by living within its boundaries. Early in the twentieth century, and just before the debunking era, Zona Gale published her popular *Friendship Village Love Stories*, in which she eulogized village life:

> In fellowship! I think that in this simple basic emotion lies my joy in living in this, my village. Here, this year long, folk have been adventuring together, knowing the details of one another's lives, striving a little but companioning far more than striving, kindling to one another's interests instead of practicing the faint morality of mere civility; . . . The ways of these primal tribal bonds are in my blood, for from my heart I felt what my neighbor felt when she told me of the donation party which the whole village has just given to Lyddy Ember:—"I declare," she said, "it wasn't so much the stuff they brought in, though that was all elegant, but it was the Togetherness of it. I couldn't get to sleep that night for thinkin' about God not havin' anybody to neighbour with."[1]

This imaginary village contained characters like "Little Child," a simple, simpering, and angelic being, and her cat, "Bless-Your-Heart." In Gale's words, "'I'm breathing,' Little Child soberly announced to me that first day of our acquaintance. And I wonder why I smiled."[2] Mark Twain would have guffawed. Miggy and Peter, romantic lovers, extended the gallery of saccharine portraits which Gale created for Friendship Village. In spite of the obvious limitations of her characters, they appealed to a wide reading audience which idealized village life.

Many small-town citizens were less enamored of the "togetherness" of their existence. When a door-to-door salesman in late summer, 1898, sold sixty dollars' worth of house numbers to Gallatin, Missouri, women, the local editor immediately criticized them for being taken in by the "numbers game," which, in his opinion, was "as covered with moss as lightning-rod deals." According to him, women who disliked to live in country towns used house numbers to show that they understood city ways.[3] Although the editor was correct in saying that not one citizen out of ten knew the names of

Gallatin streets, and that residents had no need for signs and numbers to distract them, his sharp criticism of dissatisfied women undoubtedly made them no happier over having to live in a community which assumed the prerogative of telling them how to decorate their homes.

Thoughtful writers have noted the influence of "togetherness" on small-town personalities. In his stories of Winesburg, Ohio, Sherwood Anderson included the half-witted town character, Seth Smollett, the wood chopper, who went out of his way to wheel his cart of wood down Main Street for the sheer joy of being shouted at and of returning the hoots and catcalls. They proved that he belonged and had a place in local society. Anderson also described the farm boy who, after moving to town with his father to open a store, learned to dread the attitude of Winesburg people. They called his family queer, or, at least, he thought they did. Under the circumstances, he longed to return to farm life:

> When we lived out here it was different. I worked and at night I went to bed and slept. I wasn't always seeing people and thinking as I am now. In the evening, there in town, I go to the post office or to the depot to see the train come in, and no one says anything to me. . . . Then I feel so queer that I can't talk either. I go away. I don't say anything. I can't.[4]

In Anderson's story this boy "escaped" to Cleveland and hid himself in city crowds. Solitude existed on the farm and in cities, but no one could escape the "togetherness" of village life.

Prying eyes, gossip, and pressure toward conformity, which naturally accompanied the "togetherness" of village life, could scarcely have been eliminated in a group which paid that price for membership in a neighborhood—for belonging to a society in its totality. Some loved life in the small town; others found it a severe trial. Hamlin Garland called himself an intellectual aristocrat, incapable of village life, and yet he shared for a time the unalloyed joy of his mother over returning to the village home which he purchased for her:

> As I went about the village I came to a partial understanding of her feeling. The small dark shops, the uneven sidewalks, the ricketty wooden awnings were closely in character with the easygoing citizens who moved leisurely and contentedly about their small affairs. It came to me (with a sense of amusement) that these coatless shopkeepers who dealt out sugar and kerosene while wearing their derby hats on the backs of their heads, were not only my neighbors, but members of the Board of Education. Though still primitive to my city eyes, they no longer appeared remote. Something in their names and voices touched me nearly. They were American. Their militant social democracy was at once comical and corrective.
>
> O, the peace, the sweetness of those days! To be awakened by the valiant challenge of early-rising roosters; to hear the chuckle of dawn-light worm-hunting robins brought a return of boyhood's exultation. Not only did my

muscles harden to the spade and the hoe, my soul rejoiced in a new and delightful sense of establishment. I had returned to citizenship. I was a proprietor. The clock of the seasons had resumed its beat.[5]

Village people rose early in the morning and set a pace which saw them through a long working day without exhausting their energies. A leisurely tempo with slack periods gave time to enjoy others and to engage in talk, the most pervading of all social activities. Women deserted their canning, washing, and housecleaning to gossip over the back fence or to rock in another's home while they discussed departures from routine patterns of neighborhood and town life. Marriage, birth, accidents, and death were common topics of conversation. Reports on those ill circulated each morning, and rumors of moral derelictions were passed from home to home. Retired farmers, down town for the morning mail, discussed crops and weather, which had shaped their daily activities for so many years, and then deaths and marriages. These were fitted into family and community relationships. Ancestral backgrounds, family connections, property holdings, and highlights of the career of any recently deceased member of the community were recalled and placed in their proper niche in the oral history of the village, thus giving a sense of continuity.

Town loafers who worked intermittently or not at all gathered at another spot to squat against the wall of a business building or to sit hunched over on the ledge extending from the foundation. They alone failed to speak to women passing by on shopping trips to the business section, feigning instead a blindness to matron and girl which was belied by the shifty glance of appraisal and interest in the female body.

At the post office and within the stores conversation was more general and yet more restricted because of the presence of both sexes and of all age groups. Everywhere it concerned people and things. Since art, literature, and abstract ideas were beyond the daily experience of those engaged in making conversation, individuals sought esteem by telling how they had warned another of the proper method of handling some situation which resulted badly through failure to follow seasoned experience. Illness or distress were quickly known and evoked a warmly sympathetic response because people were flesh-and-blood neighbors; wrongdoing or snobbishness aroused an equally quick condemnation for much the same reasons. Gossip served as informal judge and jury, and it sat daily to pass on every individual in the town.

Although this "togetherness" was achieved without numerous, formal social organizations, Europeans have been inclined to call us a nation of joiners and to seek explanations as to why we supposedly dote on organizational activities. In the 1830s Tocqueville suggested that an equalitarian, democratic country required associations to hold society together. In contrast, said Tocqueville, aristocratic societies were somewhat like armies, with relationships clearly defined and recognized by custom or law. In societies committed to equality, in which all were on a common level, men had to band together to accomplish their purposes. In the 1880s James Bryce said that associations were formed, extended, and operated more rapidly in the United States than elsewhere in the world. And this was true in his opinion because Americans were a sympathetic people, capable of such action in spite of nomadic habits which militated against organizational efforts.[6] Still others have traced American interest in joining to the need for associations in which individuals can build their egos by the very act of combining with others and by holding offices of honor. Many observers seem to feel that rank and recognized honors must come either from associations in the American sense or from the clearly defined status of people in aristocratic societies.

The structure and functioning of nineteenth-century midwestern village life confirm European critics in their assumptions that people must have a sense of belonging to the larger society around them and also in their convictions that a mobile, equalitarian age struggles hard to find a sense of permanence and stability. But European critics have misread American history when they assert that we have achieved such ends and must achieve them by being a nation of joiners, for nineteenth-century villagers were satisfied with a limited number of organizations which admitted *all* members of the community. Before automobiles permitted people to seek distant associations, they had to find them locally. "Togetherness" before 1900 came from a few community-wide organizations, from informal community life, and from local association. Americans are not necessarily "joiners"; they do want to "belong."

Church and Lodge

Churches and lodges were the focal points of organized social life before the 1890s, and they were open to all. Many did not belong, it is true, but only because they preferred to find their social outlets through informal, community activities. The few formal organizations had no rules which excluded a portion of the community, and since membership was a matter of choice and not of necessity, little stigma was attached to limiting one's participation to affairs involving the whole community.

On Sunday morning church bells were heard throughout the town, a reminder that religion had passed beyond the usual informality of village social life and functioned throughout the year. Morning and evening preaching services on the Sabbath, Sunday school, and midweek prayer meeting were common among Protestant sects by 1865. Unlike twentieth-century arrangements, however, Sunday school might follow preaching, and varied enough among churches as to meeting time to enable gregarious individuals like William Allen White to display their knowledge of the "Golden Text" in several different places every Sunday. Though parents sometimes left infants at home with older children or the hired girl, the basic church services stressed family worship. All could participate in Sunday school, and babies were put to sleep on back benches during evening services. Young ladies attended Sunday-night preaching and the midweek prayer services as a means of meeting their beaus. When the services ended, boys gathered at the church door or along the walk to escort their favorite girls home.[7]

Sunday school has remained fairly standardized in the smaller churches since 1865. Then, as now, the Sunday-school superintendent called the group together for opening exercises, generally a prayer and a song, and then the classes, sectioned according to age or sex, adjourned to their assigned places in the main auditorium, which in the small churches constituted the one and only meeting place. Though some churches had curtains to separate classes, they did little to deaden the low drone of voices from the various groups. As individual teachers got discussion of the lesson under way, a symphony of sound like that of several hives of bees swarming at one time rose throughout the auditorium. The secretary-treasurer moved from class to class to receive pennies and nickels. Total attendance and total contributions were announced when the superintendent brought the groups together again for a final word pointing up the lesson, another hymn, and a prayer of dismissal. Louis Bromfield remembered the Biblical pictures on the walls, the small chairs, and tiny children marching twice around the room to the tune of "Onward Christian Soldiers," but he obviously belonged to a congregation rich enough to afford separate Sunday School rooms which permitted greater individuality.[8]

Sunday-school teaching left much to be desired. All could memorize the Golden Text, and all could listen to someone comment verse by verse on the scriptural subject matter of the lesson. All were expected to carry away with them a central thought or principle, generally moralistic in nature, but this objective often failed of realization. Teachers of adult classes concentrated on colored maps of the Holy Land and translated shekels and cubits into American money and inches. But if an inquiring youngster asked who made God, he was likely to have a scriptural passage—such as, "In the beginning God created the heavens and the earth. And the earth was waste and void; and darkness was upon the face of the deep. And the Spirit of God moved upon the face of the waters"—read to him in explanation.[9]

Church women maintained a Ladies Aid or a missionary society, and supported temperance groups like the W.C.T.U. While young people's groups like Christian Endeavor and Epworth League became popular around the 1890's, churches did not begin to stress auxiliary organizations of men and boys before the turn of the century.[10]

Various fund-raising and social activities were popular everywhere. One was the donation or pound party to collect money or foodstuffs for the minister. Socials or sociables also were common. On such occasions, whole families met at some private home, at the parsonage, or in the church for entertainment and fellowship.

Churches used still another type of activity, the festival, to raise money. At Chatfield, Minnesota, in 1876, Presbyterian ladies held a centennial festival in "Ye Whytee's Halle," at which they presented "ye Courteship" of Miles Standish. Also, "Ye Musicke of ye Olden Tyme." Doors opened at "Earlie Candleliting" and admission was fifteen pennies.

The Unitarians, Universalists, Episcopalians, and Catholics often combined dancing with a church dinner as a means of raising money. In February of 1867, some 200 Chatfield people attended a festival of that type. About half of them engaged in dancing but the rest limited themselves to the "delicious refreshments." In reporting the event, the local editor said that all local churches sent delegations and that none seemed unduly shocked at the dancing going on at one end of the hall. Nevertheless, it took a generous and liberal spirit for some to approach so close to wickedness, and the editor was pleased at their courage.

"Festivals and fairs," or, simply, "fairs," as they were sometimes called, were the most ambitious of all church undertakings. On such occasions, the church women sold food, entertainment, and articles donated by members and friends. When the Ladies Sewing Circle of the Algona, Iowa, Baptist Church in 1867 staged a festival and fair to help complete their church building, they raised almost a hundred dollars on a cold, blustery day by selling tea and coffee, and a choice of oysters or meat at the Harrison hotel, and music, entertainment, and donations of quilts, clothing, books, pictures, nuts, and candies at the town hall.

Catholics and Protestants of less rigorous bent also used lotteries as a part of their fund-raising activities at festivals and fairs. The Catholic young ladies at Lacon, Illinois, in 1884 visited local political meetings to sell chances on articles which they had collected for their fair at Rose's Hall. They had donated a clock for that purpose, the Sisters of Mercy had given a set of silver teaspoons, and Father O'Brien a rug and table.[11] Many local Protestants must have grumbled at such brazen gambling being permitted within the city limits.

Fraternal organizations appeared very early on the town frontier. Masons and Odd Fellows remained most numerous, even after insurance programs of the various orders of Woodmen began to exert a strong appeal around the 1890's. Although a Masonic Eastern Star auxiliary was organized in 1867, it achieved great popularity only after social cliques and clubs began to grow in numbers a generation later. Lodge halls in second-story rooms above business buildings served as regular meeting places for the conduct of routine business and initiation of new members. Lodges were popular in part because they emphasized mutual help and accepted respectable men regardless of wealth or prominence. The religious and moralistic nature of their rituals appealed to churchmen, and even to many who believed in God and morality without being affiliated with churches.

Lodges engaged in a variety of activities. At Monroe, Wisconsin, in 1869 the Masons celebrated St. John's Day with an afternoon and evening program of speeches, toasts, a dinner, and a grand ball. The Odd Fellows of Algona, Iowa, welcomed the New Year in 1877 with a musical and dancing party, an indication of the greater liberality of lodges in regard to dancing. Lodge anniversaries called for something special. The fiftieth anniversary of the founding of Odd Fellows was commemorated at Monroe, Wisconsin, in 1869 by a street parade and banquet, at which toasts, speeches, and tableaus entertained the diners and any citizens who cared to pay twenty-five cents to look on from the gallery. Lodges frequently held public installations of officers, and lodge members occasionally attended church as a group to hear a sermon in their honor. They also made much of funeral ceremonies, one of their strongest appeals. The emphasis on fellowship and informality in modern-day service clubs, like Rotary, contrasts sharply with the dignity and solemnity which dominated nineteenth-century lodge meetings. As one writer has said, the difference is seen in the modern tendency to address a fellow member as "Bill" instead of "Worshipful Grand Master."[12]

Recognition for the Common Man

Although they deferred to the "togetherness" of village life by freely admitting applicants to membership, lodges and churches represented a beginning drift toward our highly organized, twentieth-century social life. For the time being, however, most social relations followed a simple, informal pattern. For the individual, this involved birth, marriage and death as assured moments of prominence in the life cycle. For the village, it meant adjustment to seasons of the year and to state and national holidays. For all, it meant activity involving the whole community—celebrations in which individuals participated without waiting for invitations from various inner circles to join in setting social boundaries. And for all it meant that most social life was so informal as to need no organization to make it work.

Rank-and-file citizens were honored at various times. Relatives and neighbors were invited to family birthday dinners, where they joined the honored member in eating and visiting, usually without thought of presents or candles and cakes. Although weddings were scheduled to interfere as little as possible with the groom's job and honeymoon trips were for the few, dinner with the bride's parents, an "infare" visit to the home of the groom's family, and perhaps a charivari by neighbors honored newly married couples.

Golden Wedding celebrations had great appeal partly because the death rate prevented so many couples from reaching that goal, but also because people liked to think that Golden Weddings proved the greater stability of marriages in small towns. When relatives and friends of Mr. and Mrs. Peter Berdan of Chatfield, Minnesota, gave a dinner for them in 1876, their son made a trip from Chicago to present his father with a twenty-five dollar gold-headed cane, and the mother received a silver cream pitcher and sugar bowl. Friends contributed a purse of gold coins totalling forty dollars. In reporting the affair, the local editor quoted the Berdans' son to the effect that Golden Weddings were unknown in Chicago; divorces were the order of the day there.[13]

Death touched an entire community because virtually all knew the deceased. Before undertakers built their lavish parlors, a death called for many activities on the part of relatives and friends. The corpse must be washed and laid out, with its hair combed, and in its best suit or dress. A cabinet maker got busy on a casket, unless some furniture dealer carried ready-made stock. Friends began pouring in to the bereaved home as soon as the news reached them, and members of the family seated in the living room received their condolences. Each caller tiptoed into the parlor to see the corpse, as everyone was expected to perform that rite, and all commented on how natural and peaceful it looked. Cakes and pies and meats began to appear in the kitchen in profusion, the gifts of friends and neighbors. A summer death was always easier to honor because home-grown flowers were available, but even in winter one could count on a five-dollar wreath from the lodge. Some member of the family hurriedly arranged for black-edged cards announcing the hour and place of the funeral to be run off at the printing office for display in business houses. A spray of flowers or black ribbon on the front door and small groups of neighbors sitting at night in a dimly lighted room with the corpse signified that death prevailed within.

Since custom favored large funerals, citizens generally turned out in numbers. While the bereaved family would not have had things otherwise, they were in for a rough hour. A long eulogy by the preacher and doleful hymns by a quartette only served to weaken those closest to the deceased and to leave them defenseless for the final ordeal at the grave. White gloves for pallbearers and a plumed hearse gave solemn pageantry, which often was enhanced by uniformed GAR or lodge groups participating in the funeral ceremony. Unseemly haste must be avoided at all costs, and horses in the funeral processions were not permitted to move faster than a walk. When the mourners returned home, they generally found that neighbors had swept and dusted and restored a semblance of order to the house. In return for such neighborly services they inserted a card of thanks in the local newspaper informing all of their appreciation for help in their time of trouble. Widows then donned black mourning garb for a year and widowers moved with circumspection, for the sympathy which had been so evident early in their bereavement could quickly disappear if they departed in the slightest from community customs involving respect for the dead.

Fads, Fancies, and National Holidays

Crazes or temporary fascinations appeared in country towns then as now. Enthusiasm waxed and waned for many things like croquet, hunting clubs, bicycles, roller skating, and even baseball.[14] National influences, individual leadership—a very successful baseball pitcher, for example—and ennui explain much of the variation.

Midwestern enthusiasts joined the rest of the country in pushing membership in the National League of American Wheelmen, originally created in 1880, to an all-time high just before the turn of the century. Iowa had some 1,400 members in the League in 1897, many of them from small towns, and conservative citizens deplored the popularity of divided skirts for female riders just when some had hopes of curbing the growing tendency of mail-order catalogs to include pictures of men and women in underwear.

Other fads seem to have arisen and declined primarily because of local conditions. Croquet, "the courting game," was highly popular in Greencastle, Indiana, in 1867. During the summer a group of men played daily in the courthouse yard, and the local paper mentioned the game's influence on younger people:

> Out on the lawn, in the evening gray,
> Went Willie and Kate. I said, "Which way?"
> And they both replied, "Croquet, croquet."

> I saw the scamp—it was light as day—
> Put his arm round her waist in a loving way,
> And he squeezed her hand. Was that croquet?

> Silent they sat 'neath the moon of May;
> But I knew by her blushes that she said not nay,
> And I thought in my heart, "Now *that's* croquet."

In a similar way, moonlight croquet parties became the rage in Coffeysburg, Missouri, in the late summer of 1893. Roller skating rinks had a similar history. During the fall and winter of 1884–85, citizens of Washburn, Illinois, skated in great numbers, the proprietor of the local rink encouraging the fad by giving free lessons one afternoon a week for ladies who wished to engage in the sport. During a similar peak period in Monroe, Wisconsin, the local band furnished music twice a week and masked skating parties were popular.[15]

In spite of ups and downs, a well-recognized annual calendar of events geared to national holidays and weather conditions prevailed in small-town Mid-America. Year after year from January 1 to December 31 this pattern repeated itself with varying intensity but with sufficient emphasis to enable all citizens to know what lay ahead in the way of social life and recreation.

As early as 1862, for instance, Iowa followed the national pattern in making January 1 a legal holiday, along with July 4 and December 25. In 1880 Memorial Day was added to the list, in 1890 Labor Day, and in 1897 Washington's Birthday. Not until 1909, the hundredth anniversary of his birth, was Lincoln's Birthday given the same recognition in Iowa. With the exception of Lincoln's Birthday, Iowa followed the pattern of federal statutes,[16] and other midwestern states did much the same. Of these legal holidays, only July 4, December 25, and Memorial Day were observed with any degree of consistency in small towns, and even then business houses remained open part of the day.

New Year's

New Year's Eve and Day meant little to the small fry except that they were free from school and could ice skate, go sledding, or hunt rabbits to sell to local produce dealers. For teen-agers and adults it was a different story. Drunkards continued their Christmas spree through the New Year's since winter weather and the holiday season provided only casual labor, if any at all, for the element most heavily addicted to the bottle. Respectable people could choose among a number of well-recognized activities. Retired farmers and their wives generally limited themselves to a dinner with relatives and friends on New Year's Day, although some broke over and attended the New Year's Eve watch party at a local church. Methodists most often observed this practice. Such parties kept respectable people up beyond their usual bedtime hour, however, and differed very little from the regular church services to which they were accustomed. The Monroe, Wisconsin, editor in 1884 reported that sermons, songs and prayers had kept the brethren and sisters awake at a number of watch meetings in the local churches. Though lacking in novelty or excitement, the watch party continued to have a place in village life.

Oyster suppers and dances provided a more lively time for those who had no religious scruples to the contrary. A program at Monroe, Wisconsin, in 1883 started off with musical numbers by the young people and then dancing. The Universalist ladies served supper to the group during the evening. At the hour of midnight all paused to welcome the New Year, and then, it being Leap Year, the season was inaugurated with a grand waltz, the ladies having the choice of partners. All over the Midwest church groups with liberal leanings, lodges, young ladies intent on celebrating Leap Year when they could, and even "club" dances, sponsored by temporary groups formed for that purpose alone, added to the tendency to "trip the light fantastic" on New Year's Eve. Since teen-agers from pious homes could not engage in dancing, most of them ended up at the church watch party in a disgruntled state of mind.

Fortunately, many devout church members permitted their offspring to participate in play parties. Even though group singing eliminated the need for musical instruments in party games, and the tempo of actions was somewhat less than in dancing, they came close to being an adequate substitute. "Weevily Wheat," for instance, had many of the elements of the Virginia Reel, and Texans added a stanza recognizing this:

> Take a lady by her hand,
> Lead her like a pigeon,
> Make her dance the weevily wheat,
> She loses her religion.

A whole series of party games were well known everywhere: Skip-to-My-Lou; Pig in the Parlor; Here We Go Round the Mulberry Bush; Oats, Peas, Beans, and Barley Grow; Needles' Eye; London Bridge; Miller Boys; and King William was King James's Son were among the more popular. Some were combined choosing and kissing games and others depended primarily on group rhythm for their appeal.[17] Youngsters could forget the strictures of strait-laced parents when they became immersed in these along with the partner of their choice:

> Oh, Charley, he is a fine young man;
> Charley, he is a dandy.
> Oh, Charley, he's a fine young man,
> For he buys the girls some candy.
> Oh, I won't have none of your weevily wheat,
> I won't have none of your barley,
> But I'll have some flour in half an hour
> To bake a cake for Charley.

Such games seem to have had a rural origin and were popular longest in isolated farming communities, but they also lightened the gloom of village youngsters who could not take part in outright dancing.

From George Washington's administration to January 1, 1934, when Franklin Roosevelt suspended the practice, the President always held a public reception on New Year's Day. Midwestern country towns imitated this custom with varying degrees of intensity, but it was sufficiently common to merit attention in many local papers. Printers encouraged the idea of receptions in order to sell calling cards, and some advertised that they would remain open to print orders until noon on New Year's. Most of the ladies in Lacon, Illinois, kept open house or joined with friends in doing so on New Year's in 1875. In reporting this, the local editor complimented the sobriety

of callers, the "toilettes" of the ladies, and the generous refreshments. The
custom was observed at least intermittently in Lacon as late as 1894. Generous supplies of eggnog undoubtedly contributed to the rush of callers in
Chatfield, Minnesota, in 1867 and to compliments "as thick as blackbirds."
There, too, the custom lasted for a considerable period of years.[18]

Winter and Spring

Though January and February were cold, raw months on the Middle Border, they failed to halt social life. At Coffeysburg and Jamesport, Missouri,
in 1893 the temperature dropped to twenty-one below zero, and village
boys found the daily chore of filling the wood box after school more time-
consuming than usual. Still, the correspondents of those two villages had
much to report to the county paper—marriages, deaths, chicken pox
among the children, and hog cholera. Harness makers were busy preparing
for spring trade, and one of the postmasters received a new stock of notions
to occupy his time when not handing out mail. Boys braved the cold to kill
rabbits, for which they received ten cents from the local produce dealers. A
Christian Endeavor Society was organized at one of the churches. Farm
sales were common. Burt Ford moved into Grandma Coffey's place, since
she intended to live with her children the rest of her days. The GAR gave
a bean supper; young people attended informal parties in private homes;
and a citizen captured a bald eagle measuring seven feet from tip to tip.
The ground hog failed to see his shadow on the second of February. Preaching services, lodge meetings, and an occasional itinerant lecturer helped to
vary life in the dead of winter.[19]

Valentine's Day provided an excuse for a dance and for the sending of
sentimental greetings or ugly, joshing caricatures, depending on one's age
and inclinations. Volunteer fire companies and other local organizations
gave dancing parties on Washington's Birthday, but otherwise it seems not
to have been widely observed.[20]

March and April could be bitter cold, but they also were likely to bring
sudden shifts to mild, clean-smelling days when all the earth seemed ready
to burst with lush, new vegetation. Small towns like Jamesport and
Coffeysburg, Missouri, began to turn to outdoor activities. March first was
moving day for farm renters who were thinking of sowing spring oats, and
townsmen cleared away debris so gardens could be plowed and prepared for
early vegetables. Spring thaws meant a battle with mud. People were both
amused and sympathetic toward the two sisters who suffered accidents in
the spring of 1893—one receiving a mouthful of mud kicked up by the
horse which she was driving; the other a scorched back from dropping a
curling iron with which she was frizzing her curls. Though revival meetings, oyster suppers, birthday parties, and sociables were common, the ap-

proaching termination of school left no doubt that activities were shifting to the outdoors.[21]

Easter Sunday was the only occasion consistently and widely observed in these two spring months. Some women made a practice of growing flowers to decorate their churches at the Easter season. Special music, new dresses and hats for the ladies, and sermons prepared with greater care than usual combined with callas, ferns, gloxinias, and Easter lilies to make Easter Sunday a memorable day. Even before the Civil War children looked forward to dyeing Easter eggs. William Dean Howells remembered the soft, pale green colors obtained by boiling eggs with onions, and most of all the calico eggs which resulted from boiling them wrapped in multi-colored calico cloth.[22]

Youngsters had to have their fun on April Fool's Day. In 1869 the Tiffin, Ohio, editor recommended concealing a stone under an old hat on the sidewalk for passers-by to kick. In his estimation, All Fool's Day gave every sort of license to play tricks on one's friends, and no one had any right to be angry at the custom. Some village schools celebrated Arbor Day, of Nebraska origin, and editors occasionally urged citizens to plant trees in honor of the occasion.[23]

In the Steps of Huckleberry Finn and Tom Sawyer

Most of all, people looked forward to freedom from hovering within the small areas of heat generated by stoves in homes and public buildings. During the winter it was possible to be warm in front or behind, but uniform temperatures were unknown. Approaching freedom from school and access to woods, caves, and swimming holes within walking distance of town gave the small fry a feverish itch to be about their summer business of foraging, the activity best remembered by writers who spent their childhood in midwestern villages. The antics of Huckleberry Finn and Tom Sawyer, as seen through the eyes of Mark Twain, have immortalized this phase of village life, and here indeed was the glory of small-town existence for youngsters. Farm boys had too many chores, too few companions, and too much nature to enjoy it to the limit; city boys lacked the opportunity. But no one complained of the vistas which lay before village youngsters who could be in open country or the woods in a matter of minutes.

The pattern of childhood activity within the village itself was set before the Civil War. William Dean Howells remembered the sequence of events in Ohio towns—marbles in early spring, followed by foot races, tops, and swimming, and then kites during the sweltering heat of summer. Though Howells became a literary dictator in Brahmin New England with the passage of the years, he never forgot the pets of his youth—coons, dogs, goats, rabbits, and chickens around the yard, and fish and turtles in the hogshead of rain water at the corner of the house. Howells owned a pony for a time, which he stabled in part of the family cow shed. Since guns were scarce, seven or eight boys took turns shooting a muzzle-loader on hunting trips. Howells went to the woods with others to obtain May apples, blackberries, chinquapins, red haws, pignuts, black walnuts, and sugar water from maple trees. As fall approached, boys built a cart and planned to haul in several bushels of nuts, but like all foraging activities the planning of this was more important than the execution.

Thomas Hart Benton revelled in similar pleasures at his home town of Neosho, Missouri, in the 1890's. Neosho had creeks where the gang learned to swim, and on whose banks they practiced chewing and smoking, and added to their linguistic powers. A railroad siding near Neosho enabled youngsters to steal two-mile rides on passing trains. There were caves to explore, horses to ride, cottonmouth moccasins and copperheads to kill. In the autumn, Benton took part in possum hunts west of town, where one ran with a kerosene lantern in hand, trying to beat his companions to the treed possum, with only the bark of the dogs as a guide. A large barn on the Benton lot was a magnificent place for amateur shows and circuses.

Although William Allen White was never a great outdoors man, his small-town boyhood made him fond of nature. Besides his family home, White listed three major influences on his childhood. One was the family barn, with its trapeze, haymows, ancient lores and skills. A second was the river, which provided fishing, swimming, rowing and skating. And the third was "roaming"—roaming in the timber, trapping quail and songbirds, foraging for nuts, and exploiting the changing seasons of the year.

Nostalgia for one's youthful kinship with the spirit of Tom Sawyer never departed from adults who grew up in midwestern country towns. When Herbert Hoover later spoke of the swimming hole under the willows by the railroad bridge near his boyhood home in West Branch, Iowa, of trapping rabbits with box traps, of fishing with willow poles, and of spitting on the bait to assure success, he plumbed the very heart of the Midwest.[24]

Girls were more limited in their play, but they too enjoyed the pets which inhabited outbuildings of the family home, found a ready circle of neighborhood friends, and joined the boys in the nightly game of hide-and-seek. When parents called their children in after dusk of a long summer evening, boys and girls found kinship in a common fatigue and in wondering at the unreasonableness of adults who wanted youngsters to wash their feet after a day of barefooted play.

"Take Me Out to the Ball Game"

May and June quickened the tempo of outdoor life still more for all ages. Men and older boys discussed the prospects for baseball, which had become the great American game by the 1860's. In December of 1865 delegates from

Illinois, Indiana, Michigan, and Iowa met in Chicago and adopted the name "Northwestern Baseball Convention," with the intention of obtaining for western clubs some voice in the national movement. State associations were formed in Iowa and Minnesota in 1867, and league play rapidly developed among larger towns all over the Middle West.

Though smaller places were unable to maintain regular schedules, they participated to the extent of their ability. In May of 1867, for example, the Algona, Iowa, paper asked those interested in forming a local team to meet on the public square at three the next Saturday afternoon. Before the end of the month a diamond had been laid out and practice games were under way. Plans for the summer called for games at five on Wednesdays and at two on Saturdays. By the 1870's small towns like Washburn, Illinois, were holding three-day baseball tournaments at the close of the summer season, with cash prizes for the winning team. In general, teams operated on a purely amateur basis and on the smallest possible margin of cost. In 1897 the Croswell, Michigan, Grays beat Center, Michigan, on the latter's diamond fifteen to thirteen, although earned runs stood only five to three. "Jollying, singing, and jostling" helped the Croswell team forget its muddy ride to Center for the contest. After dinner at the Center hotel and a stroll around the village, the team reached the playing grounds at three. As the contest got under way, a drummer drove by and inquired what was going on, a ball game or a yacht race, and was rewarded by a jeer from the small boys hugging the sides of the diamond—"ball, you d—d fool."

Baseball did little to cement good will among competing towns. If one can believe reports in small-town newspapers, umpiring changed little over the years, for the beaten team and its supporters almost invariably agreed that decisions had been intentionally biased. Towns accused one another of playing ringers, of employing crooked umpires, and of unfair noisemaking to rattle opponents at crucial moments. But Babe Ruth never equalled the slugging record of many a midwestern small-town team. Freeport beat Monroe, Wisconsin, on July 5, 1869, by a score of sixty-six to thirty-nine. In explaining the loss, the Monroe editor pointed out that the score was thirty-all at the end of the fifth, but since Freeport had three pitchers and Monroe only one, the latter naturally dropped behind in the later innings.[25]

Memorial Day and Fourth of July

May and June encouraged villagers to live outdoors. Churches and lodges held so many ice cream and strawberry lawn festivals that papers merely noted the hour and date. Children's day Sunday-school exercises were occasionally held as early as 1869, and had become fairly common by the 1880's. May-day customs, including baskets for sweethearts and picnics, appealed only to a scattering of towns,[26] but all observed Memorial Day.

First proclaimed in 1868 by General John A. Logan, commander-in-chief of the recently formed Grand Army of the Republic, Memorial Day rapidly developed as a major ceremonial occasion.

Two heavy fieldpieces on the river bank fired a sunrise salute at Lacon, Illinois, on Memorial Day in 1884, and shortly thereafter country people began to arrive. At one o'clock the Peru Band, a military company, fifty veterans, and citizens on foot and in carriages went in procession to the local cemetery, where eight little girls placed sprigs of evergreen on graves of Union soldiers. Prayers, songs by a quartette, and the firing of a military salute completed the cemetery program, after which the group marched to a grove to hear more band music, more singing, and the orator of the day. Several short talks were also made, one of which stressed the politically useful, time-honored theme of the Republican party—that the Democrats were traitors and that Jeff Davis should have been hanged at the close of the Civil War. Elaborate celebrations of this type were costly, flannel for the powder sacks, and powder and gun primers alone costing fifteen dollars. The program at Minonk, Illinois, the same year showed that Memorial Day celebrations were similar everywhere, and yet the variety of details that could be worked in. The Minonk precession contained a brass band, a drum corps, a wagon holding an organ and a quartette, 200 school children carrying flowers for the graves, the usual assortment of veterans, and forty carriages of civilians. An additional crowd, estimated at one thousand people, straggled along the sidewalks on foot. After visiting the cemetery, the group returned to the local opera house for music and recitations by school children and an oration by a local preacher. The day closed with an "elocutionary entertainment" to raise $150.00 to pay for the celebration.

Memorial Day rapidly surpassed even the Fourth of July as the outstanding ceremonial honoring American national traditions, partly because of the great strength of the Grand Army of the Republic and its auxiliaries like the Women's Relief Corps. Perhaps, too, the "Boys in Blue," and their honored dead, symbolized American conviction that preservation of the Union had ended the last threat to national safety. Since America, and especially the Midwest, was heading toward an era of peace and constantly increasing material growth, one needed only to honor the dead who had made this possible. An occasional citizen like William Allen White's father, irritated by the constantly increasing pension raids and GAR bias toward the Republican party, muttered that Memorial Day parades included "a lot of damn bounty jumpers." But Memorial Day remained supreme until national and world events, starting with the Spanish American War, and the thinning ranks of the GAR, encouraged Americans to divide their attention more evenly among national holidays.[27]

American seaboard villages began to observe the Fourth of July early in the nineteenth century with public prayer, a reading of the Declaration of

Independence, and a patriotic speech by an "orator of the day." Many villages also held public dinners at which leading citizens drank patriotic toasts. Although music and entertainment were not wholly eliminated, these early celebrations were basically commemorative in nature. As native-born Americans moved on into the Middle West it was only natural for them to adopt the same kind of program.

Although the effort and cost involved in serving as host on the Fourth of July encouraged towns to pass the honor around, major celebrations were usually held in sufficient numbers to enable farm families everywhere to attend. Special efforts were made to provide an outstanding program on the hundredth anniversary of the signing of the Declaration of Independence, July 4, 1876. The celebration at Algona, Iowa, in that year was typical of the many held. Anvils, cannons, and guns began to fire at sunrise, and by nine o'clock the walks were jammed with people. Township delegations in carriages and on foot milled around, hunting assigned places in the parade line. The Algona silver cornet band headed the morning parade, followed next by two floats of girls arrayed in fitting costumes, one representing the colonies and the other the states. Although muddy roads reduced the number of floats, Algona businessmen and the local newspaper entered enough to make a mile-long parade to Judge Call's grove. Between 450 and 500 vehicles and over 3,000 people were present. Although only half the crowd could be seated at the grove, the rest stood through a long sequence of prayers, band music, glee-club songs, a reading of the Declaration of Independence, an historical sketch of the county, and the oration of the day, all of which preceded the basket dinner. In spite of intermittent rain during the afternoon, the program went on—sack races, tub races, wheelbarrow races, running-and-trotting horse races, drills by a militia company, and a baseball game. Heavy rain ruined the fireworks display at night and reduced attendance at the courthouse ball and festival, sponsored by the local band for the purpose of buying new uniforms and a band wagon.

Many years later, Kin Hubbard wrote a humorous sketch based on the celebrations held in 1876. Hubbard described Alex McGee, the grand marshal of the day, with

> a calico Oregon pony an' th' fierce, stern expression o' a fiery rear admiral. "Stand back! Git back! Ever'buddy git back!" he roared as he galloped around th' public square while th' liberty pole wuz bein' raised. In times o' peace Alex wuz as tame as a kitten, but on a big day he could crush enough women an' children t' keep himself in hidin' th' year around.

Hubbard also mentioned the town drunk who had a reputation to sustain on every public occasion: "Most as many folks used t' come t' town on a big day t' see Buck Taylor taken t' jail as they did t' hear th' music an' see th' sights." In Hubbard's sketch, courtship proceeded apace between bashful country girls and the band boys. A balloon ascension and a hook-and-ladder race, staged by the local volunteer fire company, greatly pleased the crowd. And, sure enough, Buck had to be hauled off to jail with ten or fifteen fellows standing on the dray to hold him down. After this, many went home, but the young blades remained in town to see the "ten thousand dollar" fireworks display.

Elaborate celebrations were held less frequently after 1876. In 1886 Luverne, Iowa, welcomed the Fourth with a sunrise cannon salute which was audible three miles away. An oration, band music, and fireworks featured the day-long celebration. Algona repeated much the same pattern as in 1876, except that the cannon blew up from an overload of gunpowder through failure to discover that someone had choked its mouth with clay, and a "bowery dance," staged in a brush-covered arbor competed with one at the courthouse.

More and more, towns took the day at a less strenuous pace or turned to sheer amusement. At Centreville, Michigan, in 1888 people used the daylight hours for fishing and picnics, and waited until sundown to drift downtown to hear the band and see the fireworks. The Centreville program on July 4, 1897, revealed the changed emphasis when towns celebrated elaborately. The mayor issued a proclamation asking citizens to display large flags and to wear smaller ones or strips of red, white, and blue cloth in their lapels. The program consisted almost wholly of contests—running, jumping, vaulting, catching a greased pig, and egg, sack, and wheelbarrow races, with prizes for winners in each. Because of the current bicycle craze, the largest prizes were given to winners in that division.[28] Within another few years, small-town, Mid-America, responded to the national crusade for a safe-and-sane Fourth in protest against a yearly toll of youngsters maimed by exploding firecrackers and to protect adult nerves. By then, however, the whole pattern of life was shifting.

As torrid heat began to settle over the Middle Border, and more and more farm crops were laid by or harvested, farmers and townsmen alike slowed to a snail's pace in response to a brassy sun by day and humid nights. The Protestant churches of Monroe, Wisconsin, even started union services in the courthouse park for the remainder of the summer in July, 1876, but Baptists at Centreville, Michigan, in August of 1879 still boasted of "Baptists not yet on Vacation" to show that they could endure two regular Sunday preaching services in hot weather. Lawn socials and Sunday-school picnics increased in popularity at this time of year as did railroad and steamboat excursions for those who could afford the expense. Small boys found the scum and stagnant water of their favorite swimming holes less inviting and spent more time resting on the muddy banks, unwittingly storing strength to meet the penalty of illness which many of them would pay. The eastern Chautauqua movement was beginning to invade the Middle West, and citizens of Iowa and Wisconsin towns began to attend the Monona Lake Assembly, while others within easy driving distance went to the Old Salem Chautauqua grounds in Illinois to hear inspirational lectures.[29]

Old Settlers' Associations

September and October revived community activities. As graded schools became the rule, more and more youngsters found themselves back in class by early September, and adults looked forward to the three great community efforts of the early fall—the Old Settlers' Celebration, the county fair, and election campaigns.

Old Settlers' Associations appeared quickly on the agricultural frontier and had an enormous popularity with elderly people, who sensed the rapidly changing nature of life around them. The founders of such an association in Van Buren County, Iowa, in 1872, thanked Providence for sending them to Iowa and for lengthening their lives so that they might see the great advances in civilization made by their adopted state. They hoped also to "cultivate a more fraternal feeling" and to pass on to their descendants a history of their own early "trials and tribulations." The founding of numerous county organizations, and even of state federations, should have stimulated a sense of continuity, but most efforts had disappeared or were taken over by 1900 as adjuncts of county fairs or city celebrations.

They had difficulty in surviving because Middle Border ideals of progress held that everything old was inferior. In seeking "advantages" for their children and in emphasizing *growth* in size and numbers, the pioneers themselves had disdained the past. Why, then, should a new generation, swollen with conceit over its advanced civilization, do more than humor the elderly by enabling them to get together to recall the days of their youth? Some local bard wrote a long poem for the souvenir pamphlet published by the *Lacon Home Journal* in 1888 to commemorate the old settlers' meeting held on August 28. Although meant to be complimentary, the poem's jocular, patronizing tone was that of an adult preparing to help somewhat backward children have a good time:

> Nothun like the ole times now—
> Time goes back'ards anyhow!
> Ole folks mostly passed away
> With the good times o' their day,
> When we all wore homespun clothes,
> Jist as happy, I suppose
> As the young folks air to-day,
> Jist as peart, too, ever' way!

Uncle Johnny took the prize
As the oldest settler heur,
An' he dainced a hornpipe thur,
Right on the platform 'fore our eyes;
Yessir, an' 'at man knows more lies
'N any feller anywhur!
Killed more Injuns, wolves an' bear—
Built fust cabin, raised first corn,
Hult first meetin, fit first fight,
Got up the first county fair—
Brung first circus'n' side-show there,
His son Ben first sucker born,
Uncle Johnny's jist a *sight*!

Then ole Uncle Johnny got
A feller—kindo heavy sot—
Majors was his name—to play
Fiddle-chunes the rest o' the day;
Played ole "Rye Straw" an' "Gray Eagle."
'N'en the geurles commenced to giggle
When they called fur "Leather Britches,"

Lord! our feet commenced to go
'Fore he'd hardly drawed his bow!
Cur'us how a feller feels
Daincun them ole ratlun reels!
Wusht ye could'a' seen them folks
Hoppun round an' crackun jokes,
Gray ole Women an' *ole men*
Jist as young's they'd ever be'n,
Rakun up the old-time fun:

Never thinkun of the sun
Till they noticed it wus gone
An' the night wus comun on!
An' ole Johnny says to me,
As we started home, says 'e:
"Now, dog-on, ef't didn't seem
Ole times come back in a dream!"

Uncle Johnnies in their second childhood, incapable any longer of getting the truth straight, ignorant and outdated, apparently were all that the Middle Border saw in the environment from which it sprang.

While the pioneers still lived, the annual reunion attracted large crowds. Although it was occasionally held in other months, late August or September became the favorite time of meeting. People sometimes talked of erecting and equipping pioneer cabins, and old settlers occasionally baked corn pone, displayed old newspapers, and exhibited "relics" of early days, but nothing of a permanent nature resulted. In general, such gatherings took place at a county seat or village, with a morning oration, followed by a basket dinner, and then music, games, reminiscences of the past, and a reading of the names of those who had died during the preceding year. As pioneer ranks thinned, leadership passed to younger people. Algona, Iowa, solved the problem in 1898 in a common way by calling one day of the county fair "Old Settlers' Day." When Algona celebrated its Jubilee in 1904, citizens gathered pioneer relics into a temporary museum and honored the few remaining early settlers,[30] but there as elsewhere concrete remains and traditions had disappeared within a half century almost as completely as the herds of deer that once ranged the county.

The County Fair

County fairs survived because they could be modernized from time to time to meet shifting interests and changed conditions. The period preceding the 1870's has been called the golden age of midwestern fairs because of its heavy emphasis on educational activities, with amusement strictly subordinated to instruction. Midwestern county seat towns awarded generous premiums on farm exhibits,[31] and serious-minded farm folk looked forward to vying with one another for prizes and to visiting with neighbors.

Between 1870 and the turn of the century considerable change occurred. Increasing co-operation with newer educational agencies, like agricultural colleges and farmers' institutes, and more scientific methods of stock judging gained widespread approval. Other changes were more debatable. Horse racing became more prominent and racing circuits were arranged to coincide with a series of county fairs. Opponents of horse racing argued that it had nothing to do with the real business of agriculture; instead, it absorbed an undue proportion of premium funds, distracted attention from farm exhibits, and encouraged gambling. Defenders were not lacking, however, and their arguments impressed a countryside that loved horse racing. They insisted that the development of fine horses of all kinds was a legitimate branch of stock breeding, and that gambling could be controlled, if people really wanted to check it. Moreover, attendance would decline, especially among townsmen, if racing was eliminated.

A rapid growth of shows, carnivals, and other midway features aroused opposition from puritanical citizens. The secretary of the Michigan county fair association in the early 1880's vividly described existing abuses. According to him, "honest grangers" were shocked when they accidentally stumbled into the presence of the "Circassian beauty" while looking for something less exciting. The president of the Wisconsin State Fair Association in 1883 also denounced "the gaudy shows, gambling devices, organ-grinding, conjuring, mountebankism, and every species of graceless vagabondism, which we have admitted to our grounds."[32] Rural newspapers echoed similar sentiments. In spite of a successful fourteenth annual fair at Algona, Iowa, in 1886, the local paper criticized those in charge for admitting travelling shows staffed with "blacklegs and swindlers." The Preston, Minnesota, paper in 1896 even questioned whether fairs were worth while, morally or financially. On Thursday night of fair week Preston streets had been crowded with young men, many of whom were drunk. Some of them had won considerable money betting on the horse races and had drunk too much while treating their friends.

County fairs continued to draw large crowds to the turn of the century in spite of criticism. Some towns held a short, spring racing program, at which grandstand weddings, mule races, and ladies' riding contests vied with the pacers and trotters for attention. The main fair came in the early fall, with a program lasting from two to three days. Directors of the Algona, Iowa, fair in 1877 required all exhibitors to have their entries in place by Wednesday, September 12. Thursday morning was devoted to showing brood mares, jacks, and mules, and to a shooting match with glass balls as targets. The afternoon program opened with an exhibition of horses, which was followed by a pulling contest at two, and then trotting and running races. Awards on farm produce, stock and machinery were announced at ten on Friday, and the rest of the day was given over to horse racing.

Weather-beaten, high board fences enclosed the fair grounds that adjoined the city limits of virtually every county-seat town on the Middle Border. Grandstand, race course, stock pens, and a "floral hall" to shelter the exhibits entered by the ladies were common features, and all towns had hopes of financing enough buildings to shelter crowds and entries alike in bad weather.

The midway asked only for room to pitch its tents and stalls, which moved from fair to fair during the season. As early as 1875 fairs had balloon ascensions, glass works, monkey shows, shooting galleries, and minstrel troupes. In time the midway featured attractions for every age. All bought "candy cream," long strips of a sweet confection which were cut with scissors and wrapped in tissue paper as they emerged from vending machines. Music from a wheezy hand organ—often the same tune over and over—and the thin, shrill whistle of a small steam engine, which emitted puffs of black coal smoke in its efforts to move a heavy load of customers, drew attention to the merry-go-round. Burly countrymen, bashful but proud of their strength, fell easy prey to barkers who challenged them to bet a dime against a good cigar that they could sledge-hammer a lead weight into ringing a gong topping a pole.

Even the most abject gained confidence as they gave way to the frenzied spirit of the midway. Boys twirled canes won at some booth and purchased feather dusters to poke into girls' faces, and were showered with confetti in return. The more daring donned hatbands with snappy slogans and purchased soft rubber balls fastened to India-rubber strings, which enabled them to pop a girl and retrieve the balls virtually in one motion. Small boys exchanged information about sideshow freaks and the strength of the lemonade before investing their nickels and pennies. And all stood in line for access to the one shallow tin cup attached to the fairground pump, even though individuals far back in the milling mob tried to drive other parched throats away by yelling that a dead cat had been found in the well.[33]

Country people brought basket dinners with them and townsmen were sure to arrive in time for the afternoon racing. Herbert Quick has described the excitement of the crowd when horses neared the finish:

> The crowd in the grand-stand rose to their feet as the field of trotters came down the homestretch. The marshals yelled at the track-side throng to keep back and give the horses room—and when they came to the wire, with the sorrel still taking the pole, the black leading him by a neck, and roan and bay hurling themselves forward in great surges to close the gap by which they were losing, you should have heard the roar which arose from that Iowa crowd.[34]

Voting a Straight Ticket

Although elections were important any time, country towns seethed with excitement and debate in presidential-election years. As soon as national conventions announced their tickets, local ratification meetings enthusiastically endorsed the candidates and township political clubs prepared for early fall campaigning. Marching clubs performed at political rallies and in torchlight processions, their members garbed in some distinctive manner such as blue capes and blue helmets topped with white feathers, or white plug hats and canes. Bands, drum corps, blazing torches, flamboyant oratory, and victory barbecues stimulated partisan spirit.

The Monroe, Wisconsin, band played while a crowd gathered at the local Turner's Hall for a Republican rally in 1884. The campaign glee club opened the program by singing "Hold the Fort for Blaine and Logan," after which an abbreviated speech only forty minutes long was given by an embarrassed young man. A seasoned speaker from Janesville held the crowd for two hours, however. He contrasted the American laborer's favorable status under tariff protection with conditions under the caste system and free trade in Europe, compared the records of the presidential candidates, and then finished off with "clever imitations" of "dudes" in the opposing party. The Democrats won that election, and on November 26 staged a local demonstration in honor of their first President in many years. Again the cornet band was called into action to head a parade containing men carrying brooms marked "solid South." Others were dressed as tramps, intended as takeoffs on Blaine and Logan. Mottoes and transparencies, uniformed juvenile marching clubs, fireworks and prismatics on all sides of the public square, shots from improvised cannon, Chinese lanterns everywhere in the courthouse park, speeches, and then a bonfire featured the local celebration.

The Bryan-McKinley campaign aroused even more excitement than usual. An elderly retired farmer of Athens, Illinois, estimated the crowd at a local Republican rally at 5,000 people. Marching clubs from at least ten other towns, some of them as far away as Springfield, were in line. Glee clubs, women's clubs, bands, and all the other paraphernalia of political campaigning were in evidence. Everyone, of course, was excited over Bryan's campaign for free silver and against the "interests." Even youngsters could not ignore the contest when they played their annual Halloween pranks. At Wesley, Iowa, the morning after Halloween the local banker discovered a sign on the front of his bank reading, "I believe in the free and unlimited coinage of silver at the ratio of 16 to 1, G. B. Hall," and an outhouse which had been moved in front of the livery stable bore a placard reading "Free Silver Headquarters."

As soon as the voting ended, citizens began to gather in local opera houses for telegraphic returns. At Athens, Illinois, voters had been excited for months and had talked nothing but politics. By midnight Athens knew pretty well the results and the crowd became wild with excitement. People paraded the streets, shouted, tooted horns, and danced for the rest of the night. While the Republicans were receiving returns at Atlantic, Iowa, a well-known Democrat whose enthusiasm was greater than his information stuck his head in the door, and was informed by some wag that the Argentine Republic had just gone for McKinley, but, being equal to the occasion, he promptly retorted, "It's a d–d lie, for we just got word it went for Bryan."[35]

Christmas—The Major Festival

During the early fall some churches staged Harvest Home festivals to show their gratitude for bountiful crops, and lyceums and literary societies resumed their winter tempo. Sportsmen who had hunted deer and elk near Algona, Iowa, and other midwestern towns in the 1860's now turned to small game or even to trapshooting. Thanksgiving-morning union church services, turkey dinners, and visiting among relatives and friends were common from the 1860's on.[36] But Christmas remained the last and greatest festival of all the year.

William Dean Howells recalled his pleasure in Santa Claus and in hanging up his stockings on Christmas Eve in the small, pre-Civil War Ohio town where he lived as a boy, an indication of the basic continuity of the Christmas pageant. Minor variations existed from place to place, it is true, and church groups occasionally experimented with substitutes for even the Christmas tree. These included paper ships and mills loaded with presents; arches and pyramids; and even illuminated crosses, but invariably congregations used a tree the next year. An editorial in the Lacon, Illinois, paper in 1865, headed "Christmas next Monday," could appear in a country paper today without needing any change to modernize it. Christmas, the editor said, was a day for children, but all had visions of Santa Claus, peanuts, plum puddings, fat turkeys, and genial companions. Children would retire on Christmas Eve with tantalizing visions of Santa Claus in mind and would rise early on Christmas morning to explore the recesses of their stockings suspended from the branches of the family tree. And everyone should spend the day in the real spirit of the occasion, not in "guzzling rot gut."

Local schools dismissed for as much as a week, which alone would have endeared Christmas to children. College boys, schoolteachers, and distant relatives arrived to spend the vacation with their families; dances, marriages, and drinking increased; and youngsters drilled on their songs and recitations for the Christmas program. Already filled with wonder and excitement, children saw fairyland when they entered the church door holding to their parents' hands. There, at the front of the church, stood a magnificent tree, reaching almost to the ceiling, its branches strung with ropes of beauty made from threading pop corn kernels and cranberries alternately on twine. Tin-foil streamers, tapers, and a gold star at the very top added to its splendor. Even the odor of the place seemed changed, a mixture of the smell of wet snow on clothing, of evergreens, of wax and tinsel, of oranges, all nicely mixed and flavored by drafts of hot air from stove or registers and the sharply biting cold which swept inside each time the door was opened.

Children knew that they were sure to receive one of the net stockings crammed with dyed candies, nuts and oranges, and they hopefully eyed the dolls, packages, and curious parcels hanging from branches of the tree or piled at its base. But first the program. Some went through that ordeal with brazen aplomb and loud voice but more hitched at trousers or skirts and twisted handkerchiefs in knots to conceal their agony of embarrassment. The program at the Algona, Iowa, Congregational church in 1886 opened with a song by the entire Sunday school, which meant the whole audience. This was followed by the minister's invocation, and then a song by Mrs. McCoy's class. Georgie Horton gave a recitation, "What Santa Claus Saw," and Howard Robinson followed with another called "The Orphan's Christmas." Master Lee Reed recited "My First Pants," and the program went on through recitations, dialogues and songs until all children had made an appearance. At the Methodist church the program consisted of a cantata, "Catching Kriss-Kringle," but there too the parts were numerous enough to give all fond parents a chance to see their children perform.[37]

In just a few more days the annual cycle of social life would start over again and citizens would have to decide whether to attend the Methodist watch party or a dance on New Year's Eve. By the 1890's small-town social clubs were growing in numbers, state federations of women's clubs were joining the national federation, and the "togetherness" of nineteenth-century country towns was shifting toward a twentieth-century pattern. For the time being, however, citizens automatically belonged to neighborhood and to community, around which social life revolved.

NOTES

1. Zona Gale, *Friendship Village Love Stories* (New York, 1909), 6.
2. *Ibid.*, 24.
3. Gallatin, Missouri, *North Missourian,* August 5, 1898.
4. Sherwood Anderson, *Winesburg, Ohio. A Group of Tales of Ohio Small-Town Life* (New York, 1919), 237–238.
5. Hamlin Garland, *A Daughter of the Middle Border* (New York, 1921), 14–15.
6. Alexis de Tocqueville, *Democracy in America,* edited by Henry Steele Commager (New York, 1947), 323; James Bryce, *The American Commonwealth* (New York, 1891), II, 269, 281–282.
7. William Allen White, *Autobiography* (New York, 1946), 44; Rose Wilder Lane, *Old Home Town* (New York, 1935). The "Golden Text" consisted of a short scriptural passage pointing up the central idea of the lesson. All were supposed to memorize it.
8. Henry O. Severance, "The Folk of Our Town," *Michigan History Magazine,* XII (January, 1928), 51–65; Louis Bromfield, *The Farm* (New York, 1935), 145.
9. Don Marquis, *Sons of the Puritans* (New York, 1939), 41–42.
10. See, for example, a detailed analysis of the origins of such organizations in Newell L. Sims, *A Hoosier Village: A Sociological Study with Special Reference to Social Causation* (New York, 1912), 68.
11. Chatfield, Minnesota, *Chatfield Democrat,* February 26, 1876, April 1, 1876; Algona, Iowa, *The Upper Des Moines,* March 7 and 21, 1867; Lacon, Illinois, *Lacon Home Journal,* October 30, 1884.
12. Monroe, Wisconsin, *Monroe Sentinel,* April 21, 1869, June 30, 1869; Algona, Iowa, *The Upper Des Moines,* December 21, 1876, announcement of plans for New Year's; Earnest Elmo Calkins, *They Broke the Prairie: Being Some Account of the settlement of the Upper Mississippi Valley by religious and educational pioneers, told in terms of one city, Galesburg, and of one college, Knox* (New York, 1937), 25.
13. Chatfield, Minnesota, *Chatfield Democrat,* February 19, 1876.
14. A detailed study of an Indiana town has shown the extent of this pattern over a long period of years. For instance, the town had a baseball team in the years 1869–70, 1883–84, 1888–90, 1893, 1895, 1897–99, 1902–5 and 1910; a shooting club 1872–78, 1884, 1898–1902 and 1909–10; a roller skating rink 1883–85 and 1905–6; and a bicycle club 1883–85, 1888 and 1890–92. Newell L. Sims, *A Hoosier Village,* 114.

15. Dorothy W. Regur, "In the Bicycle Era," *Palimpsest*, XIV (October, 1933), 349–362; Greencastle, Indiana, *Putnam Republican Banner*, July 4 and August 7, 1867; Report of Coffeysburg correspondent in Gallatin, Missouri, *North Missourian*, September 1, 1893; Lacon, Illinois, *Lacon Home Journal*, January 1, 1885 and October 9, 1884; Monroe, Wisconsin, *Monroe Sentinel*, January 2, 9, 30, 1884.

16. William J. Peterson, "Legal Holidays in Iowa," *Iowa Journal of History and Politics*, XLIII (January, 1945), 3–68 and (April, 1945), 113–91.

17. Monroe, Wisconsin, *Monroe Sentinel*, January 2, 1884; Henry O. Severance, "The Folk of Our Town," *Michigan History Magazine*, XII (January, 1928), 51–65; Leah Jackson Wolford, *The Play Party in Indiana* (Indianapolis, 1916), 105. See also article and bibliography by Bruce E. Mahan and Pauline Grahame, "Play-Party Games," *Palimpsest*, X (February, 1929), 33–90.

18. Advertisement, Monroe, Wisconsin, *Monroe Sentinel*, December 31, 1884; Lacon, Illinois, *Illinois Gazette*, January 6, 1875; *Lacon Home Journal*, December 27, 1894; Chatfield, Minnesota, *Chatfield Democrat*, January 5, 1867 and January 2, 1886.

19. See reports of correspondents from Coffeysburg and Jamesport in Gallatin, Missouri, *North Missourian*, January–February, 1893.

20. See discussion and advertisements of ugly Valentines, Algona, Iowa, *The Upper Des Moines*, February 17, 1886, and February 12, 1896, and Croswell, Michigan, *Sanilac Jeffersonian*, January 28, 1898. Also, balls and dinners, *ibid.*, February 11, 1898, and Lacon, Illinois, *Lacon Home Journal*, February 10, 1875. See also balls and dinners, Tiffin, Ohio, *Tiffin Tribune*, February 4, 1869; Chatfield, Minnesota, *Chatfield Democrat*, February 16, 1867, and Monroe, Wisconsin, *Monroe Sentinel*, February 27, 1884.

21. See reports of correspondents from Coffeysburg and Jamesport in Gallatin, Missouri, *North Missourian*, March–April, 1893.

22. Gallatin, Missouri, *North Missourian*, April 7, 1893. See also William Dean Howells, *A Boy's Town* (New York, 1890), 113, for a description of Easter eggs before the Civil War. Also, Ruth Suckow's novel *New Hope* (New York, 1942), for an excellent description of Easter services.

23. Tiffin, Ohio, *Tiffin Tribune*, April 1, 1869; Chatfield, Minnesota, *Chatfield Democrat*, April 24, 1886; Gallatin, Missouri, *North Missourian*, April 7, 1893.

24. William Dean Howells, *A Boy's Town*, 80–92, 133–147, 152, 161–70; Thomas Hart Benton, *An Artist in America* (New York, 1937), 9–10; William Allen White, *Autobiography*, 44; Herbert Hoover, "Boyhood in Iowa," *Palimpsest*, IX (July, 1928), 269–276.

25. Writers Program of the Iowa W.P.A., "Baseball! The Story of Iowa's Early Innings," *Annals of Iowa*, XXII (January, 1941), 625–654; Cecil O. Monroe, "The Rise of Baseball in Minnesota," *Minnesota History*, XIX (June, 1938), 162–181; Harold C. Evans, "Baseball in Kansas, 1867–1940," *Kansas Historical Quarterly*, IX (May, 1940), 175–192; baseball reports in Algona, Iowa, *The Upper Des Moines*, May 16 and 23, 1867, August 11 and 25, 1886; Report of Washburn correspondent in Lacon, Illinois, *Lacon Home Journal*, August 25, 1875; Croswell, Michigan, *Sanilac Jeffersonian*, June 11, 1897; Monroe, Wisconsin, *Monroe Sentinel*, July 7, 1869.

26. Monroe, Wisconsin, *Monroe Sentinel*, June 30, 1869; Chatfield, Minnesota, *Chatfield Democrat*, June 16, 1886. See, for example, reports of the custom of hold-

ing a May-day picnic at Jamesport, Missouri, in Gallatin, Missouri, *North Missourian*, May 19, 1893.

27. Lacon, Illinois, *Lacon Home Journal*, June 5, 1884; William Allen White, *Autobiography*, 73.

28. Algona, Iowa, *The Upper Des Moines*, July 6, 1876 and July 7, 1886; for the Kin Hubbard quotation, see "Abe Martin on an Ole-Fashioned Fourth O' July," *American Magazine*, LXXIV (July, 1912), 356–358; Centreville, Michigan, *St. Joseph County Republican*, July 7, 1888 and June 11, 1897.

29. Monroe, Wisconsin, *Monroe Sentinel*, July 19, 1876 and August 5, 1896; Centreville, Michigan, *St. Joseph County Republican*, August 9, 1879; Algona, Iowa, *The Upper Des Moines*, August 18, 1886; John E. Young Diaries 1843–1994, entry August 11, 1899, Illinois Historical Society Library, Springfield.

30. "Pioneer Association of Van Buren County," *Annals of Iowa*, XI (January, 1873), 375–399; early volumes of the *Annals of Iowa* are full of material relating to Old Settlers' Associations. See also "The Michigan Pioneer and Historical Society," *Bulletin* Number 3, Michigan Historical Commission (Lansing, 1914), 12–62; "Proceedings of Old Settlers of Cass County, Indiana 1870–1888," scrapbook in Indiana State Library, Indianapolis; and *Proceedings of the Old Settlers' Meeting held at Catlin, Illinois, Saturday September Twenty-Sixty, 1885* (Danville, Illinois, 1886). See also account of founding of county society of Monroe, Wisconsin, *Monroe Sentinel*, January 13, 27 and February 3, 1869; and founding of county society at Tiffin, Ohio, *Tiffin Tribune*, February 4, 1869. See *Souvenir of the Old Settlers' Association of Marshall County*, published by the *Lacon Home Journal* (Illinois), 1888, Illinois Historical Society Library, Springfield; Benjamin F. Reed, *History of Kossuth County Iowa* (Chicago, 1913), I, Chapter 22 and pp. 470–471.

31. See lists in Algona, Iowa, *The Upper Des Moines*, July 4, 1867 and in Monroe, Wisconsin, *Monroe Sentinel*, July 21, 1869.

32. Quoted in Earle D. Ross, "The Evolution of the Agricultural Fair in the Northwest," *Iowa Journal of History and Politics*, XXIV (July, 1926), 445–481. Quotation on p. 473. Unless otherwise indicated, material relating to fairs has been taken from this study.

33. Algona, Iowa, *The Upper Des Moines*, August 9, 1877 and September 29, 1886; item from Preston paper in Chatfield, Minnesota, *Chatfield Democrat*, October 1, 1896; Maurice Thompson, *Hoosier Mosaics* (New York, 1875), story titled "Trout's Luck"; Oney Fred Sweet, "An Iowa County Seat," *Iowa Journal of History and Politics*, XXXVIII (October, 1940), 339–408.

34. Herbert Quick, *The Invisible Woman* (Indianapolis, 1924), 294.

35. See, for example, Monroe, Wisconsin, *Monroe Sentinel*, September 22, 1876, September 24 and November 26, 1884; Lacon, Illinois, *Lacon Home Journal*, September 11, October 9, 23, and November 27, 1884; Hillsboro, Ohio, *Hillsborough Gazette*, October 9, 1884; Chatfield, Minnesota, *Chatfield Gazette*, November 25, 1876; Centreville, Michigan, *St. Joseph County Republican*, June 30 and October 20, 1888; Algona, Iowa, *The Upper Des Moines*, November 4, 1896; John E. Young Diaries 1843–1904, entries October 13, 23, 30, November 3, 4, 1896. Illinois Historical Society Library, Springfield; Edwin T. Chase, "Forty Years on Main Street," *Iowa Journal of History and Politics*, XXXIV (July, 1936), 227–261.

36. Centreville, Michigan, *St. Joseph County Republican*, November 27, 1869,

November 29, 1879 and September 24, 1897. See also the description of the Harvest Home festival by Ruth Suckow, *New Hope*. See also Algona, Iowa, *The Upper Des Moines*, April 18, 1867, November 21, 1867, January 9, 1868, August 2, 1877, June 23, 1886, and November 24, 1886; Monroe, Wisconsin, *Monroe Sentinel*, November 17, 1869 and August 2, 1876; Hillsboro, Ohio, *Hillsborough Gazette*, January 3, and December 4, 1884; Lacon, Illinois, *Illinois Gazette*, November 29, 1865 and *Lacon Home Journal*, November 24, 1875; Greencastle, Indiana, *Greencastle Banner*, November 25, 1886; and Tiffin, Ohio, *Tiffin Tribune*, November 19, 1868.

37.   Centreville, Michigan, *St. Joseph County Republican*, January 4, 1879; report from Bainbridge in Greencastle, Indiana, *Greencastle Banner*, December 30, 1886; Chatfield, Minnesota, *Chatfield Democrat*, December 25, 1886; Lacon, Illinois, *Illinois Gazette*, December 20, 1865; and Algona, Iowa, *The Upper Des Moines*, December 29, 1886.

The Hired Girls

FROM *My Ántonia*

WILLA CATHER

WRITING ABOUT HIS OWN HOMETOWN in western Minnesota in an essay called "The Music of Failure," Bill Holm observes, "Minneota is a community born out of failure about 1880. By that I mean that no one ever arrived in Minneota after being a success elsewhere. It is an immigrant town, settled by European refuse, first those starved out of Ireland, then Norway, Iceland, Sweden, Holland, Belgium." Other towns—like Garrison Keillor's fictional Lake Wobegon—were founded by Yankee entrepreneurs who were quite successful at railroading, shop keeping, or the business of founding and promoting towns, but always town life involved an ethnic diversity and a social structure of at least two classes. Around the Midwest one sees the record, in the names on tombstones or on cornerstones of co-op or creamery, of a Yankee entrepreneurial class mingled with ethnic immigrants. Usually, however, the cemeteries (and churches) of the native-born American upper class—Presbyterian, Episcopal, American Lutheran—top out around 1920, while the cemeteries and churches of a vigorous, rising immigrant group—Catholic, Methodist, German or Scandinavian Lutheran—continued to grow, even into the sixties. The history of midwestern small towns is very much tied to ethnic immigration. As Holm suggests, the immigrants were not necessarily those who had been successful in the countries they left behind, but they prevailed and eventually dominated, either strengthened by the stress of immigration or winnowed by a Darwinian process of natural selection on the harsh prairies.

One common pattern of immigration, encouraged by the Homestead Act, was for a group of individuals from little town A in country B to move collectively to a cluster of homesteads in section C of township D, in county E of state F, bringing with them their cultural heritage (including their church) and founding or taking over a village. A second method was for an established farm or village family to pay passage for a young male or female from their homeland, who would work as a farm hand or domestic for a specified period of time. Another method was for the family in Europe to save enough money to buy passage to America for one older son, who would set himself up in a small town or on a farm, save enough money to buy passage for one sibling (usually a brother), and then another, until the entire family could join those they had sent before. Men farmed or worked in factories; women hired out as domestics. This method is still used today; few immigrants set up on 160 acres of land, but employment is readily available in the trucking, restaurant, food processing, and housecleaning industries. Studies indicate that despite language and cultural difficulties, immigrants match native-born Americans in earning power in about three to five years, although their work is harder and their social status lower.

As a girl of ten, somewhat unwillingly transplanted in 1883 from her native Virginia to Red Cloud, Nebraska, Willa Cather spent almost as much time chatting with the young farm wives and immigrant girls as she did organizing amateur theatricals in town. Like Meridel Le Sueur (who wrote of the Poles and Bohemians, "They freed me from severe puritan sexual rigidity, from relating pleasure to guilt and sin"), Cather found these farm girls more interesting than the Protestant town girls who belonged to the upper class. One such farm girl, a Bohemian named Annie Sadilek, became the model for Ántonia Shmirda in one of Cather's most powerful novels, *My Ántonia*. In the second section of that novel, Ántonia moves from the farm to the town (Red Cloud thinly disguised as Black Hawk), finding employment with the Harling family, neighbors of the novel's narrator, Jim Burden. Burden, like other village males, sees the hired girls as more vital, more energetic, and more intelligent than the town girls: "The older girls, who helped to break up the wild sod, learned so much from life, from poverty, from their mothers and grandmothers; they had all, like Ántonia, been early awakened and made observant by coming at a tender age from an old country to a new. . . . I can remember something engaging about each of them. Physically they were almost a race apart." They are a sharp contrast to the town girls, whose stiff bodies when they danced never moved inside their clothes, whose muscles seemed to ask but one thing—not to be disturbed. "The young men who belonged to the Progressive Euchre Club used to drop in late and risk a tiff with their sweethearts and general condemnation for a waltz with 'the hired girls,'" Cather writes.

In part seven of that section of the novel, Cather sends Jim Burden to a piano concert in Black Hawk. Cather's suggestive comments on winter (which "chills the restlessness out of people"), her frank depiction of race relationships, and the cosmopolitan atmosphere of this very small-town audience should not be overlooked, but the real cultural commentary is provided by the Bohemian hired girls who are invited to join the white males (who have been drinking!) in dancing to music played by the black pianist. This is certainly behavior of which Mrs. Gardener—hotel matron and moral watchdog—would not have approved.

o o o

Winter lies too long in country towns; hangs on until it is stale and shabby, old and sullen. On the farm the weather was the great fact, and men's affairs went on underneath it, as the streams creep under the ice. But in Black Hawk the scene of human life was spread out shrunken and pinched, frozen down to the bare stalk.

Through January and February I went to the river with the Harlings on clear nights, and we skated up to the big island and made bonfires on the frozen sand. But by March the ice was rough and choppy, and the snow on the river bluffs was gray and mournful-looking. I was tired of school, tired of winter clothes, of the rutted streets, of the dirty drifts and the piles of cinders that had lain in the yards so long. There was only one break in the dreary monotony of that month; when Blind d'Arnault, the negro pianist, came to town. He gave a concert at the Opera House on Monday night, and he and his manager spent Saturday and Sunday at our comfortable hotel. She told Ántonia she had better go to see Tiny that Saturday evening, as there would certainly be music at the Boys' Home.

Saturday night after supper I ran downtown to the hotel and slipped quietly into the parlor. The chairs and sofas were already occupied, and the air smelled pleasantly of cigar smoke. The parlor had once been two rooms, and the floor was sway-backed where the partition had been cut away. The wind from without made waves in the long carpet. A coal stove glowed at either end of the room, and the grand piano in the middle stood open.

There was an atmosphere of unusual freedom about the house that night, for Mrs. Gardener had gone to Omaha for a week. Johnnie had been having drinks with the guests until he was rather absent-minded. It was Mrs. Gardener who ran the business and looked after everything. Her husband stood at the desk and welcomed incoming travelers. He was a popular fellow, but no manager.

Mrs. Gardener was admittedly the best-dressed woman in Black Hawk, drove the best horse, and had a smart trap and a little white-and-gold sleigh. She seemed indifferent to her possessions, was not half so solicitous about them as her friends were. She was tall, dark, severe, with something Indian-like in the rigid immobility of her face. Her manner was cold, and she talked little. Guests felt that they were receiving, not conferring, a favor when they stayed at her house. Even the smartest traveling men were flattered when Mrs. Gardener stopped to chat with them for a moment. The patrons of the hotel were divided into two classes; those who had seen Mrs. Gardener's diamonds, and those who had not.

When I stole into the parlor Anson Kirkpatrick, Marshall Field's man, was at the piano, playing airs from a musical comedy then running in Chicago. He was a dapper little Irishman, very vain, homely as a monkey, with friends everywhere, and a sweetheart in every port, like a sailor. I did not know all the men who were sitting about, but I recognized a furniture salesman from Kansas City, a drug man, and Willy O'Reilly, who traveled for a jewelry house and sold musical instruments. The talk was all about good and bad hotels, actors and actresses and musical prodigies. I learned that Mrs. Gardener had gone to Omaha to hear Booth and Barrett, who were to play there next week, and that Mary Anderson was having a great success in "A Winter's Tale," in London.

The door from the office opened, and Johnnie Gardener came in, directing Blind d'Arnault,—he would never consent to be led. He was a heavy, bulky mulatto, on short legs, and he came tapping the floor in front of him with his goldheaded cane. His yellow face was lifted in the light, with a show of white teeth, all grinning, and his shrunken, papery eyelids lay motionless over his blind eyes.

"Good evening, gentlemen. No ladies here? Good-evening, gentlemen. We going to have a little music? Some of you gentlemen going to play for me this evening?" It was the soft, amiable negro voice, like those I remembered from early childhood, with the note of docile subservience in it. He had the negro head, too; almost no head at all; nothing behind the ears but folds of neck under close-clipped wool. He would have been repulsive if his face had not been so kindly and happy. It was the happiest face I had seen since I left Virginia.

He felt his way directly to the piano. The moment he sat down, I noticed the nervous infirmity of which Mrs. Harling had told me. When he was sitting, or standing still, he swayed back and forth incessantly, like a rocking toy. At the piano, he swayed in time to the music, and when he was not playing, his body kept up this motion, like an empty mill grinding on. He found the pedals and tried them, ran his yellow hands up and down the keys a few times, tinkling off scales, then turned to the company.

"She seems all right, gentlemen. Nothing happened to her since the last time I was here. Mrs. Gardener, she always has this piano tuned up before I come. Now, gentlemen, I expect you've all got grand voices. Seems like we might have some good old plantation songs to-night."

The men gathered round him, as he began to play "My Old Kentucky Home." They sang one negro melody after another, while the mulatto sat rocking himself, his head thrown back, his yellow face lifted, its shriveled eyelids never fluttering.

He was born in the Far South, on the d'Arnault plantation, where the spirit if not the fact of slavery persisted. When he was three weeks old he had an illness which left him totally blind. As soon as he was old enough to sit up alone and toddle about, another affliction, the nervous motion of his body, became apparent. His mother, a buxom young negro wench who was laundress for the d'Arnaults, concluded that her blind baby was "not right" in his head, and she was ashamed of him. She loved him devotedly, but he was so ugly, with his sunken eyes and his "fidgets," that she hid him away from people. All the dainties she brought down from the "Big House" were for the blind child, and she beat and cuffed her other children whenever she found them teasing him or trying to get his chicken-bone away from him. He began to talk early, remembered everything he heard, and his mammy said he "wasn't all wrong." She named him Samson, because he was blind, but on the plantation he was known as "yellow Martha's simple child." He was docile and obedient, but when he was six years old he began to run away from home, always taking the same direction. He felt his way through the lilacs, along the boxwood hedge, up to the south wing of the "Big House," where Miss Nellie d'Arnault practiced the piano every morning. This angered his mother more than anything else he could have done; she was so ashamed of his ugliness that she couldn't bear to have white folks see him. Whenever she caught him slipping away from the cabin, she whipped him unmercifully, and told him what dreadful things old Mr. d'Arnault would do to him if he ever found him near the "Big House." But the next time Samson had a chance, he ran away again. If Miss d'Arnault stopped practicing for a moment and went toward the window, she saw this hideous little pickaninny, dressed in an old piece of sacking, standing in the open space between the hollyhock rows, his body rocking automatically, his blind face lifted to the sun and wearing an expression of idiotic rapture. Often she was tempted to tell Martha that the child must be kept at home, but somehow the memory of his foolish, happy face deterred her. She remembered that his sense of hearing was nearly all he had,—though it did not occur to her that he might have more of it than other children.

One day Samson was standing thus while Miss Nellie was playing her lesson to her music-master. The windows were open. He heard them get up from the piano, talk a little while, and then leave the room. He heard the door close after them. He crept up to the front windows and stuck his head in: there was no one there. He could always detect the presence of any one in a room. He put one foot over the window sill and straddled it. His mother had told him over and over how his master would give him to the big mastiff if he ever found him "meddling." Samson had got too near the mastiff's kennel once, and had felt his terrible breath in his face. He thought about that, but he pulled in his other foot.

Through the dark he found his way to the Thing, to its mouth. He touched it softly, and it answered softly, kindly. He shivered and stood still. Then he began to feel it all over, ran his finger tips along the slippery sides, embraced the carved legs, tried to get some conception of its shape and size, of the space it occupied in primeval night. It was cold and hard, and like nothing else in his black universe. He went back to its mouth, began at one end of the keyboard and felt his way down into the mellow thunder, as far as he could go. He seemed to know that it must be done with the fingers, not with the fists or the feet. He approached this highly artificial instrument through a mere instinct, and coupled himself to it, as if he knew it was to piece him out and make a whole creature of him. After he had tried over all the sounds, he began to finger out passages from things Miss Nellie had been practicing, passages that were already his, that lay under the bones of his pinched, conical little skull, definite as animal desires. The door opened; Miss Nellie and her music-master stood behind it, but blind Samson, who was so sensitive to presences, did not know they were there. He was feeling out the pattern that lay all ready-made on the big and little keys. When he paused for a moment, because the sound was wrong and he wanted another, Miss Nellie spoke softly. He whirled about in a spasm of terror, leaped forward in the dark, struck his head on the open window, and fell screaming and bleeding to the floor. He had what his mother called a fit. The doctor came and gave him opium.

When Samson was well again, his young mistress led him back to the piano. Several teachers experimented with him. They found he had absolute pitch, and a remarkable memory. As a very young child he could repeat, after a fashion, any composition that was played for him. No matter how many wrong notes he struck, he never lost the intention of a passage, he brought the substance of it across by irregular and astonishing means. He wore his teachers out. He could never learn like other people, never acquired any finish. He was always a negro prodigy who played barbarously and wonderfully. As piano playing, it was perhaps abominable, but as music it was something real, vitalized by a sense of rhythm that was stronger than his other physical senses,—that not only filled his dark mind, but worried his body incessantly. To hear him, to watch him, was to see a negro enjoying himself as only a negro can. It was as if all the agreeable sensations possible to creatures of flesh and blood were heaped up on those black and white keys, and he were gloating over them and trickling them through his yellow fingers.

In the middle of a crashing waltz d'Arnault suddenly began to play softly, and, turning to one of the men who stood behind him, whispered, "Somebody dancing in there." He jerked his bullet toward the dining-room. "I hear little feet,—girls, I 'spect."

Anson Kirkpatrick mounted a chair and peeped over the transom. Springing down, he wrenched open the doors and ran out into the dining-room. Tiny and Lena, Ántonia and Mary Dusak, were waltzing in the middle of the floor. They separated and fled toward the kitchen, giggling.

Kirkpatrick caught Tiny by the elbows. "What's the matter with you girls? Dancing out here by yourselves, when there's a roomful of lonesome men on the other side of the partition! Introduce me to your friends, Tiny."

The girls, still laughing, were trying to escape. Tiny looked alarmed. "Mrs. Gardener wouldn't like it," she protested. "She'd be awful mad if you was to come out here and dance with us."

"Mrs. Gardener's in Omaha, girl. Now, you're Lena, are you?—and you're Tony and you're Mary. Have I got you all straight?"

O'Reilly and the others began to pile the chairs on the tables. Johnnie Gardener ran in from the office.

"Easy, boys, easy!" he entreated them. "You'll wake the cook, and there'll be the devil to pay for me. She won't hear the music, but she'll be down the minute anything's moved in the dining-room."

"Oh, what do you care, Johnnie? Fire the cook and wire Molly to bring another. Come along, nobody'll tell tales."

Johnnie shook his head. "'S a fact, boys," he said confidentially. "If I take a drink in Black Hawk, Molly knows it in Omaha!"

His guests laughed and slapped him on the shoulder. "Oh, we'll make it all right with Molly. Get your back up, Johnnie."

Molly was Mrs. Gardener's name, of course. "Molly Bawn" was painted in large blue letters on the glossy white side of the hotel bus, and "Molly" was engraved inside Johnnie's ring and on his watch-case—doubtless on his heart, too. He was an affectionate little man, and he thought his wife a wonderful woman; he knew that without her he would hardly be more than a clerk in some other man's hotel.

At a word from Kirkpatrick, d'Arnault spread himself out over the piano, and began to draw the dance music out of it, while the perspiration shone on his short wool and on his uplifted face. He looked like some glistening African god of pleasure, full of strong, savage blood. Whenever the dancers paused to change partners or to catch breath, he would boom out softly, "Who's that goin' back on me? One of these city gentlemen, I bet! Now, you girls, you ain't goin' to let that floor get cold?"

Ántonia seemed frightened at first, and kept looking questioningly at Lena and Tiny over Willy O'Reilly's shoulder. Tiny Soderball was trim and slender, with lively little feet and pretty ankles—she wore her dresses very short. She was quicker in speech, lighter in movement and manner than the other girls. Mary Dusak was broad and brown of countenance, slightly marked by smallpox, but handsome for all that. She had beautiful chestnut hair, coils of it; her forehead was low and smooth, and her commanding dark eyes regarded the world indifferently and fearlessly. She looked bold and resourceful and unscrupulous, and she was all of these. They were handsome girls, had the fresh color of their country upbringing, and in their eyes that brilliancy which is called,—by no metaphor, alas!—"the light of youth."

D'Arnault played until his manager came and shut the piano. Before he left us, he showed us his gold watch which struck the hours, and a topaz ring, given him by some Russian nobleman who delighted in negro melodies, and had heard d'Arnault play in New Orleans. At last he tapped his way upstairs, after bowing to everybody, docile and happy. I walked home with Ántonia. We were so excited that we dreaded to go to bed. We lingered a long while at the Harlings' gate, whispering in the cold until the restlessness was slowly chilled out of us.

The Poetry of Vachel Lindsay

Selections

VACHEL LINDSAY

Among American poets, an admittedly eccentric lot, Vachel Lindsay is unmatched for theatricality, color, and eccentricity. Son of a respectable medical doctor from Springfield, Illinois, talented painter in the modern tradition, unabashed fundamentalist Christian, tireless social critic and crusader for social justice (including temperance), performance artist in the troubadour tradition, Lindsay studied briefly in New York City before returning to Springfield to write poems, publish *The Village Magazine* (printed at his father's expense and handed out free to passers-by on the village street corners), and campaign for a better, more beautiful Springfield. Occasionally he wandered the countryside, trading poems for food and lodging, reporting his escapades in the book *Adventures While Preaching the Gospel of Beauty*. Thanks to Harriet Monroe's *Poetry* magazine, published in nearby Chicago, this unlikely approach to creating and marketing art allowed Lindsay to become world famous. Three of his poems were for many years staples of American literature and known by heart to millions of Americans. (In a motion picture set in the 1950s, students of Wilton Academy chant Lindsay's "The Congo" while leaving their underground meeting of the Dead Poets' Society.) Recently Lindsay's strong opinions and preference for traditional forms have caused him to disappear from textbooks and anthologies, and hence from the American consciousness.

In Lindsay's time, Springfield, the capital of Illinois, was halfway along the road from village to city. It was, of course, the hometown of Abraham Lincoln—who looms large in Lindsay's mind as the archetypal small-town giant—and temporary residence of other illustrious Illinois statesmen. Dissatisfied with Springfield in its middle age, Lindsay looked both backward and forward: the ghosts of Lincoln and Governor John Peter Altgeld challenge complacent burghers to a program of rigorous Village Improvement. Lindsay could shrug his shoulders and admit "a city is not builded in a day," but he was an impatient visionary. He did not imagine Springfield as a second Chicago. He sought instead an expanded village filled with peace, beauty, indigenous art, and "Lincoln-hearted men." Lindsay envisioned a community in possession of its soul, a harmony of science and art and industry—an American small town grown up.

o   o   o

On the Building of Springfield

Let not our town be large, remembering
That little Athens was the Muses' home,
That Oxford rules the heart of London still,
That Florence gave the Renaissance to Rome.

Record it for the grandson of your son—
A city is not builded in a day:
Our little town cannot complete her soul
Till countless generations pass away.

Now let each child be joined as to a church
To her perpetual hopes, each man ordained:
Let every street be made a reverent aisle
Where Music grows and Beauty is unchained.

Let Science and Machinery and Trade
Be slaves of her, and make her all in all,
Building against our blatant, restless time
An unseen, skilful, medieval wall.

Let every citizen be rich toward God.
Let Christ the beggar, teach divinity.
Let no man rule who holds his money dear.
Let this, our city, be our luxury.

We should build parks that students from afar
Would choose to starve in, rather than go home,
Fair little squares, with Phidian ornament,
Food for the spirit, milk and honeycomb.

Songs shall be sung by us in that good day,
Songs we have written, blood within the rhyme
Beatings, as when Old England still was glad,—
The purple, rich Elizabethan time.

Say, is my prophecy too fair and far?
I only know, unless her faith be high,
The soul of this, our Nineveh, is doomed,
Our little Babylon will surely die.

Some city on the breast of Illinois
No wiser and no better at the start
By faith shall rise redeemed, by faith shall rise
Bearing the western glory in her heart.

The genius of the Maple, Elm and Oak,
The secret hidden in each grain of corn,
The glory that the prairie angels sing
At night when sons of Life and Love are born,

Born but to struggle, squalid and alone,
Broken and wandering in their early years.
When will they make our dusty streets their goal,
Within our attics hide their sacred tears?

When will they start our vulgar blood athrill
With living language, words that set us free?
When will they make a path of beauty clear
Between our riches and our liberty?

We must have many Lincoln-hearted men.
A city is not builded in a day.
And they must do their work, and come and go,
While countless generations pass away.

Abraham Lincoln Walks at Midnight
(In Springfield, Illinois)

It is portentous, and a thing of state
That here at midnight, in our little town
A mourning figure walks, and will not rest,
Near the old court-house pacing up and down.

Or by his homestead, or in shadowed yards,
He lingers where his children used to play,
Or through the market, on the well-worn stones
He stalks until the dawn-stars burn away.

A bronzed, lank man! His suit of ancient black,
A famous high top-hat and plain worn shawl
Make him the quaint great figure that men love,
The prairie-lawyer, master of us all.

He cannot sleep upon his hillside now.
He is among us:—as in times before!
And we who toss and lie awake for long
Breathe deep, and start, to see him pass the door.

His head is bowed. He thinks on men and kings.
Yea, when the sick world cries, how can he sleep?
Too many peasants fight, they know not why,
Too many homesteads in black terror weep.

The sins of all the war-lords burn his heart.
He sees the dreadnaughts scouring every main.
He carries on his shawl-wrapped shoulders now
The bitterness, the folly and the pain.

He cannot rest until a spirit-dawn
Shall come;—the shining hope of Europe free:
The league of sober folk, the Workers' Earth,
Bringing long peace to Cornland, Alp and Sea.

It breaks his heart that kings must murder still,
That all his hours of travail here for men
Seem yet in vain. And who will bring white peace
That he may sleep upon his hill again?

Springfield Magical

In this, the City of my Discontent,
Sometimes there comes a whisper from the grass,
"Romance, Romance—is here. No Hindu town
Is quite so strange. No Citadel of Brass
By Sinbad found, held half such love and hate;
No picture-palace in a picture-book
Such webs of Friendship, Beauty, Greed and Fate!"

In this, the City of my Discontent,
Down from the sky, up from the smoking deep
Wild legends new and old burn round my bed
While trees and grass and men are wrapped in sleep.
Angels come down, with Christmas in their hearts,
Gentle, whimsical, laughing, heaven-sent;
And, for a day, fair Peace have given me
In this, the City of my Discontent!

The Springfield of the Far Future

Some day our town will grow old.
"She is wicked and raw," men say,
"Awkward and brash and profane."
But the years have a healing way.
The years of God are like bread,
Balm of Gilead and sweet.
And the soul of this little town
Our Father will make complete.

Some day our town will grow old,
Filled with the fullness of time,
Treasure on treasure heaped
Of beauty's tradition sublime.
Proud and gay and gray
Like Hannah with Samuel blest.
Humble and girlish and white
Like Mary, the manger guest.

Like Mary the manger queen
Bringing the God of Light
Till Christmas is here indeed
And earth has no more of night,
And hosts of Magi come,
The wisest under the sun
Bringing frankincense and praise
For her gift of the Infinite One.

Sons of the Middle West

Where, after all, is the soul of the nation?
Why do we turn to the East with yearning
When our fathers come to the West with yearning
Generation on Generation?
Live in the West! There is no returning
From the soil where buried breasts are burning.

Maybe buried after Lincoln
They lived through Freedom's second dawn.
Maybe pierced with Indian arrows
By cabins rude as the nests of sparrows
Or wagons wandering to the Sunset
On strange old plains in the days long gone
Or swept with prairie fires or floods
They died with their toiling all undone
Near the Gray Ohio or Black Missouri
Or Wan and Haunted Sangamon.

Say not—"That wild land is no more.
Whose voice was in the voice of Lincoln!"
Yea, Lincoln—how he haunteth us!
And unseen fires from buried breasts
Rise into the living hearts of us.
No other soil is haunted thus.
What has the East for us?

The Town of American Visions
(Springfield, Illinois)

Is it for naught that where the tired crowds see
Only a place for trade, a teeming square,
Doors of high portent open unto me
Carved with great eagles, and with hawthorns rare?

Doors I proclaim, for there are rooms forgot
Ripened through aeons by the good and wise:
Walls set with Art's own pearl and amethyst
Angel-wrought hangings there, and heaven-hued dyes:—

Dazzling the eye of faith, the hope-filled heart:
Rooms rich in records of old deeds sublime:
Books that hold garnered harvests of far lands,
Pictures that tableau Man's triumphant climb:

Statues so white, so counterfeiting life,
Bronze so ennobled, so with glory fraught
That the tired eyes must weep with joy to see
And the tired mind in Beauty's net be caught.

Come enter there, and meet Tomorrow's Man,
Communing with him softly day by day.
Ah, the deep vistas he reveals, the dream
Of angel-bands in infinite array—

Bright angel-bands, that dance in paths of earth
When our despairs are gone, long overpast—
When men and maidens give fair hearts to Christ
And white streets flame in righteous peace at last.

The Budding of Art

FROM *The Age of Indiscretion*

CLYDE BRION DAVIS

CLYDE BRION DAVIS was born in Nebraska in 1894. His family soon moved to Chillicothe, Missouri, and later to Kansas City. Davis dropped out of school at age fourteen to pursue a variety of odd jobs. While in the Army during World War I, Davis received training and experience in journalism, a field in which he would enjoy a distinguished career, including a stint in Europe as international correspondent during World War II. Davis wrote more than a dozen books, including two early novels, both of which described the progress of a small-town protagonist achieving success in the big world, and several later novels set in small midwestern towns. He also wrote an extended reminiscence of life in Chillicothe at the turn of the century, the glory days of this small town.

He does not romanticize the village in the manner of early Zona Gale, nor does he satirize it in the tradition of Sinclair Lewis, Sherwood Anderson, Edgar Lee Masters, or Ruth Suckow. Mostly the village offers one set of possibilities, contrasted with another set of possibilities offered by the city. Neither city nor country has an advantage. In a chapter of *The Age of Indiscretion* titled "The Good Old Days," Davis points out that even nostalgia is relative:

> If these people were venerable enough, they meant the good old days before the war—and not the Spanish-American war just finished so gloriously, but the *other* war, the war between the Blue and the Gray. The old folk in 1900 mourned for the glamorous old days before the Hannibal and St. Joe Railroad was pounded across the state, frightening the deer and bear and wild turkeys clear out of the country, when people were good neighbors and you could borrow a bucket of fire without being expected to return it with interest, when the skies were bluer and the winters colder and the girls were prettier and the young men hardier.

Davis's Chillicothe is more than anything else a place trying to define itself, educate its children and—without becoming tony or citified—develop art and culture. While culture in Chillicothe, as in any midwestern town, is a late arrival, and its rural tastes are primitive and vulgar, the local school is working on the problem, trying to develop indigenous artists who might—

like Grant Wood, Thomas Hart Benton, John Steuart Curry, and Clyde Brion Davis—escape their native environments to depict their hometowns in a manner which is simple, honest, and recognizably midwestern American.

o o o

To the best of my knowledge fine art did not exist in Chillicothe, Missouri, or in comparable Midwestern towns at the beginning of the Twentieth Century. Although I suspect oil paintings of a sort did hang on the walls of such mansions as the Mansurs' and the Miners' and in the better saloons, I am sure I never saw one until I went to Kansas City in 1908.

Pictures on the walls of most middle-class homes consisted of (1) big, bad crayon portraits of slightly cross-eyed bewhiskered men with pink cheeks, and slightly cross-eyed women with pink cheeks (those copiers of photographs seemed to have difficulty in making eyes match); (2) steel engravings of sentimental subjects, historical events and portraits of great men and Frances Willard; (3) bright lithographs, usually of German origin, of lakes and trees and hills and a waterfall and a small boat with or without sail and a humble cottage and lowing kine and birds in the sky; (4) religious chromos.

Frequently the pictures were enhanced by a spray of gilded cattails or peacock feathers arching from behind the frames.

It's my opinion that the series of world's fairs—Philadelphia, 1876; Chicago, 1893; Buffalo, 1901; St. Louis, 1904—threw the first gleam of artistic light into the cultural darkness of America.

My father and mother spent ten days or so at the Chicago fair and were fascinated by the Hall of Art—or whatever they called it. Whether the selections in the main were good, bad or indifferent, this art exhibition made them conscious at least of a wonderful world which had lain unknown beyond their horizon. The fact that my mother preferred the German section above all others is not particularly significant. The German's traditional obsession with detail would have its appeal to a meticulous housewife. I believe they both absorbed a good deal and I doubt whether it was entirely accidental that the two big French etchings my father purchased in Chicago turned out to be sound art.

Assuredly there must have been some fine American art available in 1893 and I take it for granted it was represented at the World's Columbian Exposition. But there also was some atrocious American art available and I suspect that was even better represented.

I used to know a Japanese diplomatist named Yakashira Suma who was Japanese minister to Spain in 1941. Dr. Suma came from a wealthy old family and he had with him a stack of portfolios containing photographs of his inherited art collection. Most of this extensive collection was Oriental, of course—ceramics as well as pictorial—and wonderful. There were portfolios of French, Italian, Spanish, English and German art, each example very good and representative and picked with the skill of a shrewd connoisseur.

Suma brought out his American portfolio last. "This," he said solemnly, "is our representative collection of American art purchased by my Grandfather Suma at the Chicago World's Fair in 1893."

The portfolio contained perhaps twenty photographic prints, about eleven by fourteen, of paintings which must have been perpetrated by the dunce class of the Hudson River school. They were primitive but not primitives. They were pompous, pretentious, sentimental and awful.

"Surely," I said, "your Grandpa Suma could have found better things than these."

"Oh, no doubt," he said, "but you see my grandfather was not looking for the best. He wished our collection to be representative of American art as the others are representative."

"So," I said, "he picked the worst damn daubs he could find. I don't believe, Dr. Suma, that your grandfather liked the United States very well."

He smiled and licked his lips. This, incidentally, was a few months before Pearl Harbor. "Oh," he said, "on the contrary. He often told me as a child of his visit to America with a great deal of pleasure. He enjoyed himself in America very much, and especially the Chicago World's Fair. You see, my Grandfather Suma had a great sense of humor."

I suppose it's too much to hope that the precision bombing of Tokyo and Yokohama was precise enough to destroy Suma's American collection and to spare the rest.

Well, "art" was taught in the Chillicothe public schools in the early nineteen hundreds. We had drawing books and we were supposed to copy spheres, cubes, triangles and the like. Then, as the class advanced, we would draw apples and cats.

You drew an apple by grasping the pencil backwards, resting your thumb knuckle firmly on the paper and, with this makeshift compass established, you turned the paper on the thumb pivot until the pencil drew a circle. Then, free hand, you drew a reclining parenthesis near the top of the circle with a sprig emerging from the reclining parenthesis. That was an apple. You made a cat with a big circle for the body and a smaller circle joining it at the top for the head and then drew in the ears and tail.

Being clumsy at this procedure, I thought it silly, and I didn't believe the apples looked like apples or the cats like cats. So I tried to be smart and draw free-hand apples that looked like apples and free-hand cats that looked like cats, and Miss Vivian Evans, the third grade teacher, was appalled at my rebellious stupidity. She assigned Jennie Carr, a bright little girl in pigtails, to move over with me and give me special instructions. Jennie tried and I tried, but it was no use. My thumb would slip and the pencil would cant and the running line, trying desperately to dock against adverse winds and tide, always floundered in on the wrong side of the river. I tried a slideslip and I tried a hook-slide, but Jennie would stand for neither and finally she held up her hand and spoke with exasperation, "Miss Evans, it's just hopeless. I just don't think he can learn *anything.*"

Because I admired Jennie Carr, that hurt me. I realized there was justification, but I felt she could have been more gentle in her pronouncement.

In any event, Jennie's judgment was accepted and thereafter I was ignored during "art" period, being awarded an automatic "F," and I put in the art class period drawing pictures of locomotives complete with all current appurtenances.

Later we had a teacher named Miss Belle Lowe, a slim, grave country girl who had ideas of her own. Somehow, some way, she either got permission or took it on her own initiative to have us get cheap water color outfits that came with a limp camel's-hair brush in the box. We were to try to paint still lifes—flowers and such.

My first one was a purple iris and, though I tried very hard, I simply could not achieve the impeccable neatness that my pal Chester, sitting next to me, got so easily. I was ashamed of my picture but I knew there was no way to avoid turning it in.

Miss Lowe came down our aisle, picking up the damp papers, occasionally commenting, "That's nice, Jennie," "Good, Fred."

Then she picked up mine and my face began to burn as she paused to look at it. There was a shuffling sound as the boys and girls turned in their seats waiting for the fun. Miss Lowe didn't know my "art" work, but they did.

"Clyde," she said gravely, "I think that's wonderful."

The class roared. She looked around her but didn't change expression as she held up my painting. "This, she said, "is very close to real art, I think. He's captured the spirit of the iris."

I slumped lower in my seat, burning with humiliation while the laughter beat upon me in waves. The class was delighted. They hadn't expected such delightful humor from the solemn Miss Lowe. I hated her venomously. I hated everyone. I even hated my pal next to me. At least Chester, I thought, in view of our close comradeship, might have restrained his laughter.

When she had gone Chester whispered from the side of his mouth, "Spirit of the iris."

I punched him on the thigh as hard as I could in the cramped quarters. He punched my thigh. I punched him back. He punched me back and Miss Lowe turned and called sharply, "Boys!"

We stopped punching but I whispered, "All right for you."

Realizing that things were getting on dangerous ground, we didn't follow it up after school, even though Chester's mouth did quirk when other boys called me "Iris."

I didn't even try at the next painting session, but Miss Lowe shook her head and said, "That's fine. I thought yesterday it might be an accident, but this has got something too."

There was a little laughter at that, but not much, and I began to wonder if perhaps, if just *possibly* Miss Lowe was not making fun of me after all.

I know that Chester was puzzled as well as amused, as also, no doubt, was the whole class. I was astonished but very, very pleased when it developed that Belle Lowe was actually finding merit in my lack of manual skill, in my clumsy inability to delineate detail as well as the average youngster. Maybe everyone else thought Belle Lowe was silly, bit I didn't. All along I had felt there must be a deep-lying vein of superiority of some obscure sort in me, and Belle Lowe was the first to sense the latent riches which lay so well-hidden beneath the surface.

Working, apparently, on the premise that if a person is bad enough to be outstanding, he had potentials for outstanding goodness, Miss Lowe declared before the class that I might become a real artist if I wanted to badly enough and worked at it and went away to art school when old enough.

Well, I didn't know that I wanted to be an artist. From what I had read of them they were a bunch of dern sissies, except, of course, Ernest Thompson Seton. While taking it for granted that when I grew older great purple talents would blossom from me like springtime violets in the graveyard, I had not decided whether I wanted to be Ty Cobb, Thomas A. Edison, Napoleon Bonaparte or Admiral Dewey; and there always was a specter lurking in the background in the thought that perhaps God would take heed of my father's suggestions and demand that I become a preacher. Being an artist assuredly was preferable to the life of a preacher and I was grateful to Belle Lowe for the suggestion. Maybe, in a pinch, God could be talked into a compromise.

There was another point to be considered, also. Not a soul except myself ever had remarked any similarity between me and Ty Cobb on the baseball field. As yet I had invented nothing of importance except the caterpillar tractor and a few minor things like that. And if I were to become a great military chief I'd have to develop a more dominating personality. Of course a sword at my side and a lot of gold braid would be of considerable assistance, as would a prancing charger, but attempts to be a Napoleon so far had brought me nothing better than a black eye and cut lip.

Yes, I was grateful to Belle Lowe for the suggestion. I was more than grateful because it was my first recognition of any sort. Maybe Miss Vivian Evans and all the rest were right and Miss Belle Lowe was silly in giving me public praise, but I loved her for giving it. I loved her dearly. Perhaps I should become a great artist just to prove to the world that Miss Lowe's faith in me was not misplaced. At least I wanted to do *something* for her to show my appreciation. But I didn't know how. All I ever did was virtually a betrayal.

That came about through my inordinate love for marbles, and it happened I know while my principal income still came from selling *The Saturday Evening Post,* which averaged twenty cents a week.

Through some obscure tradition the boys of Chillicothe called agate marbles "flints," and a flint was the best possible taw or shooter. At that time I was far from being an expert player, and my only flint was a miserable gray thing with a flaw, two bad nicks and numerous "moons." It was too small for a proper taw.

One spring day at the height of the marble season a new consignment of marbles appeared in the window of Clark's Pharmacy and among them was a small box in which a dozen agates rested like precious jewels on a bed of cotton. Among these was one perfect gem of rich wine color, ringed with cream, just the exact size, I thought, for my hand. Brazenly, I entered the store and asked to see it, and it was more beautiful even than it had seemed from the outside. Utterly flawless, it glowed in my hand, just the proper weight, just the proper size.

"How much is it?" I asked.

"Twenty cents," said the clerk.

Most flints of adequate beauty and utility cost a nickel. Mine, for which I had traded a handful of ordinary marbles, had probably cost three cents. Some exceptional flints cost a dime and Harry Hayden claimed he had paid fifteen cents for his tawny beauty which had won him such a weight in marbles. I never had even heard of a marble selling for twenty cents, but I admitted in my heart that this one was worth it. It was the most gorgeously voluptuous thing I had ever seen in my life.

"Well," I said to the clerk, "I'll have to think it over."

The clerk carefully replaced the magnificent agate marble on its cotton. "Don't think too long," he advised, "or somebody else will get it."

I didn't really need to think it over at all. That was merely a phrase I had picked up from adults and employed because I had only two pennies in my pocket. But I should get my *Saturday Evening Posts* Thursday evening and, if I were lucky, could sell them by Saturday noon. That would give me the necessary twenty cents, but, alas, I should be compelled to give a nickel to Sunday School.

However, with Saturday afternoon free, I could scurry around back alleys with my express wagon, picking up bits of iron and bone and rags and no doubt find enough before Rupp's junkyard closed for the night to get three cents or perhaps even a nickel.

Each day then until Saturday I checked Clark's window and the lovely thing was still there. But Saturday afternoon after the magazines were sold my plans to raise three cents were thwarted by my mother's antipathy to plantain weeds in the lawn. There was a little argument, but not much. I stayed home and cut plantain weeds from the lawn.

Monday morning I ran to Clark's before school, seething with a plan which might work in the remote event that the marble had not been sold. Steeling myself for the disappointment, I glanced at the window and the flint was still there. For a moment I stood grinning at it and that beautiful marble grinned back at me.

Then I went into the store and Mr. Clark himself was up front. I approached him and said, "Howdy, Mr. Clark-you-know-that-twenty-cent-flint-you've-got-in-the-window?"

"That what?"

So I explained and more slowly, and he went to the window and took out the box and lifted the treasure from among its poor relations.

"Mean this one?"

"Yes, sir, Mr. Clark. Well, what I wanted to say, Mr. Clark, I want to buy that flint but I haven't got enough money right now and I'm afraid somebody else will come and buy it and I wanted to say I'd be much obliged if you'd let me pay you seventeen cents right now and you take the flint out of the window so it's not for sale anymore and I'll have the other three cents next Thursday and come in and pay it and take the flint."

He looked down at me solemnly and then at the agate in his hand.

"You kind of like that marble?"

"Yes, sir."

"And you've got just seventeen cents?"

"Yes, sir. But I'll have more Thursday."

Mr. Clark smiled. "Well, son, here's a curious coincidence that's going to interest you. The price of this marble was just reduced this morning from twenty cents to seventeen cents. You give me the seventeen cents and the marble is yours right now without waiting till Thursday."

So I ran to school, but was forced to stop every block or so to take out the marble and gaze at it and fondle it and rub it against my cheek—a smoothness beyond description—and to tell myself this was the most wonderful thing that ever happened to me because it was the most beautiful flint in town and maybe in the world.

I plopped panting into my seat perhaps half a minute late but Miss Lowe did not look up from her desk. Fred Black, however, ostentatiously took out his watch and held it up at me, hoping, I thought, that Miss Lowe would look up as he did it and catch the implication.

I did not like Fred Black. He was everything I was not. He was bright and alert and knew all the answers. When a question was asked Fred Black's hand was always the first to be raised. When another pupil was wrong Fred Black always shook his head violently, groaned audibly and thrust his clean, white hand upward. He was always neat and wore a stiff, white linen collar.

His hair was always combed. He assuredly was the boy most likely to succeed.

"All right," I said to myself, "you've got a watch and ain't that fine. It keeps you from ever being late to school. But I've got something I like better than any derned old watch."

I touched Chester Grace at my side and whispered, "Lookit."

Drawing the flint from my pocket, I held it in shooting position against my thumb knuckle with my forefinger and it glowed there richer than any ruby that ever adorned a potentate's crown.

"Gosh!" Chester whispered and reached for it. But as I glanced up to see that Miss Belle Lowe was still occupied, the wondrous smoothness of my treasure betrayed me. It slipped from my grasp, banging like the crack of doom on the floor and it rolled, horribly, horribly across the worn old boards. Miss Lowe looked up. Everyone looked up. And Fred Black, with his neat hair and linen collar and watch in his pocket, leaned over quickly and then held up his hand.

"Here it is, Miss Lowe," he cried triumphantly.

"Bring it up, please," said Miss Lowe.

So Fred Black walked to the desk and gracefully handed my lovely flint to Miss Lowe and Miss Lowe, without even looking at it to admire its beauty, placed it like any ordinary old marble in the corner of her desk and Fred Black with his fool watch that nobody else would want ticking in his pocket and probably a clean handkerchief in another pocket—yes, and probably perfume on the handkerchief—went back to his seat and shot his cuffs and smoothed his hair and sat down with the air of one who has simply done his duty, but well.

Oh, I knew the rule that any marble dropped on the floor was confiscated. My treasure of treasures was gone before I had ever plumped from a taw-line with it, before I had ever banged it with back-spin against another taw with the shout, "vent-takin's and everetts!"

I sat in my seat and died. But I managed somehow to keep from bursting into tears.

Miss Lowe opened her book and started calling the roll.

"Fred Black."

"Present," said Fred, in a pleased, clear voice.

Then there was a knock on the door and Miss Lowe went to answer it. She stood with the door half-open, her back to the room. Instantly I was out of my seat and on my hands and knees, moving swiftly but softly forward. I knew I could do it because the sympathies of almost everyone would be with me, and I *did* do it. I reached around the side of Miss Lowe's desk, found my flint, grabbed it and crawled quickly back to my own seat long before Belle Lowe left the door.

Because I was living in approximately the Cro-Magnon period of my development, I was inclined to see signs, portents and omens in the most in-nocent things about me. So it was very easy for me to attribute mystic prop-erties to my beautiful new agate marble. I made a chamois bag to carry her in and I named her "Vashti the Magic Taw." When I took Vashti out of her bag, blew on her and rubbed her between my palms, the other kid was half-licked before we ever lagged for taws. She won me a fortune in marbles.

Miss Lowe never mentioned the marble, but of course she knew what happened. Of course she knew who dropped it and recovered it. She couldn't possibly have know what Vashti meant to me and it would have been logical for her to think of me as a despicable little sneak.

Perhaps it was only my imagination, perhaps it was because a guilty con-science did something to my work, but after my deliverance of Vashti a cool, intangible barrier seemed to rise between Miss Belle Lowe and me. From then on she gave my "art work" no more than perfunctory praise when she noticed it at all. Perhaps it was my imagination, but the contempt I sensed in her eyes shriveled my soul and the lonesome little flame of ambition flut-tered and retreated into a weak smoulder.

For many years now Miss Lowe has been at Iowa State College teaching not art but science. She says the only reason she ever taught "art" in Chil-licothe was that "I had had two or three courses in college, whereas the other teacher had none."

Miss Lowe has attained national distinction in the field of foods and nu-trition and is the author of a widely used textbook. She not only has no rec-ollection of the marble incident, but doesn't remember me.

What became of Fred Black, the boy most likely to succeed? The last I heard about him he was a major general in the United States Army. He *would* be.

Well, I have said fine art did not exist in Chillicothe in those days, but that was only objectively true. It did exist—in a latent form. It was exem-plified by a yearning for mystic, unknown things and it found a partial out-let in religion, needlework and maybe political oratory. Despite her denials that she ever was an artist, I believe Miss Lowe did carry the innate sense of proportion and fitness of things and rightness which could be called the spirit of art.

The law of averages being what it is, and people being what they are, so fundamentally alike whether they live and die in Tiflis or Topeka, who can say what mute inglorious Miltons or unsung Cézannes lived out their lives in Chillicothe, Missouri, trying to assuage the misinterpreted pangs of un-realized ambition with calomel and quinine?

After all, there is bound to be talent in any region. We only know of this talent when the proprietors are lucky enough or strong enough to emerge from the wilderness and find opportunity to develop their talents. In 1905 there were, for instance, such small boys as Thomas Hart Benton, Grant

Wood and John Steuart Curry in Missouri, Iowa and Kansas who escaped their native environments to paint their native environments.

It is interesting to compare the careers of these three great American artists, all born where a map of the United States folds in the middle, within eight years of each other. All found it necessary not only to go far from home for necessary training, but felt they had to go to Europe for it.

Benton, the eldest of the three, was born in Neosho, Missouri, in 1889, the son of a lawyer and politician and named for his great-uncle, Thomas Hart "Old Bullion" Benton, Missouri's first United States Senator.

Neosho was only about half the size of Chillicothe, but I gather the school systems were about the same in all of those Missouri towns and that young Thomas proved adept at drawing apples and cats by thumb-circle. At any event he could draw at an early age. But he didn't like going to school in Neosho and quit altogether in 1906 to take a job with some surveyors around the lead mines of Joplin. Shortly afterward he talked the Joplin *American* into giving him a job as cartoonist, using, I suppose, the chalk-plate process which was usually employed in those days by small-city papers. Inasmuch as I never saw a chalk-plate cartoon that wasn't pretty crude, I suspect young Benton's also looked as if they had been carved out of wood with a jackknife.

The father, Colonel Maecenus Benton, still wasn't convinced that his son shouldn't have an education and that fall the boy was sent to the Western Military Academy in Alton, Illinois. But by that time young Benton was certain he wanted to be an artist. In a couple of months he left the military school and went to Chicago to enroll in the Chicago Art Institute where within a year he convinced an instructor that his talent was exceptional and moreover persuaded the instructor to persuade Colonel Benton to send him to Paris to study.

In Paris from 1908 to 1911 Benton "wallowed in every ism that came along." He went to Italy and studied the Italian masters. Then back in New York and without his father's support, he worked as a stevedore and anything else that came his way until the first World War when he entered the Navy, as an architectural draftsman. It was there, apparently, that what he had learned in Paris and Chicago crystallized. There, he says, he was forced to observe for the first time the objective character of things and to "forget my esthetic drivelings."

With the Navy Benton discovered himself and also discovered America. Following the war Benton had a successful exhibition in New York and became an instructor at the Art Students' League. Then he married and moved back to Missouri to achieve a world reputation.

Grant Wood, born in 1892 near Anamosa, Jones County, Iowa, had no father to back him in going where he could gain the art education he desired. The boy was only nine when his father died and, because he and his mother and younger sister were unable to operate the farm, it was foreclosed and they moved to the city of Cedar Rapids. Grant worked his way through high school and helped support mother and sister, partly as a metalworker and partly as night watchman in the morgue.

I don't know whether Iowa schools taught drawing then by the thumb-circle cat and apple method, but at least young Grant Wood was skilled with his hands. He loved to draw and he wanted to paint.

At twenty-three, however, he was still a handyman around Cedar Rapids, trying to save enough money some way to go to art school. For a dollar down and a dollar a month, he bought a lot in a brush-grown thicket on the edge of town and built there a ten-by-sixteen shack. He and his mother and sister lived in this shack for two years while he continued with his odd jobs, trapped rabbits and cooked them on an outdoor fireplace and drew pictures on every scrap of paper he could pick up. He actually learned to draw by drawing—and without instruction.

The first World War interrupted this program when Wood went into the Army. There he picked up extra money (and hoarded it) by drawing portraits of other soldiers.

These pencil portraits attracted attention, enough attention so that after the war the Cedar Rapids schools gave him a job as art teacher, which he kept seven years.

Grant Wood may not have known too much about art at that time. But he could draw, and in the minds of the school board anyone who could draw was a fine artist. Grant Wood knew well that he was no fine artist then, but he also knew this job would give him opportunity to get the training and study he needed to *become* a fine artist.

Each summer for those seven years he went to Europe, studying like Benton in Paris and Italy. He learned technique. But it was in Munich, under the fascination of early German masters, that he discovered himself and discovered Iowa. It was in Munich that he found the rhythm of Iowa and his own individual interpretation.

He went back to Iowa, became artist in residence at the University of Iowa, a fine artist and without doubt a great artist.

John Steuart Curry was born in 1897 on a farm near the hamlet of Dunavant in the hills of Jefferson County in eastern Kansas.

Curiously enough, Margaret Steuart Curry, a Kansas farm wife, mother of four children besides John Steuart, working from dawn until late at night, still had the time and inclination to make a collection of reproductions of the old masters. And when John, the eldest child, showed the common love of children for drawing, she encouraged him to make copies of reproductions. From that he graduated to sketching farm animals.

Young Curry attended high school briefly in nearby Winchester, a village of less than five hundred, but there was nothing in the curriculum to interest him. He quit and got a job as section hand on the Kansas City, North-western Railroad, saved his money and went to Kansas City to attend classes of the Kansas City Art Institute.

At this time I also was attending night classes of the Kansas City Art In-stitute, and it quite definitely was fast enough company for one of my mea-ger talents. Destiny, an acute sense of discrimination or something prodded young Curry out of Kansas City quickly, however. He went to Chicago where he financed a couple of years at the Art Institute by working as a restaurant busboy and janitor. Following that, he discovered he could make a living illustrating western story magazines, but that still didn't give him what he wanted.

Borrowing a thousand dollars, he, like Benton and Wood, went to Paris. And in Paris he discovered Kansas—and John Steuart Curry.

His "Baptism in Kansas," which he painted from memory, was pur-chased by Gertrude Vanderbilt Whitney, who also subsidized him for two years at fifty dollars a week. That was all he needed to gain international fame.

These three—and particularly Wood and Curry—might be called the bootstrap boys. They lifted themselves by the bootstraps. They succeeded in the face of impossible obstacles.

Well, no reasonable claim can be made that Missouri, Iowa and Kansas are ideal spots today for the talented youngster. But I am positive that it no longer is necessary for a boy or girl to go to Europe to find himself or herself in art.

Even the Kansas City Art Institute has grown tremendously and, al-though Thomas Hart Benton quit as director after saying some harsh words, Mr. Benton is not known for his tolerance of things which fail to measure up to his conception of perfection.

Chillicothe is still no art center. As yet there isn't even much amateur painting going on in the region. But there is one marked improvement, and that is in the quality of pictures hanging on the walls of middle-class homes.

There has been practically a revolution in the buying of fine art in the last thirty-five years.

Up until the first World War the big New York galleries counted on only a few sales a year, but those sales would be to wealthy collectors at fabulous prices. There was little market for anything short of an old master.

Now the income tax has made it necessary for the wealth collectors to dip into principal if they want to pay a fortune for a famous painting, and not many are willing to dip into principal.

The typical purchaser of art today on New York's Fifty-Seventh Street is from the Midwest or Southwest and is a college graduate in his early thir-ties. He has had a course in art appreciation and knows more than the af-fluent merchant prince collectors did in 1900. He isn't buying names. He is buying art and buying it on his own surprisingly good judgment. His top price is about three hundred dollars.

This is a wonderful development from the viewpoint of the comparatively unknown contemporary artist. It's all right, also, from the viewpoint of the galleries whose volume of sales has multiplied to the extent that a number of them have opened branch galleries in midwestern cities.

I don't want to give the impression that any large proportion of midwesterners are buying good original oils and water colors because that would not be true at all. But there is a definite trend in that direction and many more are buying and hanging gelatine process reproductions of good art, modern as well as the old masters.

What is the cause of this growth in good taste? I think there are several answers.

For one thing, mechanical developments which not only have made those gelatine prints possible but have advanced photo-engraving and color printing to a point where popular magazines and book publishers can put marvelous reproductions of real art into general circulation together with dissertations by competent critics, explaining just *why* these pictures are real art. After all, a corn-fed Missourian can tell an emerald from a piece of beer bottle glass once he has the opportunity to hold them together. And, given his choice, he'll almost invariably select the emerald.

Just as important is the fact that educators in these days are better educated. They have been exposed to culture, more or less, in college. Many midwestern colleges and universities are finding places on their faculties for competent "artists in residence." And a good many educators realize what I think Miss Belle Lowe sensed, that drawing is not art although it may be *part* of art.

Teaching art in the Chillicothe High School now is Mrs. Honor Israel, a gentle and soft-spoken woman, who concentrates on teaching appreciation of art rather than on drawing. Her equipment is largely a number of books of art prints together with portfolios of color reproductions of art from Giotto through the Impressionists to the non-objective moderns, which she has clipped from various magazines over the years. She uses as a text *Art Appreciation for Junior and Senior High Schools* by Collins and Riley, and she lectures on the history and development and meaning of art over the centuries.

Mrs. Israel's students also draw and paint, of course, and while I saw little evidence of great budding talent, the work at least was quite uninhibited. The principle of the thumb-circle cat has been thrown overboard completely, even in the elementary grades.

The point is that these boys and girls are learning *appreciation* of art, and that is true advancement of culture by any definition you can dig up. The point is that Susie comes home from school and talks. And Susie says,

"Mother, *when* are you going to get rid of that *dreadful* old picture over the mantel? It just makes me cringe every time I go into the living room." And Mother says, "Why, darling, I always kind of liked that picture of the sunset on the millpond." And Susie says, "Oh, *Mother*—it's pure corn. The composition is terrible for one thing, and mostly it's crude and, well, really, Mother it's in poor *taste* and I feel just humiliated when the Spencers come in because I know they're looking at that *thing* and smiling to themselves and pitying us because we don't know any better. Mother, the Spencers have got two Van Goghs and a Cézanne." And Mother says, "Well, darling, you know we couldn't afford to buy any real fine oil paintings." And Susie says, "But they're *not* originals, Mother. The originals would cost thousands and thousands of dollars, but there are beautiful reproductions that look just like originals." And, of course, the net result is that finally some new pictures are bought. Probably they're not Van Goghs, but perhaps a reproduction of something by Edward Hopper or Charles Burchfield and good still life by some capable but not very renowned artist. And after the family has lived with the new pictures for a while they begin to see what Susie was talking about and appreciation of art has budded in the home.

After all, in my humble opinion, the principal thing Benton and Wood and Curry learned in Europe was not painting technique (although they probably learned some of that too) but a deep understanding of what art is about. That, in their day and in mine, they could not do at home or in Kansas City or Cedar Rapids or very much in Chicago or even New York.

As far as the creation of art is concerned, the WPA art projects during the early days of Franklin Roosevelt's presidency really started things. Those projects put paint brushes into the hands of thousands of young men and women who produced acre upon acre of very bad canvases, but an astonishing number of very good pictures, and to almost all of the participants came an inevitable joy of creation and an awakening to the beauties which lie so unexpectedly in line and light and shadow wherever you may be— under the old L in the Bowery or in the Great Salt Desert, above the clouds in an airplane or in a Livingston County barnyard.

I have heard that Franklin Roosevelt didn't know a hawk from a handsaw as far as art is concerned and that in approving these "boondoggling" projects he remarked merely that he supposed an artist had to eat the same as anyone else. Yet I suspect those boondoggling art projects in the long run could prove to be of as great importance in the cultural development of America as any other governmental act in the first half of the Twentieth Century.

Storm

FROM *Not Without Laughter*

LANGSTON HUGHES

WHILE NEWSPAPER COVERAGE favored the prosperous, Anglo, merchant element in small-town society, literary writers from Mark Twain onward tend to portray that class as repressed and repressing, bored and boring, middlebrow and prejudiced—if not neurotic, ignorant, and bigoted. Life on the other side of the tracks—whether represented by an ethnic minority, immigrant farmers, or blue-collar laborers—is often shown to be more enlightened, more humane, and generally more alive. Writers who came from the privileged classes may accurately be charged with romanticizing the dispossessed and with patronizing the humble poor. Writers born to poverty and hardship are usually less nostalgic about the old days, and can back up their words with experience.

Langston Hughes, one of America's most prominent African American writers, was born in Joplin, Missouri, and grew up in Lawrence, Kansas. He escaped the poverty of his youth through the magic of books. At age thirteen, he moved to Lincoln, Illinois, and a year later to Cleveland, Ohio. After graduation from high school, where he played sports and edited the yearbook, he attended Columbia University, spent time in Europe, and returned to the States to write. Hughes was writing poetry and working as a busboy in a Washington, D. C., restaurant when he met Vachel Lindsay, whose patronage and encouragement helped him establish a national reputation. As Lindsay was one of the leading lights of the so-called Chicago Renaissance, Hughes was the central figure in the Harlem Renaissance, influenced by both urban jazz and folk blues.

Hughes lived most of his adult life in New York and is most famous for his blues-based poetry and his "Jessie B. Simple" stories, but one of his most financially successful projects was an autobiographical coming-of-age novel set in Kansas and Chicago, *Not Without Laughter*. The book was well received by white and black reviewers and made the author financially independent. It provides a valuable record of black dialect in Kansas circa 1910 and—perhaps more important—a record of small-town race relations of that era. As his title suggests, Hughes is not bitter about race relations in America. He asserts that the town, from a black perspective, contains both good and bad white folks and that "All the neighborhood, white or colored,

called his grandmother when something happened." Still, the main character, Sandy, is conscious of both his color and his class. Aware of his exclu-
sion, he decides that even though his mother may be dead, "he wasn't going to cry and make a racket there by himself on the strange steps of these
white folks' house." The following excerpt, "Storm," tells us more about
small-town racial relations than about Kansas tornadoes.

o o o

Aunt Hager Williams stood in her doorway and looked out at the sun. The
western sky was sulphurous yellow and the sun a red ball dropping slowly
behind the trees and house-tops. Its setting left the rest of the heavens grey
with clouds.

"Huh! A storm's comin'," said Aunt Hager aloud.

A pullet ran across the back yard and into a square-cut hole in an unpainted piano-box which served as the roosting-house. An old hen clucked
her brood together and, with the tiny chicks, went into a small box beside
the large one. The air was very still. Not a leaf stirred on the green apple-
tree. Not a single closed flower of the morning-glories trembled on the back
fence. The air was very still and yellow. Something sultry and oppressive
made a small boy in the doorway stand closer to his grandmother, clutching her apron with his brown hands.

"Sho is a storm comin'," said Aunt Hager.

"I hope mama gets home 'fore it rains," remarked the brown child holding to the old woman's apron. "Hope she gets home."

"I does, too," said Aunt Hager. "But I's skeared she won't.

Just then great drops of water began to fall heavily into the back yard,
pounding up little clouds of dust where each drop struck the earth. For a few
moments they pattered violently on the roof like a series of hammer-
strokes; then suddenly they ceased.

"Come in, chile," said Aunt Hager.

She closed the door as the green apple-tree began to sway in the wind and
a small hard apple fell, rolling rapidly down the top of the piano-box that
sheltered the chickens. Inside the kitchen it was almost dark. While Aunt
Hager lighted an oil-lamp, the child climbed to a chair and peered through
the square window into the yard. The leaves and flowers of the morning-
glory vines on the back fence were bending with the rising wind. And across
the alley at the big house, Mrs. Kennedy's rear screen-door banged to and
fro, and Sandy saw her garbage-pail suddenly tip over and roll down into the
yard, scattering potato-peelings on the white steps.

"Sho gwine be a terrible storm" said Hager as she turned up the wick of
the light and put the chimney on. Then, glancing through the window, she

saw a black cloud twisting like a ribbon in the western sky, and the old woman screamed aloud in sudden terror: "It's a cyclone! It's gwine be a cyclone! Sandy, let's get over to Mis' Carter's quick, 'cause we ain't got no cellar here. Come on, chile, let's get! Come on, chile! . . . Come on, chile!"

Hurriedly she blew out the light, grabbed the boy's hand; and together they rushed through the little house towards the front. It was quite dark in the inner rooms, but through the parlor windows came a sort of sooty-grey-green light that was rapidly turning to blackness.

"Lawd help us, Jesus!"

Aunt Hager opened the front door, but before she or the child could move, a great roaring sound suddenly shook the world, and, with a deafening division of wood from wood, they saw their front porch rise into the air and go hurtling off into space. Sailing high in the gathering darkness, the porch was soon lost to sight. And the black wind blew with terrific force, numbing the ear-drums.

For a moment the little house trembled and swayed and creaked as though it were about to fall.

"Help me to shut this do'," Aunt Hager screamed; "help me to shut it, Lawd!" as with all her might she struggled against the open door, which the wind held back, but finally it closed and the lock caught. Then she sank to the floor with her back against the wall, while her small grandson trembled like a leaf as she took him in her lap, mumbling: "What a storm! . . . O, Lawdy! . . . O, ma chile, what a storm!"

They could hear the crackling of timbers and the rolling limbs of trees that the wind swept across the roof. Her arms tightened about the boy.

"Dear Jesus!" she said. "I wonder where is yo' mama? S'pose she started out fo' home 'fore this storm come up!" Then in a scream: "Have mercy on ma Annjee! O, Lawd, have mercy on this chile's mamma! Have mercy on all ma chillens! Ma Harriett, an' ma Tempy, an' ma Annjee, what's maybe all of 'em out in de storm! O, Lawd!"

A dry crack of lightning split the darkness, and the boy began to wail. Then the rain broke. The old woman could not see the crying child she held, nor could the boy hear the broken voice of his grandmother, who had begun to pray as the rain crashed through the inky blackness. For a long while it roared on the roof of the house and pounded at the windows, until finally the two within became silent, hushing their cries. Then only the lashing noise of the water, coupled with the feeling that something terrible was happening, or had already happened, filled the evening air.

After the rain the moon rose clear and bright and the clouds disappeared from the lately troubled sky. The stars sparkled calmly above the havoc of the storm, and it was still early evening as people emerged from their houses and began to investigate the damage brought by the twisting cyclone that had come with the sunset. Through the rubbish-filled streets men drove slowly with horse and buggy or automobile. The fire-engine was out, banging away, and the soft tang-tang-tang of the motor ambulance could be heard in the distance carrying off the injured.

Black Aunt Hager and her brown grandson put their rubbers on and stood in the water-soaked front yard looking at the porchless house where they lived. Platform, steps, pillars, roof, and all had been blown away. Not a semblance of a porch was left and the front door opened bare into the yard. It was grotesque and funny. Hager laughed.

"Cyclone sho did a good job," she said. "Looks like I ain't never had no porch."

Madam de Carter, from next door, came across the grass, her large mouth full of chattering sympathy for her neighbor.

"But praise God for sparing our lives! It might've been worse, Sister Williams! It might've been much more calamitouser! As it is, I lost nothin' more'n a chimney and two wash-tubs which was settin' in the back yard. A few trees broke down don't 'mount to nothin'. We's livin', ain't we? And we's more importanter than trees is any day!" Her gold teeth sparkled in the moonlight.

"'Deed so," agreed Hager emphatically. "Let's move on down de block, Sister, an' see what mo' de Lawd has 'stroyed or spared this evenin'. He's gin us plenty moonlight after de storm so we po' humans can see this lesson o' His'n to a sinful world."

The two elderly colored women picked their way about on the wet walk, littered with twigs and branches of broken foliage. The little brown boy followed, with his eyes wide at the sight of baby-carriages, window-sashes, shingles, and tree-limbs scattered about in the roadway. Large numbers of people were out, some standing on porches, some carrying lanterns, picking up useful articles from the streets, some wringing their hands in a daze.

Near the corner a small crowd had gathered quietly.

"Mis' Gavitt's killed," somebody said.

"Lawd help!" burst from Aunt Hager and Madam de Carter simultaneously.

"Mister and Mis' Gavitt's both dead," added a nervous young white man, bursting with the news. "We live next door to 'em, and their house turned clean over! Came near hitting us and breaking our side-wall in."

"Have mercy!" said the two women, but Sandy slipped away from his grandmother and pushed through the crowd. He ran round the corner to where he could see the overturned house of the unfortunate Gavitts.

Good white folks, the Gavitts, Aunt Hager had often said, and now their large frame dwelling lay on its side like a doll's mansion, with broken furniture strewn carelessly on the wet lawn—and they were dead. Sandy saw a piano flat on its back in the grass. Its ivory keys gleamed in the moonlight like grinning teeth, and the strange sight made his little body shiver, so he hurried back through the crowd looking for his grandmother. As he passed the corner, he heard a woman sobbing hysterically within the wide house there.

His grandmother was no longer standing where he had left her, but he found Madam de Carter and took hold of her hand. She was in the midst of a group of excited white and colored women. One frail old lady was saying in a high determined voice that she had never seen a cyclone like this in her whole life, and she had lived here in Kansas, if you please, going on seventy-three years. Madam de Carter, chattering nervously, began to tell them how she had recognized its coming and had rushed to the cellar the minute she saw the sky turn green. She had not come up until the rain stopped, so frightened had she been. She was extravagantly enjoying the telling of her fears as Sandy kept tugging at her hand.

"Where's my grandma?" he demanded. Madam de Carter, however, did not cease talking to answer his question.

"What do you want, sonny?" finally one of the white women asked, bending down when he looked as if he were about to cry. "Aunt Hager? . . . Why, she's inside helping them calm poor Mrs. Gavitt's niece. Your grand-mother's good to have around when folks are sick or grieving, you know. Run and set on the steps like a nice boy and wait until she comes out." So Sandy left the women and went to sit in the dark on the steps of the big corner house where the niece of the dead Mrs. Gavitt lived. There were some people on the porch, but they soon passed through the screen-door into the house or went away down the street. The moonlight cast weird shadows across the damp steps where Sandy sat, and it was dark there under the trees in spite of the moon, for the old house was built far back from the street in a yard full of oaks and maples, and Sandy could see the light from an upstairs window reflecting on the wet leaves of their nearest boughs. He heard a girl screaming, too, up there where the light was burning, and he knew that Aunt Hager was putting cold cloths on her head, or rubbing her hands, or driving folks out of the room, and talking kind to her so that she would soon be better.

All the neighborhood, white or colored, called his grandmother when something happened. She was a good nurse, they said, and sick folks liked her around. Aunt Hager always came when they called, too, bringing maybe a little soup that she had made or a jelly. Sometimes they paid her and sometimes they didn't. But Sandy had never had to sit outdoors in the darkness waiting for her before. He leaned his small back against the top step and rested his elbows on the porch behind him. It was growing late and the people in the streets had all disappeared.

There, in the dark, the little fellow began to think about his mother, who worked on the other side of town for a rich white lady named Mrs. J. J. Rice.

And suddenly frightful thoughts came into his mind. Suppose she had left for home just as the storm came up! Almost always his mother was home before dark—but she wasn't there tonight when the storm came—and she should have been home. This thought appalled him. She should have been there! But maybe she had been caught by the storm and blown away as she walked down Main Street! Maybe Annjee had been carried off by the great black wind that had overturned the Gavitt's house and taken his grandma's porch flying through the air! Maybe the cyclone had gotten his mother, Sandy thought. He wanted her! Where was she? Had something terrible happened to her? Where was she now?

The big tears began to roll down his cheeks—but the little fellow held back the sobs that wanted to come. He decided he wasn't going to cry and make a racket there by himself on the strange steps of these white folks' house. He wasn't going to cry like a big baby in the dark. So he wiped his eyes, kicked his heels against the cement walk, lay down on the top step, and, by and by, sniffled himself to sleep.

"Wake up, Son!" Someone was shaking him. "You'll catch your death o' cold sleeping on the wet steps like this. We're going home now. Don't want me to have to carry a big man like you, do you, boy? . . . Wake up, Sandy!" His mother stooped to lift his long little body from the wide steps. She held him against her soft heavy breasts and let his head rest on one of her shoulders while his feet, in their muddy rubbers, hung down against her dress.

"Where you been, mama?" the boy asked drowsily, tightening his arms about her neck. "I been waiting for you."

"Oh, I been home a long time, worried to death about you and ma till I heard from Madam Carter that you-all was down here nursing the sick. I stopped at your Aunt Tempy's house when I seen the storm coming."

"I was afraid you got blowed away, mama," murmured Sandy sleepily. "Let's go home, mama. I'm glad you ain't got blowed away."

On the porch Aunt Hager was talking to a pale white man and two thin white women standing at the door of the lighted hallway. "Just let Mis' Agnes sleep," she was saying. "She'll be all right now, an' I'll come back in de mawnin' to see 'bout her. . . . Good-night, you-all."

The old colored woman joined her daughter and they started home, walking through the streets filled with debris and puddles of muddy water reflecting the moon.

"You're certainly heavy, boy," remarked Sandy's mother to the child she held, but he didn't answer.

"I'm right glad you come for me, Annjee," Hager said. "I wonder is yo' sister all right out yonder at de country club. . . . An' I was so worried 'bout you I didn't know what to do—skeared you might a got caught in this twister, 'cause it were cert'ly awful!"

"I was at Tempy's!" Annjee replied. "And I was nearly crazy, but I just left everything in the hands o' God. That's all." In silence they walked on, a piece; then hesitantly, to her mother: "There wasn't any mail for me today, was there, ma?"

"Not a speck!" the old woman replied shortly. "Mail-man passed on by."

For a few minutes there was silence again as they walked. Then, "It's goin' on three weeks he's been gone, and he ain't written a line," the younger woman complained, shifting the child to her right arm. "Seems like Jimboy would let a body know where he is, ma, wouldn't it?"

"Huh! That ain't nothin'! He's been gone before this an' he ain't wrote, ain't he? Here you is worryin' 'bout a letter from that good-for-nothing husband o' your'n—an' there's ma house settin' up without a porch to its name! . . . Ain't you seed what de devil's done done on earth this evenin', chile? . . . An' yet de first thing you ask me 'bout is de mail-man! . . . Lawd! Lawd! . . . You an' that Jimboy!"

Aunt Hager lifted her heavy body over fallen tree-trunks and across puddles, but between puffs she managed to voice her indignation, so Annjee said no more concerning letters from her husband. Instead they went back to the subject of the cyclone. "I'm just thankful, ma, it didn't blow the whole house down and you with it, that's all! I was certainly worried! . . . And then you-all was gone when I got home! Gone on out—nursing that white woman. . . . It's too bad 'bout poor Mis' Gavitt, though, and old man Gavitt, ain't it?"

"Yes, indeedy!" said Aunt Hager. "It's sho too bad. They was certainly good old white folks! An' her married niece is takin' it mighty hard, po' little soul. I was nigh two hours, her husband an' me, tryin' to bring her out o' de hysterics. Tremblin' like a lamb all over, she was." They were turning into the yard. "Be careful with that chile, Annjee, you don't trip on none o' them boards nor branches an' fall with him."

"Put me down, 'cause I'm awake," said Sandy.

The old house looked queer without a porch. In the moonlight he could see the long nails that had held the porch roof to the weather-boarding. His grandmother climbed slowly over the door-sill, and his mother lifted him to the floor level as Aunt Hager lit the large oil-lamp on the parlor table. Then they went back to the bedroom, where the youngster took off his clothes, said his prayers, and climbed into the high feather bed where he slept with Annjee. Aunt Hager went to the next room, but for a long time she talked back and forth through the doorway to her daughter about the storm.

"We was just startin' out fo' Mis' Carter's cellar, me an' Sandy," she said several times. "But de Lawd was with us! He held us back! Praise His name! We ain't harmed, none of us—'ceptin' I don't know 'bout ma Harriett at de club. But you's all right. An' you say Tempy's all right, too. An' I prays that

Harriett ain't been touched out there in de country where she's workin'. Maybe de storm ain't passed that way."

Then they spoke about the white people where Annjee worked . . . and about the elder sister Tempy's prosperity. Then Sandy heard his grandmother climb into bed, and a few minutes after the springs screaked under her, she had begun to snore. Annjee closed the door between their rooms and slowly began to unlace her wet shoes.

"Sandy," she whispered, "we ain't had no word yet from your father since he left. I know he goes away and stays away like this and don't write, but I'm sure worried. Hope the cyclone ain't passed nowhere near wherever he is, and I hope ain't nothin' hurt him. . . . I'm gonna pray for him, Sandy. I'm gonna ask God right now to take care o' Jimboy. . . . The Lawd knows, I want him to come back! . . . I loves him. . . . We both loves him, don't we, child? And we want him to come on back!"

She knelt down beside the bed in her night-dress and kept her head bowed for a long time. Before she got up, Sandy had gone to sleep.

Main Street

Excerpt

E DGAR LEE MASTERS'S *Spoon River Anthology*, Sherwood Anderson's *Winesburg, Ohio*, and Sinclair Lewis's *Main Street* are the major landmarks in a literary movement identified by Anthony Hilfer as "the revolt from the village." They present a realistic critique of literary depictions of the American village as a warm, nurturing place—Zona Gale called it "Friendship Village" in a book by the same name—the egalitarian engine room of American individualism, independence, and democracy.

These three books, especially *Main Street*, depict Midwest villagers as class-conscious, complacent, petty, dull, parsimonious, sexually repressed, middle-class middlebrows incapable of real culture or even of significant cultural aspirations. Lewis speaks of "the village virus." These books forced Americans, in Clara Lee Moodie's words, to "stop and take a hard look at themselves." The fact that *Main Street* and *Spoon River Anthology* were both instant best sellers suggests that millions of Americans were already in revolt against the village and prepared for such a reassessment. Lewis warned his readers in a preface that the town of Gopher Prairie, Minnesota, is but a continuation of Main Streets all across America, from upper New York State to Montana to the Carolina hills, and his story, though set in rural Minnesota, was a story of the American small town.

Where Anderson had a gift for psychological analysis, Lewis's genius was more suited to social critique, and the characters of *Main Street* are mostly the types one finds in satire or comedy of manners: Mrs. Bogart, prominent Baptist and town gossip; her son Cyrus, town bully; Vida Sherwin, schoolteacher; Percy Bresnahan, small-town boy who made it big Out East; Miles Bjornstam, town radical, the "Red Swede"; Ezra Stowbody, bank president; Guy Pollock, failed liberal; Bea Sorenson, Swedish maid; and of course Will Kennicott, town doctor, good fellow, booster, patient husband, father figure, the true embodiment of pedestrian small-town values. The town's name is itself a cruel joke: "Gopher Prairie," a kind of underground city. Other small jabs are the lake to which wealthier townsfolk retire in the summer (Lac-qui-Meurt, or "the Lake that Dies," from Lac qui Parle, "the Lake that Talks," located in western Minnesota) and the literary club (the Thanatopsis Society, from a poem on death by William Cullen Bryant).

For all his criticism of the small town, Lewis is merely reporting a culture in which husbands have five enthusiasms (doctoring, hunting, motor cars, wife, and land investment) and wives understand neither themselves nor their communities. One of the author's major problems in this book is that he can't decide whether his heroine, Carol Kennicott, is a vehicle or a subject of satire (Lewis did recognize that Carol Kennicott was a thinly disguised "Red" Lewis), so idealist reformers are quite as much satirized as curmudgeonly small-town middlebrows.

In chapter four, Carol meets for the first time the neighbors who will circumscribe her life in Gopher Prairie. Brought together at a party thrown in her honor, they seat themselves around the room in a vast, prim circle "as though they were attending a funeral." After presenting their best public selves in answer to Carol's witty, urbane sophistication, they fall into groups segregated by gender and reveal their true natures: parochial, petty, self-absorbed. And moral in the narrowest sense of the word: "Don't get onto legs and all that immoral stuff," Carol's husband advises when the party is over. "Pretty conservative crowd."

o o o

Chapter Four

The recently built house of Sam Clark, in which was given the party to welcome Carol, was one of the largest in Gopher Prairie. It had a clean sweep of clapboards, a solid squareness, a small tower, and a large screened porch. Inside, it was as shiny, as hard, and as cheerful as a new oak upright piano.

Carol looked imploringly at Sam Clark as he rolled to the door and shouted, "Welcome, little lady! The keys of the city are yourn!"

Beyond him, in the hallway and the living-room, sitting in a vast prim circle as though they were attending a funeral, she saw the guests. They were *waiting* so! They were waiting for her! The determination to be all one pretty flowerlet of appreciation leaked away. She begged of Sam, "I don't dare face them! They expect so much. They'll swallow me in one mouthful—glump!—like that!"

"Why, sister, they're going to love you—same as I would if I didn't think the doc here would beat me up!"

"B-but—— I don't dare! Faces to the right of me, faces in front of me, volley and wonder!"

She sounded hysterical to herself; she fancied that to Sam Clark she sounded insane. But he chuckled, "Now you just cuddle under Sam's wing, and if anybody rubbers at you too long, I'll shoo 'em off. Here we go! Watch my smoke—Sam'l, the ladies' delight and the bridegrooms' terror!"

His arm about her, he led her in and bawled, "Ladies and worser halves, the bride! We won't introduce her round yet, because she'll never get your bum names straight anyway. Now bust up this star-chamber!"

They tittered politely, but they did not move from the social security of their circle, and they did not cease staring.

Carol had given creative energy to dressing for the event. Her hair was demure, low on her forehead with a parting and a coiled braid. Now she wished that she had piled it high. Her frock was an ingénue slip of lawn, with a wide gold sash and a low square neck, which gave a suggestion of throat and molded shoulders. But as they looked her over she was certain that it was all wrong. She wished alternately that she had worn a spinsterish high-necked dress, and that she had dared to shock them with a violent brick-red scarf which she had bought in Chicago.

She was led about the circle. Her voice mechanically produced safe remarks:

"Oh, I'm sure I'm going to like it here ever so much," and "Yes, we did have the best time in Colorado—mountains," and "Yes, I lived in St. Paul several years. Euclid P. Tinker? No, I don't *remember* meeting him, but I'm pretty sure I've heard of him."

Kennicott took her aside and whispered, "Now I'll introduce you to them, one at a time."

"Tell me about them first."

"Well, the nice-looking couple over there are Harry Haydock and his wife, Juanita. Harry's dad owns most of the Bon Ton, but it's Harry who runs it and gives it the pep. He's a hustler. Next to him is Dave Dyer the druggist—you met him this afternoon—mighty good duck-shot. The tall husk beyond him is Jack Elder—Jackson Elder—owns the planing-mill, and the Minniemashie House, and quite a share in the Farmers' National Bank. Him and his wife are good sports—him and Sam and I go hunting together a lot. The old cheese there is Luke Dawson, the richest man in town. Next to him is Nat Hicks, the tailor."

"Really? A tailor?"

"Sure. Why not? Maybe we're slow, but we are democratic. I go hunting with Nat same as I do with Jack Elder."

"I'm glad. I've never met a tailor socially. It must be charming to meet one and not have to think about what you owe him. And do you——Would you go hunting with your barber, too?"

"No but—— No use running this democracy thing into the ground. Besides, I've known Nat for years, and besides, he's a might good shot and —— That's the way it is, see? Next to Nat is Chet Dashaway. Great fellow for chinning. He'll talk your arm off, about religion or politics or books or anything."

Carol gazed with a polite approximation to interest at Mr. Dashaway, a tan person with a wide mouth. "Oh, I know! He's the furniture-store man!" She was much pleased with herself.

"Yump, and he's the undertaker. You'll like him. Come shake hands with him."

"Oh no, no! He doesn't—he doesn't do the embalming and all that—himself? I couldn't shake hands with an undertaker!"

"Why not? You'd be proud to shake hands with a great surgeon, just after he'd been carving up people's bellies."

She sought to regain her afternoon's calm of maturity. "Yes. You're right. I want—oh, my dear, do you know how much I want to like the people you like? I want to see people as they are."

"Well, don't forget to see people as other folks see them as they are! They have the stuff. Did you know that Percy Bresnahan came from here? Born and brought up here!"

"Bresnahan?"

"Yes—you know—president of the Velvet Motor Company of Boston, Mass.—make the Velvet Twelve—biggest automobile factory in New England."

"I think I've heard of him."

"Sure you have. Why, he's a millionaire several times over! Well, Perce comes back here for the black-bass fishing almost every summer, and he says if he could get away from business, he'd rather live here than in Boston or New York or any of those places. *He* doesn't mind Chet's undertaking."

"Please! I'll—I'll like everybody! I'll be the community sunbeam!"

He led her to the Dawsons.

Luke Dawson, lender of money on mortgages, owner of Northern cut-over land, was a hesitant man in unpressed soft gray clothes, with bulging eyes in a milky face. His wife had bleached cheeks, bleached hair, bleached voice, and a bleached manner. She wore her expensive green frock, with its passementeried bosom, bead tassels, and gaps between the buttons down the back, as though she had bought it second-hand and was afraid of meeting the former owner. They were shy. It was "Professor" George Edwin Mott, superintendent of schools, a Chinese mandarin turned brown, who held Carol's hand and made her welcome.

When the Dawsons and Mr. Mott had stated that they were "pleased to meet her," there seemed to be nothing else to say, but the conversation went on automatically.

"Do you like Gopher Prairie?" whimpered Mrs. Dawson.

"Oh, I'm sure I'm going to be ever so happy."

"There's so many nice people." Mrs. Dawson looked to Mr. Mott for social and intellectual aid. He lectured:

"There's a fine class of people. I don't like some of these retired farmers who come here to spend their last days—especially the Germans. They hate to pay school-taxes. They hate to spend a cent. But the rest are a fine class of people. Did you know that Percy Bresnahan came from here? Used to go to school right at the old building!"

"I heard he did."

"Yes. He's a prince. He and I went fishing together, last time he was here."

The Dawsons and Mr. Mott teetered upon weary feet, and smiled at Carol with crystallized expressions. She went on:

"Tell me, Mr. Mott: Have you ever tried any experiments with any of the new educational systems? The modern kindergarten methods or the Gary system?"

"Oh. Those. Most of these would-be reformers are simply notoriety-seekers. I believe in manual training, but Latin and mathematics always will be the backbone of sound Americanism, no matter what these faddists advocate—heaven knows what they do want—knitting, I suppose, and classes in wiggling the ears!"

The Dawsons smiled their appreciation of listening to a savant. Carol waited till Kennicott should rescue her. The rest of the party waited for the miracle of being amused.

Harry and Juanita Haydock, Rita Simons and Dr. Terry Gould—the young smart set of Gopher Prairie. She was led to them. Juanita Haydock flung at her in a high, cackling, friendly voice:

"Well, this is so nice to have you here. We'll have some good parties—dances and everything. You'll have to join the Jolly Seventeen. We play bridge and we have a supper once a month. You play, of course?"

"N-no, I don't."

"Really? In St. Paul?"

"I've always been such a book-worm."

"We'll have to teach you. Bridge is half the fun of life." Juanita had become patronizing, and she glanced disrespectfully at Carol's golden sash, which she had previously admired.

Harry Haydock said politely, "How do you think you're going to like the old burg?"

"I'm sure I shall like it tremendously."

"Best people on earth here. Great hustlers, too. Course I've had lots of chances to go live in Minneapolis, but we like it here. Real he-town. Did you know that Percy Bresnahan came from here?"

Carol perceived that she had been weakened in the biological struggle by disclosing her lack of bridge. Roused to nervous desire to regain her position she turned on Dr. Terry Gould, the young and pool-playing competitor of her husband. Her eyes coquetted with him while she gushed:

"I'll learn bridge. But what I really love most is the outdoors. Can't we all get up a boating party, and fish, or whatever you do, and have a picnic supper afterwards?"

"Now you're talking!" Dr. Gould affirmed. He looked rather too obviously at the cream-smooth slope of her shoulder. "Like fishing? Fishing is my middle name. I'll teach you bridge. Like cards at all?"

"I used to be rather good at bezique."

She knew that bezique was a game of cards—or a game of something else. Roulette, possibly. But her lie was a triumph. Juanita's handsome, high-colored, horsey face showed doubt. Harry stroked his nose and said humbly, "Bezique? Used to be great gambling game, wasn't it?"

While others drifted to her group, Carol snatched up the conversation. She laughed and was frivolous and rather brittle. She could not distinguish their eyes. They were a blurry theater-audience before which she self-consciously enacted the comedy of being the Clever Little Bride of Doc Kennicott:

"These-here celebrated Open Spaces, that's what I'm going out for. I'll never read anything but the sporting-page again. Will converted me on our Colorado trip. There were so many mousey tourists who were afraid to get out of the motor 'bus that I decided to be Annie Oakley, the Wild Western Wampire, and I bought oh! a vociferous skirt which revealed my perfectly nice ankles to the Presbyterian glare of all the Ioway schoolma'ams, and I leaped from peak to peak like the nimble chamoys, and—— You may think that Herr Doctor Kennicott is a Nimrod, but you ought to have seen me daring him to strip to his B. V. D.'s and go swimming in an icy mountain brook."

She knew that they were thinking of becoming shocked, but Juanita Haydock was admiring, at least. She swaggered on:

"I'm sure I'm going to ruin Will as a respectable practitioner—— Is he a good doctor, Dr. Gould?"

Kennicott's rival gasped at this insult to professional ethics, and he took an appreciable second before he recovered his social manner. "I'll tell you, Mrs. Kennicott." He smiled at Kennicott, to imply that whatever he might say in the stress of being witty was not to count against him in the commercio-medical warfare. "There's some people in town that say the doc is a fair to middlin' diagnostician and prescription-writer, but let me whisper this to you—but for heaven's sake don't tell him I said so—don't you ever go to him for anything more serious than a pendectomy of the left ear or a strabismus of the cardiograph."

No one save Kennicott knew exactly what this meant, but they laughed, and Sam Clark's party assumed a glittering lemon-yellow color of brocade panels and champagne and tulle and crystal chandeliers and sporting duchesses. Carol saw that George Edwin Mott and the blanched Mr. and Mrs. Dawson were not yet hypnotized. They looked as though they wondered whether they ought to look as though they disapproved. She concentrated on them:

"But I know whom I wouldn't have dared to go to Colorado with! Mr. Dawson there! I'm sure he's a regular heartbreaker. When we were introduced he held my hand and squeezed it frightfully."

"Haw! Haw! Haw!" The entire company applauded. Mr. Dawson was beatified. He had been called many things—loan-shark, skinflint, tightwad, pussyfoot—but he had never before been called a flirt.

"He is wicked, isn't he, Mrs. Dawson? Don't you have to lock him up?"

"Oh no, but maybe I better," attempted Mrs. Dawson, a tint on her pallid face.

For fifteen minutes Carol kept it up. She asserted that she was going to stage a musical comedy, that she preferred café parfait to beefsteak, that she hoped Dr. Kennicott would never lose his ability to make love to charming women, and that she had a pair of gold stockings. They gaped for more. But she could not keep it up. She retired to a chair behind Sam Clark's bulk. The smile-wrinkles solemnly flattened out in the faces of all the other collaborators in having a party, and again they stood about hoping but not expecting to be amused.

Carol listened. She discovered that conversation did not exist in Gopher Prairie. Even at this affair, which brought out the young smart set, the hunting squire set, the respectable intellectual set, and the solid financial set, they sat up with gaiety as with a corpse.

Juanita Haydock talked a good deal in her rattling voice but it was invariably of personalities: the rumor that Raymie Wutherspoon was going to send for a pair of patent leather shoes with gray buttoned tops; the rheumatism of Champ Perry; the state of Guy Pollock's grippe; and the dementia of Jim Howland in painting his fence salmon-pink.

Sam Clark had been talking to Carol about motor cars, but he felt his duties as host. While he droned, his brows popped up and down. He interrupted himself, "Must stir 'em up." He worried at his wife, "Don't you think I better stir 'em up?" He shouldered into the center of the room, and cried:

"Let's have some stunts, folks."

"Yes, let's!" shrieked Juanita Haydock.

"Say, Dave, give us that stunt about the Norwegian catching a hen."

"You bet; that's a slick stunt; do that, Dave!" cheered Chet Dashaway. Mr. Dave Dyer obliged.

All the guests moved their lips in anticipation of being called on for their own stunts.

"Ella, come on and recite 'Old Sweetheart of Mine,' for us," demanded Sam.

Miss Ella Stowbody, the spinster daughter of the Ionic bank, scratched her dry palms and blushed. "Oh, you don't want to hear that old thing again."

"Sure we do! You bet!" asserted Sam.

"My voice is in terrible shape tonight."

"Tut! Come on!"

Sam loudly explained to Carol, "Ella is our shark at elocuting. She's had professional training. She studied singing and oratory and dramatic art and shorthand for a year, in Milwaukee."

Miss Stowbody was reciting. As encore to "An Old Sweetheart of Mine," she gave a peculiarly optimistic poem regarding the value of smiles.

There were four other stunts: one Jewish, one Irish, one juvenile, and Nat Hicks's parody of Mark Antony's funeral oration.

During the winter Carol was to hear Dave Dyer's hen-catching impersonation seven times, "An Old Sweetheart of Mine" nine times, the Jewish story and the funeral oration twice; but now she was ardent and, because she did so want to be happy and simple-hearted, she was as disappointed as the others when the stunts were finished, and the party instantly sank back into coma.

They gave up trying to be festive; they began to talk naturally, as they did at their shops and homes.

The men and women divided, as they had been tending to do all evening. Carol was deserted by the men, left to a group of matrons who steadily pattered of children, sickness, and cooks—their own shop-talk. She was piqued. She remembered visions of herself as a smart married woman in a drawing-room, fencing with clever men. Her dejection was relieved by speculation as to what the men were discussing, in the corner between the piano and the phonograph. Did they rise from these housewifely personalities to a larger world of abstractions and affairs?

She made her best curtsy to Mrs. Dawson; she twittered, "I won't have my husband leaving me so soon! I'm going over and pull the wretch's ears." She rose with a *jeune fille* bow. She was self-absorbed and self-approving because she had attained that quality of sentimentality. She proudly dipped across the room and, to the interest and commendation of all beholders, sat on the arm of Kennicott's chair.

He was gossiping with Sam Clark, Luke Dawson, Jackson Elder of the planing-mill, Chet Dashaway, Dave Dyer, Harry Haydock, and Ezra Stowbody, president of the Ionic bank.

Ezra Stowbody was a troglodyte. He had come to Gopher Prairie in 1865. He was a distinguished bird of prey—swooping thin nose, turtle mouth, thick brows, port-wine cheeks, floss of white hair, contemptuous eyes. He was not happy in the social changes of thirty years. Three decades ago, Dr. Westlake, Julius Flickerbaugh the lawyer, Merriman Peedy the Congregational pastor and himself had been the arbiters. That was as it should be; the fine arts—medicine, law, religion, and finance—recognized as aristocratic; four Yankees democratically chatting with but ruling the Ohioans and Illini and Swedes and Germans who had ventured to follow them. But Westlake was old, almost retired; Julius Flickerbaugh had lost much of his practice to livelier attorneys; Reverend (not The Reverend) Peedy was dead; and nobody was impressed in this rotten age of automobiles by the "spanking grays" which Ezra still drove. The town was as heterogeneous as Chicago. Norwegians and Germans owned stores. The social leaders were common merchants. Selling nails was considered as sacred as banking. These upstarts—the Clarks, the Haydocks—had no dignity. They were sound and conservative in politics, but they talked about motor cars and pump-guns and heaven only knew what new-fangled fads. (Mr. Stowbody felt out of place with them.) But his brick house with the mansard roof was still the largest residence in town, and he held his position as squire by occasionally appearing among the younger men and reminding them by a wintry eye that without the banker none of them could carry on their vulgar businesses.

As Carol defied decency by sitting down with the men, Mr. Stowbody was piping to Mr. Dawson, "Say, Luke, when was't Biggins first settled in Winnebago Township? Wa'n't it in 1879?"

"Why no 'twa'n't!" Mr. Dawson was indignant. "He come out from Vermont in 1867—no, wait, in 1868, it must have been—and took a claim on the Rum River, quite a ways above Anoka."

"He did not!" roared Mr. Stowbody. "He settled first in Blue Earth County, him and his father!"

("What's the point at issue?" Carol whispered to Kennicott.

("Whether this old duck Biggins had an English setter or a Llewellyn. They've been arguing it all evening!")

Dave Dyer interrupted to give tidings, "D' tell you that Clara Biggins was in town couple days ago? She bought a hot-water bottle—expensive one, too—two dollars and thirty cents!"

"Yaaaaaah!" snarled Mr. Stowbody. "Course. She's just like her grandad was. Never save a cent. Two dollars and twenty—thirty, was it?—two dollars and thirty cents for a hot-water bottle! Brick wrapped up in a flannel petticoat just as good, anyway!"

"How's Ella's tonsils, Mr. Stowbody?" yawned Chet Dashaway.

While Mr. Stowbody gave a somatic and psychic study of them, Carol reflected, "Are they really so terribly interested in Ella's tonsils, or even in Ella's esophagus? I wonder if I could get them away from personalities? Let's risk damnation and try."

"There hasn't been much labor trouble around here, has there, Mr. Stowbody?" she asked innocently.

"No, ma'am, thank God, we've been free from that, except maybe with hired girls and farm-hands. Trouble enough with these foreign farmers; if you don't watch these Swedes they turn socialist or populist or some fool thing on you in a minute. Of course, if they have loans you can make 'em listen to reason. I just have 'em come into the bank for a talk, and tell 'em a few things. I don't mind their being democrats, so much, but I won't stand having socialists around. But thank God, we ain't got the labor trouble they have in these cities. Even Jack Elder here gets along pretty well, in the planing-mill, don't you, Jack?"

"Yep. Sure. Don't need so many skilled workmen in my place, and it's a lot of these cranky, wage-hogging, half-baked skilled mechanics that start trouble—reading a lot of this anarchist literature and union papers and all."

"Do you approve of union labor?" Carol inquired of Mr. Elder.

"Me? I should say not! It's like this: I don't mind dealing with my men if they think they've got any grievances—though Lord knows what's come over workmen, nowadays—don't appreciate a good job. But still, if they come to me honestly, as man to man, I'll talk things over with them. But I'm not going to have any outsider, any of these walking delegates, or whatever fancy names they call themselves now—bunch of rich grafters, living on the ignorant workmen! Not going to have any of those fellows butting in and telling *me* how to run *my* business!"

Mr. Elder was growing more excited, more belligerent and patriotic. "I stand for freedom and constitutional rights. If any man don't like my shop, he can get up and git. Same way, if I don't like him, he gits. And that's all there is to it. I simply can't understand all these complications and hoop-te-doodles and government reports and wage-scales and God knows what all that these fellows are balling up the labor situation with, when it's all perfectly simple. They like what I pay 'em, or they get out. That's all there is to it!"

"What do you think of profit-sharing?" Carol ventured.

Mr. Elder thundered his answer, while the others nodded, solemnly and in tune, like a shop-window of flexible toys, comic mandarins and judges and ducks and clowns, set quivering by a breeze from the open door:

"All this profit-sharing and welfare work and insurance and old-age pension is simply poppycock. Enfeebles a workman's independence—and wastes a lot of honest profit. The half-baked thinker that isn't dry behind the ears yet, and these suffragettes and God knows what all buttinskis there are that are trying to tell a business man how to run his business, and some of these college professors are just about as bad, the whole kit and bilin' of 'em are nothing in God's world but socialism in disguise! And it's my bounden duty as a producer to resist every attack on the integrity of American industry to the last ditch. Yes—SIR!"

Mr. Elder wiped his brow.

Dave Dyer added, "Sure! You bet! What they ought to do is simply to hang every one of these agitators, and that would settle the whole thing right off. Don't you think so, doc?"

"You bet," agreed Kennicott.

The conversation was at last relieved of the plague of Carol's intrusions and they settled down to the question of whether the justice of the peace had sent that hobo drunk to jail for ten days or twelve. It was a matter not readily determined. Then Dave Dyer communicated his carefree adventures on the gipsy trail:

"Yep. I get good time out of the flivver. 'Bout a week ago I motored down to New Wurttemberg. That's forty-three——No, let's see: It's seventeen miles to Belldale, and 'bout six and three-quarters, call it seven, to Torgenquist, and it's a good nineteen miles from there to New Wurttemberg—seventeen and seven and nineteen, that makes, uh, let me see: seventeen and seven 's twenty-four, plus nineteen, well say plus twenty, that makes forty-four, well anyway, say about forty-three or -four miles from here to New Wurttemberg. We got started about seven-fifteen, prob'ly seven-twenty, because I had to stop and fill the radiator, and we ran along, just keeping up a good steady gait——"

Mr. Dyer did finally, for reasons and purposes admitted and justified, attain to New Wurttemberg.

Once—only once—the presence of the alien Carol was recognized. Chet Dashaway leaned over and said asthmatically, "Say, uh, have you been reading this serial 'Two out' in *Tingling Tales?* Corking yarn! Gosh, the fellow that wrote it certainly can sling baseball slang!"

The others tried to look literary. Harry Haydock offered, "Juanita is a great hand for reading high-class stuff, like 'Mid the Magnolias' by this Sara Hetwiggin Butts, and 'Riders of Ranch Reckless.' Books. But me," he glanced about importantly, as one convinced that no other hero had ever been in so strange a plight, "I'm so darn busy I don't have much time to read."

"I never read anything I can't check against," said Sam Clark.

Thus ended the literary portion of the conversation, and for seven minutes Jackson Elder outlined reasons for believing that the pike-fishing was better on the west shore of Lake Minniemashie than on the east—though it was indeed quite true that on the east shore Nat Hicks had caught a pike altogether admirable.

The talk went on. It did go on! Their voices were monotonous, thick, emphatic. They were harshly pompous, like men in the smoking-compartments of Pullman cars. They did not bore Carol. They frightened her. She panted, "They will be cordial to me, because my man belongs to their tribe. God help me if I were an outsider!"

Smiling as changelessly as an ivory figurine she sat quiescent, avoiding thought, glancing about the living-room and hall, noting their betrayal of unimaginative commercial prosperity. Kennicott said, "Dandy interior, eh? My idea of how a place ought to be furnished. Modern." She looked polite, and observed the oiled floors, hard-wood staircase, unused fireplace with tiles which resembled brown linoleum, cut-glass vases standing upon doilies, and the barred, shut, forbidding unit bookcases that were half filled with swashbuckler novels and unread-looking sets of Dickens, Kipling, O. Henry, and Elbert Hubbard.

She perceived that even personalities were failing to hold the party. The room filled with hesitancy as with a fog. People cleared their throats, tried to choke down yawns. The men shot their cuffs and the women stuck their combs more firmly into their back hair.

Then a rattle, a daring hope in every eye, the swinging of a door, the smell of strong coffee, Dave Dyer's mewing voice in a triumphant, "The eats!" They began to chatter. They had something to do. They could escape from themselves. They fell upon the food—chicken sandwiches, maple cake, drug-store ice cream. Even when the food was gone they remained cheerful. They could go home, any time now, and go to bed!

They went, with a flutter of coats, chiffon scarfs, and good-bys.

Carol and Kennicott walked home.

"Did you like them?" he asked.

"They were terribly sweet to me."

"Uh, Carrie—— You ought to be more careful about shocking folks. Talking about gold stockings, and about showing your ankles to schoolteachers and all!" More mildly: "You gave 'em a good time, but I'd watch out for that, 'f I were you. Juanita Haydock is such a damn cat. I wouldn't give her a chance to criticize me."

"My poor effort to lift up the party! Was I wrong to try to amuse them?"

"No! No! Honey, I didn't mean—— You were the only up-and-coming person in the bunch. I just mean—— Don't get onto legs and all that immoral stuff. Pretty conservative crowd."

She was silent, raw with the shameful thought that the attentive circle might have been criticizing her, laughing at her.

"Don't, please don't worry!" he pleaded.

Silence.

"Gosh, I'm sorry I spoke about it. I just meant—— But they were crazy about you. Sam said to me, 'That little lady of yours is the slickest thing that ever came to this town,' he said; and Ma Dawson—I didn't hardly know whether she'd like you or not, she's such a dried-up old bird, but she said, 'Your bride is so quick and bright, I declare, she just wakes me up.'"

Carol liked praise, the flavor and fatness of it, but she was so energetically being sorry for herself that she could not taste this commendation.

"Please! Come on! Cheer up!" His lips said it, his anxious shoulder said it, his arm about her said it, as they halted on the obscure porch of their house.

"Do you care if they think I'm flighty, Will?"

"Me? Why, I wouldn't care if the whole world thought you were this or that or anything else. You're my—well, you're my soul!"

He was an undefined mass, as solid-seeming as rock. She found his sleeve, pinched it, cried, "I'm glad! It's sweet to be wanted! You must tolerate my frivolousness. You're all I have!"

He lifted her, carried her into the house, and with her arms about his neck she forgot Main Street.

Spoon River Anthology

Selections

EDGAR LEE MASTERS

B ECAUSE THE RISE of "modernism" coincided in the United States with the ascendancy of the midwestern small town as a social and political force, much of the literature of small towns is "modern." Literary modernism refers to a movement that reached its zenith between the two world wars. It incorporated new developments in the hard sciences and in psychology, sociology, and aesthetics. Modernism emphasized character more than plot. By recognizing multiple points of view and thus multiple truths, it tended to be morally neutral or ambivalent. It stressed unconscious motivation, subconscious connections, disjuncture of time, fidelity to place, and the value of commonplace experiences seen in new light. It saw literature not as a moral beacon drawing readers to ethical behavior, or even as a faithful chronicle of everyday life, but as a tool of cultural criticism and experiment. More than anything, it valued the new: new material, new ways of thinking, new modes of expression.

Not surprisingly, much "modern" American writing emerged outside of the literary centers of New York and Boston. Writing in 1920, H. L. Mencken observed that "a circle of two hundred miles radius around Chicago" would enclose "four-fifths of the real literature of America— particularly four-fifths of the literature of tomorrow." Many writers who comprised this so-called "Chicago Renaissance" wrote not of the city but of the small town: Hamlin Garland, Vachel Lindsay, Sherwood Anderson, and Edgar Lee Masters. They were rapidly eclipsed by later, more successful, and more international modernists, but their impact on American literature was great, especially in the area of poetry. "For these people," Lisel Mueller has written, "experience was the touchstone of knowledge," and "free verse, Midwest style, was not an European import, but an introduction of everyday common speech patterns into the province of poetry."

Edgar Lee Masters was a successful lawyer with eleven undistinguished books of poetry and prose to his name when he began publishing in the newspaper *Reedy's Mirror* the poems that would be collected into the bestselling *Spoon River Anthology*. The idea of writing an American version of the epitaphs in the *Greek Anthology* appealed to Masters, who had escaped the small towns of Petersburg and Lewistown, Illinois, and saw in epitaphs a way to dig below the façade of smug respectability which had so offended him in those villages. Masters's characters speak in death the truths they could not tell in life, and their collective testimony, frequently cross-referenced, portrays a village filled with vice and hypocrisy to rival Mark Twain's bitter story "The Man That Corrupted Hadleyburg." Unfortunately for Masters's long-term reputation, he had almost no ear for rhythm or music, his free verse was almost pure prose, he had no sense of imagism or psychological complexity, and his two great gifts to American literature—breaking the forms of traditional rhymed and metered poetry and insisting on the primacy of facts and events—were soon raised by others to heights he himself could not reach.

o o o

Daisy Fraser

Did you ever hear of Editor Whedon
Giving to the public treasury any of the money he received
For supporting candidates for office?
Or for writing up the canning factory
To get people to invest?
Or for suppressing the facts about the bank,
When it was rotten and ready to break?
Did you ever hear of the Circuit Judge
Helping anyone except the "Q" railroad,
Or the bankers? Or did Rev. Peet or Rev. Sibley
Give any part of their salary, earned by keeping still,
Or speaking out as the leaders wished them to do,
To the building of the water works?
But I—Daisy Fraser who always passed
Along the streets through rows of nods and smiles,
And coughs and words such as "there she goes,"
Never was taken before Justice Arnett
Without contributing ten dollars and costs
To the school fund of Spoon River!

Doctor Meyers

No other man, unless it was Doc Hill,
Did more for people in this town than I.
And all the weak, the halt, the improvident
And those who could not pay flocked to me.
I was good-hearted, easy Doctor Meyers.
I was healthy, happy, in comfortable fortune,
Blest with a congenial mate, my children raised,
All wedded, doing well in the world.
And then one night, Minerva, the poetess,
Came to me in her trouble, crying.
I tried to help her out—she died—
They indicted me, the newspapers disgraced me,
My wife perished of a broken heart.
And pneumonia finished me.

Roscoe Purkapile

She loved me. Oh! how she loved me!
I never had a chance to escape
From the day she first saw me.
But then after we were married I thought
She might prove her mortality and let me out,
Or she might divorce me.
But few die, none resign.
Then I ran away and was gone a year on a lark.
But she never complained. She said all would be well,
That I would return. And I did return.
I told her that while taking a row in a boat
I had been captured near Van Buren Street
By pirates on Lake Michigan,
And kept in chains, so I could not write her.
She cried and kissed me, and said it was cruel,
Outrageous, inhuman!
I then concluded our marriage
Was a divine dispensation
And could not be dissolved,
Except by death.
I was right.

Mrs. Meyers

He protested all his life long
The newspapers lied about him villainously;
That he was not at fault for Minerva's fall,
But only tried to help her.
Poor soul so sunk in sin he could not see
That even trying to help her, as he called it,
He had broken the law human and divine.
Passers by, an ancient admonition to you:
If your ways would be ways of pleasantness,
And all your pathways peace,
Love God and keep his commandments.

Mrs. Purkapile

He ran away and was gone for a year.
When he came home he told me the silly story
Of being kidnapped by pirates on Lake Michigan
And kept in chains so he could not write me.
I pretended to believe it, though I knew very well
What he was doing, and that he met
The milliner, Mrs. Williams, now and then
When she went to the city to buy goods, as she said.
But a promise is a promise
And marriage is marriage,
And out of respect for my own character
I refused to be drawn into a divorce
By the scheme of a husband who had merely grown tired
Of his marital vow and duty.

Mrs. Sibley

The secret of the stars,—gravitation.
The secret of the earth,—layers of rock.
The secret of the soil,—to receive seed.
The secret of man,—the sower.
The secret of woman,—the soil.
My secret: Under a mound that you shall never find.

Jack McGuire

They would have lynched me
Had I not been secretly hurried away
To the jail at Peoria.
And yet I was going peacefully home,
Carrying my jug, a little drunk,
When Logan, the marshal, halted me,
Called me a drunken hound and shook me,
And, when I cursed him for it, struck me
With that Prohibition loaded cane—
All this before I shot him.
They would have hanged me except for this:
My lawyer, Kinsey Keene, was helping to land
Old Thomas Rhodes for wrecking the bank,
And the judge was a friend of Rhodes
And wanted him to escape,
And Kinsey offered to quit on Rhodes
For fourteen years for me.
And the bargain was made. I served my time
And learned to read and write.

Poor White

Excerpt

SHERWOOD ANDERSON

I T'S HUMAN NATURE not to appreciate what we've got until it's gone, to rush ahead only to fall behind, to ignore the simple things in life which are, after all, the best things in life. It's also human nature to imagine the past as safer, healthier, saner, and more comfortable than the disillusioning present or the uncertain future. The small town, because it embodies certain social and ethical values, is often subject to such romanticization. Even writers who know better tend to look back upon the small town of their childhood as a Great Good Place, an age of innocence before the trauma of industrialization.

Sherwood Anderson certainly belongs to this group. His collection of interlocked short stories titled *Winesburg, Ohio* depicts the narrow, repressed lives of inarticulate small-town folk (it took decades for his hometown of Clyde, Ohio, to forgive Anderson's unflattering portrait) and the need for ambitious youngsters to escape the village. His largely Freudian analysis caused genteel readers of his day to regard his work as scandalous and inaccurate, although the book is now considered Anderson's best, one of the great achievements in American literature. As a realist and a modernist, Anderson is a major figure in twentieth-century American literature. His settings are particular, he writes in vernacular English, and his characters are psychologically complex. Plot is less important in his stories than character, and the central moment of the story is usually what the Irish short-story writer James Joyce called "an epiphany": a brief and possibly temporary moment of self-awareness.

In his novel *Poor White*, Anderson takes a more economic approach to analyzing the village's problems. He describes a small Ohio farming town, Bidwell, transformed by sudden industrialization, which brings wealth, complexity, and a national consciousness while fragmenting the self-sufficient community and reducing by comparison the stature of its small-town citizenry. Wallace Stegner has written, "The more urban [the American way of life] has become, and the more frantic with technological change, the sicker and more embittered our literature, and I believe our people, have become."

The following selection describes the town of Bidwell before the Fall. It is a cohesive rural community celebrating the agricultural rituals of harvest and courtship, tolerant of eccentrics and charitable toward all. Self-sufficient moderation is the village norm, although Anderson suggests early in his novel the agents of coming industrialization—the town's railroad lines and its reliance on distant markets. He also sounds at the close of this chapter the "new note" of industrial imperialism in the form of the four harnesses Tom Butterworth has ordered from a factory in Philadelphia, harnesses which will soon render local craftsman Joseph Wainsworth (like Anderson's own father, who was a harness maker) "technologically displaced." In this peaceful moment between the traumas of pioneering and industrialization, "everyone knew his neighbor and was known to him. . . . For the moment mankind seemed about to take time to try to understand itself."

o o o

Book Two, Chapter III

Bidwell, Ohio, was an old town as the ages of towns go in the Central West, long before Hugh McVey, in his search for a place where he could penetrate the wall that shut him off from humanity, went there to live and to try to work out his problem. It is a busy manufacturing town now and has a population of nearly a hundred thousand people; but the time for the telling of the story of its sudden and surprising growth has not yet come.

From the beginning Bidwell has been a prosperous place. The town lies in the valley of a deep, rapid-flowing river that spreads out just above the town, becomes for the time wide and shallow, and goes singing swiftly along over stones. South of the town the river not only spreads out, but the hills recede. A wide flat valley stretches away to the north. In the days before the factories came the land immediately about town was cut up into small farms devoted to fruit and berry raising, and beyond the area of small farms lay larger tracts that were immensely productive and that raised huge crops of wheat, corn, and cabbage.

When Hugh was a boy sleeping away his days in the grass beside his father's fishing shack by the Mississippi River, Bidwell had already emerged out of the hardships of pioneer days. On the farms that lay in the wide valley to the north the timber had been cut away and the stumps had all been rooted out of the ground by a generation of men that had passed. The soil was easy to cultivate and had lost little of its virgin fertility. Two railroads, the Lake Shore and Michigan Central—later a part of the great New York Central System—and a less important coal-carrying road, called the Wheeling and Lake Erie, ran through the town. Twenty-five hundred people lived then in Bidwell. They were for the most part descendants of the pioneers who had come into the country by boat through the Great Lakes or by wagon roads over the mountains from the States of New York and Pennsylvania.

The town stood on a sloping incline running up from the river, and the Lake Shore and Michigan Central Railroad had its station on the river bank at the foot of Main Street. The Wheeling Station was a mile away to the north. It was to be reached by going over a bridge and along a piked road that even then had begun to take on the semblance of a street. A dozen houses had been built facing Turner's Pike and between these were berry fields and an occasional orchard planted to cherry, peach or apple trees. A hard path went down to the distant station beside the road, and in the evening this path, wandering along under the branches of the fruit trees that extended out over the farm fences, was a favorite place for lovers.

The small farms lying close about the town of Bidwell raised berries that brought top prices in the two cities, Cleveland and Pittsburgh, reached by its two railroads, and all of the people of the town who were not engaged in one of the trades—in shoemaking, carpentry, horseshoeing, house-painting or the like—or who did not belong to the small merchant and professional classes, worked in summer on the land. On summer mornings, men, women and children went into the fields. In the early spring when planting went on and all through late May, June and early July when berries and fruit began to ripen, everyone was rushed with work and the streets of the town were deserted. Everyone went to the fields. Great hay wagons loaded with children, laughing girls, and sedate women set out from Main Street at dawn. Beside them walked tall boys, who pelted the girls with green apples and cherries from the trees along the road, and men who went along behind smoking their morning pipes and talking of the prevailing prices of the products of their fields. In the town after they had gone a Sabbath quiet prevailed. The merchants and clerks loitered in the shade of the awnings before the doors of the stores, and only their wives and the wives of the two or three rich men in town came to buy and to disturb their discussions of horse racing, politics and religion.

In the evening when the wagons came home, Bidwell awoke. The tired berry pickers walked home from the fields in the dust of the roads swinging their dinner pails. The wagons creaked at their heels, piled high with boxes of berries ready for shipment. In the stores after the evening meal crowds gathered. Old men lit their pipes and sat gossiping along the curbing at the edge of the sidewalks on Main Street; women with baskets on their arms did the marketing for the next day's living; the young men put on stiff white collars and their Sunday clothes, and girls, who all day had been crawling over the fields between the rows of berries or pushing their way among the tangled masses of raspberry bushes, put on white dresses and walked up and down before the men. Friendships begun between boys and girls in the fields ripened into love. Couples walked along residence streets under the trees and talked with subdued voices. They became silent and embarrassed. The bolder ones kissed. The end of the berry picking season brought each year a new outbreak of marriages to the town of Bidwell.

In all the towns of Midwestern America it was a time of waiting. The country having been cleared and the Indians driven away into a vast distant place spoken of vaguely as the West, the Civil War having been fought and won, and there being no great national problems that touched closely their lives, the minds of men were turned in upon themselves. The soul and its destiny was spoken of openly on the streets. Robert Ingersoll came to Bidwell to speak in Terry's Hall, and after he had gone the question of the divinity of Christ for months occupied the minds of the citizens. The ministers preached sermons on the subject and in the evening it was talked about in the stores. Everyone had something to say. Even Charley Mook, who dug ditches, who stuttered so that not a half dozen people in town could understand him, expressed his opinion.

In all the great Mississippi Valley each town came to have a character of its own, and the people who lived in the towns were to each other like members of a great family. The individual idiosyncrasies of each member of the great family stood forth. A kind of invisible roof beneath which everyone lived spread itself over each town. Beneath the roof boys and girls were born, grew up, quarreled, fought, and formed friendships with their fellows, were introduced into the mysteries of love, married, and became the fathers and mothers of children, grew old, sickened, and died.

Within the invisible circle and under the great roof everyone knew his neighbor and was known to him. Strangers did not come and go swiftly and mysteriously and there was no constant and confusing roar of machinery and of new projects afoot. For the moment mankind seemed about to take time to try to understand itself.

In Bidwell there was a man named Peter White who was a tailor and worked hard at his trade, but who once or twice a year got drunk and beat his wife. He was arrested each time and had to pay a fine, but there was a general understanding of the impulse that led to the beating. Most of the women knowing the wife sympathized with Peter. "She is a noisy thing and her jaw is never still," the wife of Henry Teeters, the grocer, said to her husband. "If he gets drunk it's only to forget he's married to her. Then he goes home to sleep it off and she begins jawing at him. He stands it as long as he can. It takes a fist to shut up that woman. If he strikes her it's the only thing he can do."

Allie Mulberry the half-wit was one of the highlights of life in the town. He lived with his mother in a tumble-down house at the edge of town on Medina Road. Besides being a half-wit he had something the matter with his legs. They were trembling and weak and he could only move them with great difficulty. On summer afternoons when the streets were deserted, he hobbled along Main Street with his lower jaw hanging down. Allie carried a large club, partly for the support of his weak legs and partly to scare off dogs and mischievous boys. He liked to sit in the shade with his back against a building and whittle, and he liked to be near people and have his talent as a whittler appreciated. He made fans out of pieces of pine, long chains of wooden beads, and he once achieved a singular mechanical triumph that won him wide renown. He made a ship that would float in a beer bottle half-filled with water and laid on its side. The ship had sails and three tiny wooden sailors who stood at attention with their hands to their caps in salute. After it was constructed and put into the bottle it was too large to be taken out through the neck. How Allie got it in no one ever knew. The clerks and merchants who crowded about to watch him at work discussed the matter for days. It became a never-ending wonder among them. In the evening they spoke of the matter to the berry pickers who came into the stores, and in the eyes of the people of Bidwell Allie Mulberry became a hero. The bottle, half-filled with water and securely corked, was laid on a cushion in the window of Hunter's Jewelry Store. As it floated about on its own little ocean crowds gathered to look at it. Over the bottle was a sign with the words—"Carved by Allie Mulberry of Bidwell"—prominently displayed. Below these words a query had been printed. "How Did He Get It Into The Bottle?" was the question asked. The bottle stayed in the window for months and merchants took the traveling men who visited them, to see it. Then they escorted their guests to where Allie, with his back against the wall of a building and his club beside him, was at work on some new creation of the whittler's art. The travelers were impressed and told the tale abroad. Allie's fame spread to other towns. "He has a good brain," the citizen of Bidwell said, shaking his head. "He don't appear to know very much, but look what he does! He must be carrying all sorts of notions around inside of his head."

Jane Orange, widow of a lawyer, and with the single exception of Thomas Butterworth, a farmer who owned over a thousand acres of land and lived with his daughter on a farm a mile south of town, the richest person in town, was known to everyone in Bidwell, but was not liked. She was called stingy and it was said that she and her husband had cheated everyone with whom they had dealings in order to get their start in life. The town ached for the privilege of doing what they called "bringing them down a peg." Jane's husband had once been the Bidwell town attorney and later had charge of the settlement of an estate belonging to Ed Lucas, a farmer who died leaving two hundred acres of land and two daughters. The farmer's daughters, everyone said, "came out at the small end of the horn," and John Orange began to grow rich. It was said he was worth fifty thousand dollars. All during the latter part of his life the lawyer went to the city of Cleveland on business every week, and when he was at home and even in the hottest weather he went about dressed in a long black coat. When she went to the stores to buy supplies for her house, Jane Orange was watched closely by the merchants. She was suspected of carrying away small articles that could be slipped into the pockets of her dress. One afternoon in Toddmore's grocery, when she thought no one was looking, she took a half dozen eggs out of a basket and looking quickly around to be sure she was unobserved, put them into her dress pocket. Harry Toddmore, the grocer's son who had seen the theft, said nothing, but went unobserved out at the back door. He got three or four clerks from other stores and they waited for Jane Orange at a corner. When she came along they hurried out and Harry Toddmore fell against her. Throwing out his hand he struck the pocket containing the eggs a quick, sharp blow. Jane Orange turned and hurried away toward home, but as she half ran through Main Street clerks and merchants came out of the stores, and from the assembled crowd a voice called attention to the fact that the contents of the stolen eggs having run down the inside of her dress and over her stockings began to make a stream on the sidewalk. A pack of town dogs excited by the shouts of the crowd ran at her heels, barking and sniffing at the yellow stream that dripped from her shoes.

An old man with a long white beard came to Bidwell to live. He had been a carpetbag Governor of a Southern state in the reconstruction days after the Civil War and had made money. He bought a house on Turner's Pike close beside the river and spent his days puttering about in a small garden. In the evening he came across the bridge into Main Street and went to loaf in Birdie Spinks' drugstore. He talked with great frankness and candor of his life in the South during the terrible time when the country was trying to emerge from the black gloom of defeat, and brought to the Bidwell men a new point of view on their old enemies, the "Rebs."

The old man—the name by which he had introduced himself in Bidwell was that of Judge Horace Hanby—believed in the manliness and honesty of purpose of the men he had for a time governed and who had fought a long grim war with the North, with the New Englanders and sons of New Englanders from the West and Northwest. "They're all right," he said with a grin. "I cheated them and made some money, but I liked them. Once a crowd of them came to my house and threatened to kill me and I told them that I did not blame them very much, so they let me alone." The judge, an ex-politician from the city of New York who had been involved in some affair that made it uncomfortable for him to return to live in that city, grew prophetic and philosophic after he came to live in Bidwell. In spite of the doubt everyone felt concerning his past, he was something of a scholar and a reader of books, and won respect by his apparent wisdom. "Well, there's going to be a new war here," he said. "It won't be like the Civil War, just shooting off guns and killing peoples' bodies. At first it's going to be a war between individuals to see to what class a man must belong; then it is going to be a long, silent war between classes, between those who have and those who can't get. It'll be the worst war of all."

The talk of Judge Hanby, carried along and elaborated almost every evening before a silent, attentive group in the drugstore, began to have an influence on the minds of Bidwell young men. At his suggestion several of the town boys, Cliff Bacon, Albert Small, Ed Prawl, and two or three others, began to save money for the purpose of going east to college. Also at his suggestion Tom Butterworth the rich farmer sent his daughter away to school. The old man made many prophecies concerning what would happen in America. "I tell you, the country isn't going to stay as it is," he said earnestly. "In eastern towns the change has already come. Factories are being built and everyone is going to work in the factories. It takes an old man like me to see how that changes their lives. Some of the men stand at one bench and do one thing not only for hours but for days and years. There are signs hung up saying they mustn't talk. Some of them make more money than they did before the factories came, but I tell you it's like being in prison. What would you say if I told you all America, all you fellows who talk so big about freedom, are going to be put in a prison, eh?

"And there's something else. In New York there are already a dozen men who are worth a million dollars. Yes, sir, I tell you it's true, a million dollars. What do you think of that, eh?"

Judge Hanby grew excited and, inspired by the absorbed attention of his audience, talked of the sweep of events. In England, he explained, the cities were constantly growing larger, and already almost everyone either worked in a factory or owned stock in a factory. "In New England it is getting the same way fast," he explained. "The same thing'll happen here. Farming'll be done with tools. Almost everything now done by hand'll be done by machinery. Some'll grow rich and some poor. The thing is to get educated, yes, sir, that's the thing, to get ready for what's coming. It's the only way. The younger generation has got to be sharper and shrewder."

The words of the old man, who had been in many places and had seen men and cities, were repeated in the streets of Bidwell. The blacksmith and the wheelwright repeated his words when they stopped to exchange news of their affairs before the post office. Ben Peeler, the carpenter, who had been saving money to buy a house and a small farm to which he could retire when he became too old to climb about on the framework of buildings, used the money instead to send his son to Cleveland to a new technical school. Steve Hunter, the son of Abraham Hunter the Bidwell jeweler, declared that he was going to get up with the times, and when he went into a factory, would go into the office, not into the shop. He went to Buffalo, New York, to attend a business college.

The air of Bidwell began to stir with talk of new times. The evil things said of the new life coming were soon forgotten. The youth and optimistic spirit of the country led it to take hold of the hand of the giant, industrialism, and lead him laughing into the land. The cry, "get on in the world," that ran all over American at that period and that still echoes in the pages of American newspapers and magazines, rang in the streets of Bidwell.

In the harness shop belonging to Joseph Wainsworth it one day struck a new note. The harness maker was a tradesman of the old school and was vastly independent. He had learned his trade after five years' service as apprentice, and had spent an additional five years in going from place to place as a journeyman workman, and felt that he knew his business. Also he owned his shop and his home and had twelve hundred dollars in the bank. At noon one day when he was alone in the shop, Tom Butterworth came in and told him he had ordered four sets of farm work harness from a factory in Philadelphia. "I came in to ask if you'll repair them if they get out of order," he said.

Joe Wainsworth began to fumble with the tools on his bench. Then he turned to look the farmer in the eye and to do what he later spoke of to his cronies as "laying down the law." "When the cheap things begin to go to pieces take them somewhere else to have them repaired," he said sharply. He grew furiously angry. "Take the damn things to Philadelphia where you got 'em," he shouted at the back of the farmer who had turned to go out of the shop.

Joe Wainsworth was upset and thought about the incident all the afternoon. When farmer-customers came in and stood about to talk of their affairs he had nothing to say. He was a talkative man and his apprentice, Will Sellinger, son of the Bidwell house painter, was puzzled by his silence.

When the boy and the man were alone in the shop, it was Joe Wainsworth's custom to talk of his days as a journeyman workman when he had gone from place to place working at his trade. If a trace were being stitched or a bridle fashioned, he told how the thing was done at a shop where he had worked in the city of Boston and in another shop at Providence, Rhode Island. Getting a piece of paper he made drawings illustrating the cuts of leather that were made in the other places and the methods of stitching. He claimed to have worked out his own method for doing things, and that his method was better than anything he had seen in all his travels. To the men who came into the shop to loaf during winter afternoons he presented a smiling front and talked of their affairs, of the price of cabbage in Cleveland or the effect of a cold snap on the winter wheat, but alone with the boy, he talked only of harness making. "I don't say anything about it. What's the good bragging? Just the same, I could learn something to all the harness makers I've ever seen, and I've seen the best of them," he declared emphatically.

During the afternoon, after he had heard of the four factory-made work harnesses brought into what he had always thought of as a trade that belonged to him by the rights of a first-class workman, Joe remained silent for two or three hours. He thought of the words of old Judge Hanby and the constant talk of the new times now coming. Turning suddenly to his apprentice, who was puzzled by his long silence and who knew nothing of the incident that had disturbed his employer, he broke forth into words. He was defiant and expressed his defiance. "Well, then, let 'em go to Philadelphia, let 'em go any damn place they please," he growled, and then, as though his own words had re-established his self-respect, he straightened his shoulders and glared at the puzzled and alarmed boy. "I know my trade and do not have to bow down to any man," he declared. He expressed the old tradesman's faith in his craft and the rights it gave the craftsman. "Learn your trade. Don't listen to talk," he said earnestly. "The man who knows his trade is a man. He can tell everyone to go to the devil."

The Resurrection

FROM *Midland Magazine*

RUTH SUCKOW

WHILE PHILIP WYLIE'S suggestion, put forth in *A Generation of Vipers*, that America has always been a matriarchy suffocating under the supervision of Victorian Moms, is more than a little far-fetched, there is probably truth to Page Smith's remarks in *As a City Upon a Hill:*

> The town, built by the man, and so often the tomb of his ambitions, was the perfect setting for the woman who emerged in time as the indomitable forerunner of today's Mom. The female presence pervaded the town's life—cooking, baking, admonishing, loyally supporting the beaten husband, sponsoring culture, maintaining the church, upholding the old values, pushing her children, plotting, planning, saving, and finally subduing the town, making it into a large mother, the place where trust and love and understanding could always be found, making the town one of America's most persistent and critical symbols—the town as mother, comforter, source of love.

Writers both male (Hamlin Garland, Sinclair Lewis) and female (Willa Cather, Meridel Le Sueur) testify that the women of America's farms and small towns wielded considerable silent power, especially in matters cultural, educational, and religious.

Ruth Suckow was the daughter of a Congregational minister who moved his family from one Iowa town to another. She attended Grinnell College in Iowa and the Curry School of Expression in Boston before returning to the Midwest to work as a writer and—with John T. Frederick at *Midland Magazine*—as an editor of Midwest writing. She eventually moved to California, but, like Cather, Suckow drew her fiction from the small midwestern towns she had known as a girl. Like Lewis and Anderson, she portrays those towns as stifling, especially for women, but also for men. Standards are old-fashioned and materialistic; work is hard and the hours long; nature is not always beautiful or rewarding. A young girl's choices seem to be escape or resignation. For those who stay, the memory of a single moment of selfish personal happiness must often suffice to sweeten a lifetime of maintaining the church, upholding the old values, and pushing her children.

In the story "The Resurrection," a lifetime of emotional containment and "doing for" others—including her husband—has so transformed a beautiful small-town girl into Mother and then Grandmother that when she relapses upon death to the remote beauty who won her husband's heart long before her daughters and granddaughters were born, her children do not recognize her. Only her husband recognizes the girl he once knew. He is shocked and a little terrified by the sudden realization that not only did she have a life before the one they shared, but she may actually have preferred that moment, brief and long buried, to all her years as Mom, Grandma, and Wife.

o o o

He whom they had always thought of as Mr. Ward, but who all this day had been a shadowy, necessary, scarcely seen, and yet alleviating presence, was at the parlor door.

"I think you may—" He nodded solemnly.

They rose stiffly, the desultory talk they had been keeping up stricken with silence.

After a moment, Clara, who was nearest the door, murmured: "Shall I go first?"

She moved on, keeping hold of her husband's arm, and the others followed.

Little Jean kept close to her father, her big, bright eyes very wide open. Helen was near them, hiding with an almost sullen look the pounding of her heart.

Grandpa walked by himself in a kind of stolid bewilderment.

His daughters glanced at him anxiously, but did not go to him. He moved ponderously in his square-toed blackened shoes—an old man's shoes. The discomfort that he had always felt on Sundays, when Grandma had made him put on his "other clothes," was intensified, ludicrously and yet tragically. Now, for a day, he had sat around the house, pitifully out of ease in his solemn best clothes, his big, scarred hands idle on his knees.

Was it Grandma who was having all this fuss made for her? That was not like her. No wonder he did not believe it.

The parlor seemed to be motionless in a strange chill. All its well-known characteristics were curiously heightened—its order, its prim propriety, its smell of Brussels carpet and painted woodwork. Every chair was strangely significant—and the stand, the fern, the bookcase, the center table with the Bible. All seemed new, and at the same time more familiar than ever before.

So the persons standing there felt themselves more than ever as individuals, and far more than ever as a family.

At once they were aware of an alien scent of flowers, breathlessly still. Reluctant, yet moved by a yearning inner necessity, they moved close about and looked upon her.

Here was the very essence of that blended familiarity and strangeness. Her crimped white hair was parted neatly, as always, held by her own shell combs. She wore her black silk dress. But the alien look of hothouse flowers upon her plain, small person that they had seemed to know so well—and, most of all, her face. . . .

Little Jean whispered: "Mama, is it *Grandma?*"

"Yes, dear, of course. Don't you know her?"

The child did not answer. Just so, on autumn mornings, she had looked out to see her whole familiar world transfigured by the silver touch of frost. This was like frost—still, white, and wonderful.

Clara made an uncontrollable murmur.

"I never saw her look so lovely," said Lil.

The sisters—Clara, Lil, and Jennie—drew together. The three sons-in-law made a murmur of assent. Then, after a decorous interval, feeling more terribly out of place than at their weddings in this same room, they stole out, one after another.

Helen, who had come afraid, and because they said she must, stood now in awe to find this still beauty where she had expected terror.

Little Jean's wonderment was in the minds of all: Is this Grandma?

Her face, like the things in the room, baffled them with its blending of the known and the unknown. The small, aged features were hers—more than ever hers. But the look. . . .

"It is not herself," the daughters thought.

"It is herself," the old man felt.

They had been used to know her as a little, gentle, fluttering-voiced woman, anxiously unobtrusive, trying always with pathetic eagerness to "do for" them. They had seen her always at work—cooking for them all, mending and sewing for them, then making things for their children, little dresses, underwear, and lastly rows and rows of knitted lace for tiny petticoats. Only a few times, when they were children, they had caught her, just at dusk, sitting alone by the kitchen window staring out at the gray light behind the apple trees, and had crept away, feeling awed and very lonely. But mostly they had never thought of her as a person in herself. She had been Mother, and then, Grandma.

Now the lonely feeling came back to them, deepened, and with a wondering hurt. The strange, inscrutable superiority of death crushed them. They had lost their mother indeed.

Her household look was gone from her; and now, at the moment of supposed extinction, her essential self, overlaid, neglected for years upon years, had taken radiant, calm possession. They were bewildered, filled with an obscure remorse. She who had been so simply Mother, had she, too, been something other than she seemed? The essential solitude of every human soul came over them with icy breath. And yet she was beautiful! They had the feeling of someone who stands upon a high mountain top and sees, with an awe transcending fear, the barren sublimity of space.

Was this Grandma?

After a silent, tearful, concentrated look, that carved that still face forever on their hearts, they touched the little girls and moved away. They could not see her again, they would have gazed forever, but the very poignancy of the moment made it end.

But Grandpa did not move. His lips, covered with a frost of beard, hung apart. There was puzzlement, rather than grief, in his eyes. Clara looked at her sisters, moved toward him, then went uncertainly away. He stayed on alone.

He could never have spoken, even to himself, the dim, strange things that moved in his clumsy brain. It meant something, he felt. That look was a sign. But he could not make it out. Some of the hurt that his daughters had felt worked at his old heart. But mostly wonderment.

He knew, half unconsciously, this look so strange to all the rest. It was the spirit of her girlhood. It was the look that she had worn to him years ago when he had first loved her. Then, too, she had seemed beautiful and far away.

And her beauty, her remoteness in her white silence, smote him. She had lived their life so long—never her own. He felt a kind of fear to see the spirit that, all these years with him, had underlain the acquiescence, the seeming patience of every day. Mother—Grandma—he struggled for the old, familiar feeling. It would not come.

Perhaps it was only her thoughtfulness to look so fair that the children might not be frightened. Or that sense of propriety at which he had often scoffed, to look her very best upon a great occasion. Or that foolish sentiment that women have—to take with her this look as her dearest keepsake.

But he felt that it was a sign. And strange things struggled in him for clearness. It seemed that she might wear this look to show that that religion of hers, which had meant nothing to him, was not so foolish after all— a woman's affair. Broken phrases of it went through his mind—*Shall be no sorrow there—All your sorrows shall be forgotten—All shall be bliss— The Resurrection and the Life—*

This look of hers . . . that vague hurt beset him. Why should she look so, instead of the familiar way of their life together? The wrinkles, the hollows, the marks of care and toil, were gone, were as if they had not been. Her virgin, untouched self shone supreme. Had their whole life counted for nothing at the final test? He was awed before the relentless artistry of death, that, putting aside the minute, daily, painful sculpturing of life, had disdained it all and found this one thing fit for immortality.

He was the one human being who had seen just this look of hers before. Something proud and tearful swelled in his dumb old heart. Perhaps he would find her so again. Thoughts of a past long gone flitted through his mind. He was lifted.

Then he was not sure. He felt, as always, baffled, ill at ease before beauty. He seemed more than ever an intruder, with his big, clumsy feet, in this small parlor. Her fine clothes, the ceremony, the flowers, bewildered him.

What did it mean? Perhaps the others knew. Or perhaps it was not true— no one else had seen. Yet he had seen.

When Helen came to the door and said: "Grandpa, mama says to come," he turned and looked at the young girl with searching, misty eyes. Something in the look stopped her—some note of awe and wistfulness in his voice as he spoke to her. For a moment they almost shared a recognition.

"Your Grandma looks—real nice—don't she, Nellie?"

A Peculiar Treasure

Excerpt

EDNA FERBER

IN THE TWENTY-FIRST CENTURY, *U.S.A. Today*, CNN news, AP and UPI wire services, the Weather Channel, and NPR reporters from the BBC and other international affiliates have pretty much wiped out the hometown newspaper and its editor. A century ago, every town needed a newspaper as much as it needed a railroad, a grain elevator, and a general store. The editor was an important and influential member of the community. The newspaper kept a careful record of select aspects of the small-town quotidian, and offered printing for handbills, posters, and projects of a more literary nature.

Of course its stories and editorials reflected the biases of the editor, and thus of the small-town merchant-advertisers on whom the editor depended. Editors tended to favor the Republican Party, small business, and the upper class of white, Anglo-Saxon, native-born citizens. Church services, social gatherings, out-of-town trips, and business enterprises were regularly and extensively reported. Stories of small-town life, like Sinclair Lewis's *Main Street* and William Gass's *In the Heart of the Heart of the Country*, often incorporate gossipy excerpts from fictional local newspapers. However, historians researching small-town vice will find no material in small-town newspapers on the local pool halls, bars, and dance halls, except by way of admonitions against entering the same. Page Smith goes so far as to suggest that the values preached by many small-town newspapers were in fact not the town's: "They did not come out of the tradition of the noble farmer, nor out of the tradition of the Protestant ethic with its emphasis on 'calling,' on frugality, and self-denial. They came from the city." In *Main Street*, Carol Kennicott overhears a farmer explaining the exploitation of farmers by town merchants and the complicity of the town's newspaper, *The Dauntless*: "Gus, that's the way these towns work all the time. They pay what they want to for our wheat, but we pay what they want us to for their clothes. Stowbody and Dawson foreclose every mortgage they can, and put in tenant farmers. *The Dauntless* lies to us about the Nonpartisan League, the lawyers sting us, the machinery-dealers hate to carry us over a bad year, and then their daughters put on swell dresses and look at us as if we were a bunch of hoboes. Man, I'd like to burn this town!"

Still, the newspaper provides a remarkable resource for local historians, and it offered wonderful training for writers. Most great pre–World War II American writers got their training in newspaper reporting. News reporting taught them to pay attention to details, to get the facts straight, to listen to the voice of small-town citizens, and, perhaps most important, to write to an audience. (This is in sharp contrast to writers after the war, who learned their craft in M.F.A. programs and spent most of the rest of their lives working inside of and writing for the academic community.)

One such writer was Edna Ferber, who in 1902 began her career at age seventeen, working for three dollars a week in the office of the *Appleton (Wisconsin) Daily Crescent*. Appleton, population 15,000, supported a newspaper staff of six including the pressman and the young girl who would become famous as the author of *Showboat, Giant,* and *So Big* and winner of a Pulitzer Prize in Literature. Her brief stint in the newspaper office, at the bottom of the newsroom's pecking order, taught Ferber a lesson she never forgot: get the story and get it right: "What do you know? What do you know? What do you know? It is the greeting of the reporter the world over. I sometimes find myself saying it still."

---

o o o

Chapter Eight

There never had been a woman reporter in Appleton. The town, broad-minded though it was, put me down as definitely cuckoo. Not crazy, but strange. Big-town newspapers, such as the *Chicago Tribune* and the *Milwaukee Sentinel,* employed women on their editorial and reportorial staffs, but usually these were what is known as special or feature writers, or they conducted question-and-answer columns, advice to the lovelorn, society columns or woman's pages. But at seventeen on the *Appleton Crescent* I found myself covering a regular news beat like any man reporter. I often was embarrassed, sometimes frightened, frequently offended and offensive, but I enjoyed it, and knowing what I know today I wouldn't swap that year and a half of small-town newspaper reporting for any four years of college education. I'm a blank when it comes to Latin, I can't bound New York State, and I count on my fingers, but in those eighteen months I learned to read what lay behind the look that veiled people's faces, I learned how to sketch in human beings with a few rapid words, I learned to see, to observe, to remember; learned, in short, the first rules of writing. And I was the town scourge.

No wonder they found me a freak. In appearance I was short and plump, my abundant hair tied at the back of the neck in a bunch of short black wiry curls held by a wide black taffeta bow. My coiffure was further enhanced by a large black ribbon *chou* nestling in one corner of a massive pompadour.

My shirtwaist with its modish broad Gibson shoulder tuck was finished at the throat with a stiff white standing collar and a tie which should have been a four-in-hand but wasn't because I never could master that intricate knot. My Ryan High School class pin naïvely ornamented the tie. The whole effect was less that of a hard-boiled newspaper reporter than it is possible to convey. After six months of scouring the town it was suggested to me by Sam Ryan that perhaps I'd present a slightly more professional appearance if I'd put my hair up. I took the hint. The more sophisticated hairdress, together with my embonpoint, emphasized by the voluminous starched umbrella drawers, the petticoats, the boned corsets and ruffled corset covers of the day changed me from a roly-poly schoolgirl into what seemed to be a plump Midwestern young matron. Dieting hadn't become a fad. I liked good food and ate what I liked. Besides, to know the fashionable figure of that time one need only dig up a photograph of that famous stage beauty, Lillian Russell, curved like a roller coaster.

Ten years of haphazard omnivorous reading served me well now. Year in, year out, I had read at least a book a day. In one long Wisconsin summer afternoon, stretched in the hammock under the cherry tree, I could gallop through *The Three Musketeers*. Now, when I needed it, I found myself equipped with a fair vocabulary. The deep reach within oneself for that right first word with which to start the paragraph miraculously brought the word to the surface.

O. Henry, the writer of short stories with the snapper ending, was the model after which every young writer patterned himself. In the magazine room of the Appleton public library I always searched the periodicals for an O. Henry story. Now, unconsciously, I copied his style; but there was a strong dash of Dickens, too; and De Maupassant, Balzac, Mark Twain, The Duchess, and Robert W. Chambers were not slighted. Readers of the *Appleton Crescent* could not complain of faring meagerly at my hands. Much of it may have been hash—but it was good rich hash.

Those three dollars per week were earned. Eight in the morning found me at my desk. Lest that should have a rich and commanding sound I hasten to add that my desk was a shaky pine table in the darkest, smallest and dustiest corner of that dark, small and dusty room which constituted the *Crescent* editorial department. We worked underground, like moles. Why, in this sunny little Wisconsin town, Sam Ryan and his father James Ryan before him had chosen to install their newspaper plant in a basement, I can't imagine. Thrift, probably. There it was below the street level at the corner of College Avenue and Morrison Street. There were five little stone steps leading down to the front office. By the very way in which a reporter hurled himself down those steps you could sense whether he had a good story or not. As the windows, dust-dimmed, were on a level with the sidewalk, we in our little cave, as we sat at our typewriters, glimpsed the passing world only from the feet to the ribs. Though we saw no faces we learned to distinguish Banker Erb by his walk and his stomach; George Baldwin by his hands, always mysteriously gloved summer and winter; Mrs. Lawrence University Professor's wife Hotchkiss by her derrière; Earl Kenyon by the way he toed in.

Stuffed into the little room were five desks. We worked in a clattering heap. Sam Ryan, editor and proprietor, kinged it at a roll-top which was marked off from the rest of the room by a chicken-wire fence, heaven knows why, unless it was to prevent him from hurling paste pots at us, or infuriated reporters from throwing scissors at him. A difficult but distinctive fellow, Sam Ryan; an irascible bachelor, bald, sarcastic, fortyish. Fishing was his passion. He would let the presses wait to talk rods and flies with a chance visitor. The newspaper business irritated him. Outside the office he was kind, humorous, companionable. During working hours he lost his temper at the slightest provocation. It must have been indigestion or an inhibition or just rebellion at finding himself in a stuffy office instead of thigh deep in a trout stream. He was a fluent curser. When he discovered a typographical error or when something went wrong in the back shop the air crackled with his star-spangled profanity. Though a vast wastebasket stood at his elbow he had a habit of throwing newspaper exchanges, old copy paper, letters and envelopes under his desk, usually crushed into a vicious wad. When he began to scuffle his feet among these papers, slam objects on his desk and mutter imprecations we knew he was in a tantrum. He would push back his chair with a squeaking of casters and make for the back room, a sheet of galley proof streaming behind him like the tail of a fiery comet. To me he was sweetness and gentleness itself, under all his scathing irony and caustic comment. He taught me much about newspaper work and writing. Through those thick-lensed spectacles his myopic pale-blue eyes saw the town stripped to the skin. His was a mordant but tangy comment. He knew writing when he saw it in others. He himself couldn't write worth a cent.

At right angles with Sam's desk, her back to the street window, sat his sister, Miss Ivy Ryan, a shrewd and witty spinster. She was the office bookkeeper, she took want ads and all paid notices for lodge and society meetings, death announcements and the like. Short, plump, birdlike, Ivy Ryan was at once a pillar of strength and a source of quiet entertainment in that fusty little hive. She never lost her temper (God knows there wasn't room for two tempers in that box); she had you classified before you so much as turned the corner of the chicken-wire fence. Her shirtwaists were always exquisitely crisp and fresh, she wore armlets to protect her immaculate sleeves, her hair was done in a psyche knot on top of her head. She taught me volumes. Lodge sisters were clay in her hands. It was before the day of the Rotarians, and the town hummed with Foresters, Masons, Odd Fellows, Knights of Pythias, Woodmen, Knights of Columbus, Elks. These were forever having suppers, dances, picnics, initiations, parades, and many of them boasted a ladies' auxiliary. One or another of these seemed constantly to be laboriously descending the precarious stone steps into the basement office to place an announcement or an ad. They called it "inserting a squib." It is a phrase that infuriates all newspaper people. Nothing so offends a newspaper reporter as to hear his story spoken of as a "squib." "I saw your little squib in the paper today"—those are fighting words.

One ladies' auxiliary in particular was active beyond belief. No sooner had they finished with a Chicken-Pie Supper than they were waist deep in a Cake Sale. They were forever "inserting a squib." Deep-bosomed ample women in eyeglasses and sensible hats and durable coats, bent on relieving the tedium of child-rearing and housekeeping by these worthy social gatherings. This feminine adjunct of the male organization was called the Venus Lodge. Ivy Ryan took a wicked enjoyment in the name. She dubbed them Wenuses. In time we of the *Crescent* office designated as Wenuses all matrons of the big-bosomed, bustling and officious type. "She's a Wenus" meant a definite breed to us, no matter what her social standing. Ivy had a news nose keener than that of any reporter or editor in town. She knew the history, inside and out, of every household in Appleton, and no family skeleton so dry that she could not have ferreted out its bones if she had chosen. With all this she wasn't a gossip. Hers was a storehouse of knowledge which added just the proper soupçon of spice to her lively and sustaining conversation.

The remaining three desks were those of the city editor, Pomeroy; the reporter, Byron Beveridge; and myself. Pomeroy was an Appleton man. Very shortly after my coming to the paper he was replaced by a big-city importation, a shy nervous young fellow named John Meyer who had been a desk man on one of the Milwaukee papers. He was an easy blusher and we used to plot to make the scarlet rush up into his fine fair skin. He was too keenly trained for his job, really. He worked hard and well, but the whole setup irked him. He had a temper, too, and was of no mind to defer to Sam Ryan. The two would glare at each other, Sam would start to scuffle his feet among the papers under his desk, slam, mutter. There never was a cub reporter more blundering and naïve than I, but Meyer never lost his temper with me, and when he left to go back to Milwaukee some months later he made me heir to his job as Appleton correspondent of the *Milwaukee Journal*.

The reporter, Byron Beveridge, was a lanky cadaverous chap who had been a lieutenant in the Spanish-American War and was a great Company G boy and man-about-town. He wasn't a warm or even an engaging personality, but he knew everyone, everyone knew him, his lank stoop-shouldered figure ranged the town at a lope.

The printing shop and pressroom were separated from the front office only by a doorway, and the door never was closed. There were the type forms and tables, the Linotype machine (a new and fearsome invention to me), the small press, the big newspaper press, the boiler plate, the trays of type, all the paraphernalia that goes to make up the heart of a small-town newspaper. The front room is its head, but without the back room it could not function or even live. The Linotype and the small press went all day, for there the advertising was set up and printed, as well as handbills, programs, all the odds and ends classified as job printing. Mac, who ruled this domain, was the perfect example of the fictional printer. He had come in, a tramp printer, years before. He was given to periodic sprees, his brown hair curled over a mild brow, the corners of his drooping walrus mustache were stained with tobacco juice, his limp shirt seemed perennial. But his eye, though sometimes bleary, was infallible, and few if any shrdlus and etaoins marred the fair sequence of Mac's copy. His voice was soft, gentle, drawling, but he was boss of the print shop from the cat to the Linotype operator. Mac seldom talked but sometimes—rarely—he appeared in the front office, a drooping figure, with a piece of news by which he had come in some devious way. Standing at the side of the city editor's desk he would deliver himself of this information, looking mild and limply romantic. It always proved to be a bombshell.

Such was the make-up of the Appleton, Wisconsin, *Daily Crescent* office.

In the past thirty years all sorts of ex-newspaper men from Richard Harding Davis to Vincent Sheean and John Gunther have written about the lure of the reporter's life, the smell of printer's ink, the adventure of reporting. It all sounds slightly sentimental and silly, but it's true—or it was, at least, in my newspaper experience. To this day I can't smell the scent of white paper, wet ink, oil, hot lead, mucilage, tobacco and cats that goes to make up the peculiar odor of any newspaper plant, be it Appleton, Wisconsin, or Cairo, Egypt, that I don't get a pang of nostalgia for the old reporting days. "I was once a newspaper man myself" has come to be a fun phrase. But practically everyone seems to have been, or to have wanted to be, a newspaper reporter.

My handwriting at that time was (and still is) that of a ten-year-old who is not quite bright. I never had used a typewriter. The city editor, the printers, the Linotype operator rebelled at trying to decipher my penciled scrawls. Out of some back-room junk heap was retrieved a vintage Oliver typewriter which in appearance, sound and action resembled a broken-down lawn mower. On this I essayed painfully to pick my way with two forefingers and a thumb. After thirty years of typewriting daily for hours I still use this method, but necessity has taught me speed. As time went on it became impossible for me to think in writing terms unless my hands were on the typewriter keyboard. A pen or pencil is like a shovel in my fingers, and the signing of my name at the bottom of a letter or a check constitutes my longhand stint from one year's end to the other. On trains or shipboard I use a portable. A pencil spells creative paralysis for me, so strong is the habit of newspaper training.

The *Appleton Crescent* was my school and workshop from the time I turned seventeen until I was eighteen and a half. It was just long enough. The whole community may sift through a reporter's fingers in that time. It always has been my contention that when a newspaper man or woman has written that Christmas story three times for the same paper he should leave his job or reconcile himself to being a hack reporter forever. I may be flattering myself, but I think I can usually spot a man or woman who has been a newspaper reporter. I don't mean merely one who has dabbled in newspaper work, sending in vague "items," dreamy articles and amateurish out-of-town correspondence. I mean a reporter who has gone through the grind and tension of a year or more of actual leg work, getting the news, and getting it all, and getting it first if possible. The alumni of this school usually are alert, laconic, devastatingly observant, debunked and astringent. They are, too—paradoxically enough—likely to be at once hard-boiled and sentimental. The career of a newspaper reporter does not make for erudition, but through it one acquires a storehouse of practical and psychological knowledge, and a ghastly gift of telling the sham from the real, of being able to read and classify the human face, on or off guard.

It makes little difference whether the paper is large or small, the town one of fifteen thousand or a million five hundred thousand. There are—in the approximate words of the Harry Leon Wilson-Booth Tarkington play, *The Man from Home*—just as many kinds of people in Kokomo as there are in Paris.

Eight o'clock found me pounding down Morrison Street on my way to the office. Before eight-thirty the city editor had handed me my assignment sheet for the day. Dull-enough stuff, usually, for I was the least important cog in the *Crescent* office machine. When it came to news stories the city editor came first. He had his regular run—the juiciest one, of course. Next came Byron Beveridge. All the really succulent bits fell to them—the Elks Club up above Wharton's China Store on College Avenue, where the gay blades of the town assembled; Moriarty's pool shack, the Sherman House, the city jail, the fire-engine house, the Hub Clothing Store, the coroner's office, the mayor's office, Peter Thom's stationery and tobacco store, Little's Drug Store, the Sherman Barber Shop—these were the rich cupboards from which the real food of the day's news was dispensed. There you found the facts and gossip of business, politic, scandal, petty crime.

To me fell the crumbs. They gave me the daily courthouse run and I wondered why until I discovered that it was up in the Chute at the far end of town, a good mile and a half distant. You could take the bumpy little local street car, but that cost five cents one way, and the office furnished no car-fare for daily scheduled runs. Sixty cents a week was too serious a bite out of a three-dollar weekly wage. I walked it. I walked miles and miles and miles, daily. At the end of that first year my plumpness had melted almost to streamline proportions.

At eight in the morning, then, I turned in any bits of news that I had accumulated since closing time the day before. I scanned my assignment sheet. I rewrote any out-of-town exchange clippings given me. Then I took up the run that I had dug up for myself. Ferber's Store (The My Store it had unfortunately been called by my father, who had fancied that as an original and distinguished name for his place of business, poor dear) furnished me with some meager odds and ends, what with Martha Gresens, the clerk who lived on the other side of the tracks, Arthur Howe from up in the Chute and Julia Ferber whose bright brown eyes saw everything. I paid a daily morning call on the Pettibone-Peabody department store, the biggest shop in town. Jo Steele, the general manager, didn't like a reporter nosing around, taking his clerks' time and making a sort of gossip center of his place of business. The other merchants didn't like my coming in for news, either. I always felt like a sneak thief when I entered Pettibone's or Peerenboom's or Ingold's. Fortunately, old man Peabody, our chief merchant and the town swell, never knew of my existence. He rarely favored Appleton with his presence. A widower and an Anglophile, he was the only man in our town who wore spats, a walking stick, and a pince-nez with a broad black ribbon. It is characteristic of the town's broad-mindedness and tolerance that it neither ridiculed this affectation of his nor deferred to it. It was simply accepted as was my newspaper gallivanting and Doc Meeker's deafening red automobile—the first in Appleton—and the immoral goings-on of the town idiot, Minnie the Hatrack. Pettibone's was rather a rich vein. Irish witty Ella Malone in the woolens, Madonna-faced Tillie Whitman in the fancy goods and notions, the wasp-waisted James girls in the silks-by-the-yard were utter darlings. They would pause in their early-morning stock arranging to give me such innocuous Personal and Local items as came to their minds—a new sidewalk being built in front of St. Patrick's Catholic church, Mr. and Mrs. Ernie Wagner going to Madison for the graduation of their son Ernest at the University of Wisconsin. Then, with a swift glance around, they would hastily, and *sotto voce,* impart a smart bit of gossip that would send me off hotfoot on the scent of a real story. A man reporter wouldn't have been permitted to enter these places of business as part of his daily news run. They were too kindhearted to throw out a girl.

It was all to be grist for my mill in the years to come, but I didn't know it then. My first short story, entitled "The Homely Heroine," starts with a brief description of the clerks in Pettibone's Dry Goods Store, and I used its atmosphere and that of Ferber's My Store for parts of any number of the Emma McChesney stories.

Another source of news, incredibly enough, was the gray stone monastery that nestled among the trees near the ravine next to the German Catholic church. My buddy was Father Basilius—Father Basil for short. He was the unofficial go-getter and publicity expert for the church. Such information as he gave me was church and parish stuff, and he was charming about it, with a real nose for news. I called at the monastery door twice a week. A plumpish brown-bearded man, Father Basil, peering with very nearsighted eyes through thick spectacles; his brown habit was tied with a stout brown ropecord about his ample waist, and his bare feet were thrust into sandals. He and I would sit on the bench under the chestnut tree in the courtyard and have a good gossip, very cozy and comfortable. What do you know, Father Basil? Waddyou know?

What do you know? What do you know? What do you know? It is the greeting of the reporter the world over. I sometimes find myself saying it still. When I hear it in greeting—whether from a senator, a millionaire or a tramp—I know that that one has been a newspaper man himself.

The courthouse, the county jail up in Chute at the other end of town, these weren't nourishing news sources, but I had to cover them. Such criminals as were housed in the tree-shaded county jail were there for crimes which already had been disposed of as news. Courthouse records were made up of dry bits such as real-estate transfers in the town and the near-by farm districts. There was nothing very exhilarating about jotting down items such as "State of Wisconsin, Winnebago County, Such-and-Such Township, sixty acres northeast section, etc." But having plodded the mile and a half up there I gleaned what I could. Bailiffs, clerks, courthouse hangers-on were a roughish tobacco-chewing crew with little enough to do. I was fair game for them. As I clattered up and down the long corridors paved with tiles, in and out of the land record office, the county clerk's office, here and there, making a lot of noise with my hurried determined step, one of the men in a group called out to me in greeting one morning, "Hi, Boots!" And Boots I remained as long as I worked on the *Appleton Crescent*.

I ranged the town, ferreting out corners too obscure or too obvious for the loftier glance of Meyer or Beveridge. Sometimes rich morsels repaid me for my pains. If space permitted I was allowed such feature or special stories as struck my fancy. This sort of half-imaginative writing turned out to be excellent practice for later fiction-writing use. I raked up tear-jerkers about the Poor Farm at the edge of town; when Barnum & Bailey's circus came to town I spent the day in the back tents with the performers. I ate dinner with the Living Skeleton, the Fat Lady, the clowns and the trapeze artists, and very good it was, too. The tents were miracles of cleanliness, the circus people friendly and warmhearted, my story was the trite and shopworn stuff about the bareback rider in the pink tights and spangles sitting in her tent just before the show sewing a fine seam on her baby's dress or mending her lion-tamer husband's socks, or some such matter. But it was all new to me, and true, so perhaps it had something of freshness, as well. . . .

Ours was, of course, an afternoon paper. The rattle and clank of the Linotype machine grew more feverish as noon passed. It had a fascination for
me, that strange and talented contraption, and to this day I stand in awe of
it. There was, for me, something human about the way in which it carried
the leads, picked them up in its long skinny arm, brought them over,
dropped them out of its metal fingers, deposited them neatly with a rattle
and clank of relief, then stretched forth for more.

By two-thirty or three the paper was put to bed, the press was rolling. The
chatter of the Linotype, the locking of the forms, the thump-thump of the
press were plain in our ears as we sat at our typewriters in the front office,
for the open door between us and the back shop made one big room of the
whole. Townspeople slammed and scuffed up and down the stone steps, in
and out of the office, all day long. I early learned that the big story isn't the
one that is brought to you. The things people want you to print in your paper usually are the things of interest to few besides themselves. One of the
angles that make newspaper reporting so chancy, exhilarating and absorbing is the chase. The person you want most to talk to frequently doesn't
want to talk to you, though it is an amazing fact that almost anyone, properly approached, will tell you almost anything. Half the people I encountered preferred not to have me discover the very thing I wanted most to
know. It wasn't long before I learned, from that quick appraising look at my
victim's face, to gauge his character and to shape my approach in accor-
dance. If he didn't want to talk he must be made to talk by wheedling, brib-
ing, cajoling, threatening, playing for sympathy. Roughly, the approach was
one of these:

1. I understand your reluctance to talk about this. But I have to turn in
some kind of story. I can't go back to the office without it. Don't you think
we'd better get it straight from you?

2. It's going to be in the newspapers anyway. Take my advice. Talk.

3. I wish you'd help me out on this. If I come back without a story I'll
lose my job.

4. I think—if you don't mind my saying so—that you've taken a wonderful stand in this matter. I'd like to be able to write it from your viewpoint,
because it seems to me to be the only one worth while.

5. Perhaps if you'll tell me all about this, frankly, we can help you.

If all this sounds revolting, it is as nothing compared to coming into the
office without your story.

During this year and a half of small-town cub reporting I formed the
habit of trained observation and memory. A good reporter sees and remembers at a glance. It is called the camera eye. If it is a supercamera eye it not
only sees, it gets a sort of X-ray impression. That kind of reporter gives
vitality to bare incidents. Perhaps I was helped by the fact that we, as a fam-

ily at home, were given to quick appraisal and decision. Perhaps it is a
Jewish trait. People who must walk in the midst of crowded and dangerous
traffic learn to see with the back of the head as well as the front. A sixth
sense develops, for protection.

I learned to see and remember details without taking notes. If I had to
take them it was done as surreptitiously as possible in the presence of the
person being interviewed, or after I had left and was on my way back to the
office. A trained reporter, in an interview, takes notes only if he must. It is
only on the stage that a reporter whips out a notebook and begins to scribble feverishly. Most newspaper people do their note-taking on a little folded
sheaf of yellow copy paper grabbed up on their way out of the office. If he
must use this homemade pad he usually lets his pencil scrawl unguided, his
gaze meeting the eye of the person speaking, and responding to it. To one
being interviewed there is something disconcerting about the sight of that
busy pencil traveling over the blank paper. His speech hesitates, falters, the
flow of revelation ceases. People tell you more when you are looking at them
with understanding or sympathy. It is a kind of hypnotism. After all, I was
not yet eighteen, not even fully grown, my mind and body were elastic. I
learned to remember whole speeches as I heard them, the phrases falling
into the proper sequence. I saw and remembered the location of doors, windows, furniture, small objects. The eye recorded the look on a face, the turn
of a hand, the style and set of clothing, the cadence of a voice. It wasn't done
consciously. Necessity brought it about. Fortunately there was little nervous or physical strain connected with working on a paper in a town the size
of Appleton. But the *Milwaukee Journal* did affect my general health for my
lifetime.

The reporter's habit of hanging around the office after hours now insidiously began. I stayed at my typewriter or sat talking when the day's grist
had long been on the press. In the evening I couldn't resist dropping into the
little basement office if I came within a block of it. The yellow light glowed
cozily through the grimy window level with the street. Someone was always
at work down there, bent over a typewriter or a desk—Beveridge or Meyer
or Ryan. . . .

It was legitimate newspaper ethics to get your story by any means short
of murder. But having got it, it must be proof against dispute or correction.
That early training now leaves me gasping at the antics of today's newspaper columnists. People's personal lives, private plans, moral history, future hopes, dearest secrets, innermost thoughts are seized on, embellished
or completely fabricated without the consent or even the knowledge of the
victim. In the naïve prewar period such a fellow would have been fired; not
only fired but no paper would have hired him. The one example of this type
of garbage dispenser was a big-bellied whiskered dodo named Colonel Mann
of New York. He ran a scandal sheet called "Town Topics" and lived on

blackmail. How he came by his military title no one seems to know, but from all accounts horsewhips writhed about his head like black-snakes; and if all the outraged victims of his method who threatened to horsewhip him actually did so he must have been striped with welts like a zebra. Perhaps George Ade, Bert Leston Taylor, Ring Lardner, Eugene Field would make dull fare for column readers today.

Newspapers were not models of integrity; but certainly competition had caused no such havoc of journalistic disintegration as can be encountered today. You advertised in a newspaper or in a magazine. There was no radio, there were few motion pictures. The advertiser could withhold his patronage, but where could he go? Certainly he often influenced a paper's policy, but he rarely dictated it, as now.

What there was to see in Appleton I saw. A lively town, decent, literate. Automobiles were beginning to be seen on the streets, scaring the farmers' horses into fits. Appleton traveled, it went to Chicago for the opera (Grand Opera it always was called) at the Auditorium; it went to Milwaukee to do important shopping and to see a play, perhaps, at the Davidson Theater. It was chic to take the 7:52 morning train, eastbound. In its green velvet upholstered parlor car sat the well-to-do of the rich little paper-mill towns along the Fox River Valley. They knew the conductor by name, they knew the porter wasn't called George. They had had their good solid breakfasts, the men read the *Milwaukee Sentinel*. The women wore quiet well-made clothes and smart—but not too smart—hats. They knew what was fashionable and bought it. At home they prided themselves on knowing what was being served and served it; their linen and silver and glass and jewelry were good. They read; they educated their children at the University of Wisconsin or at eastern schools. They went to Europe if they could manage it, and that didn't in the least mean that they were wealthy. The streets of London, Paris, Rome, Dublin, Edinburgh and Munich were known to Appleton school-ma'ams who had achieved out of their earnings the five or six hundred dollars necessary for the trip in those days. Certainly no other nation, in the half-century before the World War, could produce a traveling cross section such as America showed; and the thriving little town of Appleton, Wisconsin, was representative of this urge to be on the move. Travel—even European travel out of America—was by no means confined to the wealthy or the middling well-to-do. School teachers, artisans, small merchants, laboring men—all the countless hundreds of thousands who later were to invest their earnings in new-model automobiles now lavishly laid them at the feet and thresholds of European statues, cathedrals, museums, ruins and hotelkeepers.

It was a comfortable way of life. Women—and most men—paid not the slightest attention to politics. As for European politics and the problems of the countries of Europe, Americans would no more have dreamed of interfering with these than they would have contemplated sinking the entire continent. Europe was simply something on the other side of the Atlantic. You visited it if you were lucky; you learned about it at school. Europe was history. Europeans were people who came to America because they didn't like it over there. Appleton was full of German, Bohemian and Irish parents whose children were thorough second-generation Americans. Europe was as remote to these children as to any American whose American ancestry went back two hundred years. . . .

Now Meyer, the little blond city editor, left for his old job in Milwaukee, fed up with his small-town experience. He turned over to me his job as Appleton correspondent for the *Milwaukee Journal*. It became my duty to telegraph or telephone the briefest possible line on any local happening of consequence. This was called querying the paper. If they found the story of sufficient importance they would telephone or telegraph an order for the number of words they thought the story rated. Less immediate stuff I mailed in on the afternoon southbound train. Semi-feature stuff I pasted up and mailed in from time to time. I felt enormously important and professional. Among other things the Lawrence University football games had to be covered, as well as the Ryan High School games. This was a tough assignment for a girl. It had to be caught play by play. At first I was guilty of using such feminine adjectives as splendid and lovely, but after a bit I caught on to the sport writer's lingo, and I don't think that the *Milwaukee Journal* readers found the Appleton football correspondence too sissy.

Paul Hunter was the new city editor, imported from out of town. A moist, loose-hung man, eyeglassed, loquacious. He didn't like me. He didn't want a self-dramatizing Girl Reporter around the place. He began a systematic campaign. My run was cut down. My stories were slashed. My suggestions were ignored or pooh-poohed. I was in the doghouse. Midway through my summer vacation of two weeks I got word that I needn't return. I was fired. I can see why Hunter didn't want a girl around the place when a second man reporter could cover more varied ground. My rather embellished style of writing had no appeal for Hunter. He wanted the news and no nonsense.

The bottom had dropped right out of my world and I was left dangling in space.

The novel *Cimarron*, written in 1929, contains a vast amount of detailed description of a small-town newspaper office. The paper started by my hero, Yancey Cravat, in the land-rush village called Osage, following the famous run into the Indian Territory, was named the *Oklahoma Wigwam*. The paper and the town never existed except in my imagination, nor did Yancey Cravat and his wife, Sabra. But the newspaper stuff was newspaper stuff true of any small American town. I needed only to reach back into my mind and pull the Appleton, Wisconsin, *Crescent* days out of my memory. Mac is the Jesse Rickey of Cimarron. Sabra is partly (sorry) my own dramatizing of myself. The cases of pied type, the hand press, the little job press, the back room, the fusty little front office—all these bits of newspaper publishing description I gleaned during my Appleton reporter days.

I had been fired just in time, but I didn't know it then. My heart was broken.

That summer I tried to interest myself in Appleton life (as a layman. I! I who had once walked so proud as a newspaper reporter!). But the world was flat and flavorless.

In another six months I would be nineteen. Withered old age stared me in the face.

At the very nadir of this despair there appeared a message timed like a last-minute reprieve in a bad melodrama. It was from Henry Campbell, the managing editor of the *Milwaukee Journal*. He asked me to come to work on the *Journal* immediately at fifteen dollars a week, and to call him on the telephone in Milwaukee at once.

In order to telephone long-distance one had to go to the main office of the telephone company. I held the telegram in my hand. The family sat there, looking at me—my father, my mother, my sister. There is a curiously strong bond in Jewish families. They cling together. Jewish parents are possessive, Jewish sons and daughters are filial to the point of sentimentality. I wonder now how I ever had the courage to leave that blind invalid. It takes real courage to be selfish. Until now we had clung together, we four Ferbers. I am certain I never should have written if I had not gone. I was wrung by an agony of pity as I looked at my father's face.

"You go on, Pete," he said. "You go if you want to."

It is lucky that youth is ruthless, or the work of the world never would be done.

I walked down to the telephone company's office and put in my call for the *Journal*'s managing editor. It took some minutes to get him. As I waited in the booth, my heart beating fast, a townsman who had come into the office stood chatting with the chief operator.

"That's Ferber's girl, isn't it?"

"Yeh."

"She the one is a reporter?"

"Yeh, she's calling up Milwaukee, the *Journal* there, she says they want her to go to work for them in Milwaukee."

The other man ruminated. "Wonder a girl like that wouldn't try to do something decent, like teaching school."

Inventions Re-making Leisure

FROM *Middletown*

ROBERT S. LYND AND HELEN MERRELL LYND

I N THE LATE NINETEENTH CENTURY the average American citizen would rarely travel more than one hundred miles from the place of his or her birth during his or her lifetime. The majority of Americans lived on farms and in the thousands of small towns that provided their connection to the outside world. These tight-knit communities also provided a haven from the outside world. The political and economic systems were locally based and relatively self-sufficient. These agricultural societies, the historian Robert Wiebe writes, were essentially semi-autonomous "island communities" that provided essential services. In 1880 the average member of one of these isolated midwestern communities would bump into a national corporation only infrequently, perhaps the most common connection occurring when the two-day-old Chicago newspaper arrived on the train or when a purchase of Standard Oil kerosene was made at the general store so that the family could read the Bible after the sun went down.

By the 1920s, however, these island communities had dissolved, already swallowed up in the emerging mass markets that were national in scope. Everywhere one turned, the influence and power of the outside world were evident. This was no more dramatically demonstrated than in the invasion of Main Street early in the new century by what Indiana farmers initially denounced as the "devil wagon" because it frightened horses along the dusty town streets. But the automobile soon won over all but the most reactionary of residents. By 1930 some 29 million automobiles and trucks prowled the streets and roads of America, nearly one vehicle for every four American citizens. The automobile opened new horizons for the farmer and the resident of the towns; the town merchants, who had for decades fought competition from the big cities in the form of catalogue sales, now saw their domination of the local markets severely threatened.

The automobile was only one of many technological innovations whose impact was felt during the 1920s. The arrival of electricity not only brought the convenience of refrigerators, vacuum sweepers, and myriad other labor-saving devices, it also ushered in the new age of entertainment that largely originated in Hollywood and New York City and introduced to Main Street the values and trends of the big city. The following selection is taken from

the classic study by cultural anthropologists Robert S. Lynd and Helen Merrell Lynd that resulted from their detailed examination of life during the
1920s in "Middletown," a "typical" midwestern community that was, in
fact, Muncie, Indiana.

o o o

Although lectures, reading, music, and art are strongly intrenched in
Middletown's traditions, it is none of these that would first attract the attention of a newcomer watching Middletown at play.

"Why on earth do you need to study what's changing this country?" said
a lifelong resident and shrewd observer of the Middle West. "I can tell you
what's happening in just four letters: a-u-t-o!"

In 1890 the possession of a pony was the wildest flight of a Middletown
boy's dreams. In 1924 a Bible class teacher in a Middletown school concluded her teaching of the Creation: "And now, children, is there any of
these animals that God created that man could have got along without?"
One after another of the animals from goat to mosquito was mentioned and
for some reason rejected; finally, "The horse!" said one boy triumphantly,
and the rest of the class agreed. Ten or twelve years ago a new horse fountain was installed at the corner of the Courthouse square; now it remains
dry during most of the blazing heat of a Mid-Western summer, and no one
cares. The "horse culture" of Middletown has almost disappeared.[1] . . .

The first real automobile appeared in Middletown in 1900. About 1906
it was estimated that "there are probably 200 in the city and county." At the
close of 1923 there were 6,221 passenger cars in the city, one for every 6.1
persons, or roughly two for every three families.[2] Of these 6,221 cars, 41
percent were Fords; 54 percent of the total were cars of models of 1920 or
later, and 17 percent models earlier than 1917.[3] These cars average a bit over
5,000 miles a year.[4] For some of the workers and some of the business class,
use of the automobile is a seasonal matter, but the increase in surfaced roads
and in closed cars is rapidly making the car a year-round tool for leisure-
time as well as getting-a-living activities. As, at the turn of the century, business class people began to feel apologetic if they did not have a telephone,
so ownership of an automobile has now reached the point of being an accepted essential of normal living.

Into the equilibrium of habits which constitutes for each individual some
integration in living has come this new habit, upsetting old adjustments,
and blasting its way through such accustomed and unquestioned dicta as
"Rain or shine, I never miss a Sunday morning at church"; "A high school
boy does not need much spending money"; "I don't need exercise, walking
to the office keeps me fit"; "I wouldn't think of moving out of town and be-

ing so far from my friends"; "Parents ought always to know where their children are." The newcomer is most quickly and amicably incorporated into those regions of behavior in which men are engaged in doing impersonal, matter-of-fact things; much more contested is its advent where emotionally charged sanctions and taboos are concerned. No one questions the use of the auto for transporting groceries, getting to one's place of work or to the golf course, in place of the porch for "cooling off after supper" on a hot summer evening; however much the activities concerned with getting a living may be altered by the fact that a factory can draw from workmen within a radius of forty-five miles, or however much old labor union men resent the intrusion of this new alternate way of spending an evening,[5] these things are hardly major issues. But when auto riding tends to replace the traditional call in the family parlor as a way of approach between the unmarried, "the home is endangered," and all-day Sunday motor trips are a "threat against the church"; it is in the activities concerned with the home and religion that the automobile occasions the greatest emotional conflicts.

Group-sanctioned values are disturbed by the inroads of the automobile upon the family budget.[6] A case in point is the not uncommon practice of mortgaging a home to buy an automobile. Data on automobile ownership were secured from 123 working class families. Of these, sixty have cars. Forty-one of the sixty own their homes. Twenty-six of these forty-one families have mortgages on their homes. Forty of the sixty-three families who do not own a car own their homes. Twenty-nine of these have mortgages on their homes. Obviously other factors are involved in many of Middletown's mortgages. That the automobile does represent a real choice in the minds of some at least is suggested by the acid retort of one citizen to the question about car ownership: "No, sir, we've *not* got a car. *That's* why we've got a home." According to an officer of a Middletown automobile financing company, 75 to 90 percent of the cars purchased locally are bought on time payment, and a working man earning $35.00 a week frequently plans to use one week's pay each month as payment for his car.

The automobile has apparently unsettled the habit of careful saving for some families. "Part of the money we spend on the car would go to the bank, I suppose," said more than one working class wife. A business man explained his recent inviting of social oblivion by selling his car by saying: "My car, counting depreciation and everything, was costing mighty nearly $100.00 a month, and my wife and I sat down together the other night and just figured that we're getting along, and if we're to have anything later on, we've just got to begin to save." The "moral" aspect of the competition between the automobile and certain accepted expenditures appears in the remark of another business man, "An automobile is a luxury, and no one has a right to one if he can't afford it. I haven't the slightest sympathy for any one who is out of work if he owns a car."

Men in the clothing industry are convinced that automobiles are bought at the expense of clothing,[7] and the statements of a number of the working class wives bear this out:

"We'd rather do without clothes than give up the car," said one mother of nine children. "We used to go to his sister's to visit, but by the time we'd get the children shoed and dressed there wasn't any money left for carfare. Now no matter how they look, we just poke 'em in the car and take 'em along."

"We don't have no fancy clothes when we have the car to pay for," said another. "The car is the only pleasure we have."

Even food may suffer:

"I'll go without food before I'll see us give up the car," said one woman emphatically, and several who were out of work were apparently making precisely this adjustment.

Twenty-one of the twenty-six families owning a car for whom data on bathroom facilities happened to be secured live in homes without bathtubs. Here we obviously have a new habit cutting in ahead of an older one and slowing down the diffusion of the latter.[8]

Meanwhile, advertisements pound away at Middletown people with the tempting advice to spend money for automobiles for the sake of their homes and families:

"Hit the trail to better times!" says one such advertisement.

Another depicts a gray-haired banker lending a young couple the money to buy a car and proffering the friendly advice: "Before you can save money, you first must make money. And to make it you must have health, contentment, and full command of all your resources. . . . I have often advised customers of mine to buy cars, as I felt that the increased stimulation and opportunity of observation would enable them to earn amounts equal to the cost of their cars."

Many families feel that an automobile is justified as an agency holding the family group together. "I never feel as close to my family as when we are all together in the car," said one business class mother, and one or two spoke of giving up County Club membership or other recreations to get a car for this reason. "We don't spend anything on recreation except for the car. We save every place we can and put the money into the car. It keeps the family together," was an opinion voiced more than once. Sixty-one percent of 337 boys and 60 percent of 423 girls in the three upper years of the high school say that they motor more often with their parents than without them.[9]

But this centralizing tendency of the automobile may be only a passing phase; sets in the other direction are almost equally prominent. "Our daughters [eighteen and fifteen] don't use our car much because they are always with somebody else in their car when we go out motoring," lamented one business class mother. And another said, "The two older children [eighteen and sixteen] never go out when the family motors. They always have something else on." "In the nineties we were much more together," said another wife. "People brought chairs and cushions out of the house and sat on the lawn evenings. We rolled out a strip of carpet and put cushions on the porch step to take care of the unlimited overflow of neighbors that dropped by. We'd sit out so all evening. The younger couples perhaps would wander off for half an hour to get a soda but come back to join in the informal singing or listen while somebody strummed a mandolin or guitar." "What on earth *do* you want me to do? Just sit around home all evening!" retorted a popular high school girl of today when her father discouraged her going out motoring for the evening with a young blade in a rakish car waiting at the curb. The fact that 348 boys and 382 girls in the three upper years of the high school placed "use of the automobile" fifth and fourth respectively in a list of twelve possible sources of disagreement between them and their parents suggests that this may be an increasing decentralizing agent.

An earnest teacher in a Sunday School class of working class boys and girls in their late teens was winding up the lesson on the temptations of Jesus: "These three temptations summarize all the temptations we encounter today: physical comfort, fame, and wealth. Can you think of any temptation we have today that Jesus didn't have?" "Speed!" rejoined one boy. The unwanted interruption was quickly passed over. But the boy had mentioned a tendency underlying one of the four chief infringements of group laws in Middletown today, and the manifestations of Speed are not confined to "speeding." "Auto Polo next Sunday!!" shouts the display advertisement of an amusement park near the city. "It's motor insanity—too fast for the movies!" The boys who have cars "step on the gas," and those who haven't cars sometimes steal them: "The desire of youth to step on the gas when it has no machine of its own," said the local press, "is considered responsible for the theft of the greater part of the [154] automobiles stolen from [Middletown] during the past year."[10]

The threat which the automobile presents to some anxious parents is suggested by the fact that of thirty girls brought before the juvenile court in the twelve months preceding September 1, 1924, charged with "sex crimes," for whom the place where the offense occurred was given in the records, nineteen were listed as having committed the offense in an automobile.[11] Here again the automobile appears to some as an "enemy" of the home and society.

Sharp, also, is the resentment aroused by the elbowing new device when it interferes with old-established religious habits. The minister trying to change people's behavior in desired directions through the spoken word must compete against the strong pull of the open road strengthened by endless printed "copy" inciting to travel. Preaching to 200 people on a hot, sunny Sunday in midsummer on "The Supreme Need of Today," a leading Middletown minister denounced "automobilitis—the thing those people have who go off motoring on Sunday instead of going to church. If you want to use your car on Sunday, take it out Sunday morning and bring some shut-ins to church and Sunday School; then in the afternoon, if you choose, go out and worship God in the beauty of nature—but don't neglect to worship Him indoors too." This same month there appeared in the *Saturday Evening Post*, reaching approximately one family in six in Middletown, a two-page spread on the automobile as an "enricher of life," quoting "a bank president in a Mid-Western city" as saying, "A man who works six days a week and spends the seventh on his own doorstep certainly will not pick up the extra dimes in the great thoroughfares of life." "Some sunny Sunday very soon," said another two-page spread in the *Post*, "just drive an Overland up to your door—tell the family to hurry the packing and get aboard—and be off with smiles down the nearest road—free, loose, and happy—bound for green wonderlands." Another such advertisement urged Middletown to "Increase Your Week-End Touring Radius."[12] If we except the concentrated group pressure of war time, never perhaps since the days of the camp-meeting have the citizens of this community been subjected to such a powerfully focused stream of habit diffusion. To get the full force of this appeal, one must remember that the nearest lakes or hills are one hundred miles from Middletown in either direction and that an afternoon's motoring brings only mile upon mile of level stretches like Middletown itself. . . .

Like the automobile, the motion picture is more to Middletown than simply a new way of doing an old thing; it has added new dimensions to the city's leisure. To be sure, the spectacle-watching habit was strong upon Middletown in the nineties. Whenever they had a chance people turned out to a "show," but chances were relatively fewer. Fourteen times during January, 1890, for instance, the Opera House was opened for performances ranging from *Uncle Tom's Cabin* to *The Black Crook*, before the paper announced that "there will not be any more attractions at the Opera House for nearly two weeks." In July there were no "attractions"; a half dozen were scattered through August and September; there were twelve in October.[13]

Today nine motion picture theaters operate from 1 to 11 P.M. seven days a week summer and winter; four of the nine give three different programs a week, the other five having two a week; thus twenty-two different programs with a total of over 300 performances are available to Middletown every week in the year. In addition, during January, 1923, there were three plays in Middletown and four motion pictures in other places than the regular theaters, in July three plays and one additional movie, in October two plays and one movie.

About two and three-fourths times the city's entire population attended the nine motion picture theaters during the month of July, 1923, the "valley" month of the year, and four and one-half times the total population in the "peak" month of December.[14] Of 395 boys and 457 girls in the three upper years of the high school who stated how many times they had attended the movies in "the last seven days," a characteristic week in mid-November, 30 percent of the boys and 39 percent of the girls had not attended, 31 and 29 percent respectively had been only once, 22 and 21 percent respectively two times, 10 and 7 percent three times, and 4 and 7 percent four or more times. According to the housewives interviewed regarding the custom in their own families, in three of the forty business class families interviewed and in thirty-eight of the 122 working class families no member "goes at all" to the movies.[15] One family in ten in each group goes as an entire family once a week or oftener; the two parents go together without their children once a week or oftener in four business class families (one in ten), and in two working class families (one in sixty); in fifteen business class families and in thirty-eight working class families the children were said by their mothers to go without their parents one or more times weekly.

In short, the frequency of movie attendance of high school boys and girls is about equal, business class families tend to go more often than do working class families, and children of both groups attend more often without their parents than do all the individuals or other combinations of family members put together. The decentralizing tendency of the movies upon the family, suggested by this last, is further indicated by the fact that only 21 percent of 337 boys and 33 percent of 423 girls in the three upper years of the high school go to the movies more often with their parents than without them. On the other hand, the comment is frequently heard in Middletown that time formerly spent in lodges, saloons, and unions is now being spent in part at the movies, at least occasionally with other members of the family.[16] Like the automobile and radio, the movies, by breaking up leisure time into an individual, family, or small group affair, represent a counter movement to the trend toward organization so marked in clubs and other leisure-time pursuits.

How is life being quickened by the movies for the youngsters who bulk so large in the audiences, for the punch press operator at the end of his working day, for the wife who goes to a "picture" every week or so "while he stays home with the children," for those business class families who habitually attend?

"Go to a motion picture . . . and let yourself go," Middletown reads in a *Saturday Evening Post* advertisement. "Before you know it you are *living* the story—laughing, loving, hating, struggling, winning! All the adventure, all the romance, all the excitement you lack in your daily life are in——Pictures. They take you completely out of yourself into a wonderful new world. . . . Out of the cage of everyday existence! If only for an afternoon or an evening—escape!"

The program of the five cheaper houses is usually a "Wild West" feature, and a comedy; of the four better houses, one feature film, usually a "society" film but frequently Wild West or comedy, one short comedy, or if the feature is a comedy, an educational film (e.g., *Laying an Ocean Cable* or *Making a Telephone*), and a news film. In general, people do not go to the movies to be instructed; the Yale Press series of historical films, as noted earlier, were a flat failure and the local exhibitor discontinued them after the second picture. As in the case of the books it reads, comedy, heart interest, and adventure compose the great bulk of what Middletown enjoys in the movies. Its heroes, according to the manager of the leading theater, are, in the order named, Harold Lloyd, comedian; Gloria Swanson, heroine in modern society films; Thomas Meighan, hero in modern society films; Colleen Moore, ingénue; Douglas Fairbanks, comedian and adventurer; Mary Pickford, ingénue; and Norma Talmadge, heroine in modern society films. Harold Lloyd comedies draw the largest crowds. "Middletown is amusement hungry," says the opening sentence in a local editorial; at the comedies Middletown lives for an hour in a happy sophisticated make-believe world that leaves it, according to the advertisement of one film, "happily convinced that Life is very well worth living."

Next largest are the crowds which come to see the sensational society films. The kind of vicarious living brought to Middletown by these films may be inferred from such titles as: *"Alimony*—brilliant men, beautiful jazz babies, champagne baths, midnight revels, petting parties in the purple dawn, all ending in one terrific smashing climax that makes you gasp"; *Married Flirts*—Husbands: Do you flirt? Does your wife always know where you are? Are you faithful to your vows? *Wives:* What's your hubby doing? Do you know? Do you worry? Watch out for *Married Flirts."* So fast do these flow across the silver screen that, e.g., at one time *The Daring Years, Sinner in Silk, Women Who Give,* and *The Price She Paid* were all running synchronously, and at another *"Name the Man*—a story of betrayed womanhood," *Rouged Lips,* and *The Queen of Sin.*[17] While Western "action" films and a million-dollar spectacle like *The Covered Wagon* or *The Hunchback of Notre Dame* draw heavy houses, and while managers lament that there are too few of the popular comedy films, it is the film with burning "heart interest," that packs Middletown's motion picture houses week after week. Young Middletown enters eagerly into the vivid experience of *Flaming Youth:* "neckers, petters, white kisses, red kisses, pleasure-mad daughters, sensation-craving mothers, by an author who didn't dare sign his name; the truth bold, naked, sensational"—so ran the press advertisement—under the spell of the powerful conditioning medium of pictures presented with music and all possible heightening of the emotional content, and the added factor of sharing this experience with a "date" in a darkened room. Meanwhile, *Down to the Sea in Ships,* a costly spectacle of whaling adventure, failed at the leading theater "because," the exhibitor explained, "the whale is really the hero in the film and there wasn't enough 'heart interest' for the women." . . .

Some high school teachers are convinced that the movies are a powerful factor in bringing about the "early sophistication" of the young and relaxing of social taboos. One working class mother welcomes the movies as an aid in child rearing, saying, "I send my daughter because a girl has to learn the ways of the world somehow and the movies are a good safe way." The judge of the juvenile court lists the movies as one of the "big four" causes of local juvenile delinquency,[18] believing that the disregard of group mores by the young is definitely related to the witnessing week after week of fictitious behavior sequences that habitually link the taking of long chances and the happy ending. While the community attempts to safeguard its schools from commercially intent private hands, this powerful new educational instrument, which has taken Middletown unawares, remains in the hands of a group of men—an ex-peanut-stand proprietor, an ex-bicycle racer and race promoter, and so on—whose primary concern is making money.[19] . . .

Though less widely diffused as yet than automobile owning or movie attendance, the radio nevertheless is rapidly crowding its way in among the necessities in the family standard of living. Not the least remarkable feature of this new invention is its accessibility. Here skill and ingenuity can in part offset money as an open sesame to swift sharing of the enjoyments of the wealthy. With but little equipment one can call the life of the rest of the world from the air, and this equipment can be purchased piecemeal at the ten-cent store. Far from being simply one more means of passive enjoyment, the radio has given rise to much ingenious manipulative activity. In a count of representative sections of Middletown, it was found that, of 303 homes in twenty-eight blocks in the "best section" of town, inhabited almost entirely by the business class, 12 percent had radios; of 518 workers' homes in sixty-four blocks, 6 percent had radios.[20]

As this new tool is rolling back the horizons of Middletown for the bank clerk or the mechanic sitting at home and listening to a Philharmonic concert or a sermon by Dr. Fosdick, or to President Coolidge bidding his father good night on the eve of election,[21] and as it is wedging its way with the movie, the automobile, and other new tools into the twisted mass of habits that are living for the 38,000 people of Middletown, readjustments necessarily occur. Such comments as the following suggest their nature:

"I use time evenings listening in that I used to spend in reading."
   "The radio is hurting movie going, especially Sunday evening." (From a leading movie exhibitor.)
   "I don't use my car so much any more. The heavy traffic makes it less fun. But I spend seven nights a week on my radio. We hear fine music from Boston." (From a shabby man of fifty.)

"Sundays I take the boy to Sunday School and come straight home and tune in. I get first an eastern service, then a Cincinnati one. Then there's nothing doing till about two-thirty, when I pick up an eastern service again and follow 'em across the country till I wind up with California about ten-thirty. Last night I heard a ripping sermon from Westminster Church somewhere in California. We've no preachers here that can compare with any of them."

"One of the bad features of radio," according to a teacher, "is that children stay up late at night and are not fit for school next day."

"We've spent close on to $100 on our radio, and we built it ourselves at that," commented one of the worker's wives. "Where'd we get the money? Oh, out of our savings, like everybody else."

In the flux of competing habits that are oscillating the members of the family now towards and now away from the home, radio occupies an intermediate position. Twenty-five percent of 337 high school boys and 22 percent of 423 high school girls said that they listen more often to the radio with their parents than without them,[22] and, as pointed out above, 20 percent of 274 boys in the three upper years of the high school answered "radio" to the question, "In what thing that you are doing at home this fall are you most interested?"—more than gave any other answer.[23] More than one mother said that her family used to scatter in the evening—"but now we all sit around and listen to the radio."

Likewise the place of the radio in relation to Middletown's other leisure habits is not wholly clear. As it becomes more perfected, cheaper, and a more accepted part of life, it may cease to call forth so much active, constructive ingenuity and become one more form of passive enjoyment. Doubtless it will continue to play a might rôle in lifting Middletown out of the humdrum of every day; it is beginning to take over that function of the great political rallies or the trips by the trainload to the state capital to hear a noted speaker or to see a monument dedicated that a generation ago helped to set the average man in a wide place. But it seems not unlikely that, while furnishing a new means of diversified enjoyment, it will at the same time operate, with national advertising, syndicated newspapers, and other means of large-scale diffusion, as yet another means of standardizing many of Middletown's habits. Indeed, at no point is one brought up more sharply against the impossibility of studying Middletown as a self-contained, self-starting community than when one watches these space-binding leisure-time inventions imported from without—automobile, motion picture, and radio—reshaping the city.

NOTES

1. Two million horse-drawn carriages were manufactured in the United States in 1909 and 10,000 in 1923; 80,000 automobiles were manufactured in 1909 and 4,000,000 in 1923.

2. These numbers have undoubtedly increased greatly since the count was made.

As a matter of fact, by far the greater part of the wide diffusion of the automobile culture one observes today in Middletown has taken place within the last ten or fifteen years. There were less than 500,000 passenger automobiles registered in the entire United States in 1910 and only 5,500,000 in 1918, as over against 15,500,000 in 1924. (Cf. *Facts and Figures of the Automobile Industry, 1925 Edition*, published by the National Automobile Chamber of Commerce.)

3. Some further idea of the spread of automobiles, involving different degrees of inroad into the family budgets of the city, is afforded by the following list in order of frequency: Ford, 2,578; Chevrolet, 590; Overland, 459; Dodge, 343; Maxwell, 309; Buick, 295; Studebaker, 264; Oakland, 88; Willys-Knight, 74; Nash, 73; Interstate, 73; Durant, 65; Star, 62; Oldsmobile, 59; Saxon, 53; Reo, 50; Chalmers, 47; Franklin, 45; Essex, 45; Hudson, 44; Cadillac, 36; Chandler, 32; Monroe, 31; Paige, 31; Haynes, 29; International, 26; Sheridan 26; Hupmobile, 25. Sixty-nine other makes are represented by less than twenty-five cars each, including fifteen Marmons, fourteen Packards, one Pierce-Arrow, one Lincoln, but for the most part cheap, early models, many of them of discontinued makes.

The 6,221 cars owned in the city at the end of 1923 included models of the following years: 1924–13; 1923–901; 1922–1,053; 1921–633; 1920–746; 1919–585; 1918–447; 1917–756; 1916–517; 1915–294; 1914–154; 1913–85; earlier than 1913–37.

4. This is a rough figure based upon the total of 11,600 passenger cars and 1,768 trucks registered in the county at the close of 1924, the gasoline tax paid during the year, an arbitrary assumption that a truck used three times the gas used by a passenger car, and upon an estimate of 17.5 miles per gallon. The number of motorcycles is negligible.

5. "The Ford car has done an awful lot of harm to the unions here and everywhere else," growled one man prominent in Middletown labor circles. "As long as men have enough money to buy a second-hand Ford and tires and gasoline, they'll be out on the road and paying no attention to union meetings."

6. What a motor car means as an investment by Middletown families can be gathered from the following accepted rates of depreciation: 30 percent the first year, 20 percent more the second, 10 percent more each of the next three years. The operating cost of the lightest car of the Ford, Chevrolet, Overland type, including garage rent and depreciation, has been conservatively figured by a national automotive corporation for the country as a whole at $5.00 a week or $0.05 a mile for family use for 5,000 miles a year and replacement at the end of seven years. The cost of tires, gas, oil, and repairs of the forty-seven of the workers' families interviewed who gave expenditures on cars for the past year ranged from $8.90 to $192.00.

7. "The *National Retail Clothier* has been devoting space to trying to find out what is the matter with the clothing industry and has been inclined to blame it on the automobile. In one city, to quote an example cited in the articles, a store 'put on

a campaign that usually resulted in a business of 150 suits and overcoats on a Saturday afternoon. This season the campaign netted seventeen sales, while an automobile agency across the street sold twenty-five cars on the weekly payment plan.' In another, 'retail clothiers are unanimous in blaming the automobile for the admitted slump in the retail clothing trade.'" (*Chicago Evening Post*, December 28, 1923.)

8. This low percentage of bathtubs would not hold for the entire car-owning group. The interviewers asked about bathtubs in these twenty-six cases out of curiosity, prompted by the run-down appearance of the homes.

While inroads upon savings and the re-allocation of items of home expenditure were the readjustments most often mentioned in connection with the financing of the family automobile, others also occur: "It's prohibition that's done it," according to an officer in the Middletown Trades Council; "drink money is going into cars." The same officer, in answering the question as to what he thought most of the men he comes in contact with are working for, guessed: "Twenty-five percent are fighting to keep their heads above water; 10 percent want to own their own homes; 65 percent are working to pay for cars." "All business is suffering," says a Middletown candy manufacturer and dealer. "The candy business is poor now to what it was before the war. There is no money in it any more. People just aren't buying candy so much now. How can they? Even laboring-men put all their money into cars, and every other branch of business feels it."

9. As over against these answers regarding the automobile, 21 percent of the boys and 33 percent of the girls said that they go to the movies more often with their parents than without them, 25 percent and 22 percent respectively answered similarly as regards "listening to the radio," and 31 percent and 48 percent as regards "singing or playing a musical instrument." On the basis of these answers it would appear that the automobile is at present operating as a more active agency drawing Middletown families together than any of these other agencies.

10. In any consideration of the devotion to "speed" that accompanies the coming of the automobile, it should be borne in mind that the increased monotony for the bulk of the workers involved in the shift from the large-muscled hand-trades, including farming, to the small-muscled high-speed machine-tending jobs and the disappearance of the saloon as an easy means of "tellin' the world to go to hell" have combined with the habit-cracking, eye-opening effect of service in the late war to set the stage for the automobile as a release. The fact that serviceable second-hand cars can be bought for $75.00 and up, the simplicity of installment payment, "the fact that everybody has one"—all united to make ownership of a car relatively easy, even for boys.

11. For ten others charged with sex offenses during this same period the scene of the offense was not given.

12. Over against these appeals, the Sunday of 1890 with its fewer alternatives should be borne in mind: as a Middletown plumber described it, "There wasn't anything to do but go to church or a saloon or walk uptown and look in the shop windows. You'd go about hunting saloons that were open, or maybe, if you were a *hot* sport, rent a rig for $1.50 for the afternoon and take your girl out riding."

13. Exact counts were made for only January, July, and October. There were less than 125 performances, including matinées, for the entire year.

14. These figures are rough estimates based upon the following data: The total

Federal amusement tax paid by Middletown theaters in July was $3,002.04 and in December $4,781.47. The average tax paid per admission is about $0.0325, and the population in 1923 about 38,000. Attendance estimates secured in this way were raised by one-sixth to account for children under twelve who are tax-free. The proprietor of three representative houses said that he had seven admissions over twelve years to one aged twelve or less, and the proprietor of another house drawing many children has four over twelve to one aged twelve or less.

These attendance figures include, however, farmers and others from outlying districts.

15. The question was asked in terms of frequency of attendance "in an average month" and was checked in each case by attendance during the month just past.

Lack of money and young children needing care in the home are probably two factors influencing these families that do not attend at all; of the forty-one working class families in which all the children are twelve years or under, eighteen never go to the movies, while of the eighty-one working class families in which one or more of the children is twelve or older, only twenty reported that no member of the family ever attends.

"I haven't been anywhere in two years," said a working class wife of thirty-three, the mother of six children, the youngest twenty months. "I went to the movies once two years ago. I was over to see Mrs. —— and she says, 'Come on, let's go to the movies.' I didn't believe her. She is always ragging the men and I thought she was joking. 'Come on,' she says, 'put your things on and we'll see a show.' I thought, well, if she wanted to rag the men, I'd help her, so I got up and put my things on. And, you know, she really meant it. She paid my carfare uptown and paid my way into the movies. I was never so surprised in my life. I haven't been anywhere since."

16. Cf. N. 8 above. The ex-proprietor of one of the largest saloons in the city said, "The movies killed the saloon. They cut our business in half overnight."

17. It happens frequently that the title overplays the element of "sex adventure" in a picture. On the other hand, films less luridly advertised frequently portray more "raw situations."

18. Miriam Van Waters, referee of the juvenile court of Los Angeles and author of *Youth in Conflict*, says in a review of Cyril Burt's *The Young Delinquent:* "The cinema is recognized for what it is, the main source of excitement and of moral education for city children. Burt finds that only mental defectives take the movies seriously enough to imitate the criminal exploits portrayed therein, and only a small proportion of thefts can be traced to stealing to gain money for admittance. In no such direct way does the moving picture commonly demoralize youth. It is in the subtle way of picturing the standards of adult life, action and emotion, cheapening, debasing, distorting adults until they appear in the eyes of the young people perpetually bathed in a moral atmosphere of intrigue, jealousy, wild emotionalism, and cheap sentimentality. Burt realizes that these exhibitions stimulate children prematurely." (*The Survey*, April 15, 1926.)

19. One exhibitor in Middletown is a college-trained man interested in bringing "good films" to the city. He, like the others, however, is caught in the competitive game and matches his competitors' sensational advertisements.

20. Both percentages have undoubtedly increased notably since 1924, when the counts were made.

21. In 1890 the local press spoke of an occasional citizen's visiting "Paris, France," and "London, England," and even in 1924 a note in one of the papers recording the accident of some Middletown people finding themselves in a box at a New York theater with a group of Englishmen was captioned, "Lucky they weren't Chinese!" The rest of the world is still a long way from Middletown, but movies and radio are doing much to break down this isolation: "I've got 120 stations on my radio," gleefully announced a local working man. Meanwhile, the president of the Radio Corporation of America proclaims an era at hand when "the oldest and newest civilizations will throb together at the same intellectual appeal, and to the same artistic emotions."

22. Cf. N. 10 above.

23. Less than 1 percent of the 341 girls answered "radio."

III

Depression, War, and Resurgence
1930–60

BETWEEN 1930 AND 1960 the towns of the Midwest were buffeted by the conflicting forces of severe economic depression, a global war that introduced wrenching changes, and a postwar prosperity that intensified economic pressures emanating from the rapidly growing metropolitan areas. By the onset of the depression, evidence of an impending long-term slide was already beginning to appear. The root cause of this problem was the increased mobility made possible by the automobile. It encouraged travel to nearby cities for shopping and entertainment. Where Main Street merchants previously faced serious external competition only from the catalogues of Montgomery Ward and Sears, Roebuck, they now found themselves having to grapple with the greater variety and lower prices available in metropolitan arcades and department stores. Further, the cities also invaded the commercial districts of the larger towns in the form of chain stores. The arrival during the 1920s of such national entities as Rexall Drug, J. C. Penney's, and Great Atlantic and Pacific grocery further imperiled town merchants.

Historians have tended to emphasize the severe impact of the Great Depression upon farmers and urban workers, but the towns were also hit hard. In the Midwest the prosperity of Main Street had always been closely tied to the economic fortunes of agriculture. Farmers in the single-crop regions of the western portion of the Midwest had encountered difficult times during the 1920s, but during the 1930s the economic malaise spread rapidly through their communities. Sheriff's sales disposed of equipment, and local banks had little alternative but to foreclose on heavily mortgaged farms that fell into default. For a time angry farmers in Iowa used force to prevent fellow farmers from shipping crops and livestock to market in a failed effort to reduce supply and thereby raise prices. Banks and savings institutions everywhere were threatened, and many were forced into receivership as millions of families lost their savings. Up and down Main Street hard-pressed merchants struggled to survive. Unemployment and underemployment soared, and income and optimism plummeted.

All across the Midwest town leaders bravely mobilized their meager resources to assist those in need. Church aid societies and service clubs held fund raisers to assist the town's most needy, but these traditional sources proved inadequate. County and municipal governments were similarly incapable of meaningful action. Consequently, much-needed assistance came primarily not from local and private sources but from the federal government in the form of the New Deal administration of Franklin D. Roosevelt. Funneling moneys through state and county agencies, the New Deal hired unemployed locals to rake leaves, pave streets and roads, construct community facilities, install public water systems, build dams and bridges, and conduct youth programs. Although traditionally independent midwesterners naturally resisted accepting public assistance, the desperation of their financial plight forced them to take on employment offered by federal emergency agencies. Ironically, it was during the greatest economic crisis in the nation's history that many communities were able to accomplish more in the way of improving their infrastructure than in any previous comparable time period.

The national economic malaise was ended by military mobilization in 1940–41, and Main Street returned for a time to economic health. But ultimately the war's impact upon the towns proved severe. Full mobilization set in motion a migration to regional urban areas where good-paying defense industry jobs were plentiful; whereas during the 1920s the automobile facilitated day trips to nearby cities, now residents moved to urban locations for better jobs and never returned. Rural and small-town America lost 17 percent of its population between 1940 and 1945; many communities never recovered from that acute loss. The loss of population continued as the sustained postwar urban economic boom intensified migration away from rural and small-town America. By the year 2000 towns throughout the United States contained less than 10 percent of the national population, and the percentage of Americans engaged full time in agriculture hovered below 2 percent. In 1900 38 percent of the American work force had been engaged in farming, but during the next one hundred years the number of farmers in the United States fell from 6 million to 1.9 million.

It is difficult to generalize about the condition and fate of midwestern towns during the second half of the twentieth century because the variables are numerous. Those towns located close to urban areas were often swallowed up by the outward thrust of the suburban rings, losing in the process their sense of independence and identity. Other towns, located beyond the immediate reach of suburban developers, became bedroom communities for commuters willing to drive many miles round trip each day. These towns offered not only lower housing costs but a less frenetic lifestyle than existed in the metropolis.

For those towns located beyond commuting distance to a regional metropolis two essential rules prevailed: the further the distance from a metropolis the more vulnerable they became, and the smaller their population the greater the peril. Such relatively isolated towns with populations of a few thousand residents proved to be more stable because they had a modicum of built-in economic stability. If a town enjoyed designation as a county seat, an established core of government jobs helped it weather downward spirals in the economic cycle and resist external economic pressures. Towns with several thousand residents also were able to offer a wider variety of medical and educational services, as well as provide diverse shopping outlets, thereby protecting against a general decline. Location on an interstate or major federal highway provided additional economic stimulus, but many a town was negatively affected when it was bypassed by a highway or found itself removed several miles from a new stretch of the interstate highway system.

Whatever unique circumstances occurred in individual towns, a general downward trend became evident all across the Midwest. As early as 1954, the historian Lewis E. Atherton took note of this phenomenon. "Main Street," he wrote with prescience, "has not only lost population, but also the hope, daring, and originality necessary to fight back." Atherton pointed toward "vacant store buildings and sagging, unpainted houses, numerous old people vegetating in village homes, and boys and girls anxiously looking forward to the time when they can join the rush to the cities." Atherton's brusque summary, surprising to readers at the time of the book's publication, accurately anticipated the fate of the majority of midwestern towns in the decades to come.

The much-lamented departure of the younger generations for distant cities was merely symptomatic of deeper problems. One of these that became apparent in smaller towns during the 1950s was the decline in the quality of local medical care. It began when the beloved town "Doc" who made house calls retired; smaller communities faced great difficulty in attracting a replacement. In ensuing decades major changes in the practice of medical science and in the manner medical care was funded produced a concentration of medical personnel and facilities in larger towns and regional metropolises. Similarly, dentists and home nursing specialists became increasingly difficult to attract to small-town locales. A similar process of consolidation of essential services in larger population centers occurred in the public school systems. Towns lost one of their primary sources of local pride and identity when their high school was closed and students were bused miles away to a new "consolidated" school comprised of several previously independent districts. In Preble County, Ohio, where thirteen separate school systems existed in 1955, only four remained ten years later. In western Minnesota, some school names read like law firms: Russell-Tyler-Ruthton, Tracy-Milroy-Walnut Grove. Others are simply county names: Lincoln High, Yellow Medicine East.

The 1950s also witnessed the imminent rise of the Sunbelt, which soon

proved to be a major threat to the stability of town population. Traditionally, when prosperous farm couples retired they moved to a nearby town
where they continued to contribute to the local economy and social and cultural life. Now the lure of warmer climes in the South and West beckoned
retirees, thereby undercutting the stability of leadership and population
throughout the Midwest. Thus the population of the small towns—already
destabilized by the pull of nearby cities—was further decimated by the departure of more affluent seniors. Left behind, in increasingly noticeable
numbers, were those aging residents with limited economic resources. By
the onset of the 1960s, the business districts along Main Street reflected
these changing demographics. Movie theaters were permanently closed, victims of the popularity of television and a shrinking clientele. Television,
coupled with accessibility to the new shopping centers in nearby cities, also
helped bring to an end the unique social phenomenon of Saturday night in
town. No longer did farm families drive to town on Saturday evenings to do
their weekly shopping and to socialize. Main Street on Saturday night stood
abandoned, its merchants bewildered by their imperiled economic future,
wondering where the large crowds of shoppers had gone. The sense of community pride and involvement also was affected. One of the first victims
was the town baseball team. All across America "town ball" fell victim to
televised major league baseball games; by 1960 leagues and teams everywhere had disappeared. A similar fate befell the town band, and membership in local "Progressive Clubs" and similar booster organizations entered
a period of steady decline.

When the cultural anthropologist James West described the small Missouri town of "Plainville" in 1940, he reported on lifestyle patterns that existed within a relatively self-sufficient community that had somehow survived the devastations of the Great Depression. When another social
scientist, Art Gallaher, undertook a similar research effort in 1955 he discovered that "Plainville" had entered into a distinctly new era of economic
decline and population stagnation, highlighted by the departure of the
younger generation for the city. What was new, he discovered, was a pervasive and troubled concern about the community's future.

Growing Up in Clear Lake

Personal Reminiscence

ALAN R. WOOLWORTH

LIVING IN A MIDWESTERN TOWN provided many opportunities and options for youth, as Alan R. Woolworth explains in this reminiscence of growing up during the Great Depression in the village of Clear Lake, South Dakota, with the constant companionship of his twin brother, Arlan. His is a story of how individual, family, and community intersected to provide a broad range of experiences that contributed to his formative years. Seen here through the eyes of a young boy moving through adolescence, Clear Lake will be a familiar place for those who spent their childhoods in other midwestern towns. Unlike Sinclair Lewis or Sherwood Anderson, however, Woolworth discovers that his memories are not ones of bitterness, irony, frustration, and regret, but of a healthy appreciation for the many lessons learned and the many experiences that were afforded him and his brother.

Despite the difficulties posed by the severe economic times, there was the security and stability provided by his family, plus picnics, swimming in the creek, Saturday afternoons at the movies, baseball, school, climbing trees, Christmas celebrations, fishing and hunting, and church attendance. Woolworth's memories restore to life the inevitable town characters, the familiar interiors and scents of hardware stores and ice cream shops, the slow-paced ambience of a farm town that moved to the leisurely tempo of the changing seasons. Woolworth learned the value of a dollar doing odd jobs or running his newspaper route on cold and rainy days. Women played an important role in his development, and he perceived early on that roles were determined by one's gender and class—and that expectations were markedly different for girls and boys.

In his moving history of the Allied invasion of Normandy, the historian Stephen Ambrose observes that the soldiers who won this decisive battle were "young men born into the false prosperity of the 1920s and brought up in the bitter realities of the Depression of the 1930s. . . . None of them wanted to be part of another war. They wanted to be throwing baseballs, not hand grenades, shooting .22s at rabbits, not M-1s at other young men. But when the test came, when freedom had to be fought for or abandoned, they fought. They were the soldiers of democracy." Ambrose might as well have been writing about the Woolworth twins. As Alan matter-of-factly explains, he and his brother grew up with guns. They were a natural part of the learning experience of young boys whether they lived in town or on a farm. "This experience" he explains, "taught us to be careful with firearms and how to shoot straight, traits that were later useful to us in World War II." Alan survived the battlefields of France, but his brother was killed in 1944 in the bloodbath that was Anzio. Writing about his twin, Alan observes, "He was patriotic and had a sense of duty and love for our country." Such were the essential traits, among others, that he and his brother acquired as they grew up in the community of Clear Lake, South Dakota, population 635.

o   o   o

I write these happy memories of our childhood and youthful years for my daughters, grandchildren, relatives, and any others with an interest in life in small prairie towns in the Northern Great Plains from the late 1920s into the early 1940s. These are my reminiscences about a way of life that has long since disappeared. My twin brother, Arlan, and I enjoyed a happy privileged childhood despite the difficult economic times, a great drought, and the pending world war that confronted our parents and all other people in the Great Plains and the United States in the 1930s.

We were born on August 19, 1924, in a new two-story home our parents had erected in 1923 on an acre of land on the southwestern edge of Clear Lake, South Dakota. The house measured 24 by 26 feet, with a full basement and a large square cistern to hold rainwater from the roof. The first floor had a large living and dining room, a bedroom, and a kitchen. The second floor had two bedrooms and a bathroom. It was a relatively large, comfortable house with a warm air furnace, ample soft rainwater for washing, and bedrooms with walk-in closets. A few years later, a light airy porch was added on its front, measuring 8 by 22 feet. The porch was built about 1928, and Arlan and I gathered small stones to add to the concrete for the walls underneath it. Soon after, dad stored hives of bees in what we called the "bee cellar."

Our hometown, Clear Lake, was in the center of Deuel County, South Dakota, a dozen miles west of the Minnesota–South Dakota border. A county seat, it boasted a handsome courthouse completed in 1917. Around 1930, the county had a population of about 6,000 people that would soon shrink considerably. Clear Lake itself was a typical dusty prairie town with a population of 635 individuals. Most of their activities centered at the schools, the many churches, the courthouse, and the Main Street with small businesses along both sides of it for about three blocks. Some buildings were brick, but many were false-front wooden structures. And there were still a few horse hitching rails on side streets.

Clear Lake was laid out on a grid of square blocks 300 feet on a side with streets between them. Blocks were divided in half by narrow north-south alleys as many folks had kept a horse, buggy, and cow in a stable at the rear of their lot. Tree-shaded and grassy, alleys were quiet, enchanting places for children to explore; there were few adults around to hinder our eager young minds and bodies as we wandered along them. A tightly knit Christian community, people in our hometown cared about each other, and older folks watched out for little children.

During the long, cold winters great white drifts of snow accumulated in our backyard and snow covered the lower branches of the apple trees. On cold moonlit nights, we could look out of the frost-covered storm windows and see rabbits dancing on the snow and in the morning eagerly inspected their tracks. Food was scarce for them and at times they ate bark from our young apple trees. Then our father would take a .22 caliber rifle and hunt them so that they would not kill the trees. We felt sorry for the rabbits but knew it was a battle for survival between them and our family, and we cherished those apple trees.

Though we never thought much about it, most of our waking hours were spent out of doors playing with other children, exploring the countryside, or visiting folks in other parts of town. Everything was new and wonderful to us and we lived in a secret child's world with our playmates. In those days, small towns were great places for children because they were warm, friendly places where everybody knew everybody else and many of us were related to each other. We, for instance, had our grandparents and aunt Ruth Woolworth; our great-uncle Jesse Woolworth; the Axel Paulson family; and great-aunt Irene Artus and her older sister, Minnie Bremer nearby. Also our great-grand-uncle John Taylor's widow, whom we called "Grandma Taylor."

Many families there enjoyed friendly relations for two and three generations. At times, we played with other children as our fathers had when they were our age. Adults instinctively scolded children when they were doing something dangerous or had ventured out of their neighborhoods. Commonly we were told, "Get home or I will call your mother." Then we started for home as fast as we could run.

As I recall it now, we little boys were smelly, grubby savages and ruffians who needed to have our rough edges knocked off and to be force-fed large doses of socialization. When little boys got angry, they instinctively fought but easily made up with each other and then again played with their friends. They climbed trees, got sick by eating too many green apples, and threw stones at stray cats. I won't discuss our rudimentary social skills or eating habits. Most of all, we didn't want to be controlled by anyone and converted into "sissies."

Little girls appeared to be much easier to socialize and were led into proper modes of behavior and strove harder for social acceptance. I suppose that they instinctively imitated their mothers. When angry or frustrated, they cried and used socially approved methods to gain their ends. Our childhood girl playmates were something of a mystery to us for they would quarrel and cry and stay apart for a day or so and then be friends again. Obviously, they were more complex social creatures than boys.

Then, everything was new and different for us; life was a great, unfolding adventure to our young questing eyes. Arlan and I soon developed into adventurous tree climbers, and it was a memorable event when I found a large crooked box elder tree on the edge of the Will Kreger property that was easy to climb. I called it the "Cow Horn Tree," for it had a bare branch that resembled a cow's horn. Here, I found a mourning dove nest in a crook and kept a close watch over it till the eggs hatched. It was a common thing for us to hear mourning doves cooing and small owls hooting in the distance.

When we were about four years old, we began to watch the annual Memorial Day events, held at the end of May each year. Our family and neighbors hung large 48-star American flags on their houses or lawns. Then, many families assembled by the courthouse to participate in this sacred event. First, there was a patriotic assembly on the courthouse lawn with the high school band furnishing patriotic music. A prize pupil would recite President Abraham Lincoln's Gettysburg Address and a roll call of veterans from our community would be made. The names of those men who had died in World War I would be recited and listed on a program. Uniformed veterans carrying rifles would march to the city cemetery. We children were given little flags and went there by trucks and buses. Finally, Joe Staley would play "Taps" while all stood at attention. Then, a uniformed firing squad fired three volleys over white crosses representing veterans from all our country's wars. We went away subdued but proud of our country and feeling that we, too, had a definite part in its future.

We were four years old in 1928 and it was time for further socialization of two wild little boys. We were going to attend Sunday school at the local Congregational Church. Then, little boys had bobbed hair, short pants, and long stockings in keeping with the times. Oh, how we hated to pull on those long white stockings that were held up with round elastic garters, just like the ones little girls wore! How we longed for that great day when we would have our first pair of long pants! Now, we began to memorize the Twenty-third Psalm and the Lord's Prayer, scriptures that have remained with me all of my life. We attended Sunday school for many years, and I joined the church at age fourteen.

Southwestern Clear Lake was an interesting place with many members of the large German-American Kreger family as our neighbors. To the south was the large, imposing, William Kreger house where his widow, Kathryn, or "Aunt Kate," lived with her two wild sons, Ryalls and Stewart, and a younger daughter, Kathryn. The north and west sides of their large yard were bordered by a dense growth of lilacs that formed a shelter from the bitter northwest winter winds. They made a continuous green belt for nesting birds, and cottontail rabbits lived out their lives there, too. It was a fascinating place for small boys to explore. In winters, great high snowdrifts formed upwind from the lilacs.

When we were four or five years old, some of us had climbed on top of a bunk wagon while Dorsey Kreger and others were playing below around some wooden timbers and a steel water barrel. I had a pail full of mud and intended to throw it onto Dorsey but got too close to the edge of the roof and fell off onto the timbers. This knocked me out for a little while and our father carried me into our home. We didn't climb on them again.

At the southwest corner of the Will Kreger lilacs was a dirt road that ran west into the countryside. One time, when playing there, we startled a large hen turkey that had left its farm to nest and hatch its eggs. We were fascinated by this and also by a number of beautiful wild bumblebees that had their nests in the clay side of the road ditch. When we were about five years old, we made our first visit to the Fred Spinter pasture, being attracted by the South Creek that flowed down its center. In the creek, we saw a mysterious old gunnysack. Somehow, we pulled it out and opened it to find the skinned carcasses of three or four skunks. Shucks, no hidden treasures there!

To the rear of our house was a large garden that we boys were supposed to weed and hoe. We never enjoyed this very much but knew that it meant good eating in the long, cold winters. Mother canned fruit and vegetables avidly and would hire other women to work with her. Her goal was to have 200 quart glass Mason jars filled by fall and safely on wooden shelves in our basement. When peaches were on sale in grocery stores, our father would purchase a few wooden crates of them for canning. They were scalded for easy peeling and then cut up into slices and placed in sugar syrup in the jars. Similar methods were used with corn, peas, carrots, and tomatoes, but these vegetables were preserved in a water pack. At times, mother also made jellies and jams that were poured in small glass jars and sealed with melted paraffin. She had a heavy cast aluminum pressure cooker to use in the canning process.

My twin, Arlan, was larger and more adventurous than I. He often led us into pranks that were a bit lively. At the end of the honey season, our father stored many beehives in the rear of our land near the bridging equipment. Arlan got into the habit of luring a neighbor boy back to the hives and then lifting the lid and coaxing them to look at the bees. Then, he would kick the hive and the bees would swarm out and sting our victim. Somehow, once was enough for most of them. We were familiar with bee stings and somewhat immune to them, so thought it great fun.

A dirt road ran north and south in front of our house; for that matter, all the streets in town were dirt except perhaps Main Street, which had some gravel on it. We had a good old wooden coaster wagon and would run races up and down this street. When it rained, the street was muddy but still fun to play in. One time, an older boy visited the Kregers and threw mud all over our wagon. This made us angry, so Arlan and I made mud balls and plastered the street side end of the Kreger barn with them. They had a cow that was kept in a pasture and in evenings she was driven to the barn to be milked. Well, that evening, bossy saw the unfamiliar spotted barn wall, let out a bellow and kept running. This made the Kreger boys unhappy and they threatened us with dire revenge, but after a few days the blobs of mud fell off and all was peaceful again. At least until the next scrap.

In those days, there was no refrigeration, but some folks had well-insulated iceboxes for meat, butter, milk, and eggs. To meet this need, ice was harvested in winter at Clear Lake and stored in icehouses under sawdust. Every two or three days, in spring, summer, and fall, George and Joe Lastrico, who had a fruit store on the west side of Main Street, would load up an old Reo truck and make deliveries of ice to their customers. We knew the sound of that truck motor and when it came to the west part of town we clustered around it. Large ice blocks were pulled out at the rear of the truck and chopped down to fit into the iceboxes. We kids loved this ice and would take it home for lemonade or to our mother, who sometimes beat an egg or two into milk and cooled it with ice. Perhaps she added a few drops of vanilla extract for flavoring and sugar, too. It was a real treat for us.

Just north of our home was a fence and inside it was a row of mature willow trees planted long before by Herman Kreger. They were a great attraction to boys, for we made willow whistles from them in the spring and they also had good forked branches waiting to be made into slingshots with our pocket knives. When old enough, we also had BB guns and would shoot at the grackles or black birds that flocked there in the summer months. Nearby was an orchard with many large old apple trees. They weren't much for eating, but it was fun to swing on their branches. Little used, the orchard was filled with tall grass, and once when walking home through it I saw a grinning cat rolling wildly in the weeds. This puzzled me until someone said that it was enjoying a bed of catnip.

When we were five years old, someone took us to the city library and we began to check out books for our mother to read to us. This library dated from the 1890s and was long presided over by "Aunt Kate" Kreger, our longtime neighbor, and her daughter Kathryn. It contained a wealth of standard reference works and much fiction. I was attracted to the works of Joseph A. Altschelter, who wrote about pioneer life in Kentucky. As I grew older, the library became a fascinating place for me, and I regularly checked out two or three books a week for many years. Even now, seventy years later, I still read regularly and love it.

As the Fourth of July neared, we would go down to a baseball field near the school in the evening and watch with wonder the beautiful fireworks. There were skyrockets, spinning stars, and many other wonders to marvel at. Soon, too, we wanted our own firecrackers, and we gradually obtained them. Little children had lady fingers that often fizzed and sputtered with small noises. Far more impressive were the Zebra brand that made a powerful bang, and we put them under empty tin cans and blew them up into the air. As we grew older, many boys carried lighted punk sticks and lit and threw them away. Sooner or later, most of us got a split finger or two and a tetanus shot and learned to be more careful. We also had cap guns, cherry bombs, sparklers, and other moderately dangerous items. As we grew older, some of us would save up our money and have a short piece of half-inch pipe threaded and capped. Then, we mounted it on a wooden pistol-shaped handle and dropped lighted firecrackers down the barrel. They made impressive plumes of light and sound at night, but the neighbors were patient with us.

On summer Sundays, we would sometimes drive down to Clear Lake after a noon meal and casually fish for perch, bullheads, or sunfish. Often, many families would be there relaxing and fishing with long cane poles baited with worms. The poles were one-piece affairs and it was common to see a family crowded into an old automobile with several long poles tied to the top or side of the auto as they drove along. Some folks, like Nick and Frank Wagner, fished with a set line tied to a short wooden stake driven into the ground and with a bobber and hook well baited with wriggling worms.

When Arlan and I were about six years old, our father began taking us along with our older brother, William, and our mother to visit his brother Donald and family on Sunday afternoons. We would buy a box of fifty short .22 caliber cartridges and take along an old single-shot rimfire Hamilton rifle. After visiting the relatives, we drove out to their pasture, overrun with "flicker-tails" or Richardson's Ground Squirrels. We would sit there and one of us had a chance to shoot a gopher and then another would have his turn. At times, we got thirty to fifty of them. This experience taught us to be careful with firearms and how to shoot straight, traits that were later useful to us all in World War II.

When we were about six years old, my mother's older sister, Charlotte, or "Lottie," visited with her husband, Uncle Benny, and their four children. Their three sons were all older and more experienced in the ways of the world. They took us for a walk around the section line about one half mile west of our place and carried along a gunnysack. Some of us walked on each side of the road searching for discarded half-pint and pint flat liquor bottles. We also looked for soft drink bottles that had been "spiked" with cheap whiskey or alcohol. These bottles could be taken to the rear door of a pool hall and quietly sold to the proprietor, Ray Williams, for money. Once, we found a quart bottle worth 25 cents. These escapades were kept carefully concealed from our mother, who would have been upset to know that her sons did such things.

Some of the older boys in the neighborhood, perhaps the Walseths, had two racing wagons with two-by-four wood frames and steel wheels with spokes. They were steered with a rope turning the two front wheels. We rode them on the sidewalk downhill by Julia Laney's house about two blocks to Fred Seeger's house. The wheels made a loud clatter, and it was a little dangerous to cross two streets with no way to stop, but traffic was still light when we inherited these wagons and started to use them ourselves.

Arlan and I would often visit the amiable sheriff, August Bucholtz, and his friendly deputy, Harold Cordiner, in the courthouse. They always had time to visit with us and had tales to tell of their hairbreadth pursuits of "moonshiners" who made and sold illegal corn whiskey. One time, they made a bad mistake by raiding a roadhouse just across the Brookings County line where they had no authority. Instead, the owner and his sons beat them badly with baseball bats. Poor Harold wore a large white bandage around his head for a few weeks afterwards. They also had fascinating catalogs filled with wonderful carnival-type gadgets, games, and amusements that I loved to pore over, item by item.

We didn't get along too well with the fat courthouse janitor, Clyde Green, who knew that little boys could mark up his polished floors, kick over spittoons filled with brown tobacco juice, and generally be a bother. One time when Clyde was chasing us, Arlan accidentally knocked over a tall brass spittoon in the county auditor's office. Clyde had a fit, but we ran into a county commissioners meeting and stood behind Fred Taylor, the chairman, who was a first cousin of our grandfather Woolworth. Cousin Fred gave us sticks of chewing gum while Clyde fumed outside the commissioner's meeting room. Then Fred walked with us out of the building to fend off the angry janitor.

Dry conditions in the 1930s led to abandoned farm fields and dry sloughs filled with tall grass and weeds. Winters were not harsh, either, and the Chinese "ring-necked pheasants" flourished in great numbers. Most men had hunting licenses that cost only a dollar, and they carried shotguns in their automobiles. We boys went along to help drive the pheasants out of cornfields and to learn the sport. Many people hunted illegally from their autos by shooting birds in the road ditches. Hunters were allowed fifteen cocks or roosters a day and a possession limit of fifty-five pheasants by the late 1930s. Even today, I am not very fond of eating pheasant. As high school boys we carried shotguns in car trunks, and after school we went hunting pheasants. Now, of course, that would be highly illegal.

Often we played on the Fred Splinter farm, where we were always welcome. There were many flickertail or Richardson's Ground Squirrels to trap and shoot at with our slingshots. In those days, every red-blooded small town boy had a slingshot and a powerful rubber-band gun. Naturally, there were cattle in the pasture and a bull would chase us. It took precious time and many scratches to climb through high, tight, barbed-wire fences, so we soon learned to run up to the barbed-wire fences and then drop flat on the ground and slide under them. When a bull hit a tight five-row barbed-wire fence with good solid posts, it would stop him and, as the barbs hurt, he would shake his head and bellow. Soon, too, we learned to run up the steep hills on each side of the pasture when the bull was chasing us. This was safer than it looked, as we knew enough to run diagonally uphill while the large heavy bull tried to go straight uphill and was easily outdistanced. It amused us to see him puff and bellow in frustration while we were safely out of his reach.

Then, a large city pasture known as "Tom Law's Pasture" was behind the city schools. Beyond it, on the South Creek, was a well-known swimming hole frequented by boys of all ages. Older boys would put a dam across it each year to make the pond deeper. It was there that I learned to "dog paddle" while holding onto an old wooden fencepost floating in the pond. This was a first step in learning how to swim. Sometimes, some of us would get into a fight and throw mud or pieces of sod and yell at each other. Often, too, the older boys tried to keep the younger ones out of the pond, but we would sneak in there when they were gone. In the spring, the creek flooded and its icy waters attracted many boys who fell into it and then ran home wet, cold, and shivering. I was one of them.

During the early 1930s many families gave up trying to make a living from farms and moved into town where the men could work on WPA projects and the children would have better schooling. Clear Lake had its fiftieth anniversary in the summer of 1934, and though in the midst of a severe drought and economic depression, efforts were made by hard-pressed merchants to put on a parade down Main Street and a dance that evening. Undaunted, Elmer Knight dressed up as a fat lady and bought a bushel of candy suckers and gave them out to children. We children played near his filling station with little concern for the severe economic conditions or older folks' activities.

A severe drought impacted the Plains region in the early 1930s and was especially severe in 1934. Farming was under great stress and there was little forage for cattle and horses. The level of ground water declined so that all of the local lakes except for Lake Cochrane were dry, along with the small local creeks. Rainfall was scanty, so pastures and grain fields had little vegetation. This condition displaced the local "mud turtles" or painted box turtles that walked along the roads in search of water. Sometimes, we would catch them and place them in an old rain barrel on the Herman Kreger place where the Clarence Kallemeyn family lived.

Once, we went down to the stockyards by the Rock Island Railroad track to see diseased and injured cattle slaughtered. Sadly, there was hardly any market for cattle, so many young animals were disposed of, too. They were purchased by the federal government and at least the farmers received some small payments for them. Others were bought up cheaply and used to feed needy families. The county also operated a surplus program in the basement of the courthouse to distribute fruit and vegetables to needy folks.

Prices for well-fed live hogs had sunk to $4.00 per hundred pounds and many farmers didn't bother to haul them into town for sale. Dad once traded honey for a large dressed hog, and everyone thought it a fair trade. He also traded honey for other farm produce, and we kids sometimes sold it in our hometown. Large cornfields served as homes for thousands of wily pheasants, and we kids greatly enjoyed running down the rows when up to no good. Corn was burned as fuel by some farmers, and others with old tree groves were envied as they had plenty of free fuel for cooking and heating in cold winters.

Many youths hired out to herd cattle in the roadside ditches where moisture had collected and there was a little more grass. The dry fields were infested with Russian thistles or tumbleweeds. One year, there was also an infestation of pepper grass, so farmers cut and burned it to keep it from going to seed. Those of us who herded cattle barefooted soon learned to be careful with tumbleweeds. It was all right to run through the young green ones that were tender, but older dry weeds had stickers that were hard on our feet. You also learned to avoid fresh "cow pies."

Clear Lake went dry in 1934 as it had in 1894, and we ten-year-old boys went down there with our friends and walked over its dry bed. There, we saw battered old rowboats on its bottom and dead fish in a few drying pools. The lake was seined for fish as it went dry and many local people gathered there to obtain them. Local farmers planted sorghum and potatoes in its bed. Snow fell that winter and in the spring of 1935 the lake filled up again. The "Inlet" where the creek ran into the lake became a favorite swimming hole for many boys and a few daring girls.

During World War I, veterans had been promised a substantial bonus for their military service, and in the early 1930s angry veterans marched to Washington, D. C., and lived in shacks while demanding their payment. It was finally made by Franklin D. Roosevelt's Democratic administration about 1936 and was a considerable aid to many families. Our father received bonds worth several hundred dollars and purchased a much-needed second-hand automobile that lasted for several years. And, no doubt, there were other important needs.

Rain was scarce in the drought years, but when it came, it was in torrents. Then we kids would run out into the muddy street and play in the rain. Unfortunately, too, we had cyclones or tornadoes during these years. I believe that it was in 1934 that Uncle Benny's barn east of Brandt, South

Dakota, was demolished. Many others were, too, and our father, who had contracted with a large life insurance company to repair and rebuild buildings on farms, hired crews of men and used them to swiftly repair buildings so farming could continue. Naturally, he hired relatives such as his brother-in-law Axel Paulson, brother Donald Woolworth, brother-in-law Dan Collier, and mother's cousin Walter Rose.

There were many federal government relief programs such as the WPA and later the CCC. And the Republican local merchants and others complained that these men could find work if they weren't lazy. The sad truth was that there wasn't any work for them. We saw these men trimming road borders and later starting to build a small pond in our park on the North Creek that local cynics called "Lake Olson" after Ole Olson, our socialist mayor. Some of us went down there and got into a quarrel with the workers and, after being chased away, returned and dammed the creek, flooding the working area. That ended "Lake Olson," and hardly anyone remembers it today.

Families still on farms practiced subsistence farming by raising grain and corn and having cattle, sheep, pigs, and poultry. Their gardens were also very important to them as they tried to raise all of their own food. Saturday and Wednesday evenings in Clear Lake were lively with the sidewalks filled with farm families visiting each other and talking about the hard times. Hard though conditions were then, young people were busy courting each other.

People came to town bringing a few dozen eggs, a cream can, and perhaps poultry to sell or to "trade" as some of them called it. This was often their only source of ready cash for gasoline and staples such as salt, sugar, flour, and coffee. In the meantime, some of us naughty boys had our water pistols ready and would hide cans of water behind signs and at other strategic places. Then, it was fun to walk around squirting people that we knew. Most of them would laugh and of course the girls would scream, but they still enjoyed it. We also visited with friends from nearby farms.

The summer of 1936 was dry and scorching, with temperatures in the high 90s for days at a time, and the winter was bitter cold, with deeply buried water pipes freezing in the streets. An outside expert with an electrical heating apparatus was hired to thaw them out. The winter of 1937 saw a heavy snow with drifts that filled Main Street so that all traffic was halted. Trucks hauled the snow off, but it was a long, cold season, and we waited eagerly for signs of spring.

A new neighbor was O. A. Syverud, the county extension agent. He talked us into joining the 4-H club and planting certified seed potatoes. We did raise an acre of Bliss Triumph potatoes on the Mike Fisher farm northwest of Clear Lake for a couple of years and found that it was a good source of cash. It was common then, too, for youths from town to work at picking

potatoes in the fall for farmers. This was hard, heavy work, but you learned
to value money when it came from picking potatoes off the ground into five-
gallon pails and then carrying them to a horse-drawn wagon. Some of us
also began shocking grain bundles on local farms so that they would dry out
and be ready for threshing. Threshing was an exciting time for us, as we visited neighboring farms to see the threshing machine running and hayracks
filled with bundles being driven to the machine. Then, the bundles were
pitched into the threshing machine and grain ran out a spout into a grain
wagon and the straw went into a rapidly growing straw pile.

By the mid-1930s, the federal government actively promoted the planting of shelter belts of hardy trees and bushes on farms to check strong
winds, to hold snow for crop moisture in the spring months, and to promote
moisture retention in crop land. From 1938 to 1941 and after World War II,
the government sponsored a Rural Electrification Administration to provide
cheap electricity for farms. This program was a boon to farm families, for it
eased their lives, providing safe lighting for houses, barns, and yards and energy to pump water and run a host of appliances that made farm families'
lives much easier and more enjoyable.

Pocket money was scarce, so many boys mowed lawns and worked in
gardens to earn extra money. I did this for a few years, often for Harold
Cordiner, an old friend of our family. One summer, I worked for Jimmy
Smith, who had a good civil service job in the post office. His mother and
sisters were interesting folks and made delicious Cornish pastries for hungry boys after the lawn was neat and trimmed. Many of us also actively collected scrap metals such as aluminum, copper, brass, and lead. We sold
them to Andrew Helgerson, who was the night watchman on Main Street
and lived near our grandparents. His small barn was filled with scrap metal
of all kinds. Metals were a secure investment and during World War II commanded high prices.

When we were twelve or thirteen years old, we often went on long hikes
to the Hidewood Creek Valley south of Clear Lake and rambled through cattle pastures looking for Indian artifacts and enjoying the open air and sunshine. Usually, we did not wear shirts or hats, so we were deeply tanned. By
then, we were trapping skunks, weasels, and an occasional muskrat in the
fall. When skinning skunks, you had to be careful to not puncture the scent
bag and become covered with that telltale aroma. Usually, we skinned them
in a nearby barn, but mother well knew what we were up to as the odor
wafted to our home. Once, when it was cold in the barn, we began to skin
one in our basement, but mother noticed its odor and indignantly made us
take it outside immediately.

Arlan was more interested in farming than I and began to show carefully
chosen samples of our certified Bliss Triumph potatoes at local crop shows
and then in the state ones. Twice his entries won at a large international

show in Chicago, Illinois. I still have the blue first-class ribbons that he won from this work.

We shared a paper route and distributed the *Minneapolis Star* for a few years and learned much about human nature when making collections. This was also a source of pocket money as we were starting to be interested in driving automobiles and the darned things always needed gasoline and, all too often, repairs to keep them running. Arlan saved his earnings better than I did and in 1938 or 1939 was able to go by train to Hoopeston, Illinois, to visit our grandfather, Edward J. Rose. He also went to a few football games at the University of Minnesota and was greatly interested in them.

I was fascinated by the town's business and professional community along Main Street and the considerable variety of people, knowledge, and skills that they possessed. But Arlan was not much interested in these matters and loved the open air and freer life of farms and farming. About 1937, I worked part-time in summer for Lorraine "Tuffy" Jones, a nephew of Ralph Lavin, our long-time friend. Tuffy had a small dry cleaning place in a wooden building south of the Kohnke funeral parlor on Main Street. I pumped and carried endless pails of water from a well at the rear of the building. Next, I dumped them into a tank leading to a small upright cylindrical steam boiler. There was a small firebox underneath it that I fed with coal and from which I cleaned out ashes. Steam from this unit went into a steam press used to iron trousers, skirts, and other pieces of clothing. I made frequent trips to the City Café across the street and around a corner. This café was operated by Jack Thoelke, and I got bottles of Coca-Cola and hamburgers for Tuffy.

By 1938 or 1939, I had started to hang around the Banner Oil Station on the east side of Main Street and gradually started to fill gas tanks, add motor oil, and learn to repair rubber inner tubes. As I learned more, my responsibilities increased, and sometimes I would be left in charge of the station when the owner was out of town. This was quite a bit of responsibility for a youth of my years, but I was able to handle it adequately. By 1941, I worked at the Majestic Theater, where I vacuumed the floor and also learned to lay out and put up large sectional movie posters on an outside display facility. The pay wasn't great, but I also enjoyed free movies and an occasional box of popcorn.

We twins became janitors at the local Masonic lodge hall and would dutifully sweep and dust. Before lodge meetings, we would arrange chairs and during winters were careful to go there in the afternoon and start up the two oil stoves that heated the lodge room. They were connected by a long stovepipe filled with heavy, cold air, so we soon learned to fire up the stove close to the chimney and let it run for a while before starting the second stove. Then, the chimney drew well and heated up the cold lodge room properly. I must admit that we sometimes amused ourselves with some of the lodge regalia like the Worshipful Master's tall silk top hat and the

Tyler's sword. We knew, too, that we would someday join this lodge and learn more of its teachings so that we would lead better lives.

Both Arlan and I were active in the Boy Scout movement for a few years. In 1938 and 1939 we attended a weeklong scout camp near Hartford Beach on the west side of Big Stone Lake. Here, we met many interesting individuals who taught school and now had part-time jobs at the camp. We also met other youths from many different towns who became friends and at times saw them in later years.

By 1940, Arlan and I were old enough to drive and often would take William's old car and go out hunting with it. Once, we talked our cousin Fred Wiswall into pushing a large old Dodge that had flooded with gas that had leaked into the muffler. It ignited with a loud bang and blew a hole in the muffler. Another time, the wire disconnecting the freewheeling device broke and it kicked in with a jerk. We also met interesting girls and distant cousins in high school and enjoyed socializing with them.

Heavy snow began to fall on November 11, 1940, so the schools were closed in early afternoon, and we walked home through a blizzard while the country pupils were hurried to their farm homes by school buses. Soon, the electrical power failed and we borrowed a gallon of kerosene for an old lamp from the Mortimer Hunt family who lived in the Herman Kreger house. The streets filled with high snowdrifts, our father was stranded away from home, and schools were closed for a few days. This was the Armistice Day Blizzard of 1940 in which many hunters in Minnesota died.

During the 1930s, fascist regimes in Europe and the Pacific grew and rapidly armed for a war with the western colonial democracies. In 1939, Germany invaded Poland and World War II began. In 1940, France fell and the British retreated across the English Channel. Soon, the Battle of Britain began and countries in the western world at last began to admit that they, too, had much to lose if Fascism triumphed. For that matter, our western civilization was at stake, and we had to arm and fight to preserve it.

At the time, there simply weren't many opportunities in small towns such as Clear Lake. Many crafts, trades, and professions were open for us, but most of them required long, expensive training or years of college. As our country gradually began to arm and train a greatly enlarged army, air corps, and navy, many more opportunities opened up. Suddenly, families left for the West Coast to work in shipyards, aircraft plants, and other wartime industries. Many young men enlisted in our military forces and wrote letters back home from remote, exciting places.

After we graduated from the local high school in June 1942, a few of my friends went to South Dakota State College that fall, but it was too expensive for most of us. Others began to farm with their parents. Opportunities were fewer and more difficult to find for the young women in our graduating class. Some of them married farmers while others worked in the local bank or offices or stores. Unfortunately, none of them entered college, though many of them should have done so. I saw this as a great waste of human talent and still urge young women to obtain an education and to work for at least a few years before marriage and family responsibilities consume their time and energies.

Our brother William enlisted in the army in 1942 and by 1943 was in North Africa, Sicily, and Italy as the Allies advanced up the Italian peninsula. I went into military service in February 1943, as Arlan did in the middle of that year. My unit was stationed at Camp Cooke, California, on the Santa Maria peninsula about seventy miles north of Santa Barbara, where our uncle Lawrence Woolworth lived. Arlan was soon training at Camp Roberts in north central California. Arlan and I met there on a weekend and of course did not realize that we would never see each other again as our paths parted.

My unit shipped out from Camp Shanks, New York, bound for England, in February 1944. I was stationed in England for several months before moving across the English Channel to France and combat. Arlan's Paratroop Artillery unit was stationed near Anzio, Italy, where he died on July 19, 1944. He was buried in a military cemetery at Nettuno, Italy, and was brought home for burial in the Clear Lake Cemetery in August 1948. He would have married a local girl and farmed if he had lived through the war.

World War II brought unprecedented prosperity to our country. Anyone who wanted to work could find a job with good wages. This was noticeable when I came home on a furlough before shipping out for Europe. Farmers were smoking tailor-made cigarettes instead of rolling their own! This fortunate condition continued for many years.

Returning veterans eased back into employment and the general society, and many of us used the GI Bill to obtain a hitherto impossible higher education. We flooded colleges and universities in the fall of 1946 in unprecedented numbers, with many of us determined to enter professions. In my own instance, I entered college with a high school diploma, but in 1950 received the A.B. degree from the University of Nebraska and, a few years later, the M.A. degree from the University of Minnesota.

It was difficult for our parents to have all three of their sons serving in military units in combat zones in Europe at one time and to lose Arlan, but sacrifices were necessary to win this war, and he did not die in vain. He was patriotic and had a sense of duty and love for our country. Fascism and, later, Communism were defeated, the western democracies and their institutions were preserved, and we have lived and prospered in relative peace except for the Korean War and the Vietnam Conflict. Now, World War II, the climatic event of our lives, has faded into the distance though its results will continue to influence world events far into the future.

Compromise and Its Limits

FROM *Main Street in Crisis*

CATHERINE MCNICOL STOCK

O NE OF THE MOST POWERFUL ORGANIZATIONS in American society from the Revolutionary era to the middle of the twentieth century
was the Masonic Order. The secret lodge often stirred embittered criticism,
sometimes out of fear for the nature of its secret rituals but also because its
membership wielded great power within towns and villages across America. The historian Art McClure has correctly written that well into the
mid-twentieth century "Masons were at the core of power and money in
America." Exclusively male, its membership was restricted to the prosperous and the powerful. At least fifteen presidents, including George Washington, have been Masons. Shortly before he entered the White House
Harry S. Truman served as the Grand Master of Missouri. The lodge meeting room was a place for secret handshakes and symbolically rich rituals,
but it also was a place where men of power and influence within the community could meet, cut political and business deals, and enjoy the company of like-minded men.

In her study of the impact of the Great Depression on the northern
plains states, Catherine McNicol Stock notes that "being a Mason in North
Dakota was nearly equivalent of being successful." Hence the plight of the
North Dakota Masonic lodges of the 1930s proved excruciating, when
heretofore successful members encountered severe economic losses. The resulting problems included difficulty in collecting dues, falling attendance,
lack of support for community projects, and even declining membership.

Beyond illustrating pressing economic conditions, Stock's study of the
problems confronting North Dakota's Masonic lodges provides insights into
other cultural and social conflicts that pervaded the plains communities and
hence impinged upon the moral teachings of the Masons: conflicts including gambling, prohibition, and the Ku Klux Klan.

o o o

The Reconsecration of the North Dakota Freemasons

Of all Dakotans who struggled against hard times in the 1930s, those of the Farmers' Holiday Association (FHA) were the most visible and most vocal—and their wives were perhaps most significantly transformed. Still, the men and women who made their living from the soil were not the only Dakotans who felt the pinch of hard times. Nor were they the only Dakotans who made important changes and compromises in order to survive. Men and women who had never dreamed of joining a radical farm organization also discovered that staying loyal to their families, communities, and traditional roles meant working out new relationships with the New Deal, its agents, and other representatives of the new middle class.[1] No one escaped the harsh realities of the depression decade, just as no one escaped its dirt and grime.

Yet if any group of people could have avoided the suffering, it would have been the Masons. From the earliest days of settlement, the Grand Lodge A. F. and A. M. of North Dakota had been "the archetypical . . . as well as the most popular and prestigious"[2] secret fraternal order on the plains. Because its membership was limited to leading businessmen, professionals, and farmers, being a Mason in North Dakota was nearly equivalent to being successful.[3] Masons were not tenants, small farmers, or businessmen mortgaged to the hilt. Also, since one of their functions was to "validate and facilitate the exercise of masculine power," Masons did not include women.[4] They were, instead, members of the unacknowledged but omnipresent Yankee, Scandinavian, Protestant, Republican male elite within their class. As they liked to boast, the North Dakota Masons were "the best men" in every community.[5]

For all their wealth and worth, however, the Masons also had to struggle in the 1930s. And, for all the ways in which their concerns may seem frivolous or even self-indulgent in light of the life-and-death needs of those around them, their struggle was in fact more revealing than most. The Masons suffered dearly when dues, fees, and other expenses became difficult or impossible for members to afford. But, more importantly, they suffered from the decreasing interest in and authority of their order. Once the central actors in community affairs, the Masons had to learn to share that place with other clubs, outside experts, and government reformers. Still, they wondered: after making the changes they needed to keep members interested and involved and after accepting shared authority, would anything significant remain? In the 1930s, the Masons sought to reestablish their identity and to find a new role for the future, in part by looking for validation in the

past. As members of a club whose overarching purpose—and overwhelming
burden—was the protection and celebration of old-middle-class culture,
their response mirrored the strategies adopted by their class as a whole.

Freemasonry had come to the Dakotas with the very first white men who
ventured there.[6] Following the Civil War, the secret society founded in Great
Britain and again in the American northeast recovered from the political
campaigns against it and experienced an important rejuvenation. Thus soldiers at territorial forts and community builders along the Red River carried
the goals, ideals, and secret rituals of the "craft" with them as they traveled.
As Lynn Dumenil has written, the organization provided its members with
entertainment, sociability, prestige, single-sex camaraderie in a literally
"separate" sphere, and (most important of all) a middle-class "badge of respectability"—the declaration that the Masonic code of "temperance, sobriety, honesty, industry, and self-restraint" was also one's own.[7] Finally, the
Masonic "temple" was a place where those ideals and morals were celebrated through religious ritual and with a religious kind of seriousness.[8] On
the frontier, as elsewhere, Masonry was a "sacred asylum" where men
joined together both to promote and to protect middle-class morality and
culture.[9]

When the population in the Dakotas boomed, so did the craft.[10] In 1889,
when the North and South Dakota Grand Lodges were established, there
were already 1,300 Masons in the north. Two years later, the number had
almost doubled, and by 1909, when growth slowed somewhat, there were
nearly five times as many Masons. During and after World War I, membership surged again, profiting from expansion west of the Missouri River and
a national craze for "joining."[11] In 1922, North Dakota Grand Master Edwin Ripley made this enthusiastic, if ill-fated, prediction: "The gain during
the last three years has been 2,763 [new members] or 25 percent. It is safe
to assume that we shall have at least 50 percent growth every ten years.
That means in 1932 we shall have 22,000 members, in 1942, 33,000, in
1947 . . . no less than 40,000 Master Masons in North Dakota."[12]

It was just as the Masons reached the peak of their popularity, however,
that their troubles began. The first problems they faced were due to the
rapid growth itself.[13] Leaders worried, for example, about their ability to provide old-age assistance for so many new members and to preserve a feeling
of intimacy in large urban lodges.[14] Similarly, they were concerned that the
leaders of small rural lodges had been so overwhelmed by the business of
initiating new members that they were unable to do anything else.[15] Nevertheless, these were but the embarrassments of riches and were easily
resolved through refinancing, reorganization, and assistance from the
Grand Lodge.

Not so easy to handle were the problems associated with the changing character of the members and the different expectations they brought to the craft. It seemed to some leaders in the 1920s as if the craft were undergoing moral decay: reports of attendance, courtesy, and decorum problems, arrests, and suspensions for "unmasonly conduct" filled the record each year.[16] Other leaders, however, surmised that the new members were not actually less good men but simply less serious ones, men who were interested in the social rather than the business, the recreational rather than the ritualistic aspects of the craft.[17] In fact, Grand Master Theodore Elton suspected that some men had joined for no other purpose than to gain access to the Masons' higher orders, especially the prestigious Scottish Rite and fun-loving Shriners.[18]

That some Masons wanted a larger share of sociability and a smaller share of religiosity revealed the most critical challenge the Masons faced in the 1920s: developing a role for a "sacred" craft in an increasingly secular society.[19] Sociologists from Edmund Brunner's Office on Town and Country Affairs visited four North Dakota "agricultural villages" in the 1920s and 1930s and reported important trends.[20] Although most Dakota towns remained "fraternally crazy" until 1930 (significantly longer than in other parts of the country), the nature of club activities was nonetheless changing.[21] In Grafton, North Dakota, for example, the Masons were the most "highly respected" club in town, but they were now vying for new members with a recently organized Civic Club. This group held twice-monthly luncheon meetings, sponsored market days and other entertaining and profitable activities, and generally traded on the "personality . . . energy, and public-mindedness of those in charge."[22] At the same time, the fastest-growing clubs in Grafton were those that did no "business" whatsoever and also included women from time to time: the golf, baseball, and bridge clubs.[23] All in all, it seemed, Dakotans wanted to join clubs that did more than share secrets.

The Masons recognized the competition they faced from other clubs in the 1920s and initiated two related procedural and ideological changes to counteract it. The first was the "opening up" of the lodge through a dedication to "Service" and community affairs. As William Hutcheson explained in 1922, "Masonry is taking on an entirely new meaning . . . transforming the attitudes of Masons of this jurisdiction toward Masonry itself and toward their duties as men and citizens."[24] Broadly put, the transformation was from "speculative" (or intellectual) to "operative" Masonry—"the putting into practice the lessons learned in the lodge."[25] Walter Stockwell explained the reason behind the change in his typically candid fashion. "Masonry has work to do if it is to hold its present position."[26]

The "work" Masons chose to do varied widely according to the size and inclination of individual lodges. Lodges in Grand Forks and Fargo, for example, sponsored generous university scholarships, but those in LaMoure and Hebron sponsored Boy Scout troops.[27] In every lodge, however, the increased involvement in the community also prompted an increased desire to "transform . . . social and governmental institutions according to Masonic values."[28] Masons in Edgely and Mayville thus conducted "continuous school supervision"; the lodge in New England made sure "that the laws of the land are enforced in the community."[29] A fear of Catholics, Communists, and eastern European immigrants prompted some members to join another group that was devoted to 100 percent Americanism. In 1922, Grand Master Ripley demanded that any Mason who joined the Ku Klux Klan be expelled from the lodge.[30] In 1925, however, Grand Master Theodore Elton denied only any official affiliation of the two organizations. "Any Mason who desires to do so has every right to join the Klan," he determined.[31]

Part and parcel of the Masons' increased involvement in social and political affairs was their de-emphasis on ritualism. Prior to the 1920s, the Ritual of Freemasonry was all-important: it defined and reinforced the craft's sacredness, bonded members together with its secrets, and provided much of the lodge's allure to outsiders.[32] Moreover, its changelessness was evidence of the immutability of Masonry as a whole.[33] Over the course of the decade in North Dakota, however, nearly every leader stated the case against "ritualism for its own sake." "If Masonry is to devote itself mainly to Ritualism," said Stockwell, for example, "we confess to a feeling that we are spending our time and money in vain."[34] "Masonry means more than the wearing of a pin," agreed Ralph Miller.[35] In fact, some leaders argued that the ritual, crucial as it once was, now could be changed or even deleted from certain activities. Master Charles Starke put the case against religiosity most sharply of all, saying, "There is nothing sacred about our ritual."[36]

Throughout the 1920s, the North Dakota Masons tried to retain their prestige by secularizing themselves, or, as they described it later, "by guessing the way people [were] going and getting in front."[37] Rather than protect their secret allure as they had in the past, they traded openly upon it in the community. And, for the greater part of the decade, the strategy seemed to work. In Grafton, for example, the Masons continued to be "very strong and well-supported" and to sponsor "very successful" projects.[38] Nevertheless, all was not well. Between 1927 and 1929, membership increases slowed to a trickle, funds for projects grew scarcer and scarcer, and leaders worried that the move away from ritual might have gone too far. Now that the prestige of the Masons depended upon their ability to display it, it also depended upon opportunities for that display. Masonic leaders had more work to do than ever in the 1930s, precisely because they had so little "work" to do.

By 18 June 1930, Grand Secretary Walter Stockwell had been a Mason for so long that he thought he'd seen it all. Speaking to the annual "communication" in Fargo, Stockwell admitted that "there [had been] differences of opinion and one or two incidents that [had been] unpleasant" in the Grand Lodge's forty-year history. Overall, however, "peace and serenity" had reigned.[39] So it was that the particularly unpleasant events of the coming decade would deal Stockwell a particularly hard blow. "I have never put in a busier year," he wrote John Robinson in 1934, "or one that has tried one's soul as this one has."[40] With membership plunging, the future seemed dim indeed for his beloved brotherhood.

As they had in the 1920s, the Masons of the depression decade wrestled with two different but related sets of problems: declining membership and the future role of the craft as it lost its central place in the community. The Masons, like other members of their class, continued to make significant compromises to changing times in order to persist. But they also decided what things they could not change without ceasing to exist. For the Masons, then, the real work of the depression lay in identifying those aspects of the craft that were sacred after all; it lay in finding a way to adjust but not to change.

When in 1930 Grand Secretary Stockwell reported the first decline in membership in the history of North Dakota Freemasonry, he admitted that he had seen it coming.[41] Still, neither he nor anyone else foresaw the utter devastation that soon was visited upon their ranks. Between 1930 and 1944, the Grand Lodge of North Dakota lost nearly 5,000 members, or almost one-third of its total membership. Not since 1915 had there been so few Masons in North Dakota as there were in 1943. The smallest lodges suffered most. In 1934 the Berthold Lodge surrendered its charter altogether; between 1935 and 1943, nine others would do the same. Others merged or consolidated, admitting in effect that they "could not live up to their duties as Masons" on their own. As the Special Committee on Consolidating Lodges reported in 1937, "one cannot but admire the love that a brother has for his own lodge, and yet practicalities must be taken into account."[42]

The most important "practicality" to be taken into account was in fact each lodge's "account"—its financial standing. Every lodge had two sources of income and many lost the greater portion of them both. First, they lost their capital investments (savings, stocks, and real estate—usually the temple) to bank closings and foreclosures. At the same time, they lost income through unpaid dues and fees. In the 1920s, the number of Masons suspended for "non-payment of dues" fluctuated between 200 and 300. Beginning in 1930, however, this number more than doubled—to 459 in 1932, 623 in 1933, and 650 in 1935. The aging organization also lost large numbers of Masons (and their dues) to death or demission (the voluntary dismissal of a member in good standing). All in all, the decrease in revenue was nearly catastrophic: in 1936 the Grand Lodge itself required a "special emergency assessment" to avoid bankruptcy.[43]

As important as it was, the Masons' financial crisis was nevertheless only part of the problem they faced. A larger and more interesting problem was their continuing loss of authority and prestige within the community. By devoting themselves to service as they had in the 1920s, the Masons had banked on their ability to serve their communities as well or better than any other group or individual and thus had continued to attract well-qualified members. In the 1930s, however, they had very few opportunities to cash in on their investment. They had no buildings to dedicate and scarce funds for charitable activities.[44] Moreover, much of the work they had done in the past—caring for the aged and poor, for example—was taken over by the government.[45] Then, the government sponsored new, well-financed and extremely active organizations of its own, such as the 4-H Club, homemakers' clubs, and local farmers' clubs.[46] Finally, the Masons could not compete with the attractions of radios and movie houses. In 1938, the Masonic Lodge in Antler reported candidly what must have been true in many places: they had "not much doing" in their community.[47]

To keep those members they had, attract others, and keep them all interested and involved, the Masons continued to make the kind of secularizing compromises they had initiated in the 1920s. Between 1930 and 1934, for example, they agreed on a significant alteration of their traditional prohibition of Sabbath Day activities: several lodges had had the opportunity to increase revenues by renting temple space to other groups who met on Sundays. Others had increased the interest of their own members by sponsoring "picnics on Sundays, at which time parades, drills, band concerts, baseball games and other athletic sports were the chief features of the program."[48] At first, some leaders were strictly against such a change, but eventually desire and necessity won out.[49] In 1933 new by-laws allowed for rental arrangements and, moreover, for Masonic outings with "musical, religious, or educational" programs.[50]

After even more heated debate, the Masons also changed their policies regarding "the liquor question." In the 1920s, leaders were outraged at numerous reports of Masonic intemperance and compared drinking to "open rebellion."[51] After the repeal of the Eighteenth Amendment, however, the issue became more complicated. Didn't the traditional Masonic prohibition against the membership of any person directly or indirectly engaged in the trafficking of alcoholic beverages pose "a great injustice" to an organization already in trouble?[52] To some, even a consideration of this issue was unthinkable. "We cannot compromise with evil," John Robinson argued in 1933. "Our history and tradition mark us out as an institution anchored to certain fundamental principles which remain the same at all times, regardless of [sudden changes in] public opinion."[53] Nevertheless, by 1939 a new policy had been suggested so that a wide variety of men who worked in and around the liquor trade could be Masons after all.[54]

Perhaps the most significant of all the compromises the Masons made in the 1930s regarded qualifications for membership. The issue took two distinct forms: financial qualifications and qualifications of class or status. First, the Masons had to decide what to do about the huge number of men who were already members but who could no longer afford to belong. It was a tricky question: as Lynn Dumenil has pointed out, the elitist nature of the supposedly egalitarian craft was protected by large initiation fees and annual dues.[55] Similarly, it had traditionally been understood that the craft could not "afford" to retain those members who could no longer afford it.[56] In the 1930s, however, this connection became problematic: if no one in North Dakota could pay Masonic dues, did that really mean that no one deserved to be a Mason?

Beginning in the early 1930s, leaders of local lodges and the Grand Lodge alike worked out strategies for saving their memberships. For leaders of small lodges threatened with complete collapse, nothing mattered as much as saving those members who were currently enrolled. Year after year they lowered fees, remitted dues, and conferred the honorary "life-time Mason" degree on as many men as possible. Leaders in Fargo, however, worried that such stopgap measures might threaten the long-term "reputation of this Great Order."[57] They suggested instead that a minimum set of fees and dues be set for future members and that remittance be employed as rarely as possible.[58] Nevertheless, they also demanded that current members be saved whenever possible. "Go out and see these members [who are behind in fees], learn their circumstances . . . and above all, if the brother is worthy and is in distress financially, or by reason of sickness or other misfortune, protect his membership," advised Robinson in 1934.[59] Such a seemingly simple suggestion betrayed an important shift in Masonic thinking. On the one hand, the Masons had no intention of making Masonry "cheap."[60] Even so, they were admitting that a good man could experience financial hardship and still be good enough to be a Mason.

Some evidence suggests that the Masons also adjusted their notions of what qualified men for Masonic membership in the first place. Once a wholly middle-class, Anglo-Nordic, Protestant organization, the new liquor by-laws of 1939 named waiters, truck drivers, warehouse men, and clerks as possible initiates.[61] Similarly, by the end of the decade, members began to remark (not always happily) upon the ethnic diversity of the membership.[62] In another instance, Robinson was convinced to accept for membership a young man who could hardly have been called a good man, much less one of the best of his community, as he had been named in a notorious paternity suit.[63] Most intriguingly, however, the Masons began to include some Dakotans who were not men at all. Participating in the nationwide trend away from single-sex leisure, the North Dakota Masons oversaw the expansion of their women's auxiliary, the Eastern Star, and the participation of wives and girlfriends at banquets, festivals, and other out-of-temple activities.[64]

For all the adjustments they did make, there was one seemingly much less significant issue on which the Masons never budged—gambling. From time to time throughout the decade, entertainment- and income-starved lodges sponsored lotteries to raise money for activities in the community.[65] Lotteries varied widely in their type and appeal, but the leaders' reaction to them was always the same: gambling was the ultimate expression of "unmasonly conduct." Any activity that "appealed to the gambling instinct," they proclaimed, even a game of "count-the-beans," was strictly forbidden.[66] As Charles Milloy explained, gambling represented schemes "for making easy money [for those] who desire to live by their wits rather than by hard work . . . [and] to get something for little or nothing."[67]

For the Masons, the trouble with gambling was much the same as it had been for antigambling reformers since the early nineteenth century. First and foremost, gambling detracted from the importance of work and production to the creation of wealth; it said in essence that a man did not actually have to make or do something to reap financial reward and, further, that capitalism was not a fair and rational system but was irrational, unfair, and could be played and manipulated. Perhaps most importantly to the men on the northern plains, gambling—and lotteries in particular (because one individual literally profited at the expense of others)—betrayed the cooperative ideal of work for a common good.[68] It was one thing for a Mason to have made money through "good work, true work, and square work" and to have lost it in a momentary irregularity of the market; it was quite another for him to try and "steal" it back from his neighbors.[69]

When they forbade gambling, the Masons employed a strategy altogether different from compromise. They worked instead to demarcate those aspects of Masonry that they would *not* compromise, those things that *were* sacred and immutable after all. As we shall see, this search took the Masons in many different directions, but, most significantly, it led to a recovery of the past and a reconsecration of ritual. What they discovered in both was not what they had already deemed "old-fashioned"—not Sabbath Day prohibitions, temperance, or a promulgation of secrecy—but the secular ideals of work and community that lay at the heart of old-middle-class culture. With their other bonds becoming more and more tenuous, these ideals would provide the "cement" Masons needed for now and the days to come. Moreover, however closely they tied it to their craft, the Masons were hardly the only Dakotans returning to past triumphs in search of validation for the future.

There were a number of different reasons why the Masons found a retreat into the past to be a propitious task for the depression decade. Digging up old stories, collecting photographs, and dedicating landmarks was, for one thing, inexpensive work that kept otherwise idle Masons interested and busy. Similarly, consecrating Masonic history honored the elderly Masons who were now passing. And the lessons of the past had a purpose, too: to inspire or admonish present-day Masons whose spirits might be flagging. Masonic forefathers had faced their share of trials, leaders reminded their flocks, and had survived them—without the "uncounted comforts and conveniences" members now enjoyed.[70] If they had not failed, why should their progeny, Stockwell liked to ask. "Are we any less resourceful than they? Are we any less devoted?"[71]

Most importantly, uncovering the pioneer past helped Masons identify the "starting point" of Masonry: those ideals and standards that had always been and would always be peculiar to their craft.[72] As early as 1930, one leader explained, "It is proper sometimes to look backward so that we may better look forward."[73] In 1935 Mark Forkner elaborated on this beginning: "The great sacrifices of our pioneer Masons . . . should constitute an incentive to us of the present generation . . . to emulate the noble qualities in our . . . present day."[74] Lewis Thompson was more didactic: "The ideals of our forefathers . . . who carried Masonry's banner to the far reaches of the Dakota prairies must be, can be, and will be perpetuated."[75] What mattered most about the pioneers, then, was not so much what they had believed and professed as what they had achieved—in other words, the "noble qualities" that had bonded them together would bond Masons together forevermore.

Orin G. Libby, professor at the University of North Dakota and Grand Lodge Historian from 1929 until his death, took on the job of determining exactly who the pioneer Masons had been and what they had believed and valued.[76] To do so, he began at the beginning, trying to discover, lodge by lodge, exactly who the original founders had been. In his first report, he stressed the elite nature of the club: the pioneer Masons were "the finest men that eastern communities could send us," he reported in 1930.[77] Along the way, Libby documented the productive activities of bankers, doctors, merchants, and lawyers—always mentioning their line of work, their struggles, and their ultimate success. Of those Masons who had come down from Canada, another speaker stressed the same kinds of "qualities," saying they were "truly among the finest people on earth."[78]

It was not just the elite nature of the early Masons that Libby and others documented, however. They also went over and over the ideals and values that were associated with Masonic pioneers, recreating in effect the bond between wealth and worth, capital and character that in the 1930s had been so sorely challenged. First, they looked at early Masons as workers and, not surprisingly, found that they had been hard workers, self-reliant and resourceful men who through good character and honest labor had enjoyed considerable success.[79] Moreover, they were good, generous, and "hospitable" neighbors—people from whom "you could get a meal anytime and they were all happy to have you."[80] Last but not least, they were fiercely loyal—to their God, nation, state, community, and, yes, local lodge. As many leaders recalled, the early Masons traveled by foot along unmarked paths and roads to "improvised" lodge rooms because, at bottom, "the brethren of that day were strong men who took their Masonry seriously."[81]

Two events marked the apex of Libby's attempt to invent an immutable Masonic character by recreating the Masonic past. The first, on 21 May 1935, was the dedication of a memorial to Lewis and Clark (both of whom had been Masons) at the site of their winter campgrounds along the Missouri River near Washburn.[82] Although Libby spoke at length about the significance of their exploration,[83] it was not that accomplishment that interested his committee but the ideals they carried with them. As committee chair John Robinson put it, they hoped that the marker would stand "to the courage, the heroism, the fidelity to trust, and the enduring service to country of these distinguished Masons."[84]

The second celebration of the Masonic past took on a more local flavor, as delegations from all over the state participated in a historical display and pageant at the Golden Jubilee Anniversary celebration. Again, what was included in the celebration revealed what had become so important about Masonic history. For example, Libby had arranged displays of three historical periods of Masonry, but the pioneer display attracted the most attention and enthusiasm. There, Masons saw photographs and documents of community builders they may have known personally, as well as pictures of their own lodges in earlier times.[85] In his opening welcome, Master Everest Fowler of Grand Forks reminded "the older members of the craft" why such a display was so important. "You can with pride," he said, "pass on to the younger generation . . . the past, with the positive injunction that they carry on from where you leave off." And, to the younger men, he concluded, "[You] have been handed a heritage by your forefathers which [you] must not fail to preserve."[86] Finally, in the hymn that followed, the heritage was revealed: "labor," "duty," "faith," "trust," and, finally, work accomplished "together."[87]

It was not enough, however, for the Masons simply to dig up the lessons and examples of the past, they also had to give them life in the here and now. To do this, they returned to the ritual that they so completely, if only briefly, had forsaken. As early as 1927, William Hutcheson worried that the ritual had become "a lost art . . . in some lodges" and recommended that "the study of the Ritual [be] made one of the subjects of [next] year's program."[88] In the 1930s, the Masons would do more than study the ritual, they would perform it again and again. In fact, they were told to perform some ceremonies at least twice a month, whether there was actually any reason to do so or not.[89] Then, once every year for three years, they held "reconsecration nights" when every lodge throughout the state met at the same time on the same night, performed the same rituals, heard the same lectures, and learned the same lessons.[90]

Over and again throughout the decade, Masonic leaders repeated why they believed this return to ritual was so important. For the most part, they emphasized the lessons that ritual taught. "[Ritual] may well be compared to the lens through which Masonry projects the sublime teachings," Forkner explained at the 1935 "Sit-in-lodge Night." "If there are any flaws in the lens the candidate for light will be compelled to look upon a faulty picture."[91] Not surprisingly, the lessons they revealed in the ritual were the same ones they discovered in the past—the importance of work, faith, loyalty, neighborliness, courage, service, independence—the foundation, in other words, of their culture. For Forkner, just three words summed up what Masonry had brought and would always bring to the world. "Faith, hope, and charity," he said, are the "cement that turns ceremony and symbol into a living reality."[92]

In short, the ritual of the 1930s was far from a return to earlier religiosity or ritualism "for its own sake." It was instead a way for the ideals presented in Masonic history to be sanctified in everyday life and used as a force for the future. Ritual was no longer important in the way that it bonded men together in secrecy and sacredness, but in the way that it gave them a renewed purpose and an initiation into Masonic history and values. Even if Masons could no longer be men of action, Forkner argued, they could nevertheless be men of "vision," taking the "spiritual" lessons of Masonry "into every walk of life."[93] Simply put, Masons believe that expressing their ideals through ritual was something they could *do*. Ritual was work as important as any work Masons had ever done before.

In 1937 Stockwell looked back on the previous decade and did not mince his words. "No Grand Jurisdiction has had a larger share of misfortune . . . than has North Dakota." Since the boom years, he recalled, internal and external pressures had brought Freemasonry in North Dakota to the brink of ruin. Even so, he could find reason enough to be proud and optimistic: "Everywhere there has been a determination to adjust [ourselves] to reality, to adopt new methods and procedures suited to new conditions." Now, he believed, Masonic influence was more important than ever—so long as it did not keep on adjusting. "In a world of unrest and social change," he concluded, "it is essential that there remain some things that are stable and unchanging. These days therefore constitute Freemasonry's greatest opportunity."[94]

As utterly contradictory as it sounded, Stockwell's description of the Masons' survival strategy actually made perfect sense. For the Masons, the trick to surviving the Great Depression had been to change some things completely and other things not at all. Religiosity and secrecy for their own sakes were gone. An exclusive position of power and authority was gone. But the ideals of work and community, retrieved from the past and revived through the ritual, remained. These ideals, sanctified now as projects in themselves, were the Masons' ticket to the future. When at long last membership increases began to show on the books again, the Masons were certain of their role. What was important about the Masons in 1945 was not what they could do—rather little in the complex postwar world—but what they could say and think and believe. Their purpose was, in short, to represent a way of life and a way of living to everyone else in the world who, presumably, could no longer achieve it. "Love thy neighbor as thyself," proclaimed Grand Orator Alexander Burr in 1945, the year that would mark the end of the Dakotans' "hard times" and the beginning of an era with frustrations all its own, "this is Masonic philosophy reduced to its fundamentals."[95]

NOTES

1. Perhaps the best example here comes from Walsh County, North Dakota, where voters debated the merits of accepting Public Works Administration funds for a new courthouse. They rejected the government's first proposal in July 1935 because they did not want "to be bribed into mortgaging their own future . . . by the government offer of generous assistance" (*Walsh County Record,* 18 July 1935, p. 8). Three years later, however, they accepted an even more generous offer. This time many people believed that "if this community does not avail themselves [*sic*] of this offer, then another community will. In the end we will have to pay our share and get nothing in return for it" (*Walsh County Record,* 11 July 1935, p. 8; 22 Sept. 1938, p. 12).

2. Dumenil, *Freemasonry and American Culture,* p. xi.

3. Although the memberships of urban lodges included more men with white-collar occupations than with independent employment (Dumenil, *Freemasonry and American Culture,* pp. 11–13, 225), in rural North Dakota the Masons were still solidly old-middle-class. There, the Masonic ranks were filled by "the very best type of citizenry . . . professional men of high intelligence . . . leaders in business in their communities . . . artisans whose manual skill has given them a conspicuous place in their material constructiveness of their towns and cities, [and] farmers with an horizon besides that of their fields—in short, a worthy portion of the general community, the practical, the trained, and the cultured portion of it" (*BT,* 4 Nov. 1929, p. 4).

4. Clawson, "Nineteenth-Century Women's Auxiliaries," p. 41. See also Clawson, *Constructing Brotherhood;* Carnes, *Secret Ritual and Manhood in Victorian America.*

5. *Proceedings,* 1924, p. 69; *BT,* 4 Nov. 1929, p. 4.

6. General histories of Freemasonry in North Dakota come in a variety of forms. Individual lodges have printed their own histories, and these can be found in the collections at the University of North Dakota and the State Historical Society of North Dakota in Bismarck. Two syntheses are also available, one in manuscript form

in Box 41, File 6, Libby Papers, the other published in Pond, *Masonry in North Dakota.*

7. Dumenil, *Freemasonry and American Culture*, p. 88.

8. Ibid., pp. 31–32.

9. Ibid., pp. 38–39.

10. A complete compilation of membership figures appears in *Proceedings*, 1986, pp. 233–34.

11. Dumenil, *Freemasonry and American Culture*, p. xi.

12. *Proceedings*, 1922, p. 23.

13. Generally speaking, these difficulties were common to lodges around the country. Dumenil, *Freemasonry and American Culture*, p. xiii.

14. *Proceedings*, 1922, pp. 23, 30, 60, 89–90.

15. Ibid., 1926, p. 82.

16. Ibid., 1922, p. 89; 1927, p. 26.

17. Ibid., 1922, p. 59.

18. Ibid., 1925, p. 58.

19. For a discussion of this point on a national level, see Dumenil, *Freemasonry and American Culture*, part II.

20. Brunner's team of sociologists published three important accounts of rural life based on their 1924, 1930, and 1937 observations of 140 small towns throughout America. Brunner, Hughes, and Patten, *American Agricultural Villages*; Brunner and Kolb, *Rural Social Trends*; Brunner, *Rural Trends in Depression Years*. The manuscript surveys from three of the four North Dakota towns studied (Grafton, Mayville, Casselton, and Oakes) are available at the North Dakota Institute for Regional Studies, North Dakota State University, Fargo, N.D.

21. On changing trends in club activities, see especially Brunner and Kolb, *Rural Social Trends*, pp. 268–69. See also "Grafton, North Dakota," 1930, "Note."

22. "Grafton, North Dakota," 1924, pp. 31–32.

23. Ibid., 1930, p. 7; see also Fass, *Damned and the Beautiful*.

24. *Proceedings*, 1922, pp. 24, 68.

25. Ibid., 1924, p. 69.

26. Ibid., 1922, p. 45.

27. Ibid., 1924, p. 70.

28. Ibid., 1922, p. 44.

29. Ibid., 1924, p. 70.

30. Ibid., 1922, p. 85.

31. Ibid., 1925, p. 59.

32. Dumenil, *Freemasonry and American Culture*, pp. 37–39.

33. Ibid., p. 32.

34. *Proceedings*, 1922, p. 44.

35. Ibid., 1922, p. 45.

36. Ibid., 1931, p. 17.

37. Ibid., 1939, p. 70.

38. "Grafton, North Dakota," 1930, "Note."

39. *Proceedings*, 1930, p. 27.

40. W. L. Stockwell to John Robinson, 24 Dec. 1934, Box 1, File 19, Robinson Papers.

41. *Proceedings*, 1930, p. 27.

42. Ibid., 1937, p. 70.

43. Each annual report listed the membership losses for various categories in the General Secretary's address. See also *Proceedings*, 1937, p. 25.

44. The first discussion of how *little* Masonic work had been done appears in *Proceedings*, 1930, p. 11.

45. The Masons were particularly perplexed by the impact of the Social Security Act on their charitable activities (*Proceedings*, 1936, p. 34; 1937, pp. 27, 54–55), but their general issues of the role of Masonic relief in the age of government reform plagued them as well. Leaders were concerned, for example, that members were counting on Masonic relief too much and beginning to see Masonic relief as something they wanted to receive for themselves rather than give to others (*Proceedings*, 1937, p. 44; 1938, p. 35).

46. Brunner, *Rural Trends in Depression Years*, p. 284; Hay, "Social Organizations," pp. 23–26, 85–87.

47. *Proceedings*, 1938, p. 78. For a similar argument brought up to the recent past, see Emmett, *Freemasonry in Manitoba*, pp. 63–64.

48. *Proceedings*, 1933, p. 85.

49. Ibid., 1931, p. 10.

50. Ibid., 1933, pp. 10, 85–86.

51. Ibid., 1931, p. 11.

52. Ibid., 1938, p. 20; 1937, p. 18.

53. Ibid., 1933, p. 35.

54. Ibid., 1938, p. 20; 1939, p. 29. See also "Proclamation," (1938), Box 1, File 25, Robinson Papers.

55. Dumenil, *Freemasonry and American Culture*, pp. 12–13.

56. As Charles Starke put it, "Suspensions [for unpaid dues] . . . is [*sic*] merely an elimination of those whom we could not assimilate and no cause of worry. Our strength does not lie in numbers, but in a well organized body of good men, thinking alike on all great social and moral problems" (*Proceedings*, 1931, p. 9).

57. Ibid., 1933, p. 20.

58. Ibid., 1934, pp. 18–19.

59. J. Robinson to all members, 1 Oct. 1932, Box 1, File 28, Robinson Papers. For his own part, Robinson compiled a list of the names and addresses of delinquents from his home lodge in Garrison. The list reveals a part of the problem that leaders did not discuss openly: some of the Masons were not just delinquent—they were gone. One Garrison member, Floyd C. Agnew, for example, owed the lodge $11 but listed his current address in care of the Kenyon Beauty Parlor in Palo Alto, Ca. In some of the worst drought years, the only Grand Lodge in the country that increased its membership was the Grand Lodge of California. J. Robinson to Stockwell, 26 Oct. 1935, Box 1, File 22, Robinson Papers.

60. *Proceedings*, 1937, p. 9.

61. "Proclamation," (1938), Box 1, File 25, Robinson Papers.

62. *Proceedings*, 1938, p. 85. See also ibid., 1986, p. 235, for a list of all Masonic Grand Masters. By the 1960s and 1970s, nearly every leader, all of whom presumably joined the craft some time after 1925, has a Nordic or a German surname.

63. Harold Rease to J. Robinson, 16 Nov. 1939, Box 1, File 26, Robinson Papers.

64. I am assuming here that when the Masons said they invited "families" and other "non-members" to informal social functions, they meant to include women. See, for example, *Proceedings*, 1938, p. 20. See also the participation of the women's auxiliary in preparing meals at annual communications, including the Golden Jubilee. "Golden Jubilee," Box 1, File 28, Robinson Papers. Of course, women's auxiliaries did not just act as support structures for the male organizations; to the contrary, they sometimes had (perhaps unintended) feminist implications. See Clawson, "Nineteenth-Century Women's Auxiliaries," especially pp. 56–58; Dumenil, *Freemasonry and American Culture*, pp. 25–26, 196–97.

65. *Proceedings*, 1938, p. 19.

66. Ibid.

67. Ibid., 1932, p. 10.

68. Fabian, "Speculation and Gambling on the Chicago Board of Trade." See also Fabian, *Card Sharps, Dream Books, and Bucket Shops*.

69. *Proceedings*, 1937, p. 44.

70. Ibid., 1931, p. 25.

71. Ibid., p. 25.

72. Ibid., 1938, p. 60.

73. Ibid., 1930, p. 27.

74. Ibid., 1935, p. 20.

75. Ibid., p. 153.

76. Much of Libby's work is documented through correspondence in Box 41, Libby Papers.

77. *Proceedings*, 1930, p. 174.

78. Ibid.

79. Ibid., 1930, p. 170.

80. Ibid., p. 174.

81. Ibid., 1935, p. 148.

82. Ibid., 1935, p. 95.

83. Ibid., 1935, pp. 115–16.

84. "Lewis and Clark Memorial," Box 1, File 20, Robinson Papers.

85. *Proceedings*, 1939, pp. 141–45.

86. Ibid., p. 7.

87. Ibid., p. 8.

88. Ibid., 1927, p. 27.

89. "Important Business and Legislation," Box 1, File 28, Robinson Papers.

90. In 1935 Mark Forkner hosted "Reconsecration Night"; in 1936 L. K. Thompson held "Forward Together, Brethren Night"; and in 1937 William Hutchinson convened "Rededication Night."

91. *Proceedings*, 1935, p. 31.

92. Ibid., p. 174.

93. Ibid. As William Hutchinson put it by quoting Elihu Root, "Not what ultimate object we can attain in our short lives, but what tendencies toward higher standards of conduct we can aid in our generation is the test that determines our duty of service" (*Proceedings*, 1937, p. 20).

94. Ibid., 1936, pp. 28–29.

95. Ibid., 1945, p. 28.

POEMS

WILLIAM KLOEFKORN

NEBRASKA STATE POET William Kloefkorn grew up, ironically, in Attica, Kansas, "population more or less seven hundred, half a dozen churches, and a town ordinance extremely unfavorable to anything not white or Protestant." Although marked by family poverty and several near-tragedies, including his brother's near-death by drowning, Kloefkorn's childhood was something out of *Tom Sawyer*: skinny dipping in the pond at Ely's Sandpit, fishing with a cane pole for turtle and bullheads in Heacock's reservoir, hopping short rides on the slow freights of the Atchison, Topeka & Santa Fe Railroad, Panhandle Division. Kloefkorn delivered newspapers, hung out at the corner drug store playing pinball and reading comics, attended the Ecumenical United Brotherhood church on Sundays, smoked cigarettes, played pranks, chased girls. His experience, at least as he recalls it in an extensive series of autobiographical poems ranging across many books, is archetypal and idyllic.

Kloefkorn's language and experiences reflect life in the pool hall as well as in the church. He may quote or parody a familiar hymn, or he may quote or adapt a bit of café wisdom. Sometimes Kloefkorn dichotomizes the small-town boyhood experience into a naïve, middle-class narrator and an alter-ego from the wrong side of the tracks—some "animal at the far edge of my mind," an overly hormonal adolescent, or, more congenially, "Carlos," son of a Mexican American gandy dancer. The dark-side alter-ego gives Kloefkorn some of his best lines and most colorful phrases: "got your fat ears lowered," "clean as a Presbyterian's hands," "disaster with a dress on," "dressed fit to slaughter," "all the way from hell to breakfast," "two-timing, piss-complected son of a bitch." Kloefkorn is a poet of place and voice and of the small town in the late 1940s as seen over the shoulder of memory—fondly and from a distance.

o o o

Trading Comic Books

Tub Schmidt is a tub because
he eats too much,
and he eats too much because
he has too much to eat,
and he has too much to eat because
he has too much money,
yet he believes that someone
as beautiful as Wonder Woman
might one day jump right off the page
and pay him some attention,
so when we trade comic books
I save my Wonder Woman
until the last,
until Tub Schmidt begins to plead, then drool,
which means that for one Wonder Woman
I can expect to receive
a Submariner,
a Torch and a Toro,
a Batman and a Robin,
a Captain Marvel and a Superman,
plus all of Tub's loose change,
and just because he honestly believes
that someone as lovely and as trim
as Wonder Woman could care
for such a slob, who has
acne, too, like him.

Late Evening, and My Mother Is Calling Me In

It is late evening,
      late September, and my mother
            is calling me in,

she knows what is
      best for me, she does,
            the importance of a good

night's rest before the start
      of another week in school,
            and the dream of sleep

I'll admit appeals,
      yet the night
            likewise attracts, how

lofting the orange sphere
      into the net above the garage
            I want to compete against myself

indefinitely—but
      it is late evening, and my mother
            is calling me in,

and her voice like the arc
      of the orange ball
            transecting a full harvest moon

appeals, that and
      the ache in my bones
            from a long day doing all those

memorable ups & downs tomorrow
      I'll not remember,
            my mother's voice meanwhile

calling me in, voice
      with its history of thick concern—
            and the evening no less thick

with something I swear I love but
      must live another lifetime
            of nights alone and otherwise

to learn.

Prove It

I see Bubba Barnes
sneak a comic book
from the rack in
the Rexall drug-
store, and the next
day at recess
I tell him. He
says Prove it.

I even saw the
name of the comic,
I tell him. Sub-
mariner. Isn't
that right? He
says Prove it.

I don't have to
prove it, I say.
I know you did it
and you know you
did it. So, he
says, prove it, ass-
eyes. Just prove it.

You can go to
hell for swearing,
I say. Bubba says
Prove it. And for
stealing, I say,
and for not tell-
ing the truth. Bub-
ba says Prove it.
Prove it, you
little peckerhead,
he says. Prove it
prove it prove
it prove it
prove it.

Sunday Morning

This morning I am trotting the route,
my father not far away in the old Ford coupe,
its heater humming all the hymns
I ever knew the tunes to,
Sunday papers on the seat at his right
like a massive passenger,
and the pace from beginning to end
doesn't vary, I at a slow heavy trot,
the old Ford in low gear
growling in the clear bright icy
January air like a good large watchdog
creeping on the rollers of its haunches,
always about to lurch, yet never lurching,
my breath meanwhile in measured bursts
preceding me, fogging the eyes,
chilling the face, all things
in the early aftermath of sunrise
a most delicate syncopation, the smoke
from my father's cigarette (I'm
trotting now beside the car,
reaching for papers to fill again
that hollow in my arm) sweet
as the tune being hummed by the heater,
sweet and as warm as the tune
being hummed by the heater,
I trotting beside the open window
catching both the warmth and the song,
and my father, silent behind the wheel,
helping me this morning with the route,
giving me a hand to relieve this
impossible Sunday morning
weight, laying that hand on my shoulder
to wake me, to tell me that the bitter
cold is here, to say, without
my asking, I'll take you.

Collecting for the Wichita Beacon

The first house I step into
has this picture of a Marine corporal
atop the radio,
dungaree jacket pressed to a fare-you-well,
cap tilted back cockeyed
confident.

Tossing aside the paper,
the young woman, eyes so very dark, so
large, so downright beautiful,
says we are winning,
says that in spite of Wake Island and Guadalcanal
it is only a matter of time.
She tells me this again as, fumbling in her purse,
she comes up with three quarters and a forerunner
to the Franklin D. Roosevelt memorial dime.

Before releasing the coins into my hand
she moves the tip of an index finger
ever so lightly
against my palm. O
she has seldom been quite this frightened, never
this lonely. She thinks maybe, honestly,
this time she is going all the way
crazy. Against my face
her kiss is how much more
than a mother's.

I am not there to do any type of singing
when the telegram comes.
Sixty-seven customers, sixty-seven screen-
doors under relentless siege
hanging on.
And time to collect again.
And John Wayne shot again by a slant-eyed sniper.
And my face, where the kiss was, napalm burning.
And I cannot so much as give you the time of day,
and I cannot tell you, not even
to the nearest war,
how old I am.

William Kloefkorn

Running Home

You leave the pool hall
    walking
        but because it's a brisk evening

and you have energy enough
    to last a lifetime
        you begin to run—

slowly, at first,
    because you have plenty of time,
        and because there is yet light enough

for you to notice that
    not only are there trees,
        but also limbs and leaves

with their shapes described
    more sharply than imaginable
        against a darkening sky. Until

suddenly that darkening sky
    fulfills itself, and
        you increase the pace,

as if the darkness were itself
    a subtle premonition,
        until the pace becomes a sprint

you can't sustain,
    though you sustain it,
        the premonition now reality,

someone or something
    not far behind you, closing in,
        until the rattle of your feet

against the pine boards of the bridge
    just south of Mabel Cleveland's shanty
        seems palpable,

but looking right and left
    for the long arm of truth and mercy
        you see only the eyes of maybe animals,

beneath you the flat gravel road
    assuming a sudden curvature
        to send you laboring uphill—

O kiss my dead ass, Marvin,
    this must be a movie,
        this must be the awful climax,

over the crest if not in the ditches
    let there be cavalry—
        until fear is the taste

of your own fear
    strong as alum on the tongue
        and the last thing you hear is

the cue-ball going so smartly
    click! against the 8-ball,
        the 8-ball heavy

as any young boy's flesh, here
    or in the sweet hereafter
        going down.

Allowance

It's the quarter I take into the drugstore
for a coke and the newest issue
of Captain Marvel. What does it mean
to save? In church
I hear that someone
I never played house with
loves me,
Velma Jean meanwhile
not willing to give me the time of day. So
what?My buddy Ray
stands at the pinball machine
with a fistful of nickels. Tilt
spelled backwards is tlit. If I save
for the rest of my life
will my children love me? Ray is older:
he failed fifth grade
twice. In three or four years
he'll be gaining more yards than you can
shake a stick at. I flip
through my Captain Marvel with one eye
on Billy Batson and the other
on the lights of the Bally that
Ray with his heavy touch
tilts again. But almost single-handedly
he will win the game against Kiowa,
blood from somebody's nose
on the white of his helmet
like a smear of mascot,
and when leukemia not long thereafter
executes a perfect body-block
my buddy Ray will roll over
like the good dog he is
and play dead, two bits, four bits,
six bits, a dollar,
Captain Marvel smacking evil
squarely in the kisser,
and I still have a dime that maybe
I'll save, maybe, on second thought,
knowing what eventually
I'll live to verify,
I'll squander.

Quixotic

Carlos reads books whose pages come to him, he says,
    on the wings of small birds,
    on the unassuming backs of turtles.

Tonight he sits in a booth in the Tumbleweed Cafe,
    tilting at windmills, Susanne
    by way of absence

having become his lovely Dulcinea. In her honor
    he has ordered that the Tumbleweed—
    den of iniquity—

close its doors until further notice, those days
    between the closing and the notice
    to be devoted to a myriad

of purgings. I meanwhile order a hot-beef sandwich
    and a schooner of cold milk.
    Not far away a Coca-Cola clock

ticks down the seconds. When no one closes the doors
    Carlos turns the page. He looks up
    to tell me this and that

about Susanne, her hopes, her dreams, her potential
    whereabouts, her perfectly questionable
    rationale for being

elsewhere. When no one closes the doors we do so
    ourselves, leaving behind the clock-
    worn faces of regular customers.

Soon we are standing in the drugstore beside the Bally,
    waiting for Doc with his whisky
    to redeem the day. Carlos

touches the machine as if its form were substance
    recently restored, and human. In young man-
    hood, as in knighthood, Carlos says,

there are ways of adjusting everything.

The New Jerusalem

*... and the city was pure gold
like unto clear glass.*
REV. 21:21

What Carlos tells me
I cannot dispute,
that God is a frustrated architect

working to envision the Ideal City,
that if and when His grandiose scheme
achieves fruition

He will call His favorite servants
up from their myriad graves
to occupy the City,

both call and occupancy
occurring so swiftly that not an instant
will have passed

between Stasis and Motion—Aunt Ruth
as happy as if she had good sense
clicking her high jasper heels

through the portals of a sapphire K-Mart,
Grandfather standing at the corner
of Shall and Shall Not,

turning his hat in his hands, praying
without surcease to be delivered
across that garnished, ungodly river

back to his native shore.

Reap the Wild Wind

In the drugstore
Josephine mixes, according to Carlos
    the thickest malts
    west of the Mississippi, her helpmate
    meanwhile in a back room
    filling prescriptions,
    some of them legal. Because Doc,
    according to Carlos,
    is the local bootlegger, this town
    being drier, Carlos says,
    than a popcorn fart.

We take our drinks with us to the movie,
popcorn and Susan Hayward equally
bittersweet. Popcorn. Josephine malt.
Druscilla Alston. Giant squid. Ray
Milland. John Wayne and a bittersweet ending.

Which later somehow compels me to take Carlos
another step into my chamber of haunts:
Yesterday my father laid hands on my mother.
There was, I tell him,
some blood on the dashboard.

And so forth. After which we return
to the drugstore, Josephine gone, Doc
with a glass, his accomplice,
at the Bally.

And so forth. When we leave, Carlos says,
Amigo, if you need anything, just
give me a whistle. If I can't find it,
I'll teach you how to live
without it.

Carlos heads south, I north.

The Last Picture Show

FROM *Main Street Blues*

RICHARD O. DAVIES

A LL ACROSS THE MIDWEST the lament seemed to be the same. Life was slowly oozing out of small towns that for so long had provided the backbone of a society and economy built around the family farm. By the end of the 1920s the early warning signs were present—in the loss of business to nearby cities created by the availability of convenient automobile travel and in the departure of many young people for better opportunities in the cities. This process of decline during the decade of the Great Depression was arrested by World War II.

The economic impetus of the war carried towns into a period of false hopes and heightened expectations for a few years after the surrender of Germany and Japan, but with the powerful postwar economic and social trends—encouraging the growth of big cities and rendering the economic bases of the small towns increasingly fragile—the process of decline set in. *Colliers* reported in 1947 the "decline and decay" of small towns across the land. "The small centers in most parts of the country are dying," the magazine stated, noting the closing of shops and stores, the eroding tax base, and the loss of a younger generation to the expanding cities. The location of what it called "the single, most wholesome, democratic way of living" was facing extinction. In 1952 a writer in *Commonweal* warned that "These little towns are slowly dying, though they are hard to kill. They lose many of their young people but the older folk have nowhere to go. How they manage to exist in a world that seems to have no place for anything between the corporate farm and the city suburb perplexes even their inhabitants."

One such town was southwestern Ohio's Camden, with a population of 1,000, whose residents liked to boast that it was the birthplace of the novelist Sherwood Anderson, whose best work detailed the depressing lives of individuals living in the fictional small town of *Winesburg, Ohio*. The historian Richard O. Davies explored the fate of this town and identified a series of major blows that occurred in the fifteen years after the war to bring it to its knees. What transpired in Camden was replicated innumerable times across the Midwest; the details were different but the results all too tragically similar.

o   o   o

The years immediately following V-J Day were euphoric ones in Camden. Across the United States the economy expanded, in part owing to the stimulus derived from the enormous expenditure of federal defense dollars, but also owing to pent-up consumer demand resulting from fifteen years of depression and war. The country was about to enter a period of sustained growth that would carry American society to a level of affluence and economic strength unprecedented in history. Five years after the war ended, the economic expansion showed no signs of abating; the postwar economic boom made even the heady days of the 1920s pale in comparison.

For several years, like many similar towns scattered across the United States, Camden participated in the postwar boom. However, by the mid-1950s, although metropolitan areas continued to expand, the boom in Camden began to ebb. By the 1960s an ominous pattern of economic stagnation had set in. The contrast to nearby cities was obvious. While the urban areas of southwestern Ohio grew in size and economic diversity, Camden found itself struggling and was eventually unable even to maintain its position. Although the spectacular growth occurring across the Sun Belt received the preponderance of media attention, major urban growth also affected older sections of the country, including southwestern Ohio. Within two decades following V-J Day, Camden had been whipsawed by a series of events that undercut its economy and altered the very character of the town.

The powerful postwar economic expansion stimulated a massive urban housing construction boom. Much of the growth took place on the edge of the larger cities, and new rings of suburban developments transformed the structure of American urban life. Seldom did a month go by in Dayton or Cincinnati that yet another subdivision did not announce its "grand opening."[1] Central cities were undercut not only by residential suburbs but also by shopping centers and industrial parks as both commerce and manufacturing relocated to the urban fringes. The central city of Cincinnati, for example, grew by only 50,000 between 1940 and 1960, reaching a total of 502,000; in sharp contrast, its metropolitan area expanded by 225,000 to reach a total population of 864,000. Dayton's metropolitan area also expanded, the population of Montgomery County increasing from 295,000 before the war to 527,000 in 1960. Most of Cincinnati's new manufacturing and service enterprises were built on inexpensive land in its northern suburbs and across the Ohio River in northern Kentucky, rather than in the traditional industrial core located near the central business district. Such long established Queen City companies as Kroger Foods, Crosley Manufacturing, Procter and Gamble, Lever Brothers, and several local breweries also expanded their operations.

Dayton's traditionally large employers also participated in the national economic expansion: National Cash Register, DELCO, and General Motors, including one of its major subsidiaries, Frigidaire. Adding to Dayton's healthy economy was the enormous expansion of Wright-Patterson Air Force Base, which became home to a major wing of the Strategic Air Command, complete with B-52 bombers, sophisticated electronics, and nuclear weaponry. In Hamilton, such established firms as Mosler Safe, Ohio Casualty Insurance, Champion Paper, and Niles Machinery expanded operations, but the largest employer now was Fisher Body, which opened a modern factory that employed five thousand workers to manufacture automobile bodies for General Motors. This new plant was located just south of Hamilton in the rapidly growing suburban community of Fairfield. A few miles farther south, on the northern edge of Cincinnati, General Electric opened an industrial complex to manufacture jet aircraft engines, another major economic stimulus to the Ohio economy provided by the cold war. The huge blast furnaces and rolling mills at the Armco plant in Middletown, having been awakened from a decade-long stupor by the war, now produced the steel demanded by a booming American industrial economy. And, shrouded in secrecy, some ten miles southwest of Hamilton near the small community of Harrisonsville, a mysterious new factory opened. Its employment statistics were kept secret, but passersby noted several hundred cars in its parking lots. Located behind high chain fences and surrounded by an inordinate level of security, this subsidiary of the Renauld Corporation manufactured radioactive components for America's growing arsenal of nuclear weapons.

These and many smaller employers offered jobs that proved irresistible to the men and women of Camden. Those who had established homes in the town became part of the growing national army of long-distance commuters. With gasoline prices under twenty-five cents a gallon, they willingly drove a hundred miles round trip each workday, sometimes even farther. Those whose roots were not as well established in Camden moved to Hamilton or Middletown, or to such new suburban communities as Fairborn, Beavercreek, or Kettering near Dayton, or to Fairfield or one of the many new suburban developments clustered around Cincinnati. The younger the individuals, the more powerful the lure of the city seemed to be.

This outward migration was intensified by the growing importance of a college education. Increasing numbers of Camden High School graduates, sometimes approaching 20 percent of a senior class, now opted for college; the most popular institution was Miami University, just fifteen miles away in nearby Oxford. The majority of graduates, however, never considered college. Young women sought urban positions as typists, clerks, and receptionists, and their male counterparts frequently looked to the military as a way of making the transition between adolescence and adulthood. After spending a few years on active duty, they returned to live and work in one of the area's industrial cities.[2]

A destructive cycle thus took hold. Camden provided a secure haven in which young people were reared and educated, but on reaching adulthood they left for greater opportunities than those available in their hometown. This pattern emerged incrementally. It was masked for many years by the postwar economic expansion and the optimism it generated. During the immediate postwar years, a large number of veterans returned home, often marrying their high school sweethearts and establishing themselves locally. As veterans made the transition to civilian life, "Camden Behind the Men Behind the Guns" was replaced with a "Back From the Service" column.[3]

Some of the returning veterans, like former star high school athlete Stanley Humphrey, took advantage of the educational benefits of the GI bill. He enrolled at Ohio University and earned a degree in education. After teaching in Camden for two years, he departed for a better paying position in northeastern Ohio.[4] Most Camden veterans, however, decided to forgo their GI education benefits in order to enter the growing labor market. The pattern they confronted could be found elsewhere in America. Morrison Colladay, writing about his hometown in upstate New York, lamented what he saw as the beginnings of the "passing of the American village." He reported that there were a hundred World War II veterans unable to find work in this agricultural community. "Most of those who left Eastcamp during the war are home and they want to stay home. But how can they? What can they do to make a living?"[5] In Camden, some veterans secured jobs in service stations or stores or at Neff and Fry, but there was a dearth of good-paying jobs, especially those with the possibility of long-term advancement. The most fortunate were the young men who took over operation of their parents' farms. To many Camden-area youth, the prospect of entering farming was very attractive. Having been born and raised on a farm, they understood and enjoyed the lifestyle. The most perceptive of these young men recognized the major trends toward increased sophistication in American farming and enrolled in the College of Agriculture at Ohio State University to equip themselves with the scientific and managerial skills necessary to operate a complex farming operation.

Most veterans, however, were not going to inherit a farm and had to look elsewhere for a livelihood. Consequently, a pattern emerged which saw many of the best and the brightest depart. A common route went like this: first, a job at Champion Paper Company in Hamilton required the young husband to commute down narrow Route 127 five days a week. After his wife took a secretarial position at the home offices of the Ohio Casualty Insurance Company in the same city, the couple decided to rent an apartment in Hamilton to save time and money. A few years and two children later, using the GI bill housing benefits, the "Camden couple" purchased a tract home in a new Hamilton subdivision. They were gone.

Encouraged by an expanding economy that masked the departure of Camden's future, the town's leadership focused attention on civic improvements and community activities. That very few new houses were being constructed in town during an unprecedented national housing construction boom did not register on them. Nobody suggested a program to stimulate economic diversification and community development. The same lack of foresight could be found elsewhere. In Montana, a Rockefeller Foundation planning grant for developing a statewide strategy to encourage the economic development of small towns was allowed to expire by an unconcerned legislature. In a prescient comment, Colladay, whose essay on rural New York described a similar pattern, lamented that "now the little towns in Montana are back where they were when the experiment started. Unfortunately, their plight is shared by thousands of other little towns all over the country. Towns die slowly, but they do die, and today the blight has attacked too many of them."[6]

The housing shortage in Camden did not encourage young couples to remain. One of the most pressing of all postwar problems throughout the United States was a national housing shortage, estimated by Truman administration housing officials as exceeding twelve million units. The housing shortage produced a national political crisis of the first magnitude.[7] Veterans returned home, often to begin married life, and found few available houses or apartments, despite the financial assistance provided by Federal Housing Administration or Veterans Administration mortgage insurance. In Camden, few veterans used their benefits to build a house in town— undoubtedly a telling sign of their long-term plans—and instead moved in with their parents for a short time or rented an apartment.

Although the postwar Camden housing market supported the construction of only a few new homes, it did stimulate a substantial remodeling movement. With the cessation of wartime rationing, many residents threw themselves into the process of remodeling, often seeking to modernize houses that had been constructed in the nineteenth century. Local painters, carpenters, plumbers, electricians, and handymen found themselves with more work than they could handle, a sharp contrast from the prewar years. Those few merchants who dealt in furniture and appliances were unable to keep pace with demand as families sought to replace outmoded stoves, refrigerators, and washing machines.

For several years following V-J Day the local job market provided continuing employment opportunities for day laborers. Neff and Fry reduced its workday from twenty-four to eight hours, but its payroll stabilized at about a hundred, well above prewar levels, and Joe Gwynne's steel fabrication company and the revitalized Camden Cement and Tile Company, a small manufacturer of cement blocks and bricks, each employed about twenty men.

Little attention was paid to the most significant change in the local job market: the immediate return of the 125 working women at Neff and Fry to their traditional roles as homemakers. As soon as the defense contract for concrete bombs expired, the company immediately terminated all women laborers. Just as Rosie the Riveter left Henry Kaiser's ship-building factories in Oakland, California, for the hearth and stove, so too did Camden's version of feminism, Cindy the Cement worker.[8] Ironically, for the first three years after the war Camden's major employers struggled to find sufficient male labor. Prevailing social attitudes did not permit the retention of women in jobs considered to be for men only (at least in peacetime).

Employers were even forced to advertise for workers. Gwynne promised steady work, emphasizing that his company had had "No layoffs in Thirteen years." Neff and Fry believed that "The FUTURE LOOKS BRIGHT!" An advertisement that appeared for several months proclaimed, "We have a large backlog of essential and priority business! We have plans for plant improvement! We have much to be done and we need men to help do it. Working conditions good, work steady, pay periods weekly with overtime pay. The Neff and Fry Company is a well established, fast growing company with a good postwar future. Come into our office and talk it over—you'll like this work."[9] Given the accepted social assumptions under which it operated, the company did not need to mention that "women need not apply."

Since during the war many analysts had feared—quite wrongly, as it turned out—that the economy would tumble into recession, or worse, once the war had ended, it was with a mixture of relief and reserved optimism that Ray Simpson wrote shortly after V-J Day: "No unemployment situation exists here. Despite the fact that the public hears much these days from certain parts of the Nation regarding a pending unemployment situation, this problem does not exist in Camden . . . as there are many positions open here. Rodney Neff, president of Neff and Fry Company, stated this week that instead of an unemployment situation there is a serious labor shortage."[10] What Simpson did not mention, however, was that the shortage was due in part to the jobs created when the women laborers were sent home after the war.

In fact, Joe Gwynne and Rodney Neff could not compete with Fortune 500 companies like General Motors, Champion Paper, and Procter and Gamble—or with the federal government, which was paying top dollar as it rapidly expanded Wright-Patterson AFB to protect America from the Soviet menace. General Electric entered the employment fray in 1946 when it opened its huge jet aircraft factory in a northern suburb of Cincinnati. Its

personnel department took out large advertisements in the *Preble County
News* urging local workers to consider its total package of "Top Wages,
Scholarships, Vacation With Pay, Training for Advancement, Accident and
Sickness Insurance, Savings Plans, Retirement Pensions, Profit Sharing, and
Free Life Insurance!"[11] What ambitious small-town fellow could resist seri-
ously considering such an opportunity?

While attractive employment opportunities were opening up on a regular
basis elsewhere, in Camden a traditional form of employment was drying
up. Few persons paid much attention because the process had established
itself years earlier and had been steadily, if unspectacularly, taking its toll.
Farm labor had long provided employment for many Camden males. In
some instances these positions required considerable managerial and agricultural expertise, such as operating a farm for an absentee owner. Most
farm labor jobs placed a high demand on a strong back and an admirable tolerance for repetitious work. The work was seasonal and low paying but for
decades it had provided many Camden-area men with the rudiments of
their livelihood. Farm labor, however, was steadily being eliminated by advances in agriculture technology and science. New hybrid seeds, better crop
rotation systems, improved pesticides and fertilizers, advances in animal
science and veterinary medicine—the result of the combined efforts of the
Experiment Station and the Extension Service of Ohio State University's
College of Agriculture—not only markedly improved production levels but
also reduced the demand for unskilled labor. The universal adoption of tractors and sophisticated power equipment accelerated the declining need for
unskilled labor. Combines replaced the traditional threshing gangs. Hay
balers, power-driven corn pickers, and milking machines all reduced demand for manpower. In a distinct parallel to the changes occurring in manufacturing, on Ohio farms machines were quietly but surely replacing
humans.

A revolution was affecting American agriculture, and Camden was not
immune. "Underlying the current mechanization trend," the anthropologist Art Gallaher wrote of postwar "Plainville," "is the acceptance of a new
style of farming. The farmer now defines his role mainly as manipulator of
machines designed to do what formerly were irksome, time-consuming
agricultural tasks." Whereas not too many years earlier a farmer took great
pride in the amount of physical labor he could put forth, now he looked
upon extensive physical exertion as demeaning. "This new role involves a
redefinition of farm labor and the acceptance of new criteria for assessing
industriousness. Thus, men who a few years ago gained prestige by working long hours at physical labor are remembered today as 'slaves' to hard
work and long hours, and if one of them still manifests these qualities he is
ridiculed as 'behind the time.'"[12]

Few people paid much notice to this fundamental change in the nature of Ohio agriculture because it happened unobtrusively over several decades, but everyone recognized the pressures created by the postwar baby boom. It had begun during the early years of the war and now affected the public schools, driving enrollments in Camden up from 400 in 1940 to over 550 by 1950. Because of the hiatus created by the depression and the war, there were few certified new teachers available in the United States until the GI bill drove college graduation rates upward in 1949. Thus Camden's school administrators found themselves continually scrambling to hire even minimally qualified teachers. The high turnover rate was exacerbated by non-competitive salaries, and many of the most qualified teachers left for better-paying positions in the urban school systems of southwestern Ohio.

New classroom facilities were essential to cope with increased enrollments. In 1945, after much deliberation, the Camden school board put a bond issue to a vote and supporters mounted a low-key campaign to secure the necessary 65 percent of the vote. Because the needs were so great, there was no formal opposition, and in November a $179,000 bond issue, authorizing construction of much needed new facilities, including a modern multipurpose gymnasium, was approved by a 520–153 majority.[13] Camden's voters, traditionally suspicious of increased taxes, this time responded overwhelmingly to the needs of their youth.

The vote brought to an end the long tradition of Friday night basketball in the cramped upper floor of the Town Hall. The new gymnasium was designed to provide for a myriad of activities. With a seating capacity of 1,500, 50 percent larger than the town's population, it testified to the importance of high school basketball in Camden. This community jewel included state-of-the-art glass backboards, locker rooms with hot showers, a music room, a spacious stage for plays and concerts, and bleachers that folded against the walls to provide space for physical education classes. Included in the package was the construction of five new classrooms, including the school's first real chemistry laboratory, and a large kitchen to serve community dinners as well as provide for the school's hot lunch program. The new facility stood as a monument to the community's confident view of the future.

Opened in 1950—its completion suffered delays due to problems with the architectural design and initial cost overruns—the gymnasium became the focal point for community activities, rendering the top floor of the Town Hall obsolete; this once proud community icon soon fell into disrepair. The new gymnasium proved to be a functional multi-purpose facility, serving the community as theater, concert hall, dance floor, convention center, banquet hall, and sports arena. During the winter months on Friday evenings it rocked with the noise, enthusiasm, and tension that only a high school basketball game with a hated rival could generate. It also stimulated a modest expansion of performing arts programs and physical education classes.

* * *

The new gymnasium provided tangible evidence that Camden was a progressive town, ready for the challenges of the postwar era. This major construction project mirrored the activities of the Progressive Club, which had modified its orientation from helping individuals cope with economic depression to boosting major civic projects. In 1946 the Progressive Club made its largest contribution to the town by modernizing the high school baseball field. At a cost of $4,000, the club erected lights and constructed a grandstand and refreshment booth. More than a thousand fans were on hand on September 1, 1946, despite unseasonably cold weather, to see Camden's first night baseball game. Very few towns of its size had outdoor lighting for baseball, and a sense of pride surged through town. Even those who cared little for baseball showed up that night to watch a doubleheader, a softball game against Oxford and a baseball game between Bat Bousman's team and a collection of "all-stars" from the Central Ohio League.[14] Unfortunately, the Oxford softball team got its signals confused and failed to appear, and the "all-stars" soundly whipped the local nine.

The lighted ball park was a first for Preble County (although several other communities soon followed suit), and, as many a citizen commented, a sign of a town with good prospects. During the next four years, from May until September, a six-team fast pitch softball league used the facility five nights a week. Central Ohio Baseball League games were played on Sunday afternoons before large crowds. For a time, the spectators overflowed the eight rows of bleachers behind home plate. Some fans watched from the comfort of their cars ringing the outfield, where occupants would unobtrusively sip on a can of beer.

The year 1947 was a very good one for Camden, both for the local economy and for the town baseball team. Viewed from the perspective of half a century later, it stands out as perhaps the most upbeat and productive year in the community's history. Good economic times provided an aura of optimism and confidence not seen since the 1920s. Jobs were plentiful, agricultural commodity prices remained high, and community activity and involvement reached an all-time level.

Perhaps symbolic of this good year was the success of the town baseball team. The Merchants, as they were called, were now managed by one of the town's best longtime players, railroad maintenance foreman Bob Elston. The oft-contentious Bat Bousman now devoted his energies to the business side of this marginal operation, including maintenance of the field and the new lights. Elston's 1947 team included two future professional baseball players, both pitchers, one of whom was Elston's eighteen-year-old son, Donald, who would systematically work his way through the minor leagues and spend seven years with the Chicago Cubs.[15]

The most compelling member of the 1947 team, however, was substitute second baseman Dale Thomas. A 1942 graduate of the high school, this sandy-haired, bespectacled young man had lost a leg in the Battle of the Bulge. Nonetheless, he gamely hobbled around the infield on his artificial limb, fielding ground balls and even helping to turn an occasional double play. To some fans, Thomas's entrance into the lineup in the late innings was always a good sign that the game was well in hand; to the more reflective, however, it was a poignant reminder of the community's sacrifices in the war just ended.

The team spent the entire 1947 season in first place in the Central Ohio League, then swept undefeated through the postseason playoffs, winning the championship over a team representing the much larger community of Miamisburg. Camden's 5–4 victory was witnessed by an estimated 1,500 cheering fans.[16] This banner season came on the heels of the high school baseball's team stunning spring season, which saw them win the district tournament in Dayton and come within four games of winning the state championship.

The good fortunes of its baseball teams set the tone for the town. Every man who wanted a job could get one. Neff and Fry continued to advertise for workers, announcing that it was paying new employees the federal minimum wage of ninety-five cents an hour. Ford dealer Bill Matt struggled with the problem of not being able to get enough new automobiles to meet demand. By early 1946 he had a waiting list that was so long it took nearly eighteen months to deliver a new vehicle to impatient customers. Brownlee Borradaile, an energetic farmer turned car dealer, was now selling as many Chevrolets as Matt was Fords. Business was so good that Borradaile abandoned his small, rented Main Street location next to the Dover Theater and built a large showroom and maintenance shop on the north edge of town. At the time it was the largest commercial building in the county.[17]

Three new restaurants opened along Main Street, and Clarke Ledwell, who had repaired watches in his home for several years, felt sufficiently emboldened to open the town's second jewelry store. A new bakery, an ice cream parlor, and an additional grocery added to the action on Main Street. A large furniture store replaced the one that had closed during the depression. In October, a popular local automobile mechanic, Dave Campbell, entered the automobile competition when he opened a Kaiser-Fraser dealership on South Main Street. His opening day celebration attracted over six hundred curious visitors eager to see the new, innovatively styled automobiles produced by the now famous West Coast shipbuilder and industrial tycoon Henry Kaiser.[18]

Christmas season brought unprecedented crowds into local stores. Two years after the war, American manufacturers had overcome the shortages of most consumer items. Harry Simpson, now in the process of taking over the editorial responsibilities from his semiretired father, reported in the *Preble County News* that local stores were doing "a capacity business." More people seemed to have more money than ever before. Having endured the depression and the war, they were happy to enjoy the benefits of good times. "Most families are having a bigger Christmas this year than last," Simpson wrote. "Merchants have a bigger supply of merchandise and a wider variety to select from. More toys have been on the counters and some of the hard-to-get items have been more available this year."[19]

"Main Street is a 'little Broadway' these days." Simpson cheerfully noted. "Shoppers are jamming the streets and stores. Retailers report the volume of Christmas business has been 'exceedingly large.' Most people are still gainfully employed and making reasonably good money. This Christmas has offered them the opportunity of obtaining many things they have wanted for some time."[20]

In 1948 a Lions Club was chartered with thirty members. As one of its service projects, the club sponsored a drive to raise $1,200 to buy uniforms for the thirty-five-member high school band. The sparkling new red-and-black uniforms of the band became a source of community pride, and the high school musicians were invited to perform at many local functions. The popularity of the high school band was another sign of the changing times, as public schools assumed roles in the community previously filled by other organizations. Lou Sterzenbach's Camden Band had disbanded after its leader's death in 1948. For nearly three decades this popular group of local musicians of all ages had held its summertime Thursday evening concerts at the corner of Main and Central.[21]

And so it went. Jobs were plentiful, farm income was increasing, modern diesel engines replaced the coal-fired engines on the Pennsylvania main line, businesses were prospering, the new high school gymnasium was under construction, and the town baseball team had brought home a championship. Evidence of "progress" and success abounded. The future seemed bright along Main Street. And the newly outfitted band played on.

The ten-year-old boy walked down South Main Street as dusk turned to dark one warm May evening in 1948, a bag of groceries tucked under his arm. He was on his way home after running an errand for his mother to Ernie Jefferies's grocery store. As he approached a recently opened appliance store, he noticed a cluster of people standing on the sidewalk peering into the display window. His eyes were drawn to an unusual flickering, silvery luminescence emanating from the window. At that moment he saw, for the first time in his life, a television screen. He immediately became transfixed—almost hypnotized—by what he saw. The small ten-inch image was somewhat blurred, and more than once store owner Fred Schmidt had to crawl into the display window to fiddle with several dials to keep the picture from flipping over and over. But the small screen more than adequately portrayed the images of men engaged in a wrestling match. The young boy had never seen a wrestling match before, and the wild antics of the performers were captivating. The announcer said that the program was being "telecast" live from a studio in Cincinnati. Several times the boy told himself that it was time to return home. His parents gave him permission to explore the streets and alleys of town by foot or bicycle during the day, but like most parents in town, they also kept him on a short leash: "We want to know where you're going to be, whom you'll be with, and when you'll be home." That was the cardinal rule for him and his friends, but as the minutes, and then an hour, and even more, went by, he remained frozen in front of the flickering Philco. He knew the rule and he knew he was in serious violation, but he stood as if paralyzed. That fuzzy picture in the window was the most incredible thing he had ever seen.

By the time the boy—who would later become the author of this book—finally arrived home a little past ten o'clock, he was confronted by two very upset (and worried) parents, and even his story about the flickering black-and-white wrestling match he had watched in "Smitty's" window did not prevent a serious, one-sided conversation about obeying the rules. Given the extenuating circumstances, the young boy escaped serious punishment. Neither he nor his parents could have begun to anticipate just how much their lives would be affected by the advent of the age of television, which he had encountered for the first time that warm spring evening.[22]

By the summer of 1948 three stores sold television sets in Camden. In addition to Fred Schmidt, the Camden Hardware Store and Vernon Caskey plunged headlong into the television sales and repair business. The ever aggressive Caskey, his business stimulated by increased cash flow in his grocery store, purchased an adjoining building and opened a small furniture store, complete with a line of home electronic entertainment equipment. As a portent of things to come, his large advertisement in the *Preble County News* on September 1, 1949, proclaimed: "Be Sure and See the WORLD SERIES ON GENERAL ELECTRIC TELEVISION. Big 10" Tube only $189. 12" Tube only $289. Ohio State and Notre Dame Football Games!"[23]

Television transformed the community. Large television antennae, the ultimate status symbols, began to appear on the rooftops of the more affluent families. Firmly clamped to chimneys, antennae were aimed at Cincinnati to pick up WCPO and WLW, or at Dayton to receive the signals of WHIO. Local conversations now contained such new vocabulary as "snow," "vertical control," "contrast," and "coaxial cable." The relative merits of the wrestling prowess of Gorgeous George and Don Mohawk stimulated many an argument at Bob Barber's restaurant, and activity in town slowed during autumn afternoons when a World Series game was being telecast. Friday nights meant boxing from Madison Square Garden with Don Dunphy describing the bouts for Gillette Blue Blades, and Tuesday nights featured Milton Berle's *Texaco Star Theater*. In 1952 most sets were tuned to *I Love Lucy* on Monday evenings. The spectacle of wrestling seemed to be on some channel every evening, but overexposure led to its virtual disappearance until it was rescued by cable television in the 1980s.

During the first years of commercial television broadcasting, many Camden families could not afford their own sets. In order to tap into this market, the management of the H & H Cafe placed a television set above the bar and enjoyed the benefits of a rapidly expanding clientele. Competitors in the beer-and-sandwich trade, Ted Girton's Girt-Inn and Deem's Half-Way Tavern, soon followed suit.[24]

Families that purchased the town's initial television sets had delicate social problems coping with friends and relatives who devised ingenious ways to visit during prime evening hours. Television parties replaced evening bridge or canasta games, and the ubiquitous "TV tray" became a popular wedding gift. The traditional living room underwent substantial design change, and the television set became the focal point of the room, replacing a piano or reading area. Evening meals were often eaten in front of the black-and-white screen in a semidarkened room. Teachers observed that homework was not being completed, and town librarian Hattie Ward reported a sharp decline in patronage.

These changes in the patterns of daily life were not unique to Camden, of course. They were taking place across America, in large cities as well as isolated farming communities. Television accelerated the domination of small-town life by urban America, reflecting initially the values of New York City and later those of Los Angeles. Similarities of clothing and hairstyles, slang phrases, and music preferences were among the superficial manifestation of a much more important phenomenon—the standardization of thought and values and an accelerated diminution of unique regional and local cultures. Television intensified the erosion of local autonomy begun earlier by the railroad, automobile, radio, and motion pictures. By 1955 about 65 percent of American homes had a television set.[25]

Although Vernon Caskey made a lot of money selling Dumont and Crosley television sets, another business in Camden—the movie theater business— suffered grievously from the arrival of television. In October of 1950 the Dover Theater, which had already limited its operations to showing detective/Western double features on weekends, closed its doors forever. Later that year the Majestic Theater also ceased operations. On some weeknights owner Orville Wood could count the number of tickets sold on his fingers. Wood could recognize a bad business trend when he saw it, and he judiciously bailed out. In April of 1951 the Majestic reopened "under new management," but the competition of the "cool medium" of television was too much. Just thirteen months later it closed for good, a victim of the changing American entertainment scene. William Bendix and Kirk Douglas, starring in the forgettable film *Detective Story*, were the last Hollywood heroes to appear on the silver screen in Camden.[26]

Born in the depths of the Great Depression, the once proud Majestic Theater had been a boon to a severely wounded town, but now it was gone, a victim of the new age of television. Editor Harry Simpson lamented the passing of an era: "Closing of the theater will be quite a blow to the community, leaving Camden with no amusement center." He identified "low attendance" and, curiously, "high federal taxes" as the culprits. For some reason, perhaps not wishing to belabor the obvious, he made no mention of television. All across the country the impact was similar. In 1951, the journalist-historian David Halberstam reports, 134 motion picture theaters closed in southern California alone, the victims of television. That same year, in novelist Larry McMurtry's fictional windswept plains town of Thalia, Texas, Sony and his Korean War–bound pal Duane watched Audie Murphy in *The Kid from Texas*, that town's last picture show. By 1952 movie attendance nationwide had fallen nearly 40 percent since 1947.[27]

The inherent power of television was manifest in the waves of fear and anxiety that rushed through Camden each summer. Polio! The seasonal outbreaks of paralytic poliomyelitis produced panic throughout American society. Although its most famous victim, President Franklin D. Roosevelt, was thirty-nine years old when he was stricken, most of its victims were children. Adding to parents' fears was the fact that each year the number of victims in the United States increased. Television news, although in its infancy, recognized the value of an emotional story. Local and national television news departments exploited the drama of the disease, showing pitiful small children encapsulated in huge iron lungs or struggling heroically in a rehabilitation clinic to get their withered legs, supported by ugly metal braces, to move again. The threat of contracting the virus was undoubtedly real—it was, after all, afflicting over thirty thousand Americans a year—but television coverage intensified apprehension.

In 1937 Camden experienced its only known polio victim, seven-year-old Ruthayn Dearth. As a high school student in the late 1940s she bravely went about her life on crutches, her paralyzed, severely atrophied legs supported by fifteen pounds of metal braces. The sobering image of Ruthayn pulling herself slowly down the corridors of the high school, or on a visit to a local teen hangout with her friends, made the threat of the disease seem very real. Like towns everywhere, Camden held many benefits for the March of Dimes—donkey softball games under the new lights, church bake sales, school candy campaigns. Canisters to receive donations were on store counters near the cash register.

What worried parents did not know was that the disease often struck infants, who showed few symptoms but who, unbeknownst to parents or family physician, had thereby acquired immunity. It was those who contracted the disease later in life who endured major debilitating effects.[28]

Since they did not know the etiology of the disease, parents sometimes went to extreme lengths to protect their offspring. A few purchased "polio insurance" from William Eikenberry's general insurance agency, whose advertisement suggested that such protection "Might Come In Handy."[29] Some parents essentially restricted younger children to their homes and backyards for the duration of the summer epidemic months, permitting them to venture out only when accompanied. During the peak months of July and August, many boys were forbidden to swim in the murky waters of the Seven Mile Creek. Some were even forbidden to exert themselves in active play. Parents who could afford to do so opted to spend the time away from the hot and humid Camden summer climate, somehow convincing themselves that the cooler temperatures of a Michigan lakefront were safer.

The town council, eager to do something to help, conducted weekly sprayings to kill the unknown cause of the disease, a popular effort that continued until the Salk vaccine became available in 1954. The spraying, it was reported in the newspaper, was "a precautionary measure against any possible outbreak of polio cases in Camden."[30] Every Wednesday evening during the months of July and August, members of the volunteer fire department rode through the alleys of the town in the bed of a pickup truck, dousing everything in sight: weeds, rocks, buildings, and especially garbage and refuse cans. Unfortunately, the chemical spray of choice was the then popular pesticide DDT, now known to be a carcinogen. As the pickup maneuvered slowly down the dirt alley ways, children, for whose protection this effort was designed, often stood along the side to watch the action, sometimes getting themselves thoroughly exposed to the misty spray. Since no new cases of polio occurred, the reasoning went, the spraying might be doing some good. So the DDT campaign continued each summer until the miracle wrought by Dr. Jonas Salk eased the minds of concerned parents and city fathers. No subsequent study was ever made on the effect this carcinogen had upon the health of Camden's residents.

The closing of the Dover and Majestic theaters stands as the beginning of the end of an era. By 1952 the outburst of community activity and civic improvement that had developed after the war had run its course. The outmigration of families was evident by this time; the good jobs were in the cities, and there Camden's younger generation moved en masse. Despite earnest efforts by the Progressive Club, now attempting to act in the capacity of an economic development agency, no employers of any significance could be lured to town. Other than relatively unattractive teaching positions, there were few professional opportunities to entice college graduates to return to their hometown.

By the early 1950s most high school students perceived that their parents expected them to leave town after they completed their education.[31] Parents viewed such departures as evidence of their success in raising their children. Enrollments in the public schools leveled off at about six hundred students. The 1950 census reported 1,084 residents of the community—a 10 percent gain since 1940—but owing to the increased mechanization of farming, the population of the rural Somers Township showed no gain. Although Paul Stowe opened a small Willys Jeep dealership in 1952, Dave Campbell's Kaiser-Fraser agency had closed with the demise of that ill-fated automobile company.

Interest in civic affairs began to sag. Each summer the Homecoming carnivals drew smaller crowds, and the midway attractions seemed to grow ever more sleazy. Attendance was no longer high enough to support a lottery with a new automobile as the main prize. For a few years after the war the *Preble County News* had expanded to six pages to accommodate a spurt in advertising, but by 1952 it was back to its basic four-page format. Interest in the town baseball team declined as fans now watched their favorite team, the Cincinnati Reds, on television. In 1952 CBS introduced its Saturday "Game of the Week," featuring such baseball stars as Jackie Robinson, Mickey Mantle, and Ted Williams. The town team, the Merchants, its drab gray uniforms now showing the results of several years of wear and tear, could not compete with the antics of announcer Dizzy Dean and major league games televised live from Yankee Stadium. The Merchants played their last season in 1953.

Symbolically, the demise of town baseball was very important. For decades the team had carried the hopes and pride of the community on its shoulders. Now, without a whimper, it had died. Town ball was vanishing all across the United States, and a tradition that stretched back to the nineteenth century was coming to an end. Only occasionally did the bright lights stand out in Camden on a summer evening, usually to illuminate a youth team playing in front of parents and relatives.[32]

The sagging fortunes of the town were vividly underscored in the local elections in November of 1951. There were only two candidates for the council listed on the printed ballot, and no one filed for mayor. Informal nominating committees, including the Progressive Club, could not secure commitments from even minimally qualified persons to run for local office. Older leaders contended that they had met their responsibilities and believed that it was time for a younger generation to take its turn. (In a society dominated by men, no one apparently thought to consider women candidates.) Perhaps the apathy stemmed from the lack of compelling issues to attract candidates.[33]

The immediate crisis of securing candidates was resolved when four individuals, under heavy pressure from a hurriedly created "Committee for Camden," agreed to assume office if their names were written in on election day. The community was thus spared the embarrassment of not having a functioning local government. Three write-in candidates for the council and the two on the printed ballot were elected without opposition. High school principal William E. Browning received 173 write-in votes and became the town's forty-eighth mayor. He also was an ordained minister of the Church of the Brethren and occasionally appeared in local pulpits. A man of considerable ego, he soon became a controversial figure by ordering a crackdown on speeders, many of them out-of-towners passing through town on Route 127. A high school driver's education teacher who had become obsessed with driving safety, Browning felt little sympathy for the offenders who ended up in his mayor's court. There he presided in magisterial fashion, routinely handing down fines and sometimes a condescending sermon about automobile safety to transgressors. Browning and the new council suffered a serious political rebuff in the fall elections of 1952, however, when their revenue-generating plan of installing parking meters in the business area lost by a resounding 2–1 margin after angry residents forced a referendum election on the issue.[34]

What went unrecognized at the time was that the social fabric, which had long provided a sense of community responsibility and unity, had begun to unravel. What was happening in Camden was being replicated in many towns of similar size across the country, such as Art Gallaher's "Plainville." Television tended to isolate families inside their homes during evening hours, reducing the amount of visiting between neighbors. Instead of sitting on the front porch greeting evening strollers, residents now closeted themselves to watch Jackie Gleason. Over time, neighbors became more distant; newcomers sometimes remained strangers. Attendance at the three traditional churches became a subject of concern, while the recently established evangelical Church of God and the First Baptist Church enjoyed an influx of new members, primarily from the middle and lower classes. Saturday nights provided prime television programming, and merchants suffered a steady decline in their trade on that most important of evenings. Store owners also knew that when farmers and townsfolk went shopping now, especially for major purchases, they got into their automobiles and headed out of town. Their clientele increasingly looked to them only for the low-cost necessities of everyday life. Even local grocery stores lost market share to distant supermarkets.[35]

The growing number of residents who commuted to work extracted a heavy toll on the community; commuting loosened local ties in many ways.

It was more convenient for commuters to stop after work for groceries or other routine purchases in one of the sparkling new automobile-friendly strip malls along the highway from Hamilton or Dayton. And the daily grind of traveling up to a hundred miles a day reduced the time and energy that individuals had available to participate in community activities. When they arrived home after a long day they found themselves less inclined to attend a meeting and much more interested in simply plopping in front of the television set to watch *Leave It to Beaver*. Thus did Camden enter into the early stages of becoming another American commuter bedroom community, but one that lacked most of the modern services and conveniences of the new suburbs.

The convergence of these trends in the mid-1950s led to the melancholy sight of a near empty Main Street on Saturday nights. For decades, families had flocked to the business district, not just to shop, but also to socialize. After completing their errands, a husband and wife would often sit in their parked car on Main Street for extended periods of time, happily conversing out the window with passersby. Within a year after the arrival of commercial television, the Saturday night crowds became markedly smaller. Main Street merchants felt themselves under siege but had no way to counterattack. The enemy was too pervasive: the high volume, low-pricing policies of chain stores, new shopping malls, ever more sophisticated Sears catalogs, the automobile, television . . . the enemy was, in fact, modern America itself. Television and the automobile had combined to kill an American tradition—Saturday night along Main Street.

Life at mid-century in this small southwestern Ohio town reflected other social and economic changes occurring across the United States. The changing attitudes and behavior of local teenagers created concern in Camden even before Indiana native James Dean rebelled. Relaxed parental rules enabled some teenagers to cruise Main Street until late in the evening. Ducktail hairstyles, black leather jackets, cigarette packs arrogantly carried in rolled up T-shirt sleeves—feeble mimicry of the movies' portrayal of restless, rebellious youth—soon made their appearance in Bob Barber's restaurant, a popular teenage hangout. School officials pondered whether to permit such clothing and hairstyles in school, and the school board listened patiently to more than one parental complaint about the playing of rock 'n' roll music at postgame sock hops. An occasional late-night drag race awakened residents. In response, the council passed the community's first curfew; all persons seventeen years of age and younger had to be off the streets by 10 P.M. on weeknights, midnight on Saturdays. Enforcement by the town's only part-time law enforcement officer, however, proved to be a sham, since lack of widespread parental support for the curfew doomed its effectiveness.

Reports of increased crime also began to filter onto the pages of the local newspaper. A series of break-ins of businesses and residences stunned local citizens, who began to lock their doors even during daytime hours. Few residents considered the relationship of juvenile behavior and rising crime rates to national trends because they naturally tended to view life from the perspective of their daily lives and their local community. Also, they tended to know their neighbors less, thus increasing the level of suspicion and lowering their sense of security.[36]

This parochial view was especially true in relation to the complex issues raised by the cold war. It was a topic that seldom entered daily discussion because it was beyond the scope of most persons' understanding or interest. Camdenites' traditional view of the world—Republican, isolationist, conservative, Protestant, patriotic—provided a prism through which world affairs filtered into town. Many residents despaired at the defeats of Bob Taft at the hands of the eastern elite at the 1948 and 1952 conventions and accepted the conventional wisdom that the Soviet Union constituted a dire threat to American security. Although no one had ever known a Communist, everyone was naturally opposed to them. Social studies teachers in the high school dutifully emphasized the evils of Marxism and the Soviet threat to American security. When President Truman, who received only 35 percent of the Camden vote in 1948, fired military hero General Douglas MacArthur in the spring of 1951, the conventional wisdom at Deem's Half-Way Tavern was that Harry was leading the country down the road to oblivion.

The confusing nature of American policy as the cold war unfolded was revealed in the town's reaction to the Korean War. Although several local young men served in what Truman termed a "police action," interest in the conflict remained strangely muted.[37] There was considerable interest in the safety of Marine Lt. Bill Patton, a popular former high school athlete and student, who was among those trapped at Hagamari when massive numbers of Chinese troops flooded across the Yalu River in November of 1950. The community was cheered when news arrived that the local graduate of the U.S. Naval Academy had survived, although he suffered serious frostbite.[38] A feeble effort to revive the committee to provide moral support for Camden's servicemen that had been active during World War II died aborning; the "Camden Behind the Men Behind the Guns" column ran twice in 1951, contained little information, and disappeared. No Christmas packages were mailed from the community. The concept of a limited war seemed somehow foreign, perhaps "un-American," to the regulars sipping their morning coffee at the drugstore.

The cold war made an official appearance for a brief time in Camden in the form of the U.S. Air Force Ground Observer Corps. This program was designed to supplement the nation's radar defense system by visually observing and reporting, over a special telephone network, all flying aircraft that appeared above the United States. Only during these, the most frigid days of the cold war, could such a program have been taken seriously. Supposedly, somewhere in a supersecret command center, every airplane aloft over the continental United States would be tracked. For several weeks during the summer of 1952, a group of volunteers, primarily patriotic retirees and curious teenagers with nothing better to do, manned around the clock a tent pitched on top of Mt. Auburn, using a secret telephone number to report all Piper Cubs and other equally suspicious aircraft that penetrated Camden's air space. Presumably, all across the United States, other vigilant patriots were simultaneously reporting air traffic to the same secret command center, and somehow all of this information was being assimilated and evaluated in time to prevent a Russian sneak attack. By the time school resumed in September, however, and with no Soviet bombers yet in sight, interest in the project waned. As the first frosts of autumn tinged the maple trees in brilliant hues of red and orange, the Camden Observer Corps quietly folded its tent.[39]

Considerably more interest was expressed in stopping the speeding on local streets than in reporting enemy bombers. A concerted effort by the town council and its aggressive new mayor led to the writing of numerous traffic tickets, to the point that Camden, under the mayorality of the good Reverend Browning, developed a modest reputation as a "speed trap." However, it was the loud roar from "glass pack" exhaust pipes that local young men installed on their '46 Fords and '49 Mercs, coupled with the squeal of tires as their cars blasted away from intersections, that produced a crisis of law and order. The Methodist minister, James Misheff, recently graduated from the seminary and a popular community figure—albeit somewhat of a clerical maverick—became so angry at the flouting of local traffic laws that he got himself sworn in as a police officer and for several months in 1951 spent the evening hours in his family sedan, a red light taped to the roof, patrolling the streets and earnestly writing traffic tickets.[40]

Such shenanigans as these, of course, distracted attention from the things that really counted. The inexorable movement of young families to nearby cities and the departure of high school graduates steadily gained momentum. Another downward trend was the migration of substantial numbers of retirees to Florida, a change that over the next several decades stripped the town of affluent senior citizens while leaving those with limited retirement income behind. Well-to-do farmers were now as likely to retire to the Sun Belt as to "move to town," as had long been the custom. The Census of 1950 brought the good news that the town's population had exceeded a thousand for the first time; but it also revealed that Camden's growth had not kept pace with other Preble County communities located closer to rapidly growing Dayton. Camden now ranked as the county's fifth largest community, down from second in 1940.[41] The transformation of Camden from a relatively self-sufficient community into a bedroom community for commuters and a haven for the poor and for retired citizens living on Social Security had begun in earnest.

Not that the community did not try to fight back. In 1947 the Progressive Club worked hard to attract a garment factory that would have employed fifty persons. This deal fell through at the last minute, but in 1951 hopes rose when the Atlas Plywood Company opened operations near a railroad siding north of town to construct heavy-duty shipping boxes and components for mobile homes. For a brief time this seemed to be a major coup, but the company proved incapable of competing successfully in its markets and hired no local managers. Most of its jobs were of the minimum wage variety, and the company periodically laid off workers because of minor fluctuations in demand. The "box factory," as it was called, did not last until the end of the decade.[42]

More serious was the sharp decline in the fortunes of the Neff and Fry Company. In 1942–45 the company had operated three shifts and employed up to 175 men and women. Business remained good for a time after the war, and its construction crews roamed much of the United States and part of Canada erecting concrete silos and storage facilities. Although its silo construction business started to decline, demand for its large industrial storage bins soared. For several years Neff and Fry employed over two hundred men, who assembled bins as far away as Maine, Florida, and California, bins designed to hold such diverse commodities as cotton seed, fertilizer, coal, cinders, clay, lime, and chemicals. Some fifty employees were kept busy at the Camden plant producing cement staves. Not adverse to horizontal diversification, the company also developed its profitable line of sealed burial vaults. Company leaders attributed their success, as quoted in a national business newsletter, to "a small town location where they are near sand and gravel, where labor is steady and taxes low." By the early 1950s company revenues exceeded $2 million, a not insubstantial sum for a small-town-based firm, but it proved impossible to maintain this rate of growth.[43]

The swift decline of the company began with two deaths. In 1947 cofounder Charles Neff died at age seventy-four. Not only had he remained active in an advisory capacity as the company expanded during the 1940s, but as a member of the board of directors of the First National Bank he was a major player in the Camden business establishment. His cautious leadership and business acumen had guided the company's steady expansion since he and Merle Fry had founded it in 1916. Neff's son Rodney had already assumed the company's presidency and had demonstrated an enthusiasm and understanding of the industry that boded well for the company's future. However, in February of 1950 the fifty-five-year-old executive was killed on a business trip in Louisiana when his car smacked into a parked lumber truck in a heavy fog.[44]

The company's leadership then fell to a competent senior administrator, D. H. Herbster. But he encountered serious health problems and was unable to travel or to provide the daily stewardship the increasingly vulnerable company required. For a sustained period of time following his tragic death, Rodney Neff's large holding of company stock was tied up in a trust fund administered by a Cincinnati bank, which inserted itself into the company's internal management, thereby complicating decision making at a crucial time in the company's development.[45]

It was especially unfortunate that as Camden moved into the pivotal 1950s its primary nonagricultural employer encountered serious internal management problems that were not adequately resolved. At the same time, the company faced strong competition from two major corporations seeking to establish themselves in the storage facility business, Martin Marietta and International Harvester. Neff and Fry's weekly payrolls grew even smaller.

The company's decline had an adverse impact on other local economic interests. It led to a loss of contracts for three small local welding and steel fabricating operators, and especially to a drop in demand for aggregate from the White Gravel Company. In the end it was impossible to reverse the downward spiral. Over the next few years, the cumulative effect of these many problems contributed to the closing of local businesses.[46]

Just five years after the euphoric Christmas buying spree along Main Street, when the jingle of cash registers provided sweet music for local businessmen, the holiday season brought few reasons for cheer. Now those same cash registers remained all too quiet. By Christmas of 1952 changes in shopping patterns had become so pronounced that near panic had set in among merchants. They could not compete with the large chain stores and sophisticated department stores like Rike-Kumler's in Dayton or Shillito's in Cincinnati. The frequent appearance in the "Around Camden" personals column of brief notices like the following told the tale that Camden's shoppers were taking their business elsewhere: "Mrs. Harry Woodard and Mrs. E. L. Travis were Dayton visitors Tuesday."[47] Advertisements in the *Preble County News* by the popular Dayton department store carried a disturbing message for small-town merchants all across the Miami Valley: "Rikes is Ready for Christmas! Dazzling Toyland! Main Floor Fairy Land!" or "Plan a trip to Rike's in Dayton as a Christmas treat for your whole family."[48] Up and down Main Street store owners simply could not compete.

As they witnessed their customer base continue to erode, hard-pressed merchants launched a counterattack. Like Hitler's last ditch gambit in late 1944, it would prove to be Main Street's own Battle of the Bulge, producing a momentary gain after which they would be overrun by superior forces. In the spring of 1951, under the aegis of the Progressive Club, local merchants announced the "Camden Retail Merchants' Profit Sharing Plan." Throughout the week, tickets were given out by participating local merchants for sales of $1 or more. Then, every Saturday night at 9 P.M. a drawing was held in front of the Town Hall. Cash prizes totaling $100—two $25 prizes and the grand prize of $50—were given to winning ticket holders in attendance. For several months hundreds of people appeared at the appointed hour to check their handful of tickets when the winning numbers were announced.

Just as Art Gallaher reported about "Plainville," whose beleaguered merchants conducted a similar lottery, things did not go as planned. Parents, preferring to remain at home in front of their television sets, sent a teenager to check out the numbers, or they pooled tickets with neighbors. The ticket holders who did come appeared shortly before 9 P.M. and then quickly retreated to their homes; only a few bothered to drop by a store to make a purchase—the primary reasons for holding the drawing on Saturday evening. Initial curiosity produced large crowds and a temporary bump in sales, but interest and attendance soon fell. There was no evidence that the program slowed the surging amount of out-of-town shopping. Before a year had passed, the "Camden Retail Merchants' Profit Sharing Plan" was shelved. Even cash drawings could not revive the traditional Saturday nights of an earlier era.[49]

The fate that befell many of America's small towns in the years following World War II was cruel and ironic. Cruel because the towns suffered irreparable economic damage that would lead to stagnation and severe decline. Ironic because it happened during a time when the national economy was enjoying its greatest period of growth and expansion in history. By 1955 the fate of Camden had essentially been determined. It faced a future that offered little hope and considerable despair. By 1955 the town that erected prominent highway signs in 1949 proclaiming itself the "Birthplace of Sherwood Anderson, Famous Author" had entered into a new phase, one that constituted a significant break from its 150-year history.

Notes

1. The body of literature detailing the important expansion of metropolitan America, including suburbanization, is both large and rewarding. Among the many excellent studies are Kenneth Jackson, *The Crabgrass Frontier: The Suburbinization of the United States* (New York: Oxford University Press, 1985); Jean Gottmann, *Megalopolis: The Urbanized Northeastern Seaboard of the United States* (New York: Twentieth Century Fund, 1961); David Halberstam, *The Fifties* (New York: Villard

Books, 1993), pp. 131–79; and Herbert J. Gans, *The Levittowners: Ways of Life and Politics in a New Suburban Community* (New York: Pantheon Books, 1967).

2. This discussion is based upon observations by the author, but it is also supported by the responses to the questionnaire sent to high school graduates. More than a 20 percent response to the questionnaire—165 returned out of 595 mailed—demonstrates this phenomenon clearly.

3. *Preble County News*, December 20, 1945.

4. Humphrey's career pattern is quite typical of the returning veteran. He was drawn, as if by a magnet, to return to his hometown. After graduating from Ohio University in 1949 with a bachelor's degree in education, he taught and coached at Camden High School for two years. But once he compared pay scales and career potential, he moved to Conneaut, Ohio, where he taught social studies and physical education and coached championship baseball teams until his retirement in 1984. Stanley Humphrey, to author, November 1994.

5. Morrison Colladay, "The Passing of the American Village," *Commonweal*, July 18, 1952, pp. 363–64.

6. Ibid., p. 364.

7. Richard O. Davies, *Housing Reform during the Truman Administration* (Columbia: University of Missouri Press, 1966), pp. 40–59.

8. The expected, and apparently willing, return of Camden women to their domestic roles was part of a national phenomenon. See Loren Baritz, *The Good Life: The Meaning of Success for the American Middle Class* (New York: Harper and Row, 1982), pp. 176–88; and Susan Hartmann, *The Home Front: American Women in the 1940s* (Boston: Twayne Publishers, 1982).

9. *Preble County News*, September 20, 1945, and August 26, 1946.

10. Ibid., September 27, 1945.

11. Ibid., July 18, 1946.

12. Art Gallaher, *Plainville Fifteen Years Later* (New York: Columbia University Press, 1961), p. 56.

13. *Preble County News*, October 18, November 1, and November 8, 1945.

14. Ibid., September 5, 1946.

15. The other pitcher was Max DeCamp, whose career ended at the AA level with an injured arm. Elston was the only Camden native ever to make the "big leagues."

16. *Preble County News*, September 25, 1947.

17. Ibid., May 1, 1947.

18. Ibid., August 16, September 25, and October 23, 1947.

19. Ibid., December 25, 1947.

20. Ibid.

21. Ibid., April 29, 1948, and January 13, 1949.

22. I have re-created this episode from memory; the date is an educated guess, but the time of the year and the date are reasonably accurate based upon other oral histories and documents in the Camden Archives. In a retrospective essay that appeared on April 3, 1952, the *Preble County News* reported that "Smitty was the first television expert in Preble County and opened the Camden Radio and Television Shop in March of 1948."

23. *Preble County News*, November 27, 1947, and September 1, 1949; see also December 8, 1949.

24. For a good overview of the impact of television on American society, see Halberstam, *The Fifties*, pp. 180–202; for the impact of television on sports, see Richard O. Davies, *America's Obsession: Sports and Society since 1945* (New York: Harcourt Brace, 1994), pp. 63–101.

25. Erik Barnouw, *The Golden Web*, vol. 2 of *A History of Broadcasting in the United States* (New York: Oxford University Press, 1968), pp. 242–45, 283–303; Barnouw, *The Image Empire*, vol. 3 of *A History of Broadcasting in the United States* (New York: Oxford University Press, 1970), pp. 5–8, 65–84.

26. *Preble County News*, May 15, 1952.

27. *Preble County News*, November 3, 1950, April 19, 1951, and May 15, 1952; Halberstam, *The Fifties*, p. 185; Larry McMurtry, *The Last Picture Show* (New York: Pocket Books, 1966), pp. 291–92.

28. *Preble County News*, September 2, 1937; William L. O'Neill, *American High: The Years of Confidence, 1945–1960* (New York: Macmillan, 1986), pp. 136–39.

29. *Preble County News*, June 29, 1950.

30. Ibid., August 25, 1949.

31. This perception is strongly identified by more than fifty graduates of the high school from the years 1950–60 in a questionnaire conducted by the author.

32. Surprisingly, there is little in the historical literature regarding the phenomenon of town baseball. Lewis E. Atherton, *Main Street on the Middle Border* (Bloomington: Indiana University Press, 1954), pp. 200–202, 318–19, talks of its importance to town morale; see also Joseph A. Amato and John W. Meyer, *The Decline of Rural Minnesota* (Marshall, Minnesota: Crossings Press, 1993), pp. 52–54.

33. *Preble County News*, November 1, 1951.

34. Ibid., November 8, 1951, November 4, 1952, and March 20, 1955.

35. These observations are based on the author's memory, the general tenor of reports and advertisements in the *Preble County News*, and questionnaires distributed to high school graduates. For comparable studies that report the same phenomenon, see Gallaher, *Plainville Fifteen Years Later*, pp. 17, 25; Arthur Vidich and Joseph Bensman, *Small Town in Mass Society: Class, Power, and Religion in a Rural Community* (Princeton: Princeton University Press, 1968), pp. 299–30. Although published in 1954, Atherton's *Main Street on the Middle Border*, pp. 222–29, 348–52, perceptively identified this trend.

36. *Preble County News*, February 22, 1951. The perceptions in these two paragraphs are also based on my own memories, especially of conversations regarding teenage behavior with my father, who was superintendent of the local schools from 1946 until 1955. For a detailed analysis of a similar social phenomenon occurring at the same time in Missouri, see Gallaher, *Plainville Fifteen Years Later*, pp. 10–167.

37. *Preble County News*, December 7, 1950, and December 6, 1951.

38. Ibid., December 21, 1950.

39. Ibid., November 22, 1951. I myself was a member, however briefly, of this cold war defense system.

40. Ibid., April 27, and August 25, 1950; February 22, 1951.

41. Ibid., October 18, 1951.

42. Ibid., February 8, 1951.

43. "A Business of My Own," reprinted in ibid., February 2, 1946; January 5, 1950, April 3, 1952. "Camden's Foremost and Oldest Industry," *Forward Magazine,* December 1950.

44. *Preble County News,* January 9, 1947, and February 18, 1950.

45. Julia Deem, long-time secretary of the board of directors of Neff and Fry Company, to author, February 24, 1995.

46. Ibid.

47. *Preble County News,* February 12, 1953.

48. Ibid., November 18, 1948, and December 7, 1950.

49. Ibid., December 6, 1951.

Nothing Happened

FROM *Blooming*

SUSAN ALLEN TOTH

AMERICAN LIFE in the fifties has a well-deserved reputation for being quiet and untroubled, although we now know that beneath the placid surface profound social changes were taking place: relaxed codes of speech and sexual behavior, integration and civil rights, a more urban and more European outlook on life, the emergence of a youth-based and youth-oriented culture, and the ascendancy of radio and television. Like most social movements, these are clearer in hindsight than they were at the time. In 1955, America seemed to move with almost glacial slowness. Especially in contrast to the sixties, this was a decade when it seemed nothing was happening.

Some social critics have viewed the fifties as a return to normal, prewar, American, and isolationist attitudes after America's venture into internationalism during World War II. Others have read fifties America as the ascendancy of mainline Protestantism, the reassertion of a genteel tradition that dates to the colonial era, a polite reserve that represses anger, conflict, and sensuality as part of its Puritan heritage. Still others remember the fifties as the last moment of calm before a storm that seemed only to intensify as the twentieth century melted into the twenty-first.

Nor surprisingly, the fifties sleep is associated with suburbs and small towns, where—again depending on point of view—the old cultural cohesion survived longer or fundamental cracks in society were slower in revealing themselves. Town values did tend to be mainline Protestant, and racial tensions, ethnic divisions, and serious crime tended to be minimal or minimized. Perhaps small towns of the fifties were indeed Happy Village; perhaps there was a conspiracy of silence. Bill Holm writes of Minneota, Minnesota, "In my small town secrets disappeared. Retarded children vanished into the upstairs bedrooms of farmhouses, where someone carried food to them. . . . Pregnant, unmarried girls were not mentioned once they had been safely transported to the anonymity of Minneapolis to give birth. . . . When depression or any form of madness visited a house, someone disappeared (often a woman) who was described as resting because of 'nerves.' I spent my boyhood blissfully unaware of how many neighbors had experienced shock treatments. . . . I never heard a word about tuberculosis, though I even had an aunt dying of it. Suicide? Silence. The gay uncle? More silence. Prison? Nobody we knew."

Was life in the American small town during the fifties hell or heaven? Even those who lived it cannot say. Susan Allen Toth, whose childhood in Ames, Iowa, was as Protestant and genteel as can be imagined, finds herself ambivalent. She writes, "Even if I could change the ways in which I grew up, I would not know where to start or stop." Small-town America offered shelter and space to grow, security and innocence—and ignorance. A place where nothing much happened, Ames, Iowa, simply was.

o o o

When she was four years old, my daughter, Jennifer, began to develop a sense of history. "What was it like in the old days, Mommy? Did you wear long dresses? Did you ever ride in a covered wagon?" As I struggled with her questions, I realized that to her the "old days" encompassed a cloudy past when I was young, as well as when her grandmother was young, and whatever dim days extended beyond Gramma's childhood. I could not distinguish among these histories nor tell her exactly when the "old days" ended and the present began.

I have some of the same difficulty trying to explain to friends who did not grow up in a small Midwestern college town in the 1950s what life was like then. Those "old days" have disappeared into an irretrievable past that seems only faintly credible to those who did live it. Does any girl today have the chance to grow up as gradually and as quietly as we did? In our particular crucible we were not seared by fierce poverty, racial tensions, drug abuse, street crime; we were cosseted, gently warmed, transmuted by slow degrees. Nonetheless we were being changed, girls into women. The kind of woman we thought we would become was what Ames, Iowa, saw as the American ideal. She shimmered in our minds, familiar but removed as the glossy cover of the Sears, Roebuck catalogue. There she rolled snowballs with two smiling red-cheeked children, or unpacked a picnic lunch on emerald grass as an Irish setter lounged nearby, or led a cherubic toddler into blue water. Her tall, handsome husband hovered close, perhaps with his hand protectively on her shoulder. Pretty and well dressed, she laughed happily into the Koda-Color sunshine that flooded her future.

I do not think any of us would fit into such a simple picture today. During the past twenty years, that gleaming ideal has become tarnished, scratched and blackened as deeply as the copper bottoms on the shiny saucepans we got as wedding presents. Many of us have gone through painful reassessments that have made us question the kinds of assumptions upon which we so confidently based our lives. We look to the past to try to

discover how we got here from there. I look at my own childhood and adolescence in Ames and wonder: was such innocence constricting, or did it
give me shelter and space to grow? What do I see in that past I can still
value? What did I get for the price I paid? What was the price, anyway?

I cannot sum it up. I do not see my life as a cost-accounting sheet, this
friend a profit, that time a dead loss, cause and effect neatly balanced on a
ledger line. Instead, when Jennifer asks, "What was it like in the old days,
Mommy?" my mind begins to spin with images. I want to describe for her
the tension of the noisy, floodlit night we won the state basketball tournament; how sweat dripped down my dirty bathing suit as I detasseled corn
under a July sun; the seductive softness of my red velveteen formal; the
marble hush of the Ames Public Library; the feeling of choking on the cold
chlorinated water of Blaine's Pool when a boy cannonballed on top of me.

What will these images tell her about love, sex, pride? Self-esteem, ambition, fear? I do not know. Examining my childhood has not brought me
any easy answers. Sometimes I wish it had. Once I read aloud passages from
these memoirs to some local alumnae of an Eastern women's college I had
always feared but respected. They were intelligent listeners, and I know
many of them had grown up in times and towns like mine. When I had finished, I waited anxiously for their response. What conclusions had they
reached? Everyone was silent for a few moments, hesitant to begin the discussion. Then one intense young woman, a recent graduate, could contain
herself no longer. Her lips were drawn tight with suppressed indignation, her
voice trembled with feeling. "Where," she demanded, "is the admission that
it was hell?" She paused for effect, giving me just time to open my mouth
and close it again. "Where is your acknowledgment of the smugness, the
hypocrisy, the prejudice?"

Suddenly several women spoke at once, agreeing, disagreeing, and sharing their own stories. Underneath the clamor I thought, "But it wasn't hell.
Not for me. It wasn't perfect, but mostly I was happy. Yes, I saw provincial
smugness, but I didn't always realize what it was. I can report its effects
now, but I didn't suffer from them then. I wish I had known more about
some things, absorbed less about others, but that's the way it was. Of course
we weren't prepared for life. Who ever is? I paused, trying as I often have to
sum up, reach a judgment, and deliver a final verdict on my childhood. My
antagonist, seeing me silent, returned to the attack. "You see?" she said triumphantly, pointing her finger at me. "You're ambivalent! Admit it, you're
ambivalent!"

Of course I admit it. Even if I could change the ways in which I grew up,
I would not know where to start or stop. On the way home after that alumnae meeting, I was still arguing in my head, partly with myself, partly with
the finger-pointing moralizer. Whoever I became, who I am now, is the result of many tangled circumstances, and I cannot single one out for praise
or blame and say, "There!"

I wished I had thought to tell her about my garden. Maybe that would have been an answer. It is a small garden, carved from the back lawn of a city lot, but gradually I have replaced more and more grass with flowers, herbs and vegetables. I don't have much space, so I plant my perennials carefully: three gray-green bunches of English lavender, some Iceland poppies, one shaggy white Shasta daisy, other small clusters of plants that must be nurtured carefully in the violent Minnesota climate. I weed, water, mulch, pinch and spray. In the fall I bury the tender ones with leaves and straw. Most of my plants endure the winter; though I mourn some losses, I will try again, perhaps with a new variety or stronger seedlings. A few survivors grow and thrive with such sturdiness and vigor that I marvel at their bloom.

I have a friend who gardens too. She is cheerfully careless, scattering seeds in odd places, buying faded flats of petunias in mid-July, and accumulating clumps from whatever her neighbors want to get rid of. She weeds occasionally and waters during droughts, but otherwise she gardens lazily. She doesn't bother with winter covering. "I figure any plant of mine has got to be tough," she said to me last fall. I would like to be able to report that her garden is a disaster, but it's not. Her backyard has as much color as mine, with pink bleeding heart in spring, gaudy tiger lilies in midsummer, the yellow fire of mums in the fall. True, she doesn't have any English lavender, Iceland poppies or Shasta daisies, but she doesn't care. "I only plant what I know can make it without too much fuss," she explains.

Her flowers survive and bloom, and so do mine. We both have successful gardens. I would like to have told my moralizer that we are simply cultivating different plants. When I look at the time, the town, the customs, the people who surrounded me when I was growing up, I cannot wish I had been nurtured in a different place. It was the only garden I knew.

We huddled together in the cool spring night, whispering in hoarse voices, thrumming with the excitement that vibrated through the crowd gathering in the parking lot outside the Ames train station. All the way home from Des Moines we had hugged each other, laughed, cried, and hugged each other again. When we passed through the small farming towns between Des Moines and Ames, we rolled down the windows of the Harbingers' station wagon and shouted down the quiet streets, "We beat Marshalltown in seven overtimes! We beat Marshalltown in seven overtimes!" It had a rhythmic beat, a chant we repeated to each other in unbelieving ecstasy. We beat Marshalltown in seven overtimes! For the first time in ten years, Ames High School had won the state basketball championship. Most of us sophomores felt nothing so important could ever happen to us again.

As a string of cars began threading off the highway, filling up the lot, someone turned the lights along Main Street on full. It was close to midnight, but families were pouring down the street toward the station as though it held a George Washington's Birthday sale. We were all waiting for the team. The mayor had ordered out the two fire engines, which were waiting too, bright red and gleaming under the lights. When the bus finally came around the corner, a cheering erupted from the crowd that didn't stop until the boys had walked down the steps, grinning a little sheepishly, and climbed onto the engines. The coach rode on one, the mayor on another. Following our cheerleaders, voices gone by valiantly shrieking, who were leading the way in their whirling orange pleated skirts and black sweaters, we snake-danced down Main Street behind blowing sirens and paraded to the high-school auditorium. There we listened to speeches from the mayor, the principal, the coach, and the team captain. We would have no school tomorrow, the principal told us (we cheered again), just a pep assembly, then dismissal. Then Mr. J. J. Girton, who owned all three movie theatres in Ames, came to the mike and said that in honor of the occasion he would show a free movie at the New Ames tomorrow at two P.M. We cheered, but this time not as loudly. We knew whenever Mr. Girton showed free movies, he always picked the oldest Looney Tunes and a dull Western. The coach thanked everyone and sat down quickly; he looked tired. But when he introduced the team captain, who made his teammates rise, we jumped to our feet and clapped and stomped.

I was filled with love and admiration for all of them, for stocky little Tom Fisher, who had made a critical free throw; for tall, gangly Charlie Stokowski, who had racked up thirty points; for George Davis, who usually stood most of the game in front of the bench with his mouth hanging open, but who tonight in the midst of the team looked like a hero. Next to me Patsy Jones, George's girlfriend, looked smug and proud. We knew she was planning to meet him backstage for a few moments after the assembly. When our new celebrities filed off the stage, our parents, who had been sitting together in the last rows, took us home. Next morning at breakfast we could read all about ourselves, with headlines and pictures, in the Des Moines *Register*. Though we knew other stories would topple ours after a few days, it didn't matter.

Perhaps I remember that night so vividly because it stands out like a high hill in the flat, uneventful landscape that was both the physical and emotional setting for our town. Our lives were not dull, oh, no; but our adolescence bubbled and fermented in a kind of vacuum. In Ames, in the 1950s, as far as we were concerned, nothing happened.

Ames had once had a murder. It had happened a few years before we were in junior high, to someone we didn't know, a man who hadn't lived in Ames long. He had somehow accumulated gambling debts, probably on his travels out West, and one night he was found shot to death at the Round-up Motel. No one ever found a weapon or the murderers. After a few blurred photographs in the Ames Daily *Tribune* and interviews with the cleaning woman who'd found him, the motel owner, the county sheriff and local police, even the newspaper abandoned the story. But for many years afterward, when we drove with strangers past the Round-up, we would point it out in reverential tones. It might look just like a tidy modern bungalow, stretched out into longer wings than usual, but we knew it was a bloody place.

Other than our murder, we had little experience with violence. Sometimes there were accidents. One of my girlfriends had a brother who had lost an eye when another boy had aimed badly with a bow and arrow. We stared surreptitiously at his glass eye, which was bigger and shinier than it ought to be. Someone else's sister, much younger, had toddled in front of a truck on the highway and been killed. Her picture, done in careful pastels by an artist from Des Moines, hung over the sofa in her parents' living room. When they spoke of her, I tried not to look at the picture, which made me feel uncomfortable.

When death came to Ames, it seldom took anyone we knew. We were all shocked when one morning we saw our high-school teachers whispering together in the halls, a few of them weeping openly, over the history teacher's four-year-old daughter, who had been rushed the previous night to the hospital and who had died almost immediately of heart failure. Visitation was to be that night at the Jefferson Funeral Parlor. Those of us who felt close to Mr. Sansome wanted to go to "pay our respects," a phrase someone had heard from another teacher. We discussed solemnly what to wear, what to do, what to say. When two girlfriends came to pick me up, I was nervous, with a sinking feeling in my stomach because I did not know what to expect. I had never seen a dead person before.

We didn't stay at the funeral parlor long. The room was crowded with friends of the Sansomes. Mrs. Sansome wasn't there—home, in bed, someone said sympathetically—and Mr. Sansome stood with a glazed expression on his face, shaking hands, muttering politeness, to everyone who came up to him. We shook his hand and moved on to the coffin. Mary Sansome looked just as she always did, dressed perhaps more neatly in a Sunday dress with bright pink bows tied onto her long pigtails. As we leaned closer, I thought her skin looked rubbery and waxen, like a doll I had once had. Her eyes were shut, but she looked as though she might wake up any minute, disturbed by the murmured talk around her. I looked over at Mr. Sansome, usually a gesturing, dramatic man, standing woodenly a few feet away, staring straight ahead of him. The feeling in my stomach got worse. I wanted to cry, but I couldn't. Soon my friends and I went silently home.

The few deaths we knew in those years seemed rare and accidental. Once Mrs. Miller, an elderly neighbor, came fluttering to our house in high excitement. She didn't want my sister and me to hear what she had to tell my mother, but we hovered quietly in our room with the door open a crack and listened intently. Behind Mrs. Miller lived Sam and Martha Doyle, five children, a collie, and a tiger cat. It was a large, noisy, happy family. Mr. Doyle was like any other father, kindly, offhand, seldom home. But for some reason no one understood, not even patiently inquisitive Mrs. Miller, Mr. Doyle had tried to kill himself that morning. "I heard screams," she said breathlessly to my mother, "and when I ran to the back door, there was Martha Doyle standing in the driveway trying to open the garage door. I guess it must have stuck. Right behind her was Sam, with some kitchen towels wrapped around his wrists all covered with blood. Then she got the door open, they both got in the car and drove off."

We never heard what happened after the Doyles got to the hospital, but everything was quickly hushed up. Soon afterward the whole family moved away. I thought about Mr. Doyle for a long time. What could ever be so bad you would want to hurt yourself, make yourself bleed like that? Tragedy, as far as we knew it existed in adult lives, merely extended to freakish twists of fate, like the death of little Mary Sansome. Most of us were convinced that life was going to be wonderful.

As far as we knew, people in Ames didn't get divorced. But one woman did. Sallie Houlton, the divorcee, looked like any other grown-up. In her late twenties, she had an average figure, nondescript brown hair, a pleasant but undistinguished face. Sallie lived sometimes with her arthritic aunt, Miss Houlton, on the far side of town. Mother knew them both because an aunt of mine had taught with Miss Houlton years ago in Minnesota. Sometimes Sallie disappeared for temporary employment in other cities. She was a dietitian, Mother said, and ran hospital kitchens. All I really knew about Sallie Houlton was that she had been divorced. No one would say why, but once Mrs. Miller had been talking about Sallie to Mother and I heard her say, with disapproving fervor, "And on top of all that, he *drank*." I was very curious to know what "all that" was. Mother, usually fairly straightforward in her replies to my questions, hedged this one; she said it was very complicated, hard to explain. Many years later, when for some ignoble reason I was still curious about "all that," Mother said simply, "He was impotent." Oh, I said. Her answer was something of a letdown.

It was almost as difficult to understand what could happen to a husband and wife so terrible that they would want a divorce as it was to understand what had driven Mr. Doyle to cut his wrists. As I grew older and moved through high school, I began to have occasional focus, as though a blurred picture had suddenly sharpened, on a few of the marriages I had taken so far for granted. My first illumination took place outside our house one hot summer night, when my mother had given one of her four-to-six sherry parties. Her friends, all married couples, came to sip a little Taylor's Cocktail Sherry or ginger ale, smoke, talk, sip some more and go home at a decent hour. But at this party, four of the guests stayed until past ten. Two were

Australians, a visiting professor of agricultural economics and his pale blonde wife, who was a part-time secretary in the foreign students' office; the others were my mother's old friends, Mike and Helen Snyder, who had lived next door to her before I was born. The Snyders were probably in their forties then, the Australians in their twenties. Mike always liked to stay late at parties, and he and Helen had begun to snipe at each other about whether it was time to leave. I had heard their rapid fire before, seen Helen's mouth tighten at the corners, watched Mike defiantly pour more sherry into his glass; neither I nor anyone else ever took their bickering seriously. Mike was a sharp-tongued mathematician, and his cutting edge seemed almost professional. Tonight Mike kept his back turned to Helen as much as possible and talked vehemently to the Australian wife. Sometimes when he got particularly excited he picked up her hand and held it for a while. Finally, the Australian economist got up. His wife rose obediently, and Mother, who was looking tired, rose too to walk them to their car. I tagged along, bored with the party, and, surprisingly, found that Mike Snyder was walking beside me.

"So how's your summer going?" he asked me absentmindedly, but he was watching the light-haired woman in front of him. He swayed, bumped into me, and straightened up again. At the car, after her husband got in, he reached through the front window and patted her on the shoulder. "Lucy, Lucy, Lucy," he said in a kind of singsong. The car pulled quickly away from the curb. Mike turned to my mother. With astonishment, I could see that he had tears in his eyes. "What am I going to do, Hazel?" he said in a voice in which anguish had conquered the alcohol. "I love her so damn much. What am I going to do?" Mother put her arm around Mike and began to guide him back to the house. "It's going to be all right, Mike," I heard her say comfortingly, just as she did to me when I was overcome with despair. "It's all right. You know they're leaving soon. It's going to be all right."

Maybe for a while it *was* all right. The summer passed. The Australian visitors went back to Melbourne, and the Snyders continued to come to Mother's sherry parties. I tried not to talk to them much. I had been both confused and embarrassed by what I had seen. Four or five years later, when I was in college, one of the bits of news that Mother had for me at Christmas vacation was that the Snyders were getting a divorce. It was not the shock it would once have been. I asked Mother about the Australian woman, but Mother looked surprised. That was a long time ago, she said, and had nothing to do with it anyway.

If I knew little about love, I knew nothing about sex. The closest thing Ames had to offer as sex education was the Hudson station, a rickety gas outlet beyond the city limits that sold rubbers in a coin-operated machine in its men's room, or so we girls were told. A girl's reputation could be ruined if her date stopped for gas at the Hudson station. A lot of us had to ask more knowing friends what a rubber was. That piece of information was conveyed to me in patronizing tones by a fellow sixth-grader, Joyce Schwartz, who motioned me upstairs one day to her parents' bedroom when they were out. She carefully opened her father's top drawer, lifted up a pile of neatly folded handkerchiefs, and showed me a small cardboard box. "Those are rubbers," she said wisely. She let me open the top of the box but didn't want me to take anything out. I couldn't make much of what I saw anyway.

Not long after that, another friend, Emily Harris, also mature beyond my years, took me for a walk behind her house to an old deserted greenhouse that had once belonged to the college. There couples came sometimes at night and did things, she said. "Sometimes I find rubbers here in the grass," she added, staring intently around her feet, and I stared at my feet too, though I wasn't sure what I was looking for. I only saw bits of broken glass from long-gone windows, bottle caps, and used Kleenex. Suddenly Emily shouted, "There's one!" She looked around quickly for a stick, and then fished in the grass until she managed to hoist aloft a squishy shapeless piece of latex. It was the fleshlike color that seemed obscene to me. "Don't touch it," Emily warned. "You can get awful diseases from these things." I thought you could also get awfully cold here at night. What could drive anyone to such an uncomfortable spot to do something with that icky piece of rubber?

Besides having had a murder and a divorce, Ames had a prostitute. Her name was Nancy, and all the boys in high school joked about her. She lived near the college, but I never saw her until one dark rainy night when I was a senior in high school, almost ready to graduate. It was late in May, the kind of balmy weather that opened up the promise of a long drowsy summer ahead. My friend Charlie, who had dropped over on a dull evening just to talk awhile, agreed to walk with me in the rain all the way to Campustown, the tiny shopping district about a mile distant.

When we were dressed for outdoors, we looked like brothers in our wrinkled trenchcoats, the Penney's double-breasted poplin style that was practically unisex even in those days. I borrowed Charlie's shapeless old hat and jammed it down over my short hair. You couldn't see much of me except my nose, though I would lift my face up from time to time to catch the fresh feel of the rain. It was a lovely walk, as we sloshed through puddles, stared at the bright glowing lights in all the darkened houses, reveled in the quiet of the deserted streets. It seemed to me as if we were all alone in the world, wet and happy, with only the faint whooshing of tree branches and the occasional splash of passing cars to interrupt our intent conversation. When we got to Campustown, it too was deserted, the stores shuttered tight, a few small neon signs flashing in dark windows, "Cat's Paw," "Pop's Grill," "Cigars." Tonight we seemed to own this little main street, which echoed to our steps and low voices.

Striding along, matching Charlie's pace as best I could, I soon saw someone approaching from the other direction. I didn't bother to notice who it was until she drew abreast of us, paused for a moment, and said quickly but distinctly, "Want to fuck?" I looked up in disbelief. I caught a glimpse of a lined face, bright yellow stringy hair, garish lips, and then it was gone. Charlie, though startled, was beginning to laugh. "Did she say what I thought she said?" I asked anxiously. "Yup," he said, now laughing openly. "That was Nancy. She probably thought you were a boy. She must've been really startled when she saw you up close." I turned and looked behind me, but Nancy was gone. Charlie, who kept chuckling for a long while, couldn't understand why I seemed upset; I wasn't sure myself. But it seemed as though the interruption had broken something fragile, as evanescent as the rainbow oil slick in the gutter at our feet.

If I was vouchsafed some faint but definite glimmerings about sex in Ames, I saw little else troubling that small society. One reason I was so blind to common attitudes toward blacks was that Ames didn't have any. Or rather, like everything else, Ames had only one. For most of the years I was growing up, there was a single family in town who were black, or, to be precise, an unassuming shade of brown. The Elliotts, quiet and hardworking, lived far from the college campus in an unfashionable section where small businesses, warehouses and rundown older houses crowded together. It wasn't exactly a slum, but it wasn't a place where anyone I knew lived either. Alexander Elliott was in my class, his younger sister two classes behind me. They too were hardworking and quiet, always neatly dressed, pleasant expressions on their faces, ready to respond politely. What went on behind those carefully composed smiles no one then ever wondered.

We thought the Elliott kids were nice enough, we exchanged casual greetings with them, but Alexander was never invited to any parties. He did not belong to any social groups. I do not remember seeing him anywhere, except in a crowd cheering at a football game or sitting a little apart in school assembly. Once or twice I think I remember Alexander's bringing a date, also black—though "Negro" was what we called them, enunciating the word carefully—to the Junior-Senior Prom. Wherever she was from, it wasn't Ames. They danced by themselves all evening. Yet none of us thought we were prejudiced about Alex, and almost every year we elected him to some class office. The year Alex became student-body president, our principal pointed to Ames High proudly as an example of the way democracy really worked.

If I was unaware that Ames was prejudiced toward blacks, I could not miss the town's feelings about Catholics. I myself was fascinated by the glamour that beckoned at the door of St. Cecilia's, the imposing brick church defiantly planted right on the main road through town. Every Christmas St. Cecilia's erected a life-size nativity scene on its lawn, floodlit, Mary in blue velvet, glowing halos, real straw in the wooden manger.

None of the Methodists, Lutherans, Baptists or Presbyterians did anything quite so showy. I always begged Mother to slow down as we drove by so I could admire it. Sometimes I could see one of the nuns from the small convent behind the church billowing in her black robes down the street. If I was with my friend Peggy O'Reilly, who was Catholic, she would stop and greet the nun respectfully. She knew each one by name, though they all looked alike to me.

Peggy told me bits and pieces about Catholic doctrine, which was so different from the vague advice I was gathering haphazardly in my own Presbyterian Sunday School that I didn't know what to make of it. Catholics had exotic secrets. One of the saints—was it Bernadette?—had been given the exact date of the end of the world, Peggy said, and she on her death had bequeathed it to the Pope. Every Pope kept this secret locked in a special case, and when he was about to die, he opened it, read the date, and expired— probably, I thought, out of shock. Why didn't the Popes share this wonderful knowledge with the world, so we could all get ready for the end? I asked Peggy. Peggy couldn't say.

Even if we hadn't known from friends like Peggy that Catholics were different, our parents would have told us. One of the few rigid rules enforced on many of us was the impossibility of "getting serious" about a Catholic boy. For a Protestant to marry a Catholic in Ames produced a major social upheaval, involving parental conferences, conversions, and general disapproval on both sides. Even our liberal minister, who encouraged his Presbyterian parishioners to call him "Doctor Bob" because he didn't want to appear uppish about his advanced degree, came to our high-school fellowship group one night to lecture on Catholicism. He probably knew that one of his deacons' daughters was going very steadily with a Catholic boy. Warning us about the autocratic nature of the Catholic Church, its iron hand, its idolatry, and most of all the way it could snatch our very children from us and bring them up in the manacles of a strange faith, Doctor Bob heated with the warmth of his topic until his cheeks glowed as he clenched and unclenched his fists.

Since I never fell in love with one of the few Catholic boys in our class, I never faced such direct fire. But my friend Peggy did. Much to her parents' disapproval, she began going steadily with Alvin Barnes, a Methodist boy who had never dated at all before he discovered Peggy. He was a quiet, withdrawn boy who seldom talked about anything, let alone his feelings, but we could all tell by the way he looked at Peggy that he loved her with a single-minded devotion. Her parents tolerated the romance for a year, though we knew they often had long talks with Peggy about it. But during their senior year, when Peggy and Alvin were still holding hands in daylight, Peggy's family decided that enough was enough. They gave Peggy an ultimatum, which she repeated to us, sobbing, one night when we girls had gathered together at someone's house for popcorn and gossip. She was distraught, but she had no thought of disobeying them; she was going to tell Alvin they must break it off. We were indignant, sympathetic, but helpless; the price Peggy's parents were willing to pay was a year away at college, and no one thought Peggy could give that up instead.

A few days later Alvin was absent from school, and the whispers were alarming. After hearing Peggy's news, he had come to her house to try to argue with her parents. They had refused to let him in, had told him to go home and not to bother their daughter again. When he called their house, they wouldn't let Peggy come to the phone. So later that night, he had returned. There in the sloping driveway he had lain down behind the rear wheels of the O'Reilly family car. All night he lay there, waiting for the still-dark morning when Mr. O'Reilly would come out, start the engine, and back the car down the driveway on his way to work.

Of course, when morning finally came, Mr. O'Reilly saw Alvin at once. Horrified, he called Alvin's parents. They came and took Alvin away, and he did not come back to school until close to the end of the semester. Then he kept aloof, refusing to talk about what had happened, and hovered silently at the edges of our games and parties. Soon we all graduated, Alvin left town, and we lost track of him entirely. But I felt as though he had somehow been sacrificed, offered up to the fierce religious hatred I had seen gleaming in Doctor Bob's eyes. For several years, until even more bitter images etched over this one, I thought of the effects of prejudice as embodied in Alvin's quiet figure, lying patiently and hopelessly in the chilly darkness behind the wheels of the O'Reilly car.

Such drama, however, was rare. It was a quiet town and a quiet time. That may be why I can still hear the whispers of notebooks slapping shut and a pencil-sharpener grinding in the high-school study hall; the scratchy strains of "Blue Tango" on an overamplified record-player at the Friday dance; the persistent throb of grasshoppers in a rustling cornfield on a summer night when my boyfriend Peter parked his old Ford on a country road. In a world where nothing seemed to happen, small sounds were amplified so clearly that they still echo in my mind. So now on a hot summer night, when I sit by myself on my city steps, trying to block out nearby traffic and concentrating instead on the slightest rustle of leaves in the warm breeze, I remember the years of my growing up in Ames. Against that background of quiet, a girl could listen to her heart beating.

During the summer the long hot weekend days seemed to stretch out like the endless asphalt ribbons of highway winding into the country. We never had quite enough to do, especially on Saturday mornings. So we often drifted in and out of Olson's Bowling Alley, just a few lanes, hand-set pins, a quarter a line. Tucked on the second floor above a Spiegel catalogue order house at the end of Main Street, it was a most unlikely location for a bowling alley. Although the nearby high school hired it for occasional gym classes, I doubt that it ever paid its way. Sometimes we arrived at Olson's Alley early, by nine o'clock, when the downtown stores were opening their doors and hosing down their sidewalks. The heat was beginning to pour in the open windows, streaking sunshine across the dirty wooden floor and the three brightly gleaming lanes. We settled haphazardly into a game. Before long our hands were sweaty; we'd wipe them on our shorts, hoping the crispness of our carefully ironed blouses wouldn't wilt too much before the boys came.

Some boys always did drift through Olson's on those long hazy mornings, as aimlessly as the dusty sunshine. They banged noisily up the stairs, yelling to each other, and clambered over the church-pew benches to hoot at our self-conscious strides as we struggled to aim our bowling balls straight. The girl whose turn it was to be pin-setter, huddled behind the racks at the end of the long alley, looked through the intricate metal network at the far-away girls laughing and flirting with the boys. Even a boy who liked you was too embarrassed to walk all the way to the back of the lanes when everyone could see where he was going.

Though it seems odd to think of a bowling alley as a quiet place, Olson's was. Though we girls giggled and gossiped, the only other sounds beyond those occasional noisy interruptions of the boys were the heavy thud of the bowling balls, the clang of the pin-setting rack, and the flap of the torn shade at the open window. The morning seemed to stretch on forever. When we'd used up our quarters and given up on seeing any more boys, we'd tuck in our blouses, comb our hair, and emerge from the oppressive sweaty room into the blinding full-noon sun. Down Main Street we'd hurry to the Rainbow Cafe, newly air-conditioned, and treat ourselves to icy root-beer floats before taking the bus home.

When I plunge back into those uneventful Saturday mornings, I am once more lapped around by waves of time, repetitious, comforting, like the gentle undulations of Blaine's Pool when the late-afternoon breezes blew over its empty blue-green water. We all felt as though summer would go on forever. I would go to Olson's, or not; I would bowl a little, or not; I would see the boy I cared about, or I wouldn't. Other Saturday mornings stretched ahead like oases in the shimmering sun.

As I grew older, I began to realize that this quiet was not going to last. Time was speeding up; at some sharply definable point I would grow up and leave Ames. At odd moments in those last years I would be surprised by sadness, a strange feeling that perhaps I had missed something, that maybe life was going to pass me by. At the same time I nestled securely in the familiar landscape of streets whose every bump and jog I knew, of people who smiled and greeted me by name wherever I went, of friends who appeared at every movie, store, or swimming pool.

Nowhere did I feel this conflicting sense of security and impending loss as sharply as I did at the train station. Ames lay on some important transcontinental routes, and trains passed through daily on their way from Chicago to Portland, San Francisco, Los Angeles. I had ridden on trains for short trips, but I had never been on one overnight and I was too young to re- member clearly what the country was like west of Ames when the prairies stopped and the mountains began. From a long auto trip when I was eight, I only remembered endless spaces punctuated by the Grand Canyon. So for me the crack passenger trains, the *City of San Francisco*, the *City of Denver*, the *City of Los Angeles*, had titles that rang in my imagination like the purest romance. Big cities, the golden West, life beckoned to me from every flashing train window.

On slow spring or summer nights I would often ask my friend Charlie to take me down to the station to watch the trains come in. The *City of San Francisco* was due to pass through at ten o'clock, the *City of Denver* at eleven. Down at the deserted station we sat on an abandoned luggage cart near the tracks, staring into the darkness, listening for the first telltale hoot of a faraway whistle. The night was so quiet we whispered, hearing above our voices the grasshoppers, a squeal of brakes three blocks away at the beer parlor, the loud click of the station clock. The trains were always late, but we were in no hurry.

Eventually we'd hear a rumble on the tracks and then see a searching eye of light bearing down on us. Quickly we'd leap to our feet and get as close to the tracks as we dared, plugging our ears as the train ground to a stop in front of us, its metallic clamor deafening, its cars looming in the night like visitors from another world. As we stood there, we could see people moving back and forth inside the lighted windows. If we were outside a Pullman car, we might catch a glimpse of someone seated next to the window staring wordlessly back at us. I wondered why everyone wasn't asleep. A frowsy-haired woman with a brown felt hat pinned to her graying curls looked like someone I might know but didn't. Two young boys, jumping on their seats and pounding silently on the glass, could have been the Evans kids down the street, but weren't. They were strangers, separated from us not only by thick glass but by chance, being whisked away from their old lives to new ones. I felt the pull of the future, of adventure waiting for them and some-day for me.

After a few moments, an exchange of luggage flung by the stationmaster, who had suddenly emerged from inside the darkened hut, a few shouts, the train began to grind again. As we winced with the jarring sound of metal against metal, it picked up speed. I tried to watch the car with the frowsy-haired woman and the two jumping boys, but it was soon lost in a blur of streaming silver metal. A last long low shriek, and the train was gone, off to Denver or San Francisco.

I always felt let down when Charlie and I walked back to his car. I comforted myself with thinking that someday I too would be traveling on one of those trains, leaving Ames for college someplace far away, maybe even Denver or San Francisco. When I got on that train, I would head into a new and wonderful life. It never occurred to me that I would be taking my old self, and Ames, with me.

IV

Crisis on Main Street
1960–90

B Y THE 1960s problems in small-town America had become too wide-spread to ignore. Although the national economy was enjoying a sustained period of growth, towns were being left further and further behind. This was especially true of the smaller communities that lacked a solid economic base and could provide little in the way of cultural or social amenities. Businesses were closing at an alarming rate. Younger residents continued their mass movement to the cities. As long-established stores closed, they were sometimes replaced by a video rental or antique store or a small bar, but more often than not the store windows were boarded up and the doors chained. New construction ground to a near halt; the opening of a new trailer park, retirement home, or long-term nursing care residence was hailed as an important community event. Those businessmen who remained—the grocer, druggist, service station operator, and others who offered essential services—came to anticipate the day when Social Security checks arrived in town because it constituted one of the larger paydays of the month for town residents. Once stately residences fell into disrepair, some were abandoned altogether, others were sliced up into low-rent apartments. Potholes in the streets went untended, and weeds and grass pushed through pavement and sidewalks alike. Litter was less and less likely to be removed in a timely fashion. Apathy swept across the community as the high school was closed, and sometimes even a church or two shuttered their doors due to eroded membership.

Local governments found themselves hard pressed to respond to distant political bureaucracies. Officials chafed under an increased tendency of state and federal governments to hand down mandates they were expected to meet. By the 1970s political leaders found that their primary role was not to initiate programs to meet local needs but rather to respond to federal and state directives on such matters as environmental protection, health and safety, transportation, health care delivery, school curriculum, and law enforcement.

Of great symbolic importance was the closing of the locally owned and operated bank. For a century or more hometown banks had served the needs of farmers and townsfolk. Now these once fiercely independent institutions found themselves lacking the capital and the skills required to compete with urban-based banking giants taking advantage of new state and federal laws permitting branch banking and interstate banking conglomerates. By 1990 only a handful of small-town banks remained, the great majority having been absorbed in the bank merger frenzy that swept the nation during the 1970s and '80s.

Central to the economic devastation of the traditional Main Street business community was the arrival of the new mega-chain store. This phenomenon had begun early in the century with national and regional grocery and drug store franchises, and during the postwar years residents of larger towns had welcomed the diversity of goods and services offered by the mercantile outposts of Sears, Roebuck or J. C. Penney and the culinary delights provided by a Dairy Queen or Hardee's. However, these relatively benign invaders paved the way for the arrival of Wal-Mart. Enormous warehouse-like discount stores began to appear in the Midwest in the 1970s after having proved their profitability and popularity in the South during the previous decade. For nearly a quarter century founder Sam Walton pursued a strategy of establishing his stores in smaller cities, sometimes in communities with as few as 5,000 residents if they were strategically located to serve a substantial population located within an hour or two's drive. Using sophisticated computer-based managerial, marketing, inventory, and logistics systems, Wal-Mart offered low prices and an enormous range of goods heretofore unavailable from local merchants. It even competed with drug stores, automobile repair shops, photographers, and optometrists.

Although Wal-Mart prominently advertised its intention to be a "good neighbor" whenever it invaded a new community—evidenced by contributions to local charities and employee participation in community activities—this mass merchandising juggernaut overwhelmed local merchants. Faced with a choice between supporting traditional merchants or the new mass merchandiser, local customers overwhelmingly opted for the latter. Thus in a town where a Wal-Mart was planted, within a few years the central business district revealed the consequences: an increased number of Main Street storefronts were boarded up, while traffic patterns were refocused around the community edge where Sam Walton's mega-store was located. The Wal-Mart store also served as a magnet for a new cluster of satellite enterprises, most of which were also of the franchise variety: fast food restaurants, convenience stores, video rental shops, automobile oil and lubrication stations, pizza joints, donut shops, and coffee drive-thru stands. Located on the edge of town along a main highway within a stone's throw of the Wal-Mart store (or upon occasion a mega-store competitor like K-Mart), these new businesses were situated in bleak, nondescript strip malls, the only creative aspect of their architecture being oversized electric signs.

Larger lead towns, which were able to attract small manufacturing companies, service industries, or food processing facilities and thereby maintain and even increase their populations, also faced perplexing problems. The companies they could attract were often those seeking a labor market that lacked a trade union tradition and whose workers would accept relatively low wage scales. As new immigrant groups flooded into the United States in the post–Vietnam War era, some of these new residents opted for employment in smaller manufacturing and service industries that were located in midwestern towns.

At the heart of this economic transformation was the fundamental restructuring of American agriculture. By the end of the twentieth century, the once dominant independent family farm seemed headed for near-extinction, as major changes wrought by corporate agriculture took their toll. One of the more startling changes introduced in states such as Nebraska, Illinois, Iowa, Missouri, and Minnesota was the opening of enormous food factories in which hogs, chickens, cattle, and turkeys were raised with astounding scientific and economic efficiency. Massive feed lots accommodated thousands of beef cattle, and long single-story buildings dotted the rural landscape, each containing hogs, turkey, or chickens whose life span was coldly calculated to the hour by a new generation of agricultural scientists and economists armed with computers, market conditions, and the latest scientific research findings. These new operations required large numbers of low-wage employees, and thus into traditional Eurocentric communities came substantial numbers of recent immigrants—Vietnamese, Hmong, Thai, Mexican, Tongan, Indian, Muslim, African—whose languages, values, and social customs differed substantially from those long established in these once homogenous, tightly-knit, Eurocentric communities.

Work in food processing plants was both hard and dangerous, however, and turnover sometimes reached 5 percent a month. Thus school systems and other social agencies found themselves dealing with the difficult problems posed by heavy turnover as families moved in and others just as abruptly departed. Corporate agriculture and food processing companies might have brought a new source of much-needed economic activity to many communities, but, like the chain and franchise stores, they also tended to rotate their management teams in and out with predictable frequency; thus the professional leadership of communities remained in a perpetual state of flux. Long-time locals found themselves perplexed when local history and traditions fell by the wayside; sometimes these towns were converted into "communities of strangers" due to the constant in- and out-migration. One consequence of this phenomenon was that service clubs like Lions and Kiwanis, long exemplars of community boosterism and improvement, found their membership rosters dwindling.

In towns large and small, as externally imposed changes altered the structure of the community, long-time residents were forced to accept a diminished future. Leaders of the more fortunate towns were happy to maintain a modest level of growth by welcoming into their midst small assembly plants, regional distribution centers, penal institutions, and the like. The crisis was most pronounced in smaller towns along the western edge of the Midwest. Small communities, located many miles from even a modest-sized city, reflected most acutely the impact of large-scale agriculture upon local populations. These towns simply lacked the financial or human resources to mount a meaningful campaign to rejuvenate their economic base. Although generally less dramatic, some of the same symptoms were clearly evident as far east as Michigan and Ohio.

Not that some towns did not try. Several sought to revitalize their communities by emphasizing their uniqueness as a means of stimulating tourism. One such example was the eastern Nebraska town of Oakland, heavily populated by families whose Swedish forebears had migrated to the fertile rolling farmland in the late nineteenth century. Led by an energetic publisher of the weekly newspaper, a campaign was launched in the mid-1980s to publicize the community of 1,500 as the "Swedish capital of Nebraska." The water tower and street signs were decorated with Swedish motifs. Residents put a Swedish touch to the exteriors of their homes. And each June thousands of visitors flooded the town for a weekend of Swedish cultural and social events. Although this effort had a sustained impact on community involvement, it did not end the departure of residents for the bright lights of Lincoln and Omaha or beyond, nor did it revive the central business district, which was dotted with abandoned storefronts. Outside of town, on the fertile farmland where hundreds of family farms once sustained Oakland's economy, consolidation of contiguous independent farms continued unabated as the new realities of the modern farm economy continued to decimate the farm population.

Perhaps the most audacious example of a small town's efforts to save itself from oblivion occurred in the river town of Rising Sun, Indiana, located along the banks of the Ohio River fifty miles downstream from Cincinnati. In 1990 the town found itself with an aging, stagnant population of 1,200, with its small business center shrinking and few decent jobs available for residents. Workers were forced to commute twenty miles to the larger town of Lawrenceburg, the home of a major distillery, or even to Cincinnati for meaningful employment. At this juncture, amidst intense controversy, a few leaders launched a campaign to lure a riverboat casino to the community. Competing vigorously with several other Indiana towns for the few state licenses available, the campaign proved successful, and in 1996 the Hyatt Corporation opened an $85 million hotel and riverboat casino complex that attracted thousands of visitors each day from as far away as Cincinnati, Indianapolis, and Louisville. Population increased and new housing developments were opened to accommodate the influx of casino workers. Land values shot up and the local school district and town government found themselves awash in tax revenue. However, the many residents who had bitterly opposed the riverboat casino remained convinced that the casino would ultimately produce more social problems than the new prosperity was worth—compulsive gambling, drug and alcohol abuse, and increased antisocial and criminal behavior.

Thus as the new millennium approached, one of the great, if often ignored, issues facing the Midwest was the future of its towns. This problem, of course, was not unique to the nation's heartland, but the sense of place that is the Midwest had for so long rested on the ubiquitous small towns that here the problem seemed the most urgent. That most towns will somehow endure along the margins of American society is ensured, but whether many will thrive is problematical. Even as the "wired" society of the internet and the communication industry inundated American society at the close of the twentieth century, making it possible for a wide range of workers to commute electronically to their place of work, the lure of the city remained as powerful as ever. Few workers opted to live in a small town and telecommute.

Overwhelmed by the regional cities that have long dominated the Midwest, town leaders largely abandoned any pretext of rejuvenation. They contented themselves with maintaining local customs—a small summer carnival, an autumn cider festival, a weekend softball tournament, a winter ice-fishing tournament—and went about their daily lives that increasingly revolved around the senior citizens center, lunch on Tuesdays at the Lions Club, Wednesday mornings at the ladies' aid society, Sunday morning worship at a church whose aging membership was slowly dwindling, and television programs beamed from a regional city to which most of the high school graduates in recent decades had long since departed.

When Sinclair Lewis unleashed his sharp attack on small-town America in 1920, *Main Street* became an overnight best seller that was widely hailed by readers for exposing the allegedly shallow existence lived by the residents of America's small towns. Many other writers joined this bandwagon, which rolled through public commentary by the "smart set" for the next few decades. Following World War II, however, this condescending attitude gave way to a realization that, as the historian Catherine McNicol Stock concludes, Main Street had fallen into a state of "crisis." As that crisis deepened in the decades after the war, Sinclair Lewis's jaundiced outlook lost much of its allure. There emerged a kinder, gentler school of small-town interpreters, led by Minnesota humorist and radio narrator Garrison Keillor. His fictional Lake Wobegon, Minnesota, became the most famous town in the Midwest. In his Saturday night radio broadcasts to a National Public Radio audience he provided wry updates on the goings-on in Lake Wobegon. There all the children are "above average," the Lutheran Brotherhood keeps a tight rein on local moral issues, and everyone eats that famous midwestern delicacy, Powdermilk Biscuits.

Keillor's gentle humor introduced a new nostalgia to the way Americans viewed the midwestern town. In the real world, where fully 80 percent of all Americans lived in one of 270 metropolitan areas, where multinational corporations were increasingly dominating the American economy, and where satellites, cable television, cellular telephones, and the internet were transforming the ways in which Americans obtain their information and interact with each other and the rest of the world, the once proud small town was reduced to the verge of irrelevance. That in the year 2003 the most widely known midwestern town existed only in the vivid imaginations of its creator and his radio audience speaks eloquently about the status of things along Main Street.

Alliance, Illinois

Selections

DAVE ETTER

I N A POEM WRITTEN EARLY in the twentieth century, Robert Frost articulated the problem which would, over the course of the century, become the central concern of rural American life: "what to make of a diminished thing." By the year 2000 most Midwest villages had been reduced—by decades of population loss and the economic forces discussed elsewhere in this collection—to shadows of their former selves, some to ghost towns. Nevertheless the idea of a small town continued to exercise a mystique disproportionate to the population of small towns, and writers continued to write about midwestern villages.

Dave Etter emerged as the preeminent poet of the Midwest village, heir in Illinois to the tradition of Masters and Lindsay and in the Midwest to the tradition of Anderson and Lewis. Early in his career Etter focused on the small towns of Iowa and western Illinois: Beardstown, Quincy, Hannibal, and Clinton. A clear-eyed realist who is not afraid to admit the realities of small-town unemployment, sex, and boredom ("I'm being buried half alive / among the tired smiles of used-car salesmen"), Etter nevertheless celebrates what remains, presenting the diminished village as a foundation on which to reconstruct "our lost American souls."

In his most important collection, *Alliance, Illinois*, Etter created a fictional village located in the fictional Sunflower County and populated it with 220 fictional characters, each speaking a poem in the tradition of the epitaphs in Masters's *Spoon River Anthology*. Etter's characters of course are not dead, he is less bitter than Masters, and he has a better ear for the rhythms of spoken midwestern speech. In addition his work reflects art forms and movements which we do not normally consider part of the Midwest village. From the surrealists Etter borrowed the technique of juxtaposing apparently unrelated visual images. From jazz music he took the technique of repeating with slight improvisational variations a single phrase or sequence of vowel or consonant sounds. Like the new formalists, Etter often arranges his sounds and images into recognizable stanzaic shapes determined by syllable count, line length, or a simple device such as "I said," "she said," "he said." In short, while Etter's content may describe a provincial small town that died sometime in the early 1970s, his style is far more cosmopolitan and twenty-first century.

○ ○ ○

Wedding Day

A blackbird sulks on the windowsill
where I have carved a dozen hearts.

I am in love with gin and sleep.

Between the long shadows of red barns
a strange girl calls me to a marriage
under honeysuckle strung with bees.

High in this cupola bedroom
I drift off in a bell of leaves.

Soon I will never be seen again.

The Hometown Hero Comes Home

This train, two Illinois counties late,
slips through jungles of corn and hot leaves
and the blazing helmets of huge barns.
My head spins with too much beer and sun
and the mixed feelings of going home.
The coach window has melted my face.
I itch where a birthmark darkens my skin.
The Jewish woman who sits next to me
sheds tears for a son, dead in Vietnam.
Her full lips are the color of crushed plums.
I want to go off with her to some lost
fishing village on the Mississippi
and be quiet among stones and small boats.
My fever breaks in the Galena hills.
It's too humid. No one will meet me.
And there are no brass bands in Dubuque.

I Mean You

I mean you
in New Boston
and Cairo.
I mean you
in Beardstown
and Quincy.
I mean you,
I mean the river,
I mean the towboats,
I mean willows
at Hannibal
and Clinton.
I mean you
and sunsets
in Muscatine
and Sabula.
I mean you,
I mean laughing,
I mean boozing,
I mean fighting
in Keokuk
and Port Byron.
I mean you
and I mean me.
Me and you,
kissing it up
in La Crosse
or Nauvoo.

Noon at the Courthouse

This brick courthouse is whisky faced.
Look at all the red old granddads.

What rube drew a judge on the john wall,
then blacked him in real good?

Across the street at the Hotel Tall Corn
the witness circles a glass of milk.

Loud barbers say Ben's case is lost now
and the Negro might just maybe hang.

A farmer stuffed in pig-shit boots
squeaks down the marble stairs.

The lawyer lights one more White Owl
and jabbers away about Clarence Darrow.

Out here on the lawn, dead county leaves
are crumpled parking tickets.

Propped up by the town's Honor Roll,
I fall asleep over an apple core.

Two Beers in Argyle, Wisconsin

Birds fly in the broken windows
of the hotel in Argyle.
Their wings are the cobwebs
of abandoned lead mines.

Across the street at Skelly's
the screen door bangs against the bricks
and the card games last all day.

Another beer truck comes to town,
chased by a dog on three legs.

Batman lies drunk in the weeds.

Old Dubuque

There is no past, present and future time
here in Dubuque, there is just Dubuque time.
RICHARD BISSELL

From Grant's grave Galena
we drove down in a daze,
from two days of antiques,
to the Mississippi,
then crossed over at noon
to old, hunchbacked Dubuque,
a never-say-die town,
a gray, musty pawnshop
still doing business, while
on the bluff, blue jeans flapped
in a river wind laced
with fresh paint and dead carp.

We couldn't find the house
where she once lived and died,
at ninety, baking bread,
somewhere in the hard maze
of crusty shops and streets,
and Dubuque is a spry,
goofy-sad river gal,
lost in a patchwork haze
of tears and years gone by,
and I love this mad place
like my dead grandmother
loved her steins of Star beer.

Dave Etter

Lester Rasmussen
Jane's Blue Jeans

Hanging alone on a blue-rain clothesline,
hanging alone in a blue rain,
hanging alone:

a pair of torn blue jeans,
a pair of faded blue jeans,
a pair of Jane's blue jeans.

Blue jeans in the shape of Jane,
Jane now in another pair of blue jeans,
blue jeans that also take the shape of Jane.

Oh, Jane, my rainy blues blue-jean girl,
blue jeans without you inside
is the saddest blue I've seen all day.

Failing

A failing bank in a failing town,
the president of the bank shot dead
for foreclosing on a failing farm,
the farmer, turned fugitive, not caught yet.

The slow hound sleeps away his last days
on the railroad ties of no trains.

A big old boy they call C.W.
says to me in the Harvest Moon Cafe,
"You done using that there ketchup?"

Folks sipping coffee in the back booth
talking on what used to be in town
but isn't any longer in town.

There's the bank president's daughter out there.
She strolls down the broken sidewalk,
cool and prim as a dining-car rose.
She married safe money in another town.

The jukebox snuffs out locals' local chatter.
The jukebox plays Eddy Arnold's
(ah, yes, yes) "Make the World Go Away."

C.W. puts plenty of Heinz ketchup
in his bowl of broccoli soup,
crumbles plenty of crackers on top.

"Don't tell me about no Reaganomics
and nothing about Reagan, neither."

The banker's casket is in the ground now.
Not too many friends came around.
The day is hot and dry, corn withers.
The weather has failed and failed again.

George Maxwell
County Seat

Pushing deep into Sunflower County now,
just minutes before sunup,
the big semitrailer truck droning on
in the breezy, dew-heavy darkness;
leaving behind the cornfields,
the red barns, the windbreak trees,
snorting by the city limits sign
announcing ALLIANCE, pop. 6,428,
thumping across the railroad tracks
of the Chicago and North Western,
slipping past roadside produce stands
and hamburger and milkshake drive-ins,
bouncing and rattling again
between the bruised bodies of billboards
saying where to shop, eat, sleep,
where to fill up with gas;
LICHENWALNER'S DEPARTMENT STORE,
CARL'S MAINLINE CAFE,
HOTEL TALL CORN,
BOB'S TEXACO;
dipping toward the polluted waters
of the sluggish Ausagaunaskee River
and the once stately section of town
where neglected Victorian houses,
with their cupolas and wide porches,
are set back on maple-shaded lawns;
remembering good and bad times,
lost faces, half-forgotten names;
and then the driver taking a last drag
from his Marlboro cigarette,
poking me in the ribs
with yellow, tobacco-stained fingers,
one letter of Jesus on each knuckle,
breaking the long silence between us
by saying over the asthmatic breathing
of the great diesel engine
that we are here, this is it,
here's that town you've been asking for;
moving slowly into the Square,
with its domed and clocked courthouse,

its bandstand and Civil War monument,
its two-story brick buildings,
lawyers and doctors above,
the town's merchants below;
stopping on Main Street
next to the Farmers National Bank,
stepping down to the curb,
thanking the driver for the lift,
grabbing a U.S. Army duffel bag,
slamming the cab door with a loud bang,
then turning around to face
ALLIANCE CHAMBER OF COMMERCE
WELCOMES YOU
TO THE HYBID CORN CAPITAL OF AMERICA,
and thus knowing for dead certain
that I'm back in the hometown,
and that nothing has, nothing could have
really changed since I went away.

Roger Powell

The Talk at Rukenbrod's

I sit in the shade on the high curb
in front of Rukenbrod's grocery store.
I sip a cold Nehi Grape and listen to the talk;

"You remember Andy Gump, don't you?"

"My blue jeans are too tight, she tells me.
I feel creepy walking past the Square
with all those dirty eyes scraping my skin."

"No, I never knew Nettles. He was an Elk."

"Sure, Paul was farming in Pickaway County, Ohio,
but he got going in this spiritualism stuff.
Goes all over now, West Coast and all."

"Butterflies, you know, taste with their feet."

"The wife took the kids down to Hannibal,
Mark Twain's hometown on the Mississippi.
I told her to bring me back a nice souvenir."

"Joe Palooka I remember. My brother Jake liked him."

"Nettles ran a forklift up at the cannery.
Then he was with A&W Root Beer, nights.
Heart attack it was. In Terre Haute, I heard."

"A purple martin eats 2,000 insects per day."

"So I think I got me a modest daughter, see.
But last week I catch her with another girl.
And they weren't playing no dominoes, neither."

"Fred's cousin was formerly with Dial-a-Prayer."

"Guess what they brought me from Hannibal?
A Becky Thatcher back scratcher! No lie.
I didn't know whether to laugh or throw a fit."

"Butterflies do what? Taste with their what?"

I take my empty into Rukenbrod's grocery store.
They have run out of Nehi Grape.
I grab a Dr. Pepper and sit down again.

"You sure you don't remember Andy Gump?"

Henry Lichenwalner
Living in the Middle

Here in Alliance, Illinois,
I'm living in the middle,
standing on the Courthouse lawn
in the middle of town,
in the middle of my life,
a self-confessed middlebrow,
a member of the middle class,
and of course Middle Western,
the middle, you see, the middle,
believing in the middle way,
standing here at midday
in the middle of the year,
breathing the farm-fragrant air
of Sunflower County,
in the true-blue middle
of middle America,
in the middle of my dreams.

Emmylou Oberkfell
Fifth Grade Poem on America

America
is
a big
Christmas
pie:
the Middle West
is berries,
the rest
is
just
crust.

Stubby Payne
Stocking Tops

In June the syringa bushes bloom,
and I swear that I can smell oranges there.
That was your smell, Bee. I knew it well.

And I think of you today in Arne's Pub,
where all winter long you sipped Gordon's gin,
legs crossed, showing a bulge of creamy thigh
above those tantalizing stocking tops.

Green summer again. Rain. The warm earth steams.

You left town on a Burlington day coach
to visit an aunt in Prairie du Chien.
"She's full of money," you said, "and dying of cancer."

Toward the end of July,
Sunflower County cornfields turn blond.
Stiff tassels shake in the sexual sun.
There's a dust of pollen in the air.

How many bags of potato chips?
How many trips to the can?
Oh, how many quarters in the jukebox, Bee?

August heat. The girls go almost naked here.

Like some overworked Cinderella,
you always took off just before midnight
on the arm of Prince or Joe or Hal or Smith,
bound for your place above the shoe store.

Yes, I should have bedded down with you myself,
said so what if you were a bumbling barfly,
every drinking man's little honey bush.

Lance Boomsma
Wedding Reception

"Hey, go kiss the bride," I said to my brother Ben.
"I already done that already," Ben said.
"Where is it you're to honeymoon at?" Mother said.
"Galena," my bride said. "Up to Galena."
"You ain't sore she was once your girl?" I said to Ben.
"That's the way life goes," Uncle Ted said.
"Galena?" my sister said. "Why Galena?"
"Cold there this time of year," Aunt Flo said.
"We'll be back in a week," my bride said.
"Better take plenty of sweaters," Mother said.
"We're going via Rockford and Freeport," I said.
"How about that? First class all the way," Ben said.

Hamilton Rivers
Noon at Carl's Mainline Cafe

Talk of septic tanks, sheep dip, soap powder.
Talk just to be talking, saying something:

"Claude says the water is more than four feet deep
in those corn bottoms south the highway bridge."

"I'm gonna sell my galvanized hay loader,
my metal detector, and my *Star Wars* bedspread."

"You say he's a duck decoy carver now
and you haven't seen him since last Arbor Day?"

"Joe Webb dropped dead after this evangelist fella
got him over excited and puking his guts."

"I sure guess it needs a new transmission, boy.
Why you can't even back that heap up anymore."

"He's a loud kid in Big Smith overalls.
Fergus is his name, and it fits him to a T."

"Kay don't care much for her Kenmore washing machine.
Says never again another product from Sears."

"We cleaned out all that junk in the attic.
All them boxes with your forgotten toys in them."

"Funny thing, the area code here is 312.
Yet right across my street it's 815."

"Me and Willie we used to get us free wienies
from Rukenbrod's store when we'd stop from school."

"I unwrapped it and it was waxed fruit.
Sister ain't had no sense since she gone to Tulsa."

"Leave me inform you them wienies were good.
Seems they was better tasting than cooked ones."

"If I want to talk with Mabel Anderson,
I'm required to dial for long distance."

"It wasn't junk, it wasn't junk at all.
That was my Lionel train in there, you idiot."

"Ma's got herself an old Maytag, you know.
Pa he bought a platform rocker the very same day."

"Young Fergus is a pretty fair country jock,
but he bumbles about without benefit of brains."

"You was talkin' on rusty cars what leak.
We drove up here with water sloshing in the trunk."

"Ain't it sumpthing to go to your grave like that.
And Joe he never had a girl in bed or nothin'."

"I dropped Cousin Daisy a card from Vero Beach.
It comes back stamped RETURNED TO SENDER."

"What I need is a double-oven electric range
and maybe some new oars for the rowboat."

"Well, that's our flood for this April.
That's about per usual for Sunflower County."

Damn, I wish I hadn't heard all that nonsense.
I don't even remember what the hell I ate.

Clark Springstead
Fender Sitting

You want to learn, you got to listen:

"There are gospel words burning in my blood."

"I've got me a big snowplow on my truck
and they call me when a blizzard hits."

"Now what do you make of a strong kid
who lies around all day on his bed
writing nothing but work songs?"

"Mom's driving out to South Dakota next week.
I told her to miss the Corn Palace in Mitchell."

"Like his father before him, by God,
Father was one of them hard-sell preachers
which spend all their growed-up years
poaching in the poor fields of piety."

"I have seen that Corn Palace one time.
My, it was a disappointment, let me tell you."

"Will won't get a job, won't look for work,
and drives us all batty in the head
with his humming and banjo strumming."

"Snow's coming middle December,
but this old soldier can deal with it."

"Myself, I'm cool as gentle Jesus."

An education is where you find it.

Kirby Quackenbush
September Moon

The old houses, dusted with moonshine,
creak in the dry and dragging wind
that pokes about this town:
where potato salad and cold beans
are eaten in stuffy kitchens;
where, in tubs of tepid water,
ponytailed girls who love fast horses
slide pink soap between their thighs;
where skinny boys lift weights
in bedrooms gaudy with football stars;
where doctors read comic books
and lawyers read numbers on checks;
where sex-starved wives wait in the nude
for tipsy husbands to be bored
with beer glass and cue stick;
where children sleep like stones
and hall clocks tick and tock
and cats yowl and dogs growl,
as another hot Labor Day winds down
in the webbed and wrinkled dark;
and I, moondust on my face,
return from a long walk to the depot,
the depot of many fierce goodbyes;
and it's just this I want to say:
Luanne, my lost and lonely girl,
if you want me on this summer night,
run through the grass now and kiss me.

Quietly Thinking Over Things at Christmas

FROM *Letters from the Country*

CAROL BLY

T HE MANY ROLES ASSUMED BY WRITERS—entertainer, historian, philosopher, visionary, social and political activist, psychoanalyst, commemorator—have been appropriated by rural authors from Mark Twain and Hamlin Garland to Garrison Keillor and Dave Etter. Usually writers cloak their ideas in prose or poetry, although many writers of novels (Sinclair Lewis leaps to mind) cannot resist long passages of sermon, and midwestern poetry has always had a populist slant that drifts easily into politics. Vachel Lindsay wrote poems titled "Why I Voted the Socialist Ticket" and lines like "Where is McKinley, Mark Hanna's McKinley, / His slave, his echo, his suit of clothes?" Many poets and fiction writers also write autobiography and memoir in which they express directly their views on art and life.

Toward the close of the twentieth century, so-called "literary nonfiction" became especially prominent in American literature (perhaps in response to the market made available by college composition courses with their emphasis on the personal essay). Literary nonfiction achieved the status of an officially recognized art category—acknowledged by philanthropic foundations that fund artists—and produced a long list of important works by rural writers from Wendell Berry to John McPhee to Linda Hasselstrom. The personal essay is especially suited to rural midwesterners, who appreciate its honest, first-person plainspokenness and emphasis on hard fact. Henry Thoreau's *Walden* is the wellspring of this kind of writing, especially as it emerged in diaries and journals, but it is not surprising that *New Yorker* humorist James Thurber grew up in Columbus, Ohio.

Carol Bly has written both short stories and philosophical essays, but she is most remembered for her *Letters from the Country*. First published as letters to *Minnesota Monthly* and later collected into a book, Bly's essays grow out of the ferment of the late sixties and seventies, with their social and political activism in matters of war, race, gender, and class. Accurately or inaccurately, the small town was considered during those years to be a bastion of conservatism ("the true war party of America was in all the small towns," Norman Mailer writes in *The Armies of the Night*), which is precisely the way Bly depicts Madison, Minnesota, "a lost Swede town" intent on plastering over social and political problems with religious pieties and a lot of "Minnesota nice." Citizens of Madison "live outside their own history," she complains and suggests a return to the small town's radical roots (progressivism, populism, the co-operative movement, the Nonpartisan League, the Farm Holiday Movement) and Scandinavian radical thinkers and writers like Ole E. Rölvaag and Johan Bojer, Knut Hamsun and Thorstein Veblen.

Yet Bly also suggests that vestiges of this radical, free-thinking, pragmatic tradition remain, and the small town's distance from national trends and distractions—what makes the town remote, backwoods—provides a climate in which the old seeds of independent thought and action can germinate. Even in VFW lounges she sees, sometimes, "a look of deliberate *intelligence*" which may possibly flower into generalizations and even action. One cannot help remembering Meridel Le Sueur's line, "It will be from here that the prophets come."

o o o

The winter solstice is the ancient season of joining spirit and animal. In the old dances, people dressed as animals, the Morris men holding deer's heads before their faces and carrying a hobbyhorse for the Abbots Bromley horn dance; and a wren was hunted and killed, to make way for the new king. Swedish children, in fact, still think of Staffan (St. Stephen) as the patron saint of horses; in their archaic, beautiful carol *"Staffan var en stålledrang!"* St. Stephen has two red ponies, two white ponies, and one dappled. He is set upon and murdered in the forest, and his body arrives home on horseback. We don't celebrate Christ's resurrection at Christmas because that is the *parting* of body and spirit; we celebrate his birth, the *joining* of body and spirit. It is a terrific season in Minnesota: children left free to grow inward are remarkably dreamy from late October through Twelfth Night to the dullness of late January.

Then how doubly cruel that our Midwest society operates to deprive huge segments of the populace of quiet thinking for themselves, especially at Christmastime. Thousands are brought up to be respectful of this or that sacred object—family life, church activity, Christmastime, motherhood, the office of the American presidency. Any sacred cow is a curse in that it must be taken as a whole—its core, its history, and its aura, all in one. It is taboo to separate sacred subjects into their parts and say, this two-thirds is okay, this one-third is rot. Whenever a *whole* subject is sacred, we cannot think about it quietly. And, if we are not allowed quiet thought, the lie somewhere in the subject begins to grow inside us, and we feel the lie and become frenetic in our efforts to suppress it, and then we become distrustful of other people because they might wake up the part that is lie. We become addicted to not "rocking the boat."

When we think about it, we notice that rocking the boat—the greatest anathema in small-town life—consists nearly entirely of dividing a subject into its components and treating the several components differently one from the other. For example, when people in Madison began speaking of Nixon's crookedness, several of our town leaders remarked that they wished "they'd just drop the whole Watergate thing" before the United States was "blown wide open." I thought that was very interesting, because it meant that Nixon could not be taken as one component of the nation; the society, the presidency, the national polity and psyche, all apparently were felt to be welded together and would either survive or be "blown wide open" together. Yet we know the reverse is true: when you take a rotten potato out of the barrel, in good time, you save the barrel, you don't "blow it wide open." In other words, there is a sanity in treating parts of anything separately.

It is considered rocking the boat to say that the Lutheran Church is a drag, although we all know it is a drag; yet it is very likely that if the hypocritical and heartless elements of church life were brought out into the open, like Watergate, truth and some new strength for reform might well race in and fill the spaces.

It is rocking the boat to find that a city council has floated a crooked bond issue on a building, for example; yet we all know that every time such corruption is exposed it has helped, not destroyed, the town. The businessmen who remained honest throughout are brought closer together.

Or to take a small instance: it is rocking the boat to read Eliot's "Journey of the Magi" at Christmas to a rural study club because Christmas is a "joyous family season" and Eliot is frank, full of solitude, and "very different." He reminds us of a part of Christmas that is like death, and that Christmas presages death. Here is a poem of Auden's which is quiet and thoughtful; it doesn't break new ground—its strength is in its taking up *part* of Christmas instead of trying, frenetically, to be enthusiastic about the whole:

> There are enough
> Left-overs to do, warmed-up, for the rest of the week—
> Not that we have much appetite, having drunk such a lot,
> Stayed up so late, attempted—quite unsuccessfully—
> To love all our relatives, and in general
> Grossly overestimated our powers. Once again
> As in previous years we have seen the actual Vision and failed
> To do more than entertain it as an agreeable
> Possibility, once again we have sent Him away
> Begging though to remain His disobedient servant,
> The promising child who cannot keep His word for long.

This is quiet, and absorbing, in comparison to the frantic uplift and clean bounce of *Christmas Ideals* magazine. It is cruel to condition people against reading such poems as Eliot's or Auden's.

Inexperience with quiet thought has another side effect in Minnesota: a residual, rather habitual chill between men and women. This is the way it seems to work. Nearly all of us women feel it our job to keep up civilization; we have an ancient conviction that if we don't keep it up the men will ease backward through evolution, with their socks and their hauteur, the way Poland Chinas turn back into wild boars with such frightening speed. So if we believe that Christmas's character as a "joyous season" and "a family time" is a civilizing notion, we feel constrained to uphold it. A part of us says Yes, but why are we frenetic and miserable at Christmas then? and why is the suicide rate so high at Christmas?

The answer must be in the components of Christmas—two-thirds may be joyous family material, but at least one-third must be introversion and contemplation and animal celebration: julebokking[1] isn't an accident! We "horse around" during the days of Christmas; it is the season of horses and mischief. But Midwest housewives aren't free to do mischief! Or to consider this sacred subject in its components. So they are stuck, still sitting cold in church circle meetings saying, "Christmas is a joyous family time," feeling the partial lie of it. Meanwhile, the husband also suffers from the lie. Because he is likely not to be so conditioned to passivity as his wife, he fights the lie. He goes down to the VFW lounge or somewhere, somewhere dark and damned and against the pious tone of the town, and the hell with it: he is going to do some serious drinking; that is, he is going to recover, somehow, feelings he has repressed.

I've seen a certain expression in men's faces in places like VFW lounges, but only recently have I understood this look: it is a look of deliberate *intelligence*. You have all the rest as well, of course—the boorish leaning over the carelessly mixed drinks, the beastly canned music, the spasmodic, loud, halting conversations, which some idiot at intervals contrives to liven up with a joke by which Norway, Poland, or Israel is the loser—there is all that, of course—but there is a very common expression of true cunning and a will to see straight: the men's eyes stare and look bald. I now understand that look to mean that they have come to recover suppressed knowledge which their wives or their town won't let them uncover elsewhere, not for a moment. They have come to say the damned things: all our leaders in Washington are a bunch of bad-language nouns, and big businessmen who have control of everything have bad-language verbed the country, and this being conned into buying presents is a lot of collective bad-language noun, and in family life—in raising kids—a human being is somehow partially bad-language past participled by raising a family at all. All this is an attempt to recognize the bad fraction of sacred wholes.

If the men could succeed in recognizing that, they would win for themselves the old joy of *quietly thinking about things*. What happens, however, is that the man returns home, excited by the shadow material that has been seen and said—he drives home really excited. The sodium-lighted main street and the crescent-shaped pile of plowed snow around a car that wasn't moved off before the plow came by and the gritted railroad tracks at the level crossing—all this feels like his own country and he is intact, in a glittering, frantic way. It is what is called having had a pretty good drunk. Then he arrives home and his wife, whether she spent the evening with him or waited at home, is snapped into her civilization-upholding stance. A drunk, idol-smashing man is a threat to civilization: he will uncover the one-third sacred subject she tries to suppress under family cheer; he will force her into *thought* instead of *reverence*. In a word, she is terrified. She snaps at him. And he is so vulnerable because his spirit is freed and has climbed outward nearly to his skin—in fact, it is nearly on his surface. He wants to go on considering truths here, truths there, he wants to give just desserts to this evildoer and that evildoer, and he wants to remark that such-and-such a wretched failure around town really has a good side to him, by God! He wants to consider things in their components. So, when his wife snaps at him in her pain, she attacks part of his spiritual life.

She has no idea what a stunning blow it is. All his quiet judgments leak back down through the great crack in him, before they ever had a chance to become genuine, quiet, thought-out and talked-about judgments; it has all poured down back through the crack as water drops with lightning speed into a fissure in the earth, vanishing, and then the crack itself closes, and he is locked out of his soul again for a while. A dull anger lies over the earth of him now, like a dust cloud above all these movings; as he and his wife glide around the living room, putting out lights near the nonflammable tree, the dull anger in him paws over toward her. Either everything is sacred (the point she stuck at) or everything is a big bunk (the point he had arrived at) and they don't evolve beyond that with each other.

If we are producing this scene over and over in our countryside we have a very mean side to our society. Perhaps we can work up a community of cures for that part of Minnesota life which isn't so lovely; I want to make two suggestions here. First, let us start teaching that women need not be positive about sacred occasions; they may be thinkers and pessimists. Second, let us start teaching that whenever something new or something old is to be discussed it should be discussed in its parts, severally. Not, then: How did you like the concert? but, Which part of the concert did you like least? which most? This will increase the accuracy of people's remarks. A trendy question that is going around in Minnesota now is the identity issue that hit the East Coast in the late 1950s: "Who am I? My God, I've got to have a

clear sense of who I am!" It is astonishing that people should expect to identify the whole *I*, to come up with one answer. Any answer given to such
a question is bound to contain a lie in it which will ferment anxiety, just as
we see the anxiety in individual men and women suffering from sacredcowism. Nearly any answer ought to be, I think: it is one-third this way,
one-third that way, and there is a third I don't understand yet.

There is a casual relaxation in not pronouncing on whole subjects. If the
women of the Midwest could learn to be casual instead of pious, they could
drop those defenses; they could entertain one-third pessimism on countless
subjects, which would make possible thoughtful conversation with each
other and men. They could release themselves and men from lip service to
family life and motherhood and the holiness of being together all the time:
they could stop *upholding* this value and that value and just comment together. Then the men, in turn, could use their own homes instead of the
VFW lounge to explore unconscious material. I think it would help tremendously, because when you go to the VFW-lounge sort of place you tend to
turn *all* to bunk—which is only the flip side of holding *all* sacred. The end
result of that syndrome is the Dean Martin show, in which every single decent thing there is, from animal life to the United States Senate, even the
private life of Senator Humphrey, is compulsively attacked with the intent
of reducing it to trash. That is self-hatred, not quiet thought.

Viewing things in their component parts makes reform possible, too. If
"the whole country's going to the dogs" you can't reform anything, but if
one-third of the country is going to the dogs, you can decide precisely *which*
third (or other fraction) and work to get it out. We can't fire the whole CIA;
we could work at eliminating all those who conspired to ruin Allende, for
example.

It is interesting that the Southern white woman is conditioned, much as
is the Midwestern woman, to be cheerful and extroverted, and to honor sacred cows while a young woman. But then there comes a significant difference: In middle age the Southerner is expected to change roles: she becomes
an accurate commenter on human nature, rich in earthy metaphor even,
the one who cuts through falseness—even a *femme horrible*. It must be a
terrific relief! And there is a playfulness to it, which no one can say the
Lutheran Church encourages here. Our women, and men often, are stuck
upholding sacred cows until their fifties and sixties. I have been working
with senior citizens recently, and I have noticed with interest and surprise
that at seventy and seventy-five Midwestern women who have been conventional do finally get free of positive thinking and upholding institutions,
and they can become the most marvelous sharers of this or that tough
truth—and they gain the singular playfulness that goes with not lying to
oneself any more.

When a frank and quiet person like that *does* praise something finally, it isn't the perfunctory flagwaving kind of thing at all; when a free person comments on Christ's being made man at Christmas, for example, the effect is not the frantic theology of habitual liars.

NOTE

1. Julebokking—Christmas joking, the Norwegian equivalent of horsing around with fools' masses, etc.

poems from the sangamon

Selections

LEWIS E. ATHERTON

JOHN KNOEPFLE is a resident of Auburn, Illinois, the town that is the subject of John Mack Faragher's study of nineteenth-century Sugar Creek. A poet who taught at nearby Sangamon State University, Knoepfle is also a folklorist and historian interested in Native Americans and workers on inland rivers like the Illinois and Mississippi. Writing seventy-five years after Vachel Lindsay, he has witnessed the development not only of Springfield and Auburn, but of other villages in the Sangamon River region. Some grew to the size of small cities, supported economically by nuclear power plants, hydroponic greenhouses, franchised restaurants, and junior colleges. Others grew not at all: "trailers and shacks / and make-do living anyway you can." Still others remained country crossroads, marked by a cottonwood tree on one side of the road and a lunchroom on the other, filled with Edward Eggleston characters telling Mark Twain tall tales.

Knoepfle's tone balances nicely between elegy and optimism. Like Lindsay, he is haunted by the ghosts of Abraham Lincoln and John Peter Algeld. Like Lindsay, he is religious and a populist: "one mans tax write-off / another mans depression." In a farm poem titled "man in overalls" he muses aloud, "some damn odin / eats us up don't you think / one by one by one / he holds us upside down / by our ankles and what / can we do with him / nothing I can tell you." However, Knoepfle can be optimistic about the future: a five-year-old princess candidate from Sangamon County quotes Adlai Stevenson III, and graffiti in Ohlman echo the church fathers. "Knoepfle brings together historical past and present successes and failures to cause Americans to rediscover who we are," writes Theodore Haddin.

Knoepfle is a modernist poet, an experimenter and innovator who uses neither capital letters nor punctuation. He is grounded in high culture and philosophy, including Paul Hindemith, Kenneth Burke, and St. Augustine. He is also a realist who relies heavily on intimate details of small-town life and on the vernacular of west-central Illinois characters. Knoepfle's style, allusions, and voices make his poems difficult at first, but on second and third reading—once the pauses and shifts of voice have been straightened out—the stylistic leveling contributes effectively to that unity of past and present, success and failure, which defines all of us as Americans.

o   o   o

clinton

upright cinquefoil there is
a patch of the virgin prairie

and a new kind of storage bin
rising out of the cornfields
but it isnt that at all

chalk message on the bridge
where the creek leads to the cemetery
everybody get high

big wind comes
youre hoping the barn will go down
but it blows down the shed
barn still standing there
like it always was

camelot restaurant and lounge
out of business
windows covered up with plywood
the cooperative feast or famine
experimental corn plot
seems to be thriving however

you can boil water in a fire
or you use a reactor
on a seamless pad of concrete

and these evening primroses
flowers of an hour wild indigo
coralberry pussytoe leaves

625 fuel bundles
columns of uranium dioxide
3500 blades in the steam turbine
950,000 kilowatt generator
pipefitters eden

let us stand with anybody
who stands right
you have to pay attention
to small things
the dead will not be fooled
whatever the time

decatur

baroque towers of millikins old main
dna stretch of eldorado that drag
franchised as they are these days
and pershing old black jack
parallel and as bedight
this town surprises you
town leading into doors
that may or may not be opened
like a work of mahler
with a heart wounded in it

streets of sweat and yearning
they make everything in this
steam crowned city all these
air bearing crankshaft casings
easy ice cream scoops cardboard containers
made by hands laced with razor cuts
pasteurized ice milk and pumps and
imitation bacon bits who can say
from imitation hogs and corn sweeteners
and gear case housings stove knob inlays
creeper wheel assemblies potato chips
so many things here this very thingness
smolders in the whorls of our fingers
carburetor valve seats concentrate
vinyl and fabric cleaner
neatsfoot compound one hundred percent
natural diaper sweet blue raindrops
spider dance centipede hiphooray kites
laboring in the corridors of the air

saint johns lutheran cemetery
northeast of town
it is a verdant place
tertocha schalbe semelka karasch
schudzara brix tanzyus artz
hungarians and lithuanians
meat cutters and produce packers
sleep here among many friends
and south along this green rectangle
a siding for robin egg blue tank cars
track old and waffled
it cant last long

this town has tomatoes born for the future
that hydroponic renewal
freight cars assembled by computer
and there are golf courses a swimming pool
lake activities prospects
a ymca a good downtown library
junior college etcetera

hard business and hardball times
would that work could sweep us into heaven
rising in a chemical yeast
these old saints they want to come home
walk through an open door
as a man might enter a woman
all in his hallowed bones as if she knew
or could know who he was

John Knoepfle

lunch room, new berlin

I told him he needed
his head trimmed a shadow
he said why he was
the hometown bald eagle
where he came from
I wouldnt have believed him
what with his chinwhiskers
drizzling into his soupbowl
why he said last graduation
the superintendent of schools in his town
tripped on his own beard and broke
both ankles and now
the old timers drinking coffee
round back of the pharmacy
drape their beards on his crutches
keep them out of the cigarette butts
and stuff on the floor that way
I thought I would be polite
just give him a vague nod
but he went right at it
said anyone needed a haircut
where he lived they had to
lift up the barbers eyebrows
see if he was awake or just
standing at the window like a rock
I didnt believe that either
but he just jellied up a bun
and went on expostulating
told me where he came from
nobody went to the cemetery
but it wasnt like oklahoma
where those wheat farmers
are so lean and dehyderated
they use them for fence posts
when they die that is
except for the ones the woodpeckers get
no sir he told me
everyone is heavy in the haunch
back there in monticello
great chested good sound smiling folks
with hair all over them like pelts

when someone dies in monticello
they put him out in the yard
you can always tell which ones is shrubs
because no family lets a starling
sit in a relative
I humored him of course
because we were having lunch together
but when he wanted to know
would I like one of his hushpuppies
I said I surely would not
if it wasnt a chihuahua
I got him with that one
parted him right up the middle
when I said that dont you think

bulldog crossing

you want to get to kincaid
you drive down this road
turn west just before taylorville
you pass the dump on your left then
reach kincaid at the river
or east of it I guess

well this place does have a strange name
used to be a lot of bulldogs here
a hundred or more bulldogs
that was before the stock market crashed

they liked to sit where we are now
watching the trucks go south
trucks was new then and the road
had good pavers I think

it was something to see those dogs
with pie-pan muzzles and cropped ears
homing like magnets
whenever a truck went by

but I tell you the truth
those dogs were just like people
some days they just got tired
sitting on this side the road
and then they would all stand up
and go over to the other side

used to be a big cottonwood there
and they liked to sit in its shadow
watching the trucks roll north
must have been halfway to decatur

so you understand how it was
them going back and forth and forth and back
bulldog crossing just naturally
came to be called this place

well no the dogs are all gone now
they were all overcome by ambition
everyone of them ran for election
and they all burst forth
with healthy pluralities
as edmund burke would put it

why they made three governors
and sixty-five congressmen those were
truly honorable dogs and there were
several got on the supreme court and some
were senators and foreign ambassadors

you could say there were the best
politicians for bulldogs there ever were
except for the one was a complainer
he never went any place
but he had a flea in his ear
about something

you want to know about him
he went into writing wrote this book
portrait of the young dog as an artist
won a big prize hey wait I want to tell you
they made it a movie
john wayne had a part in it

snowflakes and recorders

lindsays house on a cold
sunday afternoon
in springfield
table laid with his service
reception sweet punch and cookies
I am disappointed my ankles freezing
but the recorder trio seems
impervious to the cold
they warm to their renaissance concert
they play an unnamed song
by king henry the eighth
and it is beautiful

this house has so many histories
lindsay his birth and death here
lincoln his sister-in-laws house
his last night in springfield here
so much of hope in these rooms
poems and political memories

snow a few flakes outside the window
fireplace needs a damper or a screen
henry the eighth this afternoon
sovereign of a clutch of talent
a crude power that took down
it seems only the best of men
and now his song
lovely and a surprise

vachel we dont know
what to do with our lives
how fill them up
how not even to be self conscious
our successes squeezed from us

despite our failings and yet
there are some like figures
on a cave wall
and when we find them
they teach us and we change

bath

and when lincoln came here
that was august 16th 1858
he felt like his age was something
hanging on him he remembered
surveying the town 22 years earlier
in deep wilderness then and river timber
how he staked out the first plat
with his own hands he said

and these old men around him
they were as young as himself
27 years ago in 1831
messmates in the black hawk war

the crowd heard him with respect
tell all of them why slavery
was an evil thing

bath is trailers and shacks
and make-do livings anyway you can
full of particular folk
who like pink flamingos in driveways
and peonies on the lawns
cradled in used tractor tires
things good for looking at
they tell you if you want to know

lincoln had six years
beyond his stump speech at bath
six years for the history of the world

this year in late spring
the children will go down the river bank
midmorning on memorial day
as they have since the civil war
and set their little boats
drifting on the illinois
with cargoes of flowers

south fork sunday

the peoples bank of rosamund is closed
greek revival empty another god dead
two burnt-out trucks side by side in a quarry
one mans tax write-off
another mans depression
they are loaded with chat
but they wont be going anywhere

the town of ohlman
wakes up dawn come sunday
everybody goes to church
or sits in the side yards on lawn chairs
or a family paints the doghouse
worth talking about a month of sundays

graffiti on the tin outhouse wall
god rides a harley
government without justice is a ripoff
someone reading his augustine

this is where the south fork rises
deep in christian county
welling through bronze cornets
hindemiths brass
the long fanfare of trumpet vine

If the Home Team Doesn't Win

FROM *The Decline of Rural Minnesota*

JOSEPH A. AMATO AND JOHN W. MEYER

T HE MIDWESTERN TOWN took shape in the nineteenth century as an economic hub for the surrounding cluster of family farms located within traveling distance by horse and wagon. Inasmuch as the towns grew with the expanding farm economy, it should be no great surprise that their decline coincided with the steady disappearance of the traditional family farm across the Midwest in the latter half of the twentieth century. Starting in the 1950s the more capable farmer-businessmen in a region consolidated themselves as owners of not just 160 or 320 acres, but of several thousand acres as they bought out their neighbors and used powerful new tractors and massive implements to handle their larger acreage. To amass the requisite acreage and to purchase and maintain the necessary heavy equipment this new version of the family farmer had to have access to large sums of capital.

By the 1970s, however, it was readily apparent that the consolidation movement was giving way to corporate agriculture. Thus the number of families still living on American farmland continued to dwindle. By the arrival of the new millennium only 1 percent of the American people remained actively engaged in agriculture. Bolstered by enormous federal subsidy programs the large farms continued to prosper, but increasingly those checks found their way into the coffers of agricultural corporations. All across the Midwest, drastic changes in the way agriculture was practiced were taking place: enormous feedlots contained thousands of cattle being fattened for market, and huge low-slung buildings popped up on abandoned family farms, efficient "factories" where pork, turkey, and chicken were "manufactured" for market. And the towns that had been founded to serve farmers and their families had fewer and fewer persons left to serve; like the townspeople before them, they too had departed out of necessity for the new frontier of modern America—the cities.

Joseph A. Amato of the Center for Rural and Regional Studies at Southwest State University in Marshall, Minnesota, has devoted the last two decades to studying the people and the institutions they have created in the prairie land of the nineteen-county area he has identified as southwest Minnesota. What he and co-author John W. Meyer find in *The Decline of Rural*

Minnesota is depressing to even the most hardened observer of social and economic change: the steady decline of a region blessed with fertile soil, abundant water, and hard-working—if oft-contentious—citizens. What Amato and Meyer describe is but a microcosm for a phenomenon that is not only pervasive across the Midwest but truly national if not international in scope.

○ ○ ○

The devastating 1980s, marked by the farm crisis, followed by the nationally depressed economy of the early 1990s, has accelerated the depopulation and aging of Minnesota's most rural towns and counties, and the long-term decline of its rural cities as civic and commercial entities. Rural Minnesota's main industry, agriculture, supports fewer and fewer families on the land. Its smaller cities no longer supply the things and the services its people need and want. Its institutions and professionals strain to keep up with the commands, the goods, and the increasing specialization of the outside world. The most severe pessimists look to the west to predict what lies ahead. "As went South Dakota, so go we." They tell proud and progressive Minnesotans that they should learn to live with decline gracefully.

Whether or not one agrees, few will dispute that the region is witnessing the breakdown of the compact established with the founding of its communities. In concert with the great bravado of railroads, entrepreneurs, and land speculators, the founders of its cities promised a "middle ground" between the nation's expanding industrial cities and the new farmers of the prairie. They assumed that they would offer the best things and embody the best that American civilization had to offer.

From the start, the enormous and accelerating growth of goods and services of the metropolitan center made light of the promises even of larger rural cities to keep up. Economic events exposed small towns and merchants as helpless, ambivalent spectators during serious crises when protesting farmers squared off against distant metropolises.

The 1890s were one such period. Afflicted by drought, disastrously low farm prices, and high railroad rates, many farmers organized themselves in the Populist party and attacked monopolies and the control of distant powers.

The poor farm economy of the 1920s and the depressed national economy of the 1930s also put small cities' promises to represent and embody advancing American civilization in abeyance. No different than the farmers—whose ranks were filled with sharecroppers—small-town merchants hunkered down and tried to survive. Not surprisingly, city services decreased; even leisure activities themselves ended, as golf courses and race tracks were plowed up and city baseball teams were abandoned. (These same forces put an end to girls' teams and sports in schools.) The League of Minnesota Cities turned its attention away from progressive and amenity issues to concern itself with matters of relief and unemployment.

After approximately 120 years, the founding promise of rural cities has been withdrawn. By accident or design, all three original parties to it have reneged on the deal. Farmers—now only two percent of the U.S. population—are a vanishing breed. Small businesses and shopkeepers are hot on their trail. Ironically, the third party, the mighty metropolitan centers, appear to be having a hard time keeping up with the world they created. This supports the notion developed by Joseph Tainter in *The Collapse of Complex Societies* that complex civilizations decline because they invest too much at their peripheries.

In any case, rural Minnesotans are on the verge of a new admission. They, who took themselves to be full members of an advancing society, are increasingly driven to acknowledge that they are merely the residents of a declining outpost. More and more, their fate resembles that of a colonial people and their civic loyalty is put in question.

At the outset, a warning has to be issued against nostalgia. Abandon any notion that the past was a matter of static communities and fixed identities. Nostalgia overlooks the large role competition, rivalry, failure, resentment, rancor, and hate played in shaping the countryside in the past. With the coming of different ethnic, social, and religious groups to the countryside came mutual suspicion and misunderstanding. Open antagonism often formed a negative axis that marked the affairs of townships and cities with anti-immigrant feelings. These feelings became unusually intense during the First World War. Concerned for national security, local groups spoke out against not just German communities but other non-English speaking communities, such as the Dutch of the Edgerton area. In the 1920s anti-foreign and anti-Catholic sentiments gave birth to chapters of the KKK in rural Minnesota.

Misunderstanding, litigation, and hate (activities not foreign to the human spirit) found a home in the countryside, where almost anything, from the selling of a sick horse . . . to the failure to keep one's fields and ditches clear of weeds . . . to an argument over the grading of roads, could turn neighbor against neighbor. Potential conflicts resided almost everywhere in the countryside—from the laying to the abandoning of a railroad track, the draining of lowlands or lakes to the formation of a farmers' association or a workers' union, which were, and still are, ill-received almost everywhere in rural America.

Cities were part of the spirit of rivalry that filled the countryside. They strongly competed with one another. One city's gain was intuitively—and most often correctly—understood as another's loss. Leaders did not soon forget long struggles to make their town the hub city of the region. They remembered fights to get the county seat, to be the dominant school district, or to house new institutions. In southwest Minnesota there are still sharp recollections of the passionate and guile-filled battles cities fought in the late 1950s and early 1960s to become the site of a new college, Southwest State.

Underlying rivalries between cities—which mirrored and even incorporated earlier township and ethnic rivalries—were also played out more innocently with volunteer fire departments, bands, school teams, Saturday-night fist fights, and Sunday baseball games.

For example, city baseball teams did not hesitate to water down a baseline, freeze balls, or pay professional ringers to get their way on the diamond. There are common stories throughout rural Minnesota of great local teams. (Milroy, Fulda, Ivanhoe, Wanda, Ghent, and Cottonwood were a few of southwest's best.) There are countless stories of great local players who quit the minor leagues because they enjoyed local baseball more and were paid better, too, for playing at home. Old-time fans of what now seems "wild and unregulated baseball" crowded fields by the hundreds and even the thousands for the biggest games. Horns blared late into the night when the hometown team won.

Baseball battles continued energetically from under the lights of the first night leagues in the 1940s well into the late 1950s and 1960s. Smaller towns continually bent their greatest energies to beat the nearby regional center which had outdone them economically but had not conquered them on the magic diamond.

Like baseball, nearly every intercity activity concealed a rivalry, as if there was a mirror on the wall in which community patriots and boosters looked, asking, "who is the greatest town of all?"

Having issued these warnings against nostalgia's tendency to find whole communities and fixed identities in the past, it is, nevertheless, necessary to acknowledge that civic patriotism is in trouble in ways it has never been before.

City governments compete poorly for their citizens' attention, even though their affairs are about such seemingly important matters as civic pride, communal well being, and money. They have done no better than baseball at holding their citizens' interest against television and the plethora of pleasurable activities that have come to the rural world since the 1950s and 1960s.

There is an obvious yet paradoxical reason for the diminished importance of local government. It has grown ever smaller by measure of power, autonomy, and discretion in relation to the worlds beyond it. Yet, at the same time, it has grown too complex—especially in fiscal matters—to captivate and hold the changing interests of its citizenry.

City government is dwarfed by state and federal government. It is increasingly overshadowed by county government which, because of the smaller numbers of counties, has often become the preferred vehicle for state programs in such important regional matters as social services, land control, and pollution. In turn, city and county government are often treated as secondary to the school board, at least by parents whose most important religion is their children's present and future happiness.

Being increasingly powerless in contesting for their pleasure-minded citizens' attention against intrusive outside forces does not exempt city government from acting on such important matters as zoning, policing, downtown revitalization, programs for the elderly, energy codes, housing, industrial development, parks and recreation, tourism, etc. Nor does diminished stature let city government escape the growing complexities of state government or the enhanced aspirations of its citizens. Even the smallest community is driven to rely on outside expertise to try to fulfill its duties.

Matters of taxation, revision of municipal codes, insurance, employee rights and benefits, water and energy supply, and waste and pollution are just some of the complicated issues city governments confront. At accelerating rates, these issues, embedded in complicated laws and complex funding formulas and subject to technical and philosophical debate, exceed the interest and intelligence of all but the most acute and interested local citizens. Here, as everywhere else in society, the complexity of government threatens to demoralize citizens who find themselves required to accept and do what they neither want, nor understand, nor are able to pay for.

Already by the 1970s many of the smallest towns responded to the larger and more complicated world of government by hiring city managers. Recently these administrators have been forced to depend on more distant administrators to understand what is happening to them, what it means, and what they must do about it.

Like a fading star in ever-greater void, city government recedes from its citizens. Civic patriotism wanes as St. Paul and Washington write a text too complicated to be deciphered locally.

The growing fragmentation of the former governing class—the class of small business owners—also contributes to the eclipse of local government and civic patriotism. Even a regional center like Marshall, for example, does not have a single businessperson on its city council. There are similar reports of a vanishing business class in other major regional centers in Minnesota and South Dakota. There appears no evidence from Marshall, Worthington, or even St. Cloud to argue that the new, growing, and often mobile group of citizens composed of state employees, local teachers, and representatives of outside companies are presently in the process of composing themselves into a new class of leaders.

The business class and the epoch of civic patriotism have gone the way of the popularity of town baseball. As the business class surrendered the reins of power over local government during the past decades, citizens distanced themselves from city affairs. Although individual citizens or groups of citizens might kick up dust over specific issues, the overall course of city affairs no longer attracts great passion. Civic identity is no longer a primary identity. Increasingly, the majority of rural citizens, like their fellow Americans, take up the new, manifold, and multiplying identities that—as Stephen Bender argues in *Community and Social Change in America*—make modern society what it is.

Rural people, whose ancestors made great migrations to come to the Minnesota prairie, are again mobile in body and mind. Farmers retire to villages and towns; community dwellers drive to nearby cities to work, to shop, and to take their children to school; and, in turn, the richer citizens of lead cities travel to yet larger and more distant cities for the sake of business, health, new tastes, and fashions. Rural identities are associated with seasonal vacation and retirement patterns.

As baseball went from being a pickup game played by township teams in pastures to an organized sport played on the more carefully manicured diamonds of cities under the rules of a state league, so the people and everything they do have become a matter of greater distances, greater rules and laws, and more distant regional identities.

In conjunction with changing regional, state, and national society, rural people assemble themselves in new associations and communities, and configure their identities accordingly. They do what their ancestors did before they came to settle the prairie, they lend their minds and passion to more distant hopes and imagined worlds. In this manner they transform themselves into migrants and change rural Minnesota from a permanent home to a way station on their own and their family's passage across time.

Announcing the eclipse of civic political identity in rural Minnesota does not mean despair about all communities and identities. People find community in, and have an identity with, their hometowns for all sorts of reasons other than economic growth. There are many things that join a person to a place, including infinite and intangible personal reasons (like one's first kiss, or the crazy squint of a cagey old neighbor) as well as singular places, clubs, groups, and those countless informal associations such as a men's hunting group, a favorite Sunday restaurant, and the local coffee klatch whose gossip and pecking order more or less keep all in their places.

Decline, furthermore, does not stop inhabitants from feeling good about themselves. Newcomers to the region, who most often are from the middle class, commonly find reasons to be here and find satisfactory identity in their new jobs. Initially, they are most preoccupied with making themselves and their families at home, whereas the afterglow of the "good old days" lightens the minds of many long-time residents. Living by memory of former accomplishments, they still take pride in recent accomplishments like a new fire hall, a flower garden in the park, or a new multiple-purpose senior center.

Traditional institutions and associations maintain citizens' sense of community and identity in the countryside. Often unobserved in this regard is the importance of ethnic groups which, in any given area, might have successfully built a church, shaped a township, or formed the basis of a cooperative, a telephone exchange, or a chapter of a farm association. In many regions of rural Minnesota, ethnic groups like the Norwegians, Swedes, Germans, Dutch, Belgians, Poles, Czechs, Danes, and others succeeded in transforming a part of this land into communities far more secure, familiar, and economically vigorous than those they had left behind in Europe.

Church is singularly important in making rural Minnesota home for its inhabitants. It baptizes the young, buries the dead, blesses fields, raises high and impressive steeples, runs schools, and does much else that is vital for establishing a primary community.

Other important associations maintaining and extending community are the school, the volunteer fire department, cooperatives of all sorts, farm and civic associations, youth and senior clubs, political parties, and sports and leisure activities—ranging from car racing, baseball, and bowling teams to golf, archery, and karate clubs to chapters of Pheasants Forever.

Although particular civic identities weaken, new, though yet inchoate, regional identities emerge. In contrast to city dwellers, many farmers' senses of community and identity always went beyond a single village. As John Radziłowski illustrates in the case of the Poles and Danes of Lincoln County in his *Out on the Wind,* from the beginning immigrant settlers found themselves in considerable numbers going to one city for church and sociability, and another for market and business. Other factors also stimulated farmers to broaden their identities beyond a single city. The more reliable their automobiles became, the further farmers and farm families traveled from home. The more their brothers and sisters, retired parents, children and cousins, ethnic kinfolk, and neighbors took up residence in nearby townships, villages, counties, and regional centers, the more their sense of identity extended to the region as a whole. Farm organizing, organizing for electrification, and defining watershed districts were some of the many steps that extended farmers' allegiances.

No doubt with more emotional hesitation, inhabitants of the small towns followed the same paths of migration farmers did. As their stores closed and their schools and newspapers were merged, with ever greater frequency they piled into their cars to go to the nearby city for work, business, medical services, entertainment, or "just for the heck of it." New migrations meant new identities.

Throughout rural Minnesota, regional communities and identities associated with work, leisure, learning, aging, health, and care of the elderly are on the rise. Even though these identities have yet to surface in regional political associations and coalitions, there is an increasing movement toward regional identities. Regional centers themselves are filled with representatives of surrounding towns. Life within these centers is a constant source of regional reunions.

Despite decline, the fabric of community is remarkably close. Conversations are always connected and attached to place, and even when the worth of gossip is discounted, they are remarkably particular and wonderfully specific about shared things, places, and people. The sense of being embedded is a great good in this era of impersonal forces and great change. It weighs heavily in the balance of affection and loyalty, community and identity, even if it is light on the scales of career and opportunity.

Nevertheless, as if one can only ascend toward the truth by switchbacks, decline penetrates even the most traditional communities and identities. Traditional churches, such as the Catholic, Lutheran, Presbyterian, and Methodist, all feel the consequences of declining numbers. The New Ulm Diocese of the Catholic Church, for example, has closed ten churches in the last ten years as a consequence of changing demography. It also faces the problem of a severe shortage of priests. (According to official predictions for the New Ulm diocese, there will only be 46 priests in the year 2005.)

The Lutheran church too faces the problems of a declining and aging population of believers. It closes churches and loses income as the old die and the young donate and sacrifice less than their parents and grandparents did. The financial stress of the church leads many ministers, ironically, to refer to themselves as CEOs—chief economic officers. The weakening of the social fabric and the family force them into the role of social workers and psychologists.

The fundamental communities of work and family also feel the effects of decline. Mirroring the nation, well-paid jobs are in short supply. Family farming remains a viable way of life only for the few and, for many, only on the condition of a spouse's willingness to work off the farm. Small-town business is not much better.

Significantly, rural people now almost universally recognize that families—at least for the great majority—can't be maintained across generations. Parents acknowledge that their children must leave the region for more opportunities, while they themselves, in considerable numbers, recognize that they are but one blue slip away from having to go elsewhere to work and live. One city official in southwest Minnesota speculated that the essential difference between living in a city in the vicinity of the Twin Cities and living in a city in rural Minnesota is the degree to which people are likely, or unlikely, to find other employment if they lose their present jobs.

In short, asking a question that touches the matters of community and identity in the whole nation: How do you put down roots where there is no long-term promise of work or home? Increasingly, rural Minnesota is a place one is more likely to leave than to stay.

How should the people of rural Minnesota compose themselves to live with decline? They might wish to console themselves with stories, not stories of permanent homes but of continuing migrations. These stories do not deny attachment to places; nor do they turn away from people's responsibility for their own well being. However, stories do something that every person, family, and region should: they explain people's experiences.

Beyond this, they should not expect too much from their city or their civic patriotism. The politics of cities, as Bender noted, "is more likely to be public than communal, and there is nothing wrong with this." They must free public life, and the political process and culture associated with it, from the hope that it will provide them with a whole community and a single identity.

Furthermore, by failing to recognize that the people of rural Minnesota are but a small and flagging region of a great, expanding, and contradictory market, nation, and world, they simply expect too much from politics and run the risk of discouragement. They can respect the region's communities, accomplishments, and diversity; they can insist on making the best of their condition. They should not expect, if they value their sanity, to feel at home in a world whose great forces assure no one lasting community or enduring progress.

Sumus Quod Sumus

FROM *Lake Wobegon Days*

GARRISON KEILLOR

Although the twentieth century has taken a toll on the Midwest village, the 1980 census registered a slight exception to the century-long trend: for the first time in the twentieth century, areas designated as "rural" experienced a modest population growth. Possibly the out-migration from city to town resulted from anxiety over urban upheavals of the late 1960s; possibly it was baby-boomers looking for cheaper housing and a safe place to raise their children; possibly it was a move not to small towns but to suburbs that slipped into the "rural" classification. In any event, it produced a renewed interest in rural American life and a third flowering of rural literature. Many important Midwest writers came to prominence during this period, including Louise Erdrich, Dave Etter, Jim Harrison, Norbert Blei, Linda Hasselstrom, William Kloefkorn, Carol Bly, Robert Bly, Bill Holm, William Stafford, Kathleen Norris, John Knoepfle, Larry Woiwode, Paul Gruchow, and Jon Hassler.

Perhaps the most prominent was a writer who was also a radio celebrity: Garrison Keillor. Keillor's *A Prairie Home Companion* began in 1974 as an experiment in live radio broadcast weekly on Minnesota Public Radio. Before long the Saturday-night variety hour was syndicated by other National Public Radio stations, and by 1980, riding renewed national interest in the small town suggested by census demographics, Keillor was internationally famous.

The highlight of each *Prairie Home Companion* broadcast was, and still is, Keillor's monologue, which begins, "It's been a quiet week in Lake Wobegon, my hometown," and concludes, always, with "and that's the news from Lake Wobegon, where all the women are handsome, all the men are strong, and all the children are above average." Over many years of monologues, Keillor created the fictional town of Lake Wobegon, peopled by Norwegian Lutherans and German Catholics, farmers and middle-class townspeople. Inevitably the monologues became a book, and then a series of books: *Lake Wobegon Days, Leaving Home, Wobegon Boy,* and *Lake Wobegon Summer, 1956.*

Nostalgia is strong in Keillor's writing, but as anyone who takes the trouble to read his stories quickly discovers, Keillor's books are far less sentimental than his radio programs. He is a humorist and a local colorist, with a wonderful sense of local history and speech, which he can parody affectionately. He is also a wise analyst of human behavior and values, especially midwestern small-town behavior and values. He can be cosmopolitan without condescension, prefers to celebrate what remains rather than mourn what is lost, and suggests a return to the past primarily (if not only) as a means of reclaiming direction for the future.

o o o

Why isn't my town on the map?—Well, back before cartographers had the benefit of an aerial view, when teams of surveyors tramped from one town to the next, mistakes were made. Sometimes those towns were farther apart than they should have been. Many maps were drawn by French explorers in the bows of canoes bucking heavy rapids, including Sieur Marine de St. Croix, who was dizzy and nauseated when he penciled in the river that bears his name. He was miles off in some places, but since the river formed the Minnesota-Wisconsin border, revision was politically impossible and the mistakes were inked in, though it left thousands of people sitting high and dry on the other side.

A worse mistake was made by the Coleman Survey of 1866, which omitted fifty square miles of central Minnesota (including Lake Wobegon), an error that lives on in the F.A.A.'s Coleman Course Correction, a sudden lurch felt by airline passengers as they descend into Minnesota air space on flights from New York or Boston.

Why the state jobbed out the survey to drunks is a puzzle. The Coleman outfit, headed by Lieutenant Michael Coleman, had been attached to Grant's army, which they misdirected time and again so that Grant's flanks kept running head-on into Lee's rear until Union officers learned to make "right face" a 120-degree turn. Governor Marshall, however, regarded the 1866 survey as preliminary—"It will provide us a good general idea of the State, a foundation upon which we can build in the future," he said— though of course it turned out to be the final word.

The map was drawn by four teams of surveyors under the direction of Finian Coleman, Michael having left for the Nebraska gold rush, who placed them at the four corners of the state and aimed them inward. The southwest and northwest contingents moved fast over level ground, while the eastern teams got bogged down in the woods, so that, when they met a little west of Lake Wobegon, the four quadrants didn't fit within the boundaries legislated by Congress in 1851. Nevertheless, Finian mailed them to St. Paul, leaving the legislature to wrestle with the discrepancy.

The legislature simply reproportioned the state by eliminating the overlap in the middle, the little quadrangle that is Mist County. "The soil of that region is unsuited to agriculture, and we doubt that its absence would be much noticed," Speaker of the House Randolph remarked.

In 1933, a legislative interim commission proposed that the state recover the lost county by collapsing the square mileage of several large lakes. The area could be removed from the centers of the lakes, elongating them slightly so as not to lose valuable shoreline. Opposition was spearheaded by the Bureau of Fisheries, which pointed out the walleye breeding grounds to be lost; and the State Map Amendment was attached as a rider to a bill requiring the instruction of evolution in all secondary schools and was defeated by voice vote.

Proponents of map change, or "accurates" as they were called, were chastised by their opponents, the so-called "moderates," who denied the existence of Mist County on the one hand—"Where is it?" a moderate cried one day on the Senate floor in St. Paul. "Can you show me one scintilla of evidence that it exists?"—and, on the other hand, denounced the county as a threat to property owners everywhere. "If this county is allowed to rear its head, then no boundary is sacred, no deed is certain," the moderates said. "We might as well reopen negotiations with the Indians."

Wobegonians took the defeat of inclusion with their usual calm. "We felt that we were a part of Minnesota by virtue of the fact that when we drove more than a few miles in any direction, we were in Minnesota," Hjalmar Ingqvist says. "It didn't matter what anyone said."

In 1980, Governor Al Quie became the first governor to set foot in Mist County, slipping quietly away from his duties to attend a ceremony dedicating a plaque attached to the Statute of the Unknown Norwegian. "We don't know where he is. He was here, then he disappeared," his aides told reporters, all the time the Governor was enjoying a hearty meatball lunch in the company of fellow Lutherans. In his brief remarks, he saluted Lake Wobegon for its patience in anonymity. "Seldom has a town made such a sacrifice in remaining unrecognized so long," he said, though other speakers were quick to assure him that it had been no sacrifice, really, but a true pleasure.

"Here in 1867 the first Norwegian settlers knelt to thank God for bringing them to this place," the plaque read, "and though noting immediately the rockiness of the soil, remained, sowing seeds of Christian love."

What's special about this town, it's pretty much like a lot of towns, isn't it? There is a perfectly good answer to that question, it only takes a moment to think of it.

For one thing, the Statue of the Unknown Norwegian. If other towns have one, we don't know about it. Sculpted by a man named O'Connell or O'Connor in 1896, the granite youth stands in a small plot at a jog in the road where a surveyor knocked off for lunch years ago and looks down Main Street to the lake. A proud figure, his back is erect, his feet are on the ground on account of no money remained for a pedestal, and his eyes—well, his eyes are a matter of question. Probably the artist meant him to exude confidence in the New World, but his eyes are set a little deep so that dark shadows appear in the late afternoon and by sunset he looks worried. His confident smile turns into a forced grin. In the morning, he is stepping forward, his right hand extended in greeting, but as the day wears on, he hesitates, and finally he appears to be about to turn back. The right hand seems to say, Wait here. I think I forgot something.

Nevertheless, he is a landmark and an asset, so it was a shame when the tornado of 1947 did damage to him. That tornado skipped in from the northeast; it blew away one house except for a dresser mirror that wasn't so much as cracked—amazing; it's in the historical society now, and people still bring their relatives to look at it. It also picked up a brand-new Chevy pickup and set it down a quarter-mile away. *On a road. In the right-hand lane.* In town, it took the roof off the Lutheran church, where nobody was, and missed the Bijou, which was packed for *Shame,* starring Cliff DeCarlo. And it blew a stalk of quackgrass about six inches into the Unknown Norwegian, in an unusual place, a place where you wouldn't expect to find grass in a person, a part of the body where you've been told to insert nothing bigger than your finger in a washcloth.

Bud, our municipal employee, pulled it out, of course, but the root was imbedded in the granite, so it keeps growing out. Bud has considered using a pre-emergent herbicide on him but is afraid it will leave a stain on the side of his head, so, when he mows, simply reaches up to the Unknown's right ear and snips off the blade with his fingernails. It's not so noticeable, really; you have to look for it to see it.

The plaque that would've been on the pedestal the town couldn't afford was bolted to a brick and set in the ground until Bud dug it out because it was dinging up his mower blade. Now in the historical society museum in the basement of the town hall, it sits next to the Lake Wobegon runestone, which proves that Viking explorers were here in 1381. Unearthed by a Professor Oftedahl or Ostenwald around 1921 alongside County Road 2, where the professor, motoring from Chicago to Seattle, had stopped to bury garbage, the small black stone is covered with Viking runic characters which read (translated by him): "8 of [us] stopped & stayed awhile to visit & have [coffee] & a short nap. Sorry [you] weren't here. Well, that's about [it] for now."

Every Columbus Day, the runestone is carried up to the school and put on a card-table in the lunchroom for the children to see, so they can know their true heritage. It saddens Norwegians that America still honors this Italian, who arrived late in the New World and by accident, who wasn't even interested in New Worlds but only in spices. Out on a spin in search of curry powder and hot peppers—a man on a voyage to the grocery—he stumbled onto the land of heroic Vikings and proceeded to get the credit for it. And then to name it *America* after Amerigo Vespucci, an Italian who never saw the New World but only sat in Italy and drew incredibly inaccurate maps of it. By rights, it should be called Erica, after Eric the Red, who did the work five hundred years earlier. The United States of Erica. Erica the Beautiful. The Erican League.

Not many children come to see the runestone where it spends the rest of the year. The museum is a locked door in the town hall, down the hall and to the left by the washroom. Viola Tordahl the clerk has the key and isn't happy to be bothered for it. "I don't know why I ever agreed to do it. You know, they don't pay me a red cent for this," she says as she digs around in a junk drawer for it.

The museum is in the basement. The light switch is halfway down the steps, to your left. The steps are concrete, narrow and steep. It's going to be very interesting, you think, to look at these many objects from olden days, and then when you put your hand on the switch, you feel something crawl on it. Not a fly. You brush the spider off, and then you smell the must from below, like bilgewater, and hear a slight movement as if a man sitting quietly in the dark for several hours had just risen slowly and the chair scraped a quarter-inch. He sighs a faint sigh, licks his upper lip, and shifts the axe from his left to his right hand so he can scratch his nose. He is left-handed, evidently. No need to find out any more about him. You turn off the light and shut the door.

What's so special about this town is not the food, though Ralph's Pretty Good Grocery has got in a case of fresh cod. Frozen, but it's fresher than what's been in his freezer for months. In the grocery business, you have to throw out stuff sometimes, but Ralph is Norwegian and it goes against his principles. People bend down and peer into the meat case. "Give me a pork loin," they say. "One of those in the back, one of the pink ones." "These in front are better," he says. "They're more aged. You get better flavor." But they want a pink one, so Ralph takes out a pink one, bites his tongue. This is the problem with being in retail; you can't say what you think.

More and more people are sneaking off to the Higgledy-Piggledy in St. Cloud, where you find two acres of food, a meat counter a block long with huge walloping roasts and steaks big enough to choke a cow, and exotic fish lying on crushed ice. Once Ralph went to his brother Benny's for dinner and Martha put baked swordfish on the table. Ralph's face burned. His own sister-in-law! "It's delicious," said Mrs. Ralph. "Yeah," Ralph said, "if it wasn't for the mercury poisoning, I'd take swordfish every day of the week." Cod, he pointed out, is farther down in the food chain, and doesn't collect the mercury that the big fish do. Forks paused in midair. He would have gone on to describe the effects of mercury on the body, how it lodges in the brain, wiping the slate clean until you wind up in bed attached to tubes and can't remember your own Zip Code, but his wife contacted him on his ankle. Later, she said, "You had no business saying that."

"I'll have no business, period," he said, "if people don't wake up."

"Well, it's a free country, and she has a perfect right to go shop where she wants to."

"Sure she does, and she can go live there, too."

When the Thanatopsis Club hit its centennial in 1982 and Mrs. Hallberg wrote to the White House and asked for an essay from the President on small-town life, she got one, two paragraphs that extolled Lake Wobegon as a model of free enterprise and individualism, which was displayed in the library under glass, although the truth is that Lake Wobegon survives to the extent that it does on a form of voluntary socialism with elements of Deism, fatalism, and nepotism. Free enterprise runs on self-interest.[1] This is socialism, and it runs on loyalty. You need a toaster, you buy it at Co-op Hardware even though you can get a deluxe model with all the toaster attachments for less money at K-Mart in St. Cloud. You buy it at Co-op because you know Otto. Glasses you will find at Clifford's which also sells shoes and ties and some gloves. (It is trying to be the department store it used to be when it was The Mercantile, which it is still called by most people because the old sign is so clear on the brick facade, clearer than the "Clifford's" in the window.) Though you might rather shop for glasses in a strange place where they'll encourage your vanity, though Clifford's selection of frames is clearly based on Scripture ("Take no thought for what you shall wear. . . .") and you might put a hideous piece of junk on your face and Clifford would say, "I think you'll like those" as if you're a person who looks like you don't care what you look like—nevertheless you should think twice before you get the Calvin Klein glasses from Vanity Vision in the St. Cloud Mall. Calvin Klein isn't going to come with the Rescue Squad and he isn't going to teach your children about redemption by grace. You couldn't find Calvin Klein to save your life.

If people were to live by comparison shopping, the town would go bust. It cannot compete with other places item by item. Nothing in town is quite as good as it appears to be somewhere else. If you live there, you have to take it as a whole. That's loyalty.

This is why Judy Ingqvist does not sing "Holy City" on Sunday morning, although everyone says she sounds great on "Holy City"—it's not her wish to sound great, though she is the leading soprano; it's her wish that all the sopranos sound at least okay. So she sings quietly. One Sunday when the Ingqvists went to the Black Hills on vacation, a young, white-knuckled seminarian filled in; he gave a forty-five minute sermon and had a lot of sermon left over when finally three deacons cleared their throats simultaneously. They sounded like German shepherds barking, and their barks meant that the congregation now knew that he was bright and he had nothing more to prove to them. The young man looked on the sermon as free enterprise.[2] You work like hell on it and come up a winner. He wanted to give it all the best that was in him, of which he had more than he needed. He was opening a Higgledy-Piggledy of theology, and the barks were meant to remind him where he was: in Lake Wobegon, where smart doesn't count for so much. A minister has to be able to read a clock. At noon, it's time to go home and turn up the pot roast and get the peas out of the freezer. Everybody gets their pot roast at Ralph's. It's not the tenderest meat in the Ninth Federal Reserve District, but after you bake it for four hours until it falls apart in shreds, what's the difference?

So what's special about this town is not smarts either. It counted zero when you worked for Bud on the road crew, as I did one summer. He said, "Don't get smart with me," and he meant it. One week I was wrestling with great ideas in dimly lit college classrooms, the next I was home shoveling gravel in the sun, just another worker. I'd studied the workers in humanities class, spent a whole week on the labor movement as it related to ideals of American individualism, and I thought it was pretty funny to sing "Solidarity Forever" while patching potholes, but he didn't, he told me to quit smarting off. Work was serious business, and everybody was supposed to do it—*hard* work, unless of course you thought you were too good for it, in which case to hell with you. Bud's wife kept telling him to retire, he said, but he wasn't going to; all the geezers he'd known who decided to take it easy were flat on their backs a few months later with all their friends commenting on how natural they looked. Bud believed that when you feel bad, you get out of bed and put your boots on. "A little hard work never killed anybody," he told us, I suppose, about fifteen thousand times. Lean on your shovel for one second to straighten your back, and there was Bud to remind you. It would have been satisfying to choke him on the spot. We had the tar right there, just throw the old coot in and cook him and use him for fill. But he was so strong he might have taken the whole bunch of us. Once he said to me, "Here, take the other end of this." It was the hoist for the backhoe. I lifted my end, and right then I went from a 34- to a 36-inch sleeve. I thought my back was going to break. "Heavy?" he said. *Nooo.* "Want to set her down?" *Nooo. That's okay.* "Well, better set her down, cause this is where she goes." *Okay.* All my bones had been reset, making me a slightly curved person. "Next time try lifting with your legs," he said.

People who visit Lake Wobegon come to see somebody, otherwise they missed the turn on the highway and are lost. *Ausländers*, the Germans call them. They don't come for Toast 'n Jelly Days, or the Germans' quadrennial Gesuffa Days, or Krazy Daze, or the Feast Day of St. Francis, or the three-day Mist County Fair with its exciting Death Leap from the top of the grandstand to the arms of the haystack for only ten cents. What's special about here isn't special enough to draw a major crowd, though Flag Day—you could drive a long way on June 14 to find another like it.

Flag Day, as we know it, was the idea of Herman Hochstetter, Rollie's dad, who ran the dry goods store and ran Armistice Day, the Fourth of July, and Flag Day. For the Fourth, he organized a double-loop parade around the block which allowed people to take turns marching and watching. On Armistice Day, everyone stepped outside at 11 A.M. and stood in silence for two minutes as Our Lady's bell tolled eleven times.

Flag Day was his favorite. For a modest price, he would install a bracket on your house to hold a pole to hang your flag on, or he would drill a hole in the sidewalk in front of your store with his drill gun powered by a .22 shell. *Bam!* And in went the flag. On patriotic days, flags flew all over; there were flags on the tall poles, flags on the short, flags in the brackets on the pillars and the porches, and if you were flagless you could expect to hear from Herman. His hairy arm around your shoulder, his poochlike face close to yours, he would say how proud he was that so many people were proud of their country, leaving you to see the obvious, that you were a gap in the ranks.

In June 1944, the day after D-Day, a salesman from Fisher Hat called on Herman and offered a good deal on red and blue baseball caps. "Do you have white also?" Herman asked. The salesman thought that white caps could be had for the same wonderful price. Herman ordered two hundred red, two hundred white, and one hundred blue. By the end of the year, he still had four hundred and eighty-six caps. The inspiration of the Living Flag was born from the overstock.

On June 14, 1945, a month after V-E Day, a good crowd assembled in front of the Central Building in response to Herman's ad in the paper:

> Honor "AMERICA" June 14 AT 4 p.m. Be proud of "Our Land & People". Be part of the "LIVING FLAG". Don't let it be said that Lake Wobegon was "Too Busy". Be on time. 4 p.m. "Sharp".

His wife Louise handed out the caps, and Herman stood on a stepladder and told people where to stand. He lined up the reds and whites into stripes, then got the blues into their square. Mr. Hanson climbed up on the roof of the Central Building and took a photograph, they sang the national anthem, and then the Living Flag dispersed. The photograph appeared in the paper the next week. Herman kept the caps.

In the flush of victory, people were happy to do as told and stand in place, but in 1946 and 1947, dissension cropped up in the ranks: people complained about the heat and about Herman—what gave *him* the idea he could order *them* around? "People! Please! I need your attention! You blue people, keep your hats on! Please! Stripe No. 4, you're sagging! You reds, you're up here! We got too many white people, we need more red ones! Let's do this without talking, people! I can't get you straight if you keep moving around! Some of you are not paying attention! Everybody shut up! Please!"

One cause of resentment was the fact that none of them got to see the Flag they were in; the picture in the paper was black and white. Only Herman and Mr. Hanson got to see the real Flag, and some boys too short to be needed down below. People wanted a chance to go up to the roof and witness the spectacle for themselves.

"How can you go up there if you're supposed to be down here?" Herman said. "You go up there to look, you got nothing to look at. Isn't it enough to know that you're doing your part?"

On Flag Day, 1949, just as Herman said, "That's it! Hold it now!" one of the reds made a break for it—dashed up four flights of stairs to the roof and leaned over and had a long look. Even with the hole he left behind, it was a magnificent sight. The Living Flag filled the street below. A perfect Flag! The reds so brilliant! He couldn't take his eyes off it. "Get down here! We need a picture!" Herman yelled up to him. "How does it look?" people yelled up to him. "Unbelievable! I can't describe it!" he said.

So then everyone had to have a look. "No!" Herman said, but they took a vote and it was unanimous. One by one, members of the Living Flag went up to the roof and admired it. It *was* marvelous! It brought tears to the eyes, it made one reflect on this great country and on Lake Wobegon's place in it. One wanted to stand up there all afternoon and just drink it in. So, as the first hour passed, and only forty of the five hundred had been to the top, the others got more and more restless. "Hurry up! Quit dawdling! *You've* seen it! Get down here and give someone else a chance!" Herman sent people up in groups of four, and then ten, but after two hours, the Living Flag became the Sitting Flag and then began to erode, as the members who had had a look thought about heading home to supper, which infuriated the ones who hadn't. "Ten more minutes!" Herman cried, but ten minutes became twenty and thirty, and people snuck off and the Flag that remained for the last viewer was a Flag shot through by cannon fire.

In 1950, the Sons of Knute took over Flag Day. Herman gave them the boxes of caps. Since then, the Knutes have achieved several good Flags, though most years the attendance was poor. You need at least four hundred to make a good one. Some years the Knutes made a "no-look" rule, other years they held a lottery. One year they experimented with a large mirror held by two men over the edge of the roof, but when people leaned back and looked up, the Flag disappeared, of course.

NOTES

1. The smoke machine at the Sidetrack Tap, if you whack it about two inches below the Camels, will pay off a couple packs for free, and some enterprising patrons find it in their interest to use this knowledge. Past a certain age, you're not supposed to do this sort of thing anymore. You're supposed to grow up. Unfortunately, that is just the age when many people start to smoke.

2. He is no longer in the ministry. He is vice-president for sales at Devotional Systems, Inc., maker of quadraphonic sanctuary speakers for higher fidelity sermons, home devotional programs on floppy disks, and individual biofeedback systems in the pews. Two wires with electrodes hang from each hymnal rack, which the faithful press to their temples as they pray, attempting to bring the needle on the biometer into the reverence zone. For some reason, prayer doesn't accomplish that so well as, say, thinking about food, but DSI is working on it and thinks this may be a breakthrough in the worship of the future.

Hardball

FROM *Grass Fires*

DAN GERBER

TIME TAKES ITS TOLL on everything: not only the Midwest village, but cities, cars, houses, and human bodies. As this paragraph is being written the leaders of organized baseball are contemplating "contracting" two of its franchises out of existence. And even though major league clubs are located in large cities, Americans tend to associate baseball with small towns and the pastoral tradition, so that to baseball fans the threat of "contraction" seems somehow an attack on the American village. That association between baseball and the small town is reinforced in countless stories and films. A rural writer like Sherwood Anderson or Garrison Keillor or Dave Etter is almost obliged to write, sometime, a baseball story or poem.

Baseball's association with the small town makes a certain sense. In his essay "A Rose Is a Rose, But Baseball Is Something Else," John Nemo writes, "Baseball was a new, agrarian game for a new world people who wanted and loved space. Outdoors. Green fields. Vistas. Order imposed upon the prairie. Nineteenth-century American ideals traced over greenswards with lime—white line—diamonds accessible to all citizens regardless of wealth, class rank, education." Baseball not only embodies American ideals of egalitarianism; as Nemo further points out, baseball reflects that quintessentially American experience, the journey away into self-awareness, followed by a triumphant return home: its goal "is to bring one full circle, to return the batter, through his own and his fellows' efforts, 'home!' " Often the baseball story is indeed the tale of a player who comes out of the small town, survives a journey through the perilous city, and returns spiritually and usually physically to the small town, and the small-town values, from which he—or, in the case of *A League of Their Own*, she—came. The theme of departure and return lends itself to baseball stories, even if the return must be engineered through some form of magical realism as in *Field of Dreams*.

Oddly, baseball—a game played outside of time (no clock ticks down the seconds of play)—is a marvelous measure of the passage of time. How quickly a player ages from hot young prospect to forty-year-old has-been! How innocent young players are of time, their enemy! How quickly social developments engulf the game itself: integration, women's sports, the shift

in American power centers—New York to the Middle West to California to
Florida and the Southwest and back to New York.

In "Hardball," Dan Gerber interweaves the effects of time on the small
town of Brainard, Michigan, on the player who was its claim to fame, and
on the girl who loved him. The passage of time makes this a sad story, because often things don't go quite the way we'd like them to. Not in life, not
in town, and not in the game of baseball.

---

o o o

There's a new McDonald's there now, asphalt drive, manicured lawn, curb
and gutter, nothing like it was then. There was poverty here and there in
Brainard but nowhere as concentrated as it was at The Oaks. Living there,
a person was part of a lower order, a separate species who, on summer
evenings, escaped to the benches in the park. Oaks People, they were called,
and they breathed in the cool night air, forgetting for a while the yellow brick
walls and lightless windows, the tarpaper roof and sagging front porch, the
rusting appliances in the unkempt yard. We wondered about life at The
Oaks, but nobody who didn't have to went in to find out.

In all the time I knew Craig Mosely, I never set foot in the place. We were
poor, but my mother drew the line. "You go in there, you get labeled," she
said. She'd let me have Craig over once in a while. She could see he was
nice. But Craig never wanted me over to his place, so it never came up. He
must have had a mother; I don't remember her at all. I remember his father
though. A lot of people my age and older remember Claude Mosely. He was
a big man who looked like he was made out of spare parts. Sometimes his
shoes wouldn't match, and his hair was stiff and matted and stuck out from
his head like the crown of a kingfisher. I remember coming out of the
movies one winter night with my friend, Carol Slocum, seeing Claude
Mosely staggering in front of Bob's Bar. "Money's no good," he said. He tore
the change from his pockets and scattered it over the icy sidewalk. He pulled
his pockets inside out and lurched toward the west end of Main. "God damn
God!" he hollered again and again, his breath smoking in the bitter cold, his
voice still frightening in the distance. Carol and I scrambled over the sidewalk and picked coins out of the ice and salt. A crumpled dollar bill had
tumbled into the gutter. I smoothed it out and dried it against my skirt. We
couldn't believe our good fortune. I didn't connect any of this with Craig. It
wasn't till I told my mother the next day that she told me my friend Craig
was Claude Mosely's son. I kept the money for a week and then gave it to
Craig. It was almost two dollars, which was a lot to us then. Claude
Mosely's son. I couldn't believe it.

When Craig grew up, people forgot about Claude. For a long time Craig was somebody in Brainard, our only professional athlete. "He used to be with the Tigers," anyone would say when they pointed him out to visitors. He had that fastball, and they brought him up from the Evansville farm club when Joe Sparma got hurt. He pitched five games for Detroit and won three of them. I remember Ernie Harwell's voice on the radio, "Craig Mosely, out of Brainard, Michigan, a hard thrower just up from Evansville. He's turned things around here for the Bengals." Then he threw out his arm against the Red Sox, and they sent him back to Indiana for reconditioning. He spent seven years trying to get it back, to get back to the majors. Then they dropped him down to double A ball in Birmingham, and he gave it up. But he'd pitched in Tiger Stadium, and that was what everyone remembered.

When he came back to Brainard, The Oaks was gone, condemned and torn down. It was just a grassy lot on the corner of Gilbert and Main, and people had mostly forgotten. Craig was a local treasure. Everyone called him by name like they were all old friends, and more often than not, the first year or so, the meals and the drinks were free. They were anxious to have him seen at Fred's Fine Foods or Antonelli's. Almost every place in town had an autographed picture on the wall, the same one of Craig in his Tiger whites. But it wore off in time. At his funeral, when the minister said, "We don't judge a life by a single act," he meant Craig's suicide of course, but I thought of that first game in Tiger Stadium when he came out of nowhere to pitch a one-hitter against the Yankees, and Ernie Harwell was hoarse with excitement. "Craig Moseley. There's a name for the books. Eleven strike-outs his first game in the majors." He had his picture in *Sports Illustrated,* and for a couple of weeks there, Craig was a star. He had groupies wherever they went. "They used to lick my arms," he told me.

The coffin was closed, and I thought of his arms. I'd had a crush on Craig when we were kids. I guess I always did. But I could play ball, and that's how he thought of me. I guess none of the guys really thought of me as a girl, once we got past playing doctor. I'm a big woman, and I was big then, and I could catch Craig's fastballs. Until we got to junior high, I was the only one brave enough. God they'd come in there. Wham! You could hear the air behind them, hissing like a rocket, right at your face. Then, Wham! You were on your toes, thrusting forward with the pitch so as not to get knocked on your butt. And Wham! You just crouched down and held out the mitt like a target. That's all you could do. You just knew they'd come in there. It was like making love. I trusted Craig. I knew he wouldn't hurt me. I was the only girl they'd let play and the only one who wanted to. A lot of girls wanted Craig though. He was good-looking and quiet like Montgomery Clift, and when you saw him pitch, you felt all that power pent up inside. "Chuck it in here Craig baby, right here baby. Burn it to me," I'd say. Stuff like that. I was his glove. I called the pitches between my legs.

Baseball was everything for Craig, and when he pitched that first no-hitter his sophomore year, it didn't matter about The Oaks. We won the State two years running, and the Chamber of Commerce put up a sign:

WELCOME TO BRAINARD
Pop. 4,262
State Class B Baseball Champs
1960
1961

Kenny Blondene was catching for him then, and he was good too, but I was there for every pitch. I felt every one that came through, and I hurt with those few that got hit. He pitched three no-hitters his junior year, and the scouts were showing up.

I looked around the church, and I wanted to puke. All those hypocrites showing up now he was dead. A week ago they wouldn't have given him the dust off their shoes. Five years after he came back to Brainard, he was no-body. They'd made a hero out of him, and he couldn't live up to it. Nobody could. They took his picture down when they remodeled at Fred's and it never went back up. Craig had started drinking, and when they said, "He used to pitch for the Tigers," it was like they were saying, "Can you believe it?" He tried insurance. He tried used cars. He got along on his name for a while, but it wasn't baseball. He ended up working production at Clark's, and the people couldn't stand it. They wouldn't leave him alone, and he got in fights. They talked about his dad again. Finally I stood up in the middle of the eulogy. "You assholes," I shouted. "You didn't know Craig Mosely. You didn't even like him." I was shaking, and nobody looked around. They just hunched in their pews, trying to pull their heads in like turtles. They wanted to pretend it wasn't happening, that I wasn't there to show them what they were. But I didn't really stand up and shout. I just thought about it, and I felt prickly all over.

I never did marry. I never got asked. I play softball, slowpitch, for Gilbert Chevrolet. We win it all, and I bowl. I sweep the halls at the high school, a custodial engineer, they call me. I never cared about any man but Craig, and he never thought of me as a woman, but that one time. It was two years ago, a warm night in April, he came to my trailer. We were buddies. He respected me as an athlete. He'd been drinking, really drinking. His face was all cut up, and he wasn't so cute anymore. There'd been trouble at Antonelli's. From what I could make out, Joe Antonelli and his two sons had pitched him out on the street. It had happened before. There were all different kinds of stories. His eye was cut and his lip, and one of his lower teeth was gone. "The Lasagna brothers jumped me," is what he said. His words were slurred, and his eyes never quite looked at any one thing. I got a wet rag, and I cleaned him up. "I feel sorry for old man Antonelli," he blubbered out. "He's gonna have to get hurt."

I put some iodine on his cut, and he started to cry. I got him out of his clothes. I put him to bed, and I crawled in with him and held him in my arms. I knew Craig Mosely, before the scouts came, before Evansville. He went on crying, and I held him to my breast. His body jerked with the sobs. "It's all gone. It's all gone," he cried again and again. I put my hand in his hair and held him to me, and I felt him drift off to sleep. I felt those muscles in his shoulders. I could feel that power still, and I held him all night long.

In the morning I felt him stir. I woke up, and he was making love to me. He was kissing my neck and my breasts, and I let him. He climbed on top of me, and I let him. I was forty years old, and I'd never been with a man, I mean really, since maybe I was thirteen. I thought about catching him again. For a few minutes he was pitching to me again. I thought about those groupies licking his arms.

And then it was over, just like that. It was like he was just waking up. He rolled out of bed and went into the bathroom. I made him some coffee, and he got dressed and left. He thanked me, and it was just like we were buddies again. I didn't know what to think. But for a while there, there was something. I don't know. I felt young again, and Craig was young, with his good fastball and all that promise.

Two-Speed

FROM *Light in the Crossing*

KENT MEYERS

THE SMALL TOWN has always enjoyed a reputation for creating, harboring, and in some cases canonizing eccentrics, cranks, and characters. A long tradition in midwestern small-town literature extends from Edward Eggleston through Sherwood Anderson (whose *Winesburg, Ohio* opens with an essay called "The Book of the Grotesque") and William Gass and Dave Etter to the writers of novels published last year and the year before.

Eccentrics make for interesting reading, but they also represent an implicit test of an article of American faith best articulated by Wallace Stegner: "that a new society striking boldly off from the old would first give up everything but axe and gun and then, as pioneering hardships were survived, would begin to shape itself in new forms. Prosperity would follow in due course. A native character would begin to emerge, a character more self-reliant and more naturally noble than any that could be formed in tired and corrupt Europe. . . ." America is a test of Rousseau's notion that civilization corrupts and nature restores, that the ills of our society are mostly social malfunctions that can be best remedied by returning human beings to their natural state of innocence. Being closer to natural innocence, the small town populace should be "more self-reliant and more naturally noble." If the small-town populace proves to be amoral, immoral, or just plain "grotesque," then a certain article of American faith has failed.

Writers like Sherwood Anderson and Sinclair Lewis suggested causal relationships between a life spent in constricting small towns and abnormal behavior. Other writers resist causal connections but seem sensationally to heighten the psychological and moral aberrations. Others, in the tradition of American realism, simply report. Kent Meyers is one such writer. His character Two-Speed Crandall is a drunk who abuses animals and children. Elsewhere in the novel we learn he has other unpleasant characteristics as well. He has a talent for driving a truck and a vaguely admirable ethic of not driving drunk. He is the stuff of which small-town legends are made, and many legends about him circulate through the small town of Cloten, Minnesota. Meyers's story of Two-Speed Crandall's funeral is told "with some fondness," if not for the man, then for the story and the community which carries always in its consciousness this and similar tales, the core of local history.

o   o   o

I went to Two-Speed Crandall's funeral not because I had any affection for the man, but because it's the kind of thing you do around here; you show if not in life, then at least in death, that the people whom you have talked about and nodded to, who have occupied a spot of ground close to your own for the years of your breathing and eating—you show that they were, after all, part of your community. Two-Speed Crandall, as far as I can see, gave nothing to this town worth having—and I've thought hard about this, and I'm trying to be fair, and I have no grudge against the man. I didn't go to his funeral to mourn him; I don't intend to miss him. But I didn't go to celebrate his dying either, and that, it seems to me, is as impartial as I need to be to fairly make a claim to it.

Two-Speed's family consisted of his wife, LouAnn, a woman hardly ever seen, and their three sons, Matthew, Mark, and Luke—names, I've thought since I was old enough to think such things, poignant enough to be painful, speaking certainly of LouAnn's, not Two-Speed's, dreams for their children, and as un-prophetic as names could be, since the boys had neither religious nor literary leanings—in fact, quite the opposite, Matt and Mark celebrating their sixteenth birthdays by staying away from school and never returning, and Luke, though finishing school, returning to Cloten to spend his nights catfishing on the river.

The boys boasted of their badness whenever they could, but in truth, they were nothing but small-town bad boys, their badness constrained by the same smallness they pretended to escape from with it, limited as much by their possibilities as by their imaginations: stealing candy from the grocery store when they were younger, throwing green apples at the sheriff's car as he did his daily patrol, setting fire to an abandoned barn in the country, which blazed like a torch on the horizon—everybody in Cloten, awakened by the fire sirens, standing on their lawns watching it, while the fire trucks sped out of town, and the knowledge of who had set the fire, though never proven, passed from lawn to lawn through the whole town before the sound of the sirens, coming back across the flat fields, had faded into the night.

These activities of Two-Speed's sons—as well as the way they flunked their classes not out of stupidity but through sheer stubbornness—were frowned upon but tolerated. But when Matthew, the oldest, came to school with a cattle prod and shocked several of the school outcasts with it—the clumsy and stringy-haired ones who were the butt of jokes by nearly everyone, forcing from their throats and chests sounds like pieces of raw meat being slapped together—the students rose in a wave of outrage that overwhelmed and subdued even the Crandall brothers, the students having seen, most of them, what a cattle prod could do, how its blue, sizzling arc jolted the slowest and dullest steer, thick in its flesh, into a snorting, slobbering, and panic-stricken lunge up the chute and onto the truck.

The stories went around for a long time afterward of how three of the football players—some said upon the advice of their coach—confronted Matthew behind the band saw in the shop and took the cattle prod from him, which he had stuffed down inside his boot and up along his leg, and they smashed and bent it and finally sawed it in half, and all the while, the stories a dozen times removed by the time they came to me, said that Matthew looked like he would weep, that he turned white and as still as cast aluminum, and stared in silence, only his lip trembling a little, as the saw whined through the prod.

For a long time the school laughed at this comeuppance, the tough and nasty one having his toy taken away. But when I asked my father about this—I was twelve at the time and thought he would rejoice in the story, and I told it to him after school with the mild euphoria of knowing I would please him—he only stopped working and looked out across the tangled cornstalks left by the combine.

"Don't you think it served him right?" I urged.

Still he said nothing. I felt my smile of expectation solidify on my face. Then I became defensive. "Everybody's laughing about it," I said, squinting.

He reached out and put one hand on the lugs of the tractor tire, then leaned his whole body into his shoulder. He looked down at the ground, then up again. His expression was so distant and turned inward that I thought he might not have heard me.

"Yeah, well," he finally said. "It was probably Two-Speed's prod."

"So?" I said.

He leaned his back against the tire, took off his gloves, beat them down once against his thigh. The leather smacked, and dust discolored the air. My father had pale eyes, and when he raised them to the horizon again, they were even paler than I knew them, and he kept them fastened out there when he spoke, to where the fall sky was almost white.

"There are lot of unpleasant people in this world," he said. "Two-Speed's one of them."

Two-Speed drove semi for Niebuhr's Trucking and often hauled cattle for us. "He spits," I said. "He swears a lot."

"He beats his kids," my father said. He looked down at me and caught my eyes. It was like something from the way-off sky had come into his. He hit his gloves against his pants leg again. "Do you think Matthew figured out how to use a cattle prod that way all by himself?"

Leaning as he was, my father was barely taller than I was, and we looked right at each other, and this was the first time he'd ever talked to me this

way, about something so serious, as one adult to another. I hardly compre-
hended it. "You mean?"

I couldn't take my eyes off his face. I searched there for some clue as to
how I ought to feel.

My father nodded, his mouth tight. "That's what I mean."

Since then I've come to know that Dad's opinion had support in rumors
both direct and indirect, and in the famous nastiness of Two-Speed's
threats, when leaving the bar late, to have it out upon his worthless sons. If
all this is true, Matt certainly had reason to tremble, his blood reason to flee
his face, upon the realization that his stealing of the cattle prod would in
due course be discovered by Two-Speed and an appropriate and punishing
justice exacted with some other implement equal to the task.

Of course it was all rumor and talk. Even if it had been proven, probably
nothing would have been done. Family matters, in those days in a town like
Cloten, had an aura of the sacred. Nevertheless, I mark that conversation
with my father as my introduction to adulthood and the dark secrets that
reside there. So now Two-Speed's death turns me back to think of him
again, and to feel an old attraction made safe, perhaps, by his passing.

He was a man who lived on the bare edge of our community, yet more
stories were told of him than of anyone else in town. Two-Speed was tolerated when he was working but otherwise avoided during the day, but at
night he entered the uneasy camaraderie of the bar, earned, even, a kind of
grudging respect there for his willingness to fly into a fighting rage over anything and with anybody, and for his unfeigned refusal to glance at a clock,
ever, or to find familial reasons to leave.

As a worker, he had the one great advantage that he was always available,
without contravening obligations, though he was not always willing or
sober, and he possessed—his greatest source of pride—a Class A driver's license. This license, the stories say, he always produced at some point along
the downward slope to drunkenness, so that people made bets on the number of drinks it would take for the license to appear, gambling that turned
out to be truly random, since the license's appearance seemed—even to
those who studied Two-Speed with the care that other men devote to a
horse-racing program—to be dependent not on the alcohol in his system,
but on the waverings of his heart and mind, waverings too complicated and
chaotic for pattern or prediction.

Two-Speed would slap the license down on the scarred surface of the bar
table and force his companions of the evening to stoop over it while one of
his fingers, wrenched outward, pointed to the "A." Then, flipping the card
over, he would read aloud the words on the back: "Classes: A: Tractor-trailer
combination." After which he would challenge anyone within hearing to
produce such a license, and when they all shrugged or ignored him, familiar with the routine, he would launch into a description of the testing, de-

tailing its difficulties, and end by claiming that he had never failed to pass it, not even the first time.

Which, I have no doubts, was true. If there was one thing in which Two-Speed's integrity was absolutely sound, it was in his knowledge and handling of a truck—so much so that he often turned down jobs, claiming with complete forthrightness that he wasn't sober enough. Two-Speed had no time for drunk drivers. He walked the mile from his house at the edge of town to the bar to ensure that when drunk, as he most surely would be later, he wouldn't be tempted to drive home. And he insulted those who staggered up from the table pulling their keys from their pockets, calling them damn fools and menaces to society, calling them bastards and killers and suicides, and went so far as to stand wobbling behind their vehicles, cursing them, daring them to back over him, the red glow from their brake lights enveloping Two-Speed's thin and crooked limbs and turning the smoke and steam from their exhausts, in the winter, into a cloud that seemed to burn internally, passing up over Two-Speed's form so that his curses, cracked and hoarse, emanated from the cloud.

His stubbornness was so great that he would, indeed, have let himself be run over, as evidenced once when Hank Tyrrell challenged him by slowly backing up until his bumper touched Two-Speed's knees. Two-Speed remained rooted, swaying as if in a strong, inconstant wind, without moving his feet. Hank backed further, and Two-Speed's knees crumpled. He fell to the pavement, into the red, glowing cloud, and remained there, damning Hank with all the obscenities at his muster. Still Hank backed up, in spite of the protestations of onlookers who, hearing the commotion, had left their drinks in the smoky bar to gather outside the door in the freezing air. Some of them waved their arms at Hank, trying to get his attention, but whether through the blinding obscurity of his stubbornness or of the frost on his windshield, he paid them no heed.

Two-Speed disappeared under the pickup until, depending on who you hear the story from, a scrap of his clothing caught on a rusted piece of metal or he grabbed onto the bumper and began to be dragged backward, his head hanging limply, scraping along. Never, though, did he shout for Hank to stop, but continued to scream like a crow that has learned to curse, his voice rising up from the exhaust, calling Hank to judgment for the menace he was to the roads, to the drivers who took their responsibilities seriously and knew driving as an honor and a privilege.

Hank backed the pickup clear into the street, reassured, though he couldn't see Two-Speed, by the health and vigor of his voice. He then put the vehicle into drive and began to leave the scene, puffed with pride, thinking Two-Speed had survived the backing-up and was out of danger and that he, Hank, had just become the first man in town to outdo Two-Speed's orneriness.

He made it a half block down the street to the stop sign at the highway before he became puzzled by two facts: first, that Two-Speed's voice was following him; second, that the herd of men milling outside the bar door was suddenly stampeding down the sidewalk parallel to his pickup, bellowing and pointing, most of them still in their shirt-sleeves, having never anticipated spending more than a few seconds in the frigid night. Hank could see them even through the layer of frost on his side window and decided not to pull onto the highway for home until he knew what had spooked them.

When he got out of his pickup to investigate, he found Two-Speed under the bumper, lying in blood that was beginning to pool from the great gash scraped in his scalp. Down the street, a steaming trail of the same blood marked Two-Speed's progress from the bar. Two-Speed did nothing to extricate himself from under the pickup, nor did he demand help or apology. Instead, looking up into Hank Tyrrell's horrified face bending over him, he accused Hank of begin so drunk he would drag a man under his pickup, down the highway and into the night—"Proof!" he screamed, "that you're too damn drunk to drive and you got no right to be on the road in the condition you're in. There might be a woman on the way to the hospital to give birth to a baby, and you'd come charging down and kill them both. The last thing she'd see'd be your headlights in the wrong lane. How'd you like that, Hank? Would you like all that blood on the road?"

It was too much for Hank. He allowed his illusions of victory over Two-Speed to evaporate and, a defeated man, for the first time ever called his wife, admitted that he was too drunk to drive and had her come into town and retrieve him, sliding into the passenger seat beside her and refusing to acknowledge the friends who, delighted at his ignominy, waved to him from the door of the bar as his wife, stonefaced, pulled away from the curb.

When they finally managed to get Two-Speed out from under the pickup and standing, they discovered a great patch of skull, white but flowing with blood, showing through the matted hair at the back of his head. He declined offers of aid, shaking off the hands held out to him, pulled a dirty stocking cap out of his coat pocket, pushed it down over his head and walked, dignified but drunk, through the cold, wavering light of the street lamps, home.

The next day people came into town and looked at the trail of blood, frozen and brown against the black asphalt. They smoked and muttered and followed it, heads down, to where it broadened and spread near the stop sign, as if confirming, each one for himself, that yes, this had happened, reading their own individual interpretations out of the spoor. I was in town with my father, and, coming out of the hardware store, I saw the men huddled near the stop sign. I asked Dad what had happened, but he only glanced at the men and walked on to where he'd parked our pickup.

I had to run to catch him, and by the time I made it around the hood and had opened the door, he had the engine running. He was staring through the windshield at the brick-and-glass front of the Woolworth store. I sat down hard on the cold vinyl, hearing it snap under me and hoping it would crack and tear, shifting my weight more than necessary and looking at Dad. He glanced over at me, then jerked his head toward the stop sign. "Two-Speed Crandall about killed himself last night," he said. "But he didn't get the job done. They're"—he jerked his head again—"looking. That's all."

"That's *all?* Wow! How did—"

His eyes stopped me. "Just stupid."

He pulled the pickup onto the street. In spite of him, I leaned forward as we approached the stop sign, looking at the knot of men. They glanced up as we came near. A few nodded to my father. He nodded back, but we didn't join them, and I craned my neck backward as we turned onto the highway, watching them grow smaller through the rear window, and wondering what Two-Speed Crandall had done. I think I remember, though I can't be sure— and in truth, it seems unlikely I would—seeing the blood under the feet of the men, oozing out, a brown stain over which they floated, somehow supported by it.

I heard the story later through my friends and their older brothers, stories like that descending stratums until they finally reached clear down to groups of elementary students huddled on the playground. The stories also said that the next day Hank Tyrrell got a phone call from, of all people, LouAnn Crandall, but since Hank was outside feeding his cattle, LouAnn berated Hank's wife, Betty, demanding that she keep her husband away from Simon—Two-Speed's real name—and informing her that Simon was sick and in bed and that Betty had no right to let her husband nearly kill LouAnn's husband. This phone call, by all accounts, did little to speed Betty's forgiveness of Hank, and he wasn't seen at the bar for several months after it.

These things are local legend. They've been filtered many times in being retold, and I remember them in the whole and connected way that we remember things from childhood, when even nursery rhymes have such reality and truth that we can ask our parents who the little boy who lived down the lane was, and where was the lane, and why did the black sheep want to give him some wool—questions that filled out and tried to make whole the disconnected phrases. If I tell these things with some fondness, it is fondness for the story, not for the man.

Or fondness, perhaps, for the enigma of the man. Or the enigma of memory. I remember Two-Speed still, sitting high in the cab of the semi when he came out to haul cattle for my father. To get to our barn, the drivers had to come into our yard, turn, and then back carefully between two grain bins, curve around a tree that my father refused to cut down, then straighten the rig out and ease up to the barn door. Most of the drivers would study the route, then, guided by someone else, would back up, get off course, go ahead, back up, gradually easing their way, by fits and starts, between the bins and around the tree. But Two-Speed would walk the route he had to take, then climb into the cab and back the trailer up, without ever going ahead or readjusting, or slowing down or riding the clutch. He would simply start, and there was something inexorable and beautiful about it, the churning engine, the diesel smoke, the crunch of gravel under the tires, the massive rectangular rig rolling backward, twisting without pause, reasserting its course, the exhausts throbbing, until the trailer, as wary and gentle as a dog meeting another, eased up to the chute and stopped with a sigh of air brakes, just touching the wood.

It mesmerized me. Done at night, as it often was so that the cattle would arrive at the stockyards in the morning, it was like waking from sleep to a bigger dream than any I could have dreamed myself, the whole semi glowing within the orange and red of its running lights, creaking and swaying over its axles. Then Two-Speed would take his eyes off the mirrors, where he had been intent and focused, and he would climb down from the cab, his pants tucked into his boots, as gaunt and stringy as a heron, with the same enigmatic glitter in his eyes, and the same careful delicacy about his walk, as if his world were one of shallow water and sucking mud, and walking in it was both risk and miracle. He'd step to the back of the trailer, and if he were more than an inch away from the chute, he'd grunt and spit and walk away, disgusted with himself.

But even before my father told me of Two-Speed's violence with his family, I was aware of a distortion that entered here. For Two-Speed would take out his disgust with himself on the cattle, wielding his prod with unnecessary vigor, shocking the steers even though they were moving well, shocking them just to see them jump, and holding the prongs against their flanks, holding them there when the cattle were jammed in the chute and couldn't move to escape the jolt. The steers would sometimes panic when he did this and fall to their knees on the slippery wood, their rear hooves booming in the barn as they struggled to rise, the blue arc from the blunt prongs of the prod sizzling in their hair, the sharp electric smell stinging my nostrils above the smell of oil and sweat and manure—and Two-Speed standing there unrelenting, a grim and dusky look on his face, the steer groaning in the closest sound to despair I've ever heard, until—it always happened, I waited for it, the tension building in me—my father, a man never given to swearing, or even to anger, would shout from across the barn: "Damnit, Two-Speed! Lay off the electricity!"

These are moments outside of time for me: the packed cattle like a live, roiling sea, and over their backs the two men staring at each other. Neither of them moved. The whole barn was moving, but the two men were stiller than posts or stone. My father's eyes, even in the diffuse yellow light of the barn, had that hard and distant cast that I'd noted as something borrowed from the horizon. I remember all this as something completely soundless, the cattle bucking and moving in silence, the chute swaying without creaking.

In Two-Speed's eyes there was the kind of look I had seen only once before, on the face of the neighbor's dog when, one night, I heard a commotion outside and, full of the exploratory courage of a young boy, took a .22 rifle and a flashlight and went to investigate. I found the dog tangled in a mass of barbed wire behind the chicken house, one of our chickens, feathers wet and bloodied, at its feet. Gashes along the dog's side materialized slowly in the tissue beam of the light I held. Its face, too, was cut, and blood flowed freely down its fur and into its mouth. I saw that even its tongue was cut; it must have been biting at the wire in its frenzy to free itself. It looked at me with the cunning and fear of a wild thing, but there was something else, too, that made me stop just as I was about to go to it and free its leg from the coil of wire. The eerie fear came suddenly upon me that this dog would kill me, or try to, should I free it. I don't know how long I stood there, the dark trees moving over me, before I put the rifle down and spoke the dog's name: Homer.

The animal relaxed, free to plead with me, to collapse into its daytime self, the pleaser of human beings. I see now that the flicker of hatred I had caught from its eyes sprang from an unbearable tension within it—its wild nature hating me for finding it helpless, its domestic nature hating me for finding it a killer. At the sound of its name, though, the dog became whole again, if not complete, and whined softly, giving in to the pain. I approached it carefully, and it waited patiently while I uncoiled the wire. Then it withdrew its legs, sniffed at the chicken lying in the barbs, looked once at me, and fled. With the light, I followed its limping form, receding between the dark trees of the grove, until it disappeared.

In Two-Speed's eyes as he stared at my father there was the same look the dog gave me, and it made me uneasy, an uneasiness I was then too young to recognize as fear for my father. But in the distant hardness of my father's eyes there was a look to oppose Two-Speed's—a steady, unwavering anger, so steady it was almost calm. I know now that his anger was concerned not only with the cattle, but also with the children, with those three boys not his own, and that he was enraged at his own helplessness, being as he was a believer in stories that were unproven and therefore impossible to act upon. Always it was Two-Speed who turned away. Always, with a show of sullenness he stuffed the prod into the pocket of his overalls, where it protruded stiff and ungainly, making him look even more like an unkempt wading bird as he stood undignified and lost in the dim, manurey air of the barn, where—in my memory—sudden sound resumes.

Two-Speed's funeral was a large forgetting. The whole town turned out for it. Men told all the old, good stories, slapping their hands down on the long church basement tables in imitation of the license that had flicked night after night from Two-Speed's pocket in the bar down the street. They laughed as they ate the hamburger-and-rice hotdish prepared by the St. Mark's ladies, and they slapped Hank Tyrrell on the shoulders as they walked behind his chair, while he, sitting next to Betty, pretended to ignore them. But everyone was grave around LouAnn and the three boys, men now like myself, who nodded their heads and accepted condolences without emotion, indifferent to all the attention being given them now that they no longer sought it. Everyone was careful, in speaking to the family, to call Two-Speed Simon, and to repeat the virtues they could be sure of—that no one drove a semi better than Simon Crandall, that the town would never see the likes of Simon Crandall's skill again.

I was there. I am, after all, one of them. I have been one of them since that day when my father brought me into adulthood by revealing the other stories. I was there, not to rejoice or mourn, but simply to remember, in the silences when the laughter died down, those stories no one told.

V

From Farm Crisis to the Present

THE SMALL TOWN is presently undergoing profound change. This became apparent in the 1990s, as the most dramatic of the demographic consequences of the 1980s farm crisis were understood to be a consequence of long-term and irreversible trends.

Beyond demographic decline associated with, first, population loss and aging and, second, reduced size and diminished functions and services of smaller towns, other significant changes were taking place. Rural economies depended less and less on agriculture and more and more on small industry and government payments (particularly from Social Security). The failing and, in many places, vanished merchant class that once governed Main Street was replaced in local government and community by public employees, the managers of new industries, and others who could be classified as newcomers. The small town relinquished more of its autonomy, as its own institutions closed, migrated, or merged—and it found itself. If it thrived, it did so as a bedroom community or some type of suburb. The smallest towns became in every sense satellites of larger townsites, while the countryside at large became economically, socially, and culturally ever more integrated into the institutions, tastes, and dictates of distant metropolises. To put this in other terms, locality and place played an ever diminishing role in the lives of small-town inhabitants as small-town cultures yielded to powerful influence from state, region, nation, and even the world.

This profound transformation accelerated certain trends that already existed in the countryside. Differences between populations, growth, functions, businesses and service area, and ever important location more sharply differentiated one town from another. And thoughtful analysis of a single contemporary small town now had to examine less tangible assets such as services and amenities, balance of business and industry, access to state and private investments, and, more subtlety, the coherence and composition of community traditions and leadership. Small towns, which once were sorted and gathered in groups by size, function, and location, had to be studied individually to be understood.

Such contemporary studies have an immediate importance in the case of "lead towns" in the countryside. In many ways, lead towns are the hinges on which the contemporary rural order turns. Or, in more dramatic terms, these ostensibly growing and viable towns constitute the last battlegrounds of rural life. Having survived demographic decline on the one hand and having escaped being swallowed up or annexed to a nearby town, they appear to be the last place in a countryside of profoundly diminished farms and small towns that offers an alternative to American urban life.

The term "lead town" permits no easy definition. Size may vary from 2,500 to 15,000, and service areas may range from twenty to sixty miles as one moves from the populous and fertile east to the arid and depopulated west. In fact, the designation is doubly problematic. Proclaiming oneself a lead town suggests victory in the past and promise for the future, while accepting the fact that one is not a lead town is fraught with negative political and psychological consequences. It signals not only surrender in century-long competition with one's neighbors to be the hub of a region but suggests an irremediable breach of the town's covenant with progress and the nation's future.

Setting aside the problematic matters of definition and designation, a lead town is the arena of a set of crucial battles that should compel the attention of contemporary rural politician and student. In play is the perennial question of the town's capacity to provide its region with the goods, services, and amenities demanded in an increasingly abundant and consumptive society and—in many cases—mandated expectations by law and legislation. Also in question is whether the lead town's growth will offset the decline and aging of the surrounding farms, villages, and towns—or will it, like an iceberg moving into warmer waters, steadily give way to an encircling entropy? And no longer escapable is a set of questions that turn on the capacity of any given town center to reach beyond itself—to enter into alliances with surrounding towns and adjacent town centers to undertake vital regional projects. Can a lead town by its comparative advantage of position, location, size, and growth actually transform itself into a regional leader, or will it invariably succumb to its own shrinking and aging service area?

As if the challenge of developing a successful foreign policy is not enough, lead towns face internal problems of an equal magnitude. Aside from meeting the multiple and illusive demands of economic development, a thriving lead town confronts the task of maintaining a coherent tradition, leadership, and vision. It encounters accelerated change and turbulence. It confronts increasing turnover in its own population and leadership while assimilating new industries, leaders, and immigrants, who arrive from ever more distant places. At the same time, the more dynamic the lead town's growth, the greater the likelihood it will come, out of both necessity and wish, to serve outside forces—and metamorphose itself into an agent of remote economic and political forces.

In simple terms, rural lead towns must learn to transform strangers into communities or become clients of distant metropolises. This challenge, in addition to other external challenges, suggests in all likelihood that lead cities over time will eventually go the way of other small towns. They will surrender to decline by virtue of their shrinking service areas and the mobility of their respective populations, or they will sacrifice autonomy and initiative (which were never pure or preponderant) to encroaching metropolitan agendas. However, this somewhat gloomy prophecy should be nuanced, perhaps even contradicted, as contemporary research takes a careful look at small towns' remarkable diversity and the potential for immensely varied futures.

Indeed, beyond the matter of the viability of lead towns, contemporary rural researchers have much to explore in the changing towns of the Midwest. Aside from the recent transformations emerging out of the late 1980s and early 1990s, researchers should inquire into changing patterns of migration, along with increased mobility and seasonal and recreational travel. Recent arrivals, be they ethnic minorities filling the ranks of labor (especially in the meat processing industries) or new levels of management (serving chains and regional industries), provide a fertile terrain of inquiry into relations between newcomers and changing host communities.

With increased travel, mobility, migration, and newcomers, on the one hand, and the mounting intrusion of outside economic, political, commercial, and cultural forces on the other, the question of identity surfaces. At issue, for both small-town political activists but also cultural historians and writers, is the meaning of contemporary attachment to place and a nest of associated topics about how identities are formed, maintained, and balanced in an era when the walls of town and village have collapsed. Have we, to put this in a single question, essentially moved beyond place and local identity—and, if so, what fresh and mediating identities and senses of home and place are emerging in small-town America? Inquiries into these pressing topics would find national and global parallels.

Alas, it must be conceded that—to the detriment of understanding contemporary small towns caught up in change—the majority of local historians focus their attention on a static distant past. Recently some local historians—almost unanimously amateurs—have shifted their attention forward in time to the 1940s and the 1950s. Here they find decades in which good and evil stood forth, the covenant between town and nation was unbroken, and they were held in the cocoon of the simpler days of their own childhood. Professional historians do counterbalance amateur historians, but in the main professional historians are not interested in either locality or rural life. They do not seek out transformations of the countryside, although an exception must be made for agricultural historians, who cannot help but confront an immense demographic revolution in farms and technological and biological revolutions of human productivity, labor, and the resulting relationship of man to land.

Help in understanding the transformation of the countryside does not readily come from other quarters. For a variety of reasons, social scientists—be they economists, sociologists, demographers, or geographers—do not offer their readers an entrance into the inner dimensions of a changing countryside. A commitment to generalization and a disposition toward abstractions (which ultimately flow from the claim to be a type of science) simply do not permit social scientists to tell a story of change composed of unique entities, singular events, and unprecedented evolution. Nor does rural literature—to indulge another type of generalization and abstraction—fill the void. Even when its practitioners focus on contemporary small towns—which is rare enough in itself—detailed insight into subject and happening are sacrificed (if ever perceived at all) to the repetition of past stereotypes, long-heard denunciation, or the playing out of universal—Greek or Shakespearean—drama. More succinctly, Main Street supplies the archetypes.

Decline and Denial

FROM *Broken Heartland*

OSHA GRAY DAVIDSON

THE "FARM CRISIS" OF THE 1980s greatly accelerated the decline of most midwestern towns and produced an immense differentiation between small towns and lead towns, and among lead towns themselves. After decades of stagnation, economic developments during the 1970s had seemed to offer reasons for renewed optimism. This resulted from a surge in commodity prices that was stimulated by increased agricultural exports and high inflation rates. The value of America's farmland more than doubled in the decade. On paper, at least, farmers benefited from an unprecedented bonanza. In Iowa, for example, during the decade of the 1970s the average price per acre of farmland rose from $409 to $2,066. But the illusion of renewed agricultural prosperity proved ephemeral at best. Federal agricultural policies encouraged mass production, which worked to the benefit of large farms and agribusiness, ultimately threatening those traditional small family farms that lacked the wherewithal to expand production. The farmer had to modernize and increase the amount of acreage under production in order to survive. This meant acquiring inordinately expensive new lines of equipment—such as $100,000 tractors and $200,000 combines—and taking out new mortgages to acquire additional acreage. Farmers had no choice but to heed the warning of Richard Nixon's secretary of agriculture, Earl Butz: "Get big or get out."

In order to "get big," however, farmers had to take on big debt. And when world market commodity prices plummeted in the early 1980s, despite greatly increased production per acre, farmers faced economic disaster. Mortgage foreclosures skyrocketed, while, ironically, large agricultural corporations enjoyed double-digit profit margins. Banks that had only a few years earlier urged farmers to take out large loans for land purchases and equipment upgrades now found themselves in the difficult business of foreclosing. The result was that those who survived were the agricultural corporations and only the very largest and most efficient family farms. By 1990, just 4 percent of the nation's farms produced nearly 50 percent of the nation's food.

The result was catastrophic to many midwestern communities, because the consolidation of farms resulted in a loss of population. With their basic clientele declining, town merchants were faced with agonizing decisions. They recognized that, in the face of the inevitable nearby Wal-Mart, they too had to "get big or get out." Most had little choice but to get out. Osha Gray Davidson concludes that the result was a Midwest that was marred by pockets of extreme poverty that existed within "rural ghettos." These numerous ghettos, diverse in their own way, both stand in opposition to and depend on regional lead towns, around which in all their variations the newly emerging American countryside appears to be taking shape.

---

o o o

It is a fundamental illusion of American culture:
the persistent celebration of rural life in the midst of its destruction.
HARLAND PADFIELD in *The Dying Community*

Mechanicsville, Iowa

This handsome town is much like any of the thousands of rural communities dotting the gently rolling hills of the Midwestern prairie. Built along a narrow mile-long ridge rising out of open lands in eastern Iowa, the town of slightly over 1,000 residents stands above unbroken fields of corn and soybeans like a ship at sea. The old-fashioned water tower at the center of town together with the augers and grain silos clustered around the nearby Farm Service Center reach into the Midwestern sky like masts and rigging. The fields surrounding Mechanicsville do, in fact, resemble an ocean—especially in the summer when the wind blows hard from the south, stirring the corn into waves that race to the horizon.

While there is no mistaking the fact that Mechanicsville is essentially a farm community, with its roots deep into the land, few people living within the town limits actually farm. Residents work at a variety of jobs, mostly low-skill, low-wage jobs in Mechanicsville or in one of the surrounding communities.

At 10:30 on a chilly Monday morning in spring, the town's business district, a two-block area of turn-of-the-century red brick buildings, is nearly deserted. A solitary car sits outside the post office, its motor running while the owner is inside picking up his mail. Across the street, a trio of beat-up pickup trucks are parked in front of the Village Inn, the downtown's one remaining cafe. Inside, four elderly men in seed-corn hats play pinochle at the bar while another group of men sit around a table drinking black coffee and telling me about their town.

Jim Cook, owner of the local hardware store, is the obvious leader of this last group. Cook is a World War II veteran with a shaggy mane of gray hair, a salt-and-pepper pencil-thin mustache, and a handshake you're not meant to forget. He is a die-hard conservative, a supporter of President Ronald Reagan from back when Reagan was still governor of California—that is, when it really meant something to be a Reagan man.

Over the next two hours Cook dominates the discussion, talking up the town's school system, volunteer fire department, and the principles that made Mechanicsville great: hard work, thrift, simple living, and, most of all, community pride.

"We want to show everybody else that we can do it better than they can," he says with a smile that shows he has no doubts about Mechanicsville's ability to always come out on top.

In the same firm tones, Cook ticks off the major evils of the day: greedy farmers, back-stabbing politicians, welfare mothers who "keep right on having kids," and people who don't shop locally. The two other men at the table exchange a quick glance over their coffee cups when Cook mentions this last ill. The issue of "buying local" is one of the town's sore points, especially with Cook, a topic that can escalate from hard words to threats of a fist fight in seconds.

The issue surfaced recently after Cook asked a local farmer why he made all his large hardware purchases 30 miles away in the city of Cedar Rapids instead of buying local at Cook's store.

"I'm really sorry," the man told Cook, "but they sell cheaper over there. I can't afford to shop at your store."

Cook said nothing. He just stared the man down and walked away. A week later the same farmer came into Cook's hardware store to buy two bolts—a purchase of about a dollar.

"Sorry," Cook told the man without a smile when the farmer laid the bolts on the counter at the cash register. "You'll have to drive over to Cedar Rapids for them. You can't buy them here."

The farmer thought Cook was joking. He wasn't. The man left the store threatening to pop Cook one in the nose and later sent his son in to buy the bolts.

"'Course, I wouldn't sell them to him either," says Cook mildly, and takes a sip of coffee.

Cook demands even more of himself. He once wanted to buy a bed but found nothing at the local furniture store that quite suited him, so he drove over to Cedar Rapids, found the bed he wanted, and went back to order it locally. The owner of the store said he wasn't interested in ordering anything other than what he had in stock. Cook tried everything he could think of to get the man to order the bed, but he wouldn't do it. But Jim Cook does not give in that easily. He called the company that distributed the bed, pretending to be the owner of the furniture store across the street from his own business. When the bed was delivered there, Cook went over and paid for it, including a healthy retail mark-up.

Throughout our conversation, Cook jumps at any suggestion that his town is anything other than a vital, thriving village. When one of the other men at the table recalls the time when every building in town had a business going and observes that "it was a very prosperous place back then," Cook leans forward in his chair and directs his words with cold precision at the man who has just spoken: "It is still."

The other man, an ex-farmer now in his seventies, blushes and fumbles for words. "Oh, sure . . . that's right. She still is. She's a prosperous place."

The most that Cook will allow is that there have been some problems lately.

"Sure, we may be seeing some troubles due to the downturn in the farm economy," he says, "but nothing different from anywhere else. Look, we've been through this before, during the Great Depression. We've been here for 150 years and we've always gotten through. And we'll get through now."

With that, the interview ends. Cook has to get back to his store, and I have other interviews. We shake hands and I promise to stop by his hardware store on my way out of town.

A few hours later, interviews completed, I go to say good-bye to Cook. His store turns out to be a combination hardware–kitchen appliance–gun shop. Back behind the crock pots and hammers is a long glass case packed with guns and ammunition. Blue steel pistols and chrome-plated six-shooters lie behind the glass; dozens of rifles line the walls. The store is modern on the inside, which is surprising because of the building's saloon-style brick and wood front, the kind you rarely see except in Hollywood westerns.

"Oh, I remodel every now and then," explains Cook. "You have to if you want to stay in business for 110 years like we have. My Dad bought the place in the summer of 1926, but it's been a hardware store since 1876. 'Course, a lot of new places in cities are remodeling to make them look like they're 110 years old. That's 'in' now. But I get sick and tired of that old-fashioned look. You've got to keep moving forward."

We're standing by the cash register still talking when an old man walks slowly in, nods to Cook, and heads for the greeting-card section.

"You should talk to Everett Ferguson," Cook says, nodding in the direction of the old man. "He's 90-something, still lives in the house he was born in. Hey, Everett," Cook calls out. "Talk to this guy. He wants to know about Mechanicsville."

I walk over and introduce myself. Ferguson is a small man, dressed in a plain green shirt that is buttoned to the top and a gray sports coat. His narrow face is surprisingly smooth, as if he has outlasted even his wrinkles, but his hands look as if they were made of wax paper that had been crumpled into a ball and then smoothed out, leaving a fine network of sharp creases.

"Everett," calls Cook, "tell him what's happening to Mechanicsville."

Ferguson doesn't say anything for some time. He stares at me through thick-lensed glasses that make his eyes appear large and liquid. I begin to wonder if he heard Cook, or, if he did, if he's capable of answering coherently.

Finally, just as I've decided that Everett Ferguson is lost in the mists of age, he answers in a voice that is slow and surprisingly deep. "What's happening to Mechanicsville?" he asks with a scorn reserved for those who ask the obvious. "It's dying."

The words seem to hang in the air. I hear Cook suck in his breath as if about to say something, and I turn to face him. Cook is standing silently at the cash register, one hand on the counter, the other in his sweater pocket. He looks out the store's large front window to where the late-afternoon sunlight cascades down the facade of an empty building across the street. His face is empty, too; suddenly gone is the mask of belligerent optimism, replaced by a new face—or a new mask—this one of studied indifference. It is as if he hadn't heard Ferguson, as if he were alone, waiting out the last few minutes until closing time in the store his father bought back in the summer of 1926.

The similarity of the prairie to an ocean (which is something of a paradox, since the Midwest is about as far as you can get from an ocean in this country) was noted immediately by the earliest white explorers and settlers who christened the region the Inland Sea. Judging from their diaries and letters, it was not so much the wave-like motion of the prairie grasses that inspired the name, but rather the emotions stirred in the settlers when confronted by something so vast it hinted at the infinite.[1]

"I had the feeling that the world was left behind, that we had got over the edge of it, and were outside man's jurisdiction," wrote novelist Willa Cather. "This was the complete dome of heaven, all there was. Between that earth and that sky I felt erased, blotted out. . . . That is happiness, to be dissolved into something complete and great."

Many of the early Europeans didn't find the experience of dissolution quite so idyllic. Some, in fact, were terrified by the dimensions of the open land—a quarter of a billion acres of shimmering chest-high grasses stretching from Illinois west to what is now Kansas, and from the Dakotas south through Oklahoma and into Texas.

"Wherever a man stands he is surrounded by the sky," wrote the stunned diarist of the conquistador Coronado in 1541, as the party of Spanish explorers huddled around the campfire on the Kansas prairie. Bewildered by the scale of the land, the group stayed only long enough to satisfy themselves that there were no "cities of gold" to be found and then hurried back to New Spain, where the vistas were more manageable.

Mechanicsville's first residents were neither as enamored by the prairie as Cather nor as frightened by it as Coronado's group. They were a hard-headed, pragmatic, nose-to-the-grindstone conglomeration of German, Scandinavian, and Scotch-Irish pioneers who drifted into the territory west of the Mississippi River in the mid-1800s. They came from both the Yankee East and the deep South to form a new society of farmers and shopkeepers whose values, culture, and even dialect showed the influence of the two strains.

The Southerners brought with them a high regard for generosity and liberty combined with an almost visceral distrust of authority. That last trait has always been particularly strong in this area. In 1931, when the government began testing all dairy cows in Iowa for tuberculosis, scores of armed area farmers vowed to shoot the first son-of-a-bitch to touch a Cedar County cow. The National Guard had to be called in to protect the veterinarians.[2]

"Not that we thought it was a bad idea to test for TB," recalled a local farmer who was a teenager during the Cow War. "In fact, most everybody thought it was a good idea. We just didn't like being told we had to do it."

Mechanicsville's residents could be as ornery with private officials as they were with public authorities. The town once had a railroad depot on the south edge of town that serviced 12 trains a day—one every two hours around the clock. In November of 1867, a spark from a passing train landed on the wooden-shingled depot roof, setting it on fire. Because many townspeople felt the railroad hadn't been very helpful hauling firewood a few winters before, they decided to pay the railroad back. People rushed down to the depot and instead of helping to put the fire out, they stood happily by, watching the building burn to the ground.[3]

But these attributes have always been tempered by a Southern respect for hospitality and good manners—attributes that are characterized in Iowans by a tendency to politeness that often borders on the absurd. When 1988 Democratic vice-presidential candidate Lloyd Bentsen received a few scattered boos from the crowd at the Iowa State Fair, a campaign spokesperson noticed that the catcalls were more subdued than at other stops. "In Iowa, even the hecklers are pretty polite," he observed.

The Yankees added respect for education, dedication to hard work, and a stern puritanical morality. A foreign visitor dubbed the resulting Midwestern amalgam "the most American part of America."[4] That observation was echoed during the 1988 presidential caucus when a visiting Italian journalist called the small-town Iowans he encountered "the original Americans, as if preserved in amber."

A visitor traveling through Mechanicsville today would probably agree with that assessment. From the straight tree-shaded streets, with their large old houses and sprawling wrap-around porches, down to the neatly trimmed front lawns edged with rows of petunias, the town looks as if it belongs to an earlier era. For generations, Mechanicsville has remained the knot tying together the lives of the farm families who till the rich black earth in this small piece of America's Heartland. They went to school here and shopped in the modest downtown. They socialized here, attending dances at the American Legion Hall and softball games at the dusty field by the railroad tracks. They were married here at one of the three churches (Catholic, Presbyterian, and Methodist), and on anniversaries they feasted on steak and potatoes at the restaurant Our Place. When the nearby farm couples grew old, they passed their farms down to their children and moved to town. And when at last they died, usually at home among family and friends, they returned to the earth here, buried beneath the prairie grasses in the Rose Hill Cemetery on the west edge of town.

Like most small towns, Mechanicsville always had trouble holding onto its young. Many felt stifled here, their possibilities too limited, the pace of life too slow. And so every year one or two of these ambitious young men and women left for the bright lights of Des Moines or the even brighter ones of Chicago, Minneapolis, St. Louis, or beyond. But many remained, settled into small-town life, and raised families. In fact, over one-quarter of Mechanicsville's residents have lived in the area for more than forty years; nearly 80% have lived there for at least a decade.[5]

Jim Cook was one of those who stayed. "When I got out of the service," he recalls, "people said, 'What the hell you come back here for?' I looked them right in the eye and said, 'I've been every place I could be, and Mechanicsville is no different from the rest of them. It's just as good as Carmel, California, or Timbuktu. Every one of them has their faults and if I'm going to have faults, it's going to be with the people I know. That's why I came home: because it's home.'"

That longing for a community that is "home," the need to feel part of a group that is larger than a family but more embraceable than a nation, is a familiar theme throughout American social history. Since the earliest days of settlement, rural communities have satisfied that desire by playing a wide variety of roles. "It is the community that cushions pain, the community that provides a context for intimacy, the community that represents morality and serves as the repository for old traditions," observes sociologist Kai Erikson.[6]

Life in the tightly knit rural community of Mechanicsville has always been profoundly different from that found just thirty miles away in Cedar Rapids, with a population of around 100,000. The main difference between the two is that while most Mechanicsville residents have always been essentially united—whatever factors happened to divide them—in Cedar

Rapids, residents have always been essentially divided—whatever factors happened to unite them.[7]

Eleanor Anstey, a professor of social work at the University of Iowa, recalls an incident from her high school days on an Iowa farm that for her sums up this experience of life in a rural community: "I telephoned the local flower store for lilies, but they said they were sold out. Suddenly, a voice on the party line said, 'Oh, I've got some nice ones you can have Eleanor.' It wouldn't have occurred to you to feel that your privacy was violated."

Of course it is easy to idealize small towns such as Mechanicsville, to forget the schisms, economic and social, that *do* exist there. It's easy, too, to ignore the currents of racism and anti-Semitism that run just below the surface, currents that appear in crude but relatively harmless jokes—or in far uglier ways in hard times. And one needn't be African-American or Jewish to feel shunned in a small town; the Yankee inheritance of puritanism allows for little deviation of any kind. For example, a woman who chooses to pursue a career while her husband stays home to raise their children can expect little support from the community for such a decision.

Besides, not everyone appreciates the kind of intimacy a small town provides. A 1981 survey revealed that almost half of Mechanicsville residents felt their neighbors interfered in their business too often. But 90% of respondents also believed their neighbors would help out in an emergency, and for most, the trade-off was worth it.[8] For all the drawbacks to small-town life, that sense of belonging to a caring community is what Heartland towns like Mechanicsville have always provided their residents.

But today that is changing. Small towns are in trouble. Strictly speaking, Mechanicsville and the thousands of rural communities like it are not dying, as Everett Ferguson put it. To use the term "dying" in this way at once overstates and understates the problem faced by small-town residents.

It overstates the problem, in literal terms, because most rural communities will survive—at least they will have residents and so will remain on the map for decades. But in many ways, the situation would be less dire if the towns simply folded up and the residents moved away. Instead, formerly healthy, mostly middle-class communities throughout the Midwest, the small towns that have given the area its distinctive character since its settlement, are being transformed into rural ghettos—pockets of poverty, unemployment, violence, and despair that are becoming more and more isolated from the rest of the country. As the coastal economies have boomed, the Heartland has collapsed. "The most American part of America" is fast becoming "America's Third World."

The dimensions of the problem are sobering. Between 54 and 60 million rural Americans, one-quarter of the country's population, are touched by the decline. Over 9 million people now live in poverty in America's rural areas.[9] In Iowa, the hardest hit of all Midwestern states, one out of six individuals falls below the federal poverty line, and in some counties the poverty rate approaches 30%.[10] With an irony that is especially bitter in this region, the nation's breadbasket, hunger has become a common problem.

"We've seen a steady and continuing increase in the need for food in the past five years," says Karen Ford, director of Food Bank of Iowa, which supplies donated food to 200 food pantries and nonprofit agencies throughout the state.

As the economy stagnates, manufacturers lay off workers or shut down completely. Hospitals, banks, and businesses close. Depression, suicides, and child-abuse rates grow. The need for foster care rises to an unmanageable level as families break up under the pressure of poverty. Towns compete for factories paying poverty-level wages. Mass migrations become commonplace. Local governments cannot afford the most basic services.

"People talk about the middle class being in jeopardy in Iowa, but that's inaccurate," says University of Iowa economist David Swenson. "A significant portion of the state is already out of the middle class. The notion of upward mobility in Iowa is gone."

It is ironic that the victims of this blight, the inhabitants of the new rural ghettos, have always been the most blindly patriotic of Americans, the keepers of the American dream. Their response to any criticism of America was summed up in the bumper sticker that was once common around here: AMERICA, LOVE IT OR LEAVE IT. That patriotic decal can still be seen on pickup trucks throughout the Heartland, but today it competes with another bumper sticker that reads: SHIT HAPPENS.

The speed with which the recent decline hit rural America has made the problem even more difficult for Midwesterners to deal with. Iowans, especially rural Iowans, are well known for their resistance to quick changes of any kind. A retired farmer once told me that his father was the first person in the area to try raising soybeans back in the early part of this century, when corn was the undisputed king.

"It probably took quite a while to catch on," I remarked.

"Oh, no," he assured me. "Why, some of the neighbors were giving the new crop a try just six or seven years later."

And so the reaction to the decline over the last few years has been, as usual, to wait it out—to endure. But this catastrophe is not like a period of drought that can be outlasted. Whatever recoveries may temporarily come this way, short of major structural changes in our economy and government, the rural problem is here to stay. According to a study prepared for the U.S. Congress's Joint Economic Committee, "Iowa could become the State that the Nation leaves behind."[11]

Despite the magnitude of the problem, the disintegration of rural America is largely an invisible crisis. Driving along Interstate 80—the way most outsiders see the state—you would never guess anything is wrong. From that narrow corridor you drive for hours passing fields of corn and beans that cover the horizon in lines as straight as a table's edge. Giant tractors or combines crisscross the land, planting in the spring, cultivating or spraying in the summer, harvesting in the fall. Everything you see speaks of abundance and prosperity.

Even for those few adventuresome souls who pull off the interstate and head into small farm towns like Mechanicsville, appearances are deceiving. The disaster that is sweeping through the Midwest is not like a tornado or a flood that leaves a trail of rubble and twisted-up cars in its path. (For this reason the rural crisis makes for poor film footage and so doesn't rate a spot on the nightly news.)

But if you look carefully at downtown Mechanicsville, you will notice that although the buildings still stand, a majority of them stand empty. At one time the town had as many as thirty Main Street businesses. There were two feed stores, two farm implement dealers, two hotels, two clothing stores. Also a pharmacy, a jewelry store, a soda fountain, a shoe store, an opera house, a pool hall, a bakery, a butcher shop, and a produce market. Today none of these remain.

Kathy Lehrman and her husband Kelvin bought the local paper, the *Pioneer Herald*, in 1979. In the spring of 1986 she stood outside her downtown office looking across the street at a row of empty storefronts.

"I don't know what's going to happen here," she confided. "In the past six months we've lost ten businesses in the three towns we cover. Maybe somebody ought to come in, buy the whole downtown, and just tear it all down."

One month later, the *Pioneer Herald* office was also dark. The Lehmans had sold the paper to a chain and were looking to try their luck somewhere else.

"People are hoping for things to get better," says 49-year-old Steve Seehusen, who runs a combination real estate firm and insurance agency from an office in what used to be a bank (until it closed in the Great Depression). "These are hard times. We used to sell houses as fast as they came on the market. Right now I've got seven houses listed, and they're just sitting there."

Even with homes that sold for $45,000 just a few years ago now selling for $25,000, there are no takers. "So many things are out of our control," says Seehusen dolefully.

The creation of rural ghettos is a complex process, and despite the rapid changes of the last decade it has been evolving over several generations for reasons that are less than obvious. To understand the decline in America's Heartland we have to start with the well-known but little-understood event associated with it: the farm crisis.

NOTES

1. There are several good sources for reading accounts of settlers, including Richard Lingeman, *Small Town America* (Boston: Houghton Mifflin Company, 1980), John Madison, *Where the Sky Began* (San Francisco: Sierra Club Books, 1982), Walter Prescott Webb, *The Great Plains* (Boston: Ginn, 1931), Russell Smith, ed., *Nebraska Policy Choices* (Omaha: University of Nebraska at Omaha, 1950), and Howard Zinn, *A People's History of the United States* (New York: Harper and Row, 1980).

2. Leland Sage, *A History of Iowa* (Ames: The Iowa State University Press, 1974), 275.

3. Stories about Mechanicsville's history came from a variety of sources including Iowa county histories and interviews with residents.

4. Russel Nye, "Has the Midwest Ceased to Protest?" in *The Midwest: Myth or Reality*, Thomas McAvoy, ed. (Notre Dame, Indiana: University of Notre Dame Press, 1961), 4.

5. Iowa State University, Cooperative Extension Service, "Mechanicsville Community Attitude Survey" (Ames: Iowa State University, 1981), 6.

6. Kai Erikson, *Everything in Its Path* (New York: Simon and Schuster, 1976), 193.

7. This difference between rural society (Gemeinschaft) and urban society (Gesellschaft) is discussed in Erikson (1976).

8. Iowa State University, "Mechanicsville Community Attitude Survey."

9. Kathryn Porter, *Poverty in Rural America: A National Overview* (Washington, D.C.: Center on Budget and Policy Priorities, 1989).

10. Christine Ross and Sheldon Danzinger, "Poverty Rates by State, 1979 and 1985: A Research Note," *Focus* (University of Wisconsin–Madison, Institute for Research on Poverty, Fall 1987), 2.

11. U.S. Congress, Joint Economic Committee, Subcommittee on Agriculture and Transportation, "New Dimensions in Rural Policy: Building Upon Our Heritage," 99th Congress, second session (Washington, D.C.: U.S. Government Printing Office, 1986), 288.

On the Cutting Edge

Changes in Midwestern Meatpacking Communities

DONALD D. STULL

URING THE LAST TWO DECADES of the twentieth century small communities searched for new solutions to the old problem of providing a solid economic base for local workers. In many states local communities considered themselves fortunate when they welcomed new food processing plants to their towns. These new facilities were one of the many consequences of the rapidly expanding corporate agricultural economy. Throughout the Midwest there appeared massive feedlots where beef cattle were fattened or where enormous numbers of milk cattle were located. Outside of many towns, long, single-story buildings appeared where thousands of turkey, chickens, and hogs were raised according to precise scientific calculations leading to their ultimate fate on the dining room tables of the expanding American population. The new mass-production agricultural methods encouraged the establishment of new meat packing and poultry dressing facilities close by the feeding stations. This permitted food companies to increase profits by avoiding the higher union wage scales of the cities where processing plants had traditionally been located. It also reduced sharply the cost of shipping live birds and animals to distant urban markets for slaughter. These new processing plants were warmly welcomed by the leaders of small towns because they offered much needed employment opportunities for local workers.

However, many unforeseen and unintended consequences occurred, raising issues and questions local communities and their leaders had not anticipated. New populations moved into these towns for the low-paying jobs, introducing a racial and cultural diversity that produced unexpected challenges. Many of these new town residents were recent immigrants from Mexico, Africa, and Asia, and their presence posed new challenges for public schools and social agencies accustomed to dealing only with traditional European populations. A very high turnover in jobs, often reaching 100 percent per year, contributed to serious problems affecting housing, public schools, health delivery systems, law enforcement, and social service agencies. All of this led to a "cutting edge" where old traditions and long-time residents were confronted by a new and startlingly diverse population. One town in which these issues surfaced was Garden City, Kansas. Its story, replicated in similar ways across the Midwest, is told in an essay by anthropologist Donald D. Stull.

---

o   o   o

Since World War Two, employment in both manufacturing and agriculture has declined in the United States, while service-sector employment has increased. Only a tiny fraction of Americans work directly in agriculture, yet economic development in many rural areas hinges on adding value to raw agricultural products (Broadway 1995).

Meatpacking and poultry dressing account for much of the rural job growth in the 1980s and 1990s. One in 16 new industrial jobs is now on a poultry line (Kwik 1991), and poultry processing has become the second fastest-growing factory job in the United States (Horwitz 1994:1). Beef processing is Nebraska's largest manufacturing employer, accounting for half the state's manufacturing jobs (Ackerman 1991). Since 1985, Kansas has ranked first in beef processing; its six major plants slaughter one-fifth the national output (Dhuyvetter and Laudert 1991).

Meatpacking has brought jobs sorely needed by rural communities, and it has brought change as well. Nowhere is this change more apparent than in Garden City, Kansas, a community I have been studying since 1987.

In 1980, Garden City had a population of 18,300: 82 percent were Anglo; 16 percent were Mexican-Americans; the remaining 2 percent were made up of African, Asian, and Native Americans.

In December of that year, IBP, Inc., opened the world's largest beef plant 10 miles west of Garden City in rural Finney County. The county commissioners provided $3.5 million in property tax relief for 10 years and helped finance the construction of the plant with $100 million in industrial revenue bonds. In 1983, another beef plant, now owned by Monfort, opened on Garden City's eastern edge (Stull, Broadway, and Erickson 1992). Today, these two plants combine to employ about 4,700 workers who slaughter and process more than 10,000 head of cattle a day.

An abundance of cattle, plenty of water, and tax incentives attracted both IBP and Monfort to Garden City. But like most small towns, Garden City did not have enough workers to meet the labor demands of such large manufacturers.

Companies like IBP and Monfort say they want to hire local workers. But work in a packinghouse is hard—and dangerous (Stull 1994; Stull and Broadway 1995). Turnover is high: 6–8 percent a month in established plants, and double that or higher when plants first open (Wood 1988; Hackenberg and Kukulka 1995). As a result, companies soon exhaust local sup-

plies of surplus labor and are forced to recruit from increasingly distant locations (Gouveia and Stull 1995).

In the five years after IBP opened in December 1980, Garden City added
6,000 people, growing by one-third. Over the course of the 1980s, the
county—Finney—grew by 39 percent, making it the fastest growing in the
state (Broadway and Stull 1991).

In 1980, less than 100 Southeast Asians—"first wave" refugees sponsored
by local churches—lived in Garden City. After IBP opened, Southeast
Asians began coming to Garden City in significant numbers. Estimated at
about 2,000 people, they now make up about 7 percent of the population.
Most are "second wave" Vietnamese, but Laotians, Cambodians, and Ethnic Chinese live there as well.

Garden City's Southeast Asians have attracted national attention, but
they are not the only new immigrants. Hispanics have also come seeking
work in packinghouses and feedyards. Most are of Mexican origin, but immigrants from six other Latin American countries have settled there (Cuba,
El Salvador, Nicaragua, Honduras, Guatemala, and the Dominican Republic). More recently, Somalis, Mayan Indians, and Mexican Mennonites have
also appeared.

Since 1980 Garden City has been transformed from a bicultural community of established Anglo and Mexican-Americans into a multicultural
one, with a dynamic mix of peoples, languages, and cultures. Today, Garden
City is arguably the most cosmopolitan community in the state. But along
with increasing cultural and linguistic diversity, Garden City's rapid growth
has also produced major social and economic impacts.

Social and Economic Changes in Garden City, 1980–1990

Building on new jobs in beefpacking, Garden City and Finney County have
sustained a prolonged period of economic growth, even as economic conditions have deteriorated throughout much of rural America. Employment in
the county rose by 55 percent (4,200 jobs) from 1980 to 1988, and the gain
in local payroll has led to growth in the service and retail sectors (Broadway
and Stull 1991:4). Garden City emerged from the 1980s as the primary trade
and service center for the surrounding region, surpassing its chief rivals,
Dodge City (Ford County) and Liberal (Seward County), for the capital of
beefpacking's "golden triangle."

But most of these new jobs pay low wages. Gross annual income for
beefpacking line workers ranges from approximately $13,500 to about
$23,500 depending on job grade and length of employment. Wages average
about $8.50 an hour, which yields an annual gross salary of $17,680 (Hackenberg and Kukulka 1995:198). Most new jobs outside the packinghouses
are in the service sector and are characterized by even lower wages and part-

Table 1
Average Monthly Caseloads in "Safety-Net" Social Services

Program	Average Monthly Caseload
Aid to Families With Dependent Children (AFDC)	1,028 persons
Low-Income Energy Assistance (LIEAP)	1,505
Food Stamps	2,475
Medicaid Eligible	4,519

Source: Hackenberg and Kukulka, 1995:202.

time employment. Many who work in these new jobs must rely on social service agencies for supplemental food, medical care, and other basic needs. The magnitude of this demand is reflected in the average monthly caseloads for AFDC, LIEAP, food stamps, and Medicaid in Garden City.

As you would expect in any rapidly growing community, school enrollment has soared in Garden City. From 1980 to 1990, it jumped by 45 percent, an increase of over 2,000 students (Stull 1994:115). Official enrollments for the 1996–1997 academic year reached 7,325, up 11 percent from 1990, and 62 percent above 1980, when Garden City's era of rapid growth began. Along with rapid growth has come increased ethnic diversity. In the 1995–1996 school year "minority" students became the majority in the Garden City public schools (51 percent overall; 56 percent of elementary students) (Meschberger 1996a:1). In the 1996–1997 school year the official count identified 54 percent of the district's students as minorities, up from 36 percent in 1989. Bilingual and English-as-a-second-language (ESL) programs have grown tremendously. Recruitment of minority and bilingual teachers is a priority, but it also remains a serious problem—only 9 percent of the district's 540 teachers are bilingual (Meschberger 1996c:1).

Soaring enrollment and increasing numbers of non-English-speaking students are significant challenges to the educational mission of the Garden City schools, but they are not the only ones. In 1990, Garden City's school district had the highest dropout rate in Kansas. Of ninth graders in 1986, 36 percent dropped out by the time their class graduated in 1990 (Broadway and Stull 1991:6). Chronic absenteeism and student turnover are problems of staggering proportions. Forty-five percent of all students—3,289—moved in or out of Garden City's schools after the first day of classes of the 1995–1996 school year (Meschberger 1996b:1).

High dropout rates, absenteeism, and turnover are related to high rates of turnover in the packinghouses. Poverty also plays a key role, as 34 percent of the district's students qualify for free school meals under the federal lunch program. Because they are poor, many students must work; two-thirds of those in high school work, one-third of them for more than 35

Table 2

Social and Educational Problems in Meatpacking's Golden Triangle

Juvenile arrests per 1,000 children	
Finney County	166
Ford County	53
Seward County	62
Kansas average	36
Births to mothers with less than a high school degree	
(as a percent of live births)	
Finney County	43%
Ford County	41%
Seward County	41%
Kansas average	17%
Births with early prenatal care	
(as a percent of total births)	
Finney County	61%
Ford County	67%
Seward County	56%
Kansas average	82%
Children approved for free school meals	
(as a percent of total enrolled students)	
Finney County	34%
Ford County	36%
Seward County	36%
Kansas average	22%
Children receiving public assistance	
(as a percent of total children)	
Finney County	22%
Ford County	22%
Seward County	30%
Kansas average	18%
Dropout rates for 1993–94 school year, grades 7–12	
(all races)	
Garden City (Finney Co.) public schools	5.6%
Dodge City (Ford Co.) public schools	7.0%
Liberal (Seward Co.) public schools	4.2%
Kansas average	3.3

Source: Dropout rates from Kansas State Board of Education, 1995; all other data from 1996 Kansas Kids Count Data Book Kansas Action for Children, Inc., as cited in the *Garden City Telegram,* May 24, 1996.

Table 3
Emmaus House Meal Statistics
1986–1995

	1986	1995	% Change
Food Boxes	8,505	11,682	+37%
No. of people fed	35,305	46,934	+33%
Hot meals at table	4,158	4,160	none
Total Meals Served	71,815	93,345	+30%

Source: Emmaus House, 1996

hours a week. Officially none of the packinghouses hire anyone under 18, but underage workers have been reported, and for a time Monfort even advertised for workers in the high school newspaper. Many students are over 18, of course, and some work the second shift, going from school to the plant floor, where they work till after midnight (Broadway and Stull 1991:6).

The nature and level of social problems typically facing meatpacking communities are strikingly portrayed in Table 2. The three counties in southwest Kansas that comprise meatpacking's golden triangle—Finney (home to two plants), Ford (two plants), and Seward (one plant)—score well above the state average for indicators of poverty, educational, and health problems. These and other social problems, such as child abuse, violent and property crime, have risen dramatically since 1980 (Broadway and Stull 1991:7).

Increased demands on service providers offer another barometer of the costs of rural industrialization for Garden City. Emmaus House opened in November, 1979, and provides temporary shelter and hot meals for indigent transients and newcomers seeking work, food boxes and commodities for the community's poor. This two-story house across from Garden City's only hospital is run by two full-time staff with the assistance of a dozen or so regular volunteers. Demand for the services provided by Emmaus House has increased one-third over the past decade.

Access to health care in Garden City is declining. In 1988 there was one physician for every 858 persons in Finney County; five years later, in 1993, there was only one physician for every 1,897 persons. Health care is even more remote for the poor: of Garden City's 16 full-time equivalent primary-care physicians, only one devotes her practice exclusively to the medically indigent. She is employed by United Methodist Western Kansas Mexican-American Ministries Care Centers and Clinic, Mexican-American Ministries for short. It is the primary, in many cases the sole, provider of health care for the indigent in the golden triangle of southwest Kansas. The clinic's caseload, already high, doubled from 1990 to 1992. It continues to rise.

Table 4

Finney County's Ranking in Health Indicators by Decile
Among the 105 Counties in Kansas (10 is the poorest ranking)

Health Indicator	Decile Rank
Percent of all births to single teens	10
Percent of births lacking early prenatal care	10
Percent of children lacking adequate immunization	10
Percent of births to mothers without high school degree	10
Juvenile arrest rate per 1,000 persons under age 18	10
Reported child abuse/neglect (children under 18)	9
Percent low-birth-weight babies	8
Percent of children receiving economic assistance	8

Source: Hackenberg and Kukulka, 1995:195

Table 5

Growth in Services, 1990–1992, Mexican-American Ministries

	Patients	Prenatal Visits	Total Visits
1990	4,617	345	6,000
1991	6,128	311	7,500
1992	8,741	484	13,865

Source: Hackenberg and Kukulka, 1995:203

Community Attitudes Toward Growth and New Immigrants

Many Anglo oldtimers—with their Mexican-American counterparts—see a deteriorating quality of life in Garden City. They bemoan increasing crime and declining availability of health care, heavier traffic and schools bursting at their seams. They shake their heads and remember the days when folks didn't bother to lock their homes and cars. They admit that the packers have brought the "progress" of new jobs, more business for local merchants, and added tax revenue. But they also blame the packers for the "urban problems" now confronting their community.

So, what has all this meant for community relations in "the Garden," as the locals like to call it. Interethnic discrimination is a fact of life in Garden City, as elsewhere in the United States. The degree of discrimination depends on the group's position on the social ladder—the lower down the group, the more they are looked down upon. Inter- and intragroup relations are diverse and complex. They are enhanced or limited by linguistic, cultural, and religious similarities and differences. Fluency in English and occupation play vital roles in social class membership and upward mobility (Stull 1990).

Garden City's ethnic groups live side by side—by and large amicably—a source of comment among newcomers and outside observers. But it is social distance that best describes the community's intergroup relations. The primary social force in Garden City, after all, is population mobility, fueled by high turnover in the packing plants.

Newcomers, especially packinghouse workers, come to Garden City to find work. Their attachment to the community is fragile. The Anglo wife of a Mexican packinghouse worker put it this way:

> I don't think they feel part of Garden City, but then Garden City could be anyplace. I don't think they would feel part of Marshalltown, Iowa, or Chicago, or anyplace. . . . They were not born here. They were not raised here. It's not their home. They don't really have any ties here (Stull interview 7/26/89:8, 80).

It is not surprising the workers feel little attachment to the area. They work long, grueling hours on the line—six days a week during much of the year. Many work the B shift from 3:00 P.M. until midnight or later; still others work cleanup on C shift from midnight to 6:00 in the morning. Little time is left to meet and socialize with people outside work. Socializing is often limited to having a beer or two after work; playing in a softball or bowling league with coworkers; shopping, doing laundry, or going to the park on Sunday—the only day off when the plants are running at capacity. Many live in trailer courts on the outskirts of town, in apartments hastily constructed to meet the demands of rapid growth, or in run-down residential motels—their neighbors most often line workers like themselves. Often they speak little or no English and must rely on children or friends to translate when they do business in the majority community.

High turnover on the job translates into high mobility in the community. Monthly turnover at IBP and Monfort is 6–8 percent. Using the lowest figure, 6 percent of the 4,700 workers at the two plants amounts to 282 persons a month, or 3,384 persons a year, who leave the industry. Most do not stay in Garden City—there are few other jobs for them and they have little attachment to the community. In turn, they are replaced by 3,384 new workers, most new to town. Thus, as many as 6,768 workers move into and out of the community each year—more than one-fourth of the town's population—and this does not take into account members of their immediate families.

Meatpacking workers are not the only ones who come and go in Garden City. Using school records, we monitored households who were new to Garden City in the 1986–1987 school year. Within one year, 44 percent of the cohort had left the community; a year later, another 20 percent were gone—two years after arrival only a third of the newcomers remained. Surprisingly, there was no statistically significant difference in the length of stay between Anglos, Hispanics, and Southeast Asians. Nor did it matter whether they worked in the beef plants. It appears that for a majority of newcomers, Garden City is just a place to stop and work for a year or two before moving on (Stull, Broadway, and Erickson 1992:59).

There are, in fact, two Garden Cities. One is a stable community of established residents, many from families who have lived there for generations. The other Garden City is highly mobile, and its residents are people who come seeking work and who stay only as long as they have a job. Their attachment to the community is a tenuous one. And when this mobility is coupled with the barriers inherent between peoples of different ethnic, cultural, and linguistic origins, stable and meaningful intergroup relations rarely form.

Relations between newcomers and established residents, between ethnic groups, and between packers and others are in many ways influenced by the packing industry. Work in the packing plants is "dirty work," and line workers are looked down upon by the larger community. While the shared stigma—and pride—of work in the packinghouses can build bonds that cross ethnic and language boundaries, the nature of the work and the workplace offsets such bonding. Interaction and communication on the line are kept to a minimum by the noise and the speed of the chain, and each worker has a specialized or unique task. While workers are expected to "pull their count," to be part of a team, they do so because "they are looking out for Number One." The "uncooperative teamwork" (Thompson 1983:223) and anonymity of the disassembly line are exacerbated by cultural and linguistic diversity.

This mobility disrupts the community while at the same time allowing many to tolerate its rapid growth and ethnic diversity. School administrators are unable to plan rationally for next year's enrollment, as they watch pupils come and go throughout the school year (Grey 1990). Crime and social problems keep going up. Yet, there is little evidence of significant overt conflict between newcomers and established residents. This seems to be in large part because newcomers are not seen as competitors for scarce economic resources. In fact, they serve a "dirty" but necessary economic function (Meara 1974).

Many people in the established community view the newcomers as transient and believe the packinghouses will one day close and the workers will move on. The plants are not likely to close, and Garden City's newcomer populations are there to stay, even if individuals do come and go at an amazing rate.

But others welcome their community's growing cultural diversity and work diligently to meet the accompanying challenges. Early on, the clergy, newspaper editors and reporters, school administrators and teachers, police, and social service providers worked hard to keep negative consequences of the influx of newcomers to a minimum. They still do. As a result, Garden

City has become a model for other communities who must also find a way to cope with rural industrialization, rapid growth, and ethnic diversity.

Garden City is not what most Americans imagine a "typical" Kansas community to be like. But it is in fact typical of the social, economic, and demographic changes that many American communities are experiencing, and what many more will experience in the years ahead.

It would be misleading to say that Garden City has successfully adjusted to the changes that meatpacking brought to the community in 1980. It would mislead you about both what has happened in Garden City and what is happening in other towns that play host to meat processing plants. The people of Garden City have traveled far since 1980, of that there is no doubt. But the road ahead is long and winding. In many ways, Garden City still belongs to the sedentary oldtimers; the newcomers, especially Hispanics and Southeast Asians, live and work there but never become fully part of the community. The beef plants, with their high turnover and dangerous working conditions, are the prime factor in community relations. They could work with the community to ameliorate the demands their industry makes on Garden City, but they choose not to do so. Until forced to change, meatpacking companies will exact the cost of economic development they bring to job-hungry rural communities on the backs of an imported and expendable labor force. And towns such as Garden City will still pay for the jobs they crave in the wages of increased socioeconomic problems and ever greater demands on community institutions.

Once set in motion, the growth and population mobility, the cultural and linguistic diversity, the increases in social costs and social needs—indeed, the change in every facet of community life—will continue. It has not ended in Garden City. It will not end in the growing number of communities that have followed its path. Communities are dynamic, or they die. That is their nature. Garden Citians live in an exciting place in an exciting time. It is not always easy, but it is always interesting. If you live in meatpacking's shadow, it will be the same for you.

References Cited

Ackerman, Pam (1991) "All Across Nebraska, Beef is Big Business." Lexington, Nebraska, *Clipper,* May 29.

Broadway, Michael J. (1995) "From City to Countryside: Recent Changes in the Structure and Location of the Meat- and Fish-Processing Industries," *Any Way You Cut It: Meat Processing and Small-Town America.* Donald D. Stull, Michael J. Broadway, and David Griffith, eds., 17–40. Lawrence: University Press of Kansas.

Gouveia, Lourdes, and Donald D. Stull (1995) "Dances With Cows: Beefpacking's Impact on Garden City, Kansas, and Lexington, Nebraska," *Any Way You Cut It,* 85–107.

Grey, Mark A. (1990) "Immigrant Students in the Heartland: Ethnic Relations in Garden City, Kansas, High School," *Urban Anthropology* 19: 409–427.

Hackenberg, Robert A., and Gary Kukulka (1995) "Industries, Immigrants, and Illness in the New Midwest," *Any Way You Cut It*, 187–211.

Horwitz, Tony (1994) "9 to Nowhere: Blues on the Chicken Line," *Wall Street Journal*, December 1:A1, A8–9.

Kwik, Phill (1991) "Poultry Workers Trapped in a Modern Jungle," *Labor Notes* 146:1, 14–15.

Meara, Hannah (1974) "Honor in Dirty Work: The Case of American Meatcutters and Turkish Butchers," *Sociology of Work and Occupations* 1:259–282.

Meschberger, Alesa (1996a) "Minorities Near School Majority," *Garden City Telegram*, August 21: 1–2.

— (1996b) "A Tale of Turnover: USD 457 Students on the Move." *Garden City Telegram*, September 21:1–2.

— (1996c) "Minorities Reach Majority Status," *Garden City Telegram*, November 9:1, 3.

Stull, Donald D. (1990) "'I Come to the Garden': Changing Ethnic Relations in Garden City, Kansas," *Urban Anthropology* 19:303–320.

— (1994) "Of Meat and (Wo)Men: Meatpacking's Consequences for Communities," *Kansas Journal of Law & Public Policy* 3(3): 112–118.

— (1994) "Knock 'Em Dead: Work on the Killfloor of a Modern Beefpacking Plant," *Newcomers in the Workplace: Immigrants and the Restructuring of the U.S. Economy*. Louise Lamphere, Alex Stepick, and Guillermo Grenier, eds., 44–77. Philadelphia: Temple University Press.

Stull, Donald D., and Michael Broadway (1995) "Killing them Softly: Work in Meatpacking Plants and What It Does to Workers," *Any Way You Cut It*, 61–83.

Stull, Donald D., Michael J. Broadway, and Ken C. Erickson (1992) "The Price of a Good Steak: Beef Packing and its Consequences for Garden City, Kansas," *Structuring Diversity: Ethnographic Perspectives on the New Immigration*. Louise Lamphere, ed., 35–64. Chicago: University of Chicago Press.

Thompson, William E. (1983) "Hanging Tongues: A Sociological Encounter with the Assembly Line," *Qualitative Sociology* 6:215–237.

Wood, Anita (1988) "The Beef Packing Industry: A Study of Three Communities in Southwestern Kansas: Dodge City, Liberal and Garden City." Final Report to the Department of Migrant Education. Flagstaff, AZ: Wood and Wood Associates.

Village Character: The Pioneer Store

FROM *Winter Book*

NORBERT BLEI

A S THEIR AGRICULTURAL BASES ERODED during the twentieth century, some midwestern towns survived and even prospered by developing alternative economies. Many were absorbed into expanding urban centers, transforming themselves from villages to suburbs. Four-lane highways allowed others not exactly contiguous with cities to prosper as safe bedroom communities for less safe business or industrial centers. Other small towns developed local industries, often value-added projects based on timber or crop resources. Still others developed tourist economies based on accidents of local history, scenic beauty, or newly constructed recreational opportunities for skiing, gambling, growing old, or listening to country music. Like any form of change, these new economies altered the village character and attracted a new kind of resident with attitudes at odds with traditional village values.

Door County forms the thumb of the mitten that the state of Wisconsin vaguely resembles. On the west side of that thumb lies Green Bay; on the east side lies Lake Michigan. Traditionally a land of dairy farms, cherry orchards, and fishing villages, Door County has for a century attracted a significant number of tourists from Chicago and Milwaukee, who came north in the summer months for cool weather, pleasant scenery, and good food. Tourism was concentrated in Egg Harbor, with its White Gull Inn; Ephraim, with Wilson's Ice Cream Parlor; and Bailey's Harbor with the Bailey's Harbor Yacht Club. Older restaurants like Al Johnson's Swedish Restaurant in Sister Bay, grand hotels like the Hotel du Nord in Ellison Bay, and—starting in mid-century—various mom-and-pop motels all catered to the summer visitors.

In the late twentieth century, the Door County tourist industry exploded as the urban middle class grew more affluent, the World War II generation reached retirement age, and the Door County dairy and fishing industries declined. Old centers of tourism, especially those on the Green Bay side of the peninsula, became clogged with cars bearing out-of-state license plates; homes and even churches were remodeled into gift shops and restaurants; complexes of condominiums, motels, and apartments sprouted where cows had once grazed. The delicate balance between an agricultural economy and tourism, between native and outsider, between local standards and imported values collapsed.

Writer Norbert Blei—himself a 1970 arrival from suburban Chicago, and neither a farmer nor a fisherman nor an orchardman—has chronicled the transformation of Door County and his adopted hometown of Ellison Bay in a series of books: *Door Way, Door Steps, Door to Door, Meditations on a Small Lake,* and most recently *Winter Book.* In "Village Character," Blei ponders the transformation of small-town character as it applies specifically to the local general store and a couple of old-timers: Lester Newman, who sold groceries, and Gust Klenke, who purchased groceries and supplied Newman with honey. Their relationship and others like it, Blei suggests, was as responsible for the special flavor of Ellison Bay as the language of the citizens and the paint on the buildings. In the book *Another Turn of the Crank,* Wendell Berry points out that "cooperation between local farmers and local consumers" is a cornerstone of community, and for both farmers and townspeople to survive "the long-broken connections between towns and cities and their surrounding landscapes will have to be restored." Blei wholeheartedly agrees.

o o o

(In Memory of a Small Shopkeeper, Lester Newman)

A death in the town of Ellison Bay a few years ago caused the writer to reflect again upon the past, present, and future of Door County—where we were as a community, where we are now as a tourist attraction, and where we're headed.

One of the local writer's main concerns then and now is the erosion of character in our small towns and villages as tourist commerce, unchecked, insidiously works its way up and down Main Street desecrating old stores, eliminating public buildings, churches, and private homes till nothing is left but a cutesy façade of upscale buildings brightly lit, catering to every tourist taste from teddies to teddy bears. Call it Boutique Blight.

Razing or remodeling structures, painting them garish colors (lavender and hot pink the favorite hues) adding flying pennants, wind socks, tiny Christmas lights, glow-in-the-dark-all-night soda pop machines, and large OPEN signs, just in case the poor tourist fails to notice that the once old local business is now US, and ain't we cute, smart, mini-malled to cater to your every whim. And as for what was once old Olafson's white painted frame house built in the early 1900s with the small front porch and the American flag hanging beside the door, well, all that's ancient history, folks. Check us out. Ain't we hot: pink, and lavender, with a large fancy sign on the front lawn: DOOR COUNTY UNIVERSITY T-SHIRTS. (Another original Door County business idea.)

Turning traditional white steepled churches in the heart of our towns, villages, and countryside into trendy little gift shops is yet another sign of our time and decline. Building brand new, super-churches just to cater to the burgeoning influx of summer worshipers is yet another. ("God's Condo" the local writer dubbed one of these edifices that began to take root and sprawl in his vicinity. What looks like a drive-thru window has more recently been installed. Along with a steeple anchored to the ground. Blessed be [not] the ministers who build monuments unto themselves.)

So much for local character. Small white churches that sang to the spirit of us all just because they were there in history, in plain view of local and tourist alike, speaking quietly of a faith we could all honor, are now marketed, face-lifted, to retain just the right touch of the old spirit (a single stained-glass window, a spotlight on the steeple after dark) to beckon the new spirit of the shop-till-you-drop-believers: Welcome to St. Bazaar, the Church of Big Bucks. How about some plastic seagulls for your front lawn? Leaving us all, tourists, transplants, and locals alike, short-changed—in the long run. Leaving us with architectural wonders, "Nouveau Door Grotesque." Leaving us hollow villages and towns, caricatures of themselves, which may as well be numbered as named, with no meaning or history of any consequence other than the sizzle of summer commerce. No real stores with real products, or buildings with any sense of why they are there for the local inhabitants. Not a single authentic shopkeeper minding the store. Gas stations to gift shops, town halls to tourist offices, churches to candle shops. Absentee ownership, any-old-salesperson. Businesses to be resold next year, transformed into yet another unique clothing store, coffeeshop, internet cafe, run by nobody-knows-my-name (or cares).

Which brings me back to the death of Lester Newman, small town shopkeeper, teacher, proprietor, along with his wife, Carol and family, of the Pioneer Store in Ellison Bay. A man and a woman and a business who fit naturally into the Door County woodwork, defining the true meaning of pride in place.

The Pioneer Store *is* Ellison Bay, as much as the old bridge *is* Sturgeon Bay, Al Johnson's Restaurant *is* Sister Bay, and Wilson's *is* Ephraim. Who can miss it? No windsocks. No pennants. No neon. No glamour, no glitz. No nothing but GENERAL STORE. The fact that it still exists, is still "operational" in the oldest and present sense, in these "tear-down-for-tourist-times" in Door is miracle enough. A genuine wooden storefront, posts and gingerbread in need of periodic coats of white paint, with large windows that reflect all the truth and beauty of small town life passing by.

A building so right-where-it-is, even Hollywood set-designers might envy it, and fail miserably to re-create what it is and what it stands for. Preservation in place, in the here and now, and functioning very well as is, thank you, without perverting its location or the character of the town around it to sudden schlocky economic factors of summer design, all for the sake of business. History in the now. Door County as it once was and is. Open—whenever you need it.

When the writer speaks of lost village character, he speaks of the inevitable loss (here in Ellison Bay and in surrounding area) of people as well—hardworking, authentic, and self-effacing Door County originals like Gust Klenke and his falling-down garage; Walter Severson, the old postmaster, who ran the office out of his house; Sid Telfer Sr. and his orchards; Iron John Fitzgerald, dock-building, earthmover; Carl (Pa) Carlson and his brother John, the local plumber on call 24-hours a day, 365 days a year (Pay what and when you can; a fella's got to help his neighbor—Pa's golden rule); all, alas, gone. And never to be replaced by tourists, transplants, condo clones, or any member of the Boutiques-R-Us-Unlimited and their attempt to sell plenty of nothing to everybody, paint the town pink, and bulldoze what is, what's left, what's real.

The writer speaks for that handful of businesses and people still here, still holding down the fort in downtown Ellison Bay: Kenny Gobel's gas station, Danny Peterson's Viking Restaurant, Kubie Luchterhand's used book store, Larry (Lighthouse) Thoreson's pottery shop, the remains of Gust Klenke's gas station, and the late Lester's Pioneer Store (now Carol's).

Long may all these business and local business people thrive, though the latest invasion of condo communities in "our town" contain within their development the seeds of destruction, the loss of what once was us. Good-bye Pioneer Store and Gobel's gas station, inevitably, and hello Quik Stop Convenience Store. So long old, locally-owned, lived-in, white-framed houses along the main road; hello gift shop, boutique, boutique-gallery-gift shop ad infinitum. And thank you, developers all, for nothing. Nothing but your personal greed.

What's gained? What's left that was once functional, meaningful, real? As real as the late Lester Newman behind the worn, wooden counter of the Pioneer, who seemed so perfectly in place you really thought you were living in Sinclair Lewis' *Main Street*, Thorton Wilder's *Our Town*, Edgar Lee Masters' *Spoon River*. Lester himself, a man of few words, his gaze always lowered to the counter, destined to remain forever, it seemed, just minding the old store. Lester of the serious disposition, the boyish demeanor, the puckish smile, the slow, staccato conversation—a bit of the trickster about him:

"Weeelll [pause], at least the Packers can't lose today," he might say, waiting for you to take the bait.

"Why's that, Lester?" Long pause.

"It's a bye week. The Packers . . . do . . . not . . . play . . . today." Followed by that Lester Newman Igotcha smile.

To have overheard a Pioneer Store conversation of the past between Lester and Gust Klenke, bee keeper, mechanic, all around handyman of fewer words than Lester on any given day, was to have been part of local color, local history.

"You got any honey, Gust?" asked Lester.

Long, long pause. "Yeeeeeeeep," the characteristic Gust Klenke response as he dug deep into the pockets of his frayed bib overalls, looking for some change to put on the counter for the loaf of bread he was buying.

Outside the store it was spring, or it was summer, or fall, but almost always winter, as I remember it. The quiet time. The lights on in the old store. The dusty grotesque looking plants struggling for warmth in the front windows, the old fashioned stove in the center of the store radiating waves of warmth, the antiques high up on the shelves near the old ceiling looking even more antique, cans and boxes and bags and crates and cartons and bottles and packages and freezers and display cases of food everywhere from floor to ceiling, front to back, yet all in a very small space. You could get everything you want at Alice's Restaurant, so that '60s song went, but you could get all that and more at Newman's Pioneer Store.

It was morning, afternoon, or night. But mostly night. Mostly winter. Snow was falling outside the big windows. There were almost no cars on the road. Gust was down to picking pennies out of his hand and laying them down on the counter to pay Lester. "I could use a few jars, if you got 'em."

A long pause. You could hear the fire crackle in the stove, the wind picking up outside and blowing fresh snow across the big front windows of the Pioneer. What a perfect moment to recall the taste of honey on fresh bread, a dollop of honey in a cup of hot tea. Gust Klenke's honey. How sweet a time it is, it was. "Yeeeeep."

Village character. Community. An unspoken love of place and people-in-place. The very soul of a county lost in time in a way that both redeems and honors that within us which needs a place to be, rather than diminish, replace, or destroy all that speaks of local culture, local life, putting in momentary place a fast-talking, quick-dollar culture that speaks only the language of "want" but never "need" or "be."

"Anytime."

"Yeeeeep."

Gust walks out of the store with a loaf of bread under his arm, pulls his cap down firmer on his forehead, unties his dog, Tragedy, leashed to the post outside, and makes his way home in the dark, snowy evening with nothing but bread and honey on his mind. While inside the Pioneer Store, Lester opens the daily paper on the wooden counter and waits for whoever may need something next, only pretending to read the news which is elsewhere, far away from Ellison Bay.

A Broken Heartland

FROM *U.S. News and World Report*

JEFF GLASSER

I N THE SPRING OF 2001 a national news magazine reported on the continuing population decline of the nation's heartland—the sprawling Great Plains that lie on the western edge of the Midwest. The story provides further documentation that the processes identified by earlier generations of journalists and social scientists continue unabated. As early as 1907 a concerned Theodore Roosevelt had recognized this trend and created a special presidential Commission on Country Life to find ways to stop the farm-to-city migration. Obviously he and many who followed failed to find ways to make life somehow appealing when the summers are searing hot, the winters blistering cold, and the wind blows all the time.

The changes that have occurred in agricultural economics during the twentieth century have made life on the Great Plains even less attractive; the result has been the making of a new generation of veritable ghost towns like Larson, North Dakota, as described in the journalistic account that follows. In 1994 a *New York Times* writer visited central Nebraska and discovered that even if jobs were plentiful in this agricultural region it would be difficult, if not impossible, to keep the brightest and most ambitious high school graduates. The lure of the city had become irresistible: "The failure of these places to retain their young people has traditionally been explained by a lack of jobs," he wrote. "But the talk among teen-agers on the Great Plains now reveals something deeper, a lament that no job in a small town is worth staying for." A local businessman summed up this new attitude: "It's a tragedy that people in small towns feel the only way they can be successful is to leave. In the age of cable television, rural kids get all these messages and images that suggest that all the exciting things are happening far away from them, and it's hard to explain that it's not necessarily the truth." Faced with worldwide gluts on the commodities markets and the escalating price of energy, the future of Larson, and thousands of farming towns like it, was bleak indeed as the new millennium began to unfold.

o   o   o

Larson, N.D.—The white steeple of St. John's German Lutheran Church lists from the weight of its rusted, half-ton church bell. The 93-year-old church's pews, pulpit, baptismal font, and, most important, congregants have vanished. At the end of a deserted Main Street, tumbleweeds obscure the Great Northern Railroad tracks where trains once routinely carried the world's finest durum wheat to the trade centers of the Midwest.

Across from the tracks stands the Larson Hotel, its paint peeling, its roof about to be patched with discarded aluminum newspaper printing plates. It is now home to a disabled construction worker and his family who moved here from Pennsylvania last fall, saying they could only afford to live in the middle of nowhere. An empty lot away sits the X-treme North Bar and Barely South Restaurant, a last-chance saloon with a rich history of bourbon and burlesque.

Welcome to Larson, population 17, the least populated place in one of the nation's fastest-declining counties. Burke County, N.D., lost 25.3 percent of its population in the past 10 years, falling from 3,002 to 2,242, according to 2000 census figures released this spring. Its neighbor, Divide County, shrank by 21 percent, from 2,899 to 2,283, during the same period. The two counties are littered with dozens of Larsons, Northgates, and Alkabos—virtual ghost towns that grew up as stops for steam trains and died along with the railroads. Larson has withered to the point where none of its residents—including the candidate—bothered to vote in last June's election for alderman. Four miles down state Highway 5 in Columbus, all that remains of the 74-year-old brick high school are 700 commemorative letter openers hand carved by the town elder out of its maple floors and given away as mementos. To the north, dozens of Canadian oil rigs, coal mines, and a SaskPower plant loom in the distance, a mirage of economic activity 25 miles away but a country apart. To the west, past forgotten little houses on the prairie, Crosby's cemeteries have so many fresh mounds that it looks like badgers have dug there all winter. "We're going to have to start importing pallbearers," jokes Crosby farmer Ole Svangstu, 55, noting there were 48 more deaths than births last year.

Ghost towns

Up and down the Great Plains, the country's spine, from the Sandhills of western Nebraska to the sea of prairie grass in eastern Montana, small towns are decaying, and in some cases, literally dying out. The remarkable prosperity of the last decade never reached this far. Nearly 60 percent (250 of 429) of the counties on the Great Plains lost population in the 1990s, according to a *U.S. News* analysis of the new census data.

The emptying out of the nation's rural breadbasket was all the more surprising considering the population resurgence in cities and suburbs. The nation as a whole grew at a robust 13 percent. The 10 states of the Plains, too, expanded by 10 percent overall, a 672,554-person increase fueled by the growth of cities like Billings, Mont., and the tremendous urban sprawl that swallowed the countryside adjacent to Denver, Austin, and San Antonio. Some larger rural areas in the Plains also blossomed from their natural beauty as recreation areas, but the picture was bleak in counties with fewer than 15,000 people, where 228 of 334 (nearly 70 percent) of the counties regressed. "It's like the parting of the Red Sea," says Fannie Mae demographer Robert Lang, a census expert. "There are rivers of people flowing out of the [rural] Plains."

The degeneration of a large swath of this country's midsection—covering a 317,320-square-mile area spread over parts of the 10 states—has not seeped into the conscience of urban America. City dwellers might still perceive small towns as refuges from society's maddening stew of gridlock, smog, and crime. Where else can a visitor leave a car unlocked, not to mention *running*, on a quick trip to the post office? Farmers in small towns are considered the ultimate entrepreneurs, "our national icon of autonomy," as Yale Prof. Kathryn Marie Dudley writes in *Debt and Dispossession: Farm Loss in America's Heartland*. But, as Dudley points out, the contemporary ideal collides with a harsh economic reality.

The problem is seemingly intractable. Once thriving mining and railroad commerce are distant memories. The farm economy has been in a state of contraction for at least 30 years. Forty-two percent of Midwestern farmers, the dominant economic group, earn less than $20,000 annually. A lack of Plains industry limits other opportunities for professionals. Jeff Peterson, 53, Burke County's sole lawyer, sighs wistfully as he explains why he's packing it in after 26 years. "There just aren't so many people for clients now," says Peterson. There aren't even enough people to justify having county judges. Nearly everyone else has already left Burke County, bailing out when their farming and oil and gas jobs dried up in the late 1980s and early 1990s. Peterson says he will have to write off his $120,000 office building. So far, he has found no takers for his $135,000 house. "This wasn't a smart place to invest in," he says.

Manifest destiny

That wasn't always the case. From Thomas Jefferson's stewardship of the Louisiana Purchase, which included present day Burke and Divide counties, sprang forth the concept of America's "Manifest Destiny" to inhabit all the nation's land. In 1862, Congress passed the Homestead Act, giving immigrants free 160-acre parcels called "quarters." Northwestern North Dakota was one of the final places homesteaded. At the turn of the 20th century, the region filled with Norwegians, Swedes, Danes, Belgians, and a few Germans. The territory was so forbidding that it had no trees, so the pioneers built sod homes on a virgin landscape described by novelist Willa Cather as "nothing but land, not a country at all, but the material out of which countries are made."

Postmaster Columbus Larson's settlement on the western tip of Burke County split in two with the coming of the railroads. Half set up in front of the Great Northern tracks at "Larson," half 4 miles to the northeast next to the Soo Line at "Columbus." By 1930, every quarter in Burke and Divide was inhabited, with what would be a peak 19,634 people on the land. Crowds gathered on Saturday nights at the Opera House in Larson to dance the polka and listen to traditional Norwegian yodeling. Colorful vaudeville troops headlined the marquee at Columbus Theater. Lawrence Welk and his dance band played his signature "champagne music" there. Bootleggers peddled liquor during Prohibition, and the Larson Opera House was the place for bawdy pantomime. Occasionally the townspeople gathered on Main Street and fearfully watched local young men test their strength against that of bears for cash prizes (provided they won).

In the "dirty Thirties," pioneer women placed wet bedsheets over windows to keep out dust. The perseverance and courage of the settlers—lionized by Cather in her novel *O Pioneers!*—were tested as the soil crumbled in a series of crop disasters. Most of Larson's 114 residents left the Dust Bowl behind in search of an easier life. Columbus continued to boom in the immediate post–World War II period, though, with coal miners, power-plant workers, farmers, and a few oil roughnecks keeping the place full. The town peaked with nearly 700 people in the early 1950s. Then the coal mines closed, and the local power plant shut down. Advances in technology improved crop yields, so far fewer people were needed to farm the land. A series of government conservation programs prompted hundreds of local farmers to retire to Arizona, exacerbating the exodus.

In 1972, Columbus still had 20 businesses. Larson was hanging on with six shops, including Witty's grocery store and Ole Johnson's gas station. Virtually all are gone today. Columbus, with just 151 residents, has one cafe and a farm tool supplier, both set to close later this year. The only eatery left in Larson is the X-treme North Bar and Barely South Restaurant, which may also close. "The handwriting's on the wall," says Harold Pasche, 80, a retired farmer from Larson who now lives in Columbus. "Every little town in this whole area here is going down." The collapse of the retail trade in Columbus and Larson mirrors a national decline. From 1977 to 1997, the

number of American grocery stores fell by 61.2 percent, men's clothing
stores dropped by 46.6 percent, and hardware stores slipped by 40.6 percent,
according to the Census of Retail Trade. Ken Stone, an Iowa State University economist specializing in rural development, says small-town Main
Streets are going the way of the railroads. "There's very little way to bring
[them] back," he says.

On the farm, net income is projected to decline 20 percent in the next
two years because of a worldwide depression in commodity prices and
higher energy costs. Without government intervention, 10 percent of farmers could not survive one year, says former Agriculture Secretary Dan Glickman. He calls federal farm subsidies "rural support" programs and fears
"economic devastation in large parts of rural America" if the government
nixes them. Yet President Bush's budget package does not allocate any disaster money for farmers, who in the past three years received $25 billion in
extra federal relief. Despite Glickman's warnings, there is little room in today's debate for Jeffersonian programs to resettle the Plains. People simply
do not want to deal with harsh winters and broiling summers. "It's still a
loser in [Plains] politics to say, 'Let them die,'" says Frank Popper, a Rutgers
University land-use expert. "You've got an ongoing aversion, a denial of
what's going on. But every year there are fewer farmers and ranchers. Every
year they are losing their kids." In 1988, Popper and his wife, Deborah, also
a professor, dreamed up a radical alternative for the rural Plains: a vast "Buffalo Commons," in which the federal government would return the territory to its pristine state before white settlement, when the buffalo roamed
and the prairie grasses grew undisturbed.

Where the buffalo roam?

Farmers hated the idea. But in the decade that followed, thousands of miles
on the Northern Plains have reverted to "wilderness" areas with buffalo
herds and fewer than two people per square mile. "I actually think this is the
last American frontier," says Larson's town treasurer, Debra Watterud, 53.

That leaves places like Larson and Columbus with even fewer totems of
their town histories. The latter held its final Columbus Day Parade in 1992,
when Pasche drove his treasured 1932 Chevrolet Roadster down Main one
last time. At the last major civic gathering in 1994, residents scooped up
bricks and floor planks from the soon-to-be-demolished high school. Doug
Graupe, 56, a Divide County farmer, argues that the remaining residents
have an obligation to their ancestors to persevere. "Economics shouldn't
drive every decision," he says. "Do you have to have money to have a good
quality of life? . . . People in small towns are always there to help others, to
raise kids. You have a sense of community." Graupe and others in the region
are excited about a $2.5 million pasta processing plant that they're planning

to build in nearby Crosby, but not everyone's confident it will succeed, given the perilous demographics and the area's previous failed attempts at renewal.

In Larson, Debra Watterud proposed shutting down the town after the no-show election because the level of interest was so low. Her father-in-law, retired farmer Myron Watterud, 76, opposed the idea. If Larson deincorporated, he said, who would pay for the lights (which consumes half the $3,000 town budget)? The town would disappear from maps. No one would ever bring it back, a possibility that's hard to fathom for a man who has spent his life here. His daughter-in-law agreed to table her suggestion, but Myron Watterud says he's "scared" to watch the town in the approaching darkness of its final demise. "If the leaders of this town saw what happened," he says, "they'd turn over in their graves."

Business First and Always

FROM *Rethinking Home*

JOSEPH A. AMATO

DURING THE PAST TWO DECADES Joseph A. Amato and his colleagues have focused scholarly attention on the southwestern corner of his adopted state of Minnesota. The result has been a series of books and articles illuminating the region's social, cultural, political, and economic life, turning it into a veritable laboratory for regional study. Ultimately, Amato's work led to the establishment at Southwest State University of the unique Center for Rural and Regional Studies.

In 2002 Amato synthesized his singular regional studies into a broad historical perspective. In *Rethinking Home: A Case for Writing Local History*, he contends that the local historian holds a key to a better understanding of American history and that intensive research into local matters, both major and mundane, illuminates both national historical events and contemporary issues. In the final chapter Amato focuses on the role of business in influencing a regional lead city.

Upon first glance a visitor to Marshall—a town of nearly 13,000 located about thirty miles from the South Dakota and eighty miles from the Iowa borders—is likely to take it to be another nondescript midwestern town. A relatively prosperous and sturdy community built around railroad, river, and highway, it serves as a regional economic, medical, and political center for a thinly populated surrounding farming area. But as Amato explains, there is much more to Marshall than meets the eye. Created as a railroad outpost in the turbulent times following the Civil War, Marshall became a microcosm for the changes that have occurred within American life ever since. Today it is a small regional center blessed or afflicted—depending upon one's viewpoint—with its own small university, home to a prosperous multinational agribusiness corporation that peddles frozen foods around the world, but held hostage by continued decline in the surrounding rural population. Its central business district has fallen upon hard times, while a strip mall on the town's edge has taken on increased importance in the daily ebb and flow of local commerce. Chain stores and franchised businesses have largely driven out local merchants, while the recent influx of immigrants from such disparate places as Somalia, Laos, and Mexico has led to new dimensions of diversity within the community. Intensified levels of in- and out-migration have produced, in a town that once prided itself on its neighborliness, a "community of strangers." The issue of diminishing local autonomy continues unabated, as local elected officials find that they more often than not are forced to follow the dictates and decrees of distant federal and state governments while attempting to mollify the increasingly conflicting demands of local citizens. Meanwhile the forces of consolidation, conflict, and change continue, producing increased turbulence in what appears on the surface to be a quiet midwestern town.

o o o

Business history throws opens the door to the history of the prairie. Every village is an economic entity whose well-being is measured by profit and loss. The country town, however much it informs American sentiment and culture, is first and foremost about business. Importing dreams and laws as well as products and goods, business forms the principal purpose and lubricant of small towns. As reluctant as a cultural historian like me might be to admit it, business makes the whole countryside go.

Business history, however, is no simple subject. Rather, it forms a network with endless branches for local and regional historians. And, to my consolation, in the end, if business history is carefully followed, one branch of it leads back to cultural history, for making money and participating in a capitalist society are undertakings of the individual and collective mind. Scratch the smallest crystal of commerce on the prairie and we find the largest economic galaxy reflected in it. In a single southwestern prairie town—my example is Marshall, Minnesota—the historian can observe the articulation of national and international markets, the growth of specialization, and the dramatic transformation of contemporary rural life.

The twentieth-century prairie story is more about turbulence and transformation than about continuity and permanence. It can even largely be seen as the onset of irreversible and overpowering decline, as Richard Davies observes in *Main Street Blues*.[1] My argument here is that decline and growth are dramatically fused in the contemporary countryside. Disrupted by economic cycles, transformed by changing technologies, altered by contracting and expanding markets, and influenced by politics, the prairie is awhirl with change. It is no place for historians to seek fixed souls and enduring communities.

A Business of Global Implications

Of course, local historians can restrict their scope to histories of individual
businesses and business owners. Main Street past offers countless stories of
the twists and turns of the fate of single-family businesses. Almost every region records the success story of a local son or daughter. In Marshall, for instance, a Russian Jew, Louis Weiner, and his two sons, Julius and Benjamin,
founded a multimillion-dollar food industry in the 1930s and 1940s. In later
decades a young Marshall-born entrepreneur named Marvin Schwan turned
a local ice cream company into a multibillion-dollar manufacturer and dis-
tributor of frozen food. Frequently, local business history mingles with the
exemplary community service of local businessmen or the idealism of their
wives, who, like Carol Kennicott in Lewis's *Main Street,* strive to make their
village the city it should be. At times, a town's growth so turns on the shared
visions of its upper class that business history seems (more to my liking) to
be an appendix to cultural history.

Like a running river, business history flows into economic history, especially railroad history, which quickly enmeshes its students in competing
economic visions of how to organize the world. Railroad magnates' dreams
of connecting farm and city, east and west ensnared farmers, merchants,
and speculators in visions of wealth. The equation that underlay the vast
railroad projects linked government and business in a symbiotic partner-
ship. Government gave the railroads vast amounts of property, which the
railroads in turn sold to recover their investment. They thrived by hauling
products out of the countryside and carrying goods and people back in.
Towns prospered by serving as exchange points between city and countryside. As railroads moved west, with more help from European capital and
the federal government (including its army), towns were founded, farms
were established, native people were removed, and vast ecological zones
were converted to agricultural lands to feed an emerging urban nation.

In this way, as suggested in chapter 3, American civilization marched
west town by town in tune with European expansion. As nations and markets took control of the European countryside, the Americas were settled.
As Africa was colonized and China nearly annexed, the great grasslands of
Russia, Latin America, and the United States were opened for agriculture.
Capitalism generalized the reign of money over land, commodities, and labor. In the smallest and newest prairie villages, people gauged their activities by the common measure of money and the success of commerce.

A century earlier, Thomas Jefferson himself—a child of the Atlantic community and the bourgeois eighteenth century—recognized the dominance
of commerce in the new republic. In 1784, he wrote George Washington, another property and economic developer:

> All the world is becoming commercial. Were it practicable to keep our new em-
> pire separated from them, we might indulge ourselves in speculation whether

commerce contributes to happiness of mankind. But we cannot separate ourselves from them. Our citizens have had too full a taste of the comforts furnished by the arts and manufactures to be debarred the use of them. We must, then, in our defence endeavor to share as large a portion as we can of this modern source of wealth and power.[2]

Before the West was settled, Ralph Waldo Emerson, in an article entitled "Wealth," declared on behalf of every American farmer that money counts out "the strokes of his labor, . . . so much rain, frost, and sunshine, . . . so much hoeing and threshing."[3] Money influences "all economic and social relationships," wrote noted historian Fernand Braudel.[4] It calculates both the greatest transactions and the purchase of a fish hook, a hatpin, a chew of tobacco, or a lollipop.

A Prairie Town

Marshall, a prairie town, a county seat, and over time a regional center, lies at the intersection of two railroads, the Chicago and Northwest and the St. Peter. Every mile of track laid in the nineteenth century linked Marshall to Minneapolis, the milling center of the upper Midwest, and beyond to the great prairie metropolis, Chicago, and to New York. Through this metal umbilical cord, Marshall was connected to the flow of capital and goods and the metropolis's plans, schemes, and visions. Marshall was birthed along these tracks into an intensely competitive world. Never swaddled, it was compelled to stand on its own infant legs.

As John Radziłowski remarked in his indispensable history of Marshall, *Prairie Town*, there could be only so many "new Chicagos" on the prairie. In fact, some towns were born to an inevitable decline.[5] Boosting could not bewitch economic reality. Like its fellow prairie towns, Marshall was quickly thrown up along the tracks on the northwestern corner of the tallgrass prairie, where the Redwood River coming down off the Coteau des Prairies reaches the floodplains. Wolves were still heard howling on the town's outskirts as buildings went up slapdash to fill in the railroad's standard grid, and at least one buffalo broached the city limits. After a few years, boasting a few streets, two thousand residents, and a county seat designation, Marshall declared itself the economic hub of the region.

While the town satisfied the abiding human need for community, its raison d'être was economic. A depot dispatching crops and importing products, it provided indispensable goods and services and the amenities of advancing civilization. Doctors and dentists offered the rudiments of medicine, a theater produced frivolity and serious productions, and a general store sold fashionable hats, harmonicas, and frilled bloomers in addition to flour, brooms, and nails.

A trip along Marshall's Main Street in 1873, four years after the town's founding, would reveal to local historians that the town's primary function was commercial. In addition to a newspaper, not uniquely named the *Prairie Schooner*, there was a railroad agent, a telegraph operator, a postmaster, and a land office. Also two hotels, a livery blacksmith, a lumberyard, and a drug store. The general store was complemented by a meat market, a confectionery, a hardware store, a furniture store, and—for those who wanted to capture themselves in their new environment at a historic juncture in the nation's life—a photographer. A Masonic lodge was formed that year, and the Congregational society built a church.[6]

Like other early Midwestern towns, Marshall housed two types of businesses: retail and artisanal. The artisans, represented by the once all-important blacksmiths, cobblers, harness makers, and wagon makers, vanished over time. Suggesting how technology and markets work a continuous transformation of local business and population, they were replaced by automobile mechanics, metal-shop workers, electricians, and others in the building trades.

Retailers had to keep pace with changing and expanding markets. Their goods were brought by the railroads from the metropolis. Whether they stocked bulk foods or complex machines, the retailers' enduring burden was knowing what and how much to buy at one price and sell at another price. This universal economic law applied to the smallest commercial undertaking. Successful business activity increasingly involved acuity in calculating the volume of potential sales in relation to profit margin, and the range of products in light of customers' evolving tastes.

Two other challenges illustrate how local historians of business are increasingly required to write of the place they care about in detail with reference to the laws of economics, as opposed to the challenges that face other types of historians, who, when writing of concrete places, often are dragged into the abstract. First, the less a merchant sold of a product, the higher his or her prices had to be; and the higher the prices, the more likely customers were inclined, given the opportunity, to buy elsewhere. The mail-order catalogue became the local merchant's rival. The U.S. Postal Service had brought catalogues to every town and farmhouse by the end of the century. Be it Montgomery Ward's catalogue or that of Sears and Roebuck, the catalogue set both a range of offerings and a price against which the town merchant had to compete.[7] After a few decades of futile struggle, local retailers, whether in Minnesota, Ohio, or Montana, signaled their surrender by placing these catalogues on prominent display right next to their cash registers.

The second general law that drove local business was that the more varied a merchant's stock, the more capital he or she risked on products that might not sell or that might have to be liquidated at steeply reduced prices. Conversely, if merchants didn't expand the variety of their stock, customers found fewer reasons to patronize their stores at all. On this count, merchants often bought certain products at great risk and others with no hope of profit at all but rather out of a need to make their stores convenient and fashionable for customers who had grown accustomed to the wide range of choices offered by the mail-order catalogues of Montgomery Ward.

Individual virtues and vices and family fortunes and misfortunes add color to local business history, but the overall picture for small-town businesses, retail and artisanal alike, was uniformly poor. A hundred years of prairie business history testify to this. Markets were small, even fragile, to begin with. Not much could help them, and almost anything could injure them. A fight between farmers and the owners of the town elevator or a clash over school districting could do irrevocable damage to community cohesion, cooperation, and commerce. The orthodoxy of Main Street rested on the truth that the merchants would sing or hang together. If the town did well, so did they. If it waned, they failed.

Competition magnified with the growth of transportation and communications. Markets shrank as the farm population decreased. Profit margins diminished as big-city merchants bought and sold in volume. Local merchants faced the puzzle of finding a balance between selling enough and offering an attractive range of fresh goods. Among the acquired tricks of the merchant's trade were keeping inventories low, starting an associated business (sellers of lumber learned to build houses, furniture merchants moonlighted as undertakers), and extending interest-free seasonal credit, which has disappeared in recent decades. (Credit, a matter of ongoing tension between retailer and customer, forms a subject of particular interest to the historians of business, as does the recent history of the growth of credit agencies.) Regardless of what small-town merchants did, they tended to go broke in one of two ways: with little or nothing to sell, or with unsold goods stacked high.

Dispelling a sentimental view of static small towns is the fact that rural business experienced change and turbulence from the beginning. Radziłowski contends that in the case of Marshall, between 1880 and 1910, businesses averaged a 45 percent turnover rate during each five-year period.[8] Across the same period, especially during the farm depression of the 1890s, farm ownership was characterized by failure, and stores' primary customers were farmers. During the decades preceding the First World War, regional centers (defined as towns of several thousand people, as distinct from the smaller prairie towns and villages) grew and expanded their business into the surrounding countryside.

The Marriage of Business and Culture

As was the case in other regional centers, Marshall's merchants played leading roles in civic affairs. Yankees—Anglo-Saxon Protestants from out east—formed the town's social elite. As fresh and comparatively wealthy immigrants from Britain, Germany, and Scandinavia joined in prairie leadership, an equation between northern European ancestry and business leadership was drawn throughout southwestern Minnesota and much of the Midwest. This tendency was reinforced, according to Radziłowski, by the railroad companies' assumption that "native-born white Protestants were the proper 'stock' for running the towns," while hardworking immigrants with large families would make better farmers.[9]

While the ambitious sons and daughters of town leaders went off to college and opportunities elsewhere, the Yankees, who dominated commerce, continued to define civic leadership. They held seats on the city council and the school and library boards. They filled the ranks and leadership of such important voluntary organizations as the Grand Army of the Republic, the Masons, and the Odd Fellows. Their wives formed and ran study circles and temperance groups that added a moral sheen to towns whose roads were just being paved and whose houses didn't yet have indoor plumbing. Membership in Episcopal, Congregational, Presbyterian, and Methodist churches added religious certitude to their economic calling. As good Christians and proud Americans, they marched into the twentieth century in stride with the nation. With prosperity beckoning, technology improving, and a holy crusade to be fought overseas, they believed that they held their fate in their own hands.

Marshall proved itself progressive after World War I as well. It succeeded in providing itself with water, sewage, electricity, and paved streets. It displayed its willingness to court commerce and support the town's economic growth by helping pay for a new Catholic church, which dwarfed the Episcopal church that stood directly behind it on Main Street. However, these efforts to commit itself to progress didn't insulate it against the forces that engulfed the nation and the world.

The late 1920s and the 1930s brought change of unprecedented magnitude. Tractor and automobile redefined farming and rural life. National financial crisis and worldwide depression followed a period of depressed farm commodity prices. Grim realities overtook Marshall. The covenant between the countryside and the advancing urban nation was broken. Yankee editors of local papers like the nearby *Cottonwood Current* vainly attempted to sustain the patriotic union of progress and nation by interpreting the depression as a crisis of morale rather than one of failed economic policies and national politics. The efforts of the editor of the *Current* fell every bit as short as those of the editor of the *Minnesota Mascot*, who had advocated isolationism during the First World War. The overwhelming dimensions of the interwar crisis years explain why small-town people of the 1920s and 1930s idealized the prewar period, and especially the pioneer days, as a time of order, certitude, and stability.

Marshall, which had begun to suffer demographic stagnation in the

1920s as the national rural economy faltered and the town's children followed opportunities elsewhere, experienced a period of population growth and turmoil in the 1930s. The town population grew by more than 40 percent as people from nearby farms and hamlets came to Marshall in search of work in processing plants and New Deal programs.[10] The poverty of these immigrants becomes clear when one recognizes that even though Marshall's population increased sizably during the decade, the town's bank deposits remained constant in the same period, at only 25 percent of the total county bank deposits. (In the 1990s, deposits reached 80 percent.) The town, which had known its traveling salesmen, peddlers, tramps, and Roma (Gypsies) in the past, was now filled with transients. Renters, hired hands, drifters, and farmers leaving the land appeared in droves, defining the poverty and mobility of the era. Not easily distinguished from hoboes, newcomers in need were more numerous than Marshall's resources could support, and they testified to Richard Lingeman's observation that during the depression, the inadequacies of small-town governments became glaringly apparent.[11]

The Unexpected Side of Success

If the 1930s taught fatalism, the 1950s and 1960s stimulated a nervous confidence. A look at the differences between these decades shows local historians how much their principalities are affected by the national economy and the moods it elicits. In the 1950s, as elsewhere in the nation, Marshall's population increased, housing starts multiplied, and the city took up such fundamental tasks as building a new sewage system.[12] The 1960s were a heyday for Marshall and towns like it. If Marshall ever was a self-determining community, it was then. The population tripled between 1965 and 1970. The economy thrived, with retail sales elevated to the national average of 22 percent or more between 1958 and 1963.[13] The assets of Marshall's banks are estimated to have increased by nearly 60 percent between 1961 and 1967.[14]

Yet the new wine didn't break the old wineskins. Established families and store names still held Main Street together. The old business gang, along with the head of the chamber of commerce and the superintendent of schools, still essentially ran the town. Eventually, however, a new generation of leaders composed of newcomers and sons and daughters who'd stayed in town took up the matter of Marshall's future. Perhaps it was only unwittingly that they remained loyal to the town's progressive tradition. Whatever the case, Marshall's commerce and politics continued to be ecumenical. Together in coffee shops and city government, Protestants, Catholics, and several prominent Jewish families ran the town. Collectively, they cast their lot with growth and were determined to find a way to differentiate Marshall from its regional town rivals in southwestern Minnesota.

Their ambition and dilemma were the same as those facing other regional centers. Each had to make its town grow while staving off the exodus of its brightest youth. And along with a dozen or so other communities in southwestern Minnesota, Marshall arrived at what for a moment seemed like a solution to both problems: encourage the Minnesota legislature to establish a four-year college, which southwestern Minnesota, alone of all the state's regions, lacked. The legislature approved the college, but left the decision about where the college would be located to a subsequent session.

Landing a four-year college constituted a crowning achievement of the town leaders' political efforts, who won their university against considerable odds. An incalculable and debatable combination of factors made the victory possible. It turned on Marshall's central geographic location, its new sewage system, and politics. But it also turned on the town leaders' political acumen, determination, and sacrifice.[15]

Marshall triumphed especially over its nearby rival, Redwood Falls. Its coup, never forgotten by Redwood Falls, meant that Marshall would double in population while surrounding towns of similar size remained static at five thousand or fewer. Pride filled the town's leaders. They had built a college in a cornfield.

But Southwest State College (later promoted by the mere change of name to University) proved the saying that historians write much of their text with irony. The new college, founded in 1967, wound up trampling the very hope that had created it. It did not retain Marshall's best and brightest young people, as planned. What's more, in most unanticipated fashion, the university's students and faculty soon paraded the shocking cultural changes and protests of the 1960s and early 1970s down Main Street. By 1971, the year the first class graduated, the town had discovered it had potted in its own soil an institution of strangers.

The college served up many bitter cultural potions to its hosts. Anti-war protests offered especially heavy draughts. On May 11, 1972, for example, 166 protesters were put in jail as Marshall joined the nation in criticizing Nixon's mining of the North Vietnamese ports.[16] Not since the Holiday Farmers had overrun the town some thirty-five years earlier had Marshall marched into the national headlines. With war protests, interracial conflicts, the burning of buildings, and a small but escalating drug trade, the town certainly got more than it bargained for. Liberal clothing styles and language daily rubbed salt in the wound of misunderstanding. Five years of aggressive and provocative activities by a unionizing faculty, who were intent on protecting their jobs and battling an unimaginative administration, both outraged and defied the understanding of a downtown business establishment that expected gratitude for its part in founding the college.

The college both declined and ascended during its first decade. Talk of its closing came and went, like the seasons themselves. The Twin Cities media had reported rumors of the school's closing before its buildings were even completed. All this did not undermine the fact that the college increased business revenues in Marshall, but it did damage the business leaders' sense of pride in their creation.

Meanwhile, with the university's drama keeping most eyes riveted, a small company in Marshall called Schwan's grew steadily, even stealthily. Throughout the 1970s, a multibillion-dollar food industry took shape, one that would eventually become the town's leading industry. Rooted in the conservative philosophy of its locally born owner, Marvin Schwan, and a collection of other local men he had gathered around himself, the company grew from a door-to-door seller of ice cream to a national supplier of frozen foods. Schwan's entered the frozen pizza business in 1970 and emerged at its top less than two decades later. (It includes the Tony's and Red Baron brands, with $542 million a year in sales.)

Despite the disruptive cultural changes of the era, Marshallites (who neither understood nor controlled the fate of either the university or Schwan's) had reason to be proud in the 1960s and 1970s. They appeared to have found the magic formula that served both economic growth and community strength. It rested on the progressive notion that good business and stable government (from which Marshall truly benefited) resulted in a good town. Local pride was enhanced by observations of the growing nationwide disillusionment with big-city life and a diffuse appreciation for "small is beautiful" and "back to the land" sentiments.[17] Boosters were often heard reiterating clichés about having "the best of both worlds."

Decline Amid Prosperity, Prosperity Amid Decline

In spite of some genuine successes, all was not roses with Marshall's economic progression. Growth implies that as some things are being born, others are dying. Thus, in the case of Marshall, as elsewhere, local historians are forced to tell a double-sided and more sensitive story as they approach the present. And autopsies on the living, as it were, are painful.

At an accelerating pace, Marshall in the 1960s began to enter into fuller and more direct contact with metropolitan markets. Census and state business reports illuminate these changes, which were occurring across the nation. The rate of change at work in all sectors of Marshall's economy and society make it "a community of strangers" and a servant of distant transforming forces.

The contrast in Marshall these days is between an expanding and mutating regional center and a surrounding ring of diminished farms and villages. This juxtaposition places a double burden on local historians. They are compelled to document two stories simultaneously. They must describe the declining countryside on the one hand and, on the other, characterize a regional center that, ever metamorphosed by the nearby metropolis, transforms the very countryside it claims to serve and represent. Each element of this reconstruction challenges historians to find numbers to confirm their hypotheses and words to broadcast their findings.

It fell to me, as a local and regional historian, to announce decline to the region. In two articles for the League of Minnesota Cities prior to the 1990 census and in a small book titled *The Decline of Rural Minnesota,* a colleague and I set forth the unwelcome message.[18] We contended that lead cities like Marshall (the last outposts of vitality in the countryside) were themselves perched on a melting iceberg.

The reasons for decline were manifest: between the 1950 and the 1990 census, national farming employment dropped from just under 8 million to a little over 3 million, and the number of farms dropped from 5.8 million to 2.1 million. The percentage of the rural workforce in agriculture dropped to 7.6 percent, as it correspondingly gained in manufacturing and services.[19] In Minnesota, between 1930 and 1960, the growth of the non-farm population in unincorporated areas grew from 78,000 to 313,000, or from 5 percent to 11 percent of the total population.[20] By the 1980s, out-migration averaged 11 percent among all nonmetro counties, or those that lay beyond the ring of suburbs circling the Twin Cities, with a 17 percent loss of their eighteen-to-thirty-four-year-old population.[21]

An elemental law was at work: As farms get bigger and farm families smaller, rural population declines and rural towns shrink. As available goods, jobs, and other opportunities vanish or fail to keep pace with those available in the city, rural children go elsewhere to seek their fortunes.

Decline cannot be isolated. It jumps from farm to town, mutating as it goes. It spreads to hamlets and villages, which lose not just population but the remnants of their Main Streets. Small towns lose their banks, newspapers, and schools while retaining only bars and junk shops. They struggle to save hardware stores, coffee shops, and restaurants, the last havens of the daily news and gossip that cement a community together. Having exchanged schools for nursing homes, many towns appear to be settlements for the dying. Between 1990 and 1995, in more than a dozen counties in southwestern Minnesota, more people died than were born.[22] The old stand witness to the twilight of their towns, and local historians find themselves having to recount the death of their homes.

Decline eventually attacks regional centers, where it manifests itself in the end of the small family business and the decline of Main Street. By the 1980s, local historians of once-thriving regional centers could document by a simple stroll downtown not just the end of a way of doing business but also the end of a social class and the traditional leadership group drawn from it. The empty storefronts prompt the question of who will rule next. The answer, in Marshall, is public employees, including college teachers. These newcomers have taken the seats of lifelong locals everywhere in town—in the mayor's office, on the city council, and on school and hospital boards. Simply by recording the obvious, by announcing the changing of the guard, local historians tread on sensitive ground. Nevertheless, if my experience is any guide, many town people will appreciate the historians' candor.

In Marshall, like so many other Midwestern towns, Main Street seriously began to flounder in the 1970s. John Radziłowski offers this general assessment: "Main Street retained its viability with a cluster of public service establishments: library, post office, museum, public utility building, municipal building, and county courthouse. Specialized businesses serving small niches in the retail market no longer formed the Main Street of yesteryear with its full complement of businesses to serve every need; that has become a thing of the past."[23] The decline of Main Street coincided with the ascent of a commercial strip along East College Drive. Characterized by food services, gas stations, banks, and a variety of convenience stores, the strip steadily grew, drawing customers from the college and the growing residential areas hearby.[24] The downtown's decline was ensured by the building of a shopping mall in the 1970s at the east end of town, across East College Drive from the college.

But a grocery store, a national department store, and a discount store failed to anchor even the mall. The volume of customers simply wasn't great enough, and many shop spaces remained empty. In the early 1990s, ShopKo and Wal-Mart, which established themselves next to each other along the southern bypass of the town, superseded the mall. These chain stores—which appear to prosper by drawing from the whole region—are the assassins of small-town businesses. On close investigation, the local historian who keeps an ear cocked might find in time that the chains too might suffer insufficient volume of business when on-line commerce reaches its prime.

The roots of decline that local historians describe in southwestern Minnesota lie in the rural world at large. The volume of trade is insufficient to support the local community's multiplying wants and tastes. Since the introduction of the automobile, larger numbers of people have been traveling greater distances to fulfill expanding desires at cheaper prices. More and more of them shop and amuse themselves in Sioux Falls, Mankato, Willmar, and the Twin Cities. Consumers increasingly are shopping by mail and electronically, as the frequently circulating delivery vans make plain.

The dawning era of on-line shopping may prove more challenging to rural commerce than even catalogue shopping. The majority of people are shoppers first and citizens second: they are more sensitive to price than anything else. Franchise managers will benefit even less from loyalty than did their Main Street predecessors. Surely these revolutionary developments add lanes to the great highway of exchange between country and city. As technology invites rural people to participate in a global system of information creation and dissemination, it also permits spatial dissemination and consolidates the metropolitan control that increasingly denies local orders their autonomy.[25] Local and regional historians must assess the truth of commerce's triumph over community, culture, and politics.

The visionary and the historian, who converge by virtue of their preoccupation with the changing present, conjure a countryside with hardly a farm and towns with nary a store, except franchises of national chains serving community members and passersby equally. One need be no Cassandra to foresee a novel time in history when we have cities without an agora—"a community" without local markets in which to exchange goods, opinions, and gossip. Only a handful of random convenience stores, along with telephones, copiers, fax machines, e-mail, and video arcades, will serve local places' physical and social needs.

More for Less, More with Less

Marshall has not escaped this aspect of decline. Accounting in 1970 for approximately fourth-fifths of county sales revenues and slightly more than half of the county's $80 million in bank deposits, the town has been running on the treadmill of regional service. It must, if it is to survive, increasingly expand the range of its goods and services to the surrounding area.

Marshall's bankers, the commercial linchpin of the town, found they had to affiliate with banking chains to minimize the cost of operations and broaden their services to incorporate investment and other services in an increasingly competitive environment. They've had to carry their business farther afield. At the same time, they've had to strive to increase volume in a limited market. To expand business with established customers, they have to discount services.

Marshall's hospital and its physicians address similar economic factors in a corresponding way. They offer more and more medical services simply to keep pace with the profession and to satisfy a population insisting on these services. Marshall's doctors have approximately tripled in number over the past two decades. The hospital has expanded, adding a wellness facility, a residential living complex for the independent elderly, and a larger nursing home for long-term medical care giving. At the same time, health providers in Marshall have joined forces with a larger, regional medical complex, Affiliated Medical Services located in Willmar, seventy miles to the northeast of Marshall.

Lawyers and accountants, likewise marking the end of the one- and two-person office, have consolidated. They offer increased expertise in a specialized environment and find that only in consolidation can they handle the rivers of paperwork contemporary law requires, complex as it is. Law seems to be the twin of every important facet of this rapidly changing society. Wherever there is change, there is potential for dispute and the need for resolution. Defying stereotypes of the countryside as a straightforward place where "one's word and a handshake" suffices, rural areas grow lawyers. Law is a fertile field for local historians wishing to grasp the change under way, as individual practices and small, local firms wane and larger, more aggressive regional firms grow in cases, clients, and wealth, reflecting the transition from the local to regional, state, and national practice.

Government and public employees cause, and are consumed by, a growing storm of paper and regulations. Each legislative session and administrative directive fuels the emergence of a more convoluted and alien order in the countryside. The public health nurse and the social worker at the courthouse, the pollution control officer and the extension officer in the field, or the special education teacher and psychologist in the school are perpetrators and victims of the same bureaucratic order. Held accountable for an ever greater number of increasingly protected and demanding clients, they are transformed into valets for the auditors, bankers, hospital workers, and farmers. (How specialization and bureaucracy spread across a community and actually form a kind of rural environment would be a lovely study. A more moderate but worthwhile study would tell the story of the growth of public agencies in a single county courthouse.)

At the university in Marshall, the same tight-fitting pants chafe. With insufficient staffing, Southwest State University nevertheless must offer a range of programs and services identical to those of any other four-year university. It must respond to students' broadening academic and non-academic desires, meeting expanding accreditation standards. Subject at all times to the whims of the governor and the legislature, it remains under the control of the state university system, which in the course of the past three decades has evolved from a single chancellor to an administrative staff of more than a hundred and a citizens' board that seeks to govern approximately forty institutions.[26]

As articulated in *The Decline of Rural Minnesota,* this rule of doing more with less commands the town:

> There is no end to requests for reports, evaluations, and implementations of new moral-social directives [in the college]. . . . There are emotionally exhausting and crippling budgetary about-faces, spawned by changing administrative orders, a fluctuating economy, and the vagaries of bi-annual state legislation. . . . One hears similar stories from regional businesses [especially those in road construction], law offices, medical clinics, and farms, especially at tax time. They too agonize as they try to keep up with an increasing flood

of laws, demands, and specialization that engulfs their professions and their lives. Some remark that they find themselves outpaced by new technologies, increased demand for paperwork, ever-refined sensibilities. . . . Few, if any, believe that innovative and labor saving devices are doing away with old functions faster than new functions are appearing. The farmer escapes being harnessed to the plow to be chained to the pencil.[27]

The need to keep up is evident throughout Marshall's economy. Schwan's illustrates well the effect of national and international markets on rural economies. Staying abreast requires the company to participate in global markets. While hiring computer programmers from Bombay, it must sell sandwiches in Prague. Now the leading frozen pizza company in America, Schwan's must continue to develop new products.[28]

The local corn processing plant, Minnesota Corn Processors, also must deal with complex global markets. It has to find ways to turn corn into multiple products. Proving not every sea that is seen can be successfully sailed, this farmers' cooperative recently beached itself when, amid a major expansion, it guaranteed the price of a finished product without having secured the price of supplies. As a consequence, a significant part of its stock now belongs to agricultural giant Archer Daniels Midland.

Increasingly, local historians discover that national and even global realities underlie local phenomena. Telling local stories requires acknowledging distant forces. The story of finite places further joins the course of civilization itself. People, as well as limited resources, are forced to keep pace with a world whose possibilities multiply exponentially. To do more with less at breakneck speed causes frenzy. The sense of falling behind, of never quite doing enough, becomes a common feature of mental life in the idyllic countryside. Efficiency hasn't banished malingering or shoddy work any more than the sun has stopped rising and setting, and the countryside not only looks more and more like the metropolis, it feels, thinks, plays, and works that way too. To read the same outside control into our past denies us a history. Retrospectively, our entire story appears to belong to someone else— to the story of rise and control of a dominating metropolis, as John Borchert told of the Twin Cities' hegemony over almost all of Minnesota, western Wisconsin, the Dakotas, and much of Montana, and William Cronon told of Chicago's creation and dominance of a whole inland empire, reaching north to Michigan and Wisconsin, south to Kansas, and west to Iowa, southern Minnesota, and beyond.[29]

Marshall cannot do what a lead city by definition should do. Not only can it not lead; it simply can't keep up. From hospital and bank to bookstores, travel agency, and coffee shop, Marshall is not equipped to meet rising expectations. It can only scramble to keep a semblance of bringing urban civilization to the countryside. How else could it be for a medium-size depot town in a global age?

The countryside's audience is small, divided, and mixed. Aside from distinct but diminished farming neighborhoods—the ethnic victors of a century of competitive farming—the countryside has lost much of its own context and continuity. Relatives and neighbors have emigrated from weakening towns. More and more strangers, willing to travel greater distances for the sake of lower housing costs, inhabit towns depleted of the businesses, organizations, and associations they once had. Closures and mergers in town and country correspond to the weakening and vanishing of traditional rural communities and cultures associated with townships, farm groups, fair boards, and co-ops.

At the same time, accelerated economic, social, and cultural transformation deny coherence in regional centers like Marshall. Increased turnover and turbulence on every front strip them of audiences to whom local and regional historians could direct their work. In fact, insofar as Marshall is the model, a question imposes itself: Have the most vibrant and hopeful places in the declining countryside—regional centers—become for all intents and purposes communities of strangers?

Local and regional historians who have not sworn themselves to irrelevance must push toward the most controversial edges of their subjects. They must inquire into the practice of power. They must check the very pulse of power, the belief that one can make things happen, and record whether such blood flows at all in rural veins. Moreover, they must inquire whether local leaders, fatalists to the bone, have become robots of administrative directives.

This epoch imposes fresh themes and questions on local and regional historians. They are compelled to think about uncertain change, endless transformations, and incomprehensible metamorphoses. Unless local historians are to miss their hour, they must respond. They must try to measure in detail and depth the irreversible mutation dramatically upon us and still make their stories count to all who cherish the sustaining values of freedom and place.

NOTES

1. Richard Davies, *Main Street Blues: The Decline of Small-Town America* (Columbus: Ohio State University Press, 1998).

2. Quoted in the *Oxford Book of Money* (Oxford: Oxford University Press, 1995), 359–60.

3. Quoted in ibid., 20.

4. Ibid., 37–38.

5. For Marshall, see John Radziłowski, *Prairie Town: A History of Marshall, Minnesota 1872–1997* (Marshall, Minn.: Lyon County Historical Society, 1997). For the birth of railroad towns, see John C. Hudson, *Plains Country Towns* (Minneapolis: University of Minnesota Press, 1985).

6. Torgny Anderson, *The Centennial History of Lyon County* (Marshall, Minn.: Henle Publishing Company, 1970), 169.

7. See Hal Barron, *Mixed Harvest: The Second Great Transformation in the Rural North, 1870–1930* (Chapel Hill: University of North Carolina Press, 1997), 155–92.

8. Radziłowski, *Prairie Town,* 91–92.

9. Ibid., 87–94, 118–19.

10. Joseph Amato and John Radziłowski, *A Community of Strangers: Change, Turnover, Turbulence, and the Transformation of a Midwestern Country Town* (Marshall, Minn.: Crossings Press, 1999), 26.

11. Richard Lingeman, *Small Town America: A Narrative History, 1620 to the Present* (New York: G. P. Putnam's Sons, 1980), 429–30.

12. Joseph Amato, *A New College on the Prairie: Southwest State University's First Twenty-Five Years, 1967–1992* (Marshall, Minn.: Crossings Press, 1992), 16–18.

13. John Borchert, *Upper Midwest Urban Change in the 1960s* (Minneapolis: Upper Midwest Research and Development, 1968), 24.

14. Ibid., 25.

15. Amato, *A New College,* 13–21.

16. Ibid., 46.

17. Lingeman, *Small Town America,* 441.

18. Joseph A. Amato and John W. Meyer, *The Decline of Rural Minnesota* (Marshall, Minn.: Crossings Press, 1993).

19. U.S. Department of Agriculture, Economic Research Service Department, "Rural Change," in *Understanding Rural America* (Washington, D.C.: United States Department of Agriculture, 1991).

20. John Borchert, *Upper Midwest Urban Change,* 16.

21. U.S. Department of Agriculture, Economic Research Service, "Rural Diversity," in *Understanding Rural America* (Washington, D.C.: United States Department of Agriculture, 1991).

22. For a discussion of this natural decline, see Amato and Meyer, *Decline of Rural Minnesota,* 39–50.

23. Radziłowski, *Prairie Town,* 287.

24. Ibid., 285. For a parallel study, see Davies, *Main Street Blues,* 137–84.

25. Amy Glasmeier and Marie Howland, *From Combines to Computers: Rural Services and Development in the Age of Information Technology* (Albany: State University of New York Press, 1995), 93.

26. Ibid.

27. Amato and Meyer, *Decline of Rural Minnesota,* 14–15.

28. Jim Tate, "It's in the Crust," *Marshall Independent,* Marshall, Minn., December 5, 1998.

29. John Borchert, *America's Northern Heartland: An Economic and Historical Geography of the Upper Midwest* (Minneapolis: University of Minnesota Press, 1987), and William Cronon, *Nature's Metropolis: Chicago and the Great West* (New York: W. W. Norton, 1991).

Suggestions for Further Reading

THE LITERATURE OF THE AMERICAN MIDWEST—previously known, of course, as "The West"—emerged late in the nineteenth century, when realism was challenging romanticism as the dominant literary mode. The Midwest village received essentially romantic treatments in Mark Twain's *The Adventures of Tom Sawyer* (1876) and Zona Gale's Friendship Village books (especially *Friendship Village*, 1908), but both Twain and Gale moved toward realism with *Adventures of Huckleberry Finn* (1884) and *Miss Lulu Bett* (1920) respectively. The two benchmark books of Midwest small-town fiction—Sinclair Lewis's *Main Street* (1920) and Sherwood Anderson's *Winesburg, Ohio* (1919)—are both realistic and highly critical descriptions of the village. Anderson tends toward psychological analysis, Lewis toward social commentary and satire. Willa Cather made famous the Red Cloud, Nebraska, of her youth in a sequence of novels which trace the pastoral Midwest from frontier (*O Pioneers!*, 1912) to heyday (*My Ántonia*, 1918) to decline (*One of Ours*, 1922). She divides her time between farm and village, as does Hamlin Garland in his collection of short stories, *Main-Travelled Roads* (1881). At present, Garrison Keillor's Lake Wobegon, Minnesota, is the most famous town in America, popularized by his weekly radio broadcast and a tetrology of books: *Lake Wobegon Days* (1985), *Leaving Home* (1987), *Wobegon Boy* (1997) and *Wobegon Summer 1956* (2001). Although it is set in northern Texas, Larry McMurtry's *The Last Picture Show* (1966) deserves mention as one of the great fictional (and cinematic) depictions of the American small town. And Thornton Wilder's enormously popular play *Our Town* (1938) reflects in many ways the playwright's childhood in Madison, Wisconsin, and school years at Oberlin College in Ohio.

Other popular novels have been set in the Midwest small town. Henry Bellaman's *King's Row* (1940) was made into a film starring Ronald Reagan; a sequel, *Parris Mitchell of King's Row* (1940), appeared in 1948. Ross Lockridge tried to write the modernist great American novel with *Raintree County* (1948), set in Indiana. His manuscript weighed twenty pounds, and the book became both a film and a number-one best seller. Helen Hooven Santmyer's equally encyclopedic (and very romantic) . . . *And Ladies of the Club* hit the best-sellers' lists in 1982, mostly because it was published in the author's eighty-seventh year. Other good reads are Glenway Westcott's *Goodbye, Wisconsin* (1928); Frederick Manfred's *The Chokecherry Tree* (1948), set in the Upper Plains during the Great Depression; Wright Morris's collage of Nebraska photos and text, *The Home Place* (1948), and his later *Ceremony in Lonetree* (1960); R. V. Cassill's tales of Iowa small-town life, *The Father and Other Stories* (1965); Larry Woiwode's *Beyond the Bedroom Wall: A Family Album* (1975), with its powerful memories of Hyatt, North Dakota; Jon Hassler's *Staggerford* (1977) and *Grand Opening* (1987), both set in Minnesota; and Jonis Agee's *Sweet Eyes* (1991), set in the fictional Divinity, Iowa.

Modernist and postmodernist fictional treatments of the Midwest village include William Gass's *In the Heart of the Heart of the Country and Other Stories* (1969), Robert Coover's *The Origin of the Brunnists* (1966), and Charles Baxter's *Believers* (1998), in which the town of Five Oaks becomes a non-descript suburb, no longer in any meaningful sense a Midwestern small town.

The benchmark collection of poems from the Midwest village remains Edgar Lee Masters's *Spoon River Anthology* (1915), a gathering of fictional epitaphs from the fictional graveyard in Spoon River, Illinois. Most of them tell dark and sometimes inter-related stories of malice, deceit, and sexual repression. Dave Etter's more recent *Alliance, Illinois* (1983) is a better book: Etter uses first-person speakers in the Edgar Lee Masters tradition, but his humor and ear for Midwestern idiom and rhythms of speech make the collection a real pleasure. John Knoepfle's *poems from the sangamon* (1985) is a smaller but equally fine collection, also from Illinois. Among William Kloefkorn's many reminiscences of life in small-town Nebraska, several stand out: *Not Such a Bad Place to Be* (1980), *Collecting for the Wichita Beacon* (1984), *A Life Like Mine* (1984), and *Welcome to Carlos* (2000).

Among nonfiction books of journalism, memoir, autobiography, editorial, and "creative nonfiction" these stand out: Hamlin Garland's *A Son of the Middle Border* (1917); August Derleth's meditations on Sac Prairie, Wisconsin, titled *Walden West* (1961) and *Return to Walden West* (1970); Carol Bly's analysis of Madison, Minnesota, in *Letters from the Country* (1981); Norbert Blei's portrait of small-town Wisconsin farmers, townsfolk, and fishermen in *Door Way* (1981); Susan Allen Toth's memoir *Blooming: A Small-Town [Iowa] Girlhood* (1981); Bill Holm's analysis of Minneota, Minnesota, titled *The Music of Failure* (1985); and Kathleen Norris's *Dakota: A Spiritual Geography* (1993).

An appreciation of the literature of the Midwest village begins with Lewis Atherton's *Main Street on the Middle Border* (1954), Page Smith's *As A City Upon a Hill: The Small Town in American Life* (1966), and Anthony C. Hilfer's *The Revolt from the Village, 1915–1930* (1969). Gerald Nemiac's *A Bibliographical Guide to Midwestern Literature* (1981) is essential: it contains bibliographies, brief essays on authors important in 1981, and briefer sketches of authors less important at that time. It may be supplemented by the many surveys of individual state literatures, especially Clarence Andrews's *A Liter-*

ary History of Iowa (1972), Richard Bray's *Rediscoveries: Literature and Place in Illinois* (1982), and Ronald Barron's *A Guide to Minnesota Writers* (1993). It should be supplemented by Philip Greasley, ed., *Dictionary of Midwest Literature* (2001). Milton Rieigelman's *The Midland: A Venture in Literary Regionalism* (1975) and John T. Frederick's anthology *Stories from the Midland* (1924) provide a good sense of *Midland* magazine's important contribution to the literature of this region, work carried on since 1970 by the Society for the Study of Midwest Literature, David Anderson, director, headquartered at Michigan State University and publisher of the annual *Midwestern Miscellany* and *MidAmerica* (which contains an annual bibliography).

Just as the contributions of novelists and poets to our understanding of the Midwest are overwhelming for their depth and richness, so too is the work of historians and social scientists. For starters, Richard Lingeman's *Small Town America* (1980) provides a historical overview that is richly grounded in primary resources as well as the many contributions of American novelists. Page Smith in *As a City Upon a Hill* focuses his attention primarily upon the "covented" towns of New England, although his narrative provides important data on the Midwest. Richard Francaviglia draws upon his expertise as a historical geographer and student of urban planning and design to make important distinctions between regional towns of the South and Southwest and the Midwest in *Main Street Revisited: Time, Space, and Image Building in Small-Town America* (1996). The early settlement period is captured well by Lingeman, but Richard Wade's *The Urban Frontier: The Rise of Western Cities, 1790–1830* (1959) remains indispensable. The complexities involved in town building are better understood if Wade is read in concert with John Mack Faragher's richly documented and creatively conceived *Sugar Creek: Life on the Illinois Prairie* (1986).

Lewis E. Atherton's pioneering *Main Street on the Middle Border* (1954) remains the standard historical work on the midwestern town, although its major strengths rest with the period from 1850 until 1930. Richard O. Davies's *Main Street Blues: The Decline of Small-Town America* (1998) seeks to describe the changing fates of American small towns from 1800 until the present through the prism of one Ohio community.

For a comparative study of Europe and one European town, see Eugen Weber's important essay, "And Man Made the Small Town," *American Scholar* (Winter 1988–89) and Gert Mak's *Jorwerd: The Death of the Village in Late 20th Century Europe* (2000). Several monographs have directed attention to the Upper Midwest. Joseph A. Amato and John W. Meyer focus their attention upon a cluster of struggling towns in *The Decline of Rural Minnesota* (1993). Also of importance is John Radziłowski's *Prairie Town: A History of Marshall, Minnesota, 1872–1997* (1997) and Amato and Radziłowski's *Community of Strangers: Change, Turnover, Turbulence, and the Transformation of a Midwestern Country Town* (1999). The latter study provides an intriguing preview of one possible twenty-first century future of many midwestern towns as the authors explore the impacts of ethnic and racial diversity, population mobility, and the new global economy that have descended full force upon one community in recent years.

Of special importance to the student of the Midwest town is Amato's *Rethinking Home: A Case for Writing Local History* (2002). This important work places rural communities within a larger context of the interaction of man and the natural environment and considers the small community as a pawn of larger social-political-economic forces that are regional, national, and even international in scope. This study makes the most powerful case for the utility of local history to date. Osha Gray Davidson explores the decline of small towns and their surrounding agricultural societies in *Broken Heartland: The Rise of America's Rural Ghettoes* (1990), while Catherine McNicol Stock examines the devastation of the economic depression of the 1930s upon the Upper Midwest in *Main Street in Crisis: The Great Depression and the Old Middle Class on the Northern Plains* (1992).

Although their subject was the modest-sized city of Muncie, Indiana, the insights provided by the cultural anthropologists Robert S. Lynd and Helen Merrill Lynd are invaluable as primary source material for the historian of the small town as well. Their two works remain essential reading three-quarters of a century after they first appeared: *Middletown: A Study in Modern American Culture* (1929) and *Middletown in Transition: A Study in Cultural Conflicts* (1937). The insights into the decline of the small town by the anthropologists Arthur Vidich and Joseph Bensman in *Small Town in Mass Society: Class, Power, and Religion in a Rural Community* (1968) remain useful. Although their study focuses on an upstate New York town, the same dynamics of change and decline are readily applicable to the Midwest. A study of a western Minnesota town replicates and validates the work of Vidich and Bensman within a midwestern setting: see Don Martindale and R. Galen Hansen's *Small Town and the Nation: The Conflict of Local and Translocal Forces* (1969). Similarly, the studies of a small Missouri town by Carl Withers, *Plainville, U. S. A.* (1945), and Art Gallaher, *Plainville Fifteen Years Later* (1961), depict in detail the manner in which small-town autonomy was overwhelmed by external economic, social, and political forces between 1930 and 1960.

Such works as these should be read within the vast historical panorama provided in William Cronon's *Nature's Metropolis: Chicago and the Great West* (1991), John C. Hudson's *Plains Country Towns* (1985), and John R. Borchert's *America's Northern Heartland* (1987). Although Cronon focuses on the impact of Chicago upon distant midwestern communities, Borchert on Minneapolis, and Hudson on the railroad's settling of North Dakota, their methodological approaches have utility when applied to any midwestern setting.

Credits

"The Economic Base," reprinted by permission of the publisher from *The Urban Frontier: The Rise of Western Cities, 1790–1830* by Richard C. Wade, Cambridge: Harvard University Press, © 1959 by the President and Fellows of Harvard College.

"It Answers Well for a Village," from *Sugar Creek: Life on the Illinois Prairie* by John Mack Faragher, © 1986 by Yale University Press. Reprinted by permission of Yale University Press.

Selections from *The Autobiography of Mark Twain,* edited by Charles Neider (New York: Washington Square Press, Inc., 1959).

"A Private Lesson from a Bulldog," from *The Hoosier School-Master: A Story of Backwoods Life in Indiana* by Edward Eggleston (New York: Grosset & Dunlap, 1871).

"Railroad Towns," from *Plains Country Towns* by John C. Hudson, © 1985 by the Regents of the University of Minnesota. Used by permission of the publisher.

"A 'Good Fellow's' Wife," from *Main-Travelled Roads* by Hamlin Garland (New York: The Macmillan Company, 1899).

"Belonging to the Community," from *Main Street on the Middle Border* by Lewis E. Atherton (Bloomington: Indiana University Press, 1954). Used by permission of the publisher.

"The Hired Girls," from *My Ántonia* by Willa Cather, © 1918 Willa Sibert Cather, renewed 1946.

Selections from *The Poetry of Vachel Lindsay: Complete and With Lindsay's Drawings* edited by Dennis Camp (Granite Falls, Minnesota: Spoon River Poetry Press, 1984). Used by permission of the publisher.

"The Budding of Art," from *The Age of Indiscretion* by Clyde Brion Davis (Philadelphia and New York: J. B. Lippincott Company, 1950). Reprinted by permission of David Brion Davis.

"Storm," from *Not Without Laughter* by Langston Hughes, © 1930 by Alfred A. Knopf, a division of Random House, Inc. Used by permission of Alfred A. Knopf, a division of Random House, Inc.

Excerpt from *Main Street* by Sinclair Lewis (New York: Harcourt, Brace and World, 1920).

Poems from *Spoon River Anthology* by Edgar Lee Masters (New York: Macmillan, 1915).

Excerpt from *Poor White* by Sherwood Anderson (New York: Viking, 1920).

About the Editors

RICHARD O. DAVIES is University Foundation Professor of History at the University of Nevada, Reno. He is the author of *Main Street Blues: The Decline of Small Town America* (Ohio State University Press, 1998) and several other books focusing on twentieth-century American history.

JOSEPH A. AMATO is Professor of Rural and Regional Studies at Southwest State University in Marshall, Minnesota. He is the author of a series of books on the Upper Midwest, including *When Father and Son Conspire: A Minnesota Farm Murder* (Iowa State University Press, 1988), *The Great Jerusalem Artichoke Circus: The Buying and Selling of the American Dream* (University of Minnesota Press, 1993), and, most recently, *Rethinking Home: A Case for Writing Local History* (University of California Press, 2002).

DAVID R. PICHASKE is Professor of English Literature at Southwest State University in Marshall, Minnesota. He is a specialist in the literature of the rural Midwest and is the editor of *Late Harvest: Rural American Writing* (Paragon Press, 1991) and author of *Beowulf to Beatles and Beyond: The Varieties of Poetry* (Free Press, 1972) and *A Generation in Motion: Popular Music and Culture in the Sixties* (Schirmer Books, 1979).

A Place Called Home
was designed by Dennis Anderson,
Duluth, Minnesota;
and set in type by Judy Gilats at Peregrine Graphics Services,
St. Paul, Minnesota.